In the days when the voyage from
Holland to her colonies took several
months, it was the custom for
Dutchmen in the East Indies to win
a bride by a 'glove' marriage. And the
results of these strange unions of chance
were sometimes happy, sometimes
tragic.

SILVER NUTMEG is the story of
such a marriage—between Evert Haan,
handsome, powerful sensualist, and
Annabet Van Goens, the young girl he
was determined to possess as his wife . . .

Also by NORAH LOFTS

JASSY
THE BRITTLE GLASS
A CALF FOR VENUS
QUEEN IN WAITING
SCENT OF CLOVES
THE LUTEPLAYER
BLESS THIS HOUSE
THE DEVIL IN CLEVELY
THE TOWN HOUSE
OUT OF THIS NETTLE
TO SEE A FINE LADY
THE ROAD TO REVELATION
THE HOUSE AT OLD VINE
THE HOUSE AT SUNSET
HESTER ROON

and published by CORGI BOOKS

Silver
Nutmeg

A DIVISION OF TRANSWORLD PUBLISHERS

SILVER NUTMEG

A CORGI BOOK 552 08292 9

Originally published in Great Britain
by Michael Joseph, Ltd.

PRINTING HISTORY
Michael Joseph Edition published 1947
Corgi edition published 1968
Corgi edition reissued 1969

This book is set in
Times 9 pt.

Corgi Books are published by Transworld Publishers, Ltd.,
Bashley Road, London, N.W.10

Made and printed in Great Britain by
Richard Clay (The Chaucer Press), Ltd., Bungay Suffolk

APOLOGY AND
ACKNOWLEDGMENT

THE irresistible desire to write a book about the nutmeg island of Banda came upon me when I was reading H. W. Ponder's book, 'In Javanese Waters.' There, in one short chapter, was outlined a romantic, blood-stained history that called for exploration. But, like all exploration, it presented great difficulties. The Dutch East Indies were in Japanese hands, all contact broken; Banda itself is no more than a speck, the size of a fly dirt on a map; no book that came my way gave any idea of the island's layout. So my geography is the geography of the imagination.

May I beg the tolerance of those who do know upon which side of the harbour the old Fort stood, the names of the flowers which bloomed in Annabet's garden, exactly how, in 1656, a native would address a white man. I admit my ignorance of these, and other details.

But there is an island called Banda, and the Dutch did settle there, and they did make fortunes and build mansions of marble. And there were 'Glove' marriages, and 'Company's Daughters,' and nutmeg smuggling, and native risings. And there were, of course, as there have been in all places, at all times, men and women who loved and hated, who schemed and lied, who suffered and rejoiced.

To the many people who have helped me out of their greater knowledge, especially to E. A. van Leent of the Netherlands and Netherlands Indies Information Bureau, and to Charles H. S. Jones of Bury St. Edmund's, I offer my most grateful thanks.

N. L.

'There they lie, these romantic exiles, in the shade of the nutmeg trees that were the cause of their exile here; whose fruit built their lordly mansions, paid for the clothes they wore, the food they ate and the hundreds of slaves who toiled for them.'

In Javanese Waters (H. W. PONDER)

'I had a little nut tree
Nothing would it bear
But a silver nutmeg . . .'

Nursery Rhyme

BOOK ONE

By the time that they reached the point of discussing women and marriage, neither Piet Odshoorn nor Evert Hann was really sober enough to tackle any subject seriously. Certainly Piet would never have taken Annabet Van Goens' name lightly upon his tongue so long as he was in complete control of his senses. But the occasion was a unique one, and they had celebrated it suitably.

Four hours previously they had met, by chance, for the first time in thirty years. They had met without recognition, though each subconsciously aware of something resembling himself in the other man, had paid his own vanity the tribute of a covert glance of admiration. Then Kaerko, the Agent, had made a formal introduction and the two big handsome men had fallen upon one another with cries of astonishment, recognition and goodwill. Kaerko would have found it hard to believe, had anyone troubled to tell him, that thirty years earlier the pair had parted upon the worst of terms, and that in the interval Evert had never given Piet a thought and that Piet had remembered Evert only with a smouldering hatred. But this sudden meeting on the far side of the globe was dramatic enough to wipe out indifference and ill-feeling alike. They had left the office with their arms linked.

Evert had dragged Piet home to his fine new house and given him a dinner fit for a king. They had talked without ceasing and drunk almost as steadily, and now Piet, whose stomach was to a dangerous extent stronger than his head, was well on the way to noisy drunkenness; and Evert, who carried his liquor better, had blunted the fine edge of his judgment and reached a confidential mood.

Outside the tropical night was full of moonshine, which sketched the outlines of Evert's new garden in ivory and ebony. The soft night wind of the islands, heavily laden with spices, blew in from the open verandah. The iron-caged lantern which swung from the nearest pillar, swayed and creaked; inside, on the littered dining-table, the wasting candles in their heavy silver sconces bowed their little pointed flames and shed pearl-coloured waxen tears.

'Well, that's my story,' said Evert with hearty complacency, ending a summary of thirty years' experience. 'And now all I need is a wife. It's time I settled down. As soon as the house is quite ready I must start looking round. The trouble is that it won't be easy to find the kind of woman I want out here. The local beauties are all too easy to resist.'

'Take a holiday and come back with me to Heydberg,' suggested Piet jovially. 'You could take your pick there. I lose my heart every time I go home. There's two Van Goens girls, lovely as lilies. . . .'

The words were meant as a joke, and at the same time as a sly dig at Evert, as one might say to a spoilt pampered child—and now would you like the moon to play with? But, even as he spoke them, something that was neither jocular nor derisive stirred in Piet's mind. He had a clear sharp vision of the two girls in the Van Goens' pew, accompanied by their young sister and old Truitje, and he had to stifle a half maudlin sigh before he could laugh to show Evert that he had not meant the suggestion seriously.

'Van Goens?' asked Evert, narrowing his eyes. 'The old Padroon's family? Why no, they'd be as old as us, older. D'you mean Adriaan's children? Why do you see them in Heydberg?'

'They live there. Adriaan's widow and three daughters.'

'So Adriaan's dead, is he? No loss to the world. By God, how I hated him. D'you remember how he took his crop to me for not doffing my cap quick enough for his liking? Damned puppy.'

For a moment time ran backwards, and the two big men, the respectable ship's captain and the wealthy nutmeg planter, were little boys again, little bare-foot farm boys in the village of Janshaven; growing up in the shadow of the big house; going in awe of the family of the Padroon who owned everything within sight—the fields which their father hired and tilled so industriously, the forge where the horses were shod, the mill where the corn was ground, everything.

Evert pushed the memory away, and with a comfortable swelling sense of his own success, poured generous measures of the best French brandy into the two glasses.

'I used to entertain myself as I worked, planning torments for Adriaan. But what happened? Why isn't his family at Janshaven. Didn't he get a son?'

'Oh yes. There's a son. Egbert. He's in the army. The Janshaven estate is all sold. If you wished Adriaan bad luck, Evert, you should be satisfied. He ruined his family and then blew his brains out.'

'Even that swaggering little sod couldn't get through that much property,' said Evert incredulously.

'But I tell you he did.' A suggestion of truculence crept into Piet's voice. 'Nobody in the world is so rich that they don't want to be richer, haven't you ever noticed? And Adriaan Van Goens was as greedy as the rest of us, I suppose.'

'What did he *do*?'

The gift of simple direct narrative was not Piet's to any marked degree at any time, and to-night he was befuddled with liquor.

'Damme if I can remember the name. Maybe you do. Everybody's heard of it. Evert ... ten, no, more, twelve years ago; what was the name of the new company that started off so grand? Threatened to drive the old company out of business, so all our pay was cut. I know the name as well as I know my own.'

'There was the United Eastern Mercantile. But that was nothing to do with Van Goens. That was Herman Heemskerk's job.'

'That's the name I was after. The United Eastern Mercantile. Heemskerk lent his name, I suppose Adriaan reckoned that looked better. But it was all his money. They made no secret about that, bless your soul. Every dockhand in Amsterdam knew it. And you think, Evert, what a ship like my *Eastern Venture* costs to build and fit out'—a note of almost fatuous pride sounded in his voice—'and then think that Adriaan laid out the cash for no fewer than seven, bigger than her, not to mention buying the con ... con ... what d'you call'ems, concessions, and the bribes, and warehouses, and all the people, including soldiers to fight *ours* whenever they came within spitting distance, and great new offices on Hoogenstraat that made ours look like a dog's kennel. It's easy to see where the estate went, and the horses, and even Mevrouw's jewels. That was afterwards, of course, when the U.E.M. was bankrupt within two years, and our company bought up everything for a song. Oh yes, the Van Goens are finished, poor as church mice.' He waved his great brown hand in a gesture that indicated the completeness of their fall, and one of Evert's Venetian crystal goblets was shattered on the red-tiled floor.

'My God, Evert, I'm sorry about that,' said Piet, embarrassed as a boy by his own clumsiness. But Evert, who loved all his possessions, hardly noticed the disaster.

'So then Adriaan shot himself. Yes, he would do that rather than face poverty. A very fitting end. Quite as good as anything I ever planned for him; in my wildest dreams I never saw him out of Janshaven. And to think that the Eastern trade that put money in my pocket—and in yours too, in a way, Piet, should have taken it out of his!' He brooded, very happily, for a moment. 'So then the family moved to Heydberg.'

Piet nodded. 'That's the place for the poor, it seems,' he said incautiously. The few bitter little words reminded Evert that it was to Heydberg that Piet and his mother had gone when Evert's father, who was also Piet's, had belatedly set his muddled house in order. He refrained from speaking for a moment, reached for a fresh glass, poured brandy into it, and pushed it gently towards his half-brother. When he did speak his voice was smooth and grave.

'You were as well off in Heydberg as I was in Janshaven after you'd gone, Piet. And that's the sober truth. The Old Man went to the Padroon and asked that I should be counted legitimate when it came to inheriting the tenant rights. But the Van Goens were always on your mother's side, as you know. No tenant rights for little Evert. So then he reckoned he'd buy a farm on some free land. And work! My God, Piet, I've worked in my time, but never like I did then. He fairly starved us too, and my mother wasn't the help out of doors that yours was. He used to bawl.... I should think you could have heard him in Heydberg at times. That's why I ran away. He meant me to have a farm if he killed me to get it, I could see that.'

Piet laughed, his momentary bitterness forgotten.

'And there was I, envying you like mad. When I was wet through and frozen, with my hands raw from hauling ropes and my belly full of salt horse, I used to think of you, snug by the fire, guzzling eggs and ham. Things do turn out queer, don't they?'

Evert made a noise of assent. 'And the Van Goens girls? What are they like? How old?'

'Oh, Klara's the oldest, seventeen, maybe eighteen now. I only see them across the church when I'm home, you know. It's a bit hard to keep count of their ages. Annabet's younger by about a year, and Maria's maybe fourteen. She was just a baby when they left Janshaven.'

'I see. And the two grown ones are pretty, eh?'

'Well, you remember Adriaan; and he married his cousin, like all Van Goens do. They looked more like brother and sister. The girls are all that colour.' He scowled at his glass for a moment, wondering at the amount of interest Evert was showing, and angry with himself because his description was so halting, so very far short of the vision his memory called up. 'Aw, Evert, you can't expect a chap who spends his life at sea to reckon off a girl's points like a farmer does a heifer's. Yellow hair, you know, real golden colour, and curly; and their skins all white where it isn't pink. And blue eyes.'

'Which is the prettiest?'

'I dunno. I tell you, I only see them across the church, or sometimes maybe at the door, coming in or out, or sometimes maybe I just pass them in the street. If you must know, Annabet's the pick of the bunch, to my mind, at least. Others mightn't agree.'

'Why do you prefer her to what's her name? Klara?' Evert asked relentlessly.

Something very nearly approaching misery clouded the candour of Piet's grey eyes. 'Damned if I know. But you look at Klara and then at her, and then you don't want to look at Klara again. Maybe her head's put on better, and when she walks...' His hands moved on the air in a smooth, undulating movement. 'And everything about her makes you ... Look here, Evert, I'm drunk, blathering on about how a girl looks.' He lifted his fresh glass and took a drink. 'I sound like a fool, I know. But I think about her at times, stuck away in that dull old house, and never a penny of dowry. Who'll she ever find to marry her?' He took a sip from his glass to cover the confusion which the sound of his own voice asking such a question roused in him, and went on in an elaborately careless way. 'Not that that's any business of mine. I can't think what put that into my head. In fact, I can't think what we're talking about the Van Goens' girls at all.' He blinked at Evert as though he might find enlightenment by staring at his kinsman's face—as indeed a shrewder man might possibly have done.

'If she isn't married by the time you get back, I'll make a bid for her,' Evert said.

Piet's stare of bewilderment changed to one of utter astonishment. Then he laughed.

'Ha, ha, what a joke that would be.'

'Why?'

'Why would it be a joke? Aw, Evert, you must know ...' He laughed again, a little less certainly, and then stopped struck dumb by the realisation that not only had Evert meant what he said, but that he was offended by the amusement with which his words had been received.

'Go on, Piet, tell me. I really want to know. Why should it be a joke?'

'Well, damn me! Surely you don't want anybody to tell you why. Old Jakob Kressle's second bastard and Adriaan Van Goens' daughter. Aw, Evert, come on, laugh, or I'll be thinking you meant it. And if it isn't a joke, you're crazy.'

'But I'm not joking and I'm not crazy, Piet. Why d'you think I'm still single at my age? Why d'you think I've waited till now to build myself a house? I've been in Banda for twenty years; the men who settled when I did have had homes of a sort and wives of a sort for almost that long. *I* lived in a four-roomed hut very little better than one of my coolie's. Why? Because I intended from the very first to marry a lady. I built this house to be fit for a lady. I'm not a man to be content with the second best. I don't want a planter's daughter or a first merchant's daughter. I want a lady of birth and breeding, and I want her to be fit to look at. This Annabet Van Goens that you describe so movingly, sounds exactly what I've had in mind.'

'But she wouldn't marry you. Mind you, I'm not denying that you can aim high, Evert. You're a fine handsome man,

11

and you've a fine handsome place. But the Van Goens ... why, if Mevrouw herself didn't remember, one of those old aunts with the parrot noses would remind her....'

'Of what?' asked Evert, leaning back in his chair and enjoying Piet's confusion.

'Of the old days, you fool. About the Old Man and our mothers and us. Why, you now said yourself that Adriaan took his crop to you for not doffing your cap.'

'I hope, quite sincerely, that they will remember all those things when they receive my proposal to make a glove marriage with Adriaan's prettiest daughter.'

'You hope...'

'Of course. And to make quite certain that there is no mistake you must carry the proposal for me, Piet.'

'Me.' Piet made a motion as though he intended to get to his feet and fly the lunatic's company; but his feet slipped on the tiles and it was only by seizing the edge of the table and sitting down again hastily that he saved himself from falling. 'Oh no, Evert,' he said, shaking his big head, after a glance had shown him that Evert was indeed in deadly earnest, 'I couldn't do that; and I wouldn't. Look here, I'll tell you something. Daft as it sounds, I'm still afraid of Mevrouw. Laugh if you like, it's God's truth. I know she's poor, I know she always buys the cheapest joints at the butcher's and she hasn't a gown that's a patch on the one I took mother home for her birthday, but if I meet Mevrouw in the street, though she's always very gracious and smiling—you know how ladies can be when they like, and she asks after my health and about my last voyage, I go dumb Evert, I twist my hat and shuffle my feet. And I bet you would too.' He brought out the last words aggressively.

Evert was not to be goaded. He looked at Piet's glass and added to the liquor that remained in it. Then he said, quite amiably: 'It is possible that Mevrouw Van Goens might have that effect upon me. I have no chance of ever knowing. *But* there is another side to the question. If they are really poor, as you say you know they are, and the girls are stuck away in Heydberg without dowries, seeing nobody likely to marry them, don't you think both Mevrouw and her daughter might be very grateful to the man who brought them an honourable proposal from his kinsman? Think of Annabet for a moment. Where would she be better off?'

Piet fell, unsuspecting, into the trap. 'Oh, there's no denying that, Evert. The whole of Holland is talking about the nutmeg princes. That's what I'm telling you. There's hardly a family in Holland that wouldn't spare a daughter for Banda ... but the Van Goens ... that is different. They know your beginnings.'

'Isn't that an advantage?' Evert was not offended. 'You have to look at these things calmly, Piet. Your Annabet sounds just

12

the person who would, given half a chance, snatch at the opportunity of marrying a man like *me*. Very well. What's she likely to get? We're all alike, more or less. Adventurers, old soldiers, rogues and vagabonds from five provinces who've made our fortunes either with our fists or our wits. The Van Goens, when they remember Jakob Kressle will remember that he was industrious and sober even if he was too lusty a man to be satisfied with one woman. He and his fathers had been in Janshaven for as long as the Van Goens themselves. They've lost a fortune, and I've made one. I'll bet they'd rather marry their daughter to *this* nutmeg prince than to one they know nothing about.'

'You always could argue,' said Piet, scowling as he concentrated. 'Many's the thing you've argued me out of in the old days. But there's truth in what you say.' He stared around the room again, taking note of the silver-laden sideboard, the silver and glass and napery upon the table. The things Evert owned were as good as any there had been in the Janshaven mansion. And if the things Evert said were true...

'Look here, if I do take a hand in this business, you'll have to make it easy for me. Make it so I don't have to say much. I know I seem to have talked my head off to-night, but I'm a dumb dog as a rule, and as I say, Mevrouw frightens me out of my wits.'

'Leave that to me. I'll get everything down on paper. All I want you to do is to carry the papers and make sure that Mevrouw understands that I am your kinsman.'

'That's odd, you know,' said Piet. His voice was thickening now and his stare was losing its focusing power. 'I never ... mind you, I'm not comparing, because anybody could see with half an eye that I haven't got on in the world like you have, but I never ... kind of thought about the Old Man as being respectable. What I mean is, if I was you I'd choose anybody in the world to carry those papers except *me*.'

Evert stared at the simpleton and wondered if it were worth while, or even possible, to try to make him understand. The idea which had dropped into his mind, whole perfect and utterly delightful, during the few minutes while Piet tried to describe Annabet Van Goens, was, perhaps, too subtle and too completely personal even to be explained to anyone. His luck—Evert believed implicitly in his luck and had every reason to do so—had brought him, by the merest accident, not only the chance of finding the kind of wife he had wanted all along, but the chance of the kind of revenge that only came, as a rule, in dreams. Adriaan Van Goens, the padroon's pampered only son, on a piebald pony with flowing hair and mane, Evert Haan, the tenant farmer's pampered second bastard bringing home the cows for milking; that clash of wills; the

13

inevitable ending; the insult that rankled more with every memory. Indoors, I am everything; out of doors, I am like the rest. Why, why? And now to be able to say, subtly, without words, to Adriaan's widow ... you see Mevrouw, I am not ashamed of my family or of my origin; I make no pretences; you see, Mevrouw, one of old Jakob Kressle's bastards brings you a proposal from the other one, and are you not glad to consider it? Ah, wasn't success sweet?

But Piet, of course, had never understood anything that couldn't be explained in words of three letters.

'Well, after all, this is a family matter and a personal matter. What better messenger could I find, Piet? Damn it, I'm proud of you. The company doesn't trust ships like the *Eastern Venture* to rogues or weaklings. We've made our way in the world, unaided. Is that anything to be ashamed of?'

The good-humoured smile which Piet remembered, slipped across his face. When Evert hadn't been thwarted, or scheming, he had been a jolly companion. He was that now.

'Come on, drink up, and let me fill your glass again. This is a great day.'

Piet took his glass from the table and leaned back, obscurely relieved to find that the Van Goens' family had dropped out of the conversation. He'd been a fool to talk about them as he had done. But most likely Evert was a little flown with drink too, and would have forgotten his hare-brained scheme by the morning.

'I c-can't think,' he said, his tongue stumbling a little, 'why, I didn't recognize you at once. You look just like Evert to me now.' He ran his hand over his own beautiful brown beard. 'There was some ex-excuse for you. I've grown this.'

'I had one, just as fine. But I shaved it. Too hot. But even with it, you look just Piet to me, now. To tell you the truth, back there in Kaerko's office I just looked at you and thought what a damned handsome fellow you were.'

'But that's just wh-what I thought, too. Funny, eh? And funny to find you here. D'you know ... all these years I never could bring myself to go back to Janshaven, not even for fishing, in case I ran into you. And now, here we are.'

He looked at Evert with maudlin affection. The slight weight which had lain upon his mind since he had spoken Annabet's name, lifted. He emptied his glass and was disproportionately proud of himself for refusing to have it refilled. His last sensible thought was that he must look at the time. Clumsily he drew out the great silver watch which was the terror of the unpunctual aboard the *Eastern Venture*, and, squinting at it to focus his eyes, discovered that it was past ten o'clock.

'Damme,' he said, stuffing the watch away and preparing to rise from his chair, 'I must be off. Got to be up in the morning.

14

Agent comes aboard at daybreak.' He rose to his feet, and as he did so Evert's dining-room tilted as though a wave had struck it. He sat down hastily.

'I'm worse than I reckoned,' he said, with another foolish grin.

'Stay the night,' Evert suggested. 'I can have a room made ready in a few minutes.' He reached for the silver handbell. Piet, exaggeratedly concerned, leaned over and gripped his hand. If once that bell rang, he thought, he would be persuaded into even greater folly.

'No, no,' he said. 'Don't do that, Evert. I can't stay. I'm damned drunk ... and if I go to bed drunk there's only Gijs can wake me in the morning. And to tell you the truth, I'm in b-bad odour with the Company as it is over my liquor. Fat-arsed directors sitting at their ease in Amsterdam—they've got no bowels of compassion for seafaring men that have to take their comfort where they can find it. Sent for me they did ... last time I landed and said one more chance. One more case of derry-derry-damn the word, neglect of duty and you're finished, Odshoorn, they said. And I'll tell you another thing, Evert old man, that Agent, what's his name? Kaerko, thanks. Kaerko was just going to come aboard and check over when you came in this afternoon. He put it off as a favour to *you,* not to me. I know that. Agents don't favour captains as a rule. So if I'm not there at daybreak he'll be mad as a pi-dog. And for all I know he may be a spy. See? It's nice of you, Evert, to ask me to stay; and it was a nice dinner and I'm sorry we haven't been better friends, and by God I'm glad to see you so prosperous and all. But please don't ask me to stay now. I gotta get back to Gijs. He'll see I'm all right in the morning.'

'I wouldn't think of stopping you,' Evert said. 'I'll walk down to the quay with you.'

'Thanks,' Piet said. He took hold of the edge of the table and gingerly levered himself to his feet, as though hoping that, if he did it gradually, his brain would not notice the change of position. Once upright he had one of the ideas which, to the drunken man, seem so shrewd and sober. He looked fiercely at Evert. 'And don't you go telling anybody I was too drunk to get home by myself. See? Because spies are everywhere. And nobody else has seen me. So if I'm called over the coals and sacked for getting drunk my first night in Banda, I shall know who to blame, and by God I'll maim you.' His mood changed again. 'Know what they said to me in that stinking office? You'll go to Banda, Odshoorn, they said; there's be less tem-temptation in a place where you haven't any boon com-panions. And then I'm hardly landed, just set foot in the Agent's office and Evert Haan walks in. Good old Evert, after all these years. Boon companions, eh? Funny, isn't it funny?'

'Very funny,' Evert agreed. He linked his arm in his kinsman's, and steered him out into the hall. There, on top of a Chinese lacquered chest lay their two hats, Piet's formal, heavy, hot, be-badged shore-going uniform one, Evert's a wide light straw of native workmanship. Piet, with his free hand clapped his on, lopsidedly, and would not have looked into the gilt-edged mirror on the wall above the chest, but his arm was linked in Evert's, and Evert turned, with the automatic action of a vain man and looked into the glass. For a moment the two faces, so like and yet so unlike, swam together in the greenish, dimly-lighted surface, and the lack of precision in the reflection seemed to exaggerate their salient features. The weakness of Piet's amiable mouth, the hard, thin strength of Evert's; the fan of little wrinkles about Piet's eyes, the result of years of facing wind and weather, the prominent muscles of Evert's jaw.

'By Heaven,' said Piet, with a foolish laugh which on a higher note would have been a giggle, 'we do look alike. I never real-realized that I was so like the Old Man.' The differences had eluded him, his blurred stare saw only the resemblances, the tough reddish-brown hair which in both men had retained its colour and thickness and would most likely remain the same until extreme old age, the slightly-hooked noses with the wide nostrils indicative of physical courage, the grey-green eyes below the thick straight brows.

'I suppose he's dead by now,' said Evert, turning towards the door. 'Did you ever hear?'

'Not a word. Never wan-wanted to. By God, I'm glad you left him, Evert. Served the old bastard right.'

He missed a step just outside the door and stumbled. Evert's grip on his arm saved him.

They walked for a little while in a comfortable silence. Then a mood of great happiness fell upon Piet. After all these years, he thought, Evert and me walking along together like good friends.

'We didn't always get on so badly, did we?' he asked in a sentimental voice. 'We had some good times together. Why, I remember going to the Fair with you, and you had money and I had none, and you treated me at every booth. And we came home together singing. D'you remember that? D'you remember any of the old songs, Evert?'

'No,' said Evert. 'And don't you start singing now, Piet. We're nearly into town, and you don't want to make an exhibition of yourself, do you?'

'Aw, come on. There's nobody about.' That was true enough, for the town of Banda Neira kept early hours. But, as Evert knew, that very fact would make any unusual noise the more noticeable. And the moon was bright. He didn't want sober citizens brought to their windows to see him, Evert Haan, escorting a drunken sea-captain through the streets.

'Come on,' Piet said again. 'Surely you re-remember the "Milkmaid's Holiday" ... about the young gallant who met the pretty milkmaid and be-begged her to stop and give him a drink from her sweet foaming pail, and she did, but it was slops. It was slops to the ditch she was carrying. "And good enough for you, fine sir, good enough for you." You must remember that one, Evert. Come on now, altogether,

> ' *'Twas on a bright fine morning*
> *The scent of hay perfuming...'*

His rich bass voice rang out in the ribald ditty. Along the street Evert heard the creak of an opened shutter. He lengthened his stride.

'How're you going to get back to your ship?' he asked loudly, trying to distract Piet's attention.

'Gijs'll be waiting for me. "Oh, she was very bonny, and he was very bold." '

'Will you shut up?' Evert said. 'Who is this Gijs?'

'My man.'

'Oh. I didn't know the Company allowed their captains a personal servant.'

'They don't, blast their meanness! I pay him myself. Damn it, Evert, don't keep disturbing me. "He said to her, Oh maiden, I take it you're a maiden ..." '

'You'll rouse the whole town,' said Evert, as another shutter opened briskly.

'They want to hear the fruity part,' said Piet, singing louder. So, bellowing at the top of his lungs, he emerged upon the quay. And there, alone in the moonlight, Gijs waited. Evert gladly surrendered his charge, said 'Good night' abruptly, and strode back towards the streets. Gijs drove a sharp elbow into Piet's diaphragm and said curtly, 'Pipe down, will you?' And as Piet hushed at the voice of authority, asked anxiously, 'Who was that? Anybody you know?'

The question struck the drunken man as being exquisitely funny. He broke into great volleys of laughter. 'Anybody I know,' he repeated. 'Why I was brought up with that jacka-lorum. Go to Banda they say, there won't be anybody there to drink with ... and before I've been in the Agent's office ten minutes Evert Haan comes walking in.'

'Well, that's all right then,' Gijs said, a little comforted. 'I was afraid it was just somebody you'd picked up in a tavern. And this is a little place. *They'd* soon hear that you was roaring drunk again.'

17

'But I haven't been in a tavern I tell you. Evert took me back to his house, a fine new place he's building. Like a palace. And what a dinner, Gijs, my lad. Not one thing I could name, but all delish-ush.'

Gijs, bent over the oars, merely grunted. Piet's mood tilted suddenly for no reason. 'But I've done a damn silly thing, Gijs. I've made a — damn silly promise.'

The even rhythm of Gijs' labouring arms faltered. For ten years he had been Piet's servant, mentor, father-confessor, and it was largely due to his skill and devotion that that interview in the Directors' office had been so long delayed. In the secret places of his heart he believed that, if he had been in Surabaya at the time of the fatal drunken bout, instead of in hospital, he could have saved his master the full result of his folly. But since the thing had happened and Piet had been reprimanded and warned—coming out of the office and weeping on Gijs' shoulder and vowing never to drink again except when he was on leave at home, Gijs had been doubly watchful. He had regarded Evert's prosperous well-dressed figure with the greatest suspicion. He did not look like a sea-captain's casual drinking acquaintance, more like some well-to-do busy-body who would remove a drunken nuisance and then report him. Evert's abrupt leave-taking had lent colour to the suspicion. Then Piet had claimed Evert as an old friend and Gijs had felt relieved; and now Piet was changing his tune and muttering about having made a promise. Gijs knew those promises made under the influence of liquor; there had been trouble about them more than once. Always, everywhere, up and down the route of the wide-travelling ships of the Company there were unscrupulous persons trying to persuade a simple, easy-going sea-faring man into some breach of the rules ... there was always a lady whose father was dying in Bandogar, and who hadn't had time to bespeak a passage; there was always the parcel which contained nothing of any importance but which could easily be stowed among the captain's personal stuff and for which strange sums—considering its unimportance—would be paid for delivery in a certain place with due discretion. Gijs was wise to them all; and so, in his sober moments, was Piet. But this was not the first time by a great many that the captain had returned to his ship saying. 'I've made a damn silly promise. . . .'

'Sir, you are incorrigible,' Gijs said. He had a fondness for long words, collecting them as men collect tangible objects, and using them when moved, as men use oaths.

'Now don't you start to swear at me, Gijs. Because I can't stand it. Old Evert said the air'd revive me, and he was right. By God, I've just realized what I've let myself in for.' He gave a great gusty sigh and a puff of wine-laden, shnapps-scented

18

breath hit Gijs in the face.

'What is it, this time?' Gijs spoke in a voice of weary patience.

'It's Evert's fault,' Piet said bitterly. 'He always could charm a bird off a tree if he wanted to. He charmed me out of my farm. And to-night I forgave him for that. And what did he do? Turn straight round and persuade me to do a thing that'll make me the laughing-stock of all Heydberg. And my mother for one'll never forgive me if I go and offend Mevrouw. Very partial to Mevrouw, my mother is on account of the old Mevrouw speaking up for her when there was nobody else to. And though many men don't set much store by their mothers, I *do*.'

The boat drew into the shadow of the *Eastern Venture*.

'Can you manage the ladder, sir?' Gijs asked, shipping his oars. He realised that Piet was in a garrulous, long-winded mood, and it might take some time to get to the heart of the matter—what Piet had promised to do, or say, or carry for the richly-dressed, red-faced man who had said 'Good night' so abruptly. Whatever it was, if it was against orders, Gijs would see that it was not done. Gijs, a son of the gutter, reared in the Leyden Foundlings' Home, had a deep natural distrust of all well-dressed, well-fed men, anyway, and if this representative of the kind thought he had only a simple, silly, drunken sea-captain to deal with he would soon learn differently. Praise be to God, wits were not the prerogative of the well-to-do, and Gijs knew that his own were needle-sharp naturally, and life had kept them well polished.

'I'll get you some coffee and your pills,' he said, when they stood together on the deck. 'Don't lie down till I come.'

Piet, like an obedient child, was standing bolt upright in his cabin when Gijs joined him; a mug of scalding, ink-black coffee in one hand, four rhubarb pills, each the size of a marble, in the other.

'You've got to be shipshape in the morning, early,' he said, quite tenderly. 'Sit down and I'll get your boots off while you drink your grog.'

'Damned funny, meeting old Evert,' Piet meandered, dropping obediently on to the side of his bunk and sticking out his legs. 'Thirty years since I last set eyes on him. Long time. But I remember the day as though it was yesterday. Pouring with rain, the sort of day you wouldn't turn a dog out. Not if it had been a good dog; and by God's eyes, my mother had served the old man well. Worked in the fields and yard like a horse, she had. And turned out to starve just like a horse at the end. And all on Evert's account. Of the two women the old man liked my mother far the best.' He brought his big hand down on the bunk and emitted a sound of disgust. 'And then, blast me, I'm

19

pleased to see him and go and eat his grub and promise him things.' He looked at Gijs with dazed misery.

At the word 'promise,' Gijs' slumbering interest revived.

'What did you promise exactly?' he asked, drawing off the second boot and setting the pair neatly side by side.

'Something that's going to make me the laughing-stock of the village,' said Piet bitterly.

'Why?' Ramblingly, between sips of coffee and what sounded to Gijs' impatient ears like interminable, irrelevant digressions, Piet told him what he had promised to do.

'Is that all?' Gijs asked, when the story at last came to an end. His relief was so profound as to be almost tangible. It was a perfectly legitimate errand. A nice errand, in fact. Gijs liked to hear of the mighty being brought low and the humble being exalted. He'd look at this Mynheer Haan with interest and respect if they ever met again.

'All? Don't you reckon that's enough?' Piet realised with dismal certainty that for once Gijs' sympathy had failed him. It was no use. Nobody could see the thing as he saw it. Nobody else could see the grotesqueness of this proposed linking of Haan and Van Goens, Except the Van Goens themselves. They'd see it fast enough. And so would his own mother. And they'd blame him. And he'd be there, shambling and embarrassed, stuttering out his excuses, and all the time feeling guilty as hell. Opening his great mouth over the wine glasses. Just what the Directors had said. Untrustworthy when in liquor. He heaved a gusty sigh and rolled over on to the bunk.

'You'll feel different about things in the morning,' said Gijs, who, though puzzled by his master's attitude, had been touched to pity by the sigh. 'I'll see you're about in good time. Good night.'

'Good night, Gijs. You're a good chap, but you're dead stupid,' said Piet. He burrowed into the pillow and was, despite his worries, instantly asleep. Gijs moved around softly, tidying the cabin, then he put out the light and went happily away. The captain had promised nothing which might not be performed with impunity; his drunken behaviour had been observed only by the man for whom he was pledged to do a favour, and here he was, safe aboard, where Gijs could be answerable for his punctuality in the morning.

In the morning he was at the bunkside again. He had been up for forty minutes, pottering about and taking peeps at the sky. As soon as the East flushed with pink and peach over the nutmeg groves that lay grey in the dawn, he had brewed more coffee, picked up the highly polished boots and gone to the cabin with an expression of severe determination upon his sallow, pug-featured face. The Captain was the very devil to wake after a bout of drunkenness; on the occasion which had brought the Company's dissatisfaction to a head he had slept soundly for three nights and two days, lost, anonymous, in some low wharfside tavern. The *Eastern Venture*, due to sail on the turn of the first day's tide, had stayed at anchor in Chilipung Bay and in the afternoon the Agent had come aboard to see what the trouble was. On the second day they had begun to fear that Piet had been murdered and the Agent was making what he called 'other arrangements' when the Captain himself, frowsy and swollen-eyed, had boarded his own ship. The Agent's report, the more virulent because he had himself suffered a good deal of anxiety during those wasted hours, had reached Amsterdam before the *Eastern Venture*, and the stern reproof and the warning had been the result. So, thought Gijs, wetting a rough towel in a bucket of sea-water, the Captain must be up and ready, spruce and bright, by the time the Banda Agent came aboard this morning.

He turned to the bunk, where Piet lay like the dead, except that the dead do not breathe heavily, and, straining every muscle in his slight frame, took his master by the shoulders and raised the leaden body so that, instead of reclining, the great form leaned back against the bulkhead. Piet's head fell forward and he slept on, undisturbed. Then Gijs took the wet towel and beat it about the sleeper's head and face. Drops of water rained about the cabin; runnels of it streamed down over the hairy chest and brawny shoulders. Piet slumbered on. A ray of sunshine fingered its way through the porthole and Gijs caught his breath in a panic. 'Daybreak' ... and day came quickly in these latitudes; oh God, he should have started earlier! A particularly vicious flip of the towel caught Piet across the cheek and he turned his head aside with a sound that was half grunt, half grown.

'Captain Odshoorn,' Gijs called in a shrill, piercing voice, much encouraged by this sign of life, 'wake up. Company's Agent will be aboard any moment.' He dropped the towel into the bucket, brought it up soaking and squeezed it over the tousled russet head. He repeated his shrill cry of warning; he took Piet's head by the ears and banged it gently at first, then quite roughly, against the bulkhead. An expression of pain crossed the big highly-coloured face, but Piet did not open his eyes. Another drenching from the resoaked towel, a few more bangs and a slap or two and he did rouse himself to mutter:

'Lemme alone, will you,' and having made that effort he leaned his head back as though against the most comfortable pillow and fell asleep again. Beads of sweat shone on Gijs' brow and upper lip, and he breathed like an over-driven horse. It *was* daylight now, and there was much to do.

'So you want to get yourself sacked, do you, you stinking lump of carrion,' he yelled. And from this mild beginning he launched upon a flood of obscene abuse—the conscious and unconscious gleanings of twenty years of dockside and sea-going life—any phrase of which, heard and understood, would be guaranteed to rouse resentment. When he could think of nothing novel enough to arrest attention he reached for the bucket and poured its remaining contents over Piet's head. That was the last resort and only used in moments of desperation, for it meant a good deal of work drying and mopping the floor.

'You little *swine*,' said Piet sleepily. Gijs' face cleared.

'Come on, sir, wake up,' he said in a different voice, still rousing, but deferential. 'Company's Agent is coming aboard at daybreak. And you're late as it is. Rouse up, sir. Drink this.'

He draped the wet towel round Piet's neck like a scarf, swung his feet over the bunk's edge and pressed them on to the boards, and then set the mug of coffee against his lips. The coffee was still hot, and to Piet, after his drenching with cool water, seemed hotter. Piet shook his head and then opened his eyes. Slowly his great brown hands went to his head.

'I've split my skull,' he said mournfully. 'You let me fall last night.'

'I did not,' said Gijs, briskly. 'But I nearly had to split it to wake you. And you weren't at your worst last night, either. Look at the time. And Mynheer Kaerko is coming at daybreak.'

'Mm. I know,' said Piet, still fingering his head. 'It seems all right, but it feels dreadful. Gimme that coffee.'

'Drink it down and you shall have some shnapps,' said Gijs, as though bribing a child. He reached for a dry towel and mopped Piet quickly. Then he held out his breeches. 'Come on, up now. That's right. We shall be in time after all. Clean shirt, make a good impression. Now here's your shnapps.' He whisked away the mug and held out the pewter measure, and as soon as Piet had taken it, snatched up a brush which he plied vigorously over the crisp, curly hair of his master's head and beard. Then, diving into his pocket he produced a hard ship's biscuit. 'There you are, chew that. It'll stay your belly and take away the smell.' He stood back with the brush still in his hand and regarded his handiwork with pride. You would never guess, he thought, complacently, that fifteen minutes ago he was just a drunken hulk, who, left to himself, would have slept on, and, sure as a gun, been sacked at the end of this voyage. Gijs derived great satisfaction from the thought. Ten years ago he had received from Piet the first really kind, humane treatment he had known in his life, and it pleased him to think that now he was the peg upon which the Captain's whole career depended. For although it was acknowledged that the big man was a peerless sailor, cool in an emergency, unruffled in the face of danger, utterly dependable in his sober moments, such virtues hardly compensated for the tendency to babble, to keep low company, and to neglect his duty which came upon him when he was drunk. Well, Gijs thought, we've foxed *Them* again, and next time he goes ashore, even if it is to the Agent's office, I go too.

Kaerko, with his army of clerks, came punctually aboard, and the routine of checking the cargo brought out from Holland for sale or exchange in the islands, went smoothly. Piet's head still ached and he talked very little. He noted that the Agent's manner had changed subtly since the afternoon of the day before when it had been the perfectly courteous, formal, slightly condescending manner of a very important official towards a lesser one. Now there was a show of personal interest, a veiled respect which puzzled Piet until his slow brain—slower than usual this morning—arrived at the conclusion that Kaerko had somehow heard gossip about him and was surprised to find everything aboard the *Eastern Venture* so very shipshape, so spick and span.

But presently Kaerko, ticking off the last item, scribbling his initials at the foot of the last page and handing all the papers over to the clerk who stood subserviently ready to receive them, said, 'I trust you had a pleasant evening, Captain Odshoorn.' His voice was that of a man who, finishing a slightly tedious duty, turns to the light social intercourse which attracts him far more. Piet, very conscious of the headache which was the result of that pleasant evening, blinked and managed a wry smile.

'Thank you, yes. Very pleasant. And very obliging of you, sir, to postpone all this business until this morning. Evert whisked me off so quickly I hadn't time to thank you yesterday.' He despised himself as he spoke. Sucking up to Agents was not in his line at all, he hated and despised the breed, landlubbers with a head for figures and an eye like a hawk's for the slightest mistake. But since that warning interview his confidence in himself had been shaken and he was willing to placate anyone who might, in certain circumstances, turn into an enemy.

'Mynheer Haan is an old friend of yours?' Kaerko asked, his tone pleasantly conversational, his eye greasy with curiosity.

'Oh, more than that—a relative; though I'm damned if I could put a name to the exact degree.' Even to please the Agent he was not going to describe the curious tangle which made him and Evert almost brothers.

'Indeed. How strange that you should run into him here! I

23

believe I am right in saying that Mynheer Haan, greeting you, mentioned that it was thirty years since you had met.'

'That's right,' Piet agreed, thinking, how he must have listened though he pretended not to. 'We moved, you see; and I went to sea and Evert came out East. As for its being queer, I dunno. I've had queerer things happen to me. Would you believe that once, when I put in for water at the Cape, the first person I laid eyes on was a fellow I'd lost, washed overboard in a storm off Aden, six years before. He'd been picked up by an Arab dhow and made a slave, got away and wandered all the way down the coast of Africa from Mozambique. And was he glad to see me? I tell you, sir, he wept like a child. And funnier still the fellow who'd taken his place—he was a gunner—had just been put overboard with a round of grape-shot at his heels, so there was his old gun waiting for him. That sounds a far-fetched yarn, but it's true as God is my witness, and there're men aboard this very ship that'd vouch for it.'

'I don't doubt it,' Kaerko said politely. 'Only a fool denies that coincidences occur, especially in these days when the speed of our ships has reduced the size of the earth.'

'Umm,' said Piet, to whom the words 'coincidences' and 'reduced' smacked of Gijs at his worst.

'Mynheer Haan is a very able man, and very popular,' said the Agent silkily.

Piet repressed the retort which rose to his lips—oh yes, Evert would be popular or die in the attempt—and said with unusual caution, 'That doesn't surprise me. And now sir, if you are satisfied, I'll get my breakfast and start unloading. The sooner we're empty the sooner we're full again, you know.'

'A true word, Captain Odshoorn,' said Kaerko in whom hunger had been warring with curiosity for some minutes. 'You'll have two busy days. Then it would give me pleasure if you would dine with me. That'll be Thursday, at six o'clock. We dine late here; the heat of the day is not conducive to appetite.'

'You forget I've been coming East for twenty years,' said Piet, who, resenting language he did not understand, had taken umbrage at 'conducive,' though its meaning was plain enough. Jumped up little ass, like all Agents.

'Have you indeed. You must tell me about your voyages. I daresay we have mutual acquaintances. Until Thursday then. Good morning, Captain Odshoorn.'

'Good morning, sir,' said Piet, more cheerfully. What with the rhubarb pills and the coffee and the early morning shnapps, he was longing for his breakfast. Mutual acquaintances, pooh, he thought, spitting into the blue water.

24

For the next two days the emptying of the *Eastern Venture*'s capacious hold kept him busy, and at night he was too tired to think much, but now and then he spared a thought for Evert, Annabet Van Goens, and the promise he had made. The more he thought about the business the less he liked it. He had made promises before this, when he was in his cups, and regretted them instantly when he was sober. But always before there was a kind of risk, a challenge to his blood attached to the performance of the promise, and very often the danger had appealed to the adventurer in him, and more often it had been impossible to retract the promise without the risk of seeming a coward, in his own eyes at least. Here there was no risk, no breach of the law, no flouting of Company rules. But he would rather have smuggled a jewel or a letter, or one of those lovely brown ladies whose fathers so often chose to die in Bandogar. At least such a job didn't make him feel an ass, and this one did. A dozen times a day he pictured himself walking up to the gaunt white house where now the Van Goens lived, facing Mevrouw in her rustling silk gown—old and frayed as it was—bringing out Evert's audacious proposal; and each time he had a qualm at his stomach and an outbreak of prickly heat along his spine. Some hours before he was due to dine at the Agent's house he had made up his mind that, next time he saw Evert, he would tell him straightly that, despite whatever he might have promised—and he was a bit vague as to how far he had committed himself, just as he would have denied having roared the last stanza of 'The Milkmaid's Holiday' over and over again—he would have nothing to do with the business. If Evert chose to let his new wealth give him a swollen head and make a fool of him, he must find somebody else to help him to display his swollen-headed folly.

He was surprised, and a trifle disconcerted to find that Evert was at the dinner, together with three or four other prosperous-looking gentlemen. 'Dining the Captains' was well known to be part of the Agents' duties all over the wide-flung routes of the Company's trade, a formality, a gesture, and nothing more. Often, as when a cargo was unsatisfactory, or the keen, inspectorial eye had discovered some fault, the occasions were very trying, with both host and guest trying to behave like ordinary human beings when both knew that they were merely cogs in a vast machine which at the moment was not working smoothly. And hardly ever was anyone else present at these ceremonial meals.

Piet, who had not yet got into words the exact form of his refusal to oblige, kept away from his kinsman without much difficulty, for everyone seemed anxious to talk to Evert, to laugh at his jokes and to flatter him openly or covertly. And Evert, in good company, surrounded by a flattering audience, did seem a very charming person. Piet, looking backwards, could remember how, in the old days, before the break-up of their curious family, he had varied his absolute loathing of his half-brother by admiring him prodigiously. Evert took such risks so coolly, enjoyed things so wholeheartedly, and was capable of large, good-humoured actions which blinded one for a moment to his utter selfishness. There had even been moments when Piet, as a youngster, had wondered whether all the rows in the little farmhouse had been Evert's fault, whether he himself, surly and grudging, had not been sometimes to blame. A similar kind of doubt visited him now as he watched Evert. It was so natural for an exile to want a woman of his own race for a wife; it was natural for a man who had got on in the world to marry a woman who would fit in with his position; it was natural for a man to entrust a delicate errand to his kinsman rather than to a stranger. Aw hell! Piet thought, taking refuge in his more usual frame of mind, he's put me in the wrong again, he always did, he always will; why the devil was I put on the Banda route just to run into Evert?

The dinner seemed to stretch out interminably. There was plenty to eat, but Piet's appetite was less keen than usual; there was plenty to drink, but he was afraid to have his glass refilled; there was plenty of conversation, but he took little part in it. With few and short-lived diversions it was all on one topic, the Nutmeg, its prices, its prospects, its peculiarities. With the exception of Piet, every man in the room depended entirely upon the produce of those graceful, feathery trees which covered the islands so thickly. To the nutmeg they owed the clothes they wore, the food they ate, the wines they drank, the houses in which they lived and the guilders that jingled in their breeches pockets. And, in their conversation, at least, they showed no sign of attempting to escape their sense of obligation to the little, shrivelled brown object.

Just before ten o'clock one of the guests rose, saying that he had left his wife alone and had promised to be home early. Men stirred and looked at their watches, but the party might have survived had not Evert risen to his feet and announced that it was time he was moving too. There was then a general movement, and in the hubbub of last greetings and hat-findings, Evert, as though sensing that Piet were about to escape, came up and slipped his arm familiarly into his.

'Wait for me. I'm coming your way, Piet. My prahau is at the quay.'

As soon as they were alone Evert said, 'I want you to come back with me. I've something to show you. The night's young yet, and it's only ten minutes by water.'

'Well,' Piet said reluctantly, 'I've something to say to you; might as well get it over.'

Evert did not bother to ask what that 'something' might be, and the short water journey was passed in trivial conversation, mainly gossip about Kaerko's guests. 'Boender's wife is going to have a baby in about eight and a half months' time, that's why he can't leave her alone for long,' Evert explained, laughing. 'And thanks to her we got away early. I find Kaerko extremely tedious, poor little man. He's a good Agent as they go, but he ought never to leave his office.'

Piet stared at his kinsman. He had heard Agents called many things, but never had he heard anyone say in that casual, pitying tone that an Agent was a tedious, poor little thing. More than the new house, or the style in which Evert lived, the words revealed how very far Evert had got on in the world. No wonder, he thought, that Evert always got his own way with the old man. And then, hard on the heels of that admiring thought came a stubborn one—but he's not going to get his own way with *me*.

'We'll go to my office,' Evert said. 'It's quite comfortable.'

It was a fair-sized square room with bare walls washed white and a floor of red tiles set in inch-wide borders of mortar. There were four articles of furniture, a big heavy desk with a flat top, two comfortable cushioned chairs with high backs, and a wooden bench along one wall. In the wall behind the desk there were several cupboards, one of them with an iron door. An oil lamp burned clearly upon one corner of the desk. Evert pulled it across as soon as he entered, so that its most direct light shone on the wall with the cupboards.

'Sit down,' he said, 'and I'll give you something to drink. Kaerko knows about as much about liquor as I do about knitting.' He unlocked a cupboard and brought out a tall, lopsided bottle of greenish glass and a couple of horn glasses with wide silver rims.

'Not for me, thanks,' Piet said, in what he intended to be a definite voice, only it came out a little wistfully.

'But it's genuine Everett,' Evert said, the bottle tilted and poised in his hand. 'You won't get that every day in Banda, let me tell you.'

'I know. It must have cost you a pretty penny.'

'It did,' Evert agreed. 'Well?'

'Just one then. To tell you the truth, Evert, I was very drunk the other night and talked a mighty lot of nonsense. *You* must have got your iron head from your mother's side. I'm just like the old man used to be at Christmas-time with a glass of shnapps inside him. D'you remember?'

'I'm not likely to forget. I got him to promise me a new pair of skates one Christmas night. And how he swore the next day when I reminded him.'

He took a sip from his glass and turned back to the wall

with the cupboards. He unlocked the iron door which swung open with a heavy squeak and reached within. When his hand came out it was gripping some sheets of paper and a parcel wrapped in a bit of muslin. He locked the door again and laid the articles on the desk. Meantime Piet, swallowing hard, had thought, this is the moment ... and as Evert turned he said firmly, 'Well, I'm just like him. I promised you something the other night. And now I'm sober I'm not going to swear, but I'm just going to say that I can't keep my promise. I'm sorry, Evert, I knew it was a daft idea from the first ... but as I say, I was drunk, and you'll have to forgive me.'

'This,' said Evert, sitting down in his chair and drawing the parcel towards him with one hand while he pushed the lamp back with the other, 'is what I wanted to show you.' He gave no sign of having heard Piet's speech. 'There's an attorney at the Fort, and I saw him the morning after I talked to you and he's drawn up everything quite properly. Here is a letter to Mevrouw Van Goens. I did wonder whether it should be addressed to Egbert, but you say he's in the army, he might be anywhere and there's no time to waste, so I sent it to her. It explains everything and makes the formal proposal. This,' he lifted the second paper, 'is a marriage contract, as made for the best families, he assures me. And here,' he touched the third paper with his finger, 'is a draft on the Bank of Amsterdam.' He pushed the papers aside and unfolded the muslin. 'Now look at that, Piet. Isn't it lovely? Go on, look at it. See if you can open it.' He handed across the desk a square box of exquisite workmanship, ivory, inlaid with silver and mother-of-pearl, and some pink stone which Piet did not recognize. There seemed to be no hinge or clasp or spring, and when Piet had turned it about in his big brown hands for a moment he handed it back.

'It beats me,' he said.

'Turn it so that the big pink flower is uppermost. Now press the centre and slide the whole top towards you. You haven't seen anything yet,' said Evert, enjoying himself. Piet obeyed the instructions and the box opened smoothly. He blinked. Inside, bedded on velvet which exactly matched the ivory, there lay, jumbled by his turning and twisting of the casket, a mass of jewels, emeralds and diamonds, some as large as his thumbnail, some no bigger than a pin's head, but all of the first quality, all catching the light and flashing it back in blinding white and rainbow rays. He knew more about precious stones than one would have imagined, for he had smuggled them in his time and the finger with which he straightened the mass into its component parts was vastly respectful. There was a ring, a great square emerald set in small diamonds; a pair of ear-rings, each a large emerald swung from a diamond chain,

28

and a necklet of emeralds and diamonds set in flexible links of the pale fine gold of Kabistan.

'But it's priceless,' he said, a little breathlessly. 'I've never seen such stones, Evert, and I've seen a few. The ring alone is worth a fortune.'

'Look well against a white skin,' Evert said. His tone was deliberately casual, but it was plain, even to Piet, that he was pleased by the impression he had made.

'Last, but not least,' he said, lifting the remaining article from the muslin and then dropping again as though unworthy of Piet's notice, 'is the glove.' It was the custom for these far-off bridegrooms to send a glove which, solemnly placed upon the hand of the bride, was the final symbol of the marriage being solemnised. This glove was ornate and obviously made for the purpose; it was of white leather with a heavily fringed cuff and coloured embroidery upon its back.

'It beats me,' said Piet, whose eyes, after one glance at the glove, had gone back to the jewels. 'I know you're rich, Evert, I can see that. But I'm not a fool, and I know there's a limit to what a man can make, even out of nutmegs. I don't see how you can afford things like these.'

Evert's thick reddish eyebrows drew together in a frown, and for a second his pale eyes looked dangerous. Then he grinned.

'Perhaps I didn't buy them,' he said pleasantly. 'Besides, you must remember that I have been here for twenty years, and I lived very simply until I decided to build this house. And I often pick up things cheaply. I have done certain favours and have friends who drop me a word where bargains are to be found. Anyway, you may be sure that I came by those honestly, and you may carry them without any conscience qualms.'

'But that's just what I don't want to do,' Piet began laboriously. 'I know you can't see why, and I can't make myself plain. But honestly, Evert, I don't want to have anything to do with it. See? You've got everything all ready, and there'll be another ship in, next week or the week after, maybe to-morrow even, and you can get somebody to do the job for you. Do that and I'll wish you all the luck in the world.'

'But I want *you* to carry these for me. Surely that's the obvious thing, Piet. Why not? Are you afraid of Mevrouw?'

'Maybe. I don't mind admitting it. You've lived here for a long time, Evert, and perhaps you've forgotten that there's a caste system at home as hard as that in India. I think maybe I could carry the things if you weren't related to me, if you were a stranger; but your being related to me, and Mevrouw knowing all about it, I *know* she'd think I was an uppity fool who'd put the idea into your head. As I did. But I told you I was drunk. Can't you see, Evert, that for me to go and carry your

29

proposal would look as though the next thing would be my making a bid for one of the girls myself. As though I thought just because they are poor now ... It's no use, Evert. I just can't do it.'

Evert's highly-coloured face darkened to crimson and seemed to swell, and once again his eyes looked dangerous. Piet prepared himself for an outburst of rage, the grown-up version of those tantrums with which his half-brother had so often shattered the tenuous peace of the old farm-house. But Evert had learnt the value of self-control since those far-off days. Without speaking he reached out and took the casket, closed it with careful fingers, laid it on the glove and folded the muslin back into place. He shuffled the papers until their edges were meticulously even. Then he said, 'Well, if that's how you feel, Piet, I must do as you say—find another messenger. I'm sorry.'

'I'm sorry too,' Piet hastened to say. 'I'm very sorry, Evert, especially as I put the notion into your head and as good as promised to carry the things. But honestly, it'll be better for me not to have a hand in it. For one thing, I'm not very lucky.'

Evert had risen and was replacing the parcel and the papers in the iron-doored cupboard. With his back to Piet he said in an easy, conversational tone, 'Not? You surprise me. You've done very well. You've got to the top in your job.'

'That wasn't luck,' Piet said, looking longingly at the lop-sided bottle. 'Damned hard work all the way along. Damme Evert, I even went to school again. No ... of course not, I don't mean the whip-arse place the old man pushed us both into. I'd had enough of *that*. No, when I was about twenty I realized that I'd never hold Captain's rank unless I could navigate and reckon. And about that time the ship I was in captured a Portuguese privateer. My share of the prize money came to a hundred and fifty guilders. My God, that seemed like a fortune in those days. But I gave it all to an old professor in Amsterdam. He'd taught mathematics at Leyden, but he was such a soak he'd lost his job. Half his time he didn't know whether it was Christmas or Easter, he was so sotted. But he could do sums, and he showed me. And a lot of other things besides. Come to think of it, the one lesson I ought to have learnt from him I didn't. To avoid that,' he nodded towards the bottle, 'like the plague. I ought to have been warned. But I wasn't. So now...' some hazy memory stirred.... 'Did I tell you what happened last time I docked?'

'About the Directors sending for you and giving you a last chance?' Evert asked, resuming his seat and lifting the bottle invitingly.

'Yes. No. I mean yes to your question, and no to the drink. I did tell you? Then you see what I mean when I say I ain't

30

lucky. There's many a man that drinks more than I do and neglects his duty more often ... but I'm the one that's caught. See? And just the other day, meeting you and coming here ... I tell you, if it hadn't been for Gijs I'd have made a mess of it next morning with Kaerko. I'm in a queer position, Evert, like a dog that has had two of his three bites. One more ill report and I'm done.' He saw that Evert was giving his words sharp attention and thought I'm an ass to let him know all this: yet went on talking because the words seemed to make a barrier between him and the business which Evert had wanted him to do. 'Thank God Gijs is with me again. You know, it's a queer thing, that poor little man is grateful to me because he thinks I'm kind to him. And really, he's a kind of talisman to me, a mascot. I knew it as soon as I set eyes on him. An orphan he was, you know how they're sent to sea willy-nilly, poor little swine. If ever a brat was unsuited to the sea he was, but the minute I saw him I knew, the same as I know whether a thing is black or white, that he was lucky for me. So I took him out of the forecastle where he was having a hell of a life and made him my servant. And by God it has paid me a thousand times. And will a thousand more, I have no doubt.'

Evert, the selfish, unfeeling devil had refilled his own glass and was sipping at it. Abruptly Piet pushed his own forward.

'I'll have one more,' he said. 'After all, I'm a free man till we sail and Gijs'll see I'm not caught. By God, Evert, I envy you. They call me a drunkard; but if I'd drunk what you have to-night I'd talk like a fool for an hour and then sleep for a week.'

'When do you sail?' Evert asked, tilting the bottle. Piet told him. 'Then dine with me again on the Friday night, and I promise that we'll both have two glasses of shnapps and no more.'

'Thank you. I will, and gladly,' Piet said. He had thought that his refusal to do the errand would have alienated Evert; and once again he had the feeling that he had wronged Evert; that he himself was the surly, unfriendly fellow.

The farewell dinner was wholly delightful, and throughout its course Piet was acutely aware that, although to be honest, he had always reckoned himself a better man than Evert, he would have found difficulty in entertaining so royally a man, a near kinsman, who had stubbornly refused to do a simple straightforward errand for him. His feelings on the subject were so sharp and so self-derogatory that had Evert broken his word and provided just one drink more than the stipulated two, he would probably have said, 'Gimme all that tackle and I'll do the job for you after all.' But Evert, although he had provided a feast of delicious food, had kept his promise, and there were two glasses of shnapps apiece, one before and one after the meal. And the Van Goens were never mentioned, even by implication. So Piet salved his conscience with the assurance that Evert would easily find another person to do his errand and one who would do it far more worthily.

'Would you rather go afoot or by prahau?' Evert asked, when Piet, after consulting his formidable timepiece said that it was time he was getting aboard.

'I'll walk,' Piet said. 'I'll have enough of the sea after tomorrow. But there's no need for you to come, Evert. I'm sober, and I know my way now.'

'I'll come a step or two. I've had little enough exercise today,' Evert said. He had suddenly the air of a man whose mind was elsewhere, and Piet, noting it, thought, there, now that's over and Evert's finished with me; he's thinking about something else; he's a man of many affairs, many friends. And he thought, humbly, that it was very good of Evert, after all this time, and considering everything in the past, to have gone to so much trouble to make his stay in Banda so agreeable.

They came out into the hall. Evert, with a superb disregard for habit or climate, had built his new house in Banda as he would have built one in Holland, and from the hall, which was wide and paved and pillared with marble, a staircase sprang, curving and graceful, to end in a wide gallery from which the bedrooms opened. There were tubs of flowering shrubs and plants between the pillars at the foot and head of the stairs and at intervals along the gallery. Piet, who had been too drunk upon his former visit to take much note of his surroundings, wondered again where on earth Evert had found the money for such building. He began a professional reckoning in his mind as to the cost of transport of the marble alone. There were no marble quarries in the islands, he knew, for the *Eastern Venture* had carried, upon this very journey, a slab of that stone intended for a tomb for the daughter of a planter. And that one slab had cost something in freightage.

He was thinking this, and at the same time—clapping his hat on his head—congratulating himself upon being able to recognize his own headwear, which he had been far from doing last time he stood on this spot, when he saw, peering from behind one of the tubs of flowers in the gallery, a face. He was surprised to see it there and wondered whether it had been there when he first swept his eyes around the hall and gallery, or whether it had just appeared. It made him uncomfortable to think that he had been watched, even though his actions, leaving the dining-room, looking about the place, putting on his hat, were innocent and ordinary enough. Then, after this feeling of shock and discomfort, he became interested in the face itself. It was very pretty, though the expression it wore—a kind

32

of mischievous malignance—was not engaging. The small, brown oval face was lighted by a pair of great brown eyes, and topped by a head of sleek hair. Below the face Piet could catch a glimpse of vivid scarlet colour, and then the figure was obliterated by a great branch of flowers, dead white with dark glossy leaves.

Evert, who had been enjoying the glances of admiration which Piet had directed about him, saw the sudden stiffening of his pose, the fixing of the glance into a stare and followed the direction of it. Unseen by Piet, a curious expression came over Evert's face, part exasperation, part an almost fatuous doting, part the 'caught-out' look which comes upon a man whose secret is discovered; the fluid expressions hardened finally into the one most natural upon Evert's countenance—a complacent possessiveness.

'That's my Isa,' he said, pronouncing the name so that Piet, if called upon to spell it would have done so with a double e. Then, raising his voice, he called, in exactly the tone one would use to a favourite puppy, 'You naughty little thing! What're you doing up there? Come down and show yourself.'

She rose up from behind the flowery tub so that her head showed above the rail of the gallery, but not very far, for she was no taller than a white child of twelve, and moved, reluctantly yet with complete self-possession to the head of the stairs, paused for a moment and then slowly descended, making each step a gesture, as though aware that merely walking downstairs is one of the most graceful things a pretty woman can do. She wore the traditional Malay female attire, the sarong and little jacket which, even to Western eyes, had proved so attractive that most of the white women in the islands adopted it for indoor wear. The sarong was patterned in gold and scarlet, the jacket was of unrelieved scarlet; heavy gold ear-rings swung from her ears and both her slim wrists were loaded with bangles; her finger-tips and her lips were touched with colour which held its own even against the vivid background of her jacket. The old envy of Evert stirred anew in Piet's heart. 'My Isa' was a toy any man might covet.

'So you just *had* to peep at my guest,' Evert said in a jocularly scolding way. 'Well, I hope you are satisfied. This is Captain Odshoorn, a kinsman of mine.' Piet, staring hard at the girl, yet spared attention to notice that Evert avoided the use of the term 'half-brother' just as he himself had done, and thought, funny that we should feel the same about that.

Isa acknowledged the introduction with a graceful movement of her head and a smile which just disturbed the sulky curves of her mouth and no more.

'I thought it was a woman,' she said, speaking good Dutch with a soft, most attractive lisp to it. 'You made such a

33

mystery.'

'I told you to keep out, if you call that making a mystery,' Evert said curtly. 'And I've told you not to go upstairs unless I'm there. What woman were you expecting to see here, pray?'

She said, with what appeared to be the most disarming simplicity, 'The new woman.' She had lowered her lids over her great brown dove's eyes when Evert had started to chide her; now she lifted them and added, with an expression of extreme hatred, mingled with sly knowingness, 'Wang Fu spoke of jewels.' The red-tipped fingers flashed, touching a finger, both ears, sketching a circle about her own throat. She stared straight at Evert, they might have been alone in the wide pillared hall and Piet a thousand miles away.

Evert swore luridly. '—— Wang Fu,' he said, 'the talkative pox-ridden son of a yellow bitch. I'll give him something else to talk about to-morrow. As for you, haven't I told you time and again that as long as you were here you weren't to gossip in the compound. It's the curse of the islands,' he added savagely, suddenly remembering Piet and turning towards him, 'Yap, yap, yap, that's all they find to do, the — rogues. And what they don't know they make up. Wang Fu made up that tale, d'you hear me, trying to stir up mischief; and you were fool enough to listen to him. You deserve a good beating. Spying and gossiping like a slave. Get away. Get out of my sight.'

She stood her ground calmly and it was plain to Piet that, whatever else she might feel for Evert, she was not afraid of him.

'Then it was a lie? There is no new woman?'

'No. But there soon will be if you behave like this.'

'Then who were the jewels for?' she asked with the relentless illogic of the Orient.

'I tell you there weren't any,' Evert shouted. 'Any more than there was a woman here to-night. Look at him ... does he look like a woman. Such a coil about nothing.'

She took a step or two forward and said stonily:

'Wang Fu said ...' Evert lost patience, and with a curse laid one of his big brown hands on her narrow shoulder, spinning her round.

'Will you be quiet and get out! I tell you Wang Fu is a liar, or else you are. There is no woman; there are no jewels. You go back to the compound and don't come near me till I send for you. I'm ashamed of you.' He gave her a push which carried her across several paces of the marble-flagged floor, but she recovered her balance quickly and with considerable dignity, without a backward glance, she walked towards the door in the shadow of the staircase.

'Come on, Piet,' said Evert, slapping his hat on to his head

34

and tearing open the front door as though it had angered him. Slamming it behind them, he said savagely, 'That's a sample of native behaviour. By God I'll give that Chinaman something to remember to-morrow. She's a good little bitch, and it'll be the best part of a year before I'm ready to get rid of her.'

'Other people run brothels for sailors,' Piet said. 'It's easier than running your own, I reckon.'

'No truer word was ever spoken,' Evert agreed, linking his arm in his half-brother's. 'But of course there isn't the choice . . .'

'You're right there. Would you believe that once in Bandagor . . .'

They enjoyed a man-to-man talk about women and brothels, cheatings, trollops and doxies until they reached the first houses of the town. Then Evert, withdrawing his arm, but laying his hand as soon as it was freed on Piet's solid shoulder, said, 'Well, I've come further than I intended. I'll say good-bye here, Piet. I'm mighty glad to have seen you, I wish you the best of luck on your voyage and I hope to see you next year.' The hand moved in an affectionate squeeze with each phrase.

'I'm mighty glad to have seen you, too, Evert. And thank you for your hospitality. I'm sure I wish you the best of luck . . . in everything.' He gave the last words a special emphasis.

'Good-bye, then,' said Evert, and with a final squeeze, dropped his hand.

'Good-bye,' said Piet. He reached for Evert's hand and shook it heartily. As he did so there came to their ears the sound of running feet, and Piet, who found this moment of parting with the man whom he had hated, and yet liked, who had treated him kindly and who had borne no grudge at the breaking of an all-out promise, rather tense and emotional, lightened it by saying, 'Somebody in the devil of a hurry.'

'Coming this way, too,' Evert said, checked in his turning.

The moon, which had on Piet's return from Evert's house been embarrassingly bright, had waned, and the street ahead was full of the velvet darkness of the tropic night. The patter of feet on the hard-beaten road was punctuated by audible. hard-drawn breath before the figure of the runner was visible.

'None of our business,' Evert said, 'good-bye, Piet,' and turned, and had taken some steps in the direction of his home when Piet, who had for some reason sensed something ominous in the hurrying feet and the harsh breathing and therefore deferred saying his last farewell until the runner should be visible, said sharply, 'It's Gijs!'

At the same instant the runner, tumbling up out of the darkness, gasped, 'Is that you, sir?' and drew a breath like a sob.

'It's me, all right, boy,' said Piet, with a sinking of the

35

stomach. 'What's the matter? Trouble?'

'Ummm,' Gijs said, bending double to ease the stitch in his side and straightening up again, fumbling for Piet's arm. 'Kaerko's aboard, sir. My God, I don't know how to tell you, sir. They've found some unlimed nuts among the others.'

Converging impressions met like arrows driven from differing directions upon Piet's mind. There was the shock of horror —it was nothing less—which Gijs' words conveyed; and at the same time he knew that Evert, who must have heard his exclamation as he recognised the runner, had, perhaps out of delicacy, hastened his step, and was now several yards away. He felt as though the one person who could help him was slipping out of reach; turning his head he bellowed in a voice accustomed to giving orders through the roar of tempestuous seas, 'Evert, Evert. Come back!'

'D'you want me?' Evert asked through the darkness.

'By God I do,' Piet shouted, and was relieved to hear Evert's feet retracing those steps.

'What's the matter?' Evert asked in an ordinary voice as he drew near.

'They've found some unlimed nuts aboard my ship,' Piet said in a wooden voice. 'You know what that means?'

Evert knew. It was the very strictest rule of the islands, the rule upon which the whole security of the monopoly rested, that no fertile nutmeg should ever be taken away. Every nutmeg ever shipped had been rendered sterile by a steeping in lime water. The most stringent precautions—which included the search of every man returning from shore leave and the final tooth-combing of every ship before sailing—were taken to avoid the possibility of a single fertile nut leaving the islands. And such rules were the more easily kept for the simple reason that the planters, the captains, the merchants and the Agents were sensible enough to know that their jobs depended upon the preservation of the monopoly, while the more ignorant people, like the common sailors, found the dangerous unlimed nut difficult to come by. On every plantation the slaves gathered the ripe nuts avidly, for their food and other perquisites depended upon their results, and the nuts, once credited and handed in went straight into the lime bath. In the whole of the town of Banda Neira, which was all that the seamen ever saw of the islands, there was not an untreated nut to be found. And so, although the English, the French and the Americans in the young colonies would have been glad enough to pay fabulous sums for the germ of a possible new product, breaches of the Company's rule were rare enough to be phenomenal; and the few there were were punished with deterrent ferocity. Piet, standing in the warm night air, felt the cold sweat crawl upon his body as he thought of the result of

Kaerko's find.

'Good God,' Evert said, and then was silent. The situation was too serious for words.

After a minute Piet, wetting his dry lips with his tongue and swallowing with difficulty, asked, 'Where, Gijs?'

'With the others. But done up together in a white bag tied with blue twine. The Agent spotted it in a minute. What's this, he says, done up so irregularly? And pulls it out and opens it. You know the different look, sir. There was nothing I could do.'

'What could anyone do?' Evert asked harshly. 'You've no idea, Piet? You ... haven't ... been tempted to ... smuggle?'

'Dear loving Christ,' Piet exploded, relieved at finding a focus for his fury, 'what kind of a fool do you take me for? I've smuggled women, I've smuggled jewels. I've doubled my own trade privileges and packed my passengers. But would I be such an almighty, crass, bloody fool as to ship unlimed nuts in a white bag tied with blue twine? Would anybody? Evert ...' his voice dropped from the furious to the pitiable, 'is there anything you can do?'

'There might be just one thing,' Evert said slowly. 'It's a long chance, and I can't promise that it'll work.' He was silent for a moment, while Piet and Gijs waited breathlessly, like children awaiting an adult's decision, and adult's orders. 'You go back to the ship, Piet. There's nothing you can do except say that you know nothing about the things ... that is true, isn't it. If Kaerko claps you into gaol at the Fort, don't resist him. I'll do what I can. I can't make any promises. Don't for God's sake count on me, Piet. But I'll do the only thing that I can think of.'

His hand reached out and touched Piet's shoulder, but whether the gesture was one of reassurance or of pity no one could have told. And Piet was past speculation. Then he turned away and his first few strides took him into the covering darkness, though they could tell, by the sound of his footsteps that he had taken a side turning and was not going back to his own place.

'We'd better get back,' Piet said. 'Thank God I'm sober at least. Though I wish I'd a drink or two inside me. To face them with ...' His voice tailed off miserably. After a moment he asked, 'Have you any ideas, Gijs?'

'They were put there, to be found to-night,' said the little man with complete conviction. 'Probably Kaerko did it.'

'But for what possible reason?'

'So he could find them and report. Show what a good watch he keeps. It wasn't anybody of ours, sir. I am certain of that. There's not a more ...' he hesitated, for although he had for Piet a feeling very nearly akin to worship, it was a feeling far more easily put into actions than into words ... 'more popular captain on the whole ocean. Or again,' he hurried on, embarrassed, 'it might be an accident. Like that time at Surabaya when the governor's lady's laundry was shipped with the tea.'

That had been very funny at the time, but now the only feeling that the memory evoked was one of nostalgia for those old happy days before he had been under a cloud, before he had been sent to Banda with its dangerous, ingrown monopoly.

'I wish to God we were dealing with tea now, Gijs,' he said.

'Well, we're not,' Gijs said literally. 'Look, sir. If they take you to the Fort as *he* said, manage to take me too. I could make things a lot easier for you.'

'Fat chance I'd get of arranging that—or anything else,' Piet grunted. And he thought, I'd rather something had gone wrong in Holland. There is the law there; out here it's all Company; and I'm a Company's servant who's broken it's strictest rule, and I'll be flung into the Company's Fort with the Company's Agent out for my blood. I'll be lucky if I ever see Janshaven again.

They had reached the waterfront and Gijs stepped down into the waiting boat, released its rope and took up its oars. Following him Piet was conscious of a hitherto unknown impulse. Why not throw himself overboard. He might as well. He was in bad odour with the Company already, and he'd get no second chance. Stolid as he seemed, he was not devoid of imagination and he could see himself wasting away in some dark, rat-infested dungeon, probably starving or thirsting to death; or, after some farce of a trial, being sentenced to a whipping, or having his cheek slit and his tongue pulled through. Better be dead. There'd be no one to mourn him except his mother. who was an old woman, and Gijs who would quickly transfer his affection to anyone who was moderately kind to him. The thought quickened his self-pity and his throat thickened.

'Mynheer Haan,' said Gijs' voice, answering his thought out of the darkness, 'had something in mind. He walked like someone who knew where he was going.'

Piet's body, unconsciously tensed for desperate action, relaxed. Of course, he must give Evert a chance. And of course to drown himself would be, not only cowardly, but almost an admission of guilt. He could imagine the gossip in the places where seamen gathered. ... 'Poor old Odshoorn! Tried to smuggle unlimed nuts and then couldn't face the music!'

The usual watch was on duty aboard the *Eastern Venture*, but there were also two soldiers, stocky little Indonesians in the Company's uniform, standing on guard by the head of the ladder.

'Your name, please,' one of them asked.

'Captain Odshoorn,' said Piet, dismally.

'Mynheer Kaerko awaits you in your cabin,' the little soldier said.

Kaerko, with an expression of determined distress upon his nondescript little face was sitting bolt upright in Piet's own chair. There were two other men with him, one, a big sallow-complexioned person, Piet recognised as a fellow-diner at Kaerko's table; he lolled very much at his ease, on the end of Piet's bunk; the other, wrinkled and brown as a nutmeg, sat on the small bench below the open porthole.

As Piet entered, blinking at the light, Kaerko rose.

'Your man volunteered to find you, Captain,' he said. 'And no doubt he told you why we are here.'

'Yes,' said Piet. 'And I want to say straight away that I had no knowledge of their being aboard. I didn't bring them myself, and I didn't...' a word he hardly knew he knew popped into his mouth, 'I didn't connive at their being brought aboard.'

The three men looked at one another with a 'what else could he be expected to say' expression. Piet felt trapped and helpless. What use were protests? Anyone, even the guiltiest, would say exactly what he had just said and exactly what he was prepared to say.

'You have no suggestion? No suspicion of anyone?' The big man asked the question with the air of one trying to be scrupulously fair, scrupulously just.

Piet shook his head. The crew were all searched when they returned from shore leave. He had no enemies in Banda that he knew of. He had supervised most of the loading himself.

'We have questioned the crew,' Kaerko said. 'No one admitted having seen or handled the bag which is distinctive enough to be memorable. In the circumstances, Captain Odshoorn, bearing in mind the rule that the captain is responsible for everything aboard his ship, we have no choice but to arrest you. I do that now, in the presence of two members of the Company's administrative staff.' He glanced towards the bunk and the bench and the nutmeg-faced man stood up smartly and spoke for the first time. 'You will accompany me to the Fort. Mynheer Kaerko will continue with his inquiries and you are assured of a fair trial.' The words rattled out like little stones. He put to his lips a small silver whistle, like a child's toy, and blew upon it. Hard, bare feet rustled on the companionway, and the two little soldiers stood at attention by the cabin door.

'To the Fort,' said the brown-faced man, nodding at Piet, who stood dumb like a cornered animal.

The little men stepped forward smartly, closing in on either

39

side. And the thought went through his head that he should have drowned himself. There was no way out of this. How the goddamned nutmegs had got aboard was a mystery, but it wasn't likely that anyone was going to explain it. Talk of a fair trial was utter rot, how could there be a trial when there was no defence? And what could Evert do? What could anyone do? A captain was responsible for everything aboard his ship ... that was the first thing a seaman learned; and the most deadly form of contraband had been found aboard his. He was not even resentful against Kaerko, or Sallow-face, or Nutmeg. They were simply doing their duty.

He turned in silence, forgetting the one favour he had been told to ask—that Gijs might accompany him. At the foot of the companionway one little soldier stepped ahead, the other waited, and Piet mounted between them. Kaerko and his two companions brought up the rear. It was the same at the ladder. Two prahaus, each with a lantern at its prow, appeared out of the darkness. One soldier descended, Piet followed, the second soldier completed the load; Kaerko, Sallow-face and Nutmeg stepped into the second craft and they shot away, one slightly ahead of the other towards the quay. Now, Piet thought, from the depths of his misery, is the time to put myself overboard; but as soon as he stirred four little iron hands gripped him, and one of the soldiers said in a lisping, but ferocious little voice, 'You will sit still, please.'

They came to the quay, which, fifteen minutes earlier, had been utterly deserted. Now, under the lantern which hung just above the landing stairs, there was something which gave the impression of movement, and the sound of women quarrelling. Piet was too sunk in his own misery to take much notice of what was going on, but he gathered that women were quarrelling because someone was sobbing and someone else was speaking in a high, shrill, reedy voice. Speaking Malay, too, of which Piet had only a smattering; but he recognized a few terms of abuse, which, for some reason are the most easily and quickly acquired in any language. The shrill voice was accusing somebody of being a rogue and a fool, a careless devil and a maker of trouble. The person who was thus accused made no reply but simply wept noisily.

The foremost prahau in which Piet was travelling drew into the steps and one soldier alighted; Piet followed, and the second soldier stepped up alongside. The trio waited until the second prahau had discharged its load.

Nutmeg immediately joined his men. 'All right, Kaerko,' he said abruptly, 'I'll go along with them and just...' A shrill, almost delirious cry from the left interrupted him.

'Mynheer Kaerko, Mynheer Kaerko,' cried the voice so recently raised in invective and now changed to abject pleading. 'A moment please. I have been to your house and no one knew where you could be found, Mynheer, please ... it is of the utmost importance. A great injustice may be done to somebody unless you listen.'

The group of moving shadows advanced, splitting up into its component parts, just distinguishable in the dim light, one bulky figure wrapped about in yards and yards of white cotton cloth which reminded Piet of grave-clothes, and two ordinary, barelegged natives.

'Shal Ahmi,' Kaerko said in a low voice and in the manner of one tried beyond all endurance. Then, in brisk, yet not disrespectful tone he said, 'Look, Shal Ahmi, I can't stop now. I'm very busy. I have business on hand. If you really want to see me about something of importance, come to my office in the morning.'

The bulky, wrapped figure, came another step forward and the womanish voice said, 'But Mynheer, this is your business. Company's business.' He brought out the significant word in long, separate syllables.

'Damned impostor,' said Nutmeg-face, moving around Piet and the little soldiers like an impatient sheepdog rounding up a flock. 'I can't wait, Kaerko. Good night. Good night. Vehmeer. Come along now, quick march.'

As Piet moved forward between his guards he heard the shrill voice saying, 'Mynheer, this fellow came to me because he dared not tell his master.... Come forward, misbegotten, and show your face.... Mynheer, perhaps you recognize him, Mynheer Hoogenbeet's trusted house-slave ... *trusted* ... and was ever trust more misplaced?'

'I can't interfere between a slave and his master, Shal Ahmi, you know that,' Kaerko said. And that was all of the conversation which was audible. Piet, the two soldiers and their commander, marched briskly towards the Fort, the ominous dark bulk of which showed dark, with slits of light here and there, against the night sky. But they had gone only a few dozen yards when there were bellows behind them. Nutmeg-face said 'halt,' and began to retrace his steps. In a few seconds his whistle sounded, and the two little soldiers, turning Piet between them and maintaining their places on either side, scuttled back. Kaerko, Vehmeer, Shal Ahmi and the soldiers' master stood in a close knot on the quay under the lantern. The two slaves hovered in the background, and the one who had been weeping was weeping again.

'A most peculiar thing,' Kaerko was saying, 'and most providential. We must get to the bottom of this. We'll go to my office.'

He began to walk, with quick, agitated steps towards the gap in the warehouse buildings that gave upon the street. The

41

sallow-visaged Vehmeer fell into step beside him; Nutmeg-face, pushing the soldiers and Piet ahead of him, followed, and Shal Ahmi with his two attendants, the one still sobbing like a child, completed the procession. Kaerko's house was only just behind the warehouses, a flat-faced building flush to the street with a front door reached by three shallow steps. Before they reached the house, Piet's dazed, battered mind had realised that, judging from that sudden recall, Shal Ahmi's errand had some connection with his own business, and just as they reached the steps he turned his head and asked, 'Is it something to do with those nutmegs?'

'How should I know?' the brown-faced man snapped.

Kaerko's office, a big square room, lined with shelves and containing three large tables all covered with papers, was just inside the front door. He took up a candlestick which stood on a chest in the hall and led the way in. Piet found himself halted upon almost the very spot where he had been standing on that day when Evert had come into the Agent's office and found him there. How long ago that seemed. Kaerko went round lighting candles, and when the room was almost as bright as by day, he waved Vehmeer and Nutmeg-face to seats by the largest table and dropped down into his own chair wearily.

'Now, Shal Ahmi, let's have the whole story again. You tell it. That snuffling fool would confuse Solomon.'

'Of your kindness give me permission to be seated, Mynheer,' Shal Ahmi said. And then, without waiting for Kaerko's confirmatory nod, he dropped to his haunches, saying, as he did so, 'I have been far to-day, and was but sitting down to my food when this squawking scourge of humanity arrived. I was half tempted to leave the matter until the morning, but as you know, the White Lords' business is very near my heart.' Very leisurely and with the greatest self-possession he arranged the folds of his spotless white clothing. Piet looked at him with burning interest. He was a stout man, almost fat, but so smooth and sleek, so symmetrically rounded that to call him fat would have wronged him. He reminded Piet of a seal. His head and face were entirely hairless, but the state looked so natural to him that he was no more truly described as bald than as fat. In colour he was a darkish olive, but his nose was aquiline and his lips thin, and his eyes entirely devoid of the Mongolian cast which distinguished so many of the mixed inhabitants of the islands. And his face was entirely without expression, smooth and blank as a clean slate.

'Cut the cackle, Shal Ahmi, and tell us everything you know,' Kaerko said. He sounded impatient, and yet, despite the 'cut the cackle' not disrespectful. And indeed, Piet thought, still staring at Shal Ahmi, there was about him something,

42

some queer dignity and power, very difficult to assess, and yet certainly capable of blunting, or even turning, the edge of any insult.

'They come to me, you know, when they are uncertain or in difficulty.' The roll of the hairless head included the two miserable creatures who had taken up positions behind him, and beyond them all the coloured people of the islands. 'And this misbegotten had done great mischief as you shall hear. Mynheer Hoogenbeet entrusted him with certain special nutmegs—how were they wrapped? Lift up your head and speak boldly, you gossiper in your master's time, you sleeper in public places. . . .'

'In a white bag, tied with blue twine,' said the man who had been weeping.

'In a white bag, tied with blue twine,' Shal Ahmi repeated. 'As is known to you all, it is a habit with the perkiniers to plant seeds from trees not their own, for so the stock is strengthened and Mynheer Hoogenbeet had entrusted this precious seed to this rogue to carry to Mynheer Vandenbosch in Lonthoir . . . for if it is good to change seed between plantation and plantation, how much better between island and island? And what does this fellow do? First, with the bag in his hand he meets this one and upon the wharf they talk for an hour under the midday sun. Then he is weary, much chatter has dulled his brain, so he puts the bag safely, as he thinks, on top of other bales on the quay and goes to sleep. When he wakes the little bag is gone. Where he does not know. But by questioning he learns that the other bales were carried aboard the ship while he slept. And what does he do then? He goes back to his gossiping fellow and says, great grief will come to me, for my master will beat me, what shall I do? And his partner in mischief, knowing Mynheer Hoogenbeet's strong arm, bids him come to me for advice. I am weary and my stomach within me is clamorous for food; but I know as perhaps these ignorant ones do not, the danger of the seed nutmegs lost between ship and shore. So I say, 'I will go to Mynheer Kaerko and perhaps, in gratitude because the thing has been reported and no time lost, he *may*—but of course I can promise nothing for who am I to say what the White Lords will do?—be lenient. *Perhaps* he will get back the bag and I myself will take it to Mynheer Vanderbosch so that no anger may be roused and no beating done. It is well known that the Honourable Company does not approve of beating. Though, were they in Mynheer Hoogenbeet's place, they too would see the value of blows. And I should say that I myself did beat him, not lightly. Because I do not like heavy business to disturb me at my supper.'

The thin, womanish voice ceased. Piet drew great breaths of relief, feeling as though an iron band, forged around his chest by Gijs' announcement an hour ago, had burst and released his lungs.

'So that's how it happened,' Kaerko said. His voice betrayed the greatness of his relief. 'It was damned carelessness, which might have had the most unfortunate results. And it's given Mynheer Vehmeer, Mynheer Knoel and me a very unpleasant evening.'

'*And me*,' said Piet, with such emphasis that everybody turned and looked at him.

'My dear fellow,' Kaerko exclaimed. 'Of course. But please believe that our sufferings were on your account. I shall have a word to say to Hoogenbeet about this.'

'Please,' Shal Ahmi interrupted. 'Mynheer, I know that this is your business, but if I may be allowed one word, to report the matter would be a mistake now. How then is this careless, long-tongued fool the better for coming to me? He came to ask my help to save himself. So many do that ... all the little foolish ones. Look back Mynheer and think how many little quiet words have reached my ear alone. If, now, either Mynheer Hoogenbeet or Mynheer Vanderbosch know how nearly those nutmegs were lost, this foolish one will be beaten. That will not matter, he will be the better for it, I have no doubt. But word will go round that to tell Shal Ahmi is to tell the world, and no more little quiet words will come to my ear. The loss, I think, will be greater than the gain. Mark, I could promise nothing, but I *did* say, "If you come with me and tell everything, it will be better for you." And how better if he is beaten after all? Is that plain. Mynheer? Would it not be better for me to take the little bag to Mynheer Vanderbosch and say that this one has a pain in his belly and could not finish the errand? You see, he must be back by sunrise, his errand apparently fulfilled. No real harm has been done. You could doubtless find the little bag if you looked carefully aboard the ship.'

Kaerko seemed to hesitate. The sallow-faced Vehmeer spoke first.

'He's right, Kaerko. They all trust him, and we benefit by their trust. This is an instance. We might drop a general hint about care in sending these sample seeds from place to place. Anything more specific would be a mistake.'

Knoel, he of the Nutmeg face, whose name had proved to be 'Turnip,' a grave misnomer, stood up and said briskly, 'You won't want me any more then?'

'No,' Kaerko said. 'I'm sorry you've had all this bother. You see the force of his argument?' He nodded towards Shal Ahmi. 'We won't say anything about this, outside....'

'You know what I think of Shal Ahmi and everything to do with him.' Knoel snapped. 'But what I think doesn't count. You gentlemen run the place and only send for me when you

44

get in a mess. Come on, you. Back to barracks.'

'They won't talk,' Kaerko said, it was more a question than a statement.

'God bless you, they never listen to anything but orders. And I don't give them time for compound gossip. Good night, Vehmeer. Good night, Kaerko.' He turned, most surprisingly, to Piet and said, with a smile that wrinkled his face more than ever, 'Good night, Captain. I'm glad you've been cleared. Personally, I never thought you looked like a smuggler. But then, as I said before, what I think doesn't count. Good voyage.'

Shal Ahmi, who was seated near the door, rose and stood aside. Knoel and his two little soldiers stepped out briskly.

'We have your leave to go?' Shal Ahmi asked. 'These are not supposed to be wandering in darkness and my supper will now be cold.'

'Stop by my kitchen,' Kaerko said, 'and eat your fill, Shal Ahmi. I am grateful to you for what you have done to-night. Give him the bag will you, Vehmeer. It won't be needed for evidence now.'

'These, also, have missed their supper. And it would be a good thing to reward frankness,' said Shal Ahmi, indicating his two companions. Kaerko laughed. 'Get along then. And say that I said you could have one drink of tapi apiece. One, no more, remember.'

'The hospitality of gratitude is very sweet. Good night, Mynheer,' Shal Ahmi said, hustling his fellows before him, much as Knoel had done.

'Good night,' Kaerko said. And then, turning to Piet and Vehmeer, he spoke in a different, relaxed, cheerful voice. 'And now I think we should drink too. I'm sorry the thing happened, Captain Odshoorn, but I'm sure you understand my position. And the outcome proves, doesn't it, that Knoel and the rest of them are wrong about Shal Ahmi. He can be very, very useful.'

He opened a cupboard as he spoke and took out a bottle of Marsala and three glasses.

'Who is he?' Piet asked curiously.

'Shal Ahmi? It's rather difficult to say. A kind of holy man, I suppose,' Kaerko said vaguely. 'The natives set a lot of store by him.'

Vehmeer, whose voice was soft and rather pleasant, said, 'To appreciate him properly you need to have lived here before he came ... as I did. You see, Captain Odshoorn, the labour situation here is unique. There are no Bandanese *natives*. Most of them died fighting Coen; a great number more Coen killed in the effort to subdue them and make them work, a few got away to the Kei islands. I'm told that they've settled in two villages called Banda Elat and Banda Eli, where they still carry

45

on with their pottery and ironwork, which they say is the best in all the East Indies. When I ... and Evert Haan and a few other old originals took up our grants, the nutmeg groves that were still standing were just rotting for lack of labour. The Company imported slaves from all over the place, Java Siauw, Amboina, anywhere they could spare a few. And there's nothing—or rather there was nothing—to hold the creatures together.' Vehmeer warmed to his subject, cradling his glass of wine between his hands and leaning forward over it, speaking eagerly. 'They weren't of the same religion, some were Hindu, some Mohammedan, some had been turned Catholic by the Portuguese, and some were just wild pagans; they weren't of the same blood or the same language. There was nothing you could get hold of, nobody you could treat with and say, "Look here, if you'll see the work's done and the rules're kept, we'll see that you get your pickings." That's how you can talk to a native chief or a Chinese headman. It makes things a lot easier. We had the devil's own job for a year or two, and then Shal Ahmi arrived. What exactly he is or where he came from, nobody really knows, but nobody cares because he has got the measure of the native foot. Even the Chinese fear and respect him. All the coloured people, whatever their private creed, firmly believe that if he curses them they're finished, and it is a remarkable fact that one or two people who have offended him have come to funny ends. I don't think I'd willingly offend him myself. I don't say I'm superstitious, but I should sort of expect things to go wrong if he really got busy against me. What d'you say, Kaerko?'

The Agent looked uncomfortable. 'It isn't that so much,' he said, after a little pause. 'But he is clever, very shrewd, and a very good friend of the Company's. Look at to-night. But for him we'd have Captain Odshoorn in the Fort and the business of finding a master for the *Eastern Venture* on our hands. Even if Hoogenbeet reported the business—supposing that little yellow fool was found out, which he wouldn't be till Hoogenbeet and Vanderbosch met, and even then Hoogenbeet mightn't bother to tell me—look at the waste of time. Over and over again I've found Shal Ahmi a very present help. Knoel hates the sight of him, and I don't think your cousin, Mynheer Haan, approves of him much, Captain Odshoorn.'

'Maybe he'll change his mind after to-night,' Piet said. Thus reminded of Evert he began to wonder what steps his kinsman had taken to help him. Was he busying and worrying himself at this moment? And from Evert his mind flew to Gijs. He must get back and put that poor little devil out of anxiety. He stood up.

'Well,' he said, 'I'll get back. I still feel a bit muddled in my head. But I'm happy to think I'm sailing in the morning after all.'

Kaerko, looking at him, thought merely what a good thing it was that a first-rate captain was not out of commission. Vehmeer, of a more fanciful turn of mind, thought that the big man looked like an ox which, after one blow from the poleaxe, had escaped from the slaughterhouse. It would be days, he thought, before the captain really realized the narrowness of his escape.

'Good night,' Piet said. The two men shook him by the hand, wished him a good voyage. He stumbled out to the waterfront and found Gijs, half demented, walking up and down on the quay.

'Holy Christ,' he exclaimed, gripping Piet's hand in his, which burned and shook as though from a consuming fever, 'I've been so worried. I went up to the Fort, but they said you weren't there, and I didn't know whether they were lying or not. Why didn't you do as I told you and ask if I could come?' Before Piet could answer the question he gabbled on, 'What happened? They've turned you loose? Did they find who put the things there?'

'Yes. It was an accident. It's all right, Gijs. Everything's all right. Let's get back to the old tub.' He was too tired to tell the whole story just then. He wanted to get back to his ship, to walk into his cabin and find it completely his own again, to wipe out, by a normal arrival, the shocking memory of Kaerko, Knoel and Vehmeer occupying his chair, his bench and his bunk.

But when a few minutes later, followed by Gijs, he descended to his cabin, there was still something strange about it. A woven basket of native workmanship tied at the top with thongs and bearing the official seal which showed that it had been inspected and passed for lading, stood on the table where, so lately, the damning bag of nutmegs had lain.

'What's this?' Piet asked.

'Oh, that came just after you'd gone. A Company runner brought it. I'd have brought it with me, but I thought if they'd got you in the Fort they might take it away from me before they let me in.'

Piet sat down at the table and drew the basket towards him. Gijs knelt at his side and began to remove his boots. The thongs untied easily. In the basket was a bottle of the Everett brandy which had cost Evert a 'pretty penny'; and a smaller basket containing some choice fruit; and below there were certain papers enclosed in stout wrapping, a muslin-wrapped bow, and a glove. At the very bottom of the basket was a single sheet of paper upon which were written these words:

'If you are at liberty to do my errand you will not, I trust, think that I ask too much.'

Piet stared at the words, but while his eyes were busy with them his ears were hearing Evert say, 'I'll do what I can.' What had Evert done? Was it possible that Shal Ahmi and the two natives with their carefully concocted tale, had been Evert's tools? Their arrival on the quay so apt and timely, their story so simple and conclusive.... He remembered suddenly Shal Ahmi's arguments against letting Hoogenbeet and Vanderbosch know of the accident. Of course ... because Hoogenbeet had never sent the sample of seed to Vanderbosch. Evert had made up the whole story, selected his actors and got them word-perfect and staged the whole thing in less than an hour.

'My God,' he said aloud.

Gijs looked up inquiringly.

'Ko-bet Haan must have been a mighty clever woman,' Piet said to Gijs' further bewilderment. 'It must be her head he inherited ... I'm sorry, boy, you must think I'm crazy and it's a wonder I'm not. Take a look at this. That ... half brother of mine I was telling you about is sending them to the lady of his choice. Aren't they wonderful?'

He worked the secret spring of the box and flashed the jewels before Gijs' eyes. The little man looked at them without interest.

'Your feet are like stones,' he said solicitously. 'That's shock. I'm going to get a bucket of hot water and you're going to put them in it.'

As soon as he was alone, Piet returned the glove, the inlaid box and the papers to the basket and tied the thongs. Then, padding on his stockinged feet, he carried them to a hiding-place under his bunk. He was too tired, too much exhausted by the events of the day to have energy enough to imagine his feelings, when, despite all his protests and doubts, he would carry them along to the bleak white house and face Mevrouw and perform Evert's errand. But he knew that he would do it.

Seven months, two weeks and three days later, dressed in his best, his beard brushed glossy and his spirit fortified by two glasses of shnapps which was as much as he dared take in case he muddled his head and brought disgrace upon his family, he set out from the trim little cottage in Heydberg and walked towards the Van Goens' house. In his hand he carried the basket with its thongs untied; the edges bulged, for, on top of the articles which Evert had committed to his care was a three-pound packet of tea and as much pepper, cinnamon, mace, cloves and nutmegs as could be bought in the grocer's shop for seventy guilders. For some years, ever since Piet had attained captain's status and gained the privilege of carrying a limited amount of merchandise for his own private disposal, he had, at each homecoming, made a little offering to Mevrouw Van Goens. The idea had been his mother's. Sophe Odshoorn had never forgotten that a Van Goens' lady had spoken up for her at the time of Jakob Kressle's decision, and gratitude, combined with pity for Mevrouw's fallen fortunes, overlaid upon the traditional, almost instinctive feeling of respect for the family, had produced an attitude almost of worship in the ex-washerwoman's heart.

Piet, aware of, and to a degree sharing, this feeling of his mother's, had forborne to mention to her anything about his errand. He had, in fact, not mentioned Evert at all. It would have given Sophe no pleasure to learn that her supplanter's bastard had made a success of life and grown to be a rich man. As for hearing that Evert planned to make an alliance with the sacred Van Goens family ... how saltily she would have cursed the upstart, how vigorously have forbidden Piet to have anything to do with such wicked nonsense. So, on this mild spring evening, she watched Piet set off on his errand with a feeling of pride that it should be *her* boy who was carrying Mevrouw enough of the best tea to last her for four months, and who was proving that, though the old feudal ties were broken, somebody still remembered his manners and his duties.

Old Truitje, the one servant who remained with Mevrouw and who did almost all the work in the bleak white house, greeted Piet as usual. She remembered him from the Janshaven days and her old eyes always twinkled as she punctiliously called him 'Captain.'

'Ha, a basket this time, too,' she said, stretching out her hand. 'Very pretty, and very useful. Thank you very much, Captain.'

Piet swung the basket out of reach. 'You can take this, and this ... he said, handing over the tea and the spices. 'And later on you can have the basket. But just at the moment, Truitje ... I ... would it be convenient ... could I speak to Mevrouw for a moment?'

'I should think so,' said Truitje, looking at him and then at the basket, curiously. 'Come in, and I'll ask.' Piet stepped over the threshold and stood in the dark passage. Through an open door he could see the kitchen, with a small fire in the great black stove and Truitje's old rocking-chair, and the cat curled up on the rag rug and the pot of almost-open hyacinths upon the windowsill. So homely-looking, and with such a homely smell too; and he remembered the kitchen quarters of the big house at Janshaven, with the menservants and maidservants tumbling over one another: he wondered if Truitje found life lonely. He thought his idle thoughts desperately, as he had been thinking for quite a long time, of any matter, however trivial and silly, which would take his mind off the fact that, at last, he must look Mevrouw in the face and hand Evert's papers to her, and watch her gracious smile wither and the look of furious anger and insulted pride take its place. Even in this last moment he was tempted to turn and slink out of the house before Truitje came back; and then he remembered the moment when Knoel and the two little soldiers had turned towards the Fort at Banda Neira, and the voice crying after them in the night, and the sweet feeling of resurrection which had come with the telling of Shal Ahmi's story. So he stood in the dim passsage, looking solid and stolid and slightly stupid when Truitje hobbled back to say that Mevrouw would be very pleased to speak to him.

He followed the old woman the length of the passage and into a square, stone-paved fall which, even on this mild spring evening struck very cold. Truitje opened a door, and Piet, with a stomach-shaking spasm of nervousness as he had ever felt in his life, stepped into the candle-lighted room, clapped his hat to his waistline and bowed above it.

Mevrouw was still some months short of forty, but grief and anxiety and what counted to the once-pampered beauty as privation, had aged her. Save at the extreme ends, where a glint of gold still lingered as though in mockery, her plentiful hair was snowy white, and the delicate pink-and-white porcelain surface of her face was scored with a myriad lines, many of them graved by discontent and peevishness. But the perfunctory social smile with which she greeted Piet and bade him be seated, was dazzlingly sweet, and the big man's stomach quaked again as he thought how quickly and completely his mission would remove it.

'Truitje tells me that you have brought me some tea, Captain Odshoorn,' Mevrouw said, seating herself upon a small, straight-backed chair and folding her slim white hands upon her silken lap. 'It is indeed very kind of you.'

'Not at all, Mevrouw. A pleasure, I assure you,' said Piet, hearing his own voice, stiff and wooden. Did she think he had pushed his way into her drawing-room merely to collect a personal word of thanks? Horrible.

'I trust you had a pleasant voyage.'

'Thank you, yes, Mevrouw. Less sickness than usual, and no accidents.' Covertly his eyes, which he averted because he was conscious of a desire to stare at her face, took in the details of the room. To his eyes, accustomed to cabins and cottage rooms, the room seemed large, and sparsely furnished. Everything in it was old and worn; and he guessed, correctly, that everything which had been of value had gone the way of the

50

other Van Goens' property. He tried to hearten himself by thinking of Evert's beautiful house, so full of comfort and evidence of its owner's wealth; but the thought made him feel worse, not better. It occurred to him that the only marketable thing left to Mevrouw was the desirability of her daughters and he had come, like a huckster's errand-boy, to make a bid for that. He cleared his throat as quietly as possible and plunged into speech before any further thoughts should come into his head to discourage him.

'Mevrouw, I have come to do an errand which I find little to my taste. Before I begin I want you to understand that it was forced upon me, and except to say the words and hand over the stuff I have no part in the business at all.'

The wary look which comes easily to those whose confidence in life has once been shattered flashed into Mevrouw's still-blue eyes. Had some creditor chosen this method of presenting his case, counting upon the big man's chance of gaining access to the house?'

'My last voyage took me to Banda, Mevrouw,' Piet plodded on. 'Do you remember Evert Haan, my father's other son?'

'Indeed I do. Your father wanted him to take on the tenant rights, but my dear husband's father never approved of that marriage you know, so he refused to make the arrangement. If it had been *you*, I think he would have overlooked the ...' she checked herself on the verge of saying 'illegitimacy' and tactfully substituted 'the little unusualness.' Then she leaned forward and said, quite sweetly, but with great earnestness, 'You do realise, don't you, Captain Odshoorn, that even if I wished to do anything for your half-brother, I am quite powerless now.'

'Oh yes, Mevrouw. That's all forgotten. Evert didn't stay in Janshaven, he didn't want to be a farmer after all. He went to Banda, and took up nutmeg planting. The long and the short of it is, Mevrouw, that Evert has made a fortune, and he ... at least I ... I mean ... look.'

Finally bogged—as he had known he would be—he gave up the effort to explain the position, opened the basket, took out the papers, the box and the glove, and laid them upon the little table which stood between the chairs upon which he and Mevrouw Van Goens were sitting.

'Evert said they made everything clear; he got an attorney to draw them up. I really only had to deliver them, but I thought you might not even remember who Evert Haan was. So I ... well, you'll see for yourself, Mevrouw, and there's no need for me to take up any more of your time.' He got to his feet, ready to bid her 'good evening' and retreat in good order. But Mevrouw, who had opened the wrapping of the papers, was reading the uppermost paper with eyes that seemed not to take in the words quickly enough. Without looking up she freed one hand and waved it in a gesture which ordered him to sit down again and not speak until she asked him to. Unwillingly he obeyed her.

Now that she was reading he was emboldened to look at her closely, studying her face, awaiting the inevitable flush of anger, the sparks of fury that would inevitably flash from those blue eyes. But Mevrouw read on, reached the bottom of the page, laid it aside, took up another. She read every word of the letter and of the marriage contract, and then absorbed the particulars of the banker's draft in one greedy stare. When she had done she touched the papers so that their edges were level, and leaned back in her chair, her head resting against its high narrow back. Upon her forehead and chin and around her nose there were patches of pallor and Piet, studying her face as he studied his compass for direction, or the sky for signs of bad weather, was afraid for a moment that the shock had made her faint. And he thought to himself that of course he had been a fool to expect her to grow red in the face, to glare and shout at him. She was a lady. She would not rail like a fishwife, she would quietly faint, or else wither him with a few controlled, icy words. How could he know that Mevrouw, leaning quietly back in her chair, was breathing up the most heartfelt prayer of thankfulness?

When she did speak she asked the question which he had secretly dreaded all along: the question he had tried to avoid by removing himself before it could be asked.

'Who brought my daughter to Mynheer Haan's attention, Captain Odshoorn?'

'I'm afraid I did, Mevrouw,' gasped Piet, sweating coldly. 'But I swear no such idea was in my mind. We were ... we were talking about Janshaven and the old days, and I said, in all innocence ... I do beg you to believe me, Mevrouw ... in all innocence I said it, that Mynheer Adriaan, whom Evert remembered, had three lovely daughters. Mevrouw, you must forgive Evert; he has lived abroad where things are very different, for a long time, and in Banda he is reckoned an important man. He is very rich. And Evert always did have big ideas, Mevrouw.'

Mevrouw's face remained inscrutable. Suddenly Piet realized that she had seen only the papers. He leaned forward, ripped the muslin wrapping from the box, fumbled with the spring, worked it at last, and then, getting to his feet, laid the open box with its glittering treasure, in her lap. He heard her draw her breath sharply. But she stared at the jewels without making any comment, and when she spoke her voice was steady. 'Show me please, how the box opens and closes.' Piet showed her. She opened and closed it several times as though to make

52

certain that she had mastered the secret and then stood the casket on the table.

'And that, I take it, is the glove.'

Piet nodded. She did not look inside the wrapping. Piet had remained standing, and Mevrouw now rose to her feet. She held out one hand.

'Captain Odshoorn, whatever comes of this, I am deeply grateful to you. Naturally a decision of such magnitude cannot be made in a hurry or by me alone. As soon as anything is decided I will let you know. Meanwhile, may I ask one favour?'

'Certainly, Mevrouw. Anything.' He was so relieved by the reception of his errand, so grateful that she had let him down thus lightly, that there was nothing he would not, at that moment, have done to repay her for her restraint.

'Then don't mention this matter to anyone. In a small place ... you know what gossip is ... and a young girl's reputation ...' She left the sentence incomplete, obscure, but Piet felt as though he had been honoured by a confidence.

'I haven't mentioned the business to anyone, even my mother. And not a word shall pass my lips. You may depend on me, Mevrouw.'

'I'm sure of that,' she said. And she gave him another smile, warm, friendly, a smile which struck away the years and the graven marks of anxiety, discontent and self-pity. 'Good night, Captain. I shall see you again.'

'Good night, Mevrouw.' He made another bow and got himself out of the presence. Dusk had fallen during the interview and outside the dark blue sky was scattered with stars and the air smelled of green things growing. For the first time since he had docked he felt the uprush of joy and well-being which always came to him on shore leave in Holland. He would have said that he loved the sea, but buried deeply in him was the farmer whom Evert had driven forth from his familiar acres and the scent of a cow byre could still rouse more feeling in him than all the Moluccas in full bloom. He was perfectly happy to-night, his task was fulfilled, his debt to Evert paid; now he could begin to enjoy himself. Mevrouw, being a lady, would probably write Evert a chilly little refusal, and if she should ask him to carry it, together with the rejected jewels and glove back to Banda on his next trip, well, that would be an errand more to his taste. Now that he had discharged his debt of honour he was free to think of Evert as a presumptuous dog who needed a good knock on the nose. In a very cheerful frame of mind he rolled into his favourite tavern with the comfortable assurance that if he were unable to walk home plenty of friendly arms and shoulders would be at his disposal; his mother would be neither surprised nor disgusted;

and the sacred Company would have no grounds for complaint.

A week passed, and four days of another, and there was no word from Mevrouw. Most likely, Piet thought, when he reckoned the speeding days and the little time left before he must return to Amsterdam to see to the *Eastern Venture*'s refitting for the new voyage, Mevrouw would scorn to return her answer by the hands of a common sea-captain. After all, the Van Goens, though fallen in fortune, were well-connected, and probably young Egbert knew somebody, high in the army or in the Company, who could convey the scornful refusal, and most likely a neat snub into the bargain.

It was with a feeling of surprise as well as disappointment that, returning home from a happy day's fishing, he received from his mother a message the Mevrouw Van Goens would be much obliged if he would call upon her at any hour between six and nine that evening.

'Truitje brought the message,' Sophe said, twittering with curiosity. 'I asked her what Mevrouw wanted to see you about, and she said she hadn't the least idea. Have you?'

'Maybe she wants something taken out, or brought back,' Piet said, avoiding his mother's eye and snatching his beautifully laundered shirt from the back of the chair upon which it had been airing before the fire, and hurrying away with it to his bedroom.

He was afraid, as he neared the house, that Mevrouw would have assembled a whole family to witness the discomfiture of Evert's messenger. A bevy of aunts and uncles, Egbert, perhaps even Annabet herself. Well, there was only one thing to say, and that he had already said to Mevrouw herself.

But Elsa Van Goens was alone, just as she had been on the evening when he had first entered her house. And her manner was even more affable.

'I hope I'm not making too many demands upon your time and your kindness,' she began, as soon as he had lowered himself cautiously into a chair. 'But in any case, as Mynheer Haan's kinsman, I feel that you will understand.'

'Yes?' Piet said. There, he thought, she's laid the fuse. Now for the spark and boom! Out on my ear I go. I knew how it would be.

'I sent for my son,' Mevrouw's sweet low voice continued. 'He, and other members of the family, talked the matter over thoroughly and advised me on the final decision. A reply was despatched to Mynheer Haan by the *Great Holland*, she sailed on Tuesday. That should, normally, have been the end of the business so far as you are concerned, Captain Odshoorn. But my daughter has taken a fancy to see you.

Quite understandable, if you come to think about it. You have actually seen, within these last few weeks, the man she is to marry . . .'

'To marry? You mean,' his blue eyes blinked at her, blank with astonishment, 'that you accepted Evert's proposal.'

Mevrouw's slim white hands moved in a little deprecating gesture.

'Not, I should tell you, without considerable misgiving. Banda is *so* far away. I shall lose my daughter so entirely. But Captain Odshoorn, *my* feelings must give way to the question of what is best for Annabet. I will be frank with you, and admit that in my place, a widow, in very straitened circumstances, with three daughters, one of my gravest worries has been the thought of what will happen to them. When I am gone . . .' She added the last words with a piteous little look, implying that while she lived the girls would lack nothing, her own self-sacrifice would see to that, but that the end was near now. Piet shifted uncomfortably in his chair. Mevrouw sighed. Then she braced herself and said more firmly. 'Mynheer Haan's proposal was properly made, acceptable in every sense. My son visited one of the Directors of the Company who gave a very favourable account of his position and character. We did not act rashly. I think'—she put her head on one side and regarded him inquiringly—'I think you feel perhaps that we have been a little rash?'

'No,' Piet said. No, he was certain that the family gathering had decided nothing in a hurry. Everything would be considered. Under all this lacy foam of mother love and anxiety, the rock of practical consideration lay firm and rooted.

Why, now that he was close to her, being offered her confidence, treated like a friend, was his feeling for Mevrouw undergoing a change? Why, when she spoke of being a widow in straitened circumstances had he felt not the expected pity, but a kind of embarrassed scorn? Why did this whole interview stink of humbug?

'I don't reckon I favour glove marriages much,' he said bluntly, answering his own questions aloud.

'I'm not sure that I do either,' said Mevrouw in instant agreement. 'But after all, this isn't quite an ordinary one. We do know something about the bridegroom. And you are here to tell us more. That is why Annabet is so set on seeing you. She wants to know what he looks like . . . all the little intimate personal things.'

Oh, but this was worse than being chucked out on his ear! He'd been steered into carrying the damned papers and the parcel for Evert; now he was being tacked into giving Evert a character.

'It's little enough I know about him. Till I saw him in Banda

55

I'd not run across him for thirty years, Mevrouw. I can't say what sort of husband he'd make.'

He had a vision of Evert's hands gripping the brown girl's little narrow shoulders. But you couldn't hold that against him. Any man, exasperated, would use that much violence. And you couldn't hold the girl's presence against him either. Any man who'd lived in the islands for twenty years would have a mistress of some sort. Or something worse, thought Piet, remembering the insolent, painted, be-jewelled little boys he had seen.

'Of course not,' Mevrouw agreed again. 'I think nobody knows what sort of a husband a man will become, except the woman who marries him. And often enough she does the making, you know.' The sweet smile flashed out and was gone again. 'You had heard, perhaps, Captain Odshoorn, that my daughter had been ill?'

'No. I'm sorry to hear that.'

'Oh, she is better now; well on the way to complete recovery. But being ill, of course, has made her fanciful and low-spirited. I look to you to cheer her up a little. You can tell her about Banda. I believe it is a beautiful place.'

'Very beautiful. And Evert has a fine establishment.'

'That's the kind of thing, Captain Odshoorn. I want her to realize that really she is a very lucky girl.'

Piet's mind, which held a certain shrewdness in its home-spun simplicity, could see through *that* well enough. The family was in favour of the match; the girl was dubious. He was to spin a yarn that would set her doubts at rest. It was disgusting. Mevrouw was a greedy humbug, and Evert was a greedy upstart. And between them the girl stood defenceless. He thought of the sweetness of the face which had beguiled the dull sermon hour for him, and something like real physical pain smote his heart. It was his fault. He'd done it. Opening his great mouth when he was drunk. Better to have got soaked in a tavern and got wrong with the Company.

Mevrouw rose and pulled the bell-rope.

'Annabet's looks have suffered through her illness,' she said, casually over her shoulder. 'But we ignore that. She'll recover them in time.'

The bell had evidently been a prearranged signal; for now the door opened quietly and somebody entered. Piet jumped to his feet and then stood, struck dumb, staring.

Later on in the interview he realized that the girl was still recognizable, just as some old people are recognizable to others who knew them in youth; but at the first glance, in that first horrified moment, he thought that, had he not been expecting Juffrouw Annabet, had he passed this apparition in the village street or seen it in church, he would have thought the poor girl

56

a stranger.

She was, literally, nothing but skin and bone, so skeleton thin that the very gristle of her nose could be traced by its pressure against the skin. Her dress, new and elaborate, ruffled and padded and much befrilled, hung limp and empty like a gown suspended from a peg. And all that marvellous wealth of down-pouring yellow hair was gone.

True, no effort to make her presentable had been spared. The hollow cheeks had been painted, the pen-sharp nose and bony forehead and stringy neck were powdered pearl colour, her mouth was as red as a rose. And upon her head she wore a little cap of velvet matching her gown, edged with lace and looped with ribbon. But—like the stiff, rich gown—the paint and the powder, the little cap all tailed in their purpose, made, in fact, grotesque what was simple tragedy.

Piet, still staring in horror, was recalled to his senses by Mevrouw's voice, even, sweet, ordinary; and realized that he was expected to take his part in this elaborate, horrible, harlequinade.

'Annabet, my dear, here is Captain Odshoorn. He has kindly come to tell you everything you want to know about Banda. Come and sit down.'

Piet bowed in his clumsy, inexpert fashion. Annabet inclined her head stiffly and came slowly across to the chair which her mother pushed forward as though to shorten that jerky wooden progress. But she's lame, Piet thought wildly. She's lame, and her head's a bit on one side; my God, it's as much as she can do to sit down. He felt sick. He wanted to get up and shout at Mevrouw, tell her to put the skeleton child to bed; ask her, with curses, how she could ever have been so mad and wicked as to contemplate for one moment sending this pitiable wreck to Banda or anywhere else as the wife of Evert or any man alive. It was obscene.

But the *Great Holland* had sailed on Tuesday, carrying Mevrouw's reply. Nothing could alter that now.

Mevrouw Van Goens felt that the silence had lasted long enough, and leaned forward ready to speak again, when Piet, also aware of it, said gruffly, 'I shall be glad to tell you anything I can, Juffrouw.'

'I shall be very grateful,' Annabet said, and gave him a half-smile, a formal, rather plaintive recognition of his desire to please. Her mouth was still pretty, he thought. Too large, of course, in that narrow wedge of a face, but pretty. She leaned back stiffly in her chair and folded her hands—no more substantial than a bird's claws, in her lap, and waited.

So I'm to begin, Piet thought frenziedly. But what do I start with? It'll be like making a speech, and I've never made a speech in my life. I could answer questions, though I don't fancy that much, either; but I can't just begin talking about Evert and Banda, out of the blue as it were.

Mevrouw leaned forward again. 'Captain Odshoorn says that Banda is a very beautiful place,' she said promptingly.

'Indeed? I am glad,' Annabet said.

'Oh yes, indeed. One of the prettiest places I've seen. And I've seen many places.'

This interview was not of the girl's seeking, he decided. And could you wonder? What room could there be in her mind for anything but the fact that she had been pretty, and was now as ugly as sin, and was going to be married off to a man she'd never seen and who was expecting a beauty? Her mother ought to know better than to imagine that anything I could say about Banda or Evert or his damned house could do anything to cheer her.

His thick brows came together in a scowl and he turned a baffled defiant, almost sulky look on Mevrouw, who countered it with a sweet smile.

'Tell her about the house, Captain Odshoorn. It sounds delightful, Annabet.'

The girl gave him grave attention as he jerked out the bald description of Coenpark, how big it was, how pretty, how quickly the garden was getting settled. Sounds as though I'm boasting about Evert's house, he thought suddenly, and stopped, embarrassed. Her eyes at least were beautiful, he realized. Such a deep blue, between dark lashes, each one just tipped with gold, the colour her hair had been. Oh what, on God's earth, could have happened to that lovely, lovely girl? What could have stripped off all the flesh, stiffened every joint, taken away all that beautiful, beautiful hair?

'And she won't be lonely, will she, Captain Odshoorn? It's a civilized place, plenty of white women, a social life of its own. Quite a gay place, I believe I remember hearing.'

A gay place. Piet felt sick again. Evert had wanted a pretty, young well-bred wife to sit at one end of his table. He'd said as much. *She* would have had a gay life. But this poor wreck. What in the name of God would he do with her ... suppose she survived the voyage? Maybe that was the answer to the whole problem. She really looked hardly able to hold together here, on firm land. Picture her in a storm ... why, she'd just fall to pieces.

'Captain Odshoorn says ...' said Mevrouw, relentlessly prodding him forward again, 'Yes, Truitje, what is it?' The door had opened an inch or two and the old woman's face, wearing an expression of urgency, was poked around its edge. Mevrouw rose and went over swiftly. All Piet caught was the hiss of a whisper, but it sounded the knell of an intolerable situation. He jumped to his feet and said with finality, 'I don't think there's much more to say. I'd best be getting along.'

'Sh,' said Mevrouw, hushing Truitje. 'No, please don't go, Captain Odshoorn. I won't be a minute. It's just that I .... All right, Truitje, I'm coming. Annabet, offer Captain Odshoorn a glass of wine. We were so engrossed in his delightful account that we forgot the wine. I must hear more about the place. I'll be back in a minute. ...'

She rustled out of the doorway. Piet, who had risen, sat down again, awkward, defeated. He glanced at Annabet and saw that, all in a minute, she had come to life. That was it. Up to that moment she had not only looked like a deathshead, she had been dead, just a stiff, wooden-jointed, painted thing with Annabet Van Goens' eyes and mouth. Now, despite everything, she looked like herself.

'You are disgusted by this whole business, aren't you?' she said. 'I'm sorry. I do apologize. Mamma—you see, she has to pretend to herself so often. It gets to be a habit. She's pretending now that everything is all right. Do forgive me speaking to you like this. Really, I get so puzzled that at times I'm almost distraught. And I'm forgetting the wine ...' She rose stiffly.

'Juffrouw, please don't bother. I don't ...'

'Ah, but please. Look, it's Truitje's very best. Rhubarb. As good as any French wine, I assure you. And Mamma meant it all so well. You were to tell me all the nice things about Banda and about Mynheer Haan—your cousin isn't he? And then we were all to drink—my health, I suppose. It just happens that you and I aren't very good at pretending, but we must try.' She gave him a smile that was quite dazzling upon that ravaged face, and Piet knew another pang. Ah, but she's lovely still, and friendly and real. But will Evert see that? Always supposing that she gets as far as Banda.

She hobbled towards him, a glass of pale yellow liquid in either hand. He accepted his, held it up, ceremoniously, and said earnestly. 'To your happiness, Juffrouw.'

'Thank you. Thank you very much.' She was silent for a moment. Then she said, 'You were shocked when you saw me. I have been very ill, you know. Entirely through my own fault, too.'

She must hang on to that belief or she would be overwhelmed again by self-pity and come to hate Klara, whom she loved. She must remember that she had gone to the Ice Fair on Whitwater of her own free will. But as she spoke the whole sequence of events flashed before her. Klara seizing upon this chance to meet her secret lover. 'Do come, Nab, you'd enjoy it, too.' And the winters so long and dull, nothing happening. Mamma saying that young ladies could not possibly go unescorted. Her own almost automatic protest, 'Surely Mamma, three of us together. In the daylight. And out of doors.'

Mamma, weakening at that, anxious really for them to be happy, seeing in her mind's eye the three girls, aloof, arms linked, skating through the torch-lighted hours of the brief afternoon. Klara's wild gratitude.... 'I'll do something for you one day, Nab.' And the brief, pitying thought, what could you do for me, you silly girl? Maria protesting that she would rather spend the afternoon by the fire, too young to be in Klara's confidence, too languid to know Annabet's desire for something, anything to vary the days. Maria overruled, bribed, Klara saying, 'You can have my coral necklace.' Herself offering her fur hood, 'You *can't* be cold in my fur hood.'

So they had gone, and in the first five minutes Klara had snapped a skate strap and retired to the bank of the Whitwater, hidden by all the booths and the people. Annabet and Maria had skated together to keep warm; and all the time Annabet had been thinking: what can she see in him? What is it that attracts her to that uncouth, hot-handed, stammering young man? Maria had worried about Klara, and Annabet had several times declared that she could see her among the crowds, now at this booth, now at that. Finally, when the early dusk was falling and the sky reddened behind the barrier of dark snow clouds, Annabet allowed Maria to leave the ice. 'I saw Klara a second ago by the roast chestnut stand,' she said untruthfully. That was the place of meeting arranged before the skate strap broke. But Klara was not there when they arrived, and it was Annabet's turn to grow anxious about her. Maria was for combing the crowd, but Annabet said, with apparently senseless obstinacy, 'No, it is better to stand still in one place.' Snow began to fall, a few annunciatory flakes at first, then a veritable storm. Maria started to cry from cold and anxiety. The crowd began to disperse; the roast-chestnut vendor packed his barrow, and without the warmth of his little brazier the dusk seemed to grow colder and more menacing. Suppose, Annabet thought, Klara has run away with her young farmer, eloped, like the heroines of the books that they read secretly in their room after Mamma had paid her good-night visit. Maria said through her tears, 'After all, your cloak is fur-lined, Nab. I'm perishing of cold.' 'Have it,' said Annabet violently, and swung the garment from her shoulders on to those of her sister. If Klara had really run away she would be glad to be dead of cold, partly because Mamma would most surely hold her to blame for leaving Klara alone for a moment, and partly because without Klara and the shared jokes and secrets, life in Heydberg would be insupportable. She stood and shivered for several moments before Maria, still snuffling and muffled to the ears, remembered that she was wearing two cloaks.

'All right, give me yours then. Would you like to run home

60

by yourself? It isn't far, and there'd be lots of people going that way.'

'But what should I say to Mamma?'

'Tell her we missed Klara in the crowd and that I waited for her.' Mamma would approve of that. Maria had not yet reached the age which made a solitary walk after dusk so undesirable.

Klara appeared, breathless and apologetic, five minutes after Maria had gone. Annabet's rebukes were forced from between chattering teeth. The shoulders and sleeves of her bodice had been wetted by the snow before she took Maria's cloak, and her feet were soaked because her shoes needed soling. But as they dashed away through the twilight in the hope of catching Maria before she reached the house, she managed to say— since Klara seemed dazed and capable only of apologies which lacked the ring of sincerity—'If anything is said, we'll say you said roast *potato*, and I mistook it for roast chestnut.'

But nothing was said, because by the time they had run home, overtaking Maria on the way, Annabet was shaking and shivering so violently that nobody in the house had time to think of anything but warm blankets, hot possets of black-currant tea and bricks wrapped in flannel. And then there had been the days of fever, the delirium, the copious bleedings, the cutting of the hair, partly to relieve the burning head, partly because it was already falling out so fast and partly because it was a recognised process in fever cases. And then there had been the awful return to life, the knowledge of beauty van-quished, the protruding bones, the cropped head, the pain and stiffness of certain joints which remained after the full tide of pain and stiffness had receded.

But she must say that it was her own fault. Because, beside the danger of self-pity and the danger of hating Klara, there was another reason. Father Vincent had spoken of the way of acceptance, and although, like many other things he had said that had been a little vague and mysterious, she knew that it meant not blaming others for the results of your own folly, it meant lying down, not rebelling, not trying to wriggle out of things.

So now she said, 'Entirely through my own fault,' and saw the look of pity upon the big weather-beaten face opposite, change to something else.

'The doctors hold out the hope that I may, in time, get really better,' she said quickly. 'It's such a pity that *this* should have happened before we had time to know. I suppose that when you were talking about me—Mamma said you were the person who spoke of me to Mynheer Haan—you said I was, well, you know ... all right ... like other girls. He'd ask you surely, what I looked like.'

'I said you were beautiful,' said Piet thickly.

She pressed her hands against her mouth, and he saw her eyes close, pressing against the tears. Oh God, this was as bad as, no, by Christ's wounds it was worse than, that moment when the nutmegs were found in the cargo. If he'd taken his bad luck, then he wouldn't have been in this position now. So brave, fighting back tears at this moment, so charming—with a charm Evert wouldn't see, handed over just because of the blasted money, and too late, too late to say anything.... Except the truth.

'Juffrouw, I said you were beautiful. And you are beautiful. You've been ill and the sickness has wasted your flesh. But your eyes haven't changed. Nor your mouth. And your smile is beautiful still.'

'But the stiffness? You mean to be kind, Captain Odshoorn, and I thank you for it. You see, I've seen no one outside my family since it happened—since this awful thing happened to me. And my family is so divided. Egbert, my brother, and my sister Klara are against it, against the marriage, I mean. Everybody else says it is a marvellous chance for me. They talk of the rest I shall have on the voyage, and of the warm climate. And the alternative which Mamma suggested, seems worse to me.'

'And that, Juffrouw? What was the alternative?'

'Mamma has a cousin, she rules a house of Poor Clares in County Down, in Ireland. She would accept me. But Captain Odshoorn, I have no vocation. It was truly, a choice between the two. Cheating God or man. My illness cost a great deal. I'm useless. Naturally Mamma is anxious to settle my future. It was Ireland or Banda. I chose. Was I wrong? Captain Odshoorn, I know this isn't what you expected, you didn't come here to deal with this kind of thing, it isn't fair to ask you ... but there is time still. I'm not married yet. I'm so puzzled and bewildered ... I don't know what to think or what to do.'

Not a convent, not a house of Poor Clares in Ireland. You'd be wasted there. You're skin and bone and stiff in your joints, but by God I'd marry you myself, to-night. Daft as it sounds, you have something better than prettiness, you make a man your friend. There's something in you that'd be wasted in a convent ... something that made me pick you from across the church ... that hasn't gone with your pink and white flesh and your yellow hair. Stripped of them all, you're still the woman that we dream of when we're hundreds of miles from any woman. The woman who meets us fairly, the friend.

He was amazed by the lucidity and force of his thoughts; and appalled too, because none of them could be put into words. He must sit like a stuck pig, thinking these true but

62

unutterable things, while the girl's eyes sought his, appealing. For what? Comforting words? Words of advice? He had none. Oh, if only he could have said, I brought you into this position, I'll get you out of it. Oh, if only he could have offered some other alternative. Something that would have been right for her mind and her body. The present choice was too harsh, too wide. The Convent would be best for that poor shattered body, there was no denying that; yet everything that was Protestant in him, as well as his own vigorous lust for life rose up and cried—no, not that! Yet there was Evert, soon to hear that his suit had found favour, soon to be preparing for a young, pink and white and golden bride.

'Juffrouw,' he said at last, thickly. 'Is there no third way? Must it all be decided in such a hurry? Given time . . .'

'I might get well. But by that time the chance of making an advantageous marriage will be gone. I do see the force of Mamma's arguments. To one in her position, daughters, even when they are sound and well, present a great problem. If only . . .' She pressed her hand to her mouth again, fought and conquered the weakness of self-pity, and then said, quite brightly, 'Haven't you noticed that directly you have made a choice the alternative seems more attractive, or at least more sensible. I'm quite sure that if I had decided upon going to Ireland I should be just as certain that I had chosen badly. Please don't look so distressed, Captain Odshoorn. I had no right to talk to you like this. I'm sure you have bothers enough of your own. And it was most kind of you to come to tell me things. Could you describe your cousin for me?'

'Well,' said Piet, gathering his scattering senses. 'He's much my build. My colouring, too, now I come to think about it. But he's much handsomer. He always was a good-looking fellow, and he's kept his looks. From what I could see during my visit, he's very popular too.' What could you say about Evert? If only you could be sure that he would be kind . . . but then, could you really count on any man being kind in such circumstances?

Mevrouw had opened the door and entered, so quietly that when she spoke Piet jumped nervously, wondering how long she had been in the room, and how much she had overheard. Only the last sentences he decided, judging from her pleased and complacent look of approval.

'If what you say is true, Mynheer Haan must be almost *too* handsome, Captain Odshoorn. Well, Annabet, it's time for you to take your last little walk around the garden. We mustn't neglect your exercise. Then Truitje will have your milk ready. We still treat her like an invalid,' she explained with a smile for Piet.

He was being dismissed, too. He rose. A sneaking feeling of

63

relief made itself felt. After all, it wasn't completely his fault. Granted he'd been drunk when he spoke of the girl to Evert, but he hadn't known what had happened to her. And the match was obviously very welcome to Mevrouw; and if the girl had been in her usual health and looks, everybody would have been head over heels with delight about it. He'd made the match, but he wasn't responsible for the flaw in it. It was stupid of him to feel so badly about it.

Annabet moved stiffly towards him and held out her hand.

'Good-bye, Captain Odshoorn, and thank you so much. I do hope that whenever you come to Banda you will look on my house as your home.'

His great brown fist closed over the little claw-like hand, and as it did so a pang that was half pain and half pleasure shot through him. And with it came a determination which made his heart hammer at the thought of his own audacity. He said good-bye, wished her a rapid recovery and great happiness, in a voice that was suddenly breathless. He watched her heart-breaking progress to the door, and then, instead of taking his leave of Mevrouw as he was plainly expected to do, closed the door and turned back.

'Mevrouw, you can't do this to her. It isn't right. It isn't decent.'

'Why, Captain Odshoorn, what are you talking about?' Her manner, her voice, remained unruffled, but the pupils of her blue eyes had narrowed to pin-points and she looked like a startled, defensive cat.

'Sending her to Banda like that. Evert's a man set in his ways and masterful, he likes to get what he wants. And what he wants, what he expects is the lovely young girl I told him about. May God forgive me for it. He'll be so shocked and disappointed, he might ... he mightn't even be kind to her.' His whole heart cried out in the last words.

'What utter nonsense,' Mevrouw said, quite lightly. 'Annabet may be perfectly well by the time she reaches Banda. And even if that is too much to hope, there is surely no reason to suppose that her husband would be unkind to her. I have known men to be devoted to extremely unattractive women. Haven't you?'

'Yes. If they chose them that way, or watched them get that way through years of living together. But, Mevrouw, put yourself in Evert's place for a minute. Wouldn't you feel cheated? And a man who's feeling cheated isn't very good company.'

Mevrouw's face hardened.

'You are saying some very strange things, Captain Odshoorn. Cheated. Why should the man feel cheated? He wished to marry my daughter, my second daughter, Annabet

64

Van Goens; there was no stipulation that she should be beautiful, or supple, or even in good health. So why should he feel cheated?'

'I put it to you the wrong way,' Piet said humbly. 'I always do put things the wrong way. I wasn't thinking about Evert's bargain being a bad one. She's too good for him. That's what I'm trying to tell you, Mevrouw. It's her happiness I'm thinking of.'

Mevrouw fenced again. 'That is a very strange thing to say, surely. You, Captain Odshoorn, are the person who suggested this marriage in the first place. If Annabet, with her superb looks and good health and high spirits wasn't too good for your cousin six months ago, how can she be too good for him now, when her looks are gone and she is moody and difficult? What exactly do you mean?'

'She'd have held her own with him, then. That's what I mean. Evert was never a one to be content with second best. He'd never handle a cracked thing or a weak thing carefully just on account of it being cracked or weak. He said to me, Mevrouw, when I said I didn't favour glove marriages, that all he wanted was a pretty, high-born wife to grace his house and do him credit. Is he going to take kindly to ... to your daughter? Will he try to make the best of a bad job? Look beyond the outside? Try to make her happy?'

'Really, Captain Odshoorn, your questions are very confusing. One takes a gamble on one's husband's disposition with any marriage. Women have to learn to make themselves agreeable; to adapt themselves. Annabet may fail to provoke the adulation to which she has been accustomed, but that, in a degree, is her own fault. Her illness was the direct result of a silly, headstrong action upon her own part. Having ruined her looks, *I* think that she is a profoundly lucky girl to have found a husband in the only way possible. Surely you agree upon that?'

'No, I don't. I reckon she's found the worst possible husband in the worst possible way at the worst possible time. But I can see there's no use talking about it now. Your mind's made up.'

'My mind *is* made up. You forget that I have the future to think of, and two other daughters. On the other hand, I have not been hard on Annabet, or forced her. There was an alternative. My cousin, Mother Francesca, was willing to overlook her Protestant upbringing and accept her as a novice. Annabet had her choice. I said to her, "If you don't want a husband, if you want to give way to your affliction and retire from the struggle, go to Ireland." She chose Banda and marriage herself.'

'But did it have to be decided now?'

'Most certainly. You brought the offer of marriage; her illness and its result had provoked sympathy and interest in my cousin. Two such offers might never come again. Refuse both, and what does the future hold?'

He could think of no answer. So he got to his feet again and stood there, a big clumsy figure, bothered, well-meaning, baffled.

Mevrouw sprang up lightly.

'I'm sure we both worry unduly, Captain Odshoorn. Marriage is always a serious step. But Annabet is gifted with a certain amount of sense, and despite the way in which we are forced to live, I have done my best to train her to take her place in the world. She can still talk amiably—when she likes. She was in a bad mood this evening. She understands housekeeping; she is musical; she embroiders beautifully. In many ways she will be an admirable wife. And the doctors assure me that fundamentally her health is good. As to her happiness'— Mevrouw made the same little gesture with her pretty hands, and her face softened into its plaintive expression again—'we all have to make our own happiness. Isn't that true?'

Hard as the nether millstone, he thought despairingly. But what could one do? And then suddenly, to his own amazement, the hasty, embarrassed, audacious words were out, audible on the startled silence of the room.

'Mevrouw, if it's a question of money ... I'm not a rich man ... but I earn good pay, and I could make more if I set my mind to it. I've nobody in the world except my old mother, who saves a penny for every halfpenny she spends. Sixty guilders a month, Mevrouw, would that be any help? I could manage it easy for a year or two, till you saw how she shaped and had time to look round. Aw, I know I'm forgetting my place, it's not for me to suggest such a thing to you ... but for the poor little girl's sake, Mevrouw, sink your pride and think it over. Nobody'd ever know.'

Now he had done it. The cold fury which he had been dreading and expecting ever since Evert laid bare his plan, was coming into action after all. Levelled, not at Evert, but at himself.

Mevrouw drew herself to her full height. Her eyes flashed, just as he had imagined them doing. The voice that came from the hard-lipped mouth was icy with hauteur.

'Captain Odshoorn, the kindest thing I can think is that you are intoxicated. I have never heard such a ludicrous proposal in my whole life. It is enough to make me wonder whether your cousin's success hasn't gone to *your* head. I prefer not to think that, so I will adhere to my original suspicion. I wish you good evening. Truitje will show you out.' She tugged at the bell and swept towards the door.

'Mevrouw, I'm dead sober, and you know it. Would you

have left me to talk to your daughter if you'd thought I was drunk? It's just that I'm speaking the truth to you; and fine ladies don't like the truth when it comes from rough seamen. I don't blame you for that. But this thing you're doing is the cruellest, wickedest, wrongest thing I ever . . .'

But Mevrouw was gone, and there was Truitje lumbering up, her face alight with curiosity and suspicion.

Within two minutes he was out in the sweet evening air again. As he walked from the gaunt white house he had a curious feeling of physical ill-ease, as though he had bruised himself, or roughly torn a nail. He wriggled his great shoulders inside the clean, freshly-ironed shirt, ran his hands down his thighs, shook each leg as he lifted it, but the uncomfortable feeling persisted.

He turned into his favourite tavern, and the men who were his cronies and sycophants, because he was on holiday and was generous and had money to spend, crowded about him. But even when he had treated everybody and become very drunk himself, when he was beating time to the songs they sang by smacking his pewter measure against the chimney breast, the feeling of ill-ease lingered. It was like nagging toothache. He shouldn't ever have mentioned the girl to Evert. He was to blame for it all.

BOOK TWO

'THAT,' said Captain Vehk, handing Annabet his glass and pointing ahead, 'is Banda. See the Fort?' Annabet nodded. 'See that little fishing boat?' He indicated a small craft with orange-coloured sails running rapidly before the wind. 'She's taking in the news of our arrival. Your husband will be ready to greet you.' He looked at the girl beside him with eyes in which curiosity and affection and another emotion, not so easily named, were mingled. By God, he thought, how I loathed the very name of her, how I laughed to myself when she first came aboard, and here I am, downright sorry to part from her. I wonder what the husband is like ... if he isn't good to her his neck should be broken, and I'd like to be the one to do it.

Annabet went on looking through the glass, holding it steady with hands which seemed too frail to support its weight. And Captain Vehk, standing ready to receive it back, let his mind run over the weeks of the voyage and the weeks which had preceded the sailing. Egbert Van Goens had gone to the Company's offices in Amsterdam and asked for a passage for his sister, and the Directors who had not yet ceased from gloating over the downfall of the U.E.M. which had transferred all the Van Goens' money into their own coffers, had taken a whim to treat the daughter of a fallen rival more than generously. They had sent for the captain of the *Java* and overwhelmed him with orders and instructions, together with so many hints on behaviour that he had thought, disgruntled, anybody'd think I'd never carried a female passenger before. Aboard the *Java* a bulkhead had been neatly removed so that young Mevrouw Haan had a cabin twice the size of his own. A special consignment of luxuries to supplement the ordinary fare was brought aboard; and, since the young lady was recovering from a serious illness, three goats, one recently kidded and the others due to kid at different dates during the voyage, were driven on to the deck and housed in a temporary pen. The Agent who thus made certain that Mevrouw would have milk every day, neglected to provide any fodder for the animals, and Vehk, who had watched and supervised all these preparations with cynical displeasure, had half a mind not to call attention to the omission but to turn the goats into a savoury stew during the early days of the voyage. But he had been in the Company's service since he was a boy of ten, and attention to duty had become ingrained into the texture of his being, and before the *Java* sailed there were some neat trusses of hay covered by a tilt on the deck, near enough to the pen for convenience and not near enough for the goats to help themselves.

He was certain in his mind that this special passenger was a spoilt darling, the kind who would weep over the least discomfort and complain over nothing at all. She would be seasick, she would make constant demands for hot water, she would encroach upon his time and attention. He hated the very thought of her.

Annabet, escorted by Egbert and the friendly Director to whom Egbert had first applied for her passage, came aboard at one o'clock in the afternoon. The *Java* was to sail with the turn of the tide at about half-past two. And as soon as the formal introduction had been made, Vehk's feeling of dislike—not dispelled—was tinged with wry humour. All that fuss about a thing like that! It was ludicrous. He had been told that Mevrouw Haan had been a participant in a 'glove marriage' and was going out to Banda to join her husband, and following the trio down to the cabin, he wondered what lay behind the apparently normal situation. Had the bethrothal been made long ago, when presumably the creature had some flesh on her bones? Or was it purely a marriage of convenience? Had she a fortune? He had heard of her first as Mevrouw Haan and did not connect her with the family which had been ruined by the U.E.M. (about which he knew plenty, for the new company had made a bid for his services which only ingrained caution had led him to reject).

Egbert and the Director had admired the cabin rather fulsomely. Annabet had stood in silence and the captain had braced himself for the reception of the first spate of complaint. But none came. After a moment or so Annabet had held out her hand and said, with a definite air of dismissal, 'Thank you, Mynheer, for all the trouble you have taken. You are far too kind. Good-bye.' Vehk had breathed a sigh of relief and had followed the Director out and received, with tolerable patience, his last instructions about taking great care of Mevrouw and seeing that he handed her over, safely and in good health to her husband. He was more certain than ever that there was something queer and fishy about the whole thing. Annabet, with her thin face carefully painted and powdered and a hat which covered the curls which were slowly growing out of the downy spikes upon her head, looked fifty at least, and it amused the cynical captain to hear her constantly referred to as 'the young lady,' and to be bid mind his language as though he were conveying a child-bride to Banda.

Egbert, with an expression of distress and uncertainty which went ill with his uniform and martial bearing, came up just before the anchor was weighed. He mumbled, 'Take good care of her,' and thrust a gold piece into the captain's hand. And Vehk, with various and conflicting speculations hovering upon the fringe of his mind, turned his attention to the *Java* and the new voyage.

Well, and now it was over and it would remain always in his memory as the happiest he had ever known or would ever know. Taking the glass as Annabet relinquished it and watching her as she went back to her cabin to change her dress, he thought about the voyage. About the first time that he saw her bareheaded and was surprised to find her hair like a child's—so she wasn't an old woman long ago betrothed, or wedded for her money. About the cool, composed and somehow honest demeanour which she had maintained all the time, uncomplaining, undemanding. About the entertainment which her conversation had afforded him. And how, when he had run a fish-hook into his hand and the silly little puncture had festered, she had turned the tables by looking after *him*. He realised with a feeling of surprise that, though his most earnest efforts and floods of goat milk had failed to put any appreciable amount of flesh on her bones, and the heat of the tropic sun had not loosened those stiffened joints, he no longer pitied or scorned the man who was shortly coming aboard to claim her. He envied him. He would have married her with joy and alacrity if it had been possible; had, in fact, in the company of this bare-boned, stiff-limbed scarecrow, experienced his first temptation to mental unfaithfulness to the buxom, giggling creature who waited for him in Zeeland and who had formerly been for him the acme of feminine charm. He sighed, as automatically he watched the island grow from a vague smudge into a solid collection of recognisable objects. The Fort first, grim and forbidding, then the little town with its brightly-washed houses, then the green waving mass of the nutmeg trees, and finally the details of the waterfront and the people moving on it. Automatically, precisely, he shouted his orders, and at last the *Java* wheeled into position; the anchor chains rattled and the graceful ship, swinging round, seemed to make a curtsey, like a lovely lady sure of her welcome.

Vehk saw the prahaus mustering, there they came, the searchers for plague, and for contraband, the men who would carry the mail, and once again he was sorry that the voyage was over.

He recognised Kaerko in the foremost prahau, and saw, sitting beside him, a big, red-faced man. At the same moment there was a rustle of silk just behind him, and Annabet's voice said, 'I suppose my husband will come to meet me. If you *could* arrange it, Captain, I would like to see him alone.'

'This may be him,' said Vehk, his eyes upon the red-faced

man. He knew, by this time, almost all the circumstances which had brought Mevrouw Haan to Banda, and, remembering how he himself had felt when he saw Annabet for the first time, was moved by a curious combination of envy, anger and pity. This unknown man, Haan, could not be expected to see at a glance what a prize the lottery of glove marriage had given him. He turned towards Annabet and saw that she was dressed much as she had been on the day when she boarded the *Java* for the first time. The dress was richer, that was all, and the hat was decorated with a plume instead of a bunch of ribbons. And it was significant of the relationship established between the captain and his passenger that he should say, with an easy familiarity that was not in the least disrespectful, 'I'll arrange that, Mevrouw. And you'd do best to take off that hat.'

'It shades my face a bit.'

'It hides your hair. Take it off and go wait in your cabin until I send for you. Mynheer Haan will be in my cabin.'

A glass or two of wine ... to blue the sharpest shock, he thought. He looked at Annabet who was turning away obediently. Suddenly he recognised the dress. She had worn it on the day when, recovered from his blood-poisoning, he had been able to dine at his own table once more. 'I'll wear my best dress,' she had said, 'and you must open a bottle of wine. We'll make it an occasion.' A feeling, burning and tender, neither pleasure nor pain, rose in his throat at the memory. He swallowed and shrugged as he turned his lean swarthy face towards the side of the ship where Evert was following Kaerko up the ladder.

The little Agent was nervous. His natural awe of Evert had been enhanced by the rumours and gossip he had heard about Evert's wife. He had taken refuge in an uneasy facetiousness, which, coming into play at this moment, jarred, could he but have known it, upon both his hearers.

'Well, well, Captain Vehk,' he began. 'I believe you have something very special in the way of cargo to-day. Plainly addressed to Mynheer Haan, I understand. This is Mynheer Haan—Captain Vehk. Come aboard to collect his consignment in person.'

The captain acknowledged the introduction with the grace that was the heritage of his strain of French blood, but his eye rested upon Evert with speculative detachment. Big, handsome, not too old—but not good enough. Not a gentleman—though how he came to that conclusion he did not know—probably one of Gomarus' jumped-up guttersnipes. But not without dignity, the captain conceded, a moment later. It was, doubtless, quite a tense moment for Haan, and it would have been easy enough for him to let Kaerko's opening words set the key for his own; but Evert said formally, 'I trust you have

71

had a good voyage, Captain. You will excuse me, I know, but I am anxious to greet my wife.'

'If you will come below, Mynheer...' Vehk said invitingly, and led the two men into his own cabin where, by his orders, a bottle of Rhenish and several glasses stood ready. Evert, with difficulty restraining his impatience, looked around the cabin. 'Mevrouw will join you in a moment,' Vehk said. 'Let us drink her health while we wait.'

'I never dared venture upon a glove marriage,' Kaerko said, tactlessly. 'I once knew a man in Surabaya who got a cross-eyed wife that way. But if the captain here delivers the goods, as ordered and conforming to description, who knows? I might be tempted to follow your example!'

The lines in Vehk's leathery face deepened. He drained his glass hastily and set it down. 'Come,' he said, turning to Kaerko, 'you'll be wanting your letters. Mynheer Haan, if you will wait here I will send Mevrouw to you.'

Left to himself Evert poured another glass of wine and gulped it impatiently. He appreciated neither the wine nor the delay. Contrary to the captain's surmise he was not nervous, he was merely filled with impatience. It was forty days since the *Great Holland* had brought him the formal acceptance of his proposal, and Mevrouw's accompanying letter had told him the suggested date of the wedding ceremony, the name of the ship upon which, all things being well, Annabet would sail, and the date—as nearly as these things could be forecast—when he might hope to see her in Banda. In that space of time his impatience had grown steadily, like a rapidly maturing plant. Actually, considering the circumstances the whole thing had been arranged with phenomenal dispatch; only a little more than fifteen months had passed since the possibility of marrying Annabet Van Goens had first occurred to him, but Evert was accustomed to having what he wanted, or at least what he was able to buy, delivered into his hands almost immediately and at times it had seemed that he simply could not wait to see his latest bargain.

Well, now at last the moment had come. He heard, first a footstep, then another, and attributed the space between them to a becoming reluctance, a hovering shyness; then there was a whisper of silk, and then Annabet stood framed in the open doorway.

After a stab of disappointment that his waiting should be prolonged any further, he looked at the woman without interest. Some other female passenger wandering about—or had Annabet brought a maid? No, too finely dressed. Vehk's wife perhaps—he'd looked the sort of dapper little cock who'd be pretty uxorious. Good God though, what a wife to cart round with you. And anyway, she was in the way, surely Annabet couldn't be long now.

'Mevrouw,' he said icily, 'if you are looking for the captain, I can tell you he's gone on deck. He has lent me this cabin for a little while.'

The creature gave a little timid smile and a little knowing nod.

'You are Evert Haan? I am Annabet.' She tried to step quickly into the cabin, stumbled stiffly, regained her balance and came to a standstill close in front of him. There she curtsied—not gracefully, but with the assurance of one who has been reared to fine manners. As she rose he saw that, from the foaming lace of her sleeve a white hand, all skin and bone, was extended. At the very back of his mind lay the knowledge that he should take it, raise it to his lips, murmur some words of welcome; but he was too stunned, too utterly overcome by his feelings to say or do anything. He stood like a stone and stared with steadily mounting horror. It just wasn't possible. Such a thing couldn't happen to him. Evert Haan. There was a horrible mistake somewhere. Or else someone was playing a trick upon him. He knew what his Annabet looked like. Hadn't Piet described her? Hadn't he said that she was a true Van Goens? And couldn't he remember the lovely pink and white, plump, golden women of the family who had gone past him so often long ago in Janshaven, riding in carriages which flung clouds of dust or spatters of mud over the envious, dazzled boy. It was one of *them* he had bid for. And what had he got? God in Heaven, what had he got? All in that same timeless minute which followed the words, 'I am Annabet,' his mind ran backwards again, reminding him of the things he had said in those first few intoxicated days after the *Great Holland* had brought him Mevrouw's letter. He had boasted, knowing that he was doing so and enjoying doing it. Now he felt a scorching shame as he remembered the things he had said, and all the vainglorious words seemed to coagulate into a ball which choked him.

Annabet broke the silence. The timidity which had shown in her first smile had no echo in her voice. The sweet assured tones rang out so clearly that he thought her loud-voiced into the bargain.

'My appearance has shocked you, Mynheer. I expected that; so please be at no pains to conceal your feelings. Shortly before your letter arrived in Holland I was very ill, and although I have fully recovered in health my looks have suffered. I did beg of Mamma to warn you in her letter, but she was certain that I should improve on the voyage. So I have, indeed, but not quite quickly enough.' She paused for a second as though expecting some reply. None came and she went on, 'I am very sorry. I assure you that what I lack in looks I will make up in

73

behaviour. My sole aim shall be to make you a good wife, Mynheer.'

The stilted, pompous words came out with the clarity and precision of a long-prepared speech. Hundreds of times she had visualized this meeting and every time she had pictured this Evert Haan as someone to be placated, and if it were possible, charmed into overlooking the all-too-obvious defects in her appearance. Sometimes she had steeled herself to face anger, the black, cursing, deadly rage such as her father had indulged when things began to go wrong. She had not antici- pated the blank, dumb depths of astonishment which now confronted her. And even as she said her long-prepared speech something furious and rebellious cried from the depths of her being—and I was the loveliest of the three; if I could have come eighteen months ago he'd have been on his knees to me. But she quelled that feeling, remembering those days shortly after her recovery when the destruction of her beauty had almost led to the destruction of her mind. Father Vincent had shown her how to go on living, had pointed out the way of acceptance and resignation ... she must remember the things he had said. And she must remember too what she had dis- covered for herself—that it was possible for men who at first looked upon her with horror to come to look with kindliness and sometimes more than that. The big sea-captain—Piet Odshoorn—had been horrified at first, but in less than an hour the horror had gone and his handclasp as he left had betrayed him. Little Vehk, too, so different in almost every way, had gone through an almost identical change. And Egbert, whose favourtie sister she had always been, unable to look at her at first, had been her slave again long before the letter which gave her a spurious importance had arrived. And this big handsome man, this husband if hers, was only a man after all. Given time and a modicum of tolerance to work upon, she would be able to establish at least a friendly relationship. And that, she thought, being innocent and gently reared, was basis enough for a marriage.

Evert had cleared his throat and made a sound which seemed to presage speech; but no words came. 'A good wife'— he didn't want a good wife! At least he did, of course, but he could attend to her goodness. He wanted a beautiful, attrac- tive, enviable wife who would grace his house and his life as a lovely figurehead would have graced a ship. He had been prepared to receive a cold and possibly resentful girl who might even despise his plebian blood. All his frenzied prepara- tions since the *Great Holland* anchored had been aimed at impressing and subduing her. He had not cared whether she loved him or not, he had not looked to her to bring him the happiness which ordinary men expected to find in the marital relationship. He had merely wanted a wife whom he could show off with pride and who would, through the mere fact of being his wife, remove his grudge against his humble beginnings. And he had got a scarecrow, something not merely plain but positively hideous, and who was promising, as a sop, to be a good wife. God Almighty, he could have had a good wife if he had wanted one, and far less ugly a one than this, any moment in the last twenty-five years. He had always found women easy game. He thought of the ones he could, at various times, have married. And he looked again at the thing whom he had married, this living scarecrow, this animated skeleton.

From somewhere out of sight he could hear Kaerko's voice and the sound seemed to bring him to his senses. Everybody who could possibly contrive some errand to bring him aboard would be here in a moment, ready with a joke and a slap on the back, avid to view the bride. The thought jerked him into speech.

'We'd better get ashore,' he said. And he thanked the private Diety who, lapsing lamentably in the great matter, had at least arranged that he should come in his own prahau. They could go straight back to the house without going into Banda. His one idea now was to get Annabet to the privacy of the plantation without being seen. After that ... he had no plan. He must have time.

'If you will get your hat and anything else that you need for the next hour or so, I'll send out for your baggage later.'

'Thank you,' she said. As she walked out of the cabin his eyes followed her with hatred. This marriage, he thought, was intended to avenge him upon the Van Goens; but by God they had won after all. How they must have laughed as they shipped off that crippled bag of bones. And then he thought of Piet. Had Piet known? Was it possible that that slow, stupid fellow with his long-cherished grudge had planned and executed so exquisite a revenge, 'Why do you prefer Annabet to Klara? ... he had asked that, hadn't he? Was it within the bounds of reason that Piet, first by avid partisanship and then by pretending not to want to have anything to do with the affair, had played a game simply staggering in its cleverness. Had Annabet been a cripple, an ugly cripple, all along? That, at least, was feasible, for what illness known to man could turn a young, beautiful girl into a stiff old woman? Well, if Piet had deceived him, he would find out and God help the swine next time he came to Banda. He'd nearly landed in the Fort this time on account of his stubbornness ... next time there would be no Shal Ahmi waiting on the quay. Evert Haan had been fooled and somebody was going to pay dearly.

'I am ready now,' Annabet said from the doorway. Evert

75

looked at her again and drew a deep breath. In a hat she looked worse. She looked like an old crone of fifty painted and dressed in horrid imitation of youth. He could not, he simply could not go to tne deck by her side and risk seeing any of the men he was likely to see. He knew what he would do, and he was going to do it without any regard for her feelings. She might merely be the instrument of her family's knavery, but after all she had come: willingly or unwillingly she had dared to face him, and sne must bear the result. Pushing past her he bellowed up the companionway, 'Captain Vehk! Come down here a moment, I must see you. It's urgent.'

'Look here,' he said, as Vehk clattered lithely down the stairs, 'had you made any plans for getting my wife off this ship?' His tone was deliberately aggressive.

'Why no,' Vehk said, taken aback. His eyes flew to Annabet who was standing by the cabin doorway, a small leather bag at her feet, her hat again on her head, her gloved hands clasped at waist level.

'I boarded in the usual way, Evert,' she said calmly. 'Please don't worry. I'm not nimble on the ladder, but I can manage.'

Evert ignored her entirely.

'Mevrouw is far from well,' he said in a voice that defied contradiction. 'I'm surprised that no one except myself has seen how very unwell she is. The idea of her going ashore in the ordinary way is preposterous. How would you land a sick man, captain . . . a man say, with two broken legs?'

'I'd rig a sling, of course,' said the captain, nettled by Evert's manner. Then the full implication of the question struck him and he said falteringly, 'But Mevrouw isn't . . . I mean . . . Mevrouw is as well as when she came aboard. Or . . .' He turned his back on Evert and took a step towards Annabet. 'Mevrouw,' he said, suddenly solicitous. 'Are you *feeling* unwell. Sometimes—I've noticed it myself—the sudden cessation of movement leads to something like seasickness. It will pass. Of course, if you don't feel like facing the ladder, I'll fix a sling. It's no trouble, but it takes a little time. Would you like to lie down while I make arrangements?'

'I'm . . .' Annabet began. She had started to say, 'I'm all right,' but a glance at Evert's face silenced her. She freed one hand and moved it in a gesture more eloquent than a shrug, a gesture which made Vehk spin round to face Evert again.

'I've no time to waste. We want to get home,' Evert said. 'Who's above there?'

'Three or four gentlemen unknown to me, the Agent and Mynheer Vehmeer.'

'Come to . . .' he was about to say 'gape,' but sensed in time the self-betrayal of the word. 'Come to be introduced and make silly jokes. My wife is in no state to be bothered with them

76

now. And a sling you say takes time to rig. Very well. Can you send me a good strong fellow, Captain? And will you then be so very kind as to go up and tell the assembly that Mevrouw Haan is not well. Say I'm anxious to get her home without any delay or excitement.'

'I should be grateful,' said Annabet clearly. 'And Captain Vehk, before you go, I want to thank you for everything you have done to make my voyage so agreeable. I won't say good-bye, because you're coming to dine with us, aren't you?'

'It would give me great pleasure, Mevrouw, just as anything I have done for your comfort has given me pleasure.' Confused, perplexed, he leaped for the companionway, and in a moment a burly, lithe sailor came tumbling down and pulled himself up short with a salute.

'Good morning, Daan,' Annabet said, forestalling whatever order Evert was going to give. 'You're going to help me up those stairs, across the deck and down the ladder. I'm villain-ously stiff to-day.'

'I could carry you easy,' he said, quite eagerly. Across his broad shoulder Annabet's eyes sought Evert for instruction.

'No,' he said. 'I think it would be better if you took one arm. I'll take the other, so. And the bag in your other hand. That's right.'

There now, if they looked—and he knew just how avidly they would look—they could see little save a drooping sick woman moving along between two stalwart supporters. From most angles even her face was hidden.

Kaerko, Vehmeer and the four planters stood in a little knot in the place where the Captain had unobtrusively herded them. Curiosity, a kind of deflated joviality and sympathy showed on their faces.

'There goes a damned lucky man,' said the Captain, almost provocatively as Evert, carefully keeping the bulk of his body between Annabet and the spectators, crossed the deck.

'What's she ill of?' Kaerko asked.

'She had a bad bout of fever just before we sailed,' Vehk said. 'And it's an exhausting voyage.'

'She's lame,' Vehmeer announced with an air of discovery.

'What about Evert's great dinner to-night?' Van Heem asked. 'Think she'll be well enough to attend? You're right, Vehmeer, she *is* lame. Look what a fist they're making about getting her down that ladder.'

'Good omen for to-night,' Hootman, another planter said with a grin. One or two of the others laughed and capped the remark. Vehk's dark face seemed to blacken. He said, irrelevantly and truculently, 'Mevrouw Haan is one of the most charming people I have ever had the pleasure of meet-ing.' And then, feeling that he had made a fool of himself, turned and walked away abruptly.

'Well,' said Vehmeer, his vast pale face settling back into lines of gravity, 'I suppose, unless we hear that Evert has cancelled the dinner, we shall have the pleasure of meeting her very soon.'

'And when you do,' said Hootman, who was not invited, 'take a good look for me and see if her legs are put on right. Myself, I doubt it.'

The prahau shot away over water as blue as a hyacinth. Glassed in its translucence, a thousand little coloured fish, lovely as butterflies, darted. Annabet studied them for a moment, and then, lifting her gaze, looked at the island. They were skirting the waterfront with its white-and-pink, cream and ochre-washed buildings and leaving the town to their left. In a moment there were only trees, masses and masses of dense, feathery-green divided from the blue water by the edge of creaming foam. And the scent, the flowery, spicy scent of the islands, of which she had first become aware some hours ago aboard the *Java* was here intensified until one might have imagined that great bowls of pot-pourri were being stirred and wafted just under one's nose. It did seem to be a very beautiful place. She contemplated saying so, for the silence in the boat was growing heavy and unendurable and she had been brought up to believe that a fund of rippling, impersonal small-talk was one of a lady's indispensable assets. But before she spoke she looked at Evert and caught the expression of cold loathing in his eyes. It was so unmistakable and so virulent that her inside turned cold. Even her breathing seemed to stop, and her lips parted, not in speech, but in a gasp for air.

Easily and rapidly as a waterfowl the prahau turned into an inlet and now there were trees on either side. Soon, upon the nearer, left-hand side there was a gap, and here, standing back a little from the water, was a collection of buildings, most of them thatched with reed and all of them washed white. From the clear space in front of them a little wooden landing-stage jutted out into the water. The prahau's head swung round towards it, and Annabet looked at the buildings. At first she imagined that one of them would be the house to which she had come, and the thought brought a feeling of relief. If one of these low, humble places were Evert's home, then she had been deceived too. She entertained for the space of a fleeting moment the mad hope that, after all, Evert was going to lead her into a hovel. Then she would make the best of it and he must make the best of her and things might work out all right. The boatman, nimble as a cat, sprang on to the landing-stage and held the prahau steady. Evert alighted, turned to face her, seemed to hesitate, and then deliberately stepped backward, speaking, as he did so, a word or two in some language she did not know. The boatman hastily rubbed his right hand upon the folds of white cloth which girded his loins and then stretched it out to her. Stiffly she climbed out of the prahau and set foot in Banda.

'The house,' said Evert in a wooden, reluctant voice, 'is a short walk away. The landing-stage was made for the convenience of loading nutmegs. On the other hand, I didn't want to live among the sheds.'

'I'm perfectly able to walk, thank you,' Annabet said, trying not to hobble too obviously, and accepting his words as though they apologised for the distance. And, since the dreadful silence was at last broken, she hurried on before it could form again. 'I'm not ill, you know. And not nearly so stiff as I was.' Evert said nothing. With obvious impatience he curbed his stride to her slower pace and they walked along a widish, well-trodden path, thick with dust, until it ended in a thick green hedge. Fifteen months ago when Piet had first visited Coenspark the bushy little shrubs had only just been planted and reached only to his waist; now they were more than six feet tall, and regular, careful cutting had so thickened and restrained their lavish growth that the hedge presented the appearance of a solid green wall. Two apertures with arched tops pierced the green surface, and Evert, ignoring the nearest one which led to the compound and the kitchen quarters, passed on and entered by the second.

Unconsciously he paused there. Now that the active, extrovertive business of annoyance and shame and of getting Annabet out of sight was over, softer, passive feeling could find a place in his mind; and as he stood for a second inside the green archway and looked upon his house and garden, he was nearer tears then he had been since his childhood. He had, as he had told Piet, lived very simply before he built the new house. The little low house stood there still among the sheds and drying lofts at which Annabet had looked so speculatively. It had been built in the first year of his ownership, when the native troubles were at their worst and nobody knew whether the young plantations were going to pay or not. And he had not troubled to alter or improve it in any way. It was not in his nature to be content with even second best, and in those early days he had had in his mind already the vision of the house he would one day rear and inhabit. Now here it was, as perfect as his taste and his means could make it; and the garden, though only eighteen months old, had, in this place of rapid maturity, already the trim, rich, settled look which he had remembered about the gardens of big houses in Holland. So often since Piet's visit his fancy had dwelt, with reserve at first, and then at last with assurance, upon the moment when he would say to

79

Annabet Van Goens, 'Well, there is the house...' He had planned to say it so, casually concealing his sense of pride and achievement. And now the moment had come. The contrast between the place and woman who was to live in and share it was too cruel. In place of the pink-and-white and golden girl whom he had pictured moving gracefully among the roses he had this hobbling, stiff-necked skeleton, this painted deaths-head. It was not to be borne. It wasn't bearable. And deep within him, in the secret places of his mind where so many schemes had been born and nurtured, something stirred. He wasn't going to try to bear it. He had got out of bad corners before, and he'd get out of this. He set his feet in motion again and, still in silence, began to walk towards the house.

'It is the most beautiful house,' Annabet said. Her voice was less assured then usual. She remembered her thoughts about the sheds and hovels by the landing-stage and her mind took note of the inevitable corollary. Evert had promised her a beautiful home, and had, no doubt, expected a wife to match and enhance it. A dreadful feeling of guilt shot through her, and she said impulsively, 'I shouldn't have let myself be persuaded. I should have gone to the Convent.'

'So that's what they've planned to do with you, is it?' Evert asked brutally. The words and the tone implied that a bundle of rubbish, destined for the midden, had been instead posted out to him in Banda, marked 'With Care.' The cold feeling shot through Annabet again. She had the sensation which comes to happier people only in dreams—of standing, ob-scenely half-clad before a throng of jeering strangers.

They walked up to the house, crossed the verandah and entered the hall. The whole place blazed with flowers. Un-certain as to the exact moment when the *Java* might anchor, Evert had the house garnished for several days, each bloom and each plant replaced the moment it passed its prime. One of his house-boys, noted for his running, was even now kicking his heels upon the quay, for it had been Evert's intention, had Annabet been what he expected, to bring his prahau close to the shore and send the boy running back to the house so that the servants should be warned and on duty, with wine and cakes and fruit ready on the verandah. As it was, the runner having not returned, the house seeemed deserted and the flower-embowered hall had the air of a church decorated for a festival and then momentarily abandoned.

Near the foot of the curving staircase Annabet came to a standstill. She had promised Father Vincent in those dark days when her tottering mind had leaned heavily upon the support of his mysticism, that she would waste no more tears over the loss of her beauty when there were so many real sorrows and evils in the world. But her eyes were brimming as, once again, she looked into Evert's face.

'It is all so very beautiful,' she said. 'And you are so disappointed in me.... Mynheer, I would give twenty years of my life to appear before you as I was.'

'But that is impossible,' Evert said coldly. 'I will show you your room.'

At the time of Piet's visit the room had been unfinished. Later, at first tentatively and then wholeheartedly, Evert had thrown himself into the business of making it, in his own words, 'fit for a queen.' It was all blue and white; the big bed had curtains and covers of blue-and-white silk, blue dragons on a white ground, a sofa covered in the same silk stood under one of the windows and the two low chairs were cushioned in the material. Under the other window stood a dressing-table bearing a silver-framed mirror fitted with candle-sockets. The wood of the table and the chairs was like nothing Annabet had ever seen, white, polished to the surface of satin. Silver-backed brushes and little silver boxes flanked the mirror. The carpet was of a deep, heavenly blue, and by the bed and before the dressing-table lay the great skins of white bears. Wang Fu, the Chinaman, taken into favour again, had made the mirror and the trinket set, and had also, through one of his numerous relatives, obtained the bear skins. Together with the bathroom which opened out of the bedroom—an original, highly expensive, and vastly imaginative arrangement—the room had cost more then even Evert could afford. But he had spent the money gladly; and that although in his heart he was almost certain that the woman who would eventually sleep in this room would, physically, afford him less pleasure than he had known in Isa's embrace. He had never expected the young beauty of Piet's description and his own imaginings to afford him great sexual satisfaction; her duty was of another kind— to flourish his prosperity, his taste, his success, like a great glittering banner in the society in which he lived, and eventually to bear him an heir.

And the woman to whom he was showing this beautiful room would, of course, do neither. Publicly she could bring him nothing but pity and derision; privately she was equally unprofitable. He had intended to offer his hand to her at the landing-stage, and then discovered, with an increase of horror, that he could not bring himself to touch her.

Annabet looked around the room. Lovely, exquisite, so plainly planned and furnished for quite another person. She felt the flood tide of despair setting in and thought desperately of Father Vincent's words. (It had been March when he had spoken them—March in Holland and the soft wind from the west had just defeated the cold blasts that blew from Russia, and the miserable little garden of the Heydberg house had been pricked all over with the spearheads of the bulbs she and Klara had planted in the autumn when life was still normal and shapely. She had looked at the thick knobby buds of the cherry tree by the gate while he spoke.)

Evert had left the door of the blue-and-white room ajar, for he had meant to call the maid he had engaged for Annabet and escape as soon as he could. Annabet now closed it quietly. And since it was *her* room and manners must be observed, said, 'Please sit down for a moment. I have something to say to you.' The tears were still in her eyes, making them larger than ever, and her voice was a little unsteady.

Evert hesitated for a second, and then, with a might-as-well-get-it-over-and-done-with air sat down in one of the low dragon-cushioned chairs. Annabet, exhausted by the walk and the emotions of the last hours, sank gratefully down in the other.

'Mynheer,' she began. Then, forcing a smile, 'I can't go on calling you that, can I? We shall have to use our given names. Evert. I would like, if you don't mind, to make everything plain to you. I know that I'm hideous, and I know that you are extremely disappointed and shocked at the sight of me. The pain that your distaste gives me is, in a way, no more than I deserve. Many things combined to persuade me to come to Banda. But this I must say—whether I was right or wrong to do so—I did determine, when I put on your glove in the church that to the best of my ability, in every way that was in my power, I would try to make up to you for having married a woman with an ugly face and stiff limbs. Also—and this had a certain influence upon my decision—it is possible, so the doctors say, that I may get better. I am appreciably less stiff than I was, and I gained two pounds on the voyage. As for my hair—it is growing, you may see for yourself. If you can possibly bring yourself to have patience and look upon me with tolerance ... I do assure you ...' Evert seized upon the opportunity given him by the slight halt in her speech.

'This is a very distasteful position,' he said, getting to his feet. 'You have been very ill, and are to be pitied. The blame lies with those who allowed you, or persuaded you to come here. For one thing, you are obviously unfit to have made the journey. If you take my advice you will go to bed at once. I have engaged a maid for you. She is native, of course, but she understands Dutch, and has been trained in a good household. I will call her.'

He went to the door, and opening it with a sharp feeling of relief, clapped his hands loudly three times. From nowhere it seemed, and in no time a stoutish, almost middle-aged woman with black hair oiled smoothly back from her brown face and beady, very observant, dark eyes, appeared from the far end of the gallery.

'You mistress has arrived,' Evert said shortly. 'Go to her.' Leaning back into the bedroom he remarked, 'She is called Katje.'

The loud handclaps had informed the household that the master had returned, and Josef, the chief house-boy, a man of some fifty years, was waiting at the foot of the staircase. From the bottom stair Evert could look straight across the hall to the dining-room where the long table glittering with silver and glass and napery, was set for twenty guests. The sight made him want to spit. The moment when his bride, young, beautiful, well-bred, should have taken her seat at one end of that table was to have been the crowning moment of his life.

'You can clear all that away,' he said sourly. 'Mevrouw has arrived in very ill-health, and must keep to her bed. Now, let me see. Juan is still in town, I suppose. I was so anxious to get Mevrouw home I forgot about him. Send Abbas for him while I write some notes. Then send him round with them. Mevrouw will dine in her room, and you can bring mine to the office.'

Swinging sharply to the right of the stairs' foot he strode away to his office. There he poured himself a glass of shnapps and observed, with an almost impersonal pang of pity, that his hand was unsteady on the bottle. He had never been so thoroughly upset and shaken in his life before. Even his confidence in his own luck—an attribute which had as much as anything else made him lucky—was tottering to a fall. It was not only the Van Goens who had foully tricked him, it was life itself. Everything had gone right with him for so long, and then, over this very special and important matter, everything had gone wrong.

It took him some time, and another glass of spirits to steady himself sufficiently to write out in a legible hand the notes which cancelled the dinner. They were identical and formally worded, but as he folded the one addressed to Cornelius Byskin, his best friend in Banda, he took up his quill again and wrote, 'Isn't it bad luck?' under his signature. Juan, recalled from the quay, was waiting outside the foor, chewing a lump of nutmeg cheese long before the notes were finished; and he was the first person upon whom Evert vented his mounting fury.

'I'll teach you not to come into my presence with your ugly mouth full of filth,' Evert said, landing him a swinging blow on the ear.

In the bedroom Annabet and Katje took stock of one another. Brother Egbert, who had a sharply-inquiring mind and a wide circle of acquaintances, and was thus knowledgeable in many matters, had given Annabet a few hints about native servants. He had gained his own information from a story told by an officer who had been stationed in Ceylon; but he believed that what was true of the Cingalese would be true of the natives in Banda. So he had warned Annabet of the danger of gossip. 'They're so quiet,' he said—meaning the house-servants—'and of course a different colour, so you're always in danger of forgetting that they are people with eyes and tongues. But there's nothing about you that they don't know, so I'm told, and through them, of course, the servants in other houses and their masters and mistresses know it too, down to how often you change your underlinen. I bet,' he said, 'that there's many a woman who wishes she had a brother to point this out to her before she went East, Annabet.'

Annabet had laughed and said, 'Well, thank you Egbert. But I'm not likely to indulge in an *affaire*, am I? Because that's what you're thinking of, isn't it?' Egbert had blushed and stammered and it was plain that for a moment he had been talking to the old, beautiful Annabet of his recollection.

Now, studying the egg-smooth, immobile face of Katje, Annabet wondered what she was thinking behind that mask, and whether she thought it strange that a man should speak so curtly to his newly-arrived bride. But that aspect of the situation had escaped Katje's notice for the moment. She was twenty-five years old and had spent fifteen years of her life in the service of white Mynheers and Mevrouws, but all their ways remained a mystery to her. She had been the mistress of two white men in her middle teens, when she was pretty with the fleeting loveliness of her race, but she was as far as a jungle woman from understanding the ways and the motives of her employers. If Evert had carried Annabet into the house pick-a-back, or dragged her in by her hair, Katje would have felt no surprise. But what did surprise her was her new mistress' appearance. Manners and customs may vary between East and West, but age and beauty are not subject to boundaries. Katje had heard—as who in Banda had not?—that the young Mevrouw was young and beautiful; and here was a woman in Mevrouw's house, in Mevrouw's very bedroom, who certainly was neither. In Katje's opinion such extreme emaciation could only result from old age, and as she turned her expressionless face with its beady eyes upon Annabet for the first time, her real interest was in her mistress' hair. It must be a wig; no old woman could possibly have such beautiful yellow curls; and if it was a wig it was a miracle of its kind. She had seen them before, coarse, lustreless things which deceived nobody; never anything in the least like this.

She asked, in soft, hesitating Dutch which sounded most attractive to Annabet's unaccustomed ear, 'Would Mevrouw like a bath?' The wife of the First Merchant in Batavia from whose service she had just come, had liked baths at all times of the day; and also, when people bathed they removed their wigs, if they wore them, and Katje was, above all things, anxious to have that mass of short curls in her hands so that she might examine it thoroughly and report upon its wonders.

'Yes,' said Annabet with the sweet smile which looked so out of keeping upon her ruined face.

Katje disappeared, Annabet, left to herself, moved stiffly about the room, looking out of the windows, one of which gave upon the garden, the other upon the dense green fastnesses of the nutmeg grove, touching the pieces of furniture and coming to a halt at last before the silver-framed mirror of the dressing-table. She stared resolutely at her reflection. It was horrible, especially in that beautiful frame, with the glimpse of the beautiful room as a background. Klara and Mamma had insisted upon the paint and powder, saying with loud confidence that the colour took off the hollowness of her cheeks and the ageing pallor of her lips. But though she had faithfully adhered to their rules of application, she thought now that they were wrong. It made her look older, not younger, and it obscured the one thing that the illness had left her, the fine rose-petal smoothness of her skin. Suddenly she drew her handkerchief from her sleeve and rubbed her face vigorously. And as she did so the thought went through her head—here I am, thinking about my face again, and I did promise Jean Marie I wouldn't. Oh dear, and I promised myself on the marriage day that I wouldn't think of him except as Father Vincent.... Oh dear, what a mess I have made of everything. She eyed her reflection again and her face looked back to her with an expression of sorrow, none the less valid because it was tinged with self-deprecatory humour. If only, she thought, I hadn't gone to that silly carnival on the ice ... if only Jean Marie hadn't been a priest.... And here I am, a wreck, a hideous wreck, in Banda, with a husband who hates me. I know he hates me, and who could blame him?

Katje, bearing a burnished water-can in each hand, followed by two small brown boys similarly laden, entered the room and passed through a door on the far side of the room. Annabet heard the sound of water pouring. The boys, silent-footed and with averted eyes, went out again. Three times the procession passed. Then Katje, her face showing no sign of the eager curiosity which devoured her—for the wig must come off in a moment—came to the dressing-table upon soft feet and with soft fingers began to remove Annabet's clothes. In a few moments, with her hair, most disappointingly, most surprisingly upon her head, the new mistress of Coenpark went into her bathroom.

There was nothing like it in Banda, or in Holland, or even in France where the refinements of life were seriously considered. Annabet owed her bathroom to the fact that once, long ago in his soldiering days, Evert had been billeted in the ruined palace of a prince of Java. It was there that he had seen, for the first time, marble used as a building material; and there he had seen a bath in which golden and amber and coffee-coloured beauties had wallowed at a time when Queens in the West had washed in little bowls of warm water. When he had built his house he had reproduced the palace bathing-place as faithfully as his memory allowed him to do, and Annabet, following Katje, stepped through the door into a scene which was like something in a dream. The room was square and lined throughout with marble of a pinkish hue. There was one window, high up in a wall. In the centre of the floor was sunk an oblong bath in which water was steaming, and at each corner of the bath, upon the kind of shelf formed by the surrounding floor, stood a marble vase filled with flowers. There were two tall pottery jars of cold water. Katje tilted one of them over the bath.

'How hot do you like it, Mevrouw?'

'Oh. Rather hot,' Annabet said, leaning down with difficulty and trying the water with her hand. When the temperature was bearable she stepped in and lay for some moments enjoying the sensation of remoteness from ordinary affairs that steeping in a warm bath bestows. It was, she thought, like lying in the heart of a pink rose, or a shell. She remembered, and the memory heightened the pleasure of the moment, the baths she had taken in the cold bedroom of the Heydberg house, little, shivering piecemeal baths that were nothing but a painful duty. How different this was. If only ... There she was, at it again. And the water was cooling. The blissful moment was over, and she must get out and dress and sooner or later face Evert again. All very well for Jean Marie ... Father Vincent ... to say that the flesh was nothing. To young women and the men who married them it was everything. She had known that all along. But she had wanted to go on living, and that, at least, Father Vincent with his mysticism had helped her to do. So she had lived and she had stayed sane, and so come to Banda. Father Vincent had said, with the most convincing air, that there was a purpose in everything. Was there a purpose in the combination of cowardice and avarice and recklessness which had brought her here?

Evert had often dined in his office on days when he was busy and not under emotional stress. Josef accordingly served up the usual meal and Evert was quite surprised to find that his ordinarily hearty appetite had altogether deserted him. His attitude towards food was the one customary to those who have not always been sure of a bellyful, and he could have counted on his fingers the number of times when he had voluntarily missed a meal—certain days when he was seasick, and other certain days when he had been in high fever. Even in his soldiering days the imminence of danger had failed to quell his zest for food; and anxiety, of which in his time he had known plenty, had certainly never made him send a dish away untasted. But what had happened to him to-day was something outside his previous experience. Even the food which, under Josef's eye, actually reached his mouth was tasteless, and after a few moments he said surlily, 'Bring the next dish and then take yourself off, Josef. I've some business to think about, and I don't want you fidgeting round.'

As soon as he was alone he gave up the pretence of eating, poured another drink and leaned back in his chair. He had been turning his problem over and over in his mind and reached no solution, but he had come to the conclusion that his action in smuggling Annabet off the ship and into the house had been mistaken. Van Heem and Vehmeer, Kaerko and the others would have had their already lively curiosity spurred, and there was the captain at hand, only too ready to satisfy it. Katje, too, had probably spread a description of her mistress all over the compound, and news like that spread like the plague. Probably by this time the whole island was gloating over the rumour that Mevrouw Haan was badly pocked, a hunchback, and had one leg shorter than the other. That was the curse of the East ... not just the gossip, but the gross exaggeration. For when news passed by mouth and needed several tongues to carry it a mile, each listener heard what he wanted to hear and then passed on the story in the form most likely to thrill, or shock, or amuse *his* listener. And the way in which Evert Haan had shuffled his bride ashore and cancelled the dinner party was, naturally, enough to give rise to some queerly embellished stories. It was his own fault. He could see that now. If he'd carried off the situation with a high hand, all the fools in the island would have been deceived, and probably by next week all the daft women would be starving themselves to attain Annabet's emaciation; walking stiff-legged in order to be in the fashion, and cutting off their hair. Annabet's own assurance would have helped, too.

But it was no use thinking about that. The harm was done. And to produce her now would simply deceive no one. They would see that he had succumbed to circumstances and was letting her be seen because there was nothing else he could think of to do.

His wretched train of thought was disturbed by a familiar sound, a scratch at the window. He leaped to his feet, crossed the room in a few swift strides and locked the door; then he strode to the window and opened it.

'You are alone?' asked a thin high voice.

'Shal Ahmi!' Evert exclaimed in a pleased voice. 'I've been thinking about you. I was coming to see you later on. Come in.'

Shal Ahmi stepped, with dignity, into the room, and Evert, having carefully adjusted the shutter again, pulled forward, with a gesture of attentive politeness, the other chair. Shal Ahmi watched him, a little quirk of amusement twisting the corner of his mouth. He sat in the chair, adjusted his white drapery, and let his eyes rest upon the meal which Evert had scarcely touched. He looked from the dishes to Evert's face, and the glance was insolent and amused. His manner was quite different from that he had used in Kaerko's office on the night of Piet's arrest. It lacked at once the superficial cringing and the underlying dignity. An observant watcher could have seen at a glance that Shal Ahmi and Evert were on old-established and familiar terms.

Evert looked at his rejected meal uneasily. He had no objection to taking Shal Ahmi into his confidence; indeed, he intended to do so, but he had a constitutional dislike for betraying himself.

'Rizplatzen, too,' said Shal Ahmi, meditatively. And Evert countered with, 'Would you like some? It could be heated in a moment.'

'Thank you, I have eaten. But you, my dear Mynheer, have not.' A sly, mocking smile crept across his smooth face. 'Can it be that the bride did not arrive on the long-awaited ship? Or did you fall in love at first sight? Love, so we are told, is the enemy of appetite.'

Evert sat down in his chair.

'Lay off, Shal Ahmi. Tell me the worst. What are they saying in the compounds?'

'Frankly, that your bride is a cripple, past the age of childbearing, and remarkable in that she wears a wig of spun gold which is so cunningly fitted that she can wear it in her bath....' He brought out the words in a voice of light, impersonal reporting; and then added, in a changed, kinder tone, 'I thought you might as well know the worst. Why did you act as you did? If only I could have advised you.'

'I ask your advice on every matter that I can foresee,' said Evert harshly. 'But who could have foreseen this?'

'The gossip of the compound is, for once, near the truth then?'

'No,' Evert snapped, 'but it might as well be. She's been ill. She's seventeen and looks fifty. Her knees and her elbows and God knows what else are set stiff. She's half a head shorter than I am, and if she weighs an ounce over eighty-four pounds

I'm surprised. Her hair, so far as I know—but I haven't investigated—is her own.' He looked at Shal Ahmi and his eyes were more abjectly miserable than he realised.

'Once,' said Shal Ahmi in a dreamy, ruminative voice, 'you gave me a glass of a very special brandy with a queer English name. Everett? Yes, that was it. If I remember rightly, under that benign influence, my thoughts were inspired....'

'I'm sorry,' said Evert, jumping to his feet. 'Very remiss of me. I'm all at sea to-night. Here you are. But is the liquor made that can inspire you to think a way out of this mess. If it is, you shall swim in it.'

'To swim in any liquid lessens its value,' said Shal Ahmi sagely. 'That is why so few people drink water except in necessity. He sipped in silence for a few moments.

'Of what nature?' he asked presently.

'Full of hardihood, or she would not have dared to come. Inclined to argument. Loud voiced. She invited the captain of the ship that brought her to dine with us without consulting me. A lady of family, Shal Ahmi, even now there is no gainsaying that; but ugly beyond words.'

'And that matters?' Shal Ahmi asked. 'So much?' Evert scorned to reply to what seemed to him an absurd question. 'Ugly women have been greatly loved....'

Evert interrupted him with a sound of disgust. Then he said fiercely, 'I am not a boy, Shal Ahmi. The question of love does not come into the matter at all. How could it? Does anyone expect love from that sort of marriage? I wanted a woman who would grace my home and my table, uphold my position and bear me a son. And I've saddled myself with one whose appearance has already made me a laughing-stock and who is physically so abhorrent to me that I couldn't bring myself to help her out of the prahau.'

'Not even for the sake of the son?' Shal Ahmi asked. The smooth, shining planes of his face did not shift, but his eyes twinkled. Evert shook his head with a grimace of disgust.

'That is very bad,' said Shal Ahmi. 'What will you do, then? Send her back to her father?'

'I couldn't do that,' said Evert, who had thought of the same thing and rejected it. 'They are ...' How could one describe the Van Goens, so that Shal Ahmi understood? 'Lords in their own land. They would make trouble for me. Even the Company would listen if they complained loudly enough. They've cheated me, damn them to hell, every single one of them, but it was a legal cheat. When I asked to marry her I did not stipulate that she should be plump or pretty, or sound of wind and limb. I asked for her, by name, in marriage. And I got her.'

'I suppose ...' Shal Ahmi's reedy voice was thinner still as

89

he put the question ... 'there could be no question of her virginity?' Evert gave the question his full consideration, and then said slowly, 'No. The illness came upon her more than a year ago. Before that she would be only a child—or so counted, in Holland. And the great families are careful of their daughters. Besides...' a note of something that was almost panic crept into his voice and for a moment the whites of his eyes showed like a startled foal's '... to bring that up I should have to go to bed with her. And I could not do it, Shal Ahmi.'

'Yet a son from an ugly woman,' said the native, almost as though he were speaking to himself, 'is as good as a son from a beautiful one. And the night is kind.' The twinkle showed in his eyes again, and was immediately quenched. 'All this I know from hearsay; for as you know I have no traffic with women. And out of what little wisdom I have stored I say, Get you your son. For whom else is your house reared and your coffer filled? The day will come when you will say, Ah, she is ugly, but my sons are many and good; and by that time your hatred will have changed to respect. I have seen it happen many times.'

'It wouldn't happen with me. I tell you that when I would have put out my hand to assist her, my arm weakened. When I speak to her my mouth is dry and my tongue is stiff. How then...?' There was no need to finish the sentence. Shal Ahmi, as though convinced, nodded his shining, hairless head.

'What then?' he asked. 'You can't send her away, you say, having no reason. She stays here, like an old, barren wife? And the sons you get elsewhere, are by your law, illegitimate, looked at a little sideways? Bearing always with them a stigma which neither wealth nor position can remove. Come, Mynheer, you are not the man to give in thus easily.'

'What alternative have I?' Evert asked bitterly. But his eyes had lost their look of frenzy and dwelt upon the native with something rather more eager than speculation as it was rather less than hope.

'I could think of many things,' said Shal Ahmi, avoiding Evert's glance and staring straight ahead of him at the wall. 'And I think you have somewhat in mind too. When I came in to-night you said you had been thinking of me, and would have come to me had I not come to you. Why? Was it to tell me of your ill-fortune? To weep, as you say, upon my shoulder? Rather had you not in mind the memory of those few times when I have been of service? Come, open your mind to me. What did you hope of Shal Ahmi?'

'I don't know,' said Evert, faced with the blunt question. 'But sometimes a fresh mind.... And anyway, Shal Ahmi, your advice is always worth having....'

90

'You have had my advice upon this matter,' Shal Ahmi said smoothly. 'It is not my advice you ask. Rather my aid. Am I not right?'

'Your aid then.' His control broke suddenly and his voice became pleading and piteous. 'Shal Ahmi, if you can think of any way out of this, any way to rid me of her, without scandal, without making me more of a laughing-stock than I am already, I shall be in your debt for ever. Even when all our business is finished, all my promises kept, I shall be for ever your debtor.' Then, slowly, the magnitude of what he asked crystallised in the words 'Rid me of her,' seeped into his mind and with it the realisation—I'm asking him to kill her—and his red face blenched and his heart began to pound heavily.

Shal Ahmi spread his smooth brown hands against the whiteness of his clothing and studied their backs with attention and interest.

'Suppose,' he said at last, 'your bride likes you as little as you like her; suppose she ran away to-night—to the Governor, and told him that she had never wanted to come to Banda and asked his help to get back to Holland. What would he do?'

'But she wouldn't do that.'

'Never mind what she would do. What would *he* do?'

'Send her back to me. She is my wife,' said Evert confidently.

'So, she goes to the Governor and tells him a story of being in love with a young man in Holland, and being forced by her family to come here. And she is beautiful as the morning, and so plainly the well-born girl of whom you have boasted. Thus is your face saved. Mynheer. And he sends her back, perhaps with an escort; maybe, since she is a lady and Mevrouw Haan, he brings her back himself. But in the morning she is gone again and an experienced boatman is gone too. A fishing boat has seen a prahau heading for the Kei islands where those few of my race remaining have taken refuge. Suppose, after a time, there are rumours of a white woman, living as a native, living with a native, in those islands, in the villages of Banda Elu and Banda Elat where the old trades flourish and the old beauty lives untarnished. What then is the position of Mynheer Haan? Can he divorce her and beget his legal issue elsewhere?'

'Of course I could,' Evert said. 'But she would never ...'

'My friend,' said Shal Ahmi, looking him in the face at last, 'in less than an hour I could send a white woman, beautiful and young—but unfortunately so far barren—to play that part with the Governor. And in another hour I could find a boatman who would carry your ugly bride further than the Kei islands at my command. Ah, and he would live with her too, if it were a matter of a friend of mine wanting a divorce.' His voice changed, dropping from the fanciful to the practical. 'All that is mere word-spinning. I have, as you know, given the

91

matter no thought at all. But in a moment, as you have seen, I have already hatched a plan that would rid you of her. Slow and cumbrous, yes. But I could think of others. There are a hundred ways.' He paused and then asked sharply, 'Do you trust me?'

'Have I not given you proof of that, over and over again?'

'Prove it again,' Shal Ahmi said lightly. 'First, of course, I must see the woman. And then ... is there any business urgent enough to take a newly-wedded man away from his sick wife's bedside?'

'Yes. Because—and thanks to you but they don't know that—I have been successful with my slaves, I have been commissioned to buy for the island. I should, by rights, be in Bandogar at the quarterly market. But as the *Java* was all but due, I decided to wait until the next. I could go to-morrow....'

'Your bride being sick and you being a man of public conscience. Good. But not to-morrow. The next day. To-morrow you will give the dinner which, with me to advise you, you would have given to-day. You will be a man completely satisfied and charmed with his bride, but unfortunately she is ill. You leave her in good hands, none other than those of Doctor Van de Lijn...'

'And when I return?'

'Then you act as you must, remembering always that she was dear to you.'

Evert's mouth was suddenly dry. He was like a child who has played innocently with some unknown thing and realised, too late, its lethal properties. He said, feebly, ridiculously, 'I don't want her to be hurt.'

'Why should I hurt her? Am I a thug? I have yet no know-ledge of what I shall do. Now, will you go and see that the way is clear so that I may see her?'

Evert rose, and moving like a man in his sleep, unlocked the door and went out, leaving the key upon the inside. Shal Ahmi turned the key again and then went and stood by the desk. Fumbling among his drapery he brought out a small bag. He untied the string which secured its neck and tipped out into his hand five stones, somewhat resembling dice, but slightly larger and more rounded at the corners. Upon each of the six faces of each stone was a cryptic symbol, cut into the stone and then filled in with colour, black, scarlet, orange, green and blue. He weighed the stones in his hand for a second and then flung them, haphazardly, on the desk top. Leaning he studied the combination, at first with impersonal, professional interest, and then with a sharp intake of breath. His sleek smooth face wore a look of intense absorption. Almost reverently he lifted the black stone and set it a little aside. The others he gathered in his hand again and flung carelessly as before. He pushed the green-marked stone to the side of the black and juggled with the other three. Orange next, then blue, and last of all the scarlet were laid in a line. Then, as though reading a few words in plain print he ran his finger along the serried stones and followed the finger with his eyes. A curious smile broke the immobility of his face; it was amused and yet incredulous, as though someone had just whispered an unbelievably funny joke, swearing that it was true. The smile lasted until he heard Evert's hand upon the door. Then, with lightning swiftness he swept the stones back into the bag and the bag into the fastnesses of his clothing. Expressionless again, he unlocked the door and joined Evert in the passage.

There were candles everywhere alight now, but in the hall and up the stairs and along the gallery which Evert had built to satisfy his pride and itch for magnificence, they did less to lighten than to point out the size, the hardly-banished darkness of the place. Here a piece of polished furniture reflected a gleam, there a bowl of flowers basked in the soft radiance, between stretched an eternity of gloom. The scent of the flowers and the potted shrubs was heavy on the warm air, and despite himself Evert thought of the candles and the flowers which were offered to the dead. He shuddered. But his feet were firm on the stairs.

Annabet had spent the hours since Evert had left her in a state of misery that was alternately dazed and clear-sighted. Katje had come up from the kitchen with the information that Mynheer had ordered Mevrouw's dinner to be served in her room, and presently, with apparent artlessness, she spoke at some length of the glories of the dinner which had been ordered and largely prepared for this day, and then abruptly cancelled. For the sake of her own pride Annabet took refuge in feigned invalidism. Intent upon demonstrating that it was her state of health which had put a stop to the festivities, she put on the nightdress which she had brought ashore with a few other essentials in the leather bag, and got into the big bed. She regretted the action as soon as it was performed, for she had experienced nights of sleeplessness immediately after her illness and knew that the energy released by the supine body flew to the brain and encouraged thought. She did not want to think. If she could have had her way she would have dressed again, limped about the house, gone into the garden, probably ventured further into the nutmeg groves, forcing herself all the time to take an impersonal interest in what she saw, following Father Vincent's advice to 'look outside yourself,' and so gained some temporary relief from the misery of spirit which beset her.

Katje pottered about the room, keeping up, for quite a length of time, the pretence at being busy, and when that failed at last she squatted down on the floor, apparently prepared to sit there for ever. She was perfectly still and quiet, because Annabet was pretending to be engrossed in her book; but her presence irked the nerves and after a short time Annabet said that she would sleep until dinner-time and would like to be alone. As soon as she was alone she turned her face into the big soft pillow and gave way to tears. True, in those days when she had been almost mad with crying and Father Vincent had come and talked her back to sanity, she had promised him that she would never gain shed a tear over her ruined looks; but strictly they, although the prime cause of course, were only part of the reason for crying. She cried for remorse, because her wilfulness had brought her to Banda; and from self-pity because no palatable alternative had been offered her, and from hurt pride because Evert had taken her so exactly at her face value and not even bothered to feign ordinary courtesy, he had allowed her no time, no margin. Also she was suffering from the ebb-flow of altruism. All along she had been much borne up by the sense of having greatly helped her family, a feeling not entirely worthy, since vanity and a lust of power were involved in it, but there had been, too, a genuine impulse of self-sacrifice. She was fond of her mother and Klara and Maria, and that draft on the Bank of Amsterdam was going to sweeten their lives. Klara and Maria could have new gowns, and Mamma could afford coach hire to take them out to places where they could be seen. So often Mamma had said, looking at her three pretty girls, 'If only there'd been a little more to spend I could marry you all yet. But girls have to go out. Nobody comes knocking at a house door asking, "Does a pretty girl live here?" ' So true, of course, like so many of Mamma's sayings. And Mamma, coming frankly into the open a few hours before they parted, had said, 'This husband of yours may be cool at first, that is to be expected; but he is your husband, bound to honour and cherish you and if you try to please him he will soon forget your looks.' And that dictum had dovetailed—though its essence was so divergent—with Father Vincent's exhortations to forget the mere body and cultivate the beauties of the spirit. If the spirit were right—and she had honestly meant well by Evert—then the colour and shape of the covering flesh did not matter.

But now she realised with a complete and abject realisation that between a worldly woman and an unworldly man she had been led utterly astray. Little as she had seen of Evert, few as were the words they had exchanged, she knew that there was nothing to hope for from him. She would never forget the cold loathing in his eyes.

She began to think about Evert and admitted, with a slight sense of shock, that he was extremely attractive. Her way of life had encouraged a fundamental innocence combined with trained technique in sexual matters, but for four years, between the ages of twelve and sixteen, she had been extremely pretty, and that had made her conscious of men. She knew that on the rare occasions when she went to the butcher's she had got far more meat for her money than Truitje ever received; her new shoes were finished before Klara's, though Klara's had been ordered first; when the roof of the hired house leaked and leaked through a wet winter and Mamma had written and made a personal appeal in vain, she, Annabet, had met the landlord and half in jest, complained of the drips in her bedroom, and next day the men arrived with ladders and new tiles. Almost, despite herself, she had developed an eye for masculine charms, and Evert's size and good looks had stirred her even while his bad manners waked her hurt resentment. He was just the husband she would have liked fifteen months ago ... fifteen months ago before this horrible thing happened to her. And here she was, back at the beginning, with a fresh spurt of tears over her lost loveliness.

She completed the circle several times before Katje peeped in to say softly that dinner was ready whenever Mevrouw liked to have it. Dusk was flooding into the room, and Annabet was glad that her tear-stained face and swollen eyes were hidden.

'I'm only just awake,' she said. 'Bring it in a quarter of an hour.'

'Shall I light the candles, Mevrouw?'

'That will do when you bring the food.'

When Katje had gone again she went barefooted across the room and bathed her face for several minutes in cool water, and then, in the dusk, coloured her cheeks and lips and brushed her hair. She imagined that she had no appetite for food, but she must eat; always, however, she felt, she must eat, in the hope of restoring some flesh to her bones. And when the dinner, profuse, exotic and delicately served appeared, she found that after all she was hungry. Presently, with two dishes already disposed of and a glass of Burgundy inside her, her spirits took an upward turn. After all, she thought, I might have been in Ireland now, in a cell, with a pallet bed and only the coarsest, nastiest food. I did it. I chose the world, and Banda and Evert Haan, I must make the best of them. ...

'It is not for lack of eating that her bones break free,' Katje reported. Evert had seen her downstairs and locked the outer door, telling her that he would call her when she was wanted again. 'And now,' she added, with a change of voice—envy, memory, and downright astonishment mingled in it— 'Mynheer has gone in to her.'

A sensuous languor fell upon all her hearers.

But Evert did not even enter the blue-and-white room, did not even bother to explain who the visitor was. He left Shal Ahmi at the door and went on to his own room and took a long drink of brandy from the flask which he kept by his bedside. He had, by this time, what with the shock, the vehemence of his feelings, his hours of thought, his lack of food and the quantity of liquor he had drunk, a feeling of complete unreality. He *knew*, because he had seen it and heard it happen, that his bride had arrived, that she was ugly beyond imagination, that he had smuggled her into the house, that Shal Ahmi had arrived and promised to rid him of her, and was even now in the blue-and-white room plotting ways and means. But none of this had any connection with the normal, ordinary life of a nutmeg planter in Banda, whose name was Evert Haan. The whole thing had the unreal, but none the less dreadful, sharpness of a nightmare. If only he could cry out and wake. But if he cried out he knew that it would be only with the remembered words, genuine enough, but fatuous in their conflicting sense. 'I don't want her hurt.' I don't want her hurt, but I want to be rid of her. How could Shal Ahmi, cunning as he was, pander to both these wants. Nobody could.

He drank again, and going to put the now-empty flask back on the table, caught a glimpse of his face in a mirror that hung on the wall. 'I'm a murderer,' he thought solemnly. And then he seemed to lose his holding in the real world, and to pass into the mirror. There—see that big man standing in that dimly-lighted room—that's Evert Haan, the poor farm boy who starved and sweated and nearly died of fever during Gomarus' campaign of 1638; he got a grant of a nutmeg plantation in Banda and made a tidy fortune ... shush ... don't say how, and built a fine house and married a lady. She was ugly and a cripple, so he did away with her. No he didn't, he had her done away with. Is there any difference? He's a murderer. Murderer. *Murderer*. What a sound that word has. A filthy word. It soils the tongue. Murder is the crime for which there is no redress. For any other wrong, if you are sorry, you can say so and make amends, but no man can call back the dead and apologise.

Overcome, he stepped back, feeling for the edge of the bed. And as he sank down upon it the mirror passed out of his range of vision. That was me! That is me! This is Evert Haan, tumbling on to this bed. I've tumbled on to the bed, but I can still move. I can go to Shal Ahmi and say I've changed my mind. He'd be glad. This—and all the other things I've made him do, so many things that I've made him do, are outside what he wants, really. But there's no need for me to move. He won't do anything to-night. My door is open, and I shall hear when he comes out of *that* room. I'll ask what he means to do. I'll . . .

But even in this moment of semi-drunkenness and maudlin sentiment he knew with the core of his mind which could never be self-deceived, that he would do nothing to stop Shal Ahmi, provided only that the plot he hatched were feasible and safe.

When Evert had opened the door and beckoned Katje away, Annabet's heart had begun to beat rapidly. She judged that he meant to return, for he had left the door ajar; and she braced herself to face what would, in any case, she imagined, be an ordeal; and in these circumstances with a man who hated her, almost certain to be terrible.

Mevrouw had, mentally, destined her daughters to marriage from their cradles, and all of them, even the young Maria, knew the little arts of pleasing men; knew that you mustn't be argumentative, or too silent, or too talkative; knew that men avoided the slightest indication of 'boldness' and abhorred, almost beyond everything else, the idea that you ever had a thought in your head other than being agreeable and pleasing. That was before marriage, of course. Afterwards one settled down, and was permitted to show a degree of intelligence over matters like running a household and keeping servants in order; afterwards, too, one cultivated virtues like obedience, loyalty, self-sacrifice and tolerance of male peculiarities. Even in her most despairing moments when it seemed unlikely that any one of her daughters would marry, except to contract a flagrant *mésalliance*, Mevrouw had never weakened, never said: be yourselves, please yourselves. So she would have said, if she had ever spoken of so private a matter, that Klara, Annabet, and in time little Maria, were perfectly fitted for matrimony, and she would have believed what she said. But of the physiological aspect of the married state she had said nothing. For one thing, she had no words in which to describe what happened in the connubial bed; for another, such information was entirely unnecessary. She herself had come from Brussels to marry her Cousin Adriaan with no conception of any caress more intimate than a kiss. She had managed very well and the girls would do the same. Innocence was as much a trapping of a bride as her veil.

But Annabet's innocence had been, not completely, but partially shattered by Klara. The undesirable young man who had met Klara in several furtive rendezvous, and whose dalliance was actually directly responsible for Annabet's rheumatic fever, had carried his love-making—not quite to a conclusion, but very near it. And before Annabet sailed for

Banda, Klara, rather hot in the face and stammering, but feeling very old and experienced, had said, 'There's more in it, Nab, than Mamma has said. And I think you ought to know...' Annabet had listened with the avid attention that she gave to most things, and had been shocked and horrified, not by the thing itself so much as by the knowledge that Klara's tutor in the business had been the red-faced, hard-breathing, and to Annabet, utterly unattractive, young farmer who had sweated so profusely at the skating. It was partly the idea that Evert Haan might also be red-faced and hard-breathing, in fact, just an older version of Klara's lover, which had made her so anxious to ask Piet Odshoorn about him. There was, of course, one man in the world with whom the business would have been possible, if slightly disillusioning, but he was a priest, and to think of him in such a connection was to risk eternal damnation—but she would have risked it, quite happily —and failing him, always supposing that this unseen husband were not definitely ugly or repulsive, she supposed she could bear it. Piet had at least put her mind to rest on that score, and she had seen for herself that he had told her the truth. Evert was, indeed, very attractive. But he hated her. Would that have any effect upon this curious relationship about which Klara had whispered so embarrassedly? Well, she would soon know.

She pulled the pillows behind her and sat up straight in the bed, glad that for Katje's benefit she had bathed and coloured her face and brushed her hair until every curl shone. She heard Evert's tread along the gallery—and no other step, for Shal Ahmi in his sandals moved as silently as any jungle creature— and then the heavy tread passed by, but the open door was pushed wide and a strange, indeed rather terrifying figure, stepped into the candlelight.

'Please,' said Shal Ahmi immediately, 'do not be frightened. I come as a friend. And your husband is within call.'

'He sent you?' She pulled the sheet upwards over her flat chest and wriggled a little lower in the bed.

Shal Ahmi nodded and closed the door.

'Why?'

'Because I am skilled in many arts; medicine among them, Mevrouw. But the good Doctor Van de Lijn, who will come to see you to-morrow, does not approve of our Eastern ways. So before I even look at you I want you to promise me that you will never mention, to him or anyone else, that Shal Ahmi has been to see you.'

'Is that your name?'

'I have many names, Mevrouw. In Banda I am known as Shal Ahmi. And if you stay here you will hear that I have many reputations as well.'

'*If* I stay here. I must stay here. This is my home now. Why

98

did you say *if*?'

'We will speak of that later, with your permission, Mevrouw. First, like a good doctor, I will ask about your illness.'

'But I am not ill. I have already tried to explain that to ... to my husband. I *was* ill. I got better, and now I ... I ... perhaps it is difficult for another person to believe it, but I am perfectly well. The flesh went from my bones and in places the stiffness remains, but I am in good health. You say you have knowledge of medicine. Perhaps you would be so good as to tell my husband that what I said to him to-day is true. I am perfectly well ... otherwise I should not have come. I eat, I sleep, I enjoyed my voyage; when Captain Vehk poisoned his hand I looked after him—he was delirious for three days and nights. I gained two pounds in weight on the way. That is not much, but it shows. By the time I'm forty, at that rate I shall be the right size again....' Her lovely, humourous, self-derisive smile flashed out, and Shal Ahmi who seldom smiled, except when he was alone, smiled back at her.

Yet his answer was unkind. 'That will be too late, Mevrouw.'

'I know. My husband has been talking to you, hasn't he?'

'I should like to explain something to you,' said Shal Ahmi, grave again. 'Your husband, like many other gentlemen in the islands disapproves of Shal Ahmi. As you see, his skin is brown; as you hear, his Dutch is not perfect. When I was young, Mevrouw, brown skin in the Malay tongue were the ordinary colours and speech in the islands. All that is changed now, and it seems that I must walk humbly because of my colour and my speech. Like you, Mevrouw, who was once very beautiful. Oh yes, I have eyes that see beyond the covering. You have the bones of beauty. But that, for the moment, is by the way. I was telling you that your husband, like the others, despises Shal Ahmi. But ... and here he is different from the rest. His mind is not closed. So, knowing that in Holland you would have had the best doctors, with all the wisdom of the West at their command, and still you are not restored ... I won't say to health, but not to the state in which you were, your husband, overcoming the prejudice of the white man for the lore of the brown, has asked me to consider your case. Now will you tell me, from the beginning, the story of your sickness.'

When she had finished, and the story stretched from the fatal visit to the ice fair to the day when the Dutch doctor had said that time and youth were on her side, and she might, possibly improve in looks, Shal Ahmi nodded his head. Then he moved, uninvited, to one of the blue-and-white chairs and sat down. Annabet said:

'I'm sorry. I should have asked you to take a chair ... I just

99

wasn't thinking.'

'I know that, Mevrouw. Now, I am going to ask you a strange question. Indeed, a number of strange questions. Suppose I said that I could cure you. Suppose that I did it. Would you then regret having come to Banda?'

'That would be base of me, seeing that I had been cured there.' The smile flashed again.

'I ask my questions badly, Mevrouw. I meant, would you, restored to health and looks, wish yourself unmarried? I noticed that in your story the affliction came before the proposal. Had it any bearing upon your decision?'

His eyes, which missed nothing, took note of the look of wariness which, visible as a cloud, crossed the shining candour of her gaze. And his ears caught the restraint beneath the formal words of her reply.

'It was my first proposal and acceptable to my family. A year earlier I should have come to Banda with more confidence, but with less gratitude.' The sentence seemed to need a conclusive word, and 'Mynheer' almost fell from her lips. But did one say 'Mynheer' to natives? On the other hand, she could not call him Shal Ahmi on so short an acquaintance. So 'gratitude,' ending the little speech, seemed to hang upon the air with a note of uncertainty in it.

'So you are content to stay here? You like the place, and the man to whom Fate assigned you? You may answer me frankly, Mevrouw. No word of any conversation we hold together will ever be repeated by me. And I ask these questions, not from impertinence, but from a desire to help. There is no other man, with whom given back the beauty of which you spoke with such becoming modesty, you would rather mate yourself?'

A shade of true colour, deeper and lovelier than the false hue of the paint, showed in her face. She had been violently and precociously in love with Cousin Jean Marie when she was ten, and for two years had derived great comfort and hope from the knowledge that within the Van Goens family marriages between cousins were the rule rather than the exception. But Jean Marie had taken orders when she was twelve. He had gone to Spain, and wounded vanity and a strange kind of repulsion had carried her through a critical year; and then, with the spiritual afflatus which so often accompanies the onset of adolescence, she had resigned herself to hopeless love. She would love him for ever, making no sign. But side by side with this feeling there had paced, through the next years, the natural emotions of her development, vanity, because she was pretty, a desire to be married because an old maid was a pitiable, scorned thing, a desire for children. And she had known, for some time before her illness, that one day, if by some extreme and improbably good fortune a likely suitor presented himself, she would marry him and make him so good and proper a wife that he would never suspect that she had ever loved her cousin who had become a priest. Then had come her illness, and after all its torments, the even deadlier misery of seeing herself in the glass for the first time. She had cried, ceasing only from exhaustion, for a whole week, refusing food, unable to sleep, well on the way to madness. She had been determined to die, and she had wanted to see Jean Marie once more. The wish, whispered to Klara, and reported to Mevrouw, had resulted, after further weeks of slow, relentless self-destruction, in Father Vincent's appearance by her bedside. He had changed so much as to be almost unrecognizable. 'I wanted to say good-bye to you,' she had said hoarsely. And he had said, 'Rubbish.' He had sat down by her bed and taken her limp fleshless hands and he had begun to talk. He had used, for the resuscitation of the life-force in this afflicted, vain little cousin of his, all the eloquence which was going to sustain and strengthen so many despairing souls before he died of pneumonia in an unheated priest-hole in Commonwealth England. He had been, to a degree, responsible for her coming to Banda, for it was he who had said, again and again, that it was not what happened to you that mattered, but what you were; the flesh was nothing, the spirit was all.

To-day she had proved him wrong, in one respect at least. She had met Evert in the right spirit, humble and placating; but he had hated the look of her and never given her spirit a thought. And now this queer brown man, all wrapped about in shrouds, was asking if there were any man she would prefer to Evert. What could it matter? She must deny Jean Marie—who was, anyway, no longer a man in the accepted meaning of the term. She did it firmly.

'There is no one else.'

'I ask that, Mevrouw, because with skill and certain arts I have, it would be possible even now to make this marriage as though it had never been; but afterwards, when with my other arts I have restored you to health and beauty, Mynheer Haan will possess you as he possesses his other treasures. It will be too late then.'

'It is too late already. I married Mynheer Haan in good faith. He is displeased with me. But *if* you can make me acceptable to him, all will be as it should be. Can you do that?'

'Of a surety. Mevrouw ... you have two evils and two only. You have no flesh upon your bones and there is a stiffness in your neck, your elbows and wrists, your hips and knees and ankles. Within fourteen days, if you place yourself fully in my hands, you shall be smooth and supple. I ask only that you shall maintain the secrecy which I shall demand, and follow my instructions faithfully. You have eaten to-day?'

'More than usual.' She leaned forward eagerly. 'It is not a question of eating. I have eaten everything put before me for fifteen months.'

'And digested nothing. Outwardly, Mevrouw, you have maintained a calm spirit, there are no marks of discontent or fretfulness upon your face. I am glad of that, they are hard to remove. You have accepted your affliction because of an influence, very powerful, working in your mind. But there has been war within you. When you would have wept you have withheld the tears, when you would have rebelled you have spoken pleasant words, you have cultivated the spirit at the expense of the flesh, Mevrouw. Thus I have seen holy men whose bones belied the brimming plenty of their begging bowls. I will say now, briefly, what I must say, and then I bid you lie down in your bed, think ... know ... that within fourteen days you will be lovelier than ever. I, Shal Ahmi, who never broke a promise save to those who first betrayed me, vow and swear that in less than that space the stiffness shall be gone from your bones. Think that, know that, as you lie in your bed. Know more than that. The signs which do not bother with a lie promise that your future shall be very bright, Mevrouw. There is much love in it. But you must have faith, Mevrouw. You see me, a stranger; I promise you great things. I ask in return only that you should trust me. Can you do that? Have I perhaps already shown that I understand something that has escaped the notice of your Western doctors? Will you believe that what I can recognise I can cure?'

She looked at him for a moment in silence. There had been an air of fantasy about the whole interview. But he had been right about what he so fancifully called 'war' within her, right about the powerful influence, right about the withheld tears. And although if she wrote a detailed account of this interview to Klara (only of course she would not do that until its results were proved) Klara would think she had come to a very strange place indeed, yet somehow this brown man and his confident promises and his insight into her mind, was really all of a piece with the happenings of the day, with the house and the blue-and-white room, with Katje and Evert.

'I *want* to believe it,' she said. 'And I will do whatever you tell me to.'

'That is good,' said Shal Ahmi. 'Now listen, carefully...'

For twenty-four hours Annabet Van Goens and the wildfire rumours regarding her appearance and her state of health usurped the ubiquitous nutmeg from prior place in the islanders' conversation. But by late afternoon of the second day Evert's few real friends were relieved and his many envious acquaintances disappointed to hear, on the authority of no less a person than Doctor Van de Lijn, that Mevrouw Haan was suffering from nothing more interesting than exhaustion and cramp due to her long voyage. He had based this opinion upon a view of Annabet's head as she lay in bed with the sheet smoothed under her chin, and upon what she had told him herself. He had advised her to take a good rest in bed, to eat all she could in order to make up for the unpalatable shipboard fare which had so reduced her flesh, and to get out into the sunshine as soon as she was rested. Actually he was not much interested in young Mevrouw Haan beyond the fact that she had lost weight on the voyage. If she had been a native woman, bedded upon a mat, he would have pounced upon her with glee, noted the prominence of her bones and looked avidly for the dry, scaly patches which spoke of insufficient food. For he was engaged in writing a vast and highly original treatise upon the effect of diet on physiology. He had been at it for five years, ever since he first came East in the Company's service, and had seen, with astonishment, the meagre monotonous diet of the natives. He had once lived for a month upon identical measures of rice and fish and fruit and taken daily note of his loss of weight, his lassitude and his final incapacity for work of any kind. He had taken two holidays in five years and had visited Java and Ceylon, wandering around compounds and native quarters observing and sometimes tasting the food. He had measured and weighed innumerable natives and prepared a table which compared these figures with those of Dutch soldiers and sailors. In his quarters at the Fort he had several cages of monkeys which he fed on different diets, and he was much chagrined because often, just as he was on the brink of drawing a conclusion from the results, the monkeys died—whether from captivity or from the food he could never be certain. But so much of his time and vital force was devoted to his hobby that he had little interest to spare for ordinary medical practice. If Annabet had been suffering from some recognisable complaint, or had been in childbed, or had a broken limb, something professional would have come to the surface and he would have treated her to the best of his ability. But a woman mildly indisposed, and one who could, in the circumstances, be neither weighed nor measured, roused little but boredom in him.

On his way back from Coenpark he looked in upon Kaerko, because he wanted to weigh and measure the members of the *Java*'s crew and needed the Agent's permission, and to Kaerko, who knew where he had been and was full of interest, he reported that Mevrouw would be perfectly all right in a day or two. Questioned further he said that the only thing he had really noticed about her had been her hair. It was very beautiful. He did not add that it was from the gloss upon it that he had adduced that Mevrouw was in good health.

Several people in the course of the morning visited Kaerko's office for one thing and another, and to each the Agent reported the latest news from Coenpark. And before midday Evert's invitation for the postponed dinner had confirmed the doctor's opinion.

At the dinner, which was lavish beyond anything ever imagined in the islands, Evert announced his intention of leaving next morning for Bandogar, and full of his meat and drink, nobody had a thought beyond the obvious one ... that Evert Haan was waiting to consummate his marriage until his beautiful bride was recovered from the effects of her voyage, and that he was, as ever, attentive to his business. There was not a man at the table, friend or foe, who did not admire and covertly envy him. Nobody noticed that Evert drank more than usual, or that his natural florid colour looked as though it were filmed with dust, or that his eyes were uneasy and his hand unsteady. For nobody knew that upstairs there lay an ugly, limb-locked, skeleton who, thanks to Shal Ahmi's machinations, would not be there when Evert came back from Bandogar. For that matter nobody knew that Shal Ahmi had ever crossed the threshold of the fine house where they sat carousing; and when at one point the conversation dwelt for a moment upon that queer person nobody guessed that for once, for the first and only time, Evert's sour remarks about him were at least half genuine. For in this moment of utter dependence upon Shal Ahmi's help, Evert was angered by his silence and secrecy. On the previous evening Shal Ahmi, escorted to the door by Evert, far from sober, had refused to give the slightest inkling of his plan.

'All will be well. When you come back from Bandogar you will be pleased. Ask me no questions.'

And Doctor Van de Lijn had come down this morning and given that so palpably false report; and Annabet, formally visited for the sake of appearance had said, 'I am quite well, thank you. When you come back from the journey I hear you are about to make, I shall be even better.' And he had looked at her impersonally for the first time and thought, 'You'll probably be dead.' And his feelings had been unenviable to say the least. Yet, because he had given Shal Ahmi complete control here were all his friends and his enemies—he flattered himself that he knew them apart—envying and admiring him as of yore. More than once, as they drank to the health of the bride and the bridegroom and the candlelight shone upon their flushed jovial faces and made the glasses in their hands shine like jewels, he had thought—suppose I took you upstairs and showed you the bride, what then? And since he was not utterly

104

a monster, but merely a vain egotist, he knew a moment of envy for any man who *could*, who dared, admit that he had been so thoroughly fooled. There were men, he knew, who would have let Annabet come stumbling to this table, who could have said, 'I drew in the lottery of glove marriage and this is what I got.' But he was not of their company. Such were ordinary fellows who accepted their fate. Good God, if he had been like that he would still have been ploughing the stiff Dutch soil, horny handed, happy if at the end of the year he could pay his rent and put a single gold crown away towards his old age. He would still have been like his Cousin Piet, sweating and stammering in the presence of a Van Goens, whatever its age and appearance. Whereas, being Evert Haan, special, elect, he had seen a Van Goens for what it was, a rotten, conscienceless cheat, a mere impediment to be swept out of his path. Who cared what happened to that fleshless scarecrow who had dared to invade his prosperity? Shal Ahmi was shrewd and cunning, hadn't that been proved again and again? Hadn't it been proved by the matter of the unlimed nutmegs? Hadn't he gone to Shal Ahmi and said, 'There is a man who will not do an errand for me'? And hadn't that worked out perfectly? At least perfectly as far as human fore-sight could see. He wouldn't worry any more. He would just take Shal Ahmi's word: 'All will be well.' But of course, all had always been well with Evert Haan; it always would be, because he was clever, and let nothing, not even sentiment, stand in his way.

'Fill the glasses,' he cried. And they filled the glasses and drained them, wishing their host well, even as they envied him. For there is something cheering and inspiring in the sight of a really successful man.

Afterwards, looking back upon the weeks which followed her arrival in Banda, it seemed to Annabet as though they had been detached from her real life and set apart. Solitude and a curious quietness, like a globe of fine glass, shut her off from the world. Outside among the nutmeg trees the doves kept up a perpetual soft grieving and sometimes she heard sounds of voices and laughter, but they emphasised rather than dispelled the quiet of the blue-and-white room. Katje moved about, soft-footed and sometimes murmured a bit of gossip or genuine news, but as the days passed she grew less talkative and seemed to develop a degree of awe for her mistress; and since there was little to employ her Annabet often sent her away so that she might be alone with her secrets. Day followed day in a trance of wonder and delight. And the nights were full of fantastic interest, waking dreams.

Evert had left for Bandogar in the early morning after the

dinner-party, and midway through the day Katje had come into the room bearing the smallest and lightest piece of the baggage Annabet had left on board the *Java*, and two of the boys had staggered in with the rest. Tied securely to one of the valises was a flat white wood box which she had never seen before, and as soon as the boys had put down their burdens and departed she had raised herself in the bed and asked Katje to bring the box to her. It was addressed to Mevrouw Haan, and she opened it with eager curiosity. Immediately under the lid was a slip of paper upon which was written, in letters curiously formed as though they had been made with a brush dipped in some thick black substance, 'These are not for you. Your kindness will bestow one on Katje each evening. So may the means to recovery come and go.' The box was full of sweetmeats, such things as Annabet had never seen before, brightly coloured sticky, moulded and cut into curious shapes. A little puzzled, she put the box aside, not without regret that the message forbade her to sample its contents. But in the evening when Katje dragged into the room a mat of woven straw, a small round bolster and a rug of many colours, she began to understand.

'What are you doing?' she asked.

'It is my bed,' Katje said simply. 'When the master is away the maid sleeps in the room of her mistress. That is the custom.' Her beady eyes looked at Annabet speculatively. In former days the custom—for it was a custom, well-established —had once or twice been a source of profit to her. The rings which hung from her ears were of real gold, less ornament than a form of insurance against old age or hard times, and they had been bought with guilders which she had earned by the simple expedient of moving her mat into another room. Here, she thought, regretfully, such easy money was unlikely to come her way. Who but a dutiful husband would ever wish to lie with this bag of bones?

Shal Ahmi knew everything, and was very clever, Annabet reflected; and presently she reached for the box of sweets and invited Katje to help herself. She made a pretence of selecting one for herself. Katje took the silver pins from her black hair and placed them for safety under the bolster. Then she said, 'Good night, Mevrouw. I shall hear you if you call me,' and with that—promise or threat?—lay down, pulling the rug over her fully-clothed body. In five minutes she was asleep. Far below in the depths of the house, Josef conscientiously went his rounds, bolting the shutters into place, locking the doors. When everything was made fast he went to his wife in the compound.

Annabet, without difficulty, for she had slept during the day, stayed awake. When Katje was sound asleep she got out of bed and put on her gown and her slippers. From the single candle which had been left burning by her bed she lighted others, and by their light, for the sixth or seventh time that day, she studied her face in the mirror. It did look less haggard. Shal Ahmi had been right. The war within her which had worn the flesh from her bones was ended, new hope, new assurance had already left their mark upon her. Impatiently she waited the sign.

It came at last, the tapping of a light bamboo cane upon the window; and though she was waiting for it, it startled her. She turned to the mat where Katje lay sleeping. Profound and peaceful slumber dwelt upon the hard bolster. She called loudly, 'Katje! Katje!' There was no response. She took a branched candlestick and held it before the sleeping face. A gout of wax fell upon the brown hand, but Katje did not stir. Of course not. Her visitor of last evening did not send sweets for fun. Moving jerkily, but without restraint, Annabet hobbled down the stairs, lighted by her candles, crossed the vast dark hall, and using both hands to the massive key, opened the door.

Then she was frightened. And for a moment—but a moment so packed with feeling that it seemed an age—she thought what a fool she had been. Indeed, the perfect prey. Misled by baseless promises of cure, she had willingly, eagerly, laid herself open to nameless horrors. She had herself drugged Katje, she had herself opened the door. Upon the night; upon Shal Ahmi of whom she knew nothing; upon these formless, faceless things which accompanied him.

The breath went out of her body and she gasped for air; she fumbled with the door as though to close it again, but her hands were weak with terror.

'Do not be alarmed, Mevrouw,' said Shal Ahmi. 'These are but women. Their eyes are darkened and their ears are deaf—but in your service. As Katje sleeps, in your service.'

The fluttering candlelight showed the two figures, slight, a little pathetic in their complete dependence upon the man who held one on either arm. He guided them towards the doorstep, and Annabet, stepping back, watched them enter the house.

'They have skill in their hands, Mevrouw. Skill I have had no time to acquire. You are suspicious. They are old and frail. See.' He twitched aside their veils one after the other and showed the faces of two old women, bound about the eyes with strips of white linen and with lumps of wool protruding from their ears. He let the veils fall again, and something in his attitude denied to the two old women any identity, any human importance. Comforted, but a little appalled, Annabet led the way to her own room where Katje still slept like the dead.

Shal Ahmi was like a person who had come to demonstrate

107

the efficiency of a machine. He pushed and pulled and guided. Only to Annabet, whose eyes and ears were unmuffled, did he use the ordinary means of communication.

'Now, if Mevrouw will lie in her bed and give herself into these hands the work may begin. Do not fear, Mevrouw, they have their orders. And I will wait outside the door as soon as I have put them in their places.'

He pushed one woman on one side of the bed, towards the foot, and the other upon the other side, towards the head. Then he muttered to himself a few words which Annabet did not understand and walked towards the door. Annabet, still wondering, lay down upon the bed.

Four hands, small hands with firm strong fingers, set to work with confidence and precision. First they pushed her bedgown down from the neck, up from the knees, up from the wrists and elbows. Then they moved the stiffened joints one after another, carefully, testingly. And then, as a sempstress might take to pieces an ill-fashioned garment, or a carpenter dismember an ill-made piece of furniture, the four little hands set to work.

Annabet, who had earlier submitted herself hopefully into old Truitje's hands and suffered several violent rubbings with horse liniment, braced herself to endure pain; but there was no pain, and no pleasure in the process. The hands neither gently stroked nor roughly wrenched. Through her skin they reached for and found the taut muscles, the stiffened places where bone touched bone, just as a child might feel for and loosen his sticky sweets through the paper bag which held them. Despite their blinded eyes and deafened ears, there seemed to be some curious accord between them, for when they wanted her position changed the four hands moved like one, lifting or rolling her body as though it were a lump of dough. And presently, as joint after joint was dealt with and laid, as it were, aside, finished, a dough-like feeling of lassitude and anonymity fell upon Annabet. The busy loosening fingers seemed to unfasten the bonds between mind and body until at last she, Annabet Haan, had no connection with the cage of flesh and bone, muscle and blood which had housed her so comfortably for sixteen years and then confined her so cruelly for nearly two. There on the bed it lay discarded, while above it, out of it, beyond it, her spirit floated peaceful and free.

She was sorry when Shal Ahmi stepped back into the room, and there was the inevitable fusion of mind and body as she hastily pulled the sheet over her limbs. The four little hands stopped working as soon as she moved, and the old women stepped back from the bed. With almost identical gestures they lifted the edges of their veils and wiped their faces. She saw with a pang of pity that what had seemed so easy and effortless must have been, in reality, hard work. Both the brown faces were wet with sweat, and the four hands which had been so firm and inhuman in their impersonal skill, were unsteady now, vibrating as though blown in an invisible wind.

'Well,' said Shal Ahmi, 'how do you feel now, Mevrouw?'

She stretched under the sheet. She had not known such ease of movement since the day when she had scampered off in hilarious high spirits to the Ice Fair.

'It's marvellous,' she said upon a gasp of wonder. 'I can never thank you enough.' She looked at him with shining eyes.

'Then we will go.' He picked her dressing-gown from the foot of the bed and laid it within reach of her hand; then, turning his back towards her he took an arm of each of the old women and began to propel them towards the door. Annabet slid her feet to the floor and stooped—without difficulty for the first time in many months—to pull her slippers on.

'I could cry with joy,' she said, stumbling across the room behind the trio. After the long time of checked and fettered motion the new freedom seemed greater than it was, and she felt so light, so loosely put together that her steps were uncertain, like a colt's. And she thought—I'm cured, I'm cured, and now I shall grow fat. Everything will be as it was.

'Oh, Shal Ahmi,' she cried again, 'how can I ever thank you?'

'No need for thanks, Mevrouw,' he said. 'My skill, like everything else in the world, has its price. Your husband will pay me—happily I hope. But I am glad to have given you back your youth.' The last words were kindly spoken. He halted by the mat where Katje lay, and looking over his shoulder at Annabet said, 'She sleeps well.' His eyes twinkled and Annabet laughed aloud.

'Do not be disappointed if to-morrow the cure does not seem as complete as it does to-night, Mevrouw,' he said, moving off again. 'Rest well to-morrow and the next day, eating all that you can. On the next night we will come again. You will remember to lock the door when we are gone.'

She slept soundly, dreamlessly, and woke to find Katje with her hair smoothly dressed and her clothing so neat that it was hard to believe that she had slept as she stood, standing by her bedside with the breakfast tray. Before she had come to full memory and a realisation of what had happened since last she looked into that broad brown face, she was aware that Katje was looking at her curiously.

'Mevrouw is better this morning?' Katje asked formally when their eyes had met and engaged one another for a full minute.

'Yes ... I believe I am. My neck ...' She put her hand to the

109

place where the short curls ended, and jerked her head backwards and forwards and then to each side. 'My neck is better.' It was that which Katje had seen ... ah, and there was so much that she could not see ... the ankles and the knees and the hips, the shoulders and elbows. Hadn't she run up the long curving stairway and down again and then up for the sheer pleasure of the movement last night after she had locked the door behind Shal Ahmi.

'Give me the mirror,' she said.

Katje handed the silver-backed, silver-framed toy which Evert had ordered from Wang Fu for his beautiful bride. Yes, there was a difference about her face; probably no one else would notice it, but the bones in her nose were less prominent and that awful monkeyish look which came from having nothing but skin over her teeth was going. And of course, being able to turn her head made her look very different.

She flung the mirror on the bed and turned to inspect her breakfast.

'I want more than that,' she said when she had reckoned the bulk of the little new bread rolls, warm and wrapped in a napkin, the slices of imported Dutch ham, the dish of native fish, the jar of mango preserve and the basket of fruit. 'I want as much again. You forget Katje that for nearly seven months I have *starved*.' For that was the story that Shal Ahmi had put into her mouth, the story that she had told Doctor Van de Lijn, the story which had been crystallised into a short entry in his book of notes under the heading, 'Haan, Mevrouw,' above the entry, 'Obviously a privileged person, but suffered loss of weight and energy due to monotonous diet devoid of fresh food.'

'I live like a Strasburg goose,' Annabet wrote to Klara on the third day. 'I lie in my bed and cry for food until I am sure that those of the servants who have not seen me must imagine me a monster. And I am getting fatter, *fatter*. But even more marvellous is the lessening of my stiffness. There are women in Banda skilled in some art for which I have no name, but with their fingers they charm the stiffness from one's bones. You had better not tell Truitje this, just tell her that I am better and say it is on account of the climate, because, dear soul, she did try so hard with her horse medicine. This is quite different and very difficult to describe, but when I say that this morning I touched my toes without bending my knees, you will rejoice with me, I am sure.

'Of my husband, Evert,' Annabet wrote, after some nibbling of her quill, 'I can tell you little because a business journey took him away before I had recovered from the effects of my voyage, so I hardly saw him at all. The *Java*, by which I hope

110

to send my letter to you, will sail before he returns. He is handsome, tall and broad, with reddish-brown hair and grey eyes, clean-shaven. He gave a great dinner-party to celebrate my arrival, and of course I should have been there, but I was too exhausted. Besides, my appetite is not a thing to expose to the public at the moment.

'Three of the Banda ladies have "called," Mevrouw Van Heem, Mevrouw Vehmeer and Mevrouw Byskin. I saw none of them. I mean to *burst* upon them when I look like myself. Do you realise, Klara, darling, that I am going to look like myself, and quite soon. It sounds like a miracle, doesn't it. And perhaps you will think that I am exaggerating and telling you a traveller's tale. But it is *true*. And do you remember when you left the French gloves that Aunt Ko-bet gave you in the coach when you had been to visit Cousin Margerite? And somebody—you always thought it was the man with the stammer—picked them up and posted them to you, because you had told him that you lived in Heydberg, and your name and Mamma said it was very indiscreet of you, but really it was fortunate, and always those gloves seemed more precious after that than they had seemed when Aunt Ko-bet gave them to you. It's like that, Klara. I lost my looks; I never hoped to have them again. And now I am going to. And I just can't wait until Evert returns. He will be so surprised, and so pleased. All the time, when he met me on the ship and brought me home (I must tell you all about the house, it is *magnificent*) I kept thinking, if only, if only all this had happened before I was ill. And now it is as though I hadn't been ill. There are still many days to go, and when he comes back I shall be *pretty*.... Oh Klara, I do wish you could be with me, to rejoice....'

She nibbled her quill again, and then, plunging it into the ink, sent it racing over the page. 'Klara, I can't write to Father Vincent, though he was so kind to me, because *I don't know where he is now*. But when Mamma writes she is sure to mention me. Will you tell her—I'll tell her in the letter I write with this, but you tell her too, to remind her, I want him to know that I was right to choose as I did, because I had *no vocation*. And if I had gone to County Down I shouldn't have been *cured*. Will you see that he knows that I am cured, please, and that I am happy. If I could write to him myself I could tell him a great deal more about the flesh and the spirit. It don't think one is much use without the other, and that must be why God gave us bodies as He did ... I mean if the spirit was enough by itself, why did we have to have arms and legs and faces? But if he knows that I am well, and cured and happy, that will be enough. I put all this in because he was so very kind to me....'

The letter ran on and on with its touches of humour and

pathos and nostalgia, and it was not until it was folded and sealed and accompanied by another to Mevrouw, less frank, less voluble, but equally affectionate, that Annabet remembered that the person who would convey the letters all the way over the sea to Holland was Captain Vehk, whom she had, in all good faith, invited to dine with her before he left.

She remembered him just as she was handing the letters over to Katje to give to Abbas to take down to the quay, and her hand flew to her mouth. He had been so very kind and had done so much to restore her shattered self-confidence. He had taken such care of her, too, and been so frankly pleased when she had gained those two poor pounds. His interest in her had even extended to giving her advice about not covering her hair before she met Evert. And he would think that she had forgotten all about him—or had never intended to invite him properly. It would be dreadful if he went back to Holland thinking like that.

'Wait a minute,' she said to Katje, and drew another sheet of paper towards her and plunged the quill into the ink.

'Dear Captain Vehk [she wrote vigorously], will you give me the pleasure of your company at dinner to-morrow? I will send a [she hesitated; what was the word they used? And how did one spell it? No matter, he would know what she meant], boat for you. The bearer will await an answer, and if to-morrow is inconvenient for you, please suggest another day.

Yours sincerely,
Annabet Haan.'

'Tell Abbas there is an answer,' she said, hastily folding the paper and not bothering to seal it.

As soon as Katje had gone she experienced a collapse of confidence so complete that it made her feel sick. She realised that she did not know anything about her house or her household; she had no idea of what to order in the way of food; the captain would require something to drink, and she knew nothing about that either. And at the back of her mind was a doubt as to whether young married women were supposed to entertain men to dinner during their husbands' absence. But the *Java* would sail before Evert returned, and whom else could she ask? After a moment she put the matter of convention aside and concentrated upon the practical aspect of her rash invitation. When Katje slipped into the room again she asked her, 'Katje, who is the most important servant here?'

'Josef is head boy.'

Annabet visualised the problem of providing an acceptable dinner with the help of a slightly more responsible edition of

Abbas and Juan and her heart quailed. But she said resolutely:
'Ask him to come and see me.'
'Has something displeased Mevrouw?'
'No. I want to make some arrangements.'

She was comforted and yet intimidated when Josef presented himself. He looked old and sensible, which was, in a way, a good thing, yet was, on the other hand, a little confusing. It was hard to have to admit complete ignorance to such a one. If only it had been Truitje to whom one could have said so frankly, 'Look Truitje, I want to give hospitality to someone who was very kind to me. What's the best we can do for five guilders?' But of course Josef was not Truitje, and the matter of cost was no longer paramount. So she frowned at him, because she was nervous and puzzled and Josef was extremely glad that he had rewound his turban—he was a Mohammedan—and washed his hands before he came into her presence. And the thought went through his mind that the young Mevrouw was far from being what Katje had described.

'You're Josef? You know all about the house? The stores? You know what food we have?'
'Yes, Mevrouw. Mevrouw desires some special dish?'
'Not for myself. But to-morrow, or another day ... I'll let you know in an hour, I shall be having a guest. I want to give him the best we have. And although I have enjoyed everything you have sent up to me, I don't know what to order.'

'There are chickens, Mevrouw, in the compound. Chang Loo has a litter of sucking pigs. There is fish. There is rizplatzen; there is marchpane; the cook is skilled in chupatti; there is fruit. Or the pudding, boiled in a cloth. Mevrouw has only to say what she desires.' He took Annabet's blank stare for disapproval and added hastily, 'The ship which brought Mevrouw brought also the cheese from Holland, and ham. Mevrouw has tasted the ham. Chopped and cooked in the egg dish it is acceptable. Mevrouw perhaps does not understand that the *roast joint* is difficult to obtain. In Banda there is no pastureland, and so no ox. It is perhaps of the dish called sirloin that Mevrouw is thinking.'

The names rattled in Annabet's ears like the stones in a fool's bladder.

'No,' she said. 'I have no idea what I want, but I want it to be the kind of dinner which will honour the guest. Look ... before he left Mynheer gave a dinner. I want something like that.'

'But, Mevrouw,' said Josef, wide-eyed. 'Not to-morrow. That dinner was extraordinary. For many months the preparations were made. The *bridecake* was twelve hours in the baking; the Chinaman, Wang Fu, had spent two days in the kitchen telling how the *birdsnestsoup* was made. It would be

113

impossible to make that meal in a day.'

Completely confused, Annabet said, 'I don't ask the impossible. I just want, to-morrow or the next day or perhaps the one after that, a meal which pleases my guest. And what about wines?'

'They are all locked, Mevrouw. Mynheer took the keys with him. They hang upon his chain.'

'Oh bother!' said Annabet, using the childish expression which dated from the days when the fire wouldn't light, or the carefully contrived renovation of some old garment proved unsatisfactory, or Mevrouw had disapproved of some high-spirited plan. 'Where are the wines kept, Josef?'

'Some are in the cupboard in the dining-room, Mevrouw.'

'I'll look at it,' said Annabet, and she rose to her feet more easily than Josef expected. Katje had certainly reported that Mevrouw seemed better, but her first reports had been so enthusiastically gloomy that 'better' had seemed to leave a good deal to be desired.

She had been in the dining-room of Evert's house, her house, before. But always—obeying Shal Ahmi's instructions, secretly and at night. She considered it a magnificent but oddly gloomy room. The walls were white, like all the walls of the house, and the floor was made of red tiles set into wide borders of mortar, coloured white. There was a table which could seat twenty, and twenty chairs with leather seats and twisted legs and high backs. On one wall the expanse of the whiteness was broken by a huge mirror, under which stood a sideboard laden with silver, and another contained the cupboard of which Josef had spoken so reverently. Perhaps with many guests ... uproarious, merry people at their ease, the room might be habitable, but it would be very gloomy holding just herself and Captain Vehk.

'I don't want my dinner served in here,' she said positively, when, followed by Josef, she had entered the room and stood looking meditatively at the cupboard in the wall. 'Where is there, otherwise?'

'A little table in the drawing-room,' Josef suggested. Annabet shuddered. She knew the drawing-room too, and privately deplored it. She had, after all, spent most of her formative years in the small, poorly furnished Heydberg house and the room which Evert had planned with the idea of some beautiful graceful lady dispensing tea to the ladies of Banda had struck her as being too large and over-magnificent. And there wasn't a chair in it in which Captain Vehk would feel comfortable.

'No,' she said positively. And then, without any warning pang of premonition, she went on, 'I'll have the dinner served in that little room off the verandah at the end of the passage.'

'Mynheer's study?'

114

'Is that what it is? You can put a small table in there, Josef, and plenty of candles. And as for the meal you must order the best that there is at the moment. I was only trying to give you an idea when I mentioned the dinner before Mynheer left. Fish, sucking-pig, chicken, marchpane, fruit and cheese. That will do. And now, will you bring me whatever it is that you would open a stout box with.'

'Mevrouw wishes a box opened?'

'No, thank you, Josef. I want the tool that you would use to open a box.'

When it came it was a perfectly ordinary chisel. She took it into the dining-room and after fifteen minutes' hard work succeeded in opening the cupboard in which some of Evert's liquor was stored. Faced with the rows of bottles she felt young and silly again, but decided that Captain Vehk could choose his own. Presently Abbas returned from his run into Banda and back, his slim, uncovered torso heaving with every deep, effortless breath and handed her the captain's acceptance for that evening. Afterwards the simple events of that morning gave her a whole series of 'ifs' to ponder over ... if she hadn't remembered and honoured that invitation; if she hadn't thought the dining-room too large and stiff; if she hadn't opened that cupboard and got at the brandy; if Captain Vehk had chosen another day ... how different everything would have been. Or wouldn't it? Would some other chain of little happenings have brought about the same results?

Jean Vehk came to Coenpark in what he imagined to be a mood of detached interest. Nobody had mentioned to him that Evert Haan had left for Bandogar two days after his bride's arrival, and since it was now some time since the pair had made that odd, furtive exit from the *Java*, the captain was anxious to see how, in his own phrase, they 'had shaken down.' It had taken him only a day or two to realise that the scrawny, ugly woman against whom he was prejudiced from the start, was a charming companion; and he hoped, for her sake, that the man she had married had not shown less perspicacity.

Any surprise he felt in finding Annabet alone was engulfed and forgotten in his astonishment at the change in her appearance. The graceful, easy, undulating movement with which she came forward to greet him, the perfect poise of the head which had been so stiffly, awkwardly held, the curves which were replacing the hollows in her cheeks and temples—all equally incredible.

'But for the dress, Mevrouw, I should hardly have recognised you,' he said in all sincerity.

'And even the dress has been let out,' said Annabet happily. And then a kind of awkwardness fell between them. Now that

115

the young lady looked like a young lady, Jean Vehk found himself remembering too late that one should not, so bluntly comment upon a lady's appearance. And Annabet, realising that she was no longer his cherished passenger, his almost-patient, sexless because of her affliction and their relative positions, judged that a lady ought not to refer to matters like her increasing girth and the consequent letting-out of her dress seams. She rushed into the stiff little silence with formal words which did credit to Mevrouw's training.

'I am so sorry, Captain Vehk, that my husband is not here to meet you. He had to go away on business, and you will have sailed before he returns. I know he would have enjoyed making your better acquaintance.'

'And I his, Mevrouw,' Jean Vehk said. And that avenue of communication was closed; and Annabet thought, if we go on like this it'll be a very tedious dinner, and he'll be sorry he came. What's happened to us? He's the same person that used to curse and swear and then apologise, nearly crying, when I put the bread poultice on his hand; and I'm the same person, though, thank God and Shal Ahmi, I look different. And she laughed and said:

'Why on earth we're talking to one another like this, I can't imagine. I'm so *glad* to see you. I've a hundred things to tell you. When do you sail?'

'The day after to-morrow, Mevrouw.'

'You could keep a secret for two days, couldn't you? Then I can tell you everything. All the marvellous things that have happened to me. I haven't had anyone to talk to, you see. And writing to people isn't the same. But first of all I want you to come here.'

She led him into the dining-room. 'You know about wines and things, don't you? Do you remember that day when you got up for the first time? Well look—there seems to be a lot of things there and I didn't know what you would like. Will you choose? That's right. And now look at this room. Isn't it horrible? By rights we should be in here to-night, but I just couldn't bear it.'

'It is rather large for two people, Mevrouw; but it is a beautiful room. An exceedingly beautiful room.'

'Is it. Why?'

'It is nobly proportioned, Mevrouw. The arch of that window; the fall of the curtains; the sheen of polish on the furniture. Your husband must be a man of taste and discernment.' He looked at the room as he spoke and then back at his hostess and wondered. This unknown once-seen and considerably disliked Mynheer Haan evidently had the eye of an artist. How that first meeting with his bride in the little cabin must have hurt him! How long had he been away? How much of

116

this remarkable transformation had he seen? He put the question into words, as, at Annabet's repeated request, he selected bottles from the cupboards.

'Oh, I hardly saw him. I do hope he will have a pleasant surprise when he comes back. He had a nasty one when he met me. You're my friend, aren't you, Captain Vehk? Can I say to you, without being misunderstood—that he made no secret of his feelings? And ask you a question? Is the change in *me* sufficient to justify me in expecting a change in *them*?'

'I should wait and see,' he said with his head in the cupboard. She was almost lovely now. At this rate, soon, she would be very lovely indeed—lovely, frank, honest, engaging, kind. What luck some men had!

'I owe it all to the most *peculiar* person called Shal Ahmi,' Annabet rattled on as he turned from the cupboard with his spoils. 'He's a native, but not a bit like those you see working or going errands. He's fat, and bald and all wrapped about in white linen cloths, but he's extremely dignified. I was very frightened of him at first. . . .' She broke off, as Josef, in his best manner, announced that dinner was ready.

Behind his bland mask, Josef, like Katje and all the other servants who knew anything about it, was avid with curiosity about Mevrouw and her guest. Mevrouw had risen, almost literally from her bed, in order to entertain this man, and it was disappointing to find that he was small and elderly and, even by the lenient standards which one must apply in judging white men, far from handsome. Why then had Mevrouw exerted herself, fussed about the food and burst open Mynheer's cupboard?

The dinner went smoothly. Jean Vehk spoke amusingly of Doctor Van de Lijn's weighings and measurings of the *Java*'s crew.

'He would have included me, Mevrouw, had I permitted. I told him bluntly that I had measured what I do now when I was fourteen years of age, and though I might not be contented with my size there was nothing either he or I could do about it now. As for my weight, I said, when I am sent—as God knows I might be any day—to carry a cargo or pick one up from the cannibal isles, then it will be of interest to others beside myself. Until then, no! But he measured and weighed a number of crew—I think Daan almost broke his scales—and he had the audacity, Mevrouw, to hint that we had sadly starved *you* on the voyage.' He looked at Annabet a little reproachfully, thinking of the goats; of the barrel of fine white flour; of the jars of honey, the cask of salted butter. 'He is quite mad, Doctor Van de Lijn.'

'He was a little misled,' Annabet said, conscience-stricken. Her story of Shal Ahmi and his devious ways was still untold.

117

'Very well, Josef. Bring us the coffee now and that will do.'

The table which Josef had judged to be small enough, and had had moved with difficulty, would have seated eight people with ease. The fine cloth, inset with lace, had been withdrawn, and now, between Annabet and her guest the dark polished top of the table lay like a lake, bearing islands of fruit and flowers and candlelight upon its glassy surface.

'Move your chair closer and then we can chat and be cosy,' said Annabet when Josef had set down the tray of coffee, made and served as Evert liked it, Turkish fashion, thick black syrupy stuff in little cups fitted into silver filegree holders. 'Don't drink it if you don't like it,' Annabet said, handing the little cup. 'I didn't at first, but I'm growing used to it. Did you bring plenty of brandy? That's right. There, now I can tell you about Shal Ahmi ...'

She had told him many stories before, making, by means of an apt word, a humorous turn of thought, a shrewdness of observation, an acceptable entertainment out of the undramatic things which had hitherto happened to her. Often Jean Vehk had arranged himself so that he could listen to her and not be obliged to watch the further havoc which vivacity wrought in that ruined face, or the little gestures which must once have been so engaging and were now so cramped and jerky. To-night no such arrangement of position was necessary; to-night, when she smiled, it was no longer a deathshead grinning when she said, 'veiled from here to here' her hands moved like birds in flight. The story of Shal Ahmi's methods lost nothing in the telling, and the captain leaned back in his chair, an excellent dinner inside him, good brandy at his elbow, part of his mind pleasantly lulled and at peace, as he followed the interesting tale, and the other part noting and wondering, drawing conclusions and rejecting them again, and feeling sorry for all the men in the world who were not married to Annabet Haan.

'That's why,' she said, rounding off her story, 'I couldn't ask anyone else to dine with us. Shal Ahmi was most insistent that I should see no one until Evert returned. That should be nine days from now....' She stopped speaking suddenly and seemed to listen. 'You aren't breathing funnily, are you? Somebody is. Listen!' He listened obediently and heard nothing. 'Open the door sharply,' Annabet said in a whisper, and in a normal voice went on, 'And that is why Doctor Van de Lijn said that you've starved me ... you see all this time I am supposed to be recovering from...' Jean Vehk had moved softly to the door and flung it open abruptly, expecting to find some startled, cringing native gabbling out some ready-made excuse about changing the candles or thinking he had been called. But outside the door the passage which led inwards to the house was bare and empty. On a bracket half-way along its

118

length a little lamp burned steadily.

'Nobody there,' he said, closing the door and returning to his place.

'My imagination,' said Annabet smiling. 'It's so quiet here, especially up in my room, that I expect I shall get into the habit of hearing things, just as people who live alone get to talking to themselves. No it isn't. There it is again.'

And that time he heard it, a curious low sound, like a breath drawn in an extremity of pain. He remembered that he was not in Holland, nor aboard his ship where every sound was known and recognisable, and a nervous crepitation, of which he was ashamed, ran along his spine. This was a place where anything might happen. He looked at the silver bell which stood near Annabet's place at the table, and had half a mind to suggest that she ring it and summon servants to make a tour outside the house. But even as the thought went through his mind, Annabet, who had been listening with her head turned slightly aside, jumped up and said, 'It's on the verandah,' and ran to the shutter which closed the window.

He snapped, 'Stand aside, Mevrouw,' and pushed her hand from the bolt which secured the shutter to the floor, and himself moved it cautiously, opened the shutter an inch or two, and staring into the blackness, asked sharply, 'Who's there?'

An unmistakable sound of distress answered him and he opened the shutter a little wider, and the candlelight, faint in itself, but brilliant against the blackness of the moonless night, revealed to his searching eyes the figure of a man ... who lifted a white face ... a *white* face towards the light and said, 'Thank God, Evert,' and then seemed to drop senseless.

Annabet by this time was at his elbow. He turned his head.

'You called your husband Evert, didn't you?'

'Yes. That is his name.' She pressed closer. 'What is it? Who is it?'

'Somebody who seems to know your husband's name. No. Wait a minute, will you stand back!' He reached into his pocket and his pistol met his hand reassuringly; then, deliberately, he drew the shutter closed behind him and stepped on to the verandah. Nothing stirred. After a few seconds his eyes became accustomed to the darkness and he could see, dimly, the posts of the verandah, the edge of its roof against the sky, the first few feet of the garden beyond. When he was satisfied that no active intruders were lurking behind the man who lay supine at his feet, he pushed the shutter open with his elbow, and bending, seized the fallen man by a handful of his clothing and pulled him into the room where Annabet waited, her face and her hands clasped together high on her chest, expressive of anxiety.

'What is it? Who is it?' she asked in a whisper.

'I know no more than you do,' he said, and dragged the body into the light. 'There. Ever seen him before.'

Easy enough to say no; Evert was the only white man in the whole of Banda whom she could have recognised by sight. And it was not Evert. It was nobody whom she had ever seen before. Yet, as she stared down at the upturned face, so still, so shuttered and so defenceless, and as her eyes and her mind pronounced their verdict of non-recognition, she was pierced by a feeling similar to that which might come to a blind man suddenly restored to sight, a man who had handled and smelt a rose in the days of his blindness and was now seeing one for the first time and knowing it for what it was. A recognition, not of touch or sight, but of essence.

For a moment, during which Jean Vehk thought her shocked into silence, she studied the man's face. Why should it have this singularly moving quality? Why should it give her a sense of fulfilment, of homecoming? In features it was ordinary enough. A squarish face, tanned by the sun but bleached now to a dirty pallor; a short, blunt nose that jutted arrogantly, straight black brows and long, rather childishly curving lashes. But even now, in the complete relaxment of unconsciousness, the features were of less significance than the expression. It was such—Annabet thought—such a very bitter-sweet face. The lines that ran midway down the slightly hollow cheeks, the lines that ran between nostril and mouth, the curve of the mouth itself were all so eloquent of bad luck borne with grim good-humor, of disillusionment accepted with resignation, and of a vast, almost fierce determination. You could see at a glance that life had gone hardly with him, that he could be gay, that he was reckless and stubborn, and that his youth had been brought to manhood oversoon. And it occurred to her that she was reading a story that might already have reached its end.

'Is he dead?'

Jean Vehk did not answer immediately. He had dropped to his knees beside the supine body and was feeling for the heart-beat of the stranger. The man wore a shirt, once white but now yellowed from the sun and bad washing, but ruffled at its front and cuffs. He pulled it out of the waistband of the buff-coloured breeches and laid his hand on the man's chest.

'No, he is alive, Mevrouw. His heart beats.' And as he spoke he saw, in the candlelight, the red pool widening about the man's shoulder. At the same instant Annabet said in a thin, frightened voice, 'He's bleeding! Can't we do something.'

'Mevrouw,' said Vehk, sitting back on his heels, 'this is no sight for you. Leave us. I will do what I can.' But she gave a kind of wordless gasp of protest and put her hands on either side of the man's head, easing it over as Vehk turned the body.

The back of the white shirt was soaked with blood. Vehk pulled it up and exposed the wound. Just behind the right shoulder was a little gash, not more than an inch in length, narrow as the blade of a knife, but bleeding steadily. Vehk put his hand over it.

'Mevrouw, he has been stabbed in the back. Please ... a lady ... If you wish me to help him, go away yourself and send me one of your servants.'

'I shan't faint,' said Annabet quickly. 'I'll stay and help. You see ... he came very secretly to the window, not to the door. And he asked specially for Evert, by name. It might ... perhaps it is something they oughtn't to know about.' As she spoke her mind shot off to Shal Ahmi and his secret comings and goings and she realised that his visits had prepared her for secrecy. Back in Heydberg, faced with such a situation—if that were imaginable—her first thought would have been to call Truitje. But not here. Not Josef. Not Katje.

'Could we bring him round and ask him first?' she suggested.

Jean Vehk looked at her curiously. She had been in the house for some time and might know something which in this crisis made her judgment more valuable than his own. It was true enough the stranger had come to the window, not to the door, and had said, 'Thank God, Evert,' and promptly lost consciousness as though, thinking that he recognised Haan, he could relax and leave the rest to him.

'As you will, Mevrouw,' he said, and bent again over the body, which now lay face downwards. His quick brown fingers pressed the lips of the wound together and the bleeding lessened. Holding it so, he fumbled one-handed for his handkerchief, and held it out to Annabet.

'Fold that into a tight hard pad. Thank you. Now, have you anything handy which would be long enough to tie round his chest?' She thought quickly and said, 'My stockings. Would they do?'

Vehk nodded and she stripped them off. 'Tie the toes,' he said. When they were knotted together he placed the knot over the folded handkerchief, and keeping it in position with his hand, turned the man over again. 'Pull the ends clear and hold them a moment, will you? Then, when the stranger's body was on its back again, handkerchief and knot pressed against the wound by its weight, he tied the ends of the stockings securely.

'When I was a boy,' he said reminiscently, 'my father cut his wrist with a bill-hook, and my mother stopped him bleeding to death with a piece of yarn and a cooking-spoon. It's the quickness that tells. There. Now we'll lift his head—otherwise

121

we'd choke him—did you know that? And now, a little brandy in that glass please.' She poured it, surprised to find her hand so steady. 'And a small spoon. Thank you.' Very gently he spooned drops of the spirit between the pale lips. He took his time now, holding the lolling head against the crook of his arm and dribbling a few drops, and then waiting, with the care and the patience of a woman feeding a sick child. Afterwards Annabet remembered the moment with gratitude. Presently, of its own accord, the inert body stirred. Jean Vehk tightened his clasp. The man moaned. His eyelids fluttered without opening, and his lips parted on a deep indrawn breath. Jean Vehk spooned in a few more drops of brandy and this time the man gulped them and opened his mouth again. He swallowed and then said, without opening his eyes, and speaking in a clear voice which mangled the Dutch words with curious delicacy, 'I thought I'd never get here.' And then, perhaps because he expected Evert to answer him and was shot into complete consciousness by the silence with which Annabet and Jean Vehk received the remark, he opened his eyes. For a moment his stare was like a young puppy's, vague and milky; then it hardened and sharpened; consciousness, fright, suspicion and caution showed in it. He lifted his head clear of the captain's shoulder and looked into his face.

'You're not Evert Haan,' he said accusingly.

'I never pretended to be,' said Jean briskly. He pulled the chair in which he had been sitting before the disturbance occurred, towards him, and propped the stranger against the edge of the seat and stood up. 'There, take your time,' he said. 'Mynheer Haan is away from home. I am the guest of his wife. This is Mevrouw Haan.'

'Don't be silly,' said the man. 'Evert isn't married.' He rolled his head against the seat of the chair and then said sharply, 'Whoever she is, get her away. I'm going to be sick.'

'I don't think you will be,' Vehk said, still in that brisk, business-like voice. 'You've been knifed in the back and lost a lot of blood. That's what gives you the feeling of nausea. Here, drink this.'

He mixed a glass of brandy and water and held it towards the man. 'Can you manage? Good. You'll be all right. It's a perfectly clean wound. Replace your leakage and you'll be all right.'

The stranger drained the glass and handed it back. Then he let his lids droop over his eyes again, but Annabet, standing slightly to one side, saw that his eyes were not closed, nor were his features relaxed. Upon that lowered face an expression of frank bewilderment gave way to one of extreme craftiness, and that gave way to a smile as he opened his eyes wide and said to Vehk, 'I could sit in this chair if you lent a hand. Thanks. Give me a drink, will you! Plain water.' She saw his eyes above the glass as he drank thirstily; they were wary, concerned, speculative.

'Thank you,' he said, returning the glass. And then, with a deliberate mustering of strength, 'I'm sorry to give you so much trouble. But I thought Haan was here. The light shows through that shutter you know, and I thought nobody else ever used this room. I'll go in just a minute, and I apologise for disturbing you.' His voice tailed off weakly, but he made another effort, straightened himself with a grimace of pain, quickly banished, and smiled. 'You're a friend of Haan's?'

'No. As I said before, I'm a guest of Mevrouw Haan. This is Mevrouw.'

'Oh, all right. I'm asking no questions. But I thought you might be a friend. Evert has a hundred of them. Understandable too. He's a grand fellow. And if you stick to it, we'll pretend it's Mevrouw Haan. Ask me no questions, and I'll ask you none. I'll go away in a minute. I had a little argument with a Chinaman and he knifed me, and I thought of Evert, he was nearest. But you're safe with me. If you say nothing, I say nothing, and the whole thing's forgotten.'

'But you wanted my husband for something. He is away. Is there anything I can do?' Annabet asked.

He looked at her seriously for the first time, frowning in an effort to concentrate, narrowing his grey eyes between their long dark lashes.

'You're Isa. I've heard about Isa. I didn't know she was ... white. Don't bother. Not a word shall pass my lips. Just let me go and we'll forget it ever happened. My God, though, you are beautiful. And Evert thinks the world and all of you. You're a very naughty little girl. But if you'll forget me, I'll forget you ... him too. Is that a bargain?'

Something snapped in Jean Vehk's brain. His face flushed. The man was hurt and wandering in his mind, doubtless; but Mevrouw was a wife of some days' durance and the most charming woman he had ever met.

'Mynheer,' he said incisively, 'this is Mevrouw Haan whom I had the honour of conveying from Holland to Banda. Mynheer Haan has gone away on business, and Mevrouw, having invited me, some time ago, to dine with her, has been obliged to entertain me alone. Mevrouw will perhaps make allowance for the fact that you are not quite yourself; but until you *are*, I should advise you to be silent.'

Annabet, puzzled and embarrassed, saw the face muscles tighten under the oddly patched white and dirty tan-coloured skin. He too, was puzzled and embarrassed. He lifted his left hand and brushed it across his brow and said, 'I hardly know what I'm saying, or where I am.' But she knew that he was

123

lying. Across the back of her mind fluttered the query—who is Isa? But most of her consciousness was pondering the problem of the man himself. Who was he? Where did he come from? Why had he been knifed? What did he want with Evert? Why, thinking that she was somebody else, had he made that bargain of secrecy? It was all extremely interesting.

Jean Vehk turned to the table. 'With your permission,' he said, and poured, first a glass of the yellow wine which she had drunk with her dinner, and then a glass of brandy for himself.

'We've had a shock, you know,' he said, handing her the glass.

'I do know,' the stranger said eagerly. 'It was unpardonable of me. But I couldn't know, could I? I thought there'd be old Evert here, brooding over his accounts, and he'd patch me up, give me a drink, and we'd curse all hasty-tempered Chinamen ... I'd no idea. I wouldn't have disturbed a dinner-party to save my life.'

Vehk took up the words. 'Be glad you didn't know, then. For we *did* save your life.'

'I am infinitely obliged.' He dropped his head and looked at the knot of stocking tops tied in a bow upon his chest. His eyes moved to Annabet, who blushed and looked away. 'I am *infinitely* obliged,' he repeated. His voice, for all its emphasis, was weakening; and as though he were aware of it, he said hastily:

'When will Evert be back?'

'In nine days' time,' Annabet said.

'Then I'll look in and explain things and apologise.' Above the grey eyes the bleached brows met as he frowned. 'Perhaps you'd better just give him a message from me. Tell him the cock had a black tail. He'll know then why I didn't buy it for him. That was what the argument was about. The Chinaman didn't like what I said about the bird. Just tell him that the bird had a black tail. Then he'll know how to look out for another. Evert ...' the weak voice became carefully explanatory, 'is very particular about his fighting cocks. And the best ones haven't black tails. Well, I think I'll go now.'

He rose from his chair, casual and easy, just as though he had come in for a moment to leave a message about a fighting-cock's tail. But as soon as his weight was on his feet he swayed, twisted to grip the back of the chair, missed it and fell to the floor. He had not lost consciousness again, for his hands scrabbled at the table-leg, then at its edge, and finally he pulled himself into a kneeling position and so stayed, looking at Annabet and Vehk with an expression at once piteous and defiant. He said, below his breath, three words which they did not understand, and his knuckles whitened as his hands gripped the smooth wood. Vehk, with something of delibera-

124

tion in his movements, took a step forward and hooked his arm under the man's and heaved him back into the chair.

'I don't think you'll go very far to-night, Mynheer,' he said, when the action was performed. 'It's no business of mine. In a few minutes I leave for my ship. You say you are a friend of Mynheer Haan. This is his house, and here is his wife. Hadn't you better explain your business and tell her who you are and ask her assistance?' He turned to Annabet. 'I think, Mevrouw, that you should ring your bell and summon Josef.'

'Don't do that,' said the stranger sharply. 'Do anything but that.'

'I won't,' said Annabet, eagerly. 'You hoped to find my husband here. He is away, but I am here in his place. You may trust me, Mynheer. Please behave as though he were here. What would he do?'

'Presumably,' said Vehk coldly, 'he would know the man's name and business. Such knowledge eases arrangements, Mevrouw. And until you know . . .'

'Just a minute,' said the man. He put his left hand upon the edge of the table and cautiously, experimentally, levered himself into a standing position. He attained it, but dropped back almost instantly. 'My God,' he said furiously, 'the spirit is willing, but the flesh is weak . . . I never realised what that meant until this moment.' He looked at Jean Vehk with a beaten, broken look. 'You're a strong fellow. Do me a favour. Drag me down to the landing-stage. There's a prahau there. Chuck me into it and set it loose. That's all I ask.'

Jean Vehk looked at Annabet. The suggestion was quite to his taste. The stranger had disturbed his last interview with Annabet, was mysterious and uncommunicative, and he would have turned him adrift in a prahau without the slightest compunction. But it was Mevrouw's house. It was for her to say.

'It would be better, surely, to ring for Josef and ask him to prepare a bed. Wouldn't that be what my husband would do?'

'Good God no!' He was silent for a moment after the emphatic statement, and Annabet, watching his face, thought what a pity it was that a person so near physical collapse should be driven to invent lies. 'Mevrouw, your husband is an eminently respectable man. I am not. Our lives only meet because he has fallen victim to the charm of cock-fighting. The Company does not quite approve of the sport. So I act for Evert; I buy his cocks and place his bets. I, myself, Mevrouw, am a notorious character. If it were known that I had spent a night beneath Mynheer Haan's roof, it would ruin his reputation. I would avoid that at all costs. He has been a good patron to me. Do you understand?'

125

'And what would the good patron do if he were here?'

'Carry me to the prahau and turn it loose, Mevrouw. I do assure you that it is the one thing to do.'

'Good patrons are more careful of their protégées, Mynheer. I think that if my husband were here he would solicit Captain Vehk's aid and convey you to his own room, see you into bed, and lock the door. I think, Mynheer, that it was not in order to be dragged to your prahau and set adrift that you came to that window. Or am I mistaken?'

'Excuse me,' said the stranger. 'I am now going to be sick.'

He stretched his left hand across to the right-hand pocket of his breeches, pulled out his handkerchief, and held it in front of his face. Jean Vehk took a quick sideways step so that he might interpose his body between Annabet and the regrettable sight. She stood, thinking quickly.

'Captain Vehk,' she said after a moment, addressing his back. 'Will you do something for me? I am sorry to give you any more trouble, but there's no one else whom I can ask.'

'I am at your service, Mevrouw. But before you decide upon any plan of action I feel that it is my duty—if only because I am older than you and more experienced in the world—to point out that you should be very careful what you do in your husband's absence. We have only this fellow's bare word to show that he has even your husband's acquaintance; he has not told us his name, and the story of his business being concerned with a fighting-cock sounds very thin to me. I agree that he is in no condition to be moved at the moment and unlikely to be of danger to you personally, but I should be very reluctant to assist you in any plan which involved harbouring him in your house secretly.'

'But reluctant or not, you would do it? Please. You see, Captain Vehk, I'm quite certain that, mysterious as he seems, he did come to see my husband, and intended his visit to be secret. So I must look after him and keep him hidden if it can be managed. With your help I think it can.'

'I wish,' said the man, and now his exhausted voice touched the syllables of the Dutch words so lightly that it sounded like a child's prattle, 'you wouldn't both talk about me as though I were deaf or insane. I've told you what to do. Get me down to the landing-stage and chuck me into my prahau.'

'But you'd just drift. You couldn't row or steer. You might die.' She said the words eagerly, forgetting to shelter behind the captain's body, staring into the man's face, oblivious to his wretched appearance.

'Well, you needn't worry about that, Mevrouw. It's better that I should drift and die than be caught here.'

He bit his lip, and something told Annabet that he regretted the implications of the word 'caught.'

Vehk pounced on it at once. 'This business of the fighting-cocks must be very serious for you to talk like that.'

'Damn you,' said the stranger in a voice so faint that there was little venom in the words. 'You're in the Company's service too. I suppose you've never done an errand that involved a few lies and a little secrecy. Evert Haan and I have been on the track of something very curious and shady for a long time. To-night I got proof—and a knife in my back. If I'm concerned with Coenpark in any way, Evert'll get a knife in *his* back as like as not. You're suspicious and bull-headed, and Mevrouw, bless her heart, is kind and sentimental. Between you you'll ruin the whole business. My God, when I think...'

'Mynheer,' Annabet said, before Vehk could find any words, 'if we could hide you here, so that no one knew, and kept you until you could leave. And swore ourselves to complete secrecy. Would that help?'

'But we don't know what we're keeping secret,' Vehk pointed out, logically. 'First it's cock-fighting; then it's secret business. Why should we trust either story? God knows, Mevrouw, it is only of you that I am thinking. You have to answer to your husband for what goes on in this house in his absence.'

'You needn't worry about that. If you could manage it, Evert'd be grateful. I can swear to that.'

'Then if Captain Vehk will help me, I will manage it,' Annabet said.

'Very well. What do you want me to do, Mevrouw?'

'Just to stay here, quite quietly, in the dark. I'll send Josef to the compound and get rid of Katje. Then I'll come back.'

She blew out the candles and locked the door of the office behind her. The passage was dimly lighted, for the little lamp was growing short of oil, but the hall was still bright with candles, long-wicked in their sockets. After a moment's deliberation she rang the bell which stood on the table near the foot of the stairs.

Josef, who had been dozing, came through the door beyond the stairs, looking sleepy and a little sullen. His turban was loosely wound and one cheek bulged with a fragment of nutmeg cheese which he had been chewing when sleep overtook him. He would not have dared answer Evert's summons, however late, in such a fashion, and somehow Annabet guessed it, and the knowledge gave her words incisiveness.

'You may lock up. The Captain has gone. I have locked the office because there is a good deal of liquor left. I will unlock it in the morning. Good night.'

He looked at her, thinking, parsimonious Dutch housewife. Whoever heard of a lady doing such a thing. But he said, very meekly, 'Good night, Mevrouw.' And shot the bolts on the big door and blew out all the candles as Annabet mounted the stairs.

Katje was dozing too; but she sprang into wakefulness and helped Annabet to undress, accepting, with something of Josef's feeling, the single sweet which her mistress offered her from the white wood box. She had never known a box of sweets to last so long. Every night one for Mevrouw and one for Katje. Her last mistress had had a fresh supply of sweets every day, and although she was greedy and getting a little fat as a result, there had always been a great many over when Mevrouw had gobbled her fill, and Katje had had them. They had been hers, either to eat gluttonously or to share with other servants. This Mevrouw would make a single box last for a lifetime.

'I shall read for a time, but the light doesn't keep you awake, does it?' Annabet asked, settling into bed.

Katje lay down on her mat and slept instantly.

Annabet timed ten minutes by the French clock which had been Egbert's wedding gift to her, and then rose and put on her gown and slippers as she had done every third night since Evert's departure.

In the study the twenty minutes which had passed since she had left Vehk and the stranger alone had seemed like an hour. They had kept silence, not so much because she had ordered it, as because the wounded man found it safe and the captain could not find words with which to break it. He had had what most people would consider an adventurous, exciting life, but he had never found himself in a situation even remotely resembling this one; and he had spent the twenty minutes in debating with himself whether he ought to offer to remain in the house for the night. The stranger certainly hardly constituted a menace even for a lone woman, he was obviously incapable of leaving his chair unaided; but at the same time there was something very mysterious about his arrival and his refusal to state his true business—and Jean Vehk had got into the habit of looking after Annabet. He perched on the edge of the table, and thought—after all my real responsibility ended twelve days ago when I handed her over to her husband; it was sheer accident that I happened to be here to-night. And he knew that part of his distrust of the stranger was due to the fact that he resented his intrusion. That dinner had been an occasion. Silly as he knew it was, Jean Vehk had meant to treasure the memory of it always—Annabet so nearly beautiful again, talking to him so freely and frankly, and he smothering down all the feelings which rose in him. He had liked her so much, she had meant something so special and unforeseen, even when she had been ugly as sin; and when she had

128

described the ministrations of the veiled women he had, for an unforgettable, unrepeatable moment or two lived in their hands ... it had been his touch which had soothed, caressed and cured. And when she had spoken of her husband's return he had experienced a vicarious voluptuousness, a jealousy that was half pain and half pleasure. He would never have such an experience again; and it had been rudely disturbed by this bleeding, vomiting mysterious person who was now to enjoy the shelter of her roof, and—since secrecy demanded it—the ministrations of her hands. And he thought back to the moment when he had been told that he was to carry a female passenger, partner in a glove marriage, on his next trip to Banda, and something of the curious mystery of life and its twists and turns made him quite dizzy. His life had followed such an established pattern; and there was his good, plump faithful wife waiting for him in the little house in Wilhelmstraat, never dreaming that this thing had happened to him. He had meant to say good-bye to Annabet, to lift one hand, and then the other and kiss them, and walk away into Banda with the sense that something very unusual and very beautiful had ended. Now, because of this man's coming, he would leave, not with a vague feeling of exaltation and sorrow, but with a kind of nagging anxiety, sordid, mundane.

Annabet opened the door, and the candle in her hand shed its light upon the room.

'Now,' she said, 'if you will help me, Captain Vehk ...' He looked at the wounded man and considered. He was, to his secret and everlasting regret, short of stature. The stranger was tall, probably, standing upright, six feet or a little more. Much as he would have liked to say, 'Mevrouw, I can carry him,' common sense checked the utterance. He was wiry and tough, he could have dragged the man without difficulty any distance, but he could not, without looking ridiculous, offer to carry him upstairs. But he could help him, unaided. Annabet had changed the candlestick from her right hand to her left and had placed herself by the side of the chair, prepared, he thought, to link her arm in the stranger's. And that seemed suddenly unpermissible.

'Mevrouw, if you carry the light and guide the way, I can attend to him.' He moved to the man's left-hand side, edging her away.

'Put your good arm across my shoulders,' he ordered. And as the man obeyed he slipped his own right arm around his body, carefully avoiding the knot of the stockings. 'Now, here we go.'

He knew by the feel of his burden that as soon as the man put his weight upon his legs faintness and nausea made themselves felt. He heard the harsh indrawing of breath; but he heard it without pity; merely with interest, wondering if this nameless person would face the stairs and what would happen if he collapsed half-way. But the man was resolute, too. He used his right hand to help himself, though the effort must have pained his wound; he clutched at the chair back, at the edge of the table at the side of the doorway, and at the passage wall. Annabet paused for a moment and locked the door of the little office, and then, edging past them, went, with a solicitous look, backwards now and then, before them across the hall and up the stairs. The candle which she carried shed a little pool of light in the pervading darkness, and there was a scent of flowers, and her long loose gown made a little whispering sound on the stairs and Jean Vehk thought—this is memorable, too! The stranger moved doggedly, using his right hand upon the stair rail, breathing in short gasps, leaning as little as possible. They managed the stairs.

Annabet turned left along the gallery at the top and opened the second door.

'This is Evert's room,' she said in an ordinary voice. 'I can lock it and keep it locked under some pretence or other. I shall say that I am moving the furniture to surprise him when he returns, or something like that.'

She carried the candle into the room and lighted others. The room was large, furnished with dark heavy pieces, rich, sombre. She pulled back the curtains of the bed and opened the covers.

'If you will help him into it,' she said, and turned aside while Vehk removed the man's breeches and boots and eased the long heavy body into the bed.

'There,' he said finally. 'That's done. What else can I do, Mevrouw?'

A voice from the bed answered him. 'Nothing else, thanks. Except hold your tongue. That is most important of all.'

'I realise that,' Vehk said coldly. 'You are now Mevrouw's guest, and as such no subject for gossip. In any case I sail for Holland the day after to-morrow and have occupations of my own to fill the time. Mevrouw, I should like to speak to you.'

'I shall come back,' she said, addressing the man in the bed and then she lifted the candlestick again and led the way from the room. She went straight down the stairs and set the candle on the table in the hall beside the bell and the bowl of flowers. She turned and faced the captain.

'I don't know how to thank you. I don't know what I should have done if I had been alone.' He thought, and almost said—you could hardly have done worse! But he checked the words, realising that her position had been difficult from the moment when the man spoke her husband's name. And all at once the resentment which he had been cherishing against the

130

stranger was shifted to Evert Haan: the man had no right to leave a young girl in a house where such intrusion could be expected, and leave her, moreover, without warning or instructions.

'I am glad I happened to be here, Mevrouw,' he said. 'And sorry that I leave you in so awkward a position. But I think, that with your permission I shall stay until daylight. It would be no trouble. In fact, it would relieve my mind to do so.'

'Really,' she said, almost overcome by this new proof of his solicitude, 'you are the *kindest* person, Captain Vehk. But it isn't necessary. I shall lock the door behind you. All the doors and windows are fast. Katje is asleep in my room, and we know the man can hardly move. Besides ... I told Josef you had gone. If you were seen leaving in the morning it ... he...' Her face reddened, but her eyes were steady and her lips smiled. 'We'd better say good-bye now. I can never thank you for all the care you took of me, or the pains you went to to make my voyage agreeable. And for all you've done this evening. And for taking my letters back. So many, many things. Please promise that you'll never come to the islands without coming to see me.'

'I promise that, Mevrouw. And you ...' his voice was suddenly, surprisingly, most shamingly husky, 'take good care of yourself. You've a beautiful home, and your health again. I hope you'll find life very happy.' And then, before he had time to censor the words there they were, spoken, audible. 'I wish you were coming back to Holland with me.' It was a cry from the heart and did not refer to his wish for company on the return voyage, but he hastened to make it sound as though it did. 'I shall miss you, Mevrouw. The two passengers I carry this trip are old, and look as though their livers have ruined their tempers. But that's the way it is. Good-bye, Mevrouw.' He lifted, as he had planned, one hand after the other and kissed her fingers. And a warm, weakening wave of feeling ran over her as she realised that there was more then mere formality in the action. That part of her mind which had noted and analysed the butcher's good measure, the shoemaker's favouritism, the landlord's instant response, sprang into action again after long abeyance. But not, to-night, with simple girlish vanity. The pleasure was weighed, on one side with sorrow— because now she was going to open the door and say 'good-bye' again, and this moment would be over, ended, sterile—and upon the other with anticipation; because now her looks were coming back and in nine days Evert would be returning, and, oh, the whole of life spread out before her, offering who knew what of interest and experience?

She set both hands to the great key and the heavy bolts. The door opened on the warm, scented night, upon the velvet sky

131

so thickly sown with stars.

'Good-bye, Captain Vehk. Good luck on the voyage.'

'Good-bye, Mevrouw. God bless you.'

'Good-bye.'

'Good-bye.'

She locked the door and bolted it and took up her candle. Half-way up the stairs she paused and clutched the rail. 'God bless you. . . .' They had been Father Vincent's parting words, too. And he had meant that he wished God to give her the strength to bear being ugly, to give her the power to look outside herself, to aid her in living the life of the spirit. But the little Captain had hoped that she would be happy; he had mentioned her beautiful house and her regained health—by which he meant, but was too polite to say, her looks. And she thought sadly, Jean Marie would call that feeling I now had, *sin*. Sin of quite a deadly kind, because it was a trespass of the spirit. I knew that little Jean was feeling amorous, and I could, quite easily, have kissed him, too. I wasn't disgusted; I was pleased. Jean Marie would say that I'm quite as wicked as though I had kissed him. But can one help what one feels and thinks? Thoughts and feelings happen so quickly, they don't wait to be invited.

She felt quite dizzy from the working of her puzzled mind. And in the morning there was a spatter of candle-grease where she had stood and asked herself the questions which had no answers.

Then suddenly she remembered the man lying in Evert's bed, and as though running to a refuge, she straightened the drooping candlestick, lifted the skirt of her long gown and sped into Evert's room.

He lay flat on his back and his eyes were closed, and for a moment she thought, what a pity. She had intended to tell him of her plans. But as she abandoned that idea and thought, I'll just have to lock him in and trust he has sense enough not to make a sound in the morning or whenever he wakes, the dark lashes fluttered and lifted.

'Mervouw,' he said, and his voice was stronger, 'I should be grateful to you. My body is. No bed has ever been so welcome. But my mind would have been easier in the drifting prahau.'

'I'm not going to ask you any questions,' she said hurriedly. 'If there is anything I can do for you, I'll do it. Then I must lock the door and leave you. Some time to-morrow, somehow, I'll bring you some food, and since you are the one who mentioned secrecy, you'll know that you mustn't make a sound. As soon as you feel well enough to go, you can go, and I promise I won't mention that you've been here, or anything about you. Does that put your mind at rest?'

'It should. But it doesn't. No, don't think that I don't trust

132

you. Curiously enough, I *do*. But it's such a *one-sided* bargain. Mevrouw, I told you the truth when I said that Evert and I had business together; but God knows what he'd say if he knew that I'd involved *you* in it. And sheltering me does involve you.'

She set the candlestick down and moved to the side of the bed.

'I said I wouldn't ask you any questions, but I will. Just one. You needn't answer it if you don't want to. If Evert had been here, would he have done what I've done?'

'Almost exactly—but I shouldn't be in *his* bed.'

'Then that's all right. Evert's business is my business; and in his absence I must act for him.'

'How long have you known him?'

'I don't really know him at all. Ours was a glove marriage, you see. Two days after I landed he had to go away on business. I expect you know him better than I do.'

The full, beautifully-shaped lips curved in a smile.

'I've known him for nearly five years. That's a long time, isn't it?' The smile faded completely. The next words came with startling bluntness, almost effrontery. 'Why on earth did *you* make a glove marriage?'

'That would take too long to tell. I'll fetch you some water from my room and then I must leave you. Would you like something to make you sleep?'

'Poppy or mandragora? No, thank you. I'm half asleep now. Water, yes.'

She went soft-footed past the sleeping Katje and fetched the water-jug from beside her own bed. Putting it down on the little table where Evert's empty brandy flask still lay, she said, 'I'm afraid I don't seem to be doing much for you. I haven't had much experience in nursing the sick. I *have* been ill myself, too. Truitje used to bathe my head with vinegar and water. Would you like your head bathed?'

There was something quite touching, he thought, about the little childish question. Dimly, for his mind seemed to be slipping down slopes into slumber, he remembered that he had called her Isa, thought she was Evert's kept woman, and tried to bargain for her secrecy. What a shame.

'No thank you, Mevrouw. I shall sleep now. And in the morning don't worry about coming to me, if it proves inconvenient. I will wait quietly. Good night.'

'Good night.'

She locked the door and went to her own room. From the bathroom she took one of the water-jars and the cloth which Katje used for wiping the bath and the floor, and went down to the study. The tiled floor was easily cleaned, but the man had bled on to the rug before Vehk rolled him over, and some mark

133

remained even when she had scoured it. She stared at the stain with despair for a moment, and then poured over it the coffee which remained in the little silver jug. The black puddle engulfed the brownish mark and the wider sweep of the water. When she had satisfied herself that nothing suspicious was left inside the room, she opened the shutter, and with some nervous qualms which it needed all her resolution to ignore, stepped on to the verandah. The night was almost menacingly silent, and she could not help thinking as she held the candle low and searched for the bloodstains, that if anything happened now there was no one for whom to call. Katje lay in drugged slumber, and the stranger was not only weak as a kitten, but locked in. Still, it must be done. The verandah was floored with wood, dark in colour, boldly grained, and here and there, between the top of the steps which led to the garden and the study window there were marks, just discernible to one who expected them and was searching for them, but the blood had soaked in, beyond the reach of her wet cloth, and on that dark surface did not look distinctive enough to be dangerous. With a little sigh of relief she emptied the water-jug over the rail into the garden, scuttled indoors, and bolted down the shutters. But fear went with her. Overstrained nerves suggested that someone, some thing, might have crept through the open window while she was bent over the trail of marks, and might now be hiding ... in the shadowy study, in the more than shadowy hall, around the curve of the stairs, even in her own room. She could visualise a disembodied smile of sly triumph greeting her from the shadow of her bed curtains, aha, I have you at last. Her skin crawled with cold when at last she gained the blue-and-white room, and found Katje sleeping on her mat, and everything as she had left it. She tumbled into bed with some muddled reflections upon the rightness of Father Vincent's arguments. Nothing had threatened her, yet she had been frightened, experienced the physical symptoms of fear because she had conjured danger from her own mind. The mind was important; it had great power. She pursued the thought until she was dizzy again, and then she slept, dreaming wildly.

Katje always brought up enough breakfast for two nowadays and without much self-denial Annabet was able to save a good deal of it, laying slices of ham, rolls and fruit in a clean handkerchief hidden in one corner of the bed. When Katje removed the tray. Annabet had her plan ready. Ordinarily the woman would carry the tray to the kitchen and then begin to bring up the bath water. Then she would make the bed, and after her bath Annabet would either return to bed for a time, while Katje tidied the room, or be dressed and go down to the

134

garden, leaving the room to Katje.

'I'm tired this morning. I shall have to go to sleep again. I don't want to be disturbed until eleven. I'll have my bath then. And there's something I want you to do for me, Katje, while I am alseep.'

'Yes, Mevrouw.'

'Go into the garden and cut some flowers. A lot. I want three bowlsful, one here, and here and here.' She pointed to three places where a bowl of flowers could stand. 'And I want those at the bottom of the stairs changed. They're badly arranged, stiff and crowded. Take them all out and put them back again.'

'But Mevrouw, Josef always does the flowers. It is part of his duty.'

'Oh, very well. I will tell him about those downstairs. But you must do mine. If he has anything to say about that he can say it to me. But not till eleven o'clock. You have my three bowls ready to bring up when you call me. Is that clear?'

'Yes, Mevrouw.'

'I must go downstairs for a moment. I'll see Josef there.'

She put on her gown and her slippers and took the study key in her hand. Going through the hall she rang the bell and then hurried along the passage and unlocked the office door. In the morning light, when she had thrown open the shutters, the bare little room and the table with fruit and wine-glasses and coffee-cups upon it made an incongruous sight. But the floor had dried clean, and if one excepted the spilled coffee, which might easily be due to an ordinary accident, there was nothing to show that anything unusual had taken place in it. She would have liked to inspect the verandah by daylight, but before she had been in the study for more than a moment Josef came in answer to the bell.

'I'm afraid you'll have to wash that rug, Josef,' she said pleasantly. 'I spilled a whole cup of coffee.' She moved to the table as Josef studied the mark on the rug. She couldn't leave him to remove the bottles, since she had made that feeble excuse for locking the door last night, and she didn't want him to know that the dining-room cupboard had had its lock forced. When the door was closed it looked as usual. Oh, bother, she thought. But she said casually, 'There's less left than I thought. This can go out, and this. The brandy I'll take to my room. I like to have a little brandy handy in case of faintness.' She had a feeling that she ought not to explain so much. And another feeling that Josef would probably drink what was left in the other bottles and be pleased. But Josef adhered strictly to the Prophet's injunction against fermented liquor and was not appeased.

From her bedroom window Annabet saw Katje, armed with

135

a rush-basket wandering along the far border, now and then gathering a bloom with the leisurely deliberation that was habitual to her. Safe for half an hour at least. She took the bundle of food and the bottle of brandy and the key of Evert's room and stepped out into the gallery.

The man lay just as she had left him last night, his eyes were closed, and in the shadow of Evert's plum-coloured bed curtains his face was waxen and yellow. He looked so ill that for a moment she had a feeling of panic. Suppose he had died—she hadn't thought of that. Suppose she found herself with a corpse on her hands. And eight days to go before Evert—the only person who could possibly be told—returned. She locked the door behind her after a first hasty glance, and then, almost running to the bed, shook the man quite roughly by the shoulder. He stirred and moaned. She could have shed tears of relief. He opened his eyes and looked at her, blankly at first, and then with recognition which merged into a smile.

'You did frighten me,' she said. 'I thought you'd be awake, waiting for me. I hope I didn't hurt you, but I couldn't call, because I didn't know what to call you.'

'What a predicament,' he said, still smiling.

'How are you this morning?'

'I've hardly had time to decide.' He moved his body cautiously. 'Ugh! Stiff and sore. But I slept well. I shall be all right. Don't worry about me.'

'I've brought you some food. I'm afraid you'll have to drink brandy or water. I couldn't hide any coffee. And this looks horribly rough and ready doesn't it. But it is a little awkward. Katje almost lives in my room, you see.' She laid the food on the table beside the bed. 'Can you reach it there?'

'Quite well, thanks.' He turned his head and looked at it, hiding the feeling of nausea which the very idea of food roused in him. 'I'll eat and drink too, presently. I'm still half asleep.'

'I ought to do something about the wound, too, oughtn't I? It ought to be bathed and have a clean bandage.' She spoke uncertainly, aware of her ignorance in such matters. Mamma had had severe headaches occasionally, and Truitje suffered from mild, chronic rheumatism, and there had, of course, been her own serious attack of the same complaint, but apart from these and the usual winter coughs and colds, there had been no illness in the Heydberg house. Captain Vehk's poisoned finger had been her first experience with a flesh wound, and although it had had a disastrous result it was in itself no more than a pinprick, easily poulticed; and she had had the whole resources of the ship at her disposal. This was very different.

The man put down the diffidence in her voice to reluctance. Women were known to be squeamish about blood and wounds and it was to her credit, he thought, that she had brought up the question at all. And he was glad that he could, in good faith, refuse the offer of bathing and bandaging.

'It'd be better left alone, thanks. If we touch it we might open it again. It's all right now, and we'll leave it.'

She looked at him dubiously, less relieved than he had expected. She accepted his answer, which sounded reasonable; but her mind had passed on to another aspect of sickness. A terribly awkward and most embarrassing aspect. But one must be sensible and face one's obligations. So, with colour (which she felt and cursed as it rose) creeping over her unpainted morning face, she said:

'Can you get out of bed?'

'Oh Lord, yes. I'm a lot better.'

'Well ... you'll find everything you need in here. And I ... I'll come back in a few minutes. And please don't mind ... I mean ... since I mustn't let the servants know ... I mean you must just take it for granted. You must pretend that I'm Evert.'

She saw that he was sharing—if anything to a greater degree —her burning embarrassment. She searched wildly for some means of relieving it. She wanted to rush from the room, but then it would be so very difficult to come back, as she must. And finally she put into words the only coherent thought which the moment's confusion brought her.

'If my Cousin Vincent had ever been really ill, he'd know that your body does matter. He spent hours convincing me to the contrary!'

The words sounded crude and ill-chosen as soon as they were uttered, and she was wildly pleased to see that the man was smiling again. And behind her relief was the startling consciousness that she had just spoken of Vincent with something approaching irreverence.

'Mevrouw, you are quite unique,' said the man from the bed. 'I wish I had made your acquaintance in happier circumstances. Please don't worry about me. I am going to sleep again. Forget me until it is dark. I shall be able to leave then.'

'Katje leaves me for my afternoon's sleep. I will come back then. You are certain that there is nothing else I can do for you.'

He seemed more than half asleep again and she had no means of knowing that his brief period of consciousness was whirling to chaotic darkness again, or that his whole night had been spent in a sea of similar fevered lightheadedness, dotted with similar islands of lucidity. He lay on the bed and spun round in violent circles which had one tiny grain of consciousness for their axis, and the tiny grain prayed that she would go, go, go, before the dizzy spinning tossed him off again into

137

nothingness. Dissatisfied with herself, she stole away quietly and locked the door.

At eleven o'clock Katje called Annabet and prepared her bath. At midday she carried up the tray of light refreshments which served to bridge the gap between the substantial breakfast and the evening meal which was the custom in Banda. When she had eaten part of the meal and hidden the rest, Annabet took out the box of sweets and held it to Katje, saying as she did so, "I may not rest to-day. I slept all the morning, and shall probably go into the garden. But I shan't want you, Katje.'

Katje selected a pale purple sweet, put it into her mouth and lifted the tray. I ought to have noticed how long they take to work, her mistress thought, watching her through the door, she might fall asleep on the stairs! She listened, there was no sound of breaking crockery, and no sign of Katje's return. She timed twenty minutes by the French clock, and then, feeling like a hunted animal, slipped into Evert's room. As she unlocked it, she remembered that she had made no excuse for having locked the door. How often did they dust it in their master's absence? Had the door been tried already? Would it be safe (as it was desirable) to say nothing for a day or two? The man had spoken of leaving this evening, but he hadn't looked fit to move. Oh, what a tangle, she thought, pushing the door open and turning to lock it again; and what a worry, just when I was feeling so happy, too.

The bedclothes were all tossed about now, and the waxen face had a curious dull flush upon its cheeks. The man's eyes were open, but they did not turn towards the door, or towards her; they stared at the ceiling and their expression was at once vacant and wild.

'You don't know me, do you?' she asked, going near to the bed and leaning over him. One lean brown hand moved across the covers with the gesture of someone brushing a fly away. Apart from this movement he lay as before. She could have wept from consternation and worry. Suppose he cried out, as people did in delirium!

Some part of her mind produced the thought that her concern should, by rights, be for the man, not for herself; and at the same time she noticed that his lips were cracked and dry. She looked at the bedside table and saw that he had touched neither the food nor the water which she had placed there. And he had spoken so bravely about leaving at nightfall. He must have been feeling so ill. Everything else gave way to a flood of pity. She remembered how often Truitje or Klara had given her water when she was too weak to reach for it. She poured some from the jug into the glass, and then, awkwardly slipped

138

her arm behind the man's head, raising it, while with her other hand she held the glass to his lips. He drank thirstily, but his wild, vacant stare did not change. She could feel the heat of his neck through the thin stuff of her sleeve. And then the heat seemed to be in her eyes and throat as tears of pity rushed upwards. He must have been feeling so very ill this morning, but he had sent her away, fooled by his brave words about leaving this evening. And he was young. She had never thought about his age before; had, indeed, hardly realised him as a person at all. Now, with the brown and bleached hair tumbling against her shoulder and the heat of his fever scorching her arm she suddenly became acutely aware of him, not as a stranger, not as an embarrassing responsibility, but as a man, young, sick, utterly dependent. With a gesture she had never used to anyone in her life before, she pushed back the tumbling hair from his forehead. He muttered something, but in such a low, slurred voice that even had the words been in Dutch she would hardly have caught them. Then he turned his face so that it rested against the still imperceptible curve of her breast. His hand moved again in that restless, fluttering way, as though he reached for something. Careful not to move her body she set the glass back on the bed-table, and then, with the hand thus freed, took his and held it. He gave a sigh. She saw the black lashes drop over the blind wildness of his eyes. He seemed to sleep.

She sat for what seemed a long time, uncomfortably perched on the edge of the bed, looking down upon his closed, secret face, and wondering about him. Her speculations had become entirely personal; she no longer wondered what might be his business with Evert or the reason for his secrecy. Instead she wondered what his name might be; how old he was; where he came from, with his delicate limping Dutch and his lapses into another tongue: most of all she wondered what any woman in her position would have wondered—whose place was she filling at this moment. To what remembered breast had he turned as though from habit, seeking a refuge from pain and weakness? To whose handclasp had his own responded, unconsciously, instinctively? Was some unknown woman in some unguessed-of place worrying herself sick because he had not come home?

The wonder opened strange vistas in her mind. She found herself imagining what he looked like when he was hale and well. Would he lie like this relaxed from loving, not from weakness, and how would it feel to hold him like this, not with a wondering pity, but with delight? Her young, untried senses strained at the leash of reason. How vile, she thought, weakly, to brood like this over a sick, senseless man. But the little mental protest was swept away like a paper boat on a flooded gutter. The breath from his parted, cracked lips, was warm on her breast, melting her very heart and all the tiny experiences of the mystery of sex which had ever been hers, rushed, like parted molecules of quicksilver, into one shining whole. Glances of admiration in the street or in church, little instances of favouritism, the long, abortive worship of Cousin Jean Marie, Klara's whispered warnings and the feeling they had roused, the despair, the emptiness of hope occasioned by Evert's hatred, the sheer joy of living restored by Shal Ahmi's magic, the moment last night when Captain Vehk had kissed her hand. They were not separate things ... widely as they differed in shape and texture they had all been steps leading to this moment, this final revelation of what it was all about.

She looked down, quite wildly, at the face, pinched, shadowed and flushed, which rested between her arm and her body, and thought—I love him ... I've fallen in love *again*. But how? Why? When I came in at that door I was half regretful, thinking him a nuisance ... he's done nothing, said nothing to change my mind.

It wasn't possible. It wasn't reasonable. It was something which had happened, apparently, simply because she had allowed herself, because of his sickness, to pass the bounds which convention imposed, very rightly, between men and women. Mamma had been right in her orders that one must never, never allow liberties. Because obviously the female body was not to be trusted. For the first time Annabet understood how Klara had fallen a victim to the red-faced, hard-breathing young man. Probably he'd just kissed her. And if holding a sick, senseless man out of kindness could work such havoc in a girl, what would a kiss from a whole, sensible one do? God, suppose she had given way to that impulse to kiss Captain Vehk in the hall last night!

I must get out of this, she thought. And very gently she loosed, first the hand which held the stranger's, and then, little by little, the arm which held him. He stirred and muttered as she laid him back upon the pillow, and something in her, too, cried out at the breaking of the bond. But at last she stood, free and separate, with pins-and-needles shooting through her arm, beside the bed. And even then she was not out of thrall. Moving jerkily, as though an imperative hand had propelled her, she stopped and kissed the place where the brown hair grew in a little V on the pale brow. Then, like a hunted creature again, she stepped out on to the gallery, looked right and left, looked down the stairs, locked the door and shot into her own room.

Once there, among surroundings which had become familiar, she was overcome with self-disgust. The man—and the fact that she did not know his name, made the whole thing seem more tawdry and shameful—was hurt and ill and probably dying. He needed God only knew what in the way of medical care and nursing; and all she could do was sit and feel lustful about him. Lust—a remarkable word; it embraced it all, the dryness, the greed, the slavering frenzy. So different from love ... which was cool ... which was what she must feel for Evert as soon as he allowed her to do so. But suppose Evert had been able to overcome the repulsion which her appearance aroused in him; suppose he had laid his face against her breast and held her hand—would the resulting response in her have been lust, then? No ... presumably because of that ceremony in the church at Heydberg when she had vowed to be a good wife to a man she had never seen. Why?

But if you started asking why you would go mad. And madness, with all its horrible trappings, lay in wait for her, she knew. She had been so nearly made before Jean Marie came with his talk about resignation, and acceptance, and the spiritual life. He had saved her. For what? You mustn't ask that either.

Resolutely she turned her mind to practical matters. The man in the next room was very ill, and there was, in the circumstances, very little that she could do for him, if at the same time she preserved the secret of his presence. But—and everything, feeling, reason, even her physical being, seemed to halt and listen as she made the decision—Shal Ahmi would come to-night, Shal Ahmi was a great dealer in secrets; he had knowledge and power. To save the life of a stranger she would confide in Shal Ahmi.

He arrived, with the muffled women at his usual time, and to-night, as soon as they were safely within the room and he had freed his hands from the women's arms, he took from among his garments a little jar of red pottery, wide at the base, narrow-necked, and stoppered.

'To-night, Mevrouw, they work to nourish not to loosen. Here are the Five Oils of Garu Sanjitji. It has been known to keep flesh on the bones and life in the bodies of men who could swallow no food because of sickness or because of spear wounds in the face. It is of all things most rare and precious.' He drew out the stopper and placed the jar in the hands of one of the women, and turned to leave, as was his custom.

'Wait,' Annabet said, 'something has happened since you were here, Shal Ahmi. And there is no one whom I can ask for help, except you.'

She looked at him and was deterred by the impassivity of his face. It betrayed neither interest, curiosity nor sympathy. The confidence which had been roused in her by his skill, the almost magical cure he had arranged and by the delicate tact with which he had conducted the secret visits, was shaken. For

141

hours, ever since she had found the sick man unconscious, she had thought of Shal Ahmi as a friend. Now she was not sure. She realised anew his utter strangeness. And the presence of the two women, standing like machines waiting to set to work, was disturbing, too. And there was Katje, sunk in her drugged slumber. It was like being surrounded by enemies and being suddenly afflicted by doubts as to the integrity of one who had seemed an ally.

'Would you come outside with me?' she asked hastily. 'Ask them to wait for a little.'

Shal Ahmi took no heed of the second request. He left the women standing on either side of the bed as though they were indeed machines whose services were temporarily unneeded. But he followed Annabet on to the gallery without protest.

Midway between the two doors, where she had set a candle before going down to let Shal Ahmi in, Annabet paused, and speaking hastily because she was nervous and uncertain of the reception of her words, said:

'Evert trusts you, or he wouldn't have asked you to help me. And in this affair I've tried to do what he would have done if he had been at home. Last night a man arrived, very secretly, asking for my husband. He didn't tell me his business, and though he's hurt, so that he couldn't leave, he wouldn't let me call the servants. So I put him in here and did what I could for him. But now he's out of his mind and in a high fever. Will you see what you can do for him? Please, Shal Ahmi.'

'Mevrouw, one of my trades is the cure of sickness. Open the door.'

The man lay in an uneasy attitude amid the tumbled bed-clothes. The flush on his face had darkened, the bleached brown hair was damp and lank with perspiration, and there was a faint, sickly scent in the room. Annabet walked straight to the bedside table and lighted the candles in the three-branched candlestick which stood there beside Evert's brandy flask, the bottle of brandy, the water-jug and the drying bits of food that she had put there in the morning. Shal Ahmi stopped for a moment at the foot of the bed, and then, pushing the red curtain far back on the other side, bent and took a close look at the patient. As he did so he shot a quick glance at Annabet on the far side of the bed and she saw the expression of his face change, not to pity, or to professional interest or even to curiosity, but to sharp, immediate concern.

'Do you know his name, Mevrouw?'

'No. Nor anything about him.'

'But he spoke to you?'

'Yes. He told us some lies ... at least that is a harsh word. He tried to make us believe that his business was secret because it was to do with cock-fighting ... not quite respectable.'

142

'*Us*, Mevrouw. Who was with you?'

'Captain Vehk, of the *Java*. You see, I had asked him to dinner, he'd been extremely kind to me on the voyage, and I wanted to show him how much better I was ... and to honour my invitation, of course. I couldn't wait until Evert was home because the *Java* sails to-morrow. We dined in the little office and just as we had finished *he* came to the window. Captain Vehk brought him in and tied up his wound. There's a gash in his back. He told us a Chinaman had knifed him in a quarrel about a cock's tail. He thought he could leave and left me a funny message for Evert, something about the cock having a black tail. Captain Vehk said it was an untrue tale. But he *is* knifed. I saw the wound. He said he'd be able to leave to-night ... and now I don't know what to do. It's so difficult. I gave Katje one of your sweets at midday and slipped in to see how he was. But I can't look after him *properly*.'

'If you worry yourself, Mevrouw, you will undo the good which we have done in the past days.' Shal Ahmi's voice was smooth and kind again. And he did seem interested. She was relieved until she looked down at the bed again and saw that the man's eyes were open, set in a glassy, senseless stare. And then her heart knew a pang of pain and she said urgently:

'*Do* help him.'

'You may leave him to me, Mevrouw. Will you go now. Empty your mind of all concern; lie on your bed and let the old women ply their trade. Then I will return them to their place and at the same time fetch the things I need. The night is yet young. I can go and come again and still do much before daylight.'

The women stood where they had been left. She touched one and then the other, and lay down on her bed, loosening her clothing, as she had done after the first visit. The Five Oils had a fragrant, musty scent, like that of dying roses; it made their hands slippery and soft. To-night they stroked her gently, and she thought that if last night had never been, as soon as they were gone she would fall asleep, more blissfully and soundly than she had done since the unremembered days of very early childhood. But she must keep awake. Shal Ahmi was coming back again, she must open the door for him, and probably help him with what he had to do.

The blind hands ceased their ministrations and she rose from the bed; with the perfect timing which he had always shown, Shal Ahmi appeared as soon as she was gowned and slippered. As usual she carried the candle down the stairs, unlocked the heavy door.

'I may be an hour, Mevrouw,' he said, as with a draped, anonymous, sightless, earless figure on either arm, he stepped into the darkness.

'I shall wait,' she assured him. And she wondered, idly, whether he guided the women all the way home in that fashion, or did he, half-way along the road, unwind their bandages and set them free to find their own path. And then she thought that in Heydberg the whole of life, with one exception, had been open and straightforward. Klara had had her secret and Annabet had shared it, half-frightened, not very inventive. If I could go back now, she reflected, I could play that game so much more cleverly.

And by that time the door was shut and barred again; and she was alone in the house.

She went straight to Evert's room. And there she stared with astonishment at Shal Ahmi's handiwork. The bed had been stripped to the lower sheet, and half-way down its length the pillow and the bolster had been laid on top of one another. The sick man lay, face downwards, across this mound, his head hanging, unsupported, towards the bed's upper end. His shirt had been removed, so had the handkerchief and the bandage of stockings. His back, with the dark gash in its whiteness, was curved over the bolster and pillow. Below the wound, covering him almost to the knees and holding him firmly in position like a vice, was the upper sheet, folded lengthways. It touched the floor on either side and was held down upon the one side by a chest which had been pulled forward, and upon the other by a chair, turned on its back and weighted by the rest of the bedclothes, two pairs of boots, a basin and ewer. The man's hands, which were free, scrabbled at the mattress, and he was moaning.

It was a cruel way to treat a sick man, she thought, and hurried forward; and then halted, remembering that she had asked Shal Ahmi's help, that he was wise where she was ignorant, and that he had cured her. She dared not touch the curious cage, but she went and sat on the bed, just above the mound of pillows, and edged inwards until her thigh was below that turning head which had no place to rest, and with her hands she lifted it into her lap and gently stroked it. And the man moaned, and then sighed, and one of his hands wandered about again until she took it in her own. And then, as before, he grew quiet.

She tried to keep her eyes from the uncovered wound in his back, but it drew her, with the fascination of horror. The edges were puffed and purple, so that it seemed twice the size that it had been last night; and all around it, for perhaps three inches in every direction was a dark crimson patch, like a great bruise. It should have been bathed and bandaged, she thought disconsolately; and she knew that she had accepted his refusal of her ministrations largely because of the difficulties in the way of

144

making them. I should have persisted, she thought, not been put off so easily. It's my fault that he's in this state. But she had meant to do something in the night, when the house was her own. In this climate everything happened so quickly. A rose had no length of life; it was bud in the morning, and by evening the petals lay scattered on the grass. A wound went wrong, a fever developed with like swiftness, but of course she hadn't thought of that.

'Darling,' she said aloud, using the word which sometimes, rarely, she had used to comfort Klara, 'you must get better. If you don't, I shall blame myself for ever.' And her fingers tightened on the hot limp hand as though pressure and tension might convey some healing virtue.

She was so busy with her conflicting thoughts and feelings that time slipped away quickly, and she was surprised to hear Shal Ahmi's cane tapping the lighted window. She loosened her hand gently and edged her way off the bed, regretting the uncomfortable position into which the man's head fell as soon as it was unsupported.

Shal Ahmi had a great basket on his arm and a bundle in his hand. He did not wait for her to lock the door, but marched straight up the stairs and into Evert's room. He had been hurrying and was breathing in short, sharp gasps, but his feet on the stairs were rapid and silent. When she had closed the door again and reached the bedroom he was on his knees in the middle of the floor, a heterogenous collection of articles spread about him. There were leaves, green and glossy, laid out on a square of white cloth, two more of the small red earthenware jars, a little pestle and mortar of grey stone, a tiny black pot with a long handle, a bundle of stuff which looked like very fine white tow, a knife with a short pointed blade, and, most startling of all, a miniature brazier, shaped like a flowerpot set on three little legs. Through its pierced sides she could see the dull red glow of charcoal.

As she entered Shal Ahmi finished his hasty unpacking, and, bending his head, breathed upon the brazier until the glow brightened. She watched him with renewed admiration for his resource and forethought. And at the same time there was a chill upon her. Such a dearth of any feeling lay at the root of his efficiency. She knew, without being told, that he had not wasted a single glance upon the patient, and that he would not look his way until all the preparations were completed.

As soon as the charcoal glowed he set the long-handled pot over the top of it and straightened himself, still kneeling. He placed the glossy green leaves in the mortar, laid the pestle upon them and handed the whole thing to her.

'Pound them into a paste. The odour will be unpleasant, but it will do you no harm.' His smooth brown hands busied

145

themselves with the black pot and the jars.

There had been truth in his words. As soon as the pestle had fallen upon the leaves, bruising them, a strange, bitter scent filled the room. Annabet's eyes stung and pricked, her nostrils felt as though they were full of acrid dust; she opened her mouth in order to breathe more easily, and instantly her mouth was dry. In a few moments it hurt her to blink her eyelids over her pricking eyes and her dry tongue moved like a dead leaf against her parched lips. But she pounded away and the big shining leaves collapsed and shrank until at last they were only a spoonful of soft moist paste at the pestle. By that time a faint steam was rising from the black pot. Shal Ahmi took the knife and held it for a moment inside the pot, and then, rising to his feet, he said:

'Keep your distance, Mevrouw, and take no notice of what you may hear.'

Then he advanced to the bed.

She told herself fiercely that Shal Ahmi knew what he was doing. He had cured her; he would cure the stranger. But the low, infinitely desolate moaning which came presently from the direction of the bed struck at her heart. She wanted to cry, 'Oh don't, please don't hurt him any more.' The man was beyond words, she wanted to cry out for him. But she stayed silent, and in a few moments Shal Ahmi came quietly to her side, took the mortar from her hand, looked at its contents critically, and went away again. Then he put the mortar, now empty, on the floor, and took up a handful of the towy substance, and then he came back for a roll of white linen which lay near the brazier.

'Now, if you wish, you can help me, Mevrouw.'

She moved to the bedside and her eyes went straight to the wound. It was bleeding again, but slowly, almost indecisively; and plugged into it was the mass of green paste which she had pounded, and even as she looked the bleeding stopped. Shal Ahmi, with the careless ease of perfect proficiency placed the handful of tow over the green paste and with his other hand gave the roll of linen a twist so that it uncurled like a white snake.

'Draw the end under, Mevrouw, and return it to me. Ah, that is right. Your fingers are nimble. And again, and again. I think the man told you the truth, Mevrouw. The knife which stabbed him was poisoned. A Chinese trick. But Shal Ahmi is skilled in such matters. I have cut away the rotten flesh, and the leaves will do the rest. Now I will fix this, so.' He caught the end of the bandage and twisted it firmly under its own folds. 'The wound is now finished, forgotten.' He lifted away the weighted chair upon his side of the bed and loosed the sheet. 'Shake the pillow, Mevrouw, and place it in position

146

while I turn him.' He lifted the man as easily as a child lifts a doll and laid him flat again. 'For the fever and weakness I have other cures, but those I can apply alone. Go to your bed now, Mevrouw, and sleep without a care. I shall stay here until nightfall to-morrow. I have all I need. And your uninvited guest will be safe with me. When Katje sleeps to-morrow, come to us. Perhaps we may leave together.'

'I can never thank you, Shal Ahmi. But please believe that I am *extremely* grateful.'

'Thanks, Mevrouw, should be kept for favours. I merely ply my trade. In your service ... in his ... it is all one. Sleep soundly, Mevrouw.'

He turned to his pots and jars. Across his bent head Annabet looked towards the bed and the sick man. He lay quiet and still like the dead. But he was going to live now, and perhaps leave with Shal Ahmi to-morrow night. She might never see him again.

She had breakfasted and was in her bath the next morning when knuckles beat loudly upon the bedroom door. Katje ran, and a moment after returned, her manner excited.

'Mevrouw, that was Josef. There is someone to see you who will not be turned away. Mynheer's orders were that you were not to be disturbed until his return, but this is Mynheer Kaerko, the Agent, and he will not leave until he has seen you.'

There was an imperativeness about the message which, in the present circumstances, sounded ominous. Horribly conscious of the inmates of the next room, Annabet, aided by Katje, whose fingers fumbled from haste, put on her best dress, coloured her face and brushed her hair.

Josef was hovering in the hall, and as soon as she stepped from the bottom stair he threw open the drawing-room door, and from quite a distance Annabet could see Kaerko, arrested in an uneasy pacing to and fro his hat clasped to his chest, his face drawn from sleeplessness and worry. She was not relieved to see his expression change to sharp curiosity as she entered the room. Across the surface of his anxious mind drifted the thought, Van de Lijn was right then, it was just a temporary indisposition and she walks as well as I do, so I can tell Hootman he was wrong about her legs. But at the moment he could not take comfort in the trivial, gossipy thought. Bowing low he said quickly, 'Mevrouw, I do indeed regret this intrusion, but my errand is serious, as you shall hear.'

He waited until she had seated herself in one of the graceful little chairs, and then, still standing, hurried on, 'I am given to understand, Mevrouw, that Captain Vehk, of the *Java* dined with you on the day before yesterday.'

'He did,' Annabet said with dry lips. Surely, surely little Vehk hadn't talked about the stranger. She remembered that she had not specially begged his silence, she had taken it for granted—but he hadn't seemed to like the man very much and had opposed her plan for hiding him.

'You must excuse this question, Mevrouw; but you will understand that in a case like this it is my duty to make every inquiry which might throw light on the case. I have my report to write for the Company.'

'Do sit down, Mynheer, and tell me what it is you want to know.' She heard the breathy, frightened sound in her own voice. If she swore that the man had gone, would he search the house? Would he break down the door of Evert's room?

'What did he eat, Mevrouw? Could you tell me that? It sounds an impertinent question. I know. But this is not Holland ... and you being new to the country ... and Mynheer Haan away ... it is possible that the servants...' He ended in complete incoherence.

'That the servants *what*, Mynheer?' she asked gently, taking courage from his confusion. Not thus were deadly accusations made.

'That they served something which should have been thrown out, Mevrouw. The carelessness of native servants passes the bounds of imagination.'

'Is Captain Vehk ill?'

'He is dead.'

'Oh no!' she cried foolishly. 'Oh, poor man.' She thought for an instant of their parting ... of the way he had kissed her hands. He couldn't be *dead*. 'He was perfectly well when he left here.'

'And when he arrived on board. I grant you that, Mevrouw. Whether during the hours of yesterday he felt indisposed or not, of course no one can say. He complained to no one. But shortly before midnight last night he was found, almost dead, in his cabin, and he died at one o'clock this morning. Doctor Van de Lijn, who was called at midnight and who stayed until he died, says that he showed all the symptoms of food poisoning. Was there a dish of shell-fish at your table, Mevrouw?'

'No. Josef served the meal. And I ate dish for dish with my guest, Mynheer. Little cutlets of white fish, steamed, I think, I do not know its name, a sucking-pig which we hardly touched, but newly killed I know, and quite good, a chicken, some little marchpane ships with rice-paper sails—in honour of the *Java,* you know; I ate three or four, Captain Vehk but one, and a cheese which had come from Holland in his own ship. A very simple meal, Mynheer. And as I say I ate it myself and have been perfectly well since.'

'No rizplatzen? Shell-fish often finds its way into rizplatzen,

148

Mevrouw.'

'We didn't have it. I had eaten it almost every day since I arrived, and I think it appeals only to people who are accustomed to it.'

'And the ship's cook gives a similarly harmless list,' said Kaerko, frowning. 'But his pans were dirty. I ordered him twenty lashes for the dirtiness of his pans. Yet the crew had eaten from them and were alive and well. Of course, there are the Chinese sellers of sweetmeats on the quay. It is possible that the deceased purchased something there. But Doctor Van de Lijn mentioned shell-fish particularly ... and he knows a great deal about food.'

'Would you like to ask Josef, Mynheer? Please do, if you doubt my word in the very slightest. About the fish I admit my ignorance. But I know it was white, little flat pieces ... like plaice but with more flavour. And there was sauce on it, Sauce Hollandaise, exactly like our old Truitje used to make at home. I remember feeling quite homesick for a moment as I tasted it. And poor Captain Vehk said, "This tastes of home," and I remember thinking that he would eat it again in Holland before I should.... Please excuse me.' She gulped, realising that little Jean Vehk would never eat anything anywhere again ... and he had kissed her hands and she had been aware of a desire to embrace him, and had afterwards chided herself. And the likelihood was that those hands, now clasped so tightly together in her silken lap, had taken his last kisses, he was dead, those warm, bearded lips stiff and cold. She granted them the meed of tears, and then, lifting her swimming eyes to the living man who faced her, said brokenly, 'I can't tell you how very *kind* to me he was.' Even offering to spend the night in the house, she thought, though he thought I was making a mistake. And two more huge tears welled up and spilled over her cheeks.

Kaerko, watching her with the observant eyes which had served the Company so well, thought his mean thoughts. Good God, she was in love with the fellow, a perfectly ordinary ship's captain ... and there was I, hardly able to believe my ears when they said he had dined here, and I knowing that Evert Haan was in Bandogar. What on earth next? I asked myself. But I'm no nearer knowing how Vehk died, damn him, and I've got to write a report and find somebody to take the *Java* back to Amsterdam, I can't sit here watching Mevrouw Haan piping her eye over her lover.

'Mevrouw,' he said, rising to his feet, 'please do not distress yourself. The fault is none of yours. I am sorry that you have been drawn into the matter at all, but you will understand that it was my duty to pursue every possible path of inquiry.' He paused and swallowed before putting his final question. 'I suppose you were not ... in any way ... in Captain Vehk's confidence? You wouldn't know whether he had an enemy in Banda?' And as the question became audible on the air a flight of wild romantic speculations thronged through his mind. Suppose the pair had been lovers ... and she had been afraid that the man might say something, carelessly, spitefully. What easier than to invite him to dinner and poison him? She looked simple enough, but you could never tell by appearances ... and now he came to think of it, before she started to cry there had been a certain easing of tension in her manner. She had been stiff and frightened to start with, but he himself had been too much confused to evaluate her manner properly. Had she been afraid that Vehk was merely ill?

'I know nothing of Captain Vehk's private affairs,' she said, controlling herself and speaking quite clearly. 'But I can't imagine anyone wanting to *poison* him. He was such a kind, nice man.'

'I have your permission, Mevrouw, to ask your servant about the fish. If I don't, Captain Knoel will.'

'Ask anybody anything you wish,' Annabet said, rising from her chair and stuffing her damp handkerchief into her sleeve. 'Josef served the food and knows that I ate my share of everything. Shall I call him? Then, if you will excuse me, I will go to my room.'

'May I say, Mevrouw, how grateful I am for the completeness and frankness with which you have answered my questions?'

The straight stare of her reddened blue eyes was a trifle disconcerting, even to Kaerko.

'Mynheer, I merely told you what I knew. If you suspect Captain Vehk of having been poisoned I am as interested as you are in bringing home the blame. Perhaps you will be so good as to let me know the result of your inquiries.'

She had her hand on the knob of the door-handle before he could leap ahead and open it. Not waiting to cross to the table where the bell stood she called 'Josef' in a loud clear voice. And when Josef scuttled into view she said simply, 'Mynheer Kaerko wants to ask you some questions. Do your best to answer them.' And then, turning, she said graciously, 'Good morning, Mynheer,' and left Kaerko wondering. Certainly she had entertained Vehk during her husband's absence, but then, according to Evert's own boasting words, she was a lady, and the higher the rank the less conventional the behaviour, so he had heard. And certainly she had wept ... but then women shed tears very easily. It was a puzzle. And he still had his report to write; and a captain for the *Java* to find, and Knoel would say acidly, did you ask this and that and the other thing. For a moment the Agent was weary of spirit, out of love with his work; but he revived at the sight of Josef, and before Annabet had reached the top of the stairs she could hear his dry brisk little voice rattling out its questions.

She stood for a moment near the tub of plants at the stairhead, conscious of feelings more sharply divided than she had often known. She was distressed about Jean Vehk and could very easily have gone on shedding tears over his death; but half-ashamedly she realised that actually Kaerko's statement about the cause of her errand had brought a feeling of relief, almost of triumph. Her secret was still safe. And overlaid upon the sorrow and the relief was a feeling of irritation. Her natural impulse was to go into Evert's room and speak of the dead man to Shal Ahmi. Had the upper floor of the house been safely deserted she knew that she would have opened the white door and said abruptly, 'Captain Vehk is dead.' And why she should desire to tell the news to that strange brown-faced man she could not understand. Not because he would sympathise— why should he? He had not known the dead man. Not because, clever as he was, there was anything he could do. There was nothing anyone could do. And yet she wanted to say those four words. And the desire, frustrated as it was by Katje's silent, but sure presence in the next room, annoyed her. So she stood for a moment, thinking, I am sorry, dreadfully sorry, and that is understandable; and I am glad that Kaerko came about that and not about the other business, and I suppose that's understandable too. But why should I want Shal Ahmi to know? Why should I want to tell him myself and look at him as I say the words? That I cannot understand. It's almost as though I had made a habit of telling him things. . . . But that did not explain it; for although she had told Shal Ahmi so many things and asked his help over the business of the stranger, she knew that there was a great deal she had no desire to tell him. It was rather—she delved deeply into her own mind—as though she *ought* to know.

All this secrecy and queerness is making me queer, she thought dispassionately, and with a last glance at the closed locked door of Evert's room, and an almost deliberate gathering together of strength she passed on to the half-closed door of her own room where Katje, in her usual fashion was twitching at the bedcovers, interminably stretching out the business of tidying the room.

She looked at Annabet as she entered, her beady eyes alert in her impassive flat face; and as she did so Annabet remembered that she had cried in the drawing-room and that her damp handkerchief was still clasped in her hand.

'Mynheer Kaerko brought me bad news,' she said, almost defensively. 'The friend who dined with me the day before yesterday, has died suddenly.'

151

'Mevrouw is sad,' Katje said in a voice which might have been sympathetic but somehow was not. Why? Nor surprised.

'I expect you had heard?' She was surprised to hear herself say that to Katje; and she remembered Egbert's warning about bedroom gossip. But this isn't gossip, she thought. She *did* know. She knew when she came back to the bathroom. And how did she know? This is interesting. And it might be useful. Kaerko wouldn't have told Josef what his errand was; so it can't be that the news came that way. Unknown to herself she bent upon the coloured woman the piercing, searching stare of the white folk which all the brown people, bond or free, did their best to avoid.

'Abbas ran down to buy fish this morning, Mevrouw,' Katje said. 'It is sad indeed that a man so young and handsome should die so soon.'

'He was not young or handsome,' said Annabet innocently. 'But he was a good captain, and he had been very kind to me. And he was so looking forward to going home. . . . And his wife . . . poor woman . . .'

He had spoken of his wife during the first few days of the voyage. Less often afterwards. And there had been that moment in the hall! She thought with a pang—you didn't think of Mevrouw Vehk *then*, what a humbug you are Annabet Van Goens. But I am sorry for her *now*, she countered. And a relentless voice argued back, yes, now the man is dead and gone, no use to either of you. And that moment in the dim hall, that sentimental moment of farewell, of emotion engendered by the way the little man had kissed her hands became confused with the other moment when she had held the stranger's head to her breast and known suddenly what the whole business was all about. She thought I'm not going crazy, I *am* crazy . . . perhaps Mamma knew that when she said either you go to Banda or to County Down. . . .

Katje, watching her mistress closely and remembering all the gossip in the kitchen about the Mevrouw who was too ill to receive anyone and then suddenly rose up and asked a man to dinner alone, was puzzled. All white people were queer, but this white woman was queerest of all. That mention of the man's wife, and then that look of sorrow. Nothing fitted. Nothing ran alongside with any other of Katje's quite varied experiences.

The long day ended at last; the short twilight gave way to darkness, and the little scented wind came coolly over the land. With surging impatience which at moments palsied her hands, Annabet waited while Katje served the long-drawn-out evening meal. From time to time she slipped aside portions of food, wishing with all her heart that she could carry in the dishes as

152

they were, hot and appetising, untouched. When the meal was over she made Katje brush her hair for half an hour, and then said that she would take a bath and go to bed early. The preparation, the bath itself, and the clearing away consumed the greater part of another slow hour. She climbed into bed and tried to fasten her attention upon her book. Katje moved about the room, yawning more from boredom than from sleepiness. She longed to go down and join the gossiping servants in the compound where the evening went all too quickly; dully she counted the days until the master would be home again and this tedious companionship with an invalid mistress would end.

Annabet counted the yawns and presently produced the box of sweets. When Katje had eaten the nightly oblation, chewing as slowly and deliberately as a cow, Annabet said, 'I think you are tired too, Katje. I shall read for a little, but you can go to bed. I'll put the candle out.'

Katje thankfully lay down on her mat.

Annabet could hardly wait until the woman's breathing changed to the rhythm of sleep. As soon as it did so she was out of bed, and with the key of Evert's room swinging from one finger, the candlestick in one hand and the parcel of food in the other, slipped along the gallery. As she fitted the key into the door she listened. There was no sound. There had been no sound from the room all day and the silence had added to the mystery.

The shutters had been closed and the last inch of candle was guttering in its sockets. The room smelt close and airless, full of warring scents, among which she recognised only the sharp acrid colour of the pounded leaves and the fragrant mustiness of the Five Oils. She looked round eagerly, her first glance towards the bed. It was empty. And from the big chair which stood between the windows the stranger, fully dressed—how had he found the clothes?—rose shakily to his feet. At the same moment. Shal Ahmi, with the air of one emerging from a trance or from deep sleep, unfolded his limbs and his draperies from the place on the floor where he had been crouching.

'All is well, Mevrouw, as you see,' he said in his thin high voice. 'I trust your day has gone smoothly.'

She nodded, her eyes upon the other man. 'Do please sit down. You must be so weak. Should you be up?'

'Thanks to you, Mevrouw, I am well again,' he said. He made a stiff, painful little bow, and, straightening himself, came forward a step as though to take either the food or the candle from her hand. The light, falling upon his face, showed its haggard pallor, the fevered brilliance of his eyes and her heart contracted sharply. 'Do please sit down,' she said again, and set the candle and the parcel upon the bedside table. Then she turned to Shal Ahmi. 'Ought he to be up, already?'

Shal Ahmi moved silently towards the food, and with his hands upon it said smoothly, 'Do not concern yourself, Mevrouw. I am his physician and without my consent he would not have left his bed. Food will be welcome to us both.'

His brown hands opened the napkin and hovered above the bits of food which looked so unpalatable, all huddled together. He selected a roll of bread and pushed the rest towards the other man. As she watched him break the bread between his long slim fingers, Annabet remembered what the sight of the sick man up and dressed had driven from the forefront of her mind. She said abruptly, 'Captain Vehk is dead. He died last night. Doctor Van de Lijn says he was poisoned.'

Over the crust which he was lifting to his mouth Shal Ahmi's eyes looked at her so blankly that she felt foolish. It was as though she had burst out with some information about someone of whom he had never heard, Truitje or Klara or Mamma. She said hurriedly, in an effort to justify herself. 'I told you about him. He helped us ...' Her glance included the stranger; and then her heart jolted. The sick man was looking at Shal Ahmi with a kind of startled malevolence. He opened his mouth to speak and closed it again. Baffled, she looked back at Shal Ahmi. The crust of bread had reached his mouth and he bit off a piece and chewed it once or twice before he said, 'Ah yes, I remember the name. He was a friend of yours, Mevrouw. I am sorry if his demise has caused you pain.'

Two emotions raced through her mind side by side: one a memory of that farewell moment in the dark hall, the other a sense of wonder that all through this interminable day she should have felt an impulse to convey the news to Shal Ahmi. He was not even interested; she had never heard words so perfunctory.

'I was,' she said, 'very sorry. And the most dreadful thing was that when Mynheer Kaerko told me the news I could think of nothing except how glad I was that he hadn't come about *you*.' She turned to the stranger again and met his eyes and felt a tremulous melting in her tones. The memory of the moments when she had held him in her arms swept over her, obliterating everything else. She dropped her eyes and a hot blush rose from her neck to her hair. Through a daze of confusion she heard the sick man's voice rap out a few words in some language she did not understand, and Shal Ahmi answer him in the same tongue, smooth and cool, yet sharp and authoritative.

For a moment there was a tense silence in the room. Then, swallowing the last fragment of his bread Shal Ahmi said pleasantly:

154

'Mevrouw, one final favour. Restored as he is, my patient is still weak and he has a journey before him. Could you provide a little more brandy?'

'Oh, easily,' she said, thinking of the burst lock on the cupboard of the dining-room.

She took up the candle and moved swiftly to the door. As she closed it behind her she heard the stranger say, 'Was that necessary, you devil?' And Shal Ahmi's voice answered him, laconically, in the foreign tongue.

When she returned with the brandy bottle the atmosphere in the room had changed again. Shal Ahmi was standing with his basket on his arm as though prepared to depart; the other man was eating, without appetite, some of the food from the napkin.

'I shall return as soon as possible, Mevrouw,' Shal Ahmi said, 'I go now to make ready a prahau. Perhaps you will be so kind as to close the door behind me and await, as usual, my tap upon the window.'

When she had let him out and returned to Evert's room, the sick man had abandoned his pretence at eating, and was sitting with his elbows resting on his knees and his head propped between his hands. It was an attitude of despair or of great weakness, and love and pity wrenched at her heart as she looked at him.

'Whatever he says, you're not fit to travel,' she said. 'Stay one more day. We've managed so far. We could manage one more day.'

He had dropped his hands hastily and now raised his head. The bitter-sweet lines of his hard young mouth struck at her imagination anew.

'Mevrouw, I was only thinking. Please don't worry about me. I am unbelievably well, considering.' He stared at her and his eyes confused her so that she took refuge in an anxious flutter of hospitality. 'You haven't touched the brandy. He said it was necessary for you.'

'That will do later. I was trying to think. And being still a little—shall we say, feeble—I was afraid of muddling my head. Mevrouw . . .' He spoke the last word on a rising note and then hesitated, looking miserable and dubious.

'My name is Annabet.'

He seemed not to notice, but with the slightly desperate air of a man who is sick of debating with himself and has at last taken a decision and means to stick to it now for better or for worse, blurted out, 'It's you I'm worried about.'

'Me? Oh, please don't. Once you are gone I shall be taking no risk at all.'

'It'll be some days before Evert is back. And didn't you speak of a glove marriage? Does he love you?'

She was startled into frankness. 'No. When he went away I think he hated me.'

His haggard, bitter young face took on an even harsher expression. His stare slid from her face, uneasy, discomfited.

'I asked because Evert might have protected you if . . . but in that case . . . and anyway, he isn't here. You stood by me. You saved my life. By God, I'm going to tell you. Listen. Evert and Shal Ahmi and I do business together. I'm English, I live in an island called Gadia. They smuggle nutmegs out to me and the fellows who work with me, and we ship them to England and America. That's a desperate business, and we're all desperate men, Annabet. And Shal Ahmi is ruthless and incalculable as well. You heard what happened to Vehk . . .'

A feeling of deathly cold came over her.

'You mean . . . he was . . . killed?' The question was a faint thread of sound in a horrified silence.

'I'm sorry. I shouldn't have blurted it out like that. But I wanted you to know that I wasn't talking idly. You see . . . you let that brown devil know that you didn't believe my story about the fighting cocks. And I have it in my mind that except for the fact that you've been indispensable . . . that once I've gone, he might . . . We've got to think up something quickly. We've got to think of a story you can appear to believe. Oh God, if only my head were clear. I think I will try the brandy after all.'

She sprang forward to pour it for him. As the glass changed hands his burning fingers brushed against her icy ones and the touch made her heart leap even at that moment.

'Look,' he said, 'could you act like a giggling fool who has discovered a silly secret?'

'I could try.'

'Then when he comes back, take him aside and pretend to be angry. Say that I told you the truth. Say that I deceived you. Say I drank too much brandy and lost my head. Tell him that I told you I came to visit a native girl and was stabbed by a rival. Could you say that, with a kind of mixture of anger at being deceived and giggling interest at having found out a secret? You could say that I was afraid that if the young man found out, through your servants, that I was still alive and in Banda, he might try again. Run that through your mind, Annabet, look at it critically. Does it cover everything? My eagerness for secrecy; my deceiving you in the first place. He's not an easy man to deceive, God help you. And he could set Evert against you. Their hides are at stake, you know. If this passes over you must never, never as long as you life, show that you know what I've just told you.'

'I won't. I won't. I promise you,' she said, anxious to ease his agony of apprehension.

156

'The devil was in this damned business from the start,' he said in a calmer, but extremely doleful voice. 'We don't meet a patrol once in a hundred times. And if only that window hadn't been lighted; if only you hadn't let Shal Ahmi see that you thought I was lying about the fighting cock. I shan't sleep of nights thinking about you and wondering...'

'I shall think, and wonder, about you, too.'

He looked at her sharply and she felt the blood flame in her face.

It was true then, the thing which he had put down to his own delirium. She had held him in her arms, had called him darling, had kissed him. He accepted the knowledge with a fresh onslaught of sick despair. Love belonged, with so many other things, like codes of honour and clean linen and good manners, either to the past, which one tried not to remember, or to the future, the remote future, about which it was better not to think too much. But, given the right time and place.... Even now, when the only thing his body craved was rest and ease from pain, and his mind must be driven by force of will to the contemplation of practical things, he could realise her sweetness. Had, indeed, done so in what he had thought to be his last moment. That gentle, delicate face with its expression of pitying concern had floated in a haze of candlelight before his failing sight and he had thought of angels. Then, of course, he had come to his senses, and thought that she was the Isa about whom Evert had boasted with such regrettable lack of reticence, and he had been astonished, as he had been astonished when he first saw Evert's new house, that such an ordinary fellow, such a clod, in fact, should have such taste, and such luck. And then he had known who she was. And then there had been the dreams.

But there was nothing that could be done, save what he had already done, take what steps were possible to ensure her safety. He thought wryly of the risks, the secrecy, the squalor that were the very fabric of his life. What part had women, or the love of women, in that?

'There is one thing more I would like to say,' he said abruptly. 'If anything ever happens to you, if you get into danger or trouble of any kind, send for me. I've given you a great deal of inconvenience; you're in danger at this moment because of me. If you'd let that poor little man chuck me out you'd have run no risk at all. So I'm in your debt, and if you send for me and I'm alive and in the islands, I'll come. There's a fisherman called Gariz, a tall, villainous-looking fellow with one eye, he has two boats painted red and black and he lives in a hut at the extreme south end of the harbour. He'd find me for you.'

'I don't even know your name.'

The simple, straightforward sentence had a plaintive sound.

'I'm a fool,' he said. 'I told you my head wasn't clear. It's Ayrton. Christy Ayrton.' He half rose and bowed swaying. 'Very much at your service,' he said and sat down again hastily.

She tried the strange, foreign-sounding name over in her mind, longing to say it aloud, afraid that, in its very strangeness, it might elude her. She had wanted something more personal than 'he' and 'him,' and now she had it. Christy, a little name, endearing. Lest she might betray herself she looked about the room with busy, unfocussed eyes, avoiding his face.

'If you are to be drunk when he comes back we should do something about the bottle. Will you drink some more, or shall I empty it?'

'A shrewd thought,' he said. 'A finger more for me.' As she poured it he asked, 'You think you can convince him that this time you are thoroughly deceived?'

'I think so. I'll try.' Standing so near to him she was conscious of an aching thrill through all her nerves. If only she could call back the moment when she had kissed him! But she mustn't think of that; she must think of deceiving Shal Ahmi. She pulled herself away and carried the bottle behind the screen which, with its panels of cherry-blossom, flowery bamboo and water lilies, concealed Evert's basin and ewer and slop jar. Within its frail privacy, hidden from Christy's eyes, she wanted to cry, to shed in two seconds the tears of a lifetime. He was going, out into the dark, to an unknown place. He would be lost for ever. And the only moments they had spent together, or would ever spend, must be wasted in anxious planning. It was cruel, unbearable. But she mustn't be weak, mustn't add to his anxiety. He was so ill; and so brave. She pressed her finger to her trembling lip and steadied it. Then she remembered the minute dribbles of brandy which Truitje had poured from a cherished little bottle in times of faintness or shock. And here was she, pouring a whole bottle away. She lifted the bottle and tipped it against her mouth, gasping.

'When I go,' he said, as she emerged from the screen's shelter and set the now half-empty bottle in a conspicuous place near the candle, 'I shall have to pretend to be drunk. Above all things, he mustn't suspect that there is any connivance between us. So I will say good-bye now. Please believe that I realise how much you have done for me, even to calling in that old devil and endangering your own life ... and all the little things beside. I shall remember you, always, with very lively gratitude....' So much, at least, he must say. Of the nostalgia, the sense of enchantment, the feeling that if things

158

had been otherwise than they were ... of these, naturally, no word.

Resolutely he rose from his chair and stretched out his hand. 'Good-bye, and thank you, from my heart.'

She put her own hand into his, the formal gesture, the handshake, used every day, friends, acquaintances, enemies. ... The last touch, withdrawn even as you held, last hold on hope, on life. ...

'Good-bye,' she said, and the word, forced through the ache in her throat brought the blinding tears with it. 'Take care of yourself. Oh Christy ... God bless you, wherever you go.'

Shal Ahmi's cane tapped at the window, gently, relentlessly. The burning hand tightened on hers with quick nervous pressure.

'You know what to say?'

She nodded. He bent his head and raised her hand towards his lips, but she lifted her face instead and their mouths met.

The jewelled moment, wrenched from the dull matrix of time, was theirs until the cane tapped again, imperatively. Shaken and breathless, Christy put her away, gently but with firmness.

'Darling, you must go. For your own sake ...'

He watched as she turned obediently and made her blind way to the door. Then he sat down heavily and gripped the arms of his chair, fighting for self-possession and calmness. An old memory stirred and he thought fiercely, not again! He remembered how he had parted from Betsy Harrison on that teeming wet August morning when he had ridden out to join the King at Nottingham. He had never seen her again, but the memory of her lint white hair and soft brown eyes and wild rose face had added the final touch of bitterness to his first three or four years of exile. He had recovered at last, and between Betsy and Annabet stood a long line of shadowy women, of many kinds and colours. He would have said, as he stumbled on to the verandah at Coenpark, that he had outlived and outgrown any sentiment about women. They had their uses, everything else was poetic fancy, pleasant enough in the right circumstances, but a useless burden to life lived as he must henceforth live it. Nevertheless ... I could have loved her, he thought; and then switched his mind to wonder, with a cold sweating sense of anxiety, how well, or how badly, she was telling the story which he had put into her mouth.

At the foot of the stairs Annabet wiped her eyes gently, not to redden them, and composed her face. Now that she must open the door to the man whom she knew to be Jean Vehk's murderer both the brandy glow and the excitement of that long bitter-sweet kiss, were swamped by a cold tide of fear. Vehk, who at worst could only be suspected of guessing at the secret, had been killed in the interest of its preservation. *She* knew everything, and as she opened the door she felt that her knowledge was written upon her face. The story which Christy had concocted for her sounded suddenly frail and incredible. She was horribly aware of facing an adversary who recognised only his own laws.

But Christy had told her what to say, and she must say it with confidence. Turning the key she remembered the times when she had helped Klara to elude Mamma's lynx-like eye. How small and innocent those deceptions seemed now.

As the door opened she burst straight into her story, hoping that the nervous breathlessness of her voice would be set down by her hearer to excitement over her discovery.

'Oh,' she said, as Shal Ahmi silently crossed the threshold, 'I'm sorry you were obliged to tap twice, Shal Ahmi. But I was hearing the *truth* about that man at last.'

She had raised the candle, as she always did when opening the door, and instead of lowering it, satisfied, as on other nights, she continued to hold it high, so that the light fell levelly upon Shal Ahmi's face. There was no change in his expression, his face remained bland and unconcerned, though she watched him close enough to notice the contraction of the pupils of his eyes in the candlelight.

'And what is the truth, Mevrouw?' he asked politely, with no more than perfunctory interest.

She lowered her voice conspiratorially and stood still, half-way across the hall.

'You told me to give him brandy, didn't you? Well, he drank more than he ought and told me everything. How I wish I'd known sooner, before I put him into my husband's room, and bothered you about him, and taken such trouble myself. But I must say that though I didn't for a moment believe those tales about fighting-cocks with black tails and such-like rubbish, I did believe that *somehow* he was connected with my husband. How shall I ever explain to him?' She pretended to look into the brown face piteously, as though searching for help and reassurance, but the interest and curiosity which she sought did not appear.

'And what was his business, Mevrouw?'

'I hardly know how to tell you—and you going to such trouble over him. He's nothing but a common philanderer, Shal Ahmi. He came sneaking into the compound to visit a *girl*, and some other man—on the same errand I expect, stabbed him. Of course I realise that he had to go *somewhere*, he was bleeding to death; but it was impertinent, to say the least of it, to come here and pretend to be Evert's friend. It

160

hasn't been easy for me, Shal Ahmi, to sneak about in my own house, but I had the satisfaction of feeling that I was considering my husband's interests. Now I learn that the reason for the secrecy was that if the servants knew he was here and alive they'd gossip and the man who did the stabbing would make another attempt....' Had she overdone her part? Explained too thoroughly? There was nothing upon that smooth brown face to guide her. 'I'm almost distraught, Shal Ahmi. What will my husband say when he knows that I took a person like that into his house, into his very bed? And I did try to act for the best.'

Deliberately she allowed her mind to dwell for one second upon the thought which she had been keeping at bay ... He's leaving me now, and I love him. Genuine tears—and a feeling of shame that they should be used as a means of self-defence shot through her—instantly filled her eyes.

Shal Ahmi waited until several of them had brimmed her lids and slid over her cheeks. He watched her take out her handkerchief and fight for control. The fight was as genuine as the tears, for once she started to cry the pent-up emotions of the last few days seized at this chance of release. Finally he said, still coolly, but with a certain kindness in his voice:

'I see no reason for your distress of mind, Mevrouw. You acted hastily, but from good motives. I do not think Mynheer Haan would blame you. But, if you prefer not to tell him anything of the affair, well, nobody shares your knowledge but me, and I ... I am not given to gossip.' Some slight shifting of the planes of his face which might have been a smile changed his expression at last.

'Oh,' she said, struggling again to master her tears—there will be hours, days and nights in which to cry, now you must feign delight and relief. 'If you *would* just say nothing, Shal Ahmi. It sounds very decitful, doesn't it, but I ... you see I haven't been here long, and I don't want my husband to think I'm stupid and credulous and careless with his lovely house, taking in such riffraff. Later on, when he knows me better I will tell him, I promise you.'

'Very well, Mevrouw. The thing is as though it had never happened. Now I must proceed. I also have been deceived, I would point out, and, acting like you in what I believed to be Mynheer Haan's interest, I have arranged for our friend to leave Banda to-night. Even in the light of our new knowledge, I think it is better to get him away. Do you agree?'

'Oh yes. Shal Ahmi, I've said before that I can never express my gratitude....'

'Time is short, Mevrouw,' he interrupted her, and began to make his silent way towards the upper floor. She followed holding the candle.

161

'It is to be hoped that you can walk,' Shal Ahmi said coldly as he entered the room. Christy laughed drunkenly.

'Walk! Of course I can walk. Why not. The brandy was just what I needed. But you wouldn't expect a woman to understand that, of course.'

He hooked his arm through the crooked elbow which Shal Ahmi proffered and rose to his feet.

'I've made an ass of myself,' he went on in a blurred thick voice, close to Shal Ahmi's ear. 'Told her the truth. Women are surely the oddest things God ever made. I tell her a lie and she's an angel of mercy; I tell her the truth and she acts as though I'd polluted the very air.'

'Your candle drips grease, Mevrouw. This is a trying moment, I realise, but it is almost ended,' said Shal Ahmi, moving towards the door.

'You agree with her I suppose,' Christy asked aggressively as they negotiated the doorway and made for the stair-head. 'Weren't you ever young and hot-blooded? Didn't you ever hunt in forbidden coverts? Oh Lord, this Haan, whoever he is, knows about brandy. I must be drunk talking about hunting to you. You've never hunted anything but fleas, have you?'

'Please, Shal Ahmi, don't take offence. He's drunk, he doesn't know what he is saying, I assure you. After you've been so *good* to him. But please don't mind. Just get him out of here, quickly.'

'You see? An hour ago she was wailing that I shouldn't be out of bed. Now it's get him away quickly. And all because of a little brown girl who smells of nutmeg cheese. It's the only thing I have against her. I've said to her a thousand times, "If only you wouldn't chew that damned stuff you'd be perfect." But I was wrong, of course. After all, it wasn't the nutmeg cheese that stabbed me.'

Shal Ahmi threw towards Annabet a glance that was almost apologetic. Christy, seeing it, knew a great lifting of the heart. So she had convinced him. And she was safe. Oh, thank God for that.

'You would do better to save your breath. You will need it,' Shal Ahmi said smoothly.

They were in the hall, across it. Annabet opened the door. Outside in the darkness something moved, came forward. A big, strong-looking fellow. Once the door was shut and she had no longer to be deceived they could probably carry him between them; Shal Ahmi would drop his mask of disapproval and be kind.

'But I must say good-bye to my hostess. Until this last moment she has been kind. So kind that I wish, honestly I do wish it, that I had come here about fighting-cocks. Why do you think she approves of fighting-cocks and not of little brown

162

girls? They're not so expensive in the long run. Don't push me, damn you. I want to say good-bye to Mevrouw properly.'

Swaying on Shal Ahmi's arm he turned to Annabet. Stretched out a hand. Her own would have flown to meet it; but Shal Ahmi was watching. Reluctantly, with a he-is-drunk-and-must-be-humoured glance at the brown man she laid her free hand in Christy's. Some virtue, a secret reassurance, flowed from it.

'Mevrouw, I salute you. I kiss your hand. Your mind may be narrow, but your heart is warm. I shall remember you and your kindness until my last day. I kiss your hand again. Good-bye, Farewell, Au Revoir, Arrivederci. Take your choice. And now, come weal come woe, I'll tell whom you've had the honour of entertaining: you wanted to know that, didn't you, Mevrouw? As of course any lady would. Shamus O'Flaherty, Mevrouw, as good an Irishman as ever said "The curse of Cromwell on ye." Good-bye, Mevrouw, and thanks for your hospitality. Tell your husband from me that his brandy is good, and if he values a quiet life to keep away from little brown girls.'

Between the drunkenly jerked-out words his lips travelled over her fingers. She felt her hand twisted and the warm kiss laid upon her palm, her wrist. Never, never in the whole history of the world did lovers part in such a fashion. Desperately she racked her brain for some last ambiguous word which would, while deceiving Shal Ahmi, convey her understanding, her love, her unfailing pledge of remembrance. But her mind failed in this final test of inventiveness.

Shal Ahmi plucked him away. At the bottom of the wide shallow steps the faceless, shadowy figure closed in and took Christy's other arm. Then they were gone. In less than a breathing space the darkness of the moonless night had engulfed the three linked figures. Was the third man Gariz?

Before she closed the door she whispered, 'God keep you,' into the darkness. The heavy handsome door swung into place and its thud of finality echoed through her mind. She leaned her arm against the door and lowered her head and wept. So this, after all the dreams and the imaginings, was love. Coming so unexpectedly, hurting so much, so soon wrenched away.

'Well,' said Christy, altering the position of his arm into a hold upon Shal Ahmi's that was more a conscious search for support and less a drunken dependence, 'do you think Mevrouw's curiosity is satisfied now?'

He spoke in English and Shal Ahmi, with less than his usual pompous fluency, replied in the same tongue.

'You cannot fault her for curiosity. It is her house, and was so useful and her own acts good. Your story was good too, because now, when remembered and contemplating she thinks disgust and thinks no more. Is it plain? This English,' he said crossly, 'is a tongue of barbarians. I return to the Dutch. He will not understand because I speak things of the mind.' He drew breath, tightened his hold upon Christy and plunged into what, by long usage, was as familiar and flexible as his own language. 'In the healthy mind, Mynheer, the memory is sensitive. It shrinks from the unpleasant as the hand shrinks from fire. I could see that your explanation disgusted Mevrouw. And only the deranged dwell upon memories which disgust them. I think that Mevrouw will very soon forget this Shamus O'Flaherty.'

'I hope so,' said Christy. I shall forget, too, he told himself. I'm not well yet; not myself. Mustn't let this longing for a woman I can never have take root in my mind. There's only one thing I want now, money. Ten thousand pounds, and then I can redeem my sequestered land. The rebels are feeling the pinch now, ten thousand pounds will buy a lot of forgetfulness. How long? Two or three years, if it lasts, if trade is as good as it has been. It might be sooner.

He stumbled along, thinking of the thready, twisted rumours which had reached even as far as Gadia. Cromwell and Commonwealth were not as popular as they had been; and Cromwell was said to be failing in health. After him ... what? Silly Dick? A military republic? Or the return of the rightful king? Better not count upon the Stuart too much; the family was unlucky. Better count upon Evert Haan with his overweening ambition, upon Shal Ahmi with his unguessable aims, upon his own clear-cut ends. God grant just one thing, that the Dutch authorities didn't go to war to root out the smugglers before he'd completed the hoard. He thought briefly of the pale sheets of oxslips in his Weybury woods in spring; of the brown October fields stretching away to the blazing beeches on his boundary.

'Mynheer,' said Gariz, speaking for the first time, 'a few paces more and you will be in the prahau. Take heart.'

Life was entirely a matter of taking heart, and a few more paces. One more victory like Edgehill and the war will be over; get to Yarmouth and you will be safe; get to Holland and Charles will find you a place; go East and you'll make a fortune. Always the future. And so far every future disappointing. But there was no choice except to press on. And though there hadn't been a ship at Yarmouth, there had been one at Grimsby; and though starving is poor fun even in good company, Charles had paid his passage to Java from his card-winnings; and though the fortune was being made in secret, crooked ways, it was gradually growing. Mustn't lose heart.

Shal Ahmi helped him, solicitously into the prahau, and

then stepped back, folding his hands away into his wide white sleeves.

'May the rest of your journey be as uneventful, Mynheer. Farewell until our next meeting.'

'Good-bye, Shal Ahmi. Thank you for all you have done. I'll live to repay you, I hope.'

'I was reckoning upon that,' said Shal Ahmi, stating the literal truth.

So true, Christy thought as the prahau slipped away through the nutmeg trees towards the open sea; he's looked after me because I am a confederate. He saved my life, but I owe him no debt. But the other ... Annabet ... He forced his mind away.

Presently Gariz, shifting one hand, fumbled with a bundle near his feet.

'Dried fish and rice cakes, Mynheer. There is enough for two. You are welcome.' The soft Malay words were inviting and sincere.

'I ate before I left, Gariz. I am not hungry, thanks.'

Gariz himself ate heartily, a little noisily, completely absorbed. He was glad that his passenger was quiet and patient. So often the white men did not understand that achievement was largely a matter of quiet rhythm, of persistent, inexhaustible patience. They were always trying to hurry things.

Evert, at the end of the stage of his journey by prahau, was inclined to hurry things by bullying his boatman to greater effort. Such impatience tingled in his veins that sometimes he felt a wild impulse to snatch the oars from the unhurrying brown hands and speed the tiny craft forward. Fools like Doctor Van de Lijn said that all the dotted islands of the Pacific had been peopled by men and women from the Malay peninsula who had, for some reason or other, set out into the unknown in vessels like that in which he, at the moment, lounged. That was rot. They'd have died of starvation before they reached land, they couldn't have carried enough food— not if they travelled as this fellow was forcing him to travel.

He had made the awkward journey many times before and never girded at its slowness, but for three weeks now he had been racked by impatience and uncertainty, and as the journey reached its end, he was almost demented. There had been moments when, for instance, the woman who kept the inn at Bandogar had rustled towards him, bright with recognition and respect, or when lot after lot was knocked down to him in the market, 'Mynheer Haan, of Banda,' when he had been brought up short by the realisation that he, Evert Haan, known and respected, had conspired with Shal Ahmi, a coloured man, a native, to make away with his wife. It was an incredible

165

thought. But then, so was the thought that Evert Haan's wife should be a stiffly-moving skeleton whom he was ashamed to acknowledge, even before those he regarded as his friends. An incredible thing had happened to him, and he had taken an incredible way out. And there would be no rest, no peace of mind for him until he had returned to Banda and heard for himself what had happened.

There was no fear in the ordinary sense mingled with his impatience. If Shal Ahmi had been clumsy—and that possibility was in itself almost inconceivable—and a scandal awaited him on his arrival, he, Evert Haan, was still safe. Nobody would dream of taking the word of Shal Ahmi against that of Evert Haan, upon that certainty he had anchored his peace of mind during the past three weeks. Sometimes, when, for instance, he woke in the bad hour of the night, between two and three and found difficulty in going to sleep again, he had entertained thoughts which held an element of self-torture. Something entirely unforeseen might have happened and Shal Ahmi, brought face to face with the vengeance of society, *might* have thought to save his hide by reporting the underlying gist of that interview in the study. But no one would believe him; partly because it was an incredible story, partly because everyone in Banda was aware of the ill-feeling between them, most of all because practically everyone in Banda regarded Shal Ahmi as a liar and a double dealer. And Evert, if he were ever forced into the open had his story ready—my wife was ill, the Dutch doctors had failed to cure her, Shal Ahmi had a reputation for skill in native physic and I thought it was worth taking a chance that he could do something for her, I was willing to bury past differences, but he was not.

That was to be, finally, the line of defence. Knoel, who had so often called Shal Ahmi a yellow charlatan, a pernicious influence, a disturber of the peace, would see to the rest. A great many people would regard with pleasure, or at any rate complete indifference, the prospect of the brown medicine man bound for the gallows by the Fort.

Evert would be neither pleased nor indifferent, even though it was his own word which put the noose around the plump neck. Action both tricky and dangerous would then be called for, but that need not be contemplated now. No use crossing bridges before you came to them. Yet, with a very queer bridge indeed just ahead of you, twelve, ten, seven, three days ahead, even a strong-nerved person could be excused for a desire to get across. And these last three days in the dawdling prahau had tested Evert's fortitude as much as anything he had ever been called upon to endure.

To Annabet, as a person apart from a problem, he gave no thought at all. She had ceased to exist before he left Banda.

166

Once there had been an Annabet, born of Piet Odshoorn's drunken babble and quickly brought to full stature by Evert's own imaginings, a thing of golden, wild-rose beauty, to be enjoyed; a thing of pride, to be humbled; a thing of value, to be displayed. But that Annabet had died in the cabin of the *Java*. For the sorry substitute, the last effrontery of the Van Goens towards Evert Haan, he had no feeling, no pity. There was only one thing he wanted now—to be met by Doctor Van de Lijn on the quay of Banda Neira, and to hear him say, 'She died, despite everything I could do.' Or, since this was impossible, since no one, not even Van de Lijn, could know the exact moment of the prahau's arrival, he would have liked the first man he saw to look at him with sympathy—real or false—lower his eyes and mumble out something about being sorry for his loss. Then he would know that he was a free man again.

Mingled with his impatience and speculations as he lay in the prahau on this last lap of the journey, was a strain of voluptuousness. He had already decided upon Annabet's successor. No more glove marriages for him! Jannetje Coster was the daughter of a First Merchant in Bandogar, and he was agreeably conscious of having impressed himself very favourably upon both the girl and her father during his brief stay. Jannetje had just come home from school in Batavia, and although she had none of the glamour of good family, she was a pretty little thing, with pleasing manners. She would not be in the market long; and as soon as he knew that all was well at Coenpark, Annabet safely dead and in the new burial-ground, he would send a special message to her father, bidding for her hand and suggesting a marriage in about six months' time. That would be long enough delay. It was not as though Annabet had been his loving faithful wife over a period of years and the new marriage make all the Banda ladies disapprove because it called up a wonder whether they, too, might be so quickly replaced. Everyone would say—it's the very best thing he could do; just as they did when a woman started up another baby soon after a miscarriage.

And on the day when he had dined at the Coster house, Jannetje had worn a dress, cut so low that the valley between her plump little breasts had been clearly visible. It had been difficult for him to keep his eyes from it. She would do very well, and as the daughter of a First Merchant would probably have a respectable dowry.

After all, one might as well think upon pleasant things as brood upon the distasteful ... if only this damned fellow would hurry ... if only the news in Banda were good.

At about four o'clock in the afternoon they were so close to land that he could see the windows of Vehmeer's office spark-

167

ling in the sun. The *Java* had gone from the anchorage. (And the Captain hadn't tasted the hospitality of Coenpark. Good thing too, surly little devil!) In her place lay the *Trade's Advance*, and between the ship and the shore the carrier boats were plying, laden so they only just cleared the water. Evert was glad to see the business going forward; it meant that there would be many people on the quay, and he would soon know.

As Evert's prahau bumped the steps of the quay, three sailors from the *Trade's Advance* were being hauled ashore. Their mates laid them carefully upon the three stretchers held by native bearers and with rough, good-humoured valedictions turned back to their own boat. Doctor Van de Lijn, with his big straw hat tilted over his eyes and his notebook already in his hand, was studying the three supine bodies. Scurvy, Evert thought automatically, as he climbed to the quay, briskly, despite his cramped limbs; and far gone at that, any fool can see that with half an eye. No need for him to lean over them and study them so attentively. Look up, can't you, you ass, and tell me what I want to know.

He went forward and touched the doctor on the shoulder. Van de Lijn, jerked back from some fascinating train of thought looked at him blankly for a moment and then gave a slight smile.

'Ah. So you're back. And anxious about your wife, naturally. Well, I've good news for you. She's perfectly well. As I suspected from the first, it was all a question of diet. You look surprised. But, Mynheer, you do not ... nobody.... Look, look at these poor devils.'

He took Evert by the arm and swung him round so that he had no choice but to look at the seamen. But the piteous, puffy, scrofulous faces made no impression upon his mind. That was wholly engaged by a vision of Annabet, that stiffly moving skeleton. Perfectly well. What did the fool mean? Able to eat and sleep. God damn her, she had been able to do that when he left. She'd said it herself, maddeningly, 'I'm not ill you know.'

'In three days,' said Doctor Van de Lijn, taking Evert's silence for interest, 'there'll be an unbelievable difference. Goats' milk, and fresh meat, goat or chicken, fruit, green vegetables ... that's what you need my lads. Take heart. I've seen dozens as bad as you, and had them walking in less than a week.' He lowered his voice. 'Dying of salt pork and salt herrings. Yet, God in Heaven, they're both food. What makes the difference? If only I could find out what makes the difference.'

His eyes took on a far-away look. Evert could have killed him.

'When did you last go to Coenpark?'

The doctor blinked. 'Oh, a week ... no more, ten days ago. She was in no need of my attention, I assure you.' Something in Evert's cold, angry stare, brought him to earth with a jolt. 'Mynheer, you are concerned for your wife, naturally. But, apart from the fact that I am a busy man, I have a conscience. My further attendance, so obviously unnecessary, would have been a needless expense to you.'

Bother the fool, he thought. Mevrouw Haan, with goats' milk and butter, fresh fruit and vegetables inside her, had been in perfect health twelve days ago. The last two visits he had made had been completely perfunctory. Now he had three dying men on his hands and no time to waste. 'All a matter of diet, as I have said before,' he announced quite snappily, and signalling to the foremost of the bearers, he turned his back on Evert, thinking, Thank God I'm a Company servant and can live without the patronage of fools.

Evert pushed back his hat and mopped his head. Ten days ago, that was quite a long time. Was it possible that Shal Ahmi had feared to begin before the doctor had finished? If so, for once his wits had failed him. It would have been better for the scarecrow to have died while in the professional man's care.

A hearty slap on the back made him stagger. Vehmeer, who had spied him from his office window, was welcoming him back, his vast face shining with pleasure.

'Good to see you back, Evert. Have a pleasant journey?'

'Slow, but uneventful. I'm glad to stretch my limbs.' Now ... now ... he would hear.

'Come in and have a drink. How's Bandogar? Do much business?'

'I want to get home,' Evert said abruptly. 'I've got some papers for Kaerko; and then I must get along.'

The smile which had faded for an instant when his invitation was so bluntly rejected, returned, wider than ever to Vehmeer's wide face. He struck his fat hand on his thigh.

'God bless me, old man, I was forgetting. Somebody waiting for you at Coenpark this time! Of course, you must get along. Oh, and by the way, I'd like you to know that my wife did call, visit of welcome and all that. But your lady wasn't up to seeing visitors. Though ...' he hastened to add at the sight of something in Evert's eyes, 'she was getting on. Oh yes, she sent down a message to say she was better, doing nicely.'

'When was that?' Evert asked.

'Oh, quite a long time ago, soon after you'd left. Jehane ought to have gone up again, I told her so only yesterday; but she said she'd leave it until you were back and could send word when visitors would be welcome.'

'Yes, I will. I'll let you know. I'll look in to-morrow and

169

have that drink with you.' Evert's words were pleasant, friendly, but his manner was a little strange, Vehmeer thought.

So there were still the twelve days unaccounted for. Why in God's name hadn't Shal Ahmi devised some means of letting him *know*? He strode around the corner and into Kaerko's office. The Agent was aboard the *Trade's Advance*, and the office was empty save for a young half-caste clerk who was dozing away the last hour of the warm afternoon. Evert laid the papers on the table which, he knew, was sacred to important business, and then, almost jumping down the steps, he turned into the street, shadowy between the houses, and began to hurry towards Coenpark. Away from the sea and the houses it was warm going. The path was dusty, and even the dust seemed to smell of nutmegs. Hundreds of marauding doves guzzled and mourned among the nutmeg boughs, ceasing their soulful lamentations in order to snatch off the ripe fruit, wrestle with it until the hard nut was separated from its luscious covering, and then, swallowing the fruit, dropping the nut like a pebble; that done, they would cry again in voices that were the very negation of greed.

Evert, striding along, hot and angry, made a mental note about birdlime.

Then, rounding a clump of trees which hugged the curve of the path, he came upon Shal Ahmi, seated upon a boulder, his back comfortably pressed against a tree trunk. His hands were folded in a manner which suggested infinite patience, his dusty feet in their toeless sandals stuck out across the path. He looked as though he had been waiting for an hour, and it would have been hard even for Evert to believe that the brown man had watched, with sardonic amusement his conversation with Van de Lijn and Vehmeer on the waterfront.

'The return of a traveller is always an occasion of joy,' Shal Ahmi said softly as Evert drew level with him. Despite his urgent desire for news, Evert looked up and down the path and into the groves of nutmeg trees as far as he could see on either side before halting and speaking. He had always been careful in his dealings with Shal Ahmi and now, more than ever, was care essential.

'Tell me quickly,' he said.

'Your trust in me was justified, Mynheer. It is pleasant to think that such complete trust has met with such complete justification.'

'I don't want any of your riddles and crooked answers,' Evert snapped, relieved to be able to show his ragged temper. 'Is she alive or dead?'

'But alive, Mynheer. What else did you expect?' His dark eyes widened as his hairless brows, climbing his forehead, wrinkled it in simulated astonishment.

170

Evert was speechless for a moment. When he could shape his lips and control his tongue he spluttered out, 'But you ... I trusted you. You said you would ... could; may the devil take you, you yellow traitor, you promised you'd rid me of her.'

No sign of annoyance showed upon the bland brown face. Only the eyes twinkled briefly, the corners of the thin mouth twitched.

'I have rid you of her, Mynheer—as effectually as though I had throttled her. Go along. Go up to your house and see for yourself.'

He rose from the boulder and gathered his garments about him with dignity, flicking off with a fastidious finger a fragment of bark which had caught in one of his many folds. Evert, lowering his head like an angry bull, moved to face him, prepared, it seemed, to oppose his going. Shal Ahmi stared at him without speaking. Then as Evert fell back he moved forward and turned his face toward the town.

He had taken six of his pompous, noiseless steps when Evert called him.

'Shal Ahmi. I'm sorry I spoke as I did. Listen, I ... I ... damn it man, I asked you not to speak in riddles. I lost my temper. I apologise.'

'Sometimes I wonder,' said Shal Ahmi placidly, 'how, with a temper so easily lost the head is kept.' Then, seeing that the significance of the rebuke had not been lost upon the white man he softened. 'Mynheer. I have many other things to tell you. Life has not been uneventful in your absence. But all that will do later. Perhaps to-morrow night. I think that then you will greet me as a friend.'

He turned his back resolutely and moved away. Evert stared at the wide white back for a moment, and then, impelled by such curiosity as he had never known before, swung round and ran along the path towards Coenpark.

Everything in his beautiful house was ready for him; upstairs and down, from the whitened steps of the front door to the last tile of the passage that led to the kitchen quarters, everything that could be polished and scoured and dusted shone with cleanliness.

Annabet had attempted to share in this work of preparing for the master's return, for she was in that state of nervous tension when she would have found relief in some physical activity, but Josef, without actual rudeness, had soon made it plain that even by taking an interest in the arrangement of the flowers she was insulting him; and when, tired of aimlessly fidgetting about the house and the garden she had passed through the green hedge with the archways, intending to retrace the steps of the one walk she had taken with Evert,

Katje, breathless and cross, joined her within four minutes. 'It is not a right thing for Mevrouw to go out of the garden unaccompanied.'

She had walked for a little way, and then turned back, taken a leisurely bath and put on the blue gown with the ruffles of lace which had come from Mamma's wedding dress. Then, with a towel pinned over her shoulders she sat down at the dressing-table before the silver-framed mirror and coloured her cheeks and lips carefully. The result was not like a painted deathshead any longer; some of her own natural colour was coming back; and confidence was returning too, so that she painted less desperately, to enhance, not to hide. When she had finished, Katje came forward and took up the brush and comb. She brushed vigorously, a hundred strokes, as she had been taught to do, and then wound the curls, one by one, about her fingers. They had grown very quickly, and clustered upon each temple, shining behind each ear added to the increased fullness of her face.

Throughout the lengthy toilette, as indeed throughout the hours of every day and night which had passed since she had made her momentous decision, little tremors passed at intervals along her nerves, making her heart flutter as though a butterfly had been trapped in her chest, making her face go red and then white, making her fingers unsteady. Sometimes she had a sharp clear vision of Evert's look of cold hatred, a memory of the contemptuous way in which he spoke the few words he had addressed to her. Anger flamed in her then, and a feeling of reborn confidence came with it. At least her looks were coming back. Still too thin, of course; and since Christy's going she had not continued to fatten as she had been doing. But her head sat squarely on her shoulders once more, and all her limbs were supple.

And that was Evert's doing! Nothing must be allowed to obscure that fact. It was Evert who had fetched Shal Ahmi to see her. In a very special way this new beauty of hers belonged to her husband. Well, she was doubly bound to deal honourably with him; and that she was prepared to do.

She looked at the French clock and rose from the dressing-table. She had no idea of the exact time of Evert's arrival, but it could not be long delayed now. Josef had said that Mynheer always returned from such trips before dark. It would be better for them to meet in the parlour; bedrooms were always invested with an idea of intimacy.

She was half-way down the stairs when the heavy front door was flung open, and Evert, pushing back his hat and mopping his forehead as he came, strode into the hall and toward the staircase. His shirt was unfastened at the collar and its ruffles hung limply. His face was red and hot, and his breathing was

172

quick and heavy.

After the sunset brilliance of the outer world the hall was dim. He slammed the door behind him by a backward thrust of his arm and hurried towards the stair foot, finding his way more from habit than from actual sight. He had reached the bottom step and had his foot on it before he saw her. One of those nervous spasms had come upon her at the sight of him, and she had gripped the banister, standing still, waiting for it to pass.

For a moment he looked upwards with a stunned, stupid look on his face. Through the back of his guilty mind flashed the thought that Shal Ahmi had murdered her, and that this was her ghost on the stairs. For, altered as she was, so very, very different from the crooked, ugly, starveling creature he had left, he recognised the hair, and the dress. The submerged artist in him, which made him so ruthless and so susceptible, which had enabled him to collect loveliness as a miser collects gold, gave him a sharp, unerring eye for detail, and even in that confused, uncertain, terrified moment, he realised that standing there on the stairs, one hand gripping the banister, the other pressed against her bosom, she fulfilled all the dreams he had ever cherished about the lovely woman in the lovely house.

'Annabet,' he said. And it was more a question than a greeting.

'Yes,' she said. 'You see, I am better.'

The stupid superstitious fear—God, he could laugh at it now—fled away at the sound of her voice. Hastily he removed his hat, his other hand flew to the open-neck of his shirt, pulling the ruffles together.

'I ran, all the way from the quay,' he said. 'I saw Doctor Van de Lijñ and he told me he hadn't been near you for twelve days ... I couldn't wait to see how you were.'

The tremor had passed, the moment of compensating confidence had come. She began to descend the stairs. He watched her take two supple easy steps, and then, tossing away his hat, leaped towards her, hand outstretched.

'You're better. I could hardly believe my eyes,' he babbled, raising the hand to his lips and then letting it fall. The heavy warm arm went round her shoulders, the hot red face pressed against hers. 'Now,' he said, between kisses, 'I can give you a proper welcome. I was afraid to touch you before. Afraid of hurting you. Well, haven't you a kiss for your husband? Not shy of me, are you? You'll soon get over that.' He was like a great blustering boy, granted at the last moment a longed-for treat which he had thought withheld.

'I'll go and tidy myself,' he said at last, releasing her. He clapped his hands together loudly and Josef came running.

'Wait for me in the drawing-room. You'd laugh if you knew how often I've pictured you in that room. I'll be down in ten minutes. Josef, you rogue, bring me some hot water and a long cool drink. And I want a clean shirt. And light all the candles. And tell them in the kitchen that I want dinner in half an hour; and see that it's good.'

He went leaping up the stairs, two at a time. From the top he looked back and saw the straight slim figure of his wife in the doorway of the drawing-room which he had furnished and planned with only his eye and his imagination to guide him. Lovely, exquisite. Just what he had hoped for. Bless Piet Odshoorn; and bless Shal Ahmi. What had the old devil said? 'I have rid you of her, Mynheer, as effectually as though I had throttled her.' And he hadn't even guessed.

As he washed and changed his clothing his blood cooled, and it occurred to him that his behaviour on the stairs had been crude and boisterous. Well, what of it? he asked, shrugging his shoulders under the fresh linen. He had, perhaps, been a little carried away, but that was a good thing, because if he had been given time to think he would have remembered his behaviour to her on her arrival and that would have made him uncomfortable. She had probably forgotten it; she was ill, and would now remember only that he conducted her to a comfortable bed in a beautiful room and left her in good hands, Katje's and Shal Ahmi's. Ah, the cleverness of the old stoat, to cure the infirmities, to see that hasty action would result in the waste of good material. There wasn't a white man to match him. But to go back to that meeting on the stairs, when, hot and dusty, he had drawn her close and kissed her ... wasn't that the kind of thing he had planned, ever since Piet said, 'Two Van Goens girls, lovely as lilies.' From that moment he had planned the subjection of Van Goens to Haan. That had been the idea all along, to enjoy the Van Goens beauty and subject the Van Goens pride. And by God, he had done it. In one instant. Hot and dirty, he, Evert Haan, had kissed a Van Goens lady. A dizzying thought. And even more dizzying was the one that if, as she was now, she had arrived upon the *Java* some lees of diffidence and respectfulness would have hampered him. Heavens, how carefully he had dressed himself that morning, how mindful of his manners he had been as he descended the companionway.

Better so, he thought. It's worked out for the best after all. The familiar sense of being lucky, almost elect, came upon him. Now, he thought, with a pint of well-cooled arrack inside him, I will go down and show her that I know the way to behave. I'll give her two glasses of my best Madeira, that's a lady's drink, I'll pay her a few compliments ... and then I'll take her to bed. ...

174

She had accepted the Madeira. And she had managed to eat her dinner. It was, after all, despite anything Father Vincent believed, food and drink which kept people alive, gave them vigour. And the kind of thing which she had to say needed vigour. This big, red-faced man who was her husband was obviously so delighted with her that it was hard to believe that he was the very same person who had said, 'So that's what they'd planned to do with you, is it?' and 'This is a very distasteful position.' Had he forgotten those words as completely as he appeared to have done? Yet, there was to his credit, and she must not, *must* not forget it, the fact that he had sent Shal Ahmi to cure her.

Therefore, as the long meal ended, she called up all the courage that was in her and said:

'There is something that I must say to you. Shall I say it here or in the drawing-room?'

He laughed, unrestrainedly, like an excited boy.

'We'll not trouble the drawing-room to-night, my dear. I've had a long journey. I intend to retire early.'

His eyes ran over her with cheerful possessiveness. In his mind he thumped himself upon the back with hearty congratulations. He, Evert Haan, had actually said those words, with all they implied, to a Van Goens. Never had his vanity savoured a sweeter titbit. But the realisation was unlucky, for the mental process lent to his possessive stare another quality, less frank, less excusable, and there came to his face a look with which Annabet was familiar, a covert, sheepish lecherousness. Occasionally young yokels had worn it in Heydberg, meeting Klara and her in the street or on a field path.

'Then I must say it now,' she said. Her voice was almost icy in its extreme clarity, though one of those nervous spasms had set her heart fluttering and her cheeks reddened and whitened behind the thin cover of the paint.

'I told you when we first met that I would try to make up for my ugliness by being a good wife to you, didn't I? I meant it. I owed you that ... if only in the material sense. You had sent money to my Mamma. You must have known that what you sent was far more than was needed for my expenses. And though I know, I could *see*, that you felt yourself cheated— and I *was* sorry for you—you hadn't really been. There was no clause in the marriage contract about my being beautiful, you know. But now ...'

'Look,' said Evert, interrupting her, 'let's forget all about that, can't we? If there was money over and your family found it useful, I'm glad. And if I was a bit stunned that day, well, partly it was because you looked so *ill*! I proved that, didn't I?' His voice, embarrassed to begin with, grew truculent. 'Didn't I get you to bed, with every comfort? And call in Shal

175

Ahmi, who did what all the grand doctors in Holland had failed to do?'

'That was what I wanted to say. Because of that I feel that I owe you a *different* sort of loyalty. And—since I have been here I have realised that being a good wife means something more than I meant on that first day. *Willing* isn't enough. There should be some feeling behind it. And so I'm forced to tell you that I don't *love* you.'

He looked at her, amused, enjoying the little scene.

'That doesn't bother me a bit, my dear. How could you love me? You don't know me. We'll talk about this in a month's time ... eh?'

'But I shall never love you, not in that way. That's what I've got to make clear. Even if it means that you drive me off, out of the house to-night, *because* you asked Shal Ahmi to cure me, and therefore I am grateful to you, I must make clear that never, not in twenty years, should I ever be able to love you properly.'

'Because,' said Evert, as though speaking for her, 'you love *somebody else*? That's it, isn't it?' He smiled with good-natured tolerance, almost smugly.

'Yes,' she said, and was glad that he had understood so quickly; and had a sharp painful memory of Christy's lips on her wrist.

Some dressed up, flowery young sprig of nobility who hadn't the guts to take her without a dowry, Evert thought delightedly. There were people like the Van Goens in every village in Holland, families who thought themselves too good to breathe the same air as people like himself—as he was. Now with one stroke he had humbled two of them instead of one. He hoped the young fool was eating his heart out!

'Well,' he said, in the fatuous tone one uses to a child, 'what are we going to do about that? Send you back to Holland?'

She had wondered about that herself ... endlessly wondering through the hours of the days and nights which had passed since Christy disappeared into the night.

'I will do whatever you say. I felt that I ought to tell you. I would ... make it easy for you. Say that I couldn't bear Banda, or something like that. I would take the blame. You had me cured. So I want to be fair to you.'

(And there had been moments, hours, when he would have been so dizzied with delight to hear the accommodating words. God, what luck that she hadn't spoken them before. She'd have gone back in the *Java* and he'd have missed the triumph of a lifetime.)

'You are fair to me. You're more than that, you're beautiful to me. I don't care,' he said, pushing back his chair, rising and going round to the place where she was sitting at the other end of the long table. 'I don't care whether you love—as you call it—one other man or twenty other men.' Standing above her he could see the sheen on the soft hair, the fluttering shadow of her long lashes. 'You belong to me,' he said, his voice hoarse with genuine emotion. 'That's enough for me. You're my wife.'

He loomed over her, making her feel small and helpless. She rose hastily and turned to face him.

'But, Evert, you should listen, and think about this. I'm trying to make you understand something important. I am your wife, and you have a right to hope that I shall love you. But I never shall. I shall love this other man until I die. . . .' She could hear her own voice losing its assurance in the face of his sustained, amused, misunderstanding tolerance. Falteringly she brought out the final awkward words, the words she had promised herself that she would say, because she was grateful to him. 'And if . . . if ever I saw him again, or if it ever happened that he . . . he sent for me, I'm afraid I wouldn't let anything stand between us.'

Of the whole speech only the words 'if ever he sent for me' made any real impact upon Evert's mind. So the luckless young gentleman had been left in Holland. And still she thought that he might send for her! What a forlorn hope! His hard thin mouth curved with amusement. Other men might have heard those words with anger, or dismay, or pity, according to their nature. To Evert they brought only an enhanced sense of triumph.

'D'you think I'd let you go?' he asked, good-humouredly. He put his right arm around her, cupping her breast in his hand. 'You'll forget all about this girlish hankering,' he said thickly. The warmth and softness of her flesh under the thin silk sent the blood pounding through his veins. With his left hand he tilted her face and, bending his head, set his mouth against hers. And even as he stopped, with kisses, her last vain bid of understanding, an emotion sharper and more dizzying even than lustfulness, rocked his being. Once the Van Goens women, in their silks and their laces, had gone by in their carriages, impervious, untouchable, noticing only whether he doffed his cap and stood still as they rattled past. And the detested family had shipped him their rubbish, their scarecrow cripple whom nobody else wanted, just as, in the old days, Mevrouw had given away her candle ends and her kitchen scraps. But he had defeated them. Shal Ahmi's magic had transformed the rubbish into this lovely warm flowery thing whose flesh was now contracting and throbbing beneath his fingers. Truly there seemed no limit to the luck of Evert Haan. He had only to will a thing and it was. By God, she was as beautiful, as soft, as maddening as Isa.

177

He dropped his head until his lips moved against the edge of the lace of her bodice. And he altered his hold, swinging her from her feet into his arms. 'You talk of love, but you don't know what you're talking about,' he said. 'I'll show you what love is.'

But Father Vincent, adored so long, and then discredited, and now never to be thought about without a guilty pang, had come into his own. He had dragged his poor little cousin back from the brink of madness with his talk about the supremacy of the mind over the body. And, half a world away, the poor little cousin, restored to health and sanity, more lovely than ever, petted and pampered, wandered through her cool, lovely house, or walked in her flowery lovely garden, brooding over the truth of his words, twisting their truth to fit her case.

For, if the flesh mattered, she should have been the most enviable woman living. She lacked nothing. And there remained with her enough of the memory of the bleak years in Heydberg to sharpen her appreciation of the luxuries she now enjoyed. From the moment when Katje drew the curtains, pushing the blue dragons into indistinguishable blobs of colour among the folds and letting the bright morning light into the room, until the moment when she said, 'Good night, Mevrouw,' and padded away to her own sleeping place, every one of Annabet's moments was hung about with comfort, with wishes granted, or forestalled, with leisure, beauty, adulation.

And after that ... when the night, so cool, after the day's heat, so spicily scented, flowed into the room, there was Evert, changed in a moment's space, from a good, indulgent husband, into a lover, not only ardent, but skilled. She was often amazed by her own lack of response to Evert. Night after night, when he had gone back to his own room, or had fallen asleep beside her in the big blue-and-white bed, she lay awake, wondering at herself, thinking of Father Vincent and of Christy.

Here she was, bound by vows, and by gratitude to Evert, who was kind, generous, amorous. Every bit of food that she put into her mouth, everything she touched or used or wore was provided by him. She belonged to him, as he said, always with pride, if a little too frequently; and yet, as soon as he had left her or fallen asleep, she was thinking of Christy again ... living through the experience just past but with Christy in Evert's place. And then, by a trick of thought which had become a habit, thinking of Father Vincent, remembering what he had said about the flesh and the spirit. And knowing, knowing that he had been right. The passage of love, the kisses, the most intimate caress of Evert, were nothing, less than nothing compared with the lonely, unreturned, unrecognised kiss which Christy had laid in her palm under cover of that

178

drunken leavetaking.

A thousand times she asked herself *why*? She knew so little of Christy, was bound to him by no ties which could be named. For all she knew he might be a far less estimable character than Evert. As she moved about her house and her garden her mind was often occupied by futile, fruitless speculations. If Christy had made a glove marriage and been confronted by a twisted scarecrow, he might ... who could say? ... but he *might* have behaved far less generously than Evert had done. Evert had put her to bed, arranged for her comfort and called in the one person who could cure her. Would Christy, in similar circumstances, have done more? as much? Often, when she thought in this way, the answer came that Christy would never have made a glove marriage. But that was purely supposition. Perhaps he *had* made a glove marriage ... or lived with native women.... How could she tell? She knew nothing about him except the one fact that she loved him, and, loving him, cared nothing for what he did.

Sometimes, with a feeling of panic, she wondered whether she were simply in the grip of another infatuation, similar to the one she felt, as a girl. If that were so, then she was spoiling her own life and the life of the man who appeared to love her, by her blind chasing after a dream. And at that moment, sharply aware of the passing of the days which piled up so quickly into weeks, which in their turn became months, she tried, with all the vigour of her mind and body, to forget Christy and love Evert. But that was no good. Such efforts were always followed by a feeling of degradation, as though she had been a traitor. And finally, when she had been married for about six months she resigned herself to a life which held two sharply divergent realities; the one her smooth, rounded, normal existence as Mevrouw Haan of Coenpark, the other her secret hungry existence as the yearning lover of Christy Ayrton.

And at exactly the same time, when the marriage was half a year old, Evert began to experience his first serious feelings of dissatisfaction with it. Perhaps he sensed her final withdrawal into compromise; or the first joy of possession was staling, his sense of being almost miraculously lucky sinking into commonplace acceptance. For six months he had been delighted with his bargain; then suddenly he began to see flaws in it.

Outwardly everything had gone exactly as he had planned during that boastful, self-congratulatory interval between the arrival of Mevrouw's letter and the arrival of Annabet herself. As soon as possible after his return from Bandogar he had reissued his invitations to dinner and had the satisfaction of seeing Annabet take her place at the end of his table around which were gathered all the most important people in Banda.

The postponement of the dinner, the period of speculation, rumour and counter-rumour which had elapsed since Mevrouw Haan's arrival had heightened the feeling of curiosity provoked by Evert's complacent boasting, and although it took all Annabet's training in composure to face and ignore the stares, frank or covert, which were directed at her throughout the whole evening, Evert enjoyed himself thoroughly. There wasn't a woman in the room to touch this woman, who belonged to him. Even Jehane Vehmeer, hitherto the undisputed belle of the white community looked faded and a trifle overblown compared with Annabet. And that was as it should be. Evert Haan was the cleverest man in the islands, he had the best plantation, the finest house, and now the prettiest wife.

Hardly a man left Coenpark that evening without some feeling of envy for their host; hardly a woman without some comment about the paint and powder and hair-curlers which had gone to make Annabet look so pretty. Only Mevrouw Van Heem, past all competitive feeling, stout, grey-haired, so lost to vanity that even on festive occasions she still appeared with her figure uncorsetted, pointed out that Annabet was not to blame for the things Evert had said about her before her arrival, nor for the fashion which made paint and powder and curls *de rigeur* in Holland at the moment.

'For it must be fashionable,' said Mevrouw Van Heem flatly, 'or she wouldn't do it. She's been well brought up. I've been here a long time, I've seen a lot of brides...' Her small bright eyes moved above the fat cushions of her cheeks, surveying some of the women, now married women of some standing, whose first parties she had attended, '... and I've never seen a first dinner party go off so well. Her mother reared her for better things than Evert Haan and his Coenpark.'

This pronouncement reached Evert's ears quite quickly, and did not surprise him. Trudi Van Heem and he had lived in a state of undeclared war for many years. Nor did it displease him. On the contrary, it flattered his vanity so much that there and then he decided that, if things turned out well, he would send Mevrouw Van Goens a token of his gratitude for her training of Annabet. A piece of jewellery perhaps, or another draft on the Bank of Amsterdam.

But the gift was never despatched, for, as the days ran into weeks, and the weeks, with incredible swiftness, mounted into months, his vast complacency and satisfaction with his bride began to shrink and collapse.

It was not, he told himself furiously, a hundred times, that he had expected Annabet to love him. He was past the age of romantic fancies; and nobody but a fool of the first water would expect a glove marriage to turn into a love match. He had been perfectly honest when he had told Piet Odshoorn that he had wanted a wife to decorate his home; and again perfectly honest when he had told Annabet that he didn't care whether she was in love with one other man or twenty other men. But, at the root of this non-caring there had been the certainty that, given complete possession of any woman for six months he could bring her, if not to a state of infatuation—though that was almost certain—at least to a state of subjection. And with Annabet that was just what he had failed to do.

How he knew that he had failed puzzled him. There was no proof, no evidence; but he knew it just as he knew that a blue thing was blue, not red or green. She was, in every way a man could name, a perfect wife, always amiable, agreeable to his wishes. She had never once in six months withheld a smile, failed to respond to his mood, repelled a caress. When he gave her presents—and he loaded her with gifts in those first months—she thanked him prettily, kissed him, admired the offerings and praised his taste. On those few occasions when things went wrong outside the house and he returned to her preoccupied or irritable she was at pains to dispel the mood. And of course on the round of return hospitality which followed his big dinner party she looked and was exactly the superb possession which he had intended her to be.

But something was lacking, and though he could not have given a name to the thing he missed, the lack of it piqued his vanity and his egotism. He found himself thinking and wondering and puzzling about her at moments when his mind should have been concentrated upon other matters. Going back from the landing-stage he would come to the place where the arched opening pierced the solidity of the living green wall, and with the beauty of his house and garden spread before him he would think of the moment when he stood there beside the twisted scarecrow, and he would think of Shal Ahmi's magic, and of the lovely woman who was waiting to greet him, and he would move his big shoulders in an impatient gesture. You goddamned fool, he would say to himself, you've got everything you wanted, what's the matter with you? Why aren't you satisfied?

The artistic strain which ran through his hard nature like a flaw in a rock would lead him sometimes to think, suppose this had happened to another man, Kaerko, Van de Lijn ... what should I tell them to do? The answer came easily ... take the wench to bed and let her see who is master there. And that should have been the answer. But it wasn't.

And at last, on one of those occasions when he was soothing his vanity with the reiterated assurance that he had, after all, got the wife that he wanted, a question fell, like a drop of icy water, into his mind—But have you got her? And he knew the answer to that. Knew that between kiss and kiss she eluded him; knew that, even from the most intimate embrace something escaped, unpossessable, unpossessed.

He began to think, seriously, about that stupid young gallant back in Holland, that imaginary young man over whose failure he had gloated. He had hardly listened on that evening of surprise and delight to the words which Annabet had spoken; yet now they came back to his mind, clear, significant, barbed. 'I shall love this other man until I die.' And he remembered how, for a night or two, the thought of that futile, robbed love had lent an extra zest to his own love-making. But now, quite gradually, but inexorably, the despised young man began to gather strength and substance. Began to take on the significance and the hatefulness which had, at various times belonged to other men who stood between Evert Haan and the full attainment of his wishes.

The complete singlemindedness which, combined with a growing ruthlessness, had been so largely responsible for his spectacular success in life, rendered him singularly easy prey to obsessions. There was emotions to which he was a stranger for the compass of his mind had swung almost entirely between two points, his wants and his hatreds. He had wanted old Jacob Kressle's favour and hated Piet Odshoorn; he had wanted the Janshaven farm and hated the Van Goens; then he had hated the grind of farm life and wanted more scope for his abilities; and after that he had hated the army while at the same time wanting to find favour with his superiors so that the rewards which were tumbling like ripe plums from the shaken tree of the conquered islands should drop into his hands. And he had wanted money, and hated the limits which the rules of the Company imposed upon making it; he had wanted Annabet Van Goens, and hated the ugly creature who bore her name. Finally, he found himself wanting something more than this nominal, outward possession of a woman, and hating the nameless, unknown man who, simply by existing, baulked him.

The imaginary young Dutchman became his companion in all those moments of the day when his mind was not actively engaged upon some practical problem. Evert's inward eye, which had called up the beauties of Coenpark before a stone of the house was laid, which had enjoyed Annabet's beauty even as Piet had fumbled over its description, now dwelt with loathing upon the lineaments of a young man, inevitably his own antithesis: dark, slim, soft from easy living, his useless hands smooth and white under their lace ruffles. Silky-tongued, of course—women liked quips and compliments. And his character was despicable. Evert knew all about that. He hadn't the guts to marry a girl of a fallen family, a girl who had no dowry, on the other hand, he had made her love him. He had let her come to Banda—had seen her sold like a heifer in the market; but he had made some frail, senseless promise about sending for her one day. And this poor, worthless, spineless dummy lay, night after night, like a drawn sword, between Evert and Annabet. Evert's hands clenched as he thought of it. He would have given a thousand English pounds to have that puppy's throat between his hands.

It never occurred to Evert to wonder *why* the complete subjection of Annabet mattered so much. His mind, so hard that even its imaginative faculty was concerned solely with tangible things, never once probed to the real root of his discontent. He would have rejected with scorn the notion that he was, at last, in his middle age, as much in love as his nature permitted him to be, and that this feeling of frustrated possessiveness was actually simple jealousy. He had married because he wanted a wife, beautiful, well-bred, one who would stamp him in the eyes of his world as a successful man. He had chosen Annabet Van Goens because, reported beautiful and known to be well bred, she would bring him the additional pleasure of knowing himself avenged upon the family he had hated. All that was very clear, and he would—indeed he had—admitted it. But he did not realise that his treatment of Annabet, once the disappointment and repulsion caused by her appearance had been removed, had not in any way conformed to his original plans. He had planned to overwhelm this daughter of the Van Goens with evidences of his wealth and generosity; planned to humiliate her in small, subtle ways; planned to keep her as a beautiful adjunct of his beautiful house while he sought satisfaction with Isa or Isa's successors. But actually everything he had given to Annabet had been given in the hope that it would break down the barrier between them; the idea of humiliating her had entirely left his mind; and as for Isa or any other little brown beauty, he had never given them an amorous thought since the night of his return to Banda from Bandogar.

Yet now, in his blindness, instead of realising that he was in love with his wife, and longed merely to be loved in return, he concentrated upon this unknown young Dutchman as an enemy who stood between him and something that he wanted, rather than as a rival who had been given something which he himself could never attain. But, as enemy or rival the unknown young gallant assumed such reality that when, finally he blurted out a question about him he was not conscious of any absurdity.

He had flung himself, baffled again and furious, from the blue-and-white bed, and Annabet had said, as usual, 'Good night, Evert.' And then suddenly he had turned, his hands came down heavily upon her shoulders and he blurted out in a thick, tense voice:

'Who is he? I will know. Tell me his name.'

She was startled, but not at all bewildered. She knew at once what he meant. But the question, shot out with such vehemence at such a moment, left her speechless. Six months ago Evert had dismissed the words which had cost her so much to say, with a smile, an almost contemptuous tolerance; and in the interval he had seemed to have forgotten, if he had ever noticed, them. And she had tried so hard to behave as though she had come straight from the cabin of the *Java* to Evert's bed, with no enlightening experience between. How had she failed? Through what unsuspected crack had Evert glimpsed her secret life?

Thrusting against the pressure of his hands, she rose on one elbow.

'Who is who? Whom are you asking about?' she said.

He shook her as though she were a talking doll whose mechanism of speech depended upon violent wagging to and fro.

'That man you spoke of. The one who stands between us. That puppy you left in Holland. Tell me his name.'

She raised her hands, gripping his wrists, forcing him away.

'Evert! Stop shaking me. What do you mean? "Stands between us." Was anything between us just now? Or last night? Have I given you any reason for saying such a thing?'

'Yes,' he said savagely, and repeated the word even more loudly. 'Yes. You told me about him yourself. You said you loved him and would love him until you died. What do you expect a man to make of that?'

She pushed against his hands again and threw herself across the bed, scrambling to her feet on the far side of it. Standing upright, with the voluminous white bedgown which Klara and Maria and Truitje had all taken turns in stitching and embroidering, she felt better, less overwhelmed now that the flushed red face and pale angry eyes no longer loomed over her.

'You made what you liked of it, then, Evert,' she said, her voice small, but steady. 'I told you because I felt I must be honest with you. I hoped you'd send me away. But you laughed and said it didn't matter. Why does it matter now?'

'Because you still love him, don't you? *Don't* you?'

Say no, and end this scene. Say no, since I have come to know you better, Evert, I have ceased even to think of anyone else. So easy. Why not? A lie was a lie; you had told lies to Mamma, a whole string of them, in the endeavour to help Klara; you had told lie upon lie to Shal Ahmi in those last minutes before he led Christy away. Why boggle now at a lie

184

which would ease this situation and send Evert happy to his bed?

The word was there, ripe, thrusting, ready for birth, just behind her teeth when the memory of Christy, swaying with weakness, saying, 'Darling, you must go,' bore in upon her. This was different, this was important. If she hoped ever to see him again upon this earth she must be honest now. Unheeding that the move brought her once more within the reach of those heavy hands, into the glare of those coldly angry eyes, she walked around the foot of the bed.

'Yes, I do,' she said. 'You see, I am still honest with you. And I'm speaking the truth when I say that I'm sorry. I have tried, Evert, not to ... not to let it make any difference. But if I haven't been satisfactory, you must get rid of me. You could say what you liked about me. I wouldn't contradict.'

The pang which he felt at the very mention of getting rid of her might have warned him, but he was without self-know-ledge. Fury made him blind and senseless.

'You talk like a fool," he said. 'You're my wife; you belong to me. I'd never let you go, not if the devil himself had a claim on you. As well he might, you saucy, cantankerous little bag-gage. So you're honest, are you? That for your honesty!' And Evert, who never gestured, made a gesture of ineffable con-tempt. 'What's this young puppy ever done for you? Tell me that. You came to me a beggarly cripple, your head on one side, no flesh on your bones; going to be pushed into a convent to save you from begging in the gutter. And after all I've done for you, you have the gall to stand there and tell me that you can't love me because of some dressed-up mawkin who hadn't the guts to take you without a dowry. And you don't need to tell me,' he added in a sharper voice. 'I know. I don't have to be told whether a key fits a door or not. I can feel that for myself. You've tried not to let it make any difference,' he re-peated her words contemptuously, 'but every time you've kissed me you've grudged it; every time I've ...'

'I never grudged you anything,' she said sharply. 'That's a lie. You must know that.' A hot wave of colour mounted from her neck to her hair. 'It's the other way round, Evert. Very often I think ... afterwards ... that because of the way I ... because I am so weak ... *he* should be the one to be jealous. If he knew.'

He had no idea that these starkly honest words were the pronouncement of his own doom; that they could never have been uttered save by a woman whose absent lover seemed real enough to have established rights. He could not read, behind the faltering words, their intrinsic meaning, 'Evert Haan, it often seems that I have committed adultery with you.'

Instead he was pleased, delighted. His fury evaporated.

185

Vanity and passion took its place. Somehow, without conscious movement, he was there at the foot of the bed, his arms around her, his lips moving over her face and neck. Between kisses he muttered, 'I'll make you forget him. You're going to belong to me. Forget the things I said. I didn't mean them. I was angry.'

Accepting the sudden change of mood, the kisses and the apology, Annabet in turn had no notion of their real significance. She still, after six months of marriage, knew too little of Evert's character to realise that he was behaving in a way completely unlike himself. It was only afterwards that she could look back and understand that this scene—which was to be repeated, sometimes identically, sometimes with slight variations, many, many times—was the result of a genuine passion coming late in life to a man in whom were blended a fiery temper and a cold, stubborn selfishness.

Evert appeared to have forgotten the scene by the next morning. But at some time during the day he ordered from the ubiquitous Wang Fu a silk coat, deep blue in colour, embroidered all over with white dragons which imitated in their posture the pattern of the curtains in her room. Six of Wang Fu's countrywomen worked for five days and nights, stopping for rest only when they could no longer see their needles, crouched in the stuffy, cramped room at the back of the Chinaman's house in the back street of Banda. On the evening of the sixth day Evert carried it home, and only a shrewd observer, indeed, would have seen that a thread of wistfulness ran through the complacent pride with which he watched Annabet array herself in the beautiful garment. He was pleased by her expressions of gratitude and by her praise of the design which had been his own idea, but a little disappointed because, after one glance at herself in the mirror, she had turned away from her own quite dazzling reflection. (Isa, given some trifling ornament, would have admired herself for hours.) But later on, alone in her room, Annabet put on the coat again and turned to the mirror, searching, with half-reluctant curiosity for the confirmation of the knowledge which that earlier hurried glance had conveyed. The fleeting impression had been only too accurate. With the stiff embroidered folds of the silk falling about her she had lost all identity; she looked like an image; like a dressed-up doll.

She thought suddenly of the crushed eggshells which old Truitje had dropped into soup, 'to clear it'. The Chinese coat was like them. It laid clear the fact that, petted and pampered, living with one man and loving another, the memory of whom was sometimes sharp and sometimes clouded, she was losing reality.

186

Still wearing the coat she sat down on the stool, put her elbows on the white dressing-table among the silver things and stared, almost unseeing, at her own reflection. A body ... a pleasing arrangement of bone and flesh and hair; bathed, scented, fed, brushed, kissed, taken to bed, caressed. That was what she had become. And that was happening to Annabet who had once been called back from the brink of the grave, or of madness, by words which proved that the flesh was unimportant, the soul all that mattered. A shattering, awful thought.

But it was only the rarest, strongest soul, she reflected dismally, which could survive the wearing process of daily pretence. For the others, the ordinary people, of whom she was one, the constant practice of pretence must be the slow death of reality. And one day the moment would come when she would offer to Evert the words his vanity (and you couldn't blame him for that, any husband would have felt the same!) demanded. 'I love you,' she would say. And that would be the end of Annabet. After that she would be as good as dead, though years and years might elapse before they buried her.

Why was that such a dismal prospect? It would be so much more comfortable and easy than this divided existence, this constant warfare between what was, and what might be. Why then did she shrink from it so? The answer came in the nasal whine which had so often announced the texts in the Heydberg church. 'What shall it profit a man if he gain the whole world and lose his own soul?' Fancy, she thought wryly, Mamma, conscious that the whole of Heydberg suspected her Catholic leanings, was most punctilious that we should attend the Protestant church, and I hated it, because of Vincent, and was bored every minute, and yet I remember that! And it's so dreadfully true. I am losing my soul. Because Christy, and loving Christy is part of it. Though that is very hard to understand ... because to be honest, that love started with the flesh, too. It was his face, as poor little Vehk turned him over, that made it impossible for me to let him be turned adrift to take his chance in the prahau. His face then; and later on his body when I held him in my arms. Where's the difference? Why is living with Evert, and pretending—and sometimes not so much pretending—making me less myself, whereas just remembering that I love Christy makes me more myself and more real altogether? The right, the *moral* thing would be for me to pretend to love Evert until I really did ... and then I shouldn't exist at all. I should be just like the furniture of the house. But why?

There was no answer to the question. One might as well ask why is the night dark, the day light? Why do we find some things hot, others cold? Certain facts must be accepted. And sitting there in the coat which Evert had given her as an apology, the coat which had made her look like one of the images carved over the door of the Hindu temple which one passed on one's way to the Van Heem house, she accepted, with a sad certainty that, cut off from Christy and spending all her days and nights under the impact of Evert's personality, she was like a leaf on an autumn tree, cut off from the flow of sap, and exposed to the merciless buffeting of the wind. It might hang, tenuously, determinedly for a time, but at last the stem would snap, and the leaf, dry and lifeless, would go whirling away, the plaything of the wind.

If only, she thought desperately, I could see Christy sometimes; just see him, even from a distance; or hear his voice from behind a closed door as I sometimes hear the voices of the men who come to talk to Evert in his office. Or if I could hear some news of him, as I used to hear news of Father Vincent when his mother wrote to mine. Anything, any little thing which would bring him near, make the whole of those three days less unreal and dreamlike.

She got up restlessly and slipped her arms out of the wide silken sleeves, letting the coat drop to the floor for Katje to put away with reverent, envious hands. As she did so something happened within her mind, less a matter of slow constructive thought than a blinding flash of revelation. Within her orbit, she suddenly realised, there were two people who knew of Christy's existence—Evert and Shal Ahmi. The perilous business in which they were partners must involve some meetings, some conversation. Openly, Evert had no dealings with the brown man. Shal Ahmi himself had said that when he arranged for his visits to be made so secretly, and since she had partaken of the social life in the islands she had heard in a dozen drawing-rooms, the Banda ladies end a discussion about the 'queer creature,' as they called him, with the words, 'Of course my husband is like yours, Mevrouw Haan, detests the very name of the man.' But the ladies themselves were full of curiosity and speculation. Shal Ahmi had a reputation as a spell-maker; it was said that he could give you back the shapely contours of your youth, lost through over-eating and lack of exercise; it was whispered that he had spells which would remove the curse of barrenness, or, conversely, avert an unwanted pregnancy. It was all compound gossip, relayed during those hours when the ladies were having their hair brushed, or washed, their baths prepared, their bodices hooked or buttoned; and never once, in any of the conversations did any one of them weigh in with evidence of a conclusive nature such as Annabet herself might have supplied. But over and over again she had been given to understand that Evert ... like most of the other husbands, had nothing but derision for Shal Ahmi, and that was what, in the main, had prevented the ladies from testing his skill.

So now she thought, logically, then Shal Ahmi and Evert meet secretly, and what meeting-place is more likely than this house? And if Christy does business with them, perhaps he comes too. He knew the way to the office window, he expected to find Evert there. Perhaps ... perhaps ... Her heart began to bump as she dwelt upon the possibility that on many an evening when Evert had left her with her embroidery in the drawing-room and gone to his office, Christy had stepped on to the verandah and tapped at the window and been admitted.

Why hadn't she thought of it before? Because her brain, as well as her emotions, was withering in this atmosphere of pretence and idle lassitude. With a pang she remembered the quick-wittedness which she had devoted to Klara's clandestine affair, the apparently perfect performance of the part which had served to divert Shal Ahmi's suspicions. Ah, she had been alert and intelligent at those times; but in the last six months she had slipped away into a maze of loving the memory of Christy with her mind, and pretending to love Evert with her body, and she hadn't even had the sense to seek out the one means of contact that had, perhaps, been offering itself all this time. If the Chinese coat hadn't shown her that her body was atrophying along with her mind she would never have realised that Christy might, quite possibly, have been in Evert's study several times during the last six months, while she sat in the drawing-room, a stone's throw away, pushing a stupid needle in and out of an idiotic piece of embroidery, waiting for Evert to come back and give the word for bed.

But her wits, once awakened, showed something of their pristine sharpness. Twice during the next day she mentioned the heat, three or four times complained of the stuffiness of the drawing-room after the candles had been lighted. Evert, remembering with some difficulty, the discomfort which he had felt during his early days in the islands, was sympathetic and full of helpful suggestions. Many white women, he said, had abandoned the full-skirted, full-sleeved Western dresses, with their tight waists and petticoats, for the native sarong and little jacket. Would she find them cooler? He would order some to-morrow; they could be finished by evening. What colour would she fancy? Would she like Juan and Abbas to take turns with a fan? A fan of peacock's feathers he suggested. His eye swept around the pale-coloured room and his voice was eager, with something that was almost greed in it, as he said, 'Yes, peacock's feathers ... and the sarong peacock-blue and a jacket the colour of apricots.' Aware, with disappointment, of her indifference to these suggestions, he spoke of the tryingness of the climate just before the rains broke. 'In three weeks or a fortnight, there'll be a change. Not like the winter in Holland, of course; but I bet there'll be evenings when you'll think you'd like a fire. You wouldn't really. Trudi Van Heem tried having one the first rainy season she was here. It isn't cold enough for a fire really, it's more like the weather you get with a thunderstorm at the end of a hot day at home, but you'll be glad to have a shawl.'

'But *now*,' she said, relentlessly, wondering whether her voice betrayed her obstinate determination, 'couldn't we sit on the verandah. I'm sure it would be cooler there.'

'We'd be bitten to death,' he explained tolerantly.

'I'd rather be bitten than stifled, Evert.'

'You'll learn,' he said, losing his patience suddenly. But he raised no further objections and before the week was out, Annabet, with a gauzy shawl over her neck and arms, and with the oil-lamp placed at a distance because it was found to attract the swarm of little buzzing insects, was spending her evenings on the verandah just outside the dining-room windows. And upon the evening when Evert said, 'I shall be busy for an hour or two, don't go to bed unless you're very tired. I shan't be late,' she was seated in what had become her usual place, with only the corner of the house between her and the window of the little office.

As soon as she was certain that Evert would be in the office she pulled her chair forward until it was around the corner, and with the lamp no longer visible her eyes became accustomed to the darkness. Midway between the place where she now sat and the office window was the flight of steps leading to the garden. And before she had been in her new position for ten minutes a figure, looking quite vast in its white wrappings, moved like a pale shadow, noiselessly up the steps and towards the window. She heard the gentle tapping, the sound of the shutter opening and being closed again. So she had been right. Shal Ahmi did come to Coenpark under cover of darkness. And Christy might come too.

Now that the moment might at any beat of the heart be upon her, a dreadful quaking emptiness came upon her stomach; for some seconds she felt as though there was nothing between her madly racing heart and her unsteady knees. If Evert had at that moment opened the study window and stepped on to the verandah she could not have pushed back her chair as she had planned; if Christy had walked up the steps and by some miracle have become conscious of her presence and held out his arms to her she could not have taken a step towards him. But as time passed and nothing happened, her nerves steadied themselves and the wild beating of her heart changed to the dull thumping of disappointment. She waited until the pale silent shadow which was Shal Ahmi had

190

rolled down the steps and disappeared into the shadowy garden, then, swift and nervous, she pushed her chair back to the place where Evert had left her. And there, three minutes later he found her, apparently asleep.

There had not gone through her mind on that evening, nor at any previous time, any thought of eavesdropping by the study window. If Christy had appeared she would have been irresistibly drawn to listen on the chance of hearing his voice. But the details of the business, interesting as her intelligence told her they must be, which lay between Evert and the native whom he pretended to hate and despise had, at that point, no intrinsic attraction for her. And it was as well that, upon this occasion, she had maintained her watch on the garden and the steps for, behind the unglazed shuttered window, Evert, having disposed in a few sentences of the business which had brought Shal Ahmi on one of his clandestine visits had turned to the subject which interested him almost, if not quite, as closely.

The hard-headed Dutchman who had made his way in a hard world was not precisely superstitious. But his mind's armour had chinks labelled with other names. He laughed at the suggestion that Shal Ahmi was a spellmaker, yet he trusted the brown man's medicines. And it was with some idea of pill or potion in his mind that he broached to Shal Ahmi the subject of Annabet's failure to produce an heir. There was not another living soul on earth to whom he would, or could, have mentioned the matter. There was not another living soul on earth from whom, having brought himself to mention it, he would have expected anything but wordy sympathy and senseless admonitions to patience.

And at first Shal Ahmi, in his disconcerting way, behaved like any other person.

'Mynheer, the time is young. It is what, seven months and eleven days since you returned from Bandogar and found your wife desirable. You despair too soon. One wonders why, since in other matters you await with patience a late harvest. Is there, in this matter, a doubt within your mind?

That was what made Shal Ahmi so easy to confide in, Evert thought. He did not await your explanations, he forestalled them. Easily, easily he found himself telling Shal Ahmi that Annabet did not love him, telling him about the young gallant in Holland from whom his most earnest efforts, his most passionate love-making, had failed to loosen her memory.

Shal Ahmi listened attentively, his face giving no sign of the cynical amusement, the half-pitying scorn which the story roused in him. The white men were all little boys at heart. The wonder, the amazing thing was they should all have such supreme confidence in their superiority, and should manage to preserve it despite the fact that whenever they were called

191

upon to deal with any adult emotion they broke down immediately. Here was Mynheer Haan, the most confident, the most cocksure of them all, so able, so bold, so reliable in all the little-boy aspects of life, complaining, appealing, shameless as a child, 'My pretty new toy won't work. Mend it for me, Shal Ahmi.'

And talking about some young Dutchman in Holland as though he actually existed; when he, Shal Ahmi, knew ... but he was never one to waste a piece of knowledge.

Aloud he said, 'But, my son, women have been raped by the highway and borne issue. Sons are not begotten upon the mind and memory of a woman. Would a prostitute ever quicken, to the loss of her livelihood, had the mind any say in the matter? No. The cause lies elsewhere. She is barren; or you are impotent. Upon the one side you can answer.'

'Isa bore me a son. He did not live. But he was mine.'

'And between Isa and this woman—in what meadows did you pasture?'

'In none. I am whole and clean, Shal Ahmi. And she came to me virgin. But seven months have passed.'

'Ah well, that is but a short time for the enjoyment of beauty; but I understand your impatience. All men look eagerly for their heirs; and you more eagerly than most since the child would cure this wandering fancy. Yes?' He moved his heavy shoulders under the voluminous wrappings. 'I think that I can help you. By midday to-morrow there will be upon the table of your office in Banda, a little package. Place a pinch, between the fingers, thus, and no more, in the bottom of a cup and fill up with good wine. Towards evening. If within a month you do not greet me with a shining face, there are other devices. And now, with your mind easy upon that matter, let us return to business.'

Wine had been almost unknown in the Heydberg household. Egbert, when he came home, would bring his own supply, and there had been Truitje's cowslip, and dandelion and blackberry for occasions like birthdays or Christmas. But aboard the *Java*, Annabet had drunk wine every day, for it was as plentiful as—and in the later days, since it travelled better, better than water, and in Banda she had accepted, without question, the Madeira or light Rhenish which Evert poured for her each evening. Except that it lightened her spirits and helped the flow of easy chatter which it was one of a wife's duties to provide, it had had no noticeable effect. But on the evening following her abortive vigil outside the study window, she was appalled to find that she was intoxicated. She rose from the dinner-table feeling light as a bubble; the automatic censorship which lies between the conceived speech and the audible word went out of action, she talked and laughed with abandon; for the first time she found herself meeting Evert's stripping desirous stare with something like boldness, and when on the way upstairs he put his heavy arm around her she learned back against it amorously.

Once alone with Katje in the blue-and-white room, she had a sudden reversal of feeling. She began to think about Christy with a depth and darkness of passion of which she would not have thought herself capable. Her flesh, her very entrails crawled with desire. She sent Katje away hastily, and went dizzily to the window and leaned out into the sweet night air, trying desperately to command her thoughts and hoping that Evert would not come to-night.

But Evert came. Her drugged mind laid down its arms and slept. It was a night of triumph for Evert and the flesh.

In the morning she woke from heavy slumber to an instant sense of disgust and remorse and betrayal. The very thought of facing Evert filled her with repulsion, and instead of rising and going to pour the coffee for his early breakfast she sent word by Katje that she was still tired and wished to sleep. Evert ate his solitary meal with elation. Before he went out to the plantation he climbed the stairs and stood for a few moments by her door, covering the greedy triumph of his mood with jocular talk. After a glance and a sick perfunctory smile of greeting she avoided looking at him. There was compunction in her disgust, too, which did not make it any easier to stomach. None of this was Evert's fault. She, and she alone, was to blame. She had married a man whom she did not love; she had fallen in love with another man, and she had drunk so much wine that in her confusion she had mistaken one for the other. Was ever a woman guilty of such depravity?

After Evert had strutted away she left her bed and went through the actions of bathing and dressing in a mood of complete abstraction. She thought back to the days before she had ever heard of Banda, living in her mind the simple, unluxurious life in the bare chilly house in Heydberg. Even then she had been a weak character, she reflected, always eager for the least excitement, discontent because she had no nice clothes, filled with vanity because she was the prettiest of the sisters. But she had not been utterly base. Solemnly she weighed her few little virtues in the scale. She had always helped Truitje more than she had been expected to do; she had been sympathetic, and to a degree self-sacrificing over Klara's clandestine affair; she had concealed her own discontent and often made the others laugh over their pitiful shifts in the matter of keeping up appearances; and above all, her girlish infatuation for Jean Marie had been utterly unstrained by any sensual

193

thought. She could look back and remember—and it seemed always to be the evening of a cold, reluctant Northern spring, with an apple-green sky behind the frigidly blooming cherry trees—and her thoughts of him had all been, somehow, connected with God, and the white blossom, and immortality and the cool, far-reaching fields of the sunset. It seemed incredible that the girl who had stood under the cherry tree, between the stiff lines of reluctantly opening tulips, shivering with cold and with the profundity of her own thoughts, should have become this Annabet Haan, lost in this fleshly maze.

But she could reach down and touch the very root of the matter. Selfishness and self-indulgence, hitherto held in check by the very form and substance of her way of life, had been given a chance to flower, rapidly, profusely, by her change of circumstances. Here in Banda she was so pampered and so sheltered that she had never been asked to give a thought to anything outside herself. And the whole fabric of her nature had rotted. She was drunken and lustful, unfaithful alike to husband and to lover; if she was not careful she would end in being as indiscriminate as a prostitute.

Thank God last night had given her a glimpse of the spiritual abyss upon whose edge she stood. And thank God she knew the remedy. Abstinence, and thought for others. All the good women of Heydberg engaged in acts of what they called 'charity,' which meant a care for the poor. Even Mamma who, Heaven knew, was poor enough herself, visited a few cottages regularly, carrying some of Truitje's horehound cough cure, a jar of soup, a flannel petticoat past further mending, even a spoonful of hoarded brandy for an old woman not expected to last through the night. And Annabet, her daughter, had lived here, among people infinitely more degraded, people openly referred to as 'slaves', for more than seven months, without once, without once giving a single thought to their welfare.

The compound lay between the jutting-out kitchen quarters of Evert's house, and the edge of the nutmeg plantation. It consisted of a number of reed-thatched huts, roughly ranged in a circle, about an expanse of trodden earth in the centre of which was a well. The well was a refinement not found on all plantations, and Evert had installed it upon Shal Ahmi's advice. 'I have noticed, Mynheer, that in times of sickness, communities served by a well suffer less than those who dip up water from a pool or a stream. Open water collects filth, and though the connection is not easily explained, my eyes tell me that those who drink clean water from an enclosed source, do not sicken so freely as the others. Also the digging of a well costs little, the sickness of slaves loses much profit.'

So Evert had had the well dug, and had felt satisfied about it

194

until he had by chance discovered that the slaves regarded it as a handy receptacle for any unwanted rubbish. On the day when he had chanced to see an old half-blind woman throw into it the feathers and entrails of her son's fighting-cock— killed in action, and quite edible after ten hours' simmering— he had ordered the well to be dredged and a perpetual guard to be kept over it. So, on the morning when Annabet, intent upon saving her soul by acts of charity, stepped into the clearing, there was, seated upon the well's edge, a small brown boy, the gap between his diminutive size and the vastness of his authority bridged by a long, stout stick. He was chewing vigorously upon some substance which she did not recognise, and at intervals he spat mouthfuls of non-digestible debris into the well itself. He got to his feet at the sight of a white woman and his small brown face became alight with interest. Like everyone else in the Coenpark compound he had heard of the new Mevrouw with the wonderful hair, and next time it was mentioned he could speak about it with the sweet assurance that he had seen what only the privileged house servants had seen. The curls showed quite plainly under the shallow-crowned broad-brimmed straw hat which, Evert had impressed upon her, Annabet must always wear when out of doors.

Annabet smiled at the little brown boy, and his face split in a grin which showed reddish brown, stained teeth and tongue. Then he began to circle round her like a dog, pointing with his hand to a path which led away through the bushes, and gabbling some words which, meaningless to her, sounded explanatory and slightly admonitory. After a moment of bewilderment she guessed his meaning. He thought she had wandered from the garden and lost her way and was pointing the nearest exit from the compound.

She said in Dutch, 'It's all right, I haven't lost myself,' and smiled again. Thwarted, he jabbered and pointed anew, almost dancing in the effort to make himself understood; then, as Annabet turned from him and began to walk steadily in the direction of the cabins, he called aloud in his shrill little voice and from one of the low doorways a skinny old woman with big brass ear-rings slapping against her withered cheeks, emerged. She stared in astonishment at Annabet, and her thin, veined old hands pulled the edges of her dirty jacket together defensively. The little boy gabbled.

'Mevrouw,' said the crone in high quavering voice, 'you have mistaken the path. See, I will show you.' She began to shuffle her bare feet over the hard-trodden ground.

'No. I wanted to see the compound. . . .' That didn't sound right; it sounded as though she were sightseeing, and it was, after all, the place where those people lived. It was their home. For the first time she saw, suddenly, from quite a new angle, this business of 'visiting the poor,' always regarded as such a worthy, virtuous thing. How would she herself feel if some being, much richer, much better-dressed than herself, came bursting in saying, 'I wanted to see Coenpark?' And the old woman's eyes, still bright between the wrinkled lids were looking at her, not exactly maliciously, but with such complete lack of understanding, and such a half-timorous defensiveness that they increased her lack of composure.

'I mean ... I wondered whether anyone was sick ... or in need of anything ... whether there was anything I could do to help.'

'It would be better if Mevrouw returned to her own place. The sick are attended. I myself...'

'Oh yes, of course. I didn't want to interfere. I just ... I only...'

Attempts to explain were futile. But she must expect difficulties on this first visit. She wasn't experienced. Once or twice she had gone into cottages with Mamma, and there had been respectful, apparently welcoming greetings, women dusting chair seats with the corner of an apron, little murmurings about young William's cough or Gretchen's ringworm, promises of soup or something of that sort from Mamma. However, that a thing was difficult was no reason, in her present mood, for not doing it.

'Your own family,' she said firmly. 'Are they all well?'

'I have no family,' said the old woman. Her voice was suddenly humble. 'There is a sick woman in the cabin from which the boy called me. Her child was born two days ago, and we cannot move the...' She checked herself; her old eyes travelled over Annabet's body, slowly, speculatively.

'Mevrouw, please do not enter the house. Allow me to show you the way back. It is not for you to see a woman so sick for such a reason, Mynheer...'

For a moment Annabet was tempted to obey her. The edge of reality seemed to open before her, raw, horrible. But she knew that if she flinched now she would lose the last remnant of her self-respect. She moved towards the low doorway and ducking her head, entered. A hen, squawking loudly, fluttered past her as she did so.

She had been prepared to find the cabin very different from even a poor cottage home in Heydberg. She had not expected the chairs and the table, the fireplace, the window, or the little bits of crockery and pewter that even the poor owned and treasured. But nothing had prepared her for the darkness, the extreme squalor, the filth and above all the horrible stench of the little enclosed space which somebody called home, in which some woman had borne her child.

There was nothing immediately recognisable in the room

save some embers of a smoky wood fire, a cooking-pot hung on a tripod above it, and a bowl or two, yet the constricted space seemed cluttered. Vague heaps—clothing? rags? firewood? lay against the walls; filth made the floor soft and spongy. There was no bed, no sick woman visible, but, upon the side of the hut opposite the doorway there was an opening, a kind of rough, unsymmetrical archway, above which Annabet, as her eyes became accustomed to the gloom, could see tacked into the wall some twigs and coloured rags. As she stared she heard a piteous moaning.

The old woman, nervous and uneasy, was close behind her. She turned.

'The sick woman, is she within?' The crone, with an air of defeat nodded her head. Annabet stared at the opening, a little incredulous that anyone, least of all a pregnant woman, could have entered by that low, awkward entrance.

'Childbirth,' said the old woman, dully, yet with the assurance of one who states a known truth, 'defiles the house. The place is, even now, unsuitable; it should be apart. But placed as we are we have no room. Therefore the opening was made and the shelter constructed. We trust that the ceremony of purification...'

But Annabet was no longer listening; hands and knees on the filthy floor, in the only posture it was possible to adopt, she was crawling into the space behind the cabin.

There was no window, no opening of any kind save the low archway through which she had crawled, and it was impossible for anyone of her height to stand upright in the little, lean-to space. Very dimly, in the twilight, she could make out the heap of rags or straw or twigs upon a body, a female body, fashioned like her own, as susceptible to pleasure or to pain, tossed in torment. There was no air in the place, and the stench which had affronted her nostrils in the cabin itself was intensified, as though much of the foetid odour had its origin here. And the moaning, the dreadful, wracked moaning, rose from knee-level as she crouched, eyes straining, nose assaulted, mind aghast, heart eager and pitiful.

The old woman had crawled in after her and was whining, definitely whining now. 'I have done everything that the law commends. Balls of grass first did I try, then the sacred cow-hair, so precious in this land where the cow lives not. Ah, all the way from Seringa-patam in India itself did that cow-hair come; it has been in his family for four generations. But "Try it," he said, "it may save my wife for me." "What use?" I asked him. For I know what he would fain conceal, the woman is not a good Hindu. With my own eyes I saw her kill a hen to make broth for him when he had a fever. "What is this?" he asked. With my own ears I heard him, for I was

197

tending him too. "It is a medicine we knew in Bandogar," she said, deceiving him. And he drank it. Therefore is her sin brought home to her now, in the moment of her extremity, and the sacred cow-hair that came with him from Seringa-patam to Java and from Java to Bandogar and from Bandogar to Banda will not work for her. And the afterbirth will remain in her and she will die.'

'Not if I can help it,' said Annabet between her teeth. 'Anybody, however healthy, would die in this atmosphere. We must get her into the cabin, where we can *see*. And I'll send for Doctor Van de Lijn. You must help me. Have you a sleeping-mat?'

'Any sleeping-mat upon which she lay, in that state, Mevrouw, would be defiled.'

'I will give you others,' said Annabet. 'Spread the mat, as I bid you, near to the door, out there.' Another thought struck her. 'Where is the child?'

'By his mother. That is the more unfortunate. A male, the first-born, who should have split his father's skull upon the day when the gods called. There is no milk for his sustenance. Ah ... the gods are displeased, make no mistake about that. The woman is accursed and her child with her. Just as I told him in the hour when his belly was swelling with the forbidden broth.'

'Listen,' said Annabet sharply. 'That boy by the well. Call him. Tell him to fetch Josef from the house. Just tell him to run as quickly as he can and fetch Josef. Tell him that Josef is to stop whatever he is doing, and to come here to me, as quickly as he can.' She drew a deep breath of the thick, stinking stuff which served as air in this place and beat down a feeling of her own impotence. 'Then you come straight back here and help me to move the woman and the child.' There had been no sound from the child, she realised. Two days ... without food. He was probably dead. How could they know in this darkness? She realised that her own crouched bulk blocked what light would otherwise have come through the rough opening, and kneeling down again peered into the dimness.

Now she could just discern the figure of a woman stretched out in a rigid, agonised posture, upon a heap of rags. She was quite naked save for two cords, one of which, loosely slung round her neck supported a bead or a locket of some sort, while the other, tightly tied around her distorted figure made a deep groove in the flesh. As Annabet gazed at her she moaned again and her body moved in a convulsive straining. Her eyes were wide open, but they rested upon Annabet sightlessly. The white girl, feeling sick and impotent, did the one thing that occurred to her, slipped her hand into that of the sufferer and said—as she would have said to Klara or Maria:

198

'You'll be better soon. I'll send for the doctor. He'll help you.'

The hard, hot little fingers closed on her hand like a vice which tightened when the next tremor of pain racked the woman. How long would it take the little boy to fetch Josef? Ought she to have gone herself? Where was the old woman?

It seemed an hour before a shuffling sound in the outer room announced the crone's return. The place darkened again as the old woman stood by the archway.

'Mevrouw,' she said, in a voice that relegated all responsibility, 'I have done your errand. Soon your servant will be here.'

'That is well,' said Annabet, and a corner of her mind found time to wonder why she had not said 'Good,' or 'That's right'; the old woman's formal usage of an alien tongue was infectious it seemed. 'Now, help me to lift her out. Doctor Van de Lijn, who will be here presently, is a big man, there would be no room for him to work in this place. Also there is nowhere to stand a lamp. It will probably hurt her, but we must get her out.'

There was no protest in the old woman's reply, merely the plain statement of fact. It was clear that, obeying the orders of Mevrouw Haan, she considered herself exonerated from all blame in the matter, and yet felt that, on account of Mevrouw's indescribable ignorance she found it necessary to explain, half hoping that the order might be withdrawn.

'The whole house will thus be defiled, Mevrouw. Neither the man nor his brother will be able to eat rice or sleep within it.'

'Then they must eat and sleep elsewhere,' said Annabet, crawling through filth towards the woman's head. 'Reach in and take her legs, carefully, above the knees. Lift when I tell you. You set the mat ready, as I told you? Now, lift and move backwards slowly. Remember that I must move upon my knees.'

Considering the difficulties the move was made with astonishing despatch. The outer cabin, which had seemed so dark and so malodorous, seemed incredibly light and airy as Annabet, straightening her cramped limbs at last, looked down upon the woman, safely laid upon the sleeping-mat just under the primitive, unglazed window.

After one glance she averted her horrified eyes. And at that moment Josef, with a nervous hand upon his newly-wound turban, hurried to the cabin door, closely followed by the panting little brown boy. He checked his hasty step at the doorway.

'Mevrouw,' he gasped. 'I am here. All is well. This is no place for you. Come, come!'

He appeared to think that his mere presence had rescued her from some overwhelming danger.

'Josef ... which is the boy who can run fastest?'

'Juan, Mevrouw.'

'I want you to tell him to run as fast as he can to Doctor Van de Lijn and tell him that I ... the Mevrouw Haan wants him at once. At the same time I want you to fetch me some goat milk, and a clean rag. Run, Josef, do you understand, send Juan for the Doctor Van de Lijn and then come yourself with the milk and the rag. There is a baby here, dying of starvation,. if it isn't already dead. Warm the milk, Josef ... just warm it. And run, run.'

She had never seen anyone look so utterly astonished, so stunned by astonishment, Josef's flat-tipped mouth opened and shut several times before he brought out a word.

'Mevrouw, if I leave you here, in this place, Mynheer will kill me.'

'I'll kill you myself if you don't do exactly what I say as quickly as you can.' Behind her the woman moaned again. 'And I'll kill Juan if Doctor Van de Lijn isn't here within an hour.'

What a stupid statement, a couple of stupid statements; but you had to match melodrama with melodrama.

'Go along, Josef. Do what I tell you. Are you my house-boy or aren't you? Are you supposed to take my orders?'

'If Mevrouw would come away ... back to the house ...'

'I shall stay here until Doctor Van de Lijn comes. So how long I stay here depends upon you and Juan. Run, Josef, run.'

He's flat-footed, she thought irrevelantly, as Josef turned and pounded across the clearing, I'd never noticed that before. She turned back to the sick woman and noticed the tight cord again.

'Give me a knife,' she said to the old woman. 'And then fetch out the baby.'

She did not notice that, in the interval between handing her the knife and crawling through the archway the old woman jerked out a few words to the little brown well-guarder who had been waiting, an interested spectator, just outside the doorway of the hut. She was too busy severing the cord—it was thick and stout, coloured red and marked here and there with black smudges. It had eaten into the woman's swollen belly and the mark of it remained after the cord itself had been casually thrown on to the cluttered, hen-dung spattered floor. As she flung it aside Annabet murmured to the woman, 'There, that's better, isn't it?' and the wide, tortured eyes had seemed to look back at her with understanding.

The old woman entered with the baby, a limp, incredibly tiny

200

thing, dusky purple in colour, quite still, but alive, for its little mouth opened and shut with a regular movement, like a pulse beating, and Annabet could see the small, weak flutter of its breathing.

'If she had fed it,' said the old woman accusingly, 'it would have been a fine boy.' She laid it, with a gesture of awful finality, upon the mat.

'You should have fed it,' said Annabet.

'With what, Mevrouw? Rice?' Scorn struggled with respect in the old woman's thin voice.

'Goat milk, as I shall do, if it comes in time.'

'They own no goats, this woman and her husband.'

'A wet nurse, then. Is there in the whole place no woman who has a baby and milk to spare?'

'Two,' said the old woman, softly. 'One is a follower of Mahomet, the other a wild woman, caught from among the head-hunters of Borneo. Should the child drink from such sources, Mevrouw? Or should I trap a monkey? The one would be as clean as the other to the eyes of his father. And to my eyes, Mevrouw.' She added the last words with a respectful firmness which was not without its own integrity.

At that moment, Josef, accompanied by Katje and Abbas, came hurrying into the compound. Abbas carried a jug and stayed, even when all three had halted, a pace behind Katje, just as Katje stayed a pace behind Josef. But at the doorway, after the procession had come to a standstill, Josef stepped aside and signed to Katje to come forward.

She did it at once. 'Mevrouw, I have come to take you back to the house. See ... Juan has run upon your errand and Abbas has brought the milk for which you asked. All is done. Mevrouw ... please come back with me now. If Mynheer learns of your presence here, Josef and I will smart for it.'

Mynheer? Evert? Why should Evert mind her visiting the compound and doing what she could to help? She brushed the thought aside as unworthy of attention and said, quite sharply, 'Don't talk nonsense, Katje. Pass me that milk. Did you remember the clean rag, Josef?'

'I forgot it, Mevrouw.' His tone was not exactly apologetic, but it was sincere. He prided himself on being able to carry complicated orders in his mind and was annoyed to realise that in his haste and anxiety to enlist Katje's assistance and get back to the compound he had forgotten one of the two things his mistress seemed to desire. Why a rag, of all things? Of course, there was no sense in the order, that was why it had slipped out of his mind. He was consoled by that reflection.

'Mevrouw, what Katje says is true. There will be great trouble for her and for me if we leave you here. Please come back to the house.'

'You can stay outside and go when I go, if you like. And you won't get into any trouble. But be quiet now, please.' They watched, puzzled, and a little frightened as, handing the old woman the jug of milk to hold, their mistress reached for the knife and hacked off a piece of the clean white fichu which Katje had ironed last night and tacked into the neck of the lilac coloured gown that very morning. She must be mad.

But worse was to come. They stood and saw the pretty white woman upon whom their master doted, the great rich Dutch lady who had never even had to dress herself unaided, crouch down on the filthy floor and take the naked, unwashed little baby into the lap of her gown. They saw her dip the severed end of the fichu into the warm milk and hold it, soaked and dripping against the little mouth which opened and shut in mute, ceaseless appeal. They saw Annabet's anxious face clear to an expression of pleasure and triumph as the baby took the rag into its mouth and sucked it, vaguely at first, and then with a growing intensity of purpose.

Annabet was unconscious of their presence. She was thinking how fortunate it was that she had been forced by circumstances to help Truitje in the kitchen, and that Truitje's mind, weakening with age, had occasionally slackened its rules about what was and what was not, fit for a young girl's hearing. And once, in such a relaxed moment she had talked of her cousin who, before Cromwell's cruel Navigation Laws, had been master of a cargo boat plying between London and Amsterdam. He had taken his wife with him on one trip, expecting to be back home some days before the baby was due. But there had been a violent storm, and the woman, flung against a bulkhead, had borne her baby untimely, and died. Between her death and the time when the battered little vessel had limped into harbour five days had elapsed, and Truitje's cousin had kept the baby alive with drips of sugar-water administered by means of a rag. 'It was a boy,' said Truitje in conclusion, 'he probably wouldn't have bothered with a girl.' And Annabet, listening with only half her attention to the long-drawn story which Truitje made of this little saga of the sea, had long ago forgotten even the fact that the old woman had a cousin. Yet, in the moment of extremity, the apparently useless piece of information, unknowingly stored away, had sprung to life, vital, indestructible, important.

At the moment when the satiated infant turned away from the proffered rag, Juan reached Doctor Van de Lijn and gasped out all that he knew of his errand. 'Mevrouw Haan is in the compound of Coenpark with a sick woman and she sent me to tell you to come at once.' So far as the wretched woman on the mat was concerned the message was most fortunately

202

worded. Doctor Van de Lijn, among the Dutch community whom he served, enjoyed great popularity and suffered great unpopularity at one and the same time. The planters and their families and the Company's officials knew and approved of him as a good doctor; but outside their own sick chambers they knew and disapproved of him as a damned, interfering old nuisance and busybody, for ever bleating about what the slaves had to eat, or didn't have to eat; always apt, in the case of epidemic, to blame the diet upon which the slaves supported life. One planter, indeed, a man named Rikshalt, who enjoyed unfailing good health himself, a bachelor with no dependants, had gone so far as to demand from the Company's head-quarters in Batavia a clear ruling upon the doctor's sphere of activities, and had received exactly what he wanted, an official statement which set out, beyond shadow of doubt, the exact limits of Van de Lijn's authority. He was appointed and paid by the Company to attend to the health of the Company's servants resident in the islands or arriving in sea-going vessels. His contract allowed him to attend anyone in the islands who sought his services and whose claims did not conflict with the terms of his appointment, as see above. Private individuals who profited by his professional skill were to remunerate him at their own expense. Over the slaves who worked on the plantations he had no authority whatever; if planters sought his services on their behalf that was a private affair between planter and doctor. The Company was interested in Doctor Van de Lijn's researches, naturally, since they might have some bearing upon the production of nutmegs, but whether Mynheer Rikshalt allowed these researches to be pursued upon his plantation was entirely a matter for him to decide.

'So there you are,' Rikshalt had said, waving this communication in the doctor's face. 'I asked for it clear, and I got it. So you keep off my place. And if the whole lot die of overeating or scurvy I'll get Haan to buy me some fresh ones and thank you not to go scribbling a lot of scandalous rubbish about *me*.'

'And if you break your leg in the brush, Rikshalt, or get an apoplexy through stuffing your gut too full, I won't set the bone or bleed you,' Van de Lijn retorted.

It had been a sturdy-spirited answer; but Rikshalt's appeal and the answer had had an effect. Gradually the doctor had found himself cut off from the compounds where his studies had been so extremely interesting. His notes upon purely native diet had been made of late during his holidays away from Banda itself.

Now he found himself actually asked to visit a compound. Mevrouw Haan ... yes, he remembered her, a skinny, rather self-centred woman who had arrived from aboard the *Java*;

203

obviously a pampered creature who had found ship's diet at first unpalatable and then indigestible; she had suffered stiffness of the joints, which was unusual and probably largely imaginary and she had lost weight to an extraordinary extent; but she had shown no recognisable signs of malnutrition, no abrasions of the skin, no shrinkage of the gums. But she had, he remembered, been quite sensible to talk to, and he had talked to her about the importance of food. How long ago had he visited her? About seven months. And perhaps in the meantime she had heard that he was engaged in writing this great, important thesis about the relation of food to health. Perhaps she had come across a case she thought might interest him— and being grateful that his advice had profited her, had gone against the general trend of opinion and asked him to look at a sick slave.

But one should not, of course, hope too much, or too easily. It was possibly something quite different. Mevrouw might have indulged in a fit of temper and injured some slave seriously, and learned too late that the Company—so impervious in matters of diet—did occasionally express disapproval of gross physical brutality. It might well be that, arrived at Coenpark he would find that Mevrouw had gouged out some girl's eye on account of an ill-ironed petticoat.

Cynicism warred with hope as he hurried along the path that linked Coenpark with Banda Neira. Not for the first time he longed for a pony. The Company had decreed that, since the whole island could be crossed from side to side in twenty-five minutes, no means of transport save the human foot was needed. And there was no pasture for any animal save the goats which planters kept for domestic purposes. But there were times when a pony's pace could exceed that of a middle-aged man burdened with a notebook (Juan carried the bag of tools and drugs). Still, the doctor reflected, mopping his brow … if I were allowed to keep a pony, Evert Haan would have a carriage and pair I suppose, and all the others would copy him, and they'd either sacrifice some plantation space for pasture, or use a lot of shipping to bring them corn. It's just as well.

Annabet, having fed the baby, looked about for somewhere to lay it. The sleeping-mat was narrow and the suffering woman tossed from side to side of it during the spasms of pain, so, although it seemed the obvious, indeed the only place in the cabin, it was impossible to lay the baby upon it. With the child still in her arms she went to the door and called Josef who had retired to a little distance, though still in sight of the doorway, and was sitting upon the stump of a felled tree.

'Go up to the house and fetch me a basket, Josef; a big one, big enough to hold this baby. Put a cushion in it.'

The passive surliness of the man's face shifted into an expression of active malevolence. He was a house-servant, not a slave. For more than twenty years he had served white masters, and being efficient when it suited him to be, and deceitful at all times, had garnered quite a harvest of esteem. To-day, as soon as Mynheer returned home and heard of Mevrouw's adventure, his first thought would be to blame Josef. He would say that Mevrouw was new to the country, she didn't understand, and that it had been Josef's duty to get her out of the compound. And, as though this were not enough, Mevrouw must send him up to the house to fetch milk for some unbeliever's bastard, and been too blind, or too sense-less to realise that, by making Abbas carry the milk, he, Josef, was asserting his right to refuse to wait upon slave trash. Now she wanted a basket, and a cushion. A fine load for the house-boy of Mynheer Haan of Coenpark to carry into the compound. If she wanted to demean herself that was her business —a fine tale would be on the rounds by this afternoon—but she was not going to involve him any further in this affair. He felt safe in defying her, for already he had, unjustly, incurred his master's displeasure.

He rose from the tree-stump and stood respectfully as he said:

'Mevrouw, the baskets that are in the house, and the cushions, are the property of my master. I dare not, without his permission, remove them. A cupful of milk is easily replaced, but who would want back a cushion or a basket in which *that* had lain. If Mynheer had desired to provide cradles for the brats of his slaves he would have given orders to that effect. I stay here to see that you yourself incur as little danger as possible from your folly; but I go no more errands on behalf of rubbish like *that*.'

Annabet looked down at the baby. Nobody had washed it; it was scaly and stained as it had come from the womb. The roughly-dressed fragment of navel cord was unsightly and the child itself was far from beautiful; but it had lived, too weak to cry any more it had made those mute piteous appeals with its little mouth; it had accepted the strange alien substance she had offered it, and now, mouth and eyes closed, it rested, with touching confidence, against her arm. And Josef, standing there so well-fed and confident, called it names.

She was furious, the more easily angered because her own nerves were strained; without fully realising it, part of her, the inescapable, feminine, vulnerable part, was sharing the pain of the woman on the sleeping-mat. She wanted to shriek out, 'You're sacked, Josef. We'll see what Mynheer thinks of a servant who disobeys *me*!' But something, blood, or training, or innate good sense came to her aid. She said, with dignity, 'Very well, Josef. Go and sit down again. Perhaps Katje will

205

fetch me the things I want. If not, when Doctor Van de Lijn comes, I can get them myself. Well, Katje?'

Katje had remained nearer to the cabin door. Not from any greater sense of duty, but from a more lively feeling of curiosity. For quite a long time now Katje had been absolutely certain in her own mind that her mistress was raving mad. Hitherto all evidence of her mental derangement had been confined to the blue-and-white room where Katje's beady, blank-looking eyes had seen many queer things, grimaces in the mirror, silent trances, bouts of crying—all for no reason at all; now it had come out into the open and Katje was most interested in seeing what form it would take next.

And, oddly woven into this interest were two other strands. Katje had often resented Josef's air of superiority: it could never have arisen, she thought, in a proper household, and only occurred now because Mynheer had lived as a bachelor so long. In a rightly-constituted family the Mevrouw's personal maid had precedence over every other servant because, finally, upon the surface at least, the Mevrouw was the most important person in the household. The present moment offered a chance to prove whether the lady's maid or the gentleman's man carried more weight.

And also, Katje remembered, for all her madness, Mevrouw was oddly generous. Not with money, for she seemed to have none, and in seven months Katje had never received a guilder above her wages. But with other things, trinkets and bits of clothing and free hours and kind words and smiles Mevrouw had far exceeded the standard set by the wife of the First Merchant in Batavia. Perhaps if she obeyed promptly and pleasantly now, it might be to her advantage. For although Josef still acted as though Mynheer were a bachelor, Katje knew that there were moments when Mevrouw held the supremacy. So now she said meekly:

'A basket and a cushion, Mevrouw. I will fetch them, knowing that in Josef's keeping you will be safe.'

Not even Mynheer could find fault with *that*. And Mevrouw looked pleased. Protected upon all sides, Katje departed.

Nobody had noticed that the old woman with the shuffling gait and the swinging ear-rings had disappeared as soon as she had handed back to Annabet the jug of goat milk. Or that the little guardian of the well had not returned to his post. Josef sulked upon his tree-trunk. A curious—and to an experienced observer—unnatural quietude had fallen upon the compound. If the other huts were occupied the occupants gave no sign of their presence. Nobody took advantage of the little boy's absence to throw anything into the well. Annabet, still holding the small body which she did not like to lay down on the filthy floor, the woman, still moaning and writhing upon the sleeping-mat, Josef nursing his dignity and his grievance upon the tree-stump, appeared to be the only living people within the compound. At a distance there were sounds of life, for in the plantation the slaves, working against time, since the rains would set in at any moment now, snatched off the plump, peach-like fruits of the nutmegs, chattering and singing as they worked, or silent, according to their natures, and reckoned their hauls upon their fingers, twenty at a time, both hands twice, one for each foot. And the overseer went round taking the tally. And the doves which had escaped Evert's bird-lime gobbled and mourned.

And then, quite suddenly, the compound sprang into life. The little well guard, obeying the old woman's instructions, having sighted the white man of medicine hurrying along followed by the easily recognisable Juan, dashed into the space between the huts and whistled. Immediately, from another cabin, the old crone with the ear-rings emerged, a strange, doomed look upon her face. Four old women, two of them more decrepit than herself, joined her, and stretching the sensitive hands of the blind, a middle-aged woman, guided by a toddler, hurried into the midst of them, followed by another, big with child. Seven of them, all exempt for some reason from work in the plantation, but all ready to give their lives for the sanctity of the laws by which they had lived.

At almost the same moment other cabins spewed forth their occupants and their principles. From one came a big brown woman with a child at her breast; from another a curious, rather beautiful, long-throated creature with a number of brass rings between her chin and her breastbone; from yet a third a squat brown woman with a sleeping baby slung upon her back; and proceeding slowly, but with great determination, from a cabin in an isolated position, set a little back, came two yellow women, one hardly able to walk upon her cramped tiny feet in highly-coloured shoes, the other barefooted, but hampered, like the brown woman, by the child in her womb.

A curious, subdued murmur rose and broke the stillness of the compound as the women massed into two separate groups; it sounded to Annabet like the murmur of bees in a summer garden, and she came to the door of the cabin again, the child, asleep now, still in her arms. At the same moment Josef rose from the tree-stump and thrust his way between the cabin wall and the old women who were moving doggedly towards Annabet and the door.

'Mevrouw,' he said in a voice that was suddenly shrill and frightened, 'put down that baby and come away now. At once. These are going to make trouble when the doctor arrives. Come away before he gets here.'

The old woman with the brass ear-rings moved quite quickly

and placed herself in the doorway so that her back was to Annabet and her claw-like hands, extended to the full length of her arms, pushed against Josef's chest. 'Don't come nearer,' she cried in Dutch, and then spat out another word or two which Annabet could not understand before edging herself sideways and addressing the white woman in a manner which held an odd mixture of servility and menace.

'He is right, Mevrouw. You should go now. Then when the Mynheer Doctor comes I will explain what you have done in ignorance and all will be well.'

'What will you explain?'

'That by our law only women assist in childbirth.'

'And send him away?'

'Yes, Mevrouw. Give me the baby and go.'

'I shall stay here,' said Annabet quite clearly. 'And Doctor Van de Lijn, when he comes, will help this woman. Already she is out of her mind with pain and fever. Do you want her to die?'

'Life and death are matters for the gods, Mevrouw,' retorted the crone seriously. 'Such concerns are not for us. But the woman's husband is a man of caste. She herself is nothing, and it is a thousand pities that he should have taken such a creature for his wife. But if another man crosses that threshold Ramjit is shamed for ever. It must not be, Mevrouw.'

The blind woman, bracing herself upon the shoulder of her child guide, burst into passionate speech in the unknown tongue.

'Aah,' sighed the old woman as soon as she had finished. 'She says truly, Mevrouw. She says that, slaves though we may be, brought out of our own countries and forced to labour as we are, even the white men who have enslaved us, know better than to flaunt the wishes of the gods. It was written in the laws, Mevrouw, a thousand years ago, that no man save the husband should look upon the nakedness of a woman; and that in childbirth she should be kept even from his sight.' The old eyes which had been gazing earnestly, almost hypnotically into Annabet's, shifted their stare for a second and surveyed the group of brown and yellow women who stood slightly apart, muttering. 'Mevrouw,' she said, quite pleadingly, 'give heed to what I say. Look upon those, the lawless ones, the debauched, the outcast ones. Have they not gathered to gloat upon our discomfiture? Are they not here to witness the enforced breaking of our laws? Would you have them triumph over us, this scum which has never known or has long forgotten the rules by which their unknown fathers lived.' Suddenly the bright old eyes were lost among their wrinkles and two slow difficult tears were squeezed out and travelled, infinitely pitiable, down the withered brown cheeks. 'Mevrouw, our lives are hard; our bodies are not our own any more, but a few of us have suffered great hardships to keep the laws and preserve our souls. Ramjit—apart from eating the soup which the false woman within forced upon him in his sickness—has always adhered to the rules of his caste. He trusted his wife to me—he himself tied the sacred cord which you so rashly, in ignorance, Mevrouw, I admit in ignorance—severed. He trusted me to bring forth his son according to sacred custom. And that I had done when you ... when you...' She put her thin old hands to her face and the tears, no longer separate and to be counted, spouted between her fingers. A long moan went up from the old woman, the blind woman and the mother about to be, and accompanying it a jeer from the group which stood apart. The old woman with the ear-rings sobbed for a moment, and then, raising her tear-wet face, said brokenly, 'Even the white masters have always respected our laws. Ten years have I worked here, gathering the nutmegs until I could gather no more, and never until this day have I known the white masters demand more than the labours of our hands. Aah, this is a bad day, a day of ill-omen. This is a day that the gods will remember and curse.'

Afterwards Annabet remembered with shame that her hold upon the little brown baby was loosening and she was almost, almost upon the point of handing it to the old woman at this point. They were slaves, after all; life in this world was for them a thin and sterile matter of toil and endurance; there could be no comfort in it, no hope. It would be cruel, cruel to force them to sacrifice their hope of heaven—was it heaven that they hoped for? And she had thought of Mamma who had been so meticulous not to eat meat on Fridays, because she had been born and reared a Sieberg and had chanced to marry her Protestant cousin, a Van Goens. Mamma—and time and distance had softened her idiosyncracies while at the same time making her nearer and dearer, had adhered, as far as possible to the rules, the laws. Was this queer brown woman so different? God, Elsa Sieberg's God, would be offended if she ate beef on certain days of the week, certain days of the year; and this old hag's gods (why did one think of one with a capital, one with a small letter?) would be offended if a competent, male doctor came to remove that stubborn after-birth from the body of the woman who still tossed and moaned upon the sleeping-mat. Could you distinguish between them? You, who had in any case no claim to even ordinary virtue, far less holiness. You who were probably, between Christy and Evert, far more damned than anybody in this compound.

But, and as she thought this her face hardened and her feet seemed to take a more determined stand upon the floor, this was, when all was said and done, a bodily, fleshly world. And just behind her, on the sleeping-mat, there was a mass of suffering human flesh. We can't know, she thought, we can't really *know* about Mamma's fish on Fridays and during Lent or about this old hag's ritual of birth, but we can tell, in our own bodies, which we do know something about, that pain is a bad thing and that pain which is severe enough to send us out of our minds must be displeasing to any god or gods there are ... what does that poor woman care about gods?

She had actually opened the mouth to repeat her intention of staying on until Doctor Van de Lijn's arrival, when a quiet, dry voice sounded across the compound.

'Mevrouw Haan? You mean to say she is *here*?'

He had been steering towards the path which the little well-guarder had so recently pointed out to Annabet as being the shortest way to the house; and he was surprised when Juan plucked him by the sleeve and pointed in the other direction. He had expected to find Annabet in her own house and the slave—subject of interest or victim of temper—waiting in the kitchen quarters.

He swung round towards the cabins and as he did so a kind of low moaning went up from the old woman's party and the women who composed it shuffled and stirred, so that between Annabet, gazing eagerly out of the doorway and the doctor bending his steps towards it, the old and the hampered bodies of the women formed a living barrier. At the same time the women in the other party began to shuffle and stir in much the same manner, yet apparently without purpose.

Annabet called clearly, 'It was good of you to come so quickly, Doctor Van de Lijn. The sick woman is in here.' She lowered her voice a little and spoke again to the old crone. 'I mean the doctor to come in here and help this woman, so you might as well get out of the way and tell these others to do the same. You're not to blame in the least. I'll take all the responsibility.'

The old woman looked round over her shoulder and there was for a second an expression of intense rancour and hatred upon her withered face; but it was swamped almost immediately by a look of sorrowful fanaticism, quite impersonal, as though at this fatal moment there was no room for lesser emotions.

'Mevrouw, we are bound to obey the gods. Perhaps the doctor will understand.' Without moving from her position of defence she bent her old body in a deep obeisance and began to gabble as Doctor Van de Lijn approached. Her Malay was more fluent and more emphatic than her Dutch; and within a minute Annabet saw, with astonishment, that the doctor had halted and was giving the old woman his serious attention. As soon as her spate of words ceased, and before he could make

210

any reply, the brown woman with the baby, in the other group, called in a low, musical voice, speaking almost unintelligibly broken Dutch:

'The Mevrouw is right. The woman has been in agony for two long days. Our God himself touched the sick and healed them, men and women alike. We...' she waved the baby in a circle to include the whole of her little group, 'will help you, Mevrouw, to push the heathen aside and let the doctor in. You have only to give the word.'

And then, before anyone else could speak or move, Josef snaked forward, and with a lightning gesture smote the palm of his hand on the ground just in front of Doctor Van de Lijn's toes, carried the hand to his own forehead and cried earnestly:

'Mynheer, get Mevrouw away. Tell her to leave. Perhaps she will heed you. I have asked and begged, explained and beseeched, but she will not listen to me.'

Doctor Van de Lijn, conscious that every eye in the compound was upon him, cleared his throat.

'Mevrouw,' he said over the heads of the women, 'I would like to speak to you—in private.'

'Come in, then,' said Annabet. 'If I come out *she* will close the door. And the woman is dying.'

'What is the matter with her?'

Brass ear-rings, in Malay, explained in great detail. As she did so, with many sidelong references to her unchallenged position as ritual midwife and many immodest testimonials to her own skill and nursing, Doctor Van de Lijn's mind took rapid stock of the position. Nothing of interest here, nothing which would add a line of value to his thesis. Actually he had been a fool to hope that it might. Retention of the placenta ... two days ... and after everything the old hag with the earrings had done the wretched creature would probably die, anyway. He felt his professional interest wither. There remained what might be called the social issue. The position had all the makings of a nice little religious brawl. Hindu against Christian. His agnostic mind gave a snarl of mirth. Very little to choose between them from what he knew. The brand of Christianity which the Portuguese had disseminated in the islands during their era of power was as superstition-ridden as the Hinduism and Mahommetanism against which it warred. Basically, both the parties in the compound were bad neighbours, boiling up for a row; and if he happened to be involved in it his reputation would suffer and his already narrowing field of contact with the natives would be further restricted and more deeply suspect.

He endeavoured to act with diplomacy. For, besides the other considerations he must remember that Mevrouw was a

211

patient, the wife of the most powerful and influential planter in this island. He must avoid offending her if it were in any way possible. So, with an apologetic glance in Annabet's direction, he addressed himself to the old woman who was fighting the battle of Shiv and Krishna and the rest of the oligarchy. He said, in Malay, that he perfectly understood her views and would respect them, that he was, however, bound to respect also, Mevrouw's ill-advised kindheartedness. If Mevrouw stepped out to speak to him would the old woman promise not to go into the cabin, not to close the door. Certainly the crone replied with a sly nudge at the old woman on her right, she would not move from this spot.

Doctor Van de Lijn, his boredom with the whole business assuaged by the feeling that he was being very astute, translated the promise to Annabet and repeated his invitation to her to step outside and talk to him. Once she was outside he could take one arm, and if necessary Josef could take the other, and they would hustle her away, explaining this apparently ruthless behaviour by saying, not completely untruthfully, that they were concerned for her personal safety. Evert Haan would appreciate that.

But Annabet, being behind the barrier, had seen the nudge, and the only just perceptible nod of understanding which its recipient had given. Brass ear-rings would not stir, but the other old hag would, and the door would be closed, and the woman, whose moans and writhings had been growing progressively weaker as time went on, would die.

'I said I would stay here until you came to relieve the woman, Doctor Van de Lijn. I don't want to upset anybody; but the old woman has done her best and failed, and the poor woman is dying. Isn't it your duty, as a doctor, to come in here and see what you can do to help?'

'It isn't as simple as that, Mevrouw, unfortunately.'

The brown woman, spokeswoman for the Christians, called again, musically. 'Give the order, Mevrouw, and we will clear the way.'

'You see,' Van de Lijn said, 'this matter goes deeper than the question of you and I, Mevrouw, endeavouring to help a suffering creature. Fanaticism of the wildest kind is involved. There may easily be bloodshed. Not merely between these few women, Mevrouw; but spreading first to their menfolk and then to the slaves in other compounds. I am willing to bring my skill to the woman's service, but I am forbidden, because of her husband's religion, to cross the cabin threshold. I have lived among these people long enough to respect the tabu, Mevrouw, and I strongly advise you to do likewise. Lay the child beside its mother and leave the old woman to do her worst. The life of one woman must not count against the peace

212

of the compound.'

Annabet looked at him across the living barrier and horror began to dawn in her eyes.

'You mean you won't ... you daren't...? Oh, if only I could really talk to them. Doctor Van de Lijn ... all the others are guided by what that one old woman says, and she is *jealous* in case you may be able to do what she couldn't. You speak their language, can't you explain, can't you reason with them? Do they understand that the woman is dying?'

'Mevrouw, they understand, and they believe that she is suffering and dying because she had displeased their gods. Her very plight proves to them that their gods are omnipotent and revengeful. As for reason—if that had anything to do with the matter, Hinduism would have been swept away a thousand years ago. I might as well talk to the wind. But you, Mevrouw, are different. I hope that you will be reasonable. Please do as I say. Put down the baby and leave the woman to her fate.'

The brown woman who called herself a Christian, said something in that oddly, incongruously musical voice about idol worship, and called upon the Blessed Virgin to witness that here were five women ready to spit in the face of the graven images. But Van de Lijn hardly heard her; the whole of his attention was riveted upon the woman whose misplaced charity had brought about the whole embarrassing situation. Annabet had turned so pale that the faint bloom of false colour which from custom she had brushed upon her cheeks looked harsh and garish in contrast. If she faints now, he thought, there'll be the devil to pay, for either Josef or I must haul her out of the damned place and how can we do that without polluting the whole cabin.

But Annabet was, despite the ghastly pallor, as far from fainting as she had ever been in her life. Her heart had certainly performed some peculiar antics, seeming to leap into her throat and then to sink to her pelvis and she had that deadly, deserted, lonely feeling which more fortunate people encounter only in dreams, of seeing one's trusted allies desert, one's supposed friends turn away, of being left alone, frightened and weak, to stand against dark, terrifying peril. But there was a stubborn streak in her character. Across the black heads of the old, the blind, the pregnant fanatics, she said in a voice that was quite clear, though tremulous:

'Very well, Doctor Van de Lijn, perhaps you know best about these things. But will you tell me what to do ... what to try. Can you tell me, in simple language, what you would have done if they had let you in.'

He hesitated for a moment, and then deliberately took a step or two which brought him so close to the cabin that there was only the line of women, stiffening defensively, between him

213

and the doorway. In the space of time which it took him to take the few paces he realised that he had misjudged Mevrouw Haan, and possibly, all women. His eyes in the service of the Company had taught him to despise the wives and daughters of the planters and merchants in the islands, limp, spineless, selfish creatures who never gave a thought to anything outside their clothes, their looks, their social aspirations and their ailments. And during his professional visits to Mevrouw Haan he had never detected anything which distinguished her from the general run ... yet she was different, and perhaps they were all different only he had been too blind or too busy to notice.

'If you really mean that, Mevrouw, and if your stomach is strong enough ... then I should have...' he hesitated for a moment, trying to put into terms which an ignorant layman would understand, the exact description of the procedure. When he had succeeded—and it was far more difficult than translating from Dutch to Malay—he shouted out his directions.

'Stay there, so that I can consult you,' Annabet called back. And as though the gods themselves were on her side, at that moment when she was thinking that after all she would have to lay the baby upon the filthy floor so that she could roll back her sleeves and set to work, Katje arrived panting with the basket. The breathlessness was genuine, for Katje had been eager to see what new development had taken place in her absence.

One of the old women stepped, shuffling, aside and collided with the blind one. Katje stepped up to the gap thus made and held out the basket at arm's length. Annabet seized, not the basket but Katje's plump wrist. 'You can come in and help me. At least, you will understand what I say.'

Swiftly she set the basket in the far corner of the cabin and laid the baby in it. As she did so, and straightening herself, turned back to the woman on the mat, her mind, almost without her volition, framed the plea, 'God help me. Help me to do it right.' And with the same rapidity and the same lack of deliberate thinking, doubt followed the prayer. Was God likely to listen to her *now*, after all the lies, the deceit, the lustfulness? And before she could even bend and turn the woman into the position which Doctor Van de Lijn had advised, confidence had followed the doubt. Jacob, of all the Old Testament heroes the most favoured by God, had been untruthful, deceitful and lustful too.

She had actually laid her hands upon the woman's shoulders and was on the verge of telling Katje to lift her by the knees, when a stir, which was soundless and motionless, merely a nervous commotion which to some sixth sense was tangible as

214

noise or movement, took hold of the compound and swayed every person in it. Annabet lifted her eyes and saw Evert standing between the two groups of women, just behind Doctor Van de Lijn.

She stared at her husband for a moment, astonished by the colour of his face. She had never seen Evert pale before; his face was naturally florid, and every emotion, anger, passion, pleasure, served simply to heighten his colour. But now his face was the colour of spinet keys, and his grey eyes were clear and colourless as grass.

Even as she stared, his face altered, became more normal. She realised that she was glad to see him. He would understand; he would help her; drive the old women away: bid Doctor Van de Lijn do his duty. But just as she was about to speak to him, explain, ask his aid, Evert spoke sharply in Malay, and the old women shuffled so eagerly from side to side in their haste to obey him that there was a moment's confusion. She waited for it to subside and before she spoke Evert rapped out another order.

'Come out.'

'Me?'

'Who else? Come out here to me. Katje, take Mevrouw's arm and help her out.'

'I can walk,' Annabet said, avoiding the eager Katje, and hating herself for feeling frightened, she walked out of the doorway, now so suddenly unobstructed, and up to the spot where Evert stood.

'Evert ... there's a woman in there, dying. Doctor Van de Lijn told me what to do for her. They wouldn't let him in. But I think I ...'

Evert interrupted her, His eyes were as cold as the water under the ice of Whitwater and his voice made her feel small and impotent.

'Go along up the the house. I'll be with you in a moment. Josef ... Katje ... take your mistress home.'

'But, Evert, please, please listen to me. Don't send me away just at this moment. I can help ... the old woman is useless and Doctor Van de Lijn daren't go in. Let me stay and do what I can. Please, Evert.'

The colour had flooded back into his face as soon as he had realised that she was safe. Now it deepened suddenly, and Annabet could see that it was only by an effort of restraint that he forced himself to speak civilly to her.

'Will you kindly go back to the house without further argument,' he said in that same tight, cold voice. She saw him look towards Josef and Katje, saw them, officiously obedient, closing in. She glanced wildly at Doctor Van de Lijn—surely he would speak now, support her, explain. But the doctor's

215

eyes avoided hers. He stood, in fact, looking rather silly, staring at the tops of the nutmeg trees above the cabin roofs, as though he hoped, by maintaining silence and withdrawing his attention to render himself invisible.

For a second she meditated the possibility of dashing back into the cabin, doing what she had braced herself to do and risking whatever Evert might say or do afterwards. If she once got inside the cabin Evert could not follow her, the old women would see to that. Fool ever to have come out! A glance at the doorway showed her the folly of her thought. The old women had closed their line again, and Brass ear-rings, under her meek, downtrodden look, wore a sneaky expression of complacency. And meanwhile Evert was waiting, and Josef and Katje were ready, at another nod, to lead her away by brute force. Stupid and useless to risk the ignominy. She turned abruptly and went swiftly along the path.

Now the woman will die, she thought, and perhaps I could have saved her. I could, with God's help, have saved her. I wanted to; I meant to. Now she will die. Tears, some of them springing from pity and some from anger, began to run down her face, smudging the paint and the powder. Sniffing as she cried, she became conscious, as she had not been for a month or two, of the smell of nutmeg in the air. And now for the first time it smelt of evil, of oppression, and pain, superstition and fear.

She had seen Evert angered before—for the scene which had led to the gift of the blue-and-white Chinese coat had been repeated in almost identical detail several times in the last few weeks; but always before his anger had been hot and loud and, in a degree pitiable, since he himself had not known exactly against whom his fury was directed. Hitherto his shafts had struck her obliquely and she had remained, in a way, mistress of the situation. But this was different. For the first time she encountered an Evert cold, reasonable and triumphant, and within five minutes of their argument she realised, with a sinking heart and puzzled mind that he was, at the very root, enjoying her discomfiture.

The interview had begun in a way that surprised her. Evert, flushed from hurrying had arrived in the house before she had checked her tears and had said, 'Thank God you're safe. When I got back and Abbas gabbled about you being in the compound with Josef and Katje and Doctor Damn Fool Van de Lijn and some woman who was ill, honestly, it's a wonder I didn't have a stroke on the path between the house and the compound. What on earth *possessed* you to go there?'

Something within her recognised the truth of his words. He had been white as paper when she looked up and saw him, across the heads of those awful old women.

'I'm sorry, Evert. I just went to see if there was anything I could do. I'd been thinking ... about Mamma, visiting people ... I realised that I'd been here quite a long time and hadn't ... hadn't had a thought outside myself. And it just happened that I could have done something this morning. Evert, if you hadn't arrived just then I could have saved that woman ... perhaps. At least I could have tried. Doctor Van de Lijn...'

'*He's* going to get a flea in his ear,' Evert said. 'Rikshalt nearly got him transferred, and now I *shall* get him moved. Giving my wife instructions on how to act as midwife to scum ... he's mad. I'll get him locked up.'

'But, Evert, I sent for him. If I had had my way I'd have him in that cabin, helping the woman. He daren't go against the old women, so I asked him to tell me what to do. He isn't to blame at all; if there is any blame ... if it is wrong to try to help a fellow creature out of agony ... then the blame is mine. I asked him to help and I was prepared to do what he said. And then you came...'

That was the point where Evert changed his attitude.

'Yes, I came. And only just in time. In five minutes there'd have been a riot. You don't believe me, do you? No. You come to a country about which you know nothing; you burst into a place full of people you don't understand, and when I save you from the natural result of your ignorant folly you're not grateful, you're resentful.'

'Not resentful, Evert, sorry. The woman will die now. I might have saved her.'

'Women are cheap. On my last trip to Bandogar I bought eighty at a hundred guilders each.'

She looked at him with horror. 'But, Evert, that isn't what matters. Suppose you can. Suppose you can replace her for so little as a hundred guilders. She's alive, she's a person, you shouldn't think of her in terms of money. And she's dying now. Doctor Van de Lijn could have saved her. His directions were so clear and precise, even I, ignorant as I am, could have followed them. Evert, let me go back and try...'

His eyes sparkled with anger and enjoyment.

'You still don't understand ... or is it that you are trying to act like a fool? Listen. Interference like yours this morning is dangerous. Those women who wouldn't let Doctor Tom Fool in are Hindus. They live and move, eat and sleep and think according to a set of rules as rigid as iron. Any one of those old hags would die ... not just willingly but gladly, rather than go against one word of their ridiculous law. The other trollops are anything, nothing, dregs of the Portuguese Missions; that creature with the rings round her neck is plain heathen ... they'd have rejoiced to see you cut through a bit of sacred red string or put your right hand over your left when you touched

217

the woman. Then the old women would have laid hands on you and the others would have attacked them, glad of an excuse, and there'd have been bloodshed. Their menfolk would have been involved and the thing would have spread, everybody taking the chance of avenging slights and insults and old grudges. It wouldn't even have ended in this compound, my dear silly girl. Your Mamma probably did go visiting the sick with soup and gruel. . . .' He gave a bark of mocking laughter. 'But the people whose sufferings were thus so much eased were white, reasonable, human beings. Out there they're not; they're animals, pretty tame on the surface, but capable of being very dangerous. I want you to get into your pretty little noddle that you are never, at any time, to go into the compound again.'

She was impressed by the fact that he had repeated, almost in the same words, much that Doctor Van de Lijn had said. But she felt compelled to utter some protest.

'Somebody should, Evert. They're your people . . . they belong to you even more than even the people on the estate belonged to Mamma when she lived at Janshaven. You—I don't mean you specially—but all the white people who own the plantations ought to have seen that a thing like this Hinduism was rooted out . . . long ago. They should be taught, shown, explained to. Doctor Van de Lijn ought to have had enough courage to go into that cabin and do his job. Then if the woman got better they'd all realise that our ways were better than theirs.'

'There are two arguments against that which, with your permission, I will explain to you,' said Evert coldly. 'One, the thing isn't possible. You might as well try to change the colour of their skin. Even the Portuguese admitted finally that only the riffraff who were nothing anyway, ever professed to be converted. And secondly, it isn't desirable. They're not here to be converted; they're here to tend the nutmeg groves, and a certain amount of dissension among themselves makes them easier to rule. To-day, because it was a question of Hindu ritual you had a mob of so-called Christians, brown, black and yellow, uniting together; but to-morrow, if some different squabble crops up, you'll find the Chinese, even the Christian ones, against all the others. The mixture makes for safety, because it means that they can never all get together long enough to start any real trouble. Have you ever thought, when you were bothering your head about matters which you don't understand, how many white men there are in the islands, compared with the others? Suppose we acted on your admirable advice and swept away all their differences . . . how long should we last? Not a day. Do you know, I feel so strongly in this matter that when I go to Bandogar, commissioned to buy shall we say fifty slaves, I don't go by sex, or size or age. I buy by religion, so many Hindus, so many Mahommedans, so many Mission mongrels, so many Ethiopian Christians—you'd hardly believe how different they are from the others and the tribal wars keep the supplies up, thank God—and I mix in a few Chinese, a head-hunter or two, and as many plain heathen as I can lay hands on. I only wish some merchant would offer me a few Jews and genuine Catholics. . . .' He laughed again, enjoying the look of shocked distaste upon her face. He waited for her to speak. But there was nothing to say. She thought of the woman moaning with pain, out of her mind with pain; of the baby for whom there had been no milk, of his piteous, unconscious confidence.

'So keep out of the compound,' Evert went on in a kinder voice. 'I must admit that I never said that to you. But damme, I've been here twenty years, and there've been women here almost as long as that and I never heard of one going into a compound before. I no more thought of telling you not to than of telling you not to drink poison or not to poke a stick into a wasp's nest. But you understand now. Or don't you? Do you plan, as soon as my back is turned to go running back there? Because if you do, I warn you . . . I'll give you a damned good thrashing if you ever set foot on that path again.'

And he means it, she thought . . . he'd enjoy that. She pushed the thought aside.

'Evert, I won't go near the compound. But may I send milk for that baby, if the woman dies, as she's almost sure to do?'

A most curious look came over Evert's face.

'You liked the baby, eh?'

She felt her face go hot with embarrassment. She said stiffly:

'To the extent of not wanting to think of it dying of starvation, while we have milk to spare.'

'What you want,' said Evert, 'is a baby of your own. That'd give you something to think about. That'd be the . . .'

He broke off suddenly, reached out and seized her in his arms. Easily, as though she weighed no more than the little brown baby he carried her upstairs, into the bedroom. The shutters were closed against the heat of the midday sun.

It is true, she thought wildly with that part of her mind which was not submerged, with her body in the flood of Evert's angry, jealous, tender possessiveness, I do want a baby. I knew that this morning when that little thing lay in my arms. But it's yours I want, Christy, yours, yours. . . .

That evening, when Evert poured the wine she refused it. The wine had led to the fit of conscience which had taken her to the compound, and that visit had resulted merely in what had been, to all intents and purposes, a repetition of what had

219

led to the fit of conscience. At midday too, which somehow seemed worse. Though why it was difficult to say. It had never been laid down by anybody, anywhere that love-making should take place in the darkness.

'Why?' Evert demanded, conscious of the pinch of Shal Ahmi's powder which was already dissolved in the glass of Madeira. 'You liked it last night.'

'But it made my head ache. I'm not really accustomed to wine, you know.'

'You've been long enough finding that out,' Evert said, disagreeably. Over the glasses he shot her a look of sharp suspicion. Shal Ahmi's medicine had worked last night—by God, how it had worked! Had she noticed, suspected anything? Annabet stared back at him with the cool, calm expression which she always adopted when he took that tone to her without provocation. But behind the mask she was conscious of a wry amusement. Suppose—the thought flashed through her mind—suppose I explained and said, Evert, I daren't drink wine any more because I find that it makes me lustful. How shocked he would be; how astonished; how pleased!

'Yes,' she agreed, 'I have been a long time finding out. But now I'm sure. I'll drink some fruit juice.'

Evert turned his back to her and moved a candlestick. When he handed her the innocuous glass he was pleased and smiling again. The glass of Madeira which she had refused stood on the sideboard until the end of the meal, when Annabet's Heydberg thrift made her ask, at the risk of reawakening Evert's annoyance, 'Couldn't you pour that back into the bottle?'

'It would be most unlucky,' he said, and began to laugh. The suggestion and the possibilities it called up struck him at the exact level where what sense of humour he possessed functioned best. He laughed so heartily that he choked. Damn him, if the thing worked before the supply of powder was exhausted he'd doctor several bottles and send them round to various ladies for a Christmas present. Just imagine old Trudi Van Heem behaving as Annabet had behaved last night! He laughed until he choked and had to beat himself upon his broad chest. Eventually the joke palled, and he came to himself to see Annabet watching him, puzzled, but ready to share the fun if only she knew what it was about. 'Excuse me, my dear,' he gasped, 'but your suggestion reminded me of a funny story. Not for lady's ears, I'm afraid.'

Now was perhaps a good moment.

'Evert, this afternoon I told Josef to send milk down for that baby, and to do so every day. I thought I ought to tell you.'

Evert got out of his chair and came and threw his heavy hot arm across her shoulders.

'I don't care what you send into the compound—so long as you don't go yourself.'

And it was not, despite the whining nasal warning of the Heydberg meeting-house, the wine which was to blame. For to-night was only a repetition of last night with its horrible, shattering merging of the loved and the unloved, of desire and duty, of the imaginary and the real. This was worse than the moment when Shal Ahmi dragged Christy away into the night. Then he was only lost in space and darkness; now he was being swallowed up by something vaster than distance and blackness, lost in the unexplored fastnesses of the mind, lost in the hideous, unimaginable convolutions of the flesh.

Three days after her visit to the compound the rains broke. To Annabet, accustomed to wet days, sudden showers, the drizzling, indecisive 'bad weather' of the west of Europe, the steady, relentless downpour of the wet monsoon was only slightly less trying than the heat which preceded it. Evert was jubilant. The rains were right, normal, something upon which the planters counted. If she had once lived, as he had, through a season when the rains had failed, she would appreciate the meaning of this downpour, he told her. She had expected all life to stop, all work to be suspended, all social intercourse to be at standstill. She was astounded at the way in which Evert would, five and six times a day, plunge out into the dripping, hissing world, return soaked to the skin and change uncomplainingly into dry clothes. In her own cupboards the row of shoes, some made by the old cobbler in Heydberg, some ordered by Evert and far more delicately constructed by some unknown, unnamed craftsman in Banda, bloomed with a fine blue-and-white mould. Overnight her sweat-soaked dresses rotted on their pegs. And she herself, hoping for coolness and relief at the change of season, found conditions worse rather than better. At least in the hot weather one could sweat; now the dampness of the air seemed to preclude that dubious comfort. It was, she thought, like being enclosed in a small room wherein a hundred kettles were boiling all day.

Desperately, after the first days and her first disappointment in what Evert had called 'cooler weather,' she tried to find some interest outside herself and the steaming stuffiness of the house. The garden, she noticed, was flourishing in a way which to her, experienced only to the slow cold springs of Europe, seemed little short of miraculous. Hassan, the old gardener, squatted about all day, naked save for a cloth around his loins, and the things which he planted had rooted themselves, sent forth shoots and buds almost overnight. The grass, which despite careful watering had been turning brown, was, after two days, greener than the meadows on either side the Whit-

221

water and the roses and flowering shrubs held their coloured petals to the downpour with joyous abandon. There were always more buds and blooms next morning.

After a week of it, Annabet donned the white hood and cape which Evert had thoughtfully provided against this season and stepped out into the downpour. Once out of the house, she felt better. You could, she thought, almost see and hear things growing. She walked as far as the green wall which bordered the garden and for a few moments watched Hassan who, with a pair of oddly-shaped shears, was snipping back the lush growth of the bushes which made it.

She stood idly watching him, her thoughts far away when suddenly there was a commotion. Something touched her foot, and as she stared down startled and recoiling, Hassan, with the sinister curved hook in his hand, yelled and ran forward. The man at her feet—for it was a man, very thin and brown and dripping with water as though he had just been taken out of the sea, broke into a pitiable whining gabble of which she understood no word. His eyeballs, prominent with terror, rolled towards her face and then towards Hassan's. Hassan, maintaining a threatening attitude, gasped out in broken Dutch:

'Do not be frightened, Mevrouw. He means no harm. And I am here.' The prostrate man spoke again, more firmly.

'He begs leave to touch your feet, Mevrouw. Do you permit?'

'What does he want?'

'To give you thanks, Mevrouw. It is Ramjit, the man from Seringa-patam. He thanks you, with his head on your feet for saving the life of his child. It is of goat milk that he speaks.'

Oh, she thought, this intolerable barrier of language, this old, confusing curse of Babel. It was only with the utmost difficulty that she could understand Hassan; between her and the grateful father no words were possible. She smiled and shook her head deprecatingly, thinking the things she would have said had it been of any use.

'Tell him that I am glad the child lived; glad that I had the milk to send.'

Hassan spoke, barely concealing his scorn. The man in the mud crawled forward and solemnly laid his forehead against her feet, one after the other.

'For four days, he says, he has waited here,' said Hassan, his bad Dutch taking an explanatory tone. The man, backing away, still on his knees, lifted his head at last and looked into Annabet's face. Like a dog, she thought, trying to express an emotion without speaking. She had a curious, slightly ludicrous impulse to touch him, either on the smooth black rain-soaked hair or on the thin brown shoulder.

The odd scene seemed to demand some suitable conclusion. She was glad when she thought of something to say.

'Tell him to go in peace, Hassan.'

Hassan muttered the formula. The man retreated, put his head to the mud again, rose, backed through the archway and disappeared. Hassan stared after him for a moment, and then said, sanctimoniously:

'He should not have come here, Mevrouw. But his intention was good. It is his first-born, and he is very ignorant.'

'I'm very glad he came. And I am glad you were here to speak to us both, Hassan. I should never have understood what he wanted.'

So the baby had lived. She had wondered often and had, for a few days asked questions about it of Katje and Josef who were her sole links with that outer, forbidden world. They had both been either actually or deliberately ignorant. Josef had invariably replied that the milk was being sent every day; but that had been intended to inform her that her orders were being carried out, nothing more.

Now she knew. But going back to the house through the rain and the scent of soaked earth and green things growing, she thought dejectedly, so the child lived ... and will grow up in the compound; will pick nutmegs and live in a cabin; that tuft of filthy cow-hair will be sacred to *him,* and he'll come to believe that it is better his wife should die than that a man should bring his skill to her bedside. So why did I bother, and why am I glad that he is alive?

A little burst of music answered her. As she stepped on to the verandah and kicked off her muddy shoes, there came from the compound, muted by distance and the humid air, the monotonous, yet queerly satisfying notes of the gamelans.

They're alive, she thought, and no doubt they find certain pleasures, the cessation of work, the company of their fellows, satisfaction even in the keeping of their rules of behaviour. I mustn't pity them too much, or I shall go crazy. I must accept things ... as Jean Marie said, and that means not only the things that happen to me, but the things that happen to other people. Only where does accepting things end? I might have accepted the fact that that baby's mother was dead, and therefore he must die too, for sheer lack of nourishment. And that would have been wrong. And really I ought to have told Hassan to say that that man's wife might have lived too if the old women hadn't stopped Doctor Van de Lijn from going in. Yes, I ought to have said that. It was my duty to say it. That's the kind of thing all the white people in these islands ought to say without ceasing.

On the other hand, she thought, anxious to be just, how

should I feel if I were a slave and that Ramjit, we'll say, were my master, and came around trying to make me believe that the Ten Commandments and the Sermon on the Mount were all rubbish and superstition?

The Ten Commandments—they were what slipped hastily into the mind in such an argument as this. And before she went any further with this comparison of religions it might be as well to run through and see whether she had been as faithful to her beliefs as those awful old women had been to theirs. No other gods; keeping the Sabbath; no stealing; no murder; no adultery.

But for the Christian ... and she would call herself a Christian, wouldn't she? ... the commandments carried some remarkable riders. 'But I say unto ye, whosoever looketh on a woman and lusteth after her committeth adultery in his heart.' And wasn't that perfectly true? Breathtakingly true. Wasn't she, Annabel Haan, committing adultery almost every hour of her waking day, and so frequently in the night as well. Oh Christy! Not just between me and Evert, but between me and God as well, if we abide by the letter of the law.

She slipped on the shoes which Katje had placed ready, threw down the soaked hood and cloak. Lost, she thought, with a curious feeling of detachment. Lost, body and soul. I should have gone to County Clare. This is judgment on me.

For a moment she felt important and doomed. Then sense reasserted itself, and as she walked along the passage and into the drawing-room she thought again of Jean Marie's talk about resignation and acceptance. If I could give Evert a baby, she thought, everything would be different. He would be pleased, and I should have something to love and to live for ... apart from Christy. If only I could have a baby; please God forgive my folly and my sinfulness and let me have a baby. I didn't go to County Down, oh God, because I hadn't a vocation. I came here instead, and even if that were wrong, please do try to forgive me and let me not spoil Evert's life too. Let me have a baby and I will try to forget those moments with Christy ... I'll try to be a good wife and mother ... I'll try ... I'll try ...

BOOK THREE

PIET, like most Captains in the Company's service, disliked all Agents on principle, and the fact that Kaerko, since the discovery of his relationship to Evert, had treated him with unusual civility, merely served to tinge his dislike with contempt; so he watched, without sympathy, how Kaerko's hands fluttered as soon as he had taken in the contents of that sealed cargo list; and how his face changed colour, and how his rather prominent yellow upper teeth caught at his lower lip.

Neither man made a comment upon the unusual nature of the cargo, but awareness of it lay heavily between them throughout the routine business of checking; and Kaerko's face still bore marks of concern when he left the ship to go up to the Fort to carry the Governor his despatches and to make arrangements for the unloading of the surprising items. Evert, rushing out to see Piet immediately, halted at the sight of Kaerko's expression and asked anxiously. 'What's the matter? Plague aboard?' Kaerko shook his head and muttered. 'No, perfectly clean bill of health,' in as glum a voice as he would have used if the answer had been the exact opposite.

Evert, bent upon his own business, showed no further curiosity. He would not, voluntarily, have rushed into the range of infection, but short of that nothing would have stopped him from getting hold of Piet and taking him home to dinner with him. For weeks now he had been looking forward to Piet's next visit to Banda. Piet would know the name of the fellow whom Annabet had wanted to marry; he would be able to give the phantom a name; and although he might be stubborn and reluctant to part with his information, Evert had had proof that Piet's tongue could be loosened by a sufficiency of liquor.

Piet had seen Kaerko down the ladder, and with the thought, 'Well, that's given him something to think about,' had turned back to his own cabin, where his best shirt and breeches lay on his bunk side by side with two sealed packages addressed to Annabet. He had promised both Mevrouw and Klara that he would deliver the letters with his own hand, and that he would at the same time see for himself exactly how far Annabet's report of her health was to be believed.

It had been such an easy, obvious thing to promise, but now that the *Eastern Venture* actually lay at anchor in Banda harbour, he found himself wishing that he had not done it. He was, in a way, anxious enough and curious enough to see

225

Annabet; but something deep within him shrank from the prospect of seeing her in Evert's house, in Evert's presence, in Evert's possession.

He had heard, of course, about her marvellous recovery. Mevrouw herself, very gracious, having apparently forgiven and forgotten his lapse of manners, had herself conveyed the news, 'I was right, you see,' she had said, quite sweetly, 'the change of climate was the one thing that could benefit her.' But there had been a doubt behind her confidence, and on the later occasion when she had entrusted him with her letter she had asked him to bring back a full report. Klara had been more forthright. 'She says she's been cured, but I can't really believe it. I'm afraid she exaggerated to put our minds at ease. Please find out and tell me all about it when you get back.'

On account of his promise to Klara alone, he must go to Coenpark. But not to-night, he decided suddenly. He'd send along the letters, but he wouldn't go himself. He'd find a tavern and drink a little, not much, just enough to lighten his spirits, and then he'd find himself a woman. He'd been fairly sober and completely chaste for seven months and that was a long time. Enough to make any man have queer thoughts.

With the caution of experience he laid out exactly as much money as he wished to spend on his evening's pleasure and locked the rest away. From the same motive he refrained from getting into his better clothes. He took up the letters, intending to give them to Gijs to deliver, and was about to call him when there was a sound of nimble, impetuous steps on the companionway and Evert's bulk blocked the cabin door. With a little sinking of the stomach Piet realised that his evening was no longer at his own disposal.

The girl seen across the Heydberg church had been young, immature, dressed in made-over, earnestly-contrived garments, and as remote and beautiful as an angel; the girl in the Heydberg parlour had been very ugly, emaciated, stiff, grotesque, finely dressed, and so friendly and intimate that he had actually dared to offer money for her support. Now, in the oddest way, the woman who rose from the low chair in the lovely room at Coenpark, combined the most seductive qualities of both.

He was paralysed with shyness as he handed her the letters, and replied, with a few wooden words, to her animated greeting and inquiries. Annabet, standing with the letters in her hand and feeling for a moment very near to Mamma and Klara and Truitje, near to the cold bare house and the flat landscape and coolly flowering cherry tree and the stiff tulips, remembered very sharply the details of their last meeting and put his shyness down to embarrassment. She had been over-frank with him then. And he had been very kind. So she restrained herself, though her fingers ached to open the letters and her mind hungered for news of home, especially for Klara's news; and exerted herself for a moment or two to set him at his ease. Before Evert could suggest it, she said, 'We must drink to this happy reunion.' And Evert threw her a sardonic glance and she was momentarily embarrassed herself and was driven to say, 'Oh yes, I'll risk a headache to-night. This is an occasion.' Evert poured wine for her, schnapps for Piet and himself, and she raised her glass and said, 'Many lucky voyages, Captain Odshoorn,' and then, after a moment, seeing that Piet, with a glass in his hand, had relaxed a little, set hers aside and said, 'Now please don't mind me; I must just look at my letters.'

Despite her eagerness for Klara's news, she opened Mamma's letter first from an almost automatic sense of fitness. But after scanning the first few sentences she laid it down and ripped open Klara's. The hasty, blotted, jubilant words sent stab after stab into her heart. 'So happy, I can't tell you. Don't mind anything Mamma writes, she sees only my outside. Just think, by the time you have this I shall have my baby, our baby. I am so looking forward. I do so hope it'll be a boy, with Jan's eyes and the same funny little nose. Jan would rather it was a girl, like me. So anyway, one of us will be pleased. Nab, I love him more every day, he's so kind to me. I'd do it again, a hundred times, if I had to. Though it was awful when I first knew what had happened, and there was no one to tell, and for six weeks, Nab, six whole weeks I couldn't even get out to tell *him*. Suppose he'd found another girl in that time. Truly, darling, that six weeks aged me by six years.... The house is small and rather poky, but cosy and comfortable compared with ours. All the furniture has been there since the Flood, I think, and Jan and I have the old people's bed. I did protest about that, but Jan's mother said, "Bless you, child, where Klaus and I sleep now doesn't matter." But if the harvest is good this year, Jan says he will build another room.... Mamma passed me in the street the day before yesterday, not looking, and with a face like stone. I suppose I should mind. But I don't. I didn't begin to live till I found Jan, and I was never happy until I came here.... I'm learning to milk a cow, you would laugh to see me, but I do want to be as good a wife as any farm girl he might have married....'

On and on, reiterative, incoherent, but vital and ecstatic, the account poured itself over six pages of poor thin paper. Annabet read to the end and then folded the sheets carefully and put them aside. Klara had married for love, she was spending her days and her nights ... oh God, her nights ... with somebody who roused in her the feelings which Christy

227

had roused in Annabet. I'd have lived in discomfort too. I'd have learned to smuggle nutmegs, just as Klara is learning to milk a cow, she thought. And I would have been happy too. I understand now all the things about Klara and Jan Mulder that puzzled me before. The one person. Nothing else matters. But I mustn't think about that now. I have a guest in my house.

She glanced quickly through Mamma's letter, with its fierce derogatory, coldly scornful sentences about Klara, its smooth civilised dealing with less painful subjects, its warm inquiries and good wishes. Then she laid that aside too.

'My sister, Klara, is married,' she said to Evert. And to Piet, 'I suppose you haven't happened to see her, since.'

Embarrassment had made Piet reckless and he had drunk three glasses of schnapps while Annabet read her two letters. He felt the better for them. But the question was awkward. He had seen Mevrow Mulder; she had brought the letter to his cottage herself. And she had been wearing the cloak and the hood and the wooden shoes of the ordinary tenant farmer's wife, and she had been pregnant as the devil, and as sleek and shining and happy as a woman could well be. And the whole of Heydberg had been talking about her. But young Mulder had come with her as far as the gate and had hovered while she gave Piet her letter and asked him to see for himself how Annabet was, and when she had clattered away down the path in her wooden shoes he had taken her arm ... very lover-like.

But they were made for love, and that was the truth of it. Annabet and Klara too. Any man ...

'Oh yes, I've seen her. She looked well, and happy,' he said cautiously.

'We must send her a present,' said Evert, in his genial, blustering way. 'Who's the lucky man?'

'His name is Jan Mulder, and he's a farmer,' said Annabet clearly, seeing that Piet looked confused and uncomfortable. 'Mamma is disgusted by the match, but if Klara is happy, that is all that matters.'

'Well said,' said Evert, dropping his heavy arm around his wife's shoulders. 'Now, Piet, tell me. How d'you think she looks? Does Banda suit her better than Heydberg?'

Must you maul her, under my very eyes?

'Mevrouw looks very well,' said Piet stiffly. 'And so do you, Evert.'

But that was a lie. Evert looked less well than he had done when they parted. It wasn't, Piet thought, puzzledly, that he was obviously aged, the year or so which had passed had touched him lightly, if at all. But his expression had altered. Complacent was a word outside Piet's range, otherwise he might have reckoned that the complacent expression had been wiped from Evert's face. As it was, he finally wrestled through to the thought that Evert looked as though somebody had given him a good rap on the nose.

They went in to dinner, and Evert kept Piet's glass well replenished, cunningly varying the liquors. Towards the end of the meal Piet had got the better of his nervousness and could look at Annabet calmly. The liveliness, the frank look, the friendliness, which the angel of the church had lacked and which had so startlingly shown themselves in the piteous wreck of the parlour were still there, now set in beauty. And the beauty itself had increased. The full, immature curves of girlhood had gone, replaced by something even more subtle and breathtaking. And the lovely hair had grown a darker gold. But now and then, when she had sat in silence for a moment and Evert had held Piet's attention, turning back to her suddenly he surprised a look of—not sadness, exactly, but of something almost as disquieting, upon that lovely face. And then, turning back to Evert, he realised, vaguely, through a haze of liquor, that Evert wore much the same expression. A kind of hungry, yearning look.

He was blissfully unaware that every time he looked at Annabet his own face wore the identical expression.

Annabet went away, with a whisper of silk, and Evert pulled his chair closer and poured brandy into two glasses.

'Go steady, Evert,' he said, thinking of Kaerko and Gijs, and all he had to do to-morrow.

'I'll see you safely aboard,' Evert said amiably, and leaned back in his chair, planning his next move.

A lightness of touch was essential; he didn't want Piet's sympathy. Better begin by thanking him for having made the match, and then go on, 'And I'm the more indebted to you for taking the proposal so promptly because if I hadn't grabbed her just when it'd have been too late, wouldn't it?' That would start Piet's gossiping tongue and within a few minutes Evert would have what he wanted.

'You know,' he began, 'I never thanked you properly, Piet; but I hope you'll believe that I'm damned grateful for all you did. I often look at Annabet and think that but for you ... well, you know what I mean. We aren't the sort to make flowery speeches to one another, but if there's ever a chance for me to do anything for you, remember I'm in your debt.' That was good. The word 'debt' would lead on easily to the other thing he wanted to say.

'Aw, nonsense,' said Piet, twirling his wine-glass violently, and bringing his rust-coloured brows together in a frown. 'The boot was on the other leg.' He spoke sincerely. In his present

229

mellow mood he was capable of seeing Evert as an unrewarded benefactor. He had helped Piet in a matter of life and death; Piet had only done for him—and that with extreme reluctance —a thing which anyone else could have done equally well.

'I'm going to tell you something,' he said, leaning forward suddenly.

'Yes,' said Evert, carefully controlled. By Heaven Piet was going to blurt it out on his own accord. He wouldn't have to ask, even.

'Something you ought to know. Something secret. Might be useful to you.'

'Yes,' said Evert again.

'There's going to be a war. Here, in the islands.'

The colour went out of Evert's face and Piet heard his gasp of astonishment.

'Are you sure? How d'you know? Who told you?'

'I brought the stuff. Cannon, muskets, powder and shot. They mean it to be a surprise this time. They swore me to secrecy and everything was packed to look like something else. But Kaerko knows now, so does his Excellency. And I don't see why you shouldn't know too, Evert. In businesses a little bit of information in good time sometimes comes in handy.'

'By God, you're right,' said Evert. He had recovered his colour and his eyes were clear and steady. 'It's a bit sudden, but it was bound to come. Been brewing up ever since the Navigation Act.'

'The smuggling,' Piet corrected him.

'What smuggling?' Evert asked sharply.

'Out here. Oh, I know they don't admit it; always talking about the patrol boats and the care they take. But at the other end they make no bones about it. Why, just three weeks before I sailed this time a ship reached the port of London with nearly a million guildersworth on board. They knew in Amsterdam within three days, prices dropped so steeply. The English market dropped to nothing. The Company's been forced into action.'

'I'm glad you told me. This'll send the price up. Look, Piet, I'm going to act at once. I was sending in a consignment in the morning. Now I shan't. I'll hold it back and take advantage of the price later. And I'll split the profit with you, old man. I must go out, now. You go and talk to Annabet about Heydberg. Tell her I was called away for a few minutes. I won't be long.'

He stood up and drained his glass. Piet, glad that his bit of information had proved so immediately useful, sat back contented.

The house to which Evert hurried, stood by itself outside the

230

town of Banda Neira on the side opposite the Fort. At some time, not so long ago, geologically speaking, the piece of land upon which it was built had been submerged by the sea. Neither the wild jungle nor the nutmeg trees would grow upon it, and since the Dutch, with their ideals of at least superficial cleanliness had come to power in the island, the waste ground had been made into a rubbish dump. It was an offence to throw refuse elsewhere in Banda, and periodically a gang of coolies was sent down from the Fort with orders to set fire to the revolting heaps of refuse which had collected in this place. The refuse itself stank, and the fires which consumed it stank, if possible, more abominably. At the first sign of the blue smoke rising all the housewives in Banda closed their shutters, and even the coolie women in the nearest compound—Byskin's—shut their doors and hung mats over the unglazed opening that served their cabins for windows.

Between the town itself and the municipal rubbish heap a belt of shrubs had been planted, so that the place, though malodorous, might not be an eyesore. A winding path threaded its way through the bushes, and though in the early morning, and sometimes again just before sunset the path was populous, dotted by refuse carriers, the lowest of the house servants from the white people's houses, the oldest non-working members of the native families, each carrying a reeking load, at night it was deserted. Evert strode along boldly, taking out his handkerchief in order to have it ready to clap to his nose as soon as he emerged from the path into the open. Already a sourish, sweetish, smoky, altogether disgusting odour was borne upon the spicy night air.

Shal Ahmi's house, however, looked to seaward. Its one door and its single window looked out upon a strip of beach, deserted because between it and the deep water of the harbour ran a ridge of sharp and dangerous rocks, and because its hinterland was occupied by the refuse heaps. Further to the south, where the land grew fertile again, Byskin's plantation began, and Byskin's landing-stage ran out into the sea.

Despite its unsalubrious situation the little one-roomed house was perfectly clean, and the only scent in it came from the handfuls of mysterious herbs and other substances which the occupant flung upon his little charcoal brazier as soon as he had completed the cooking of his simple meals.

Shal Ahmi opened the door himself. He showed no surprise at seeing Evert upon his threshold, though, in the whole course of their long dealings Evert had visited the house only twice before. Most of their business had been transacted during apparently unplanned meetings upon the path to Coenpark, or in the seclusion of Evert's study.

231

'You save me a journey, Mynheer. I was about to visit you.'

He closed the door and Evert stood for the third time in the room which, for the third time, struck him as being more bleak and comfortless than any slave cabin in his compound.

The floor was of earth, hard-beaten and quite bare. Along one wall was a long wooden box, along the other a shelf upon which stood some neatly arranged pots and jars and bowls. In the centre of the floor was the charcoal brazier. It was not glowing, and the pungent, slightly astringent scent in the cabin suggested that Shal Ahmi had recently extinguished it with one of his handfuls of herbs. Presumably his clothes and his sleeping-mat were enclosed in the wooden box, presumably he slept, either upon its top or on the floor beside it.

Evert, passing into the enclosed space, became aware that he was out of breath. He had walked quickly after eating a heavy meal and had held his breath as he passed the rubbish heaps. He sat down heavily upon the box and opened his mouth and breathed deeply before he spoke.

'The prahau,' he said, after a moment. 'Has it gone?'

'It goes with the tide, Mynheer. Two hours yet.'

'Of course. I need not have hurried.' He breathed deeply again. 'It mustn't go to-night, Shal Ahmi. Apparently their suspicions were aroused by a bit of news the *Eastern Venture* brought in, and they're doubling the patrols. We mustn't take any risks. The load will keep until this activity dies down.'

'So,' said Shal Ahmi, dropping down upon his haunches. 'And thus the game ends.'

Evert, through whose mind the very words had been passing, looked startled.

'What d'you mean by that?'

'I told you, Mynheer. I was about to visit you. I had news ... not of doubled patrols, Mynheer. I was coming to ask your advice and assistance. You have often had mine.'

There was, for the first time in Evert's experience, a glimmer of expression upon the bland brown face. The light of the little brass oil lamp which stood on the shelf among the bowls and jars fell full upon Shal Ahmi's countenance, but the expression, though plain and noticeable, was unfathomable.

'What news have you had? What advice did you want?' It couldn't be that Shal Ahmi knew what Piet had whispered.

'Tell me first, Mynheer, why was it so urgent that the prahau should not sail to-night?'

'I told you. Didn't you hear me? They're doubling the patrol. Think of the risk.'

Shal Ahmi made a gesture with which Evert was familiar. He turned his hands, palms upwards, in his white lap and studied them closely.

'Mynheer, for many years now we have done business together; business of many kinds; for many years. I ask you to consider this, have I ever failed in discretion; ever betrayed your trust; ever uttered a word when I should have kept silent; ever grudged you the utmost service within my power to render? Answer those questions, Mynheer, and then tell me—why should the prahau not leave to-night?'

'I have already told you twice, Shal Ahmi,' said Evert, beginning to bluster.

'Twice you have lied to me, Mynheer. Unwittingly? One of the patrol boats is dragged ashore, being caulked. The other has not yet returned from its search at Tal Arin. What liar spoke to you of double patrols, Mynheer, when such a thing is impossible?'

'I had reliable information. My kinsman, in to-day on the *Eastern Venture*, and in the Agent's company all afternoon, told me that the smuggling was causing alarm in Holland, and that as a result of the orders he carried, patrols were to be doubled. I didn't ask any questions or test his information. I just hurried straight to you.'

'He forebore to mention that many extremely heavy pieces of furniture, bulky too, had lain in his forehold? Spinets, and harps in large wooden cases, to enliven the tedium of the ladies in the Fort. Boxes of great weight, labelled "Cooking Pots," and bundles of tools, wrapped in straw and sewn in sacking. Of these he said nothing?'

'He never mentioned such things.'

Shal Ahmi raised his eyes and looked at Evert in a way which made the big man strangely uncomfortable. Then he studied his hands again, saying in a gentle, reminiscent voice: 'Mynheer, it is many years now since the Dutch came to Banda, many years since I saw muskets in any number or cannon dismantled and carried ashore piece by piece. But so clear is my memory of those distant days that if the weapons of war were nailed into coffins, draped with flags, and followed by a hundred weeping mourners, I should not be deceived. The coolies believe that they carried tools and musical instruments and cooking-pots ashore this afternoon. But I know differently. Mynheer, war came to the islands to-day. And the moment has come when you and I must face our obligations.'

Evert had recovered from the shock of having been called a liar and contradicted by Shal Ahmi, and behind his cool level stare his brain was working smoothly and swiftly as was its habit in an emergency.

'Well,' he said jocularly, 'if you know so much, you know more than I did, and more than the man who carried the cargo ever suspected, I'll warrant. War, eh? That's serious. Where, I wonder. Against whom?'

233

'Mynheer,' said Shal Ahmi, rebukingly, 'you trifle with me still. You and I, who more than anyone else know in what way the Company has been offended, need not, surely, waste time in speculations as to the direction of its vengeance.'

The little flame of the oil lamp flickered and began to subside. Shal Ahmi rose silently and padded across to the shelf and replenished it. He did not sit down again. Folding his arms in his wide sleeves he stood and looked down at Evert.

'I was coming to you, Mynheer, to discuss this situation. The English in the islands have been our good friends. Now they are threatened. . . .'

'Well?'

Evert's cold, stubborn stare met Shal Ahmi's inscrutable one. For a moment neither man spoke. Then Shal Ahmi gave an almost imperceptible shrug of the shoulders.

'So,' he said, and there was a wealth of finality in the one small word, 'their gold has lined your pocket, their offences against your honourable Company have been directly aided and connived at by you. I have been your trusted associate and friend. But the first breath of war has fired all the Dutch blood in your veins, Mynheer. When I speak of obligations you pretend not to understand me.'

'I understand you.' Evert obeyed the impulse to stand up and take advantage of his greater height in order to look down upon the brown man. 'You're suggesting that now, because we have traded with them, we should warn them of an impending attack. And I tell you straight away that I wouldn't do it for anything in the world. Granted I've smuggled out nutmegs and thereby cheated the Company of some thousands of guilders—that doesn't make me a traitor. They were my nutmegs, produced on my land, by labour I'd paid for and supported. In a properly constituted business they'd have all been mine to sell in a free and open market for the best price I could command. But no, the Company must preserve its damned monopoly, fix the prices to suit itself, fix even the number of nuts to be produced in one year. Nobody but a gutless fool would lie down under such treatment without protest. Selling my surplus to the people who paid the best price was my protest against the monopoly. I squared that with my conscience before ever I started. But that's a very different thing from warning the English now. That'd be treason.'

He threw out the ugly word truculently, expecting argument. But Shal Ahmi, after regarding him thoughtfully for a second or two, nodded his head.

'I see, Mynheer. These little shades of difference are too subtle for me. But then I am not Dutch. As a man without a country I could hardly be expected to understand things like patriotism and treason. I admit that my first thought when I

234

made my discovery this afternoon was to take some steps to ensure the safety of those who have treated me well.'

'And haven't *we* treated you well?' Evert demanded. 'The English swine have paid for what they had—why? Because that was the only way to get what they wanted. Let me tell you, Shal Ahmi, that if you'd lived in an English island you wouldn't have had the liberty you've had here. They may pay a fair price for nutmegs, but they don't treat native people softly. You've no call to entertain sentimental feelings about *them*. Your allegiance is to the country upon whose soil you live, or, if it comes to that, to me, who put you in the way of making money easily, and to ... Kaerko who always treats you with civility and protects your liberty.'

'And to Captain Knoel who is always trying to put me into gaol without reason?'

'And never succeeds because the Dutch laws are so just and equitable. No, no, Shal Ahmi. Let the English take a good trouncing. We owe them nothing. They've had value for their money. We'll let Knoel pounce on them and wipe them out. They've served their purpose so far as you and I are concerned. And the ordinary price of nutmegs will jump with the firing of the first musket.'

'You have convinced me, Mynheer,' said Shal Ahmi, dropping his hands from his sleeves in a gesture of resignation, 'It now remains to cancel the prahau's orders and return its load. The English will all be dead before it could reach the market, and if the home prices rise ...'

'That's it, exactly.'

Shal Ahmi went to the shelf and lifted from it a square of ruby-coloured glass. He propped it upright upon the ledge of his window and stood the little lamp behind it. The prahaus carrying the contraband always set off from the desolate, dangerous strip of beach that fronted his house, and the boatman, coming down to make ready, could not fail to see the warning signal.

'That's settled then,' said Evert. He walked to the door and then turned suddenly. 'One thing more, Shal Ahmi. If the Company has gone to the lengths you describe in order to conceal their intention, they want the secret kept. You know, and you've told me, what was in those crates and bales. Don't tell anyone else.'

'How loudly the Dutch blood speaks, Mynheer. How quickly it forgets the old bonds and remembers only that I am brown and therefore suspect. But rest content. For that matter, to whom else could I say, with safety, what I know? No word shall pass my lips. Good night, Mynheer.'

'Good night, Shal Ahmi,' mumbled Evert from behind the protection of his handkerchief.

He walked swiftly until he was out of range of the effluvia of the refuse heaps, then he slackened his pace, and moved thoughtfully, almost indecisively.

Strange, it had never occurred to him to imagine that Shal Ahmi might regard the English other than as he did himself—as tools to be used, a source of profit to be exploited and then abandoned as soon as it ceased to be profitable. Nor had he imagined that any person, leave alone so intelligent a person as Shal Ahmi, could possibly confuse the ethics of a little smuggling in the face of a shockingly unjust monopoly and an act of downright treachery.

He broke a twig from a bush beside the path and walked along, slowly stripping off the leaves and tearing them into little shreds. The action helped him to think clearly.

Shal Ahmi knew what the Company evidently intended to keep secret for a time. He wished to pass on his information. He had allowed himself to appear to be argued out of the intention, but—and this no one in Banda knew better than Evert Haan—Shal Ahmi was a very devious creature. He had been supremely useful. If it had ever occurred to the Company to tackle the business of the smuggling at its root, and every native in the island had been put to the torture, with an idea of extracting information, not one, in an extremity of pain would have gasped out the name Evert Haan. Within the island Shal Ahmi had organised the business, made plans, issued orders, and paid out the piteously small rewards. Evert had made the original contact with the English and organised all the outside business. He had also handled all the money, receiving it from a French tavern-keeper in Bandogar who was content to exact his ten per cent. and ask no questions. Evert had also provided the one thing without which the business could not have even started—the precious nutmegs.

And that—Evert thought, reviewing the whole situation—had been growing increasingly difficult. Year by year the Company had grown more possessive, more inquisitive, more restrictive. Almost before the storehouses were cleared there was Kaerko with his papers, demanding the estimated prospect for the next consignment; and woe betide the planter if the actuality did not match the forecast. The Company knew just how many young trees were planted each year, how many of those no-longer-profitable ones were destroyed, and just when each young tree would come into full bearing. For years Evert's keeping of accounts had been a matter of juggling. Now it was over. He had made a great deal of money, had a great deal of excitement, and enjoyed to the full the reflection that the Company, which thought it was exploiting Evert Haan, was actually being exploited by him. Now it was over; and there remained only the problem of Shal Ahmi. If the old

236

brute succeeded in warning the English it would be because he had been Evert's associate in the smuggling; so Evert would feel responsible, and when Evert had pointed out the difference between smuggling and treachery he had spoken from his heart. Walking away and leaving Shal Ahmi in possession of that dangerous piece of knowledge made him acutely uncomfortable. Besides, Shal Ahmi had said several things that rankled.

He had also said, 'And to Captain Knoel who is always trying to put me in gaol without reason.' Knoel had certainly a deep-rooted prejudice against the man. Could it be used? Not easily. For obvious reasons he could not go and lodge a complaint, or mention his suspicions. Even if he could think of some accusation, he mustn't appear as the accuser. Shal Ahmi's guile was too deep, his vengeance too certain. But ... if only he could place Shal Ahmi in Knoel's keeping for a few days he would feel that he had done his country a service. And Evert was, in his own way, completely patriotic.

Quite suddenly a thought struck him. The idea it presented was so akin to the practical jokes he had played upon Piet long ago, that he burst out laughing. It was safe enough too. Because if anything went wrong before the culmination of the scheme he could easily say he was merely playing a joke on old Byskin.

Cornelius Byskin reared, as a hobby, the decorative white fowls of Cochin China. Evert, through Wang Fu, had actually procured for him the original cock and hen. Their progeny now lived in an enclosure at the end of Byskin's garden, and were quite as dear to him as any child could have been. He fed them himself, every morning after breakfast and again just before sunset. Every visitor of any consequence was solemnly taken along to visit the clean, freshly-sanded pen. Cornelis knew the strutting fluffy white puff-balls apart and could call each by its name. To praise his eggs, to admire his fowls was a sure way to the old man's heart.

They were tame, and used to their master's handling, and although when Evert reached into the roosting-place and withdrew the nearest fowl that came to hand, they squawked and shuffled a little, they made nothing like the outcry that the similar number of ordinary barnyard fowls would have made in like circumstances. Once over the wall again. Evert wrung the neck of his captive, inexpertly, but with a certain clumsy despatch and skill. He scattered a few of the distinctive white feathers in a trail leading back along the path towards the refuse heaps. At a turn in the path he dropped a few more. A veritable snowstorm of down littered the place where the path debouched into the desolate place; and then, holding his nose, he began to move cautiously back towards Shal Ahmi's house.

He approached it from the rear this time and dropped the half-denuded body of the dead fowl upon the edge of the rubbish dump nearest the blank back wall. It would look, he thought, as though Shal Ahmi, leaping ahead of his pursuers and certain at last of discovery, had thrown away his prize upon the last inch of safe, neutral ground.

Back in the Byskins' garden he reached into the roosting-place again, this time bent upon disturbing the fowls. He threw them roughly from their perches, flapped his handkerchief among them and made hissing snake-like noises. Once their lethargy and pampered confidence was overcome they screeched and squawked like mad. The cock, making a noise like an unoiled winch, launched himself at Evert's face and pecked at his eyes. Evert beat him off and retreated. As he leaped the wall again he heard sounds of a very similar commotion emerging from the house. Cornelis' voice, a little reedy now, but loud enough, was raised in furious shouting; his boys yelled; his dog barked. Evert, rubbing his hands with his handkerchief, sprinted back along the path towards Coen-park. He hadn't thought of the dog!

But old Byskin had seen the trail of feathers and had held the hound's nose to them for a second. The pursuit went off in the direction Evert had planned. Presently he slackened pace and wiped his hot face. Not a very clever plan, but it might, just possibly serve. Byskin would be vicious enough. The circumstantial evidence was there, and Knoel was not the man to give Shal Ahmi the benefit of the doubt. And anyway, he, Evert Haan, had done what he could.

With one of those sudden switches of his whole attention which had helped to make him so successful, he stopped thinking of the war and the English and Shal Ahmi, and reverted to Annabet and Piet. I never asked him what I meant to. No matter. I'll ask him to-morrow. A man can't think of two things at once.

After Evert had left him, Piet sat on in the dining-room. He had imagined that Evert would just step down to the sheds and lofts by the jetty, give an order, and walk back. Twenty minutes perhaps. He poured himself another glass of brandy and sipped it slowly, intending to make it last until Evert's return. But the reckless, greedy demon which walked in him after the first few drinks, was soon in full charge. He filled and emptied the glass again. Then he remembered that Evert had entrusted him with a message for Annabet; she would be sitting alone, wondering. And he was in no state to go and talk to a lady. But he must. He took another drink to give him courage, and then, after another period of desperate waiting during which he almost prayed for Evert's return, he rose, and

238

lurching, made his way into the drawing-room where Annabet sat with her embroidery.

Except for occasional glimpses of Vehmeer or old Byskin at the very end of dinner parties, she had never seen anyone drunk in quite that way before. Little Vehk—ah, poor little Vehk—had occasionally become excitable and talkative when he had taken wine, but it had made him seem like a gay little boy; Evert could drink great quantities of liquor, without changing his mood at all. He became either more good-humoured or more bad-tempered according to how he had been feeling before. But he was always Evert. This great stumbling man had changed altogether, and when, as he entered the room he said, 'Evert had to go out for a bit,' she wondered what she was going to talk to him about until Evert returned. Suppose he fell down, fell out of his chair. She'd heard of men doing that.

She gave no sign of her concern. With a smile as sweet and almost as false as Mevrouw's, she said, 'Then come and sit down, Captain Odshoorn, and tell me some more about Heydberg. How is your mother? I should have asked that before, but I was so engrossed in hearing about Klara.'

'My mother's very well,' said Piet carefully, lowering himself into a chair and fixing her with a disconcerting stare. 'I'm glad to see you looking so much better. I've had you very heavy on my mind all these months.' Even his blurred voice and set stare could not disguise the kindness of his tone and his eyes, and she realised that, except for Trudi Van Heem, it was a long time since anyone had looked at her with kindness.

'I hope you haven't been thinking about the things I said last time we met. I shouldn't have bothered you with my problems. I was just nervous ... and silly, you know.'

'And are you glad now that you came? It was my fault you know. I put the notion into Evert's head. But for me he'd not have heard of you. It was my fault you came here.'

'But I'm glad to be here, Captain Odshoorn. I got better here. I've been very fortunate. I'm extremely grateful to you for any part you had in bringing me here.'

I should never have met Christy; never known those few heavenly moments that were worth all the rest of life put together.

'Then why,' Piet asked savagely, putting into words the question that had been nagging at him for an hour, 'don't you look *happier*? Heaven knows I shouldn't ask you such a question, but I tell you, I feel responsible for you on account of what I said and did, though I tried to put that right, afterwards. But what I want to know, what's been bothering me all the time is this ... Is Evert good to you?'

'I don't think anybody could have been kinder.'

239

One couldn't say less. He'd arranged for Shal Ahmi to cure her. He'd been endlessly generous, attentive, affectionate. And if he had been all these things a little too late, if she had slipped into loving Christy at a moment when Evert had seemed to hate her, you couldn't really blame him for that. She'd been so very ugly; he'd been so very disappointed. And it might not have made any difference. However Evert had welcomed her, one glance at Christy. . . . So the fact that their relationship had been poisoned from the very outset wasn't Evert's fault. It was giving him less than his due to say that he had been kind.

'I'm very glad to hear that,' said Piet. 'You see, I never can make up my mind about Evert. Things that happened a long time ago make me inclined to think badly of him whenever I get half a chance. And you know, I used to sit in church the times I was home in Heydberg and sort of make plans for you. I never reckoned then that I'd open my big mouth when I was drunk and set Evert Haan to marrying you, and that's the truth. I'm a little drunk now, you know.' He added the last sentence in explanation.

She had a curious flashing feeling about destiny, gone before it could be crystallised into such a slow thing as a thought. Herself, going to church, cross because she must appear in such makeshift finery, and—purely on Father Vincent's account—resentful of the Protestant service. And somewhere, unseen and unnoticed this big man gathering up his impressions, and coming across the seas and getting drunk and talking about her, and Evert asking to marry her, so that she came here and saw Christy. . . . A curious sequence, leading where? Her young, romantic mind could provide only one answer. To Christy. Sooner or later, by some means or another, she and Christy would meet again and all would be well. Why else had she come to Banda?

'Please,' she said earnestly, 'whenever you think about it again remember that I am most extremely grateful and indebted to you.'

That was almost exactly what Evert had said too. But if she was glad to be here and Evert was glad to have her here, why did they both have that queer hungry look on their faces? Why didn't they look like Klara and young Mulder? God, he thought, if I'd had Evert's luck and married you, I'd want you to have that sleek shining look. I'd have . . . I'd have . . .

Even in his present drunken state he could dimly realise the danger of those thoughts. Not knowing what he might say next, he relapsed into silence. Afraid to look at her because of the wild thoughts that would come unbidden, he stared fixedly at the wall opposite him.

Annabet pushed her needle in and out and thought about

Klara, and love, and Christy. She wished that there were just one person to whom she might speak his name, sharpen his remembered image by a description of his features, relive those few short moments by meticulous recapitulation. She had the lover's impulse to talk about the loved one; the mere projection of the mental vision upon another mind gave it reality. But there was no one to whom the name might be spoken; absence and distance and silence had sealed Christy away, as though into a tomb, and with every passing day the journey which her mind must take to reach him seemed to increase.

Bowed over the silly bit of embroidery she felt hope shrink again, she looked ahead and saw life stretching away; thousands and thousands of days spent in trivial occupations; thousands of evenings spent in making precise, purposeless stitches; thousands of nights spent with Evert, pretending and pretending. . . .

Next day the silence was broken.

It began like every other day. She breakfasted with Evert. He took the meal early and seriously, and had more than once, in a genial moment, urged her to breakfast later, in bed, as a lady should. But she knew that he was pleased by her presence at the meal, and in her eagerness to mollify him in every possible way, had made it a rule to rise early.

Evert went by prahau into Banda Neira as soon as he had made his morning round. Acutely aware of his moods as she always was, she thought that he had seemed silent and preoccupied that morning, but he had come into the house again on his way to the landing-stage, had kissed her, and said that he would be home by five o'clock. When he had gone she went, as she usually did, into the garden, catching at the short time of early morning freshness, so soon to be lost in the scorching heat of the day. Hassan, the gardener, was already at work, busy with the interminable job of rooting out the fast-growing weeds from a border. As she came near he straightened himself and stood, nervously shifting his bare feet, nervously plucking a weed into shreds between his big, earth-soiled hands. She wondered if some precious plant had withered, some wild thing come into the garden and worked havoc, for as a rule the old man greeted her with a smile. They were on friendly terms by this time, and except when something had gone wrong and justly or unjustly he assumed the blame for it, their morning chat together was one of the most cheerful moments of the day.

'What's the matter, Hassan?' she asked, when she was close enough to see the flutter of his heart behind the prominent bones of his thin brown chest. He looked from side to side before he answered.

241

'Nothing, Mevrouw. In the garden, nothing. But I have a message for Mevrouw. Just a message. Mevrouw will please understand that I pass on what was told me. As I was bidden.' He looked at her with eyes in which terror showed plainly.

'All right, Hassan. You were told to give me a message. I understand. What is it?'

For no known reason her own heart had begun to flutter too.

Hassan looked right and left again, then, lowering his voice until it was the merest thread of sound, said:

'Shal Ahmi is in the gaol, Mevrouw. He sent you a message. It concerns a fighting-cock with a black tail and an Irish name, Mevrouw.'

'Yes, yes. I understand. Go on.'

'He has news of the bird. Also he is anxious about your health. If you would visit him, Mevrouw, and ask his advice upon your sickness, he would give that and also the news.'

'Is that all?'

'They are the words as they were given to me, Mevrouw.' The old man drew a deep, steadying breath. 'Mynheer is no friend to Shal Ahmi. That is known to Mevrouw? And eyes are everywhere.'

'I know. Thank you, Hassan. I will be very careful.'

She turned away and walked quickly back to the house. She was trembling with excitement and agitation. Shal Ahmi, in gaol of all places, had news of Christy. To get it, she must go to the gaol, and eyes were everywhere. Even Hassan had felt it necessary to warn her of that.

News. What could it be? Had Christy enlisted Shal Ahmi's help to arrange a meeting? Would there be a message for her? Why had Christy chosen Shal Ahmi whom he distrusted so profoundly? Was there some trick in it, and she too blind and excited to see it?

Speculations were just a waste of time. She must take the risk and go to the gaol at once. But she had been repeatedly forbidden to leave the house alone. Take Katje to the gaol? Take Katje into her confidence? Pretend to be seeking Shal Ahmi's aid for some complaint, as yet undisclosed to Evert. Oh no. The very idea was distasteful. Must get out of the house. Must get rid of Katje. Must get to the gaol. News. News of Christy.

Katje was dawdling about the bedroom. At the doorway Annabet steadied herself and forced her quivering lungs to take their fill of air.

'Katje, I want you to pack my yellow muslin with the slashed sleeves. Stuff the sleeves with paper and pack it carefully. Mevrouw Van Heem wants to take a pattern of it. We're going there this morning. You can help Nina with the cutting-

242

out and basting, while I talk to Mevrouw.'

Trudi Van Heem was friendly, and sensible. And her house was close to the Fort, though Van Heem's plantation lay on the other side of the island. Told some feasible story Trudi would keep Katje occupied and allow Annabet to slip away; and although Evert did not personally like Trudi, he approved of her as an associate for his wife. A sudden, spontaneous visit to her house would cause no comment.

'I was a fool ever to ask you for the pattern,' said Trudi, when the yellow dress and the pattern paper were laid out on the big dining-table. 'I shall look as broad as I'm long in a gown like that. But it was sweet of you, Annabet, to bring it, and to come yourself, and offer your girl to help. I do appreciate it.' She put her soft, warm fat arm around Annabet's neck and kissed her.

'I want you to do something for me in return,' said Annabet, trying to speak lightly. From a distance it had seemed a good idea to half-confide in Trudi and ask her help; but now, face to face with the woman, misgivings made themselves felt.

Trudi had been, from the very first, both friendly and gracious; but she could, at times, assume a frightening dignity, and at other times make remarks that were lacerating in their frankness. Suppose, when you had blurted out your request, she chose to be affronted by your assumption that she would lend countenance to deceit; or roundly told you what she thought of your folly; or, worst of all, sent for Evert and handed you over. But the risk must be taken. Shal Ahmi had news of Christy.

'Come along,' said Trudi Van Heem, slipping her arm through Annabet's. 'We'll leave the girls to their work. Now, what do you want me to do for you? Don't look so worried, child. If it's humanly possible I'll help you.' Her small bright eyes dwelt upon Annabet's face with a look of kindness mingled with intense curiosity. Homesick? Evert? Pregnant? Lover?

It was no use beating about the bush, Annabet thought. That would be just a waste of time. If Trudi would help she would help; if she refused no amount of pretty preparatory speeches would serve.

'It's just this. I want to consult Shal Ahmi. And he's in gaol. I've got to go there, and I don't want Katje to come with me. Do you mind if I go while I'm supposed to be with you? You know how Evert feels about Shal Ahmi.'

'It's about the only thing your husband and I have in common,' said Trudi brusquely. 'Is the rogue in gaol? I didn't know. I'm glad. I hope they keep him there. But that's all by the way. What do *you* want with that brown devil?' She saw the embarrassed colour mount in Annabet's face and jumped to her own conclusion. 'My dear,' she said earnestly, leaning forward and laying her hand on Annabet's knee, 'has somebody been telling you how to get a baby? Jehane Vehmeer, I'll be bound. Don't, I do beg of you, listen to her. Oh yes, I know it works. I know of two cases. But I know how it works, too. Nights of vigil at that old shrine of his, prayers and fastings and spell-binding. Then an opium dream, timed to coincide with a ship's arrival, and a drunken sailor earning two guilders very easily. There, now I've shocked you. But it's true, Annabet. As God's in His Heaven, that's the kind of thing Shal Ahmi does. I hate him. The sight of him makes me shudder. Don't you go near him, my dear. Have patience, and that husband of yours—let him have patience too.'

To lie to this kind earnest woman was horrible. But there was nothing else for it.

'It isn't that, Trudi. I'd, I'd like a baby of course, but I'm not worried about that *yet*. It's just my hair. I lost it all when I was ill, you know, and Shal Ahmi made some stuff that grew it again, very quickly. Now it's beginning to fall again.'

'But my dear child,' said Trudi, with her eyes on the thick, lustrous cascade of golden curls, 'that's not a thing to go pushing into the gaol to see *him* about. He'll be out in a day or two. He never stays more than a day or two. In and out like a hen on a nesting-box. Captain Knoel loathes him and is always trumping up charges against him, but nothing ever comes of it. Besides, do you really have faith in him? Don't you think your hair would have grown in any case? And don't you think it's falling again on account of the hot weather? To my mind, he's a charlatan. And dangerous.'

'Dangerous he may be. But he isn't a charlatan, Trudi. I don't like him. But he did do me good, in other ways besides my hair. And I do want to see him. You needn't feel responsible. It's only that Evert won't let me go out alone, and Katje sticks to me like a burr. If I could just go now, while she's busy and thinks I'm with you . . .'

'But, my dear child, you can't just walk up to the gaol and ask to see that old devil and think Evert won't know. It'd be all over Banda in fifteen minutes. Wait till he's free. And look, I've got some real rosemary water in my room. I'll give you some for your hair. I've found that a real help in the hot weather, it cools the scalp and strengthens the hair.'

'You're so kind. But, Trudi, I must see him. Nothing else . . .'

The stout little woman's kindly expression faded. Irritability brightened her eyes. And something else. Suspicion. Well, who could wonder, Annabet asked herself. Falling hair seemed such a trivial excuse for such obstinacy. Yet she had deliberately

244

chosen a frivolous reason for the consultation, feeling that the suggestion of anything more serious would provoke more earnest protest from Trudi's prejudices.

'I believe there's something behind all this,' said Trudi Van Heem with one of the devastating flashes of frankness which Evert found so intolerable. 'You're not a superstitious fool like Jehane Vehmeer. Come along, tell me. I'm your friend, am I not? Did that old devil treat you unbeknownst to Evert and then blackmail you? That's another of his tricks. Are you taking money to the gaol for him?'

Annabet felt dizzy. And all this time the news of Christy was waiting! She could have screamed with impatience.

'No, it isn't blackmail; it isn't money; it isn't anything to do with his spells; nor with my hair, if you must know. More than that I can't tell you. I'm sorry I ever mentioned the matter. I shall just order Katje to go home alone and go to the gaol by myself. If you think you ought to tell Evert, well, you must. I have to see Shal Ahmi, to-day, as soon as possible.'

Trudi was silent for a moment. Then she said:

'In that case you must wait until evening. The gaol is in the Fort, and from this door to the gate you would be seen by everybody in Banda. I'll send word to Evert that you are staying to dine here and he can come up and fetch you. At dusk, in cloaks and veils we might pass unnoticed.'

'You are . . . you will come with me?'

'Of course. I may not see eye to eye with Evert upon many subjects, but I agree with him about Shal Ahmi, and about your walking about alone. Now, shall we see how those two idle wenches are getting on?'

An interminable day to spend in futile speculations and plans. Attempt to slip away during Trudi's siesta? Take Trudi into full confidence? Abandon the attempt to reach Shal Ahmi to-day?

Trudi whose distrust of all natives was rooted upon an evil memory of childhood, was determined that, since her young innocent friend was determined to make the visit, it should be made under her own supervision; gently, inexorably, she circumvented every transparent ruse. Just before dusk she and Annabet left the house, ostensibly to take a little walk along the shore, leaving a message for Gert Van Heem, and for Evert if he should come with him, that they would be back within an hour.

By this time Annabet was resigned to failure, apathetic, almost dumb with resignation. If Trudi insisted upon accompanying her into the actual presence of Shal Ahmi she must bear the torture of being so near to the source of news and still not hear it. She must waste the precious interview in trivial, false talk. Trudi, she decided, could not be trusted fully; not because she was malicious, or likely to tell Evert, or for any of the more obvious reasons, but because her concern for Annabet's welfare would impel her to further argument and interference. And dimly she realised, now that it came to the point of making confidences, that this infatuation would not stand up to the test of facing Trudi's practical common-sense.

Once out of sight of her own house, Trudi whipped out two lengths of thin soft veiling, one grey, one blue. With their faces hidden, the two women turned through the rapidly deepening twilight and made for the Fort. Trudi seemed to know the way, avoiding the big guarded entrance and making for a side door. Annabet was content to follow, to stand aside, to remain silent; even glad that the ordeal of facing the Dutch sergeant who was on guard, of announcing the desire to see Shal Ahmi, of discreetly slipping the sweetening coin from palm to palm, had not been left to her to bear alone. But once they were actually inside the place, following the guard down the long, malodorous passage with cells on either side her resentment against Trudi quickened. At this point a true friend would have paused, have said, I'll wait here, you go on alone. But Trudi actually went ahead, directly behind the guard, until he paused at the furthermost door and drummed on the grill which composed its upper half with his knuckles.

'He sleeps all the time,' he explained genially. 'There you are, Mevrouw. I can't let him out, or you in, because I don't carry the cell keys. But you can ask him whatever it is you want to know.'

Almost indiscernible in the faint light, Shal Ahmi's dark face appeared behind the grill. Then, and only then, Trudi stepped back. Annabet, still undecided as to the exact nature of the 'secret' errand she must pretend had lain behind her feigned concern for her hair, stepped forward, and swallowing the stiffness in her throat, said in a low voice, 'Good evening, Shal Ahmi. I am Mevrouw Haan.'

'Ah yes,' he said, in his smooth thin voice. He looked, not at her, but at Trudi, lingering in the background, but well within earshot. 'Let me see, Mevrouw Haan. Forgive me, much has happened since you sought my help and advice . . . as you see, my own life has suffered some disturbance. But I recall it all now. Ah yes, Mevrouw, I used all my skill, and all my influence in an endeavour to trace the missing articles. But I failed. I am afraid that you must allow good sense to overrule your kind heart, Mevrouw, and tell your husband, and let justice take its course.'

'But justice is so harsh, Shal Ahmi. And the offender so young.'

'More hope of his benefiting by a sharp lesson, Mevrouw.

246

However, since your heart is still tender towards the rogue, there is one road on inquiry which might lead to results. I thought of it only this morning, after I was incarcerated here. Too late. If you would really rather take further trouble than hand over the matter to your husband I could outline what you should do. But I still hold to the opinion that you are too kind, Mevrouw.'

'I would do anything. Please tell me what you have in mind.'

He stepped back from the grilled door, and Annabet caught sight of his little charcoal brazier, dimly red, burning away in the far corner.

'Excuse me, Mevrouw. We prisoners cook our own food, and my supper is ready to stand aside to cool. That is well, for now I can sweeten this foetid air. Mevrouw, you force from me the remark that no other Dutch lady in Banda would visit this pest-hole, this plague spot with its lice and its stinks, in order to save a little thief from his just punishment. This in your honour, Mevrouw.' He took a handful of something and laid it on the glowing charcoal, and almost instantly there burst from the grill of the cell a thick cloud of vapour, pungent, stinging, choking. Annabet caught her breath and her eyes filled with water. Behind her Trudi began to cough like a cow with the husk.

'It is nothing; it will pass; it sweetens the air,' said Shal Ahmi, fanning the cloud past Annabet and into the passage.

'Mevrouw, if you intend to let your heart rule you the best thing to do ... dear me, this is really a little overpowering, even to me. I must, in the poor light have thrown on more than I thought. Quite stifling. I ask your forgiveness, Mevrouw. Does it make you feel faint?' He fanned energetically, and Trudi, turning to protest, took the cloud full in her face.

'I must ... get some ... air,' she gasped. 'Come, Annabet. This place ... was bad enough ... before.' She broke off in a paroxysm of coughing and spluttering. 'He shouldn't ... be allowed ... to bring ... his filth...' She turned and hurried, gasping along the passage. Out of range of Shal Ahmi's sweetener of the air she stopped, and leaning against the wall, mopped her streaming eyes. Foul old devil, she thought. How could Annabet *breathe*? But of course, by stepping backward, Annabet had escaped the full force of it, the draught seemed to carry the cloud along the passage. Well, anyway, it didn't matter. She had heard enough to rest assured that Annabet, bless her innocent little heart, wasn't playing with fire, seeking a love philtre, or a fertility charm. Just trying to protect a horrid little brown thief from Evert's just wrath. The innocence and the folly of her. She'd have something to say to her about native servants and their ways!

'Now, Mevrouw,' said Shal Ahmi, coming close to the grill and speaking rapidly, 'we must waste no more time. Your presence here speaks of your interest in the young Englishman whose life we saved. He is in danger again, great and deadly danger. I have here,' he fumbled among his crumpled white clothing and produced a folded paper, bound with red twine and sealed with great blobs of beeswax, 'a letter of warning. If you would take it, Mevrouw, and write upon the cover the man's real name and give it to Gariz to carry, you may save his life. You would wish to do that, I think. I regret that I must drag you into this business. But first, he did not entrust me with his name; and second, though I managed, on my way to the gaol to whisper a message to you, it is not possible for me to find a willing and reliable bearer of the letter. You will take it? Turn your back to the passage and lean towards me. It will pass unobserved.'

'But my husband ... he is the one the Englishman sought. He could act so much more quickly and freely. You see ...' she jerked her head backwards ... 'how I am placed.'

'Your husband,' said Shal Ahmi, 'has worked with me and the English. Now he is content to see them taken and murdered. I cannot explain. He has made his profit and does not mind if the patrol overtakes them. But I care, Mevrouw. And so do you, for the sake of the one man. I was not deceived, Mevrouw. I witnessed your parting. The Dutch take fierce vengeance. They torture before they kill. This paper, dispatched by Gariz the boatman who has the boats striped white and red will save the young man. The patrol, when it pounces, will find the English islands deserted, the victims flown. Turn your back, Mevrouw, and lean forward as though I gave you information. There. That is well. He will owe you his life again, Mevrouw. Such debts the gods are eager to honour.' He raised his voice. 'That is all I can suggest, Mevrouw. If it fails, you must let justice take its course.' Then suddenly the expression of the brown face, pressed against the grill, changed, from conspiratorial guile to something real and urgent. 'One thing more, Mevrouw, and now I speak from the heart. By all the signs there is unmistakable evidence that the Fire Mountain will shortly spout again. If it could be arranged it would be well for you to take a holiday. A little visit to Batavia, Mevrouw, while the earth shakes and the lava pours. Good night.' He turned abruptly and was lost in the gloom of his cell. The little brazier was extinguished.

Trudi, still a little breathless, pattered along the passage and took Annabet by the arm. 'Really, my dear, you're a bigger fool than I suspected. Making all that mystery and dragging me here to this foul place and getting half-choked yourself for the

248

sake of some wretched little thieving boy.'

Oh, Trudi, don't credit me with charitable motives. And don't chatter. I've got to send Christy away . . . away, I shan't ever know where.

'I know, Trudi. It is silly. That is why I didn't want anyone to know. But if I could get the things back . . .'

'Which you never will, my dear. And I'll wager that old devil could put his hand on them to-night. It's a curious thing, but he can always find a stolen article, provided enough pressure is brought to bear. He's done it often. There was one prime example. Did you ever hear about the unlimed nutmegs that were found aboard a ship, supposed to have been lost between Hoogenbeet and Vanderbosch . . . or the other way round, I forget. Kaerko told Gert about it, trying to prove how useful Shal Ahmi was. But I had quite another thought. I wouldn't be at all surprised if it were an attempt of his own to smuggle the nuts out. I wouldn't be at all surprised if he does half the smuggling that they make all this fuss about. What exactly did the little wretch steal?'

'Oh, nothing much.' Really, at the end of this racking day she could not be bothered to invent a list of articles. 'Just some stuff of Evert's. I wanted to get them back if I could and not have any trouble.'

'But, my dear, that's just the *worst* way. If they find that you shield them, they'll . . .' Trudi was off on one of her tirades against native behaviour. So long as that lasted, Annabet was free to think and plan. But very soon the spate of questions began again. How had Annabet traced the thief? How long ago was the theft committed? What steps had Shal Ahmi actually taken? With what results?

Suddenly Annabet thought—I know how to change the subject and make her quiet.

'Shal Ahmi did tell me something else,' she said brutally. 'He says the Fire Mountain will spout shortly. All the signs point that way.'

She had lived in Banda long enough to know that any inadvertent mention of the volcano would provoke silence in any gathering. The Fire Mountain, for those who lived within range of its fury, must be resolutely ignored, otherwise its terror would dominate the thoughts of everyone in its vicinity as inescapably as its physical presence dominated the land-scape. Now and then somebody careless would speak its name, often in tracking an elusive date . . . 'just before, or just after the last eruption.' And there would be a shocked silence before everyone within hearing shrugged away the memory and the fear as deliberately as they would have moved a source of physical discomfort. The Fire Mountain must be ignored. That was the only attitude which made life supportable in such a place.

The only signs which anyone in the islands accepted as significant were the favourable ones. These certainly were noted and commented upon with an interest and fervour which betrayed the hidden fear. Some of the signs were natural and possibly valid. It was good when trees and bushes grew high on the slopes of the mountain; better still when birds and monkeys were plentiful in its vicinity. Settlers would sometimes mention—at seasons when favourable signs made such conversation acceptable—how, six years ago, just before a frightful burst of activity, a man might walk all day about the foot of the mountain and see neither flitting bird nor chattering monkey. The trees and bushes had retreated too, and withered, as though by the gathering heat underground.

Other signs were purely superstitious. Pieter Verhoven and his forty companions, the original settlers, murdered long ago by the native Bandanese, were said to walk before an outbreak in the grove where they had been killed. They carried torches and sang songs of old Holland. And if three ships in succession put into port, each reporting the recent death of a man, that was a bad sign. Three ships with such reports had put in just before the outbreak of 1629, and another three before the memorable eruption two years later. The belief had gained such a hold that each captain, afraid of being the third to bear news of a man's death, and not wishing to forego a hearty welcome, would pop the dead man overboard and lessen the ship's pace.

Thoughts of these things went through Trudi's mind for a moment or two, while Annabet, with other things to think of, blessed the little interlude of silence. Then Trudi said sturdily, 'How should he know? All the signs are favourable this year.' As they walked the few remaining yards towards the house she recounted the good signs. Annabet did not listen. Good or bad, she could feel no concern with them. She must think out some way of conveying her message to Gariz; and then, in a few hours, Christy would be gone. The blank future which she had envisaged last night became actual, came close, became the present and engulfed her. Never until this moment had she realised how large a part hope had played even in her moods of despair and resignation. Always there had been a chance, frail, far-fetched, but still a possible chance that the unexpected, the almost incredible, might happen. Evert might die, or tire of her; and she knew where Christy was and how to reach him. Now that last, forlornest link was about to be broken. Gariz would carry a message out into the vast of blue water, and the glow which had rested upon that unknown island, Gadia, would fade. Christy would be lost; her mind, searching for him, would wander the whole world undirected.

250

She forced back the despair and the tears which the thought brought and tautened the arm which was still linked in Trudi's.

'Thank you so much for coming with me, Trudi. I'd have hated to have gone alone.'

'I only came from vulgar curiosity,' said Trudi.

Evert came back with Gert Van Heem, and the four sat down to dinner. Despite Trudi's efforts it was a more silent meal than the four usually shared. Evert was less easily provoked by Trudi's sallies than usual, and Annabet had reached that stage of mental exhaustion where she heard everything she said before she said it, analysed it and decided that it was not worth saying. Her inward agitation was not soothed by the sight of Evert in a thoughtful almost glum mood. It wasn't possible, it couldn't be possible, she told herself, that he had heard already of her visit to the gaol. Of course not; only a guilty conscience could suggest such a thing. But he was brooding over something.

However, though rather silent, he seemed amiable enough, and on the way home she was glad of his silence. Once inside the house she made an effort to banish her melancholy by thinking of practical things and was glad to find something which ought to be dealt with at once. Klara's wedding present.

'Evert,' she said, taking up the piece of embroidery which she had put down last evening when Evert returned, last evening which now seemed such ages ago, 'would you mind very much if I sent Klara some of my clothes for a wedding present? You give me so many, I don't need them all. And silk is very expensive at home.' Klara had never had nice things since she was old enough to appreciate them; and, loving her young farmer, wouldn't she rejoice to be seen in such shifts and petticoats and nightdresses as Annabet owned in such plenty.

Evert had poured himself a glass of schnapps and was sipping it with less than his usual enjoyment, almost absent-mindedly. Was it possible, she wondered, that he was secretly worried about the situation between the Dutch and his erstwhile partners?

'Do as you wish,' he said. His voice was genial, but lacked some of its usual bluffness. 'As a matter of fact, I'd been thinking about a present. I looked in on Wang Fu and ordered a set of things for a dressing-table. Silver. like yours, but plainer. More suitable for a farmhouse bedroom. Piet can take them back. They'll be ready at the end of the week.'

'Oh, Evert, how very kind. I wasn't thinking of anything so grand. She'll love them.'

But that wasn't true. Any woman who knew about being poor would know that the steel comb and the worn brush could

251

be concealed in a drawer, whereas drab and shabby under-clothes ... But a man wouldn't know; and obviously Evert had meant to make a spectacular and generous gesture. Still, he had said, 'Do as you wish,' so perhaps she could send the silk things as well; and though they would wear out in time the dressing-table set would last ... could even be sold if Klara ever found herself in need of more money than her husband could give her.

'It really is extremely generous of you, Evert. Such a gift to somebody you've never even seen.'

He looked at her and saw that she was genuinely moved by gratitude, and he thought of all the presents he had showered upon her, and of all the times when he had been disappointed, thinking that her reception of them had been cool and forced. His mind slipped away to the narrow, stuffy cabin of the *Eastern Venture* and the interview which he had forced upon Piet. But he must make some reply before he began to brood and remember and plan again. So he said:

'She's your sister. I'd like you to send her a present that was suitable.' Then he was silent again.

He had gone out to the ship at the end of the day and Piet had not seemed very pleased to see him, despite the fact that they had parted on friendly, indeed intimate terms, on the previous evening. Piet had recovered his senses as he grew sober again and was in the mood to regret his breach of the Company's confidence. But Evert was not to be deterred from his purpose. It had taken a few hours for his mind to absorb and accept the news about the imminence of war; but as soon as it had done so there had come to him, side by side with immense satisfaction that the cargo of contraband had been saved, the realisation that all this was Company's business, not Evert Haan's. And at once he had regretted that, startled by the news, he had rushed out to Shal Ahmi; and then, alarmed by Shal Ahmi's attitude, he had made his plot; and then he had gone home, found Piet maudlin and almost incapable and taken him back to his ship without broaching the subject which had regained its pre-eminence in his mind.

He stepped into Piet's cabin determined to rectify his mistake. And this time he would allow nothing to divert him.

'I've come to drink with you, for a change, old man,' he had said, in such a way that Piet, who had spent the hours of daylight in renewed vows of perpetual abstinence, was bound to bring out a bottle.

After his second glass—for a man must drink with his guest, particularly if the guest has been noticeably free with his liquor on previous occasions—the sharpest pangs of Piet's alcoholic remorse were deadened, and he could look at Evert without regret and even think that, had the warning not been given last night he would have spoken now.

'Well, one more, then I must be getting back,' said Evert, accepting an invitation which had not yet been given, and Piet filled the glasses again.

Evert began to work round to the speech he had prepared last night.

'You really thought Annabet looked well ... and happy, Piet?'

Piet remembered that Annabet had said that she was happy and that Evert was kind to her; that she had thanked him for having been the cause of her coming to Banda. You couldn't believe your own stupid drunken eyes against a lady's given word!

'Indeed I did. What's more, Evert, I asked her, as an old acquaintance, whether she was happy and she said she was. She thanked me for my part in the business. More than I deserved ... but I didn't go into that.' He gave a foolish laugh.

'Ah,' said Evert. He set down his glass and put his fingertips together while his eyes went meditatively to the porthole. 'I was lucky, thanks to you; and a good many people would think Annabet lucky too. The one I can't help being sorry for is that poor young sod she deserted. How did he take the business?'

Oh, admirable! Casual, gossipy, perfect.

'What poor young sod? Who d'you mean, Evert?'

'The name has slipped my mind, if I ever knew it. But you'd know it I reckon. I gather that he was very devoted.' He gave a falsely genial laugh. 'You know, I've always imagined him as a young sprig of nobility, afraid to take a wench without a dowry; but since this news of Klara, I've wondered. Probably another young Mulder lifting his head too high. Bad matches run in families. And I'll tell you something else, Piet, that'll make you grin—if he *is* a poor chap I'd like to send him some money, anonymously of course, enough to buy a cow or a horse. That's how sentimental marriage has made me.'

Piet knit his brows and ran his hand over his beard. The lure of gossip and a slight mystery, allied to three glasses of schnapps made him an ideal collaborator in Evert's scheme. He would have been quite prepared to tell what he knew had he known anything. But he didn't. He had never heard one word of scandal or rumour concerning Juffrouw Annabet, though Juffrouw Klara had been a rallying point of gossip for full two years more. And if there'd been any chatter his mother would have heard it, there wasn't a woman in all Heydberg with a keener eye, a sharper ear, a more daring imagination or a more retentive memory, especially for anything concerning the Van Goens.

'I don't believe there was anybody else,' he said firmly after five minutes' slow reflection. 'Mother'd have known, and she'd have told me, especially after you ... well after the young lady'd kind of become one of the family so to speak. I reckon you don't need to have any pining young chap on your conscience, Evert. Nobody special, that is. There was a dozen or so used to look at her with calves' eyes through the service. Like me!' He added the last words jocularly with a burst of schnapps-born laughter which ended abruptly like a severed string. Nothing to laugh about in that; the thing wasn't a joke any more. Not after last night, and the fight he'd had to keep his daft tongue quiet and his daft hands nailed to his knees.

Evert laughed too, accepting the joke. But he went back to the point stubbornly.

'All the same, there was somebody special. She as good as told me so once. I didn't pay much attention at the time, and it's not a matter I'd care to raise with her again—she's probably forgotten him now herself. But it stuck in my mind somehow, and I felt sorry for the chap. And last night, when you were talking about Klara and young Mulder, I thought, as I told you, that if it was a similar case I'd like to do what I could to make up.'

There you are again, Piet said to himself; who'd have suspected Evert of such sympathy and generous feeling? Not a man in a thousand would feel that way; more like to be jealous. No doubt about it, Evert was one of the best. Poor old Evert, worrying about a fellow who didn't exist. He wished he could put his mind at rest. And with the wish, inspiration came. He laughed and slapped his thigh.

'I've got it. By God, Evert, I know who she meant. But you needn't worry about taking her away from *him*. He couldn't have had her if there'd been no other man on earth. Not rightly, that is. Ha-ha, that's funny, you thinking about making up for his loss. The compensation will be paid in other coin than yours, old man, God forgive for joking about it. But it is a joke, all the same.'

He laughed while Evert looked at him with scarcely concealed impatient hatred. But Piet's tongue was loosed again, and he must hand over his information in his own long-winded way.

'Mevrouw was a Sieberg, wasn't she, from Brussels. Well, her sister had a boy, nice-looking, fair-haired boy, the image of the old Padroon. You'll remember that the old man's second daughter, the tall one, married her cousin, the Sieberg one, well that's her grandson I'm talking about, and you'll see that makes him first cousin to your Annabet. Jean-Marie they called him. He used to stay at Janshaven and later on at Heydberg. My mother used to grizzle and say that he looked hungry all the time he was there because Mevrouw starved him, having had only girls to feed. Egbert had gone by that time.'

'Yes,' said Evert, and with difficulty refrained from adding— get on, you garrulous blockhead.

'Well, maybe she did like him a lot; you know what the Van Goens are for marrying their cousins. And just now when I said "I've got it," I saw the whole thing clear. Their old Truitje told my mother that when your Annabet was ill and looked like dying she kept crying and asking for him. He was away in Spain or some such place, and it took weeks to get him, but he did come and he stayed, and she did get better. But bless your soul, you didn't take her away from him. He'd given her up getting on for ten years before that.'

'Why, had he married? What made them send for him then?' Evert asked sharply.

'Didn't I make that plain? Aw, what a bumble-footed fool I am with a yarn. He'd gone into the Church. He's a priest. They don't call him Jean-Marie any more. He's Father Vincent, all shaven and shorn. That's what she was talking about if she told you she'd had a fancy for somebody before. Cousin Jean-Marie. And from a girl's point of view he'd been as good as dead for years before you sent your proposal. *Now* d'you see why I laughed?'

'Of course,' said Evert, and laughed himself. For a few moments the cabin was filled with a strong Protestant savour. The two men elaborated the joke; Evert viciously, Piet with a hidden feeling that, this being concerned with Annabet, lovely Annabet who looked so unhappy when she was not smiling, he would regret later the things he now enjoyed saying.

'Well,' said Evert, ending the session, 'I don't worry about *him* any more.'

But the knowledge of the identity of the man who stood between him and complete possession of Annabet had not brought the relief which he had anticipated. Now that he had it he began to wonder why he had ever thought it worth so much bother and guile to obtain. The phantom now had a name, two names, in fact, with both Jean-Marie Sieberg and Father Vincent; and it had a face, the typical oval, fair-skinned, blue-eyed face which Evert loathed in the Van Goens and loved in Annabet Haan. And the phantom was a priest, tonsured, emasculate, ludicrous. And immune. Utterly, by virtue of his office, immune from the vengeance which Evert had planned as soon as he knew the man's name. His mind had toyed with many schemes. There was one delightful one. He had meant to ask Annabet, casually, if she had ever met So-and-So. She might say yes or no, but he would know the truth and proceed, with pretended reserves of delicacy, to tell her that the unfortunate young man had married and that his wife was moaning through four provinces about his impotence. That would surely have been enough to kill an infatuation. Last night, after hearing about Klara and young Mulder he had imagined that Annabet, too, might have lost her heart to a young farmer, and his mind had toyed with the notion of a nasty tale concerning a cow.

After all, he thought, defending himself from the attacks of what was left of his conscience, he was not supposed to know that a filthy report of somebody unknown could hurt her. Besides, she was a married woman now; and all married men agreed that though, in public, women must be shielded, their pretences at innocence and fastidiousness deferred to, within the privacy of the connubial chamber no subject was barred.

But now he was clever enough to see that no story of physical abnormality could suddenly, with a word, turn Annabet's mind from the phantom. A priest was a physical abnormality—to a woman; and this phantom had been a priest for years. There was nothing one could say about a priest which would not make him more human. The report of the grossest irregularity would merely bring the abnormal down into the plane of the normal and aggravate the position.

Walking home, eating his dinner, sitting opposite Annabet in the drawing-room, Evert understood, with a feeling of utter frustration, that, long ago, ten years ago, when she was only a child, all idea of physical contact must have been purged from her mind. In one thing, and only one, he had been right. And that was in seeing the unknown as a phantom; and as a barrier.

All these thoughts and memories and angers rushed through his mind during the moment which followed Annabet's words of gratitude. And with them ran the poignant realisation of how sweet she had looked with that warm, surprised, delighted expression on her face. No reserve, no barrier just then. If only it could always be like that!

His mood turned two wild somersaults. For one moment he wondered whether he hadn't imagined his own frustrations. After all, there wasn't a thing he could put his finger on and say with any truth ... there she has failed me ... or there. He couldn't honestly accuse her even of coldness. Wasn't his best plan to ignore the whole business and be thankful for what he had, a lovely, kind, acquiescent wife of the kind he had always wanted, dismissing everything else as the product of his own fancy.

Next moment he was philosophic. Well, suppose it wasn't all fancy; allow that in all their intercourse, even at the most intimate moments, she was looking beyond him, hankering. What was she hankering for? A priest, all shaven and shorn,

vowed to continence. Couldn't Evert Haan who had got everything he wanted out of life, afford to pity and smile. Poor
bastard, what good would Annabet's thoughts do him?

But in the next moment the real Evert came to the surface
again; the weathercock of his mind steadied and swung between the old fixed points of his hatred and his desires. The
egomania which had made the Janshaven farm boy fight his
way into the ranks of the nutmeg princes and eclipse them all,
forbade that he should now accept the second best. He wanted
Annabet, the whole Annabet, with no reserves and no evasions.
He'd never had that yet. But he must have it. Even at the risk
of losing what he had, the kindness, the affection, the gratitude, he must make a bid for all the rest. He would, by sheer
force of his will, root that damned priest out of her mind. And
that, he realised, with a suddenness which shook his heart a
little, would be, in a double sense, the triumph of Haan over
Van Goens. He saw, a little dimly, misted by the experiences
of their months together and his own changes of feeling, all
those plans he had made for this girl's humiliation and subjection. Somehow, for some reason which he did not clearly
know, not one of them had been put into action. If anything,
he had been the humiliated and subjected one. Now he would
put that right.

He looked at her again. The soft golden light of the lamp
made a halo of her hair as she bent over her embroidery.
Below it her face looked shadowy, delicate oval of cheek,
sweet sensitive mouth, long lashes fluttering over the down-
looking eyes. Mine, mine, Evert shouted to himself greedily,
all mine, it must be, it shall be, entirely mine.

He got up so abruptly that Annabet thought he had sighted a
mosquito or some crawling pest and had leaped to kill it. He
paused by her chair and laid his hand for a second on her
head, feeling the silkiness of her hair, the warmth of her
scalp.

'We'll send Klara the silver and as many silk things as you
like. But there's one thing we didn't do. We forgot to drink her
health. We'll do that now!' He looked down at her quite
fiercely.

'You'll risk a headache to drink you own sister's health, I
suppose.'

'Why, yes. Yes, Evert, of course.'

And I'll drink to Christy's safe escape and wish him well
wherever, wherever he goes.

Evert marched into the dining-room. He swallowed two
glasses of schnapps hastily and filled the glass again. Then
from its hiding-place he took the powder which Shal Ahmi
had given him and placed a generous pinch in the bottom of a
fresh glass. He thought for a moment and added another

portion. He filled the glass with Madeira and was annoyed to see that the liquid turned cloudy. But it cleared almost at once, and carrying the two brimming glasses he returned to Annabet.

'Well,' he said in a loud bluff voice, 'here's to your sister. I don't know her, but I admire her spirit. All for love and the world well lost, as they say.'

'I hope she'll be happy,' said Annabet, rising and raising her glass.

'If she loves him, she will.' Evert spoke aggressively.

'Oh, she loves him,' Annabet said, bursting into nervous chatter because Evert seemed so strange to-night. No harm, anyway, in telling it now, with Klara safely married and Mamma powerless. She told him the story of Klara's clandestine love-making; her own share in it; the escapade to Whitwater with its well-nigh tragic result.

The story, when she started it, had lain out clear and plain in her mind, like a road often travelled or a song often sung. But before the end her mind had clouded. Identities merged, and Klara, slinking out to meet the young farmer, had become Annabet slinking out to keep tryst with Christy. *Then* I didn't know how she felt, I wondered at her. I thought I knew about love because of the way I had felt about Jean-Marie; but of course I didn't. I never thought of Jean-Marie in that way at all. That was why I couldn't understand Klara. Now I do. And I am glad, glad, glad that I helped her. In my ignorance I helped her. Oh, if only there were someone to help me, now. If only someone would scheme and plan and lie so that I could say good-bye to him. Just good-bye.

Very hard, after a brimming glass of wine, to talk about one thing and think of another. Once, in saying *Klara*, she heard her tongue slip, the soft 'l' hardened, and she almost said *Christy*.

And Evert had been prepared to let Christy be killed by the patrol. Evert had been colder-hearted, less honourable than Shal Ahmi. Evert became a patriot as soon as his pocket was lined.

Evert is my husband, and presently we shall go upstairs.

'And that's where I got my rheumatic fever.'

'And Klara her husband. Well, well, what a story,' said Evert tolerantly. 'It's getting late and I must be early in the morning. Come along.'

The night seemed cool after the burning brightness of the day, yet enough of the swooning warmth remained to make covers unnecessary and clothes merely an adornment; inside the room was the stored scent of spices and flowers, outside only the soft rustling of the nutmeg leaves and the distance-hushed soughing of the sea.

And here, in the heart of the night was that closeness of

258

flesh, that mysterious sharing of feeling in a relationship so unique that, when the early Fathers sought for some way to illustrate the unity of Christ and His Church, they could find nothing better than the metaphor of the Groom and Bride.

Here are the two oddly-shaped collections of corporeal matter, recognisable to anybody as man and woman, known to their little world as Evert and Annabet, joined by the blessing of the Church, by the custom of the law, by their own recognition of their unity. And here are two minds, housed in heads which share a pillow, operating in brain cells which at the moment are only separated by two thin cases of contingent bone, yet so opposed, so irrevocably at odds with one another that even out upon the open common ground of speech they miss communion.

'D'you remember what you told me that night I came back from Bandogar?'

'Oh, Evert, need we go over all that again?'

'Well, *need* we? Not if you've changed your mind.'

Give in now; lie and surrender. Always before the truth has seemed vital and important, concerned in some mysterious fashion with the possibility of seeing Christy again; a bribe to God ... see, I am truthful when it would pay me to lie, reward me! Tell the lie now, boldly; it will make Evert happy and your life will be easier. But why should I wish him to be happy? He was willing to let the patrol pounce upon Christy unawares. Ah, but to you he has been kind; only this evening, over the matter of Klara's present, he startled you by his kindness.

'Does it matter so much? It didn't at first, Evert. You laughed when I told you.' Gain time to think. Think quickly.

'I'm not laughing now,' Evert said unnecessarily. 'I had to give you a chance. I took you for what you were, a raw young girl, with a head full of fancies. It's different now. Oh, I know we've been over this time and again, you always say you grudge me nothing; you're grateful; you're affectionate. What's that worth? What woman wouldn't be, treated as you are treated? There's hot blood in you, too. But it doesn't work for me. I'm not foxed. I can feel the change come over you. I know when I stop being myself. And I know how you feel afterwards. That surprises you, doesn't it?'

She was indeed surprised by his perspicacity into unguarded retort.

'Then why do you ask if I've changed?' She was ashamed of the sharp, bickering quality in her own voice.

'Because something has got to be done about it.'

'I'll do whatever you suggest, Evert.' She spoke meekly in an attempt to make amends for the sharp question a second since. But the acquiescence was genuine enough. At the beginning

259

she had almost hoped that Evert would send her away; had he done so she would have taken a chance with Gariz, gone to Gadia and said simply, 'Here I am if you want me; if not I'll go away.' But now there was no hovering halo of hopeful light over Gadia, and Gariz had gone on his errand and Christy was lost in the dark. Yet still, if Evert was dissatisfied, she would accept banishment. She was indifferent to what happened to her now.

Evert sensed the genuine, bleak acceptance of the statement and was silenced. His twin passions of wanting and hating made tumult in his mind. Some physical outlet became essential. He put his hands, large peasant's hands softened by years of easy living, round her throat. He could kill her so easily; it would have been an assuagement to kill her; an end of the thing that defied him. But it would have been bereavement too. Even as his fingers tightened a little he could see the years stretching ahead, with no Annabet, no conflict, nothing to hope for. In real agony of spirit he cried out:

'What's the matter with you? Why do you hanker for something you could never have? You must be crazy. Even if he hadn't been a priest what could he ever have given you that I haven't? I want you, he didn't; he chose God, didn't he? Doesn't that show what sort of husband he'd have made? Maybe he was your cousin, and maybe it's in your family to fall in love with your cousins, but you're too good to be caught up in that sort of old-fashioned jumble. He left you; I married you. Haven't I done everything a man could? Can't you forget him and love me, me, me?'

Talking to Piet Odshoorn. Poor Evert. Jealous of Jean-Marie, who, more than anyone else, had been instrumental in sending her here. It would have been funny if anything in the world had been funny just now. Jean-Marie, Father Vincent, with his talk about the flesh and the spirit which she had, finally, interpreted so capriciously. Jean-Marie; the flowering cherry; the green sunsets, God, and the cold stiff tulips.

There was no end, no escape. Christy was gone and all hope. Even her own mind was clouding and failing. The whole of the world and the whole of life was narrowing down to the physical nearness of this big, fleshy, heated man with his wrongly-directed jealousy and his insatiable demands. And now that nothing mattered to her, now that life held no hope what did honesty matter? Honesty was a tribute to one's self-respect. When one's self didn't matter any more . . .

'Do *you* love *me*, Evert?'

So many answers: 'Haven't I proved it?' 'How can I when you're engrossed with this self-made eunuch?' 'By God, I do, damn you, I do'—rushed into his mind that, choosing between them, he hesitated.

260

'I shouldn't have asked that,' she said penitently. 'I've never done anything to make you love me, have I?' Ah, but now she was speaking Evert's language, using the word as he understood it. The initiated knew that love could neither be bought nor exchanged nor willed; like the wind, it blew where it listed. 'But I will try again, Evert. It's all past and done with. I know now that I shall never see him again. And I will try to forget. I'll be a better wife, I swear I will.'

When I arrived I said I'd try to be a good wife; now I'm vowing to be better. Good, better, best, like the grammar books. But I'll never be a best wife, I'm lying at this moment; and cheating. What else can I do? This is the only thing left to me in the whole world; there's nothing else I can do with my life except try to make this man happy.

With Shal Ahmi's aphrodisiac at work, sharpening her senses and dimming her mind, the job seemed very easy. Only the small indestructible core of her spirit pressed out into the night: Oh, Christy, were are you now? I love you. Good-bye.

Some time during the next day the Governor's circular reached Coenpark. It demanded, in the name of the Company, that Mynheer Evert Haan, should forthwith send up to the Fort at Banda Neira, any number up to twenty of specially selected slaves. They were to be male, between the ages of twenty and thirty, physically sound, with good eyesight, not natives, nor descended of natives, nor married to natives of Banda, Lonthoir, Ay, Lu or any adjacent island. They were to be provided with food for one day, and before leaving Mynheer Haan was to make certain that each one understood the purpose of their call-up which was: The Company's standing forces in the island, having fallen below the level deemed necessary for safety and the keeping of order, one hundred recruits were being sought. Those of the slaves whose response to training and general demeanour rendered them most suitable for military life would be, at the end of a month, manumitted and enlisted. The accompanying pamphlet set out the conditions of service and the rates of compensation to be paid to the owners of the slaves thus removed from the plantations.

Evert, taking the papers from the hand of the smart young Lieutenant, suppressed a smile. Very clever, he thought. Had I not known I should not have guessed. Some such scheme was put into operation every second or third year; but ordinarily the number demanded never exceeded five, and the rate of compensation was always exactly based on the Bandogar market price. Now Knoel wanted twenty and the compensation was calculated to induce the planters to send their best men. Usually the recruiting station received those who, outwardly conforming to the letter of the demand, actually could well be spared; men, in fact, for whom the market price was unlikely to be obtainable elsewhere. There was one other difference. The paper setting out the rates of pay referred to Colonel, not Captain Knoel. And that in itself was significant. Quick, easy promotion was one of the fruits of war. And although the islands were still unaware of it, the Company had been at war with the English ever since that shipload of spices had reached London.

'Very well. I'll attend to it. I'll send my batch along in the morning.'

'The selection takes time, Mynheer,' the Lieutenant ventured. The least time any other planter had asked for this inspection of nationality, antecedents and matrimonial tangles, had been forty-eight hours.

'Oh, I know mine like the palm of my hand,' Evert said casually; and it was true. Some of his knowledge he owed to the fact that he was the Company's agent in the matter of purchasing slaves; a good deal more from his association with Shal Ahmi, who could look at a hundred new arrivals and divide them into racial, and religious groupings without hesitation and without error. Even that miserable, long-necked deformity whom Evert had taken as a 'make-weight' and the like of whom even the slave-dealer in Bandogar admitted never to have seen before, presented no puzzle to Shal Ahmi. 'Burmese,' he said, after a fleeting glance. 'She was stolen, doubtless, and much mourned.'

Also, in addition to his knowledge of his slaves, Evert had had at the back of his mind, the possibility of a call-up. The regular soldiers would be sent to attack the English strongholds and the new ones would, with a few of the others, serve to uphold the authority of the Company in the islands. He had already selected his men. The highly inflated rate of compensation would induce him to make a few rearrangements, that was all. The young Lieutenant, however, was much impressed, and being earnest and efficient himself, was pleased to observe that Mynheer Haan's reputation as the most successful planter in the islands, rested upon actual, imitable qualities.

And now how long before we are informed and taken into confidence, Evert wondered as he went to collect and address the men he had selected.

It was less than a fortnight.

Before the last load of nutmegs and the last cask of water had disappeared into the hold of the *Eastern Venture*, three little schooners, taking advantage of their shallower draw, sailed in and anchored between her and the quay. They were, Piet noticed with interest, in tip-top condition; all their paint was fresh, every inch of canvas, every thread of cordage about them was brand-new. The brasswork of their cannon—they carried three apiece—glistened in the sun. The Company's pennant fluttered at each masthead. Even if Piet had not had knowledge of the nature and significance of his late cargo he would have suspected something, for the schooners were of the kind reserved for work of important and imperative nature. The Company maintained nine of them; their headquarters were at Batavia, and they were used to carry messages which could not await the slower, regular service, or for the transport of important officials, the overhauling of suspected vessels, and, more rarely, as troop carriers. Never in all his experience had Piet seen three together anywhere out of Batavia, and never anywhere had he seen three all freshly fitted out. One of the little vessels lowered a boat and two white-clad officers were rowed rapidly across the narrow stretch of water. No doubt, Piet thought, they carried the final orders.

Later in the day he received a request which, politely framed, was nevertheless a command. Would he make it convenient to return by way of Java and carry back one of the officers who had brought the schooners to Banda? Despite the loss of time which the diversion would cause him, he was pleased. His time was the Company's; and he had friends in Batavia. He promptly ordered the emptying of the greater part of his water supply. It was stupid to carry water to a watering-place, and every few days made a difference to the state of the casks at the end of a journey.

On his last day in the island he went to dine, by invitation, with Evert and Annabet; and although the food had obviously been chosen with the greatest care and generosity as an offering to one who would, very shortly, be faring monotonously, there was very little to drink, which showed great thoughtfulness upon Evert's part. Piet, with his erratic faculty of observation unimpaired, thought that his half-brother seemed happier, to have regained the full measure of that blustering, overwhelming confidence and self-esteem which was either admirable or abominable according to whether you were liking him or hating him. Annabet was a little less animated : but that Piet put down, in his simple way, to reserve. He felt badly about it. She had welcomed him very warmly last time, and had been gay, full of chatter through the dinner. Then he had blurted out his tactless questions about her happiness and Evert's kindness, and after that, alarmed by the violence of his own emotions he had been obliged to feign a somnolence he did not feel. Naturally she thought him a lout. And yet, though he had dreaded this invitation and hoped that Evert would forget the sailing date of the *Eastern Venture*, he had looked forward to it too. Perfectly sober, in full possession of his senses, liking

Evert, who was so generous and hospitable and yet thoughtful, glad that he looked happy, envying him more than ever, hating him like hell and loving Annabet like a crazy man, he spent a mad, miserable, but delightful evening. When Annabet had left the table, Evert and he, over their single glass of wine, talked about the war, and about the schooners, agreeing that the secret had been well kept. The English would be taken completely by surprise. The whole thing would be over in a few hours. They talked as all men talk, all the world over, before the first shot is fired.

'But if—mind I'm only saying *if*—if it didn't turn out to be so easy, Evert. If they started to look up old soldiers, and so on. Have you made any plans? Have you made any use of my giving you the nod?'

'Indeed I have,' Evert said firmly. He was willing that Piet should go away happy about his breach of confidence. Piet was his friend. He had brought him Annabet; and he had given him the key to the knowledge which, used discreetly, had made a vital change in her. The last ten days had been the most triumphant (he meant the happiest) of his life. And it was all due to Piet. Useless to tell him now that the only use to which the information had been put was the saving of a cargo of smuggled nutmegs. And perhaps the strengthening of Evert's self-esteem—for it had been pleasant to be able to see so clearly through the Governor's discreet circular, and it had been pleasant to-day, when everyone else was speculating about the meaning of the schooners' arrival to hug one's secret knowledge. But towards avoiding military service in the case of the standing army's failure, Evert had made no move. His faith in his star was so strong that he would have welcomed, rather than feared, another call to arms. It would have offered him a further chance to distinguish himself. If anything, he was sorry that his age and his importance as a planter precluded his taking part in the actual physical assault. He would have enjoyed showing Knoel and the rest of them how Gomarus had waged war. He was, in fact, too vain, too much in love with life, too unimaginative, despite his artistic eye, to fear death or maiming. He would have plunged into a fight as confidently, as insensitively, as he had plunged into marriage.

'I won't waste your time by describing my precautions, Piet, but they're made. and they're watertight. I'm very grateful to you, old man. And as I said, if I make money on that withdrawal I spoke of, I'll remember you.'

They parted upon the warmest terms. And next morning Piet upanchored and sailed for Java. And in the afternoon Evert, with other planters all over the islands, was summoned to the Fort, ostensibly to take dinner with the Governor; actually to hear that within twenty-four hours the assault against the English in Gadia, Ay and Lu, would be launched.

The Governor was thin, dry, old, unsociable, acutely, but not unhappily, conscious of being nothing but a figurehead, the puppet of the remote Board of Directors in Amsterdam and of the more closely-revealed powers in Batavia. He knew, and he was aware that everyone in the islands knew, that Mynheer Kaerko, Colonel—he must remember not to call him Captain —Colonel Knoel, Mynheer Haan, and Mynheer Van Heem and probably half a dozen others were actually far more irreplaceable than he was himself. He knew nothing about business, nothing about soldiers, less than nothing about growing nutmegs. He was here in Banda, treated with respect, ostensibly deferred to because in the islands there were the Company's direct representatives, like Kaerko, the soldiers, represented by Colonel, *Colonel* Knoel, and the men who actually grew the nutmegs. Left to themselves each might think himself primarily important. So a Governor was appointed, a kind of perpetual weighing-machine, a thick blob of quietening oil cast upon the turmoil of the active waters. He had no illusions, no ambitions.

He gave his guests an indifferent dinner, nothing like the meal Kaerko or Knoel or Evert would have offered to him, and at the end of it he said in his dry, old voice, 'Gentlemen, doubtless you have guessed that there is something behind this gathering. Some of you know already, and the rest of you are still to be informed that the Company has decided to clear out the English. The operation can hardly be dignified by the name of war.' Knoel bridled like an insulted girl; he had been waiting for a war for six long years. 'The presence of the English on the islands of Gadia, Ay and Lu, constitutes a perpetual threat to our trade. I have been asked to call you together and explain the circumstances. The Company does not, for one instant, doubt your allegiance and your co-operation. Your own interests are at stake. But if any of you are sufficiently disinterested in·the matter of profits, I should like to point out to you that these Englishmen are serving the cause of that arch-traitor, Oliver Cromwell, who by his Navigation Acts has crippled our carrying trade. The legitimate King of England has been the guest of our native land. The men against whom we move to-morrow are traitors to their own land and the enemies of ours. They deserve no quarter. That is all I have to say. Colonel Knoel has, I believe, something to say to you.'

Knoel, with his wrinkled brown nutmeg face alight with fervour, rose as soon as the Governor ceased speaking. He was enjoying his moment. But his speech was practical and to the point. He explained that when the schooners sailed to-morrow there would be left in the islands only a few regular soldiers, the recently enlisted draft and the planters themselves. The one thing to beware of was trouble among the slaves. Almost a negligible matter, but one to be borne in mind. Apart from that the planters could rest with easy minds. The English intruders were unprepared, he and his men were fully ready; and what was more they had right on their side. There was no doubt of the issue.

He paused for a second after that comfortable assertion, and then, with a glance of cold disapproval, nicely-shaded by deference, towards the Governor, went on: 'Nevertheless, confident as we are of the issue, I think I should point out that to-morrow's business is not a game. I am only a simple soldier, but it seems to me that when men go out to fight, when muskets are loaded and cannon fired and swords drawn, that is war. And the men against whom we move are not to be discounted as fighters. As recent events in England have shown, they are a breed which can fight fiercely even among themselves, and many of the men in Gadia, Lu and Ay, are old Royalists, experienced fighters, hardened by defeat. They will know defeat again; but blood will be shed and men will be killed. If I may not call this war, I am at a loss for a name.'

The Governor realised, without any very definite emotion, that he had made another verbal error. With rather more interest he wondered whether he or Colonel Knoel were right about the political identity of the men in the islands. If they were, as Knoel had just asserted, Royalists, then surely some pressure, short of force of arms, could have been brought to bear upon them through Charles Stuart. Didn't it seem strange that he should be living in Holland, and his adherents should be making the lives of the Dutch officials in Banda a misery by their smuggling activities? Personally he did not believe in the anomaly. Whatever Knoel might say he would still believe that these English had been directly inspired by Cromwell. But he would not argue. He would accept both snub and contradiction with dignity.

Knoel went on, in even a crisper voice. 'Some of you gentlemen have lived in the islands longer than I have. I cannot speak to you out of greater experience. But I have studied my trade, and among the things I have read is Colonel Kraemer's own account of his campaign against the Moorish pirates in Sulaya, twenty-five years ago. During that campaign, gentlemen, he was obliged, no fewer than four times, to cease his operations against the enemy and return to quell disturbances at home. The campaign, planned to take a few weeks at most, lasted, on this account, for eighteen months. I am not anticipating a repetition of this catastrophe. Things are very different from what they were in Kraemer's time. But I do ask you, very solemnly, to be alert and wary. Overlook nothing, however trivial, that is at variance with the usual routine on your plantations. Lieutenant de Klerk,' he turned towards his subordinate, the smart young man who had presented Evert with the circular which called in the draft, 'Will be at the Fort ready for action at the slightest sign of trouble. And each of you, I know, has his own methods of keeping order. I do beg of you gentlemen not to call me and my men back from Gadia to save you from being burnt in your beds.' He sat down, smiling, but the thrust went home.

Evert, like every other planter at the table, began to reckon the number of men who could, in an emergency, be trusted. Unlike some of them, Hoogenbeet, for example, had turned greenish under his tan and Vanderbosch was picking nervously at his nails, Evert made his reckoning with all the confidence of his boisterous, sanguine temperament. Why, he and Josef, Toeg the foreman, and Hassan with a musket apiece could keep the whole mob at bay. It was like Knoel to make mountains out of molehills, exaggerating this trifling assault into a war, and the remote possibility of a little trouble on a plantation into a threat of mutiny.

Piet and the young naval officer talked about the war all the way to Java. There was no need for secrecy now and added to the delight of discussing the campaign as such, was the pleasure in talking openly of what had been a matter for brooding inwardly. The young officer was of a thoughtful, slightly pessimistic turn of mind. He distrusted, not wholly without reason, the ability of his immediate superior to whom the seafaring part of the expedition had been entrusted; and even more he doubted the wisdom of the Company in recalling him to Java and allowing his place to be taken by somebody from the Fort at Banda. So his favourite topic of conversation was the welfare of the schooners, and he conducted, for hours on end, a kind of nagging, fretting dissertation upon the little vessels' idiosyncracies and the peculiar perils of the islands' sea-roads. But occasionally he indulged in wider speculations. Sometimes he wondered, he said, whether the English were as unprepared as the Company imagined. 'After all,' he would say, 'they knew that some day or other we'd take action. They must have some defences. One cannon, say. Surely they'd have one cannon, Captain. Well, say they did. A cannon, properly mounted and skilfully handled, could sink one of those schooners. Look...'

He drew with his forefinger on the table and indicated exactly to Piet where a well-directed cannon ball could strike one of his little darlings with fatal results. His long, big-nosed face turned pale. He was, Piet thought, like a father who has left three beloved children in a dangerous place. He worried

267

until it became a habit; and the scope of his worry widened, like the ripple of a stone flung into a pond. It reached the matter of native risings.

'I had to read Kraemer's report of his campaign when I was training,' he said one evening. 'D'you know, as soon as the soldiers left the island the damned natives rose and carried bloody murder and fire through the whole place. Women and children slaughtered and burned in their beds. Suppose that happened again.'

Piet, who had listened with equanimity to his dire forebodings about the fate of his schooners, felt his heart turn over. Annabet, he thought. For a moment the whole of his big body was subjected to a wild prickling impulse which, if it could have miraculously been translated into action would have resulted in his flying through the air and landing bodily in the house at Coenpark with a pistol in either hand. Since action was impossible, he was forced, as all men are forced when faced with intolerable thought, to argue it down.

'Nonsense,' he said sharply. 'There hasn't been a rising in Banda since Coen rooted out the last of the native strongholds. The coolies there are noted for their good behaviour.' He saw that the young officer was staring at him; and, not knowing that he had spoken violently, put the surprise in the stare down to his listener's wonder at his knowledge. 'I know,' he said more quietly, 'because a kinsman of mine is one of the biggest perkiniers in Banda. I've talked to him. And there's another thing to remember. There are no real Bandanese. All the slaves and servants in Banda are of mixed blood and mixed religions. . . .' Where had he heard somebody saying that? Oh, on the night when he'd been arrested. The sallow-faced fellow had spoken at some length on the subject. 'It stands to reason, doesn't it? Years ago, as soon as the soldiers withdrew the natives revolted. Why? Because they wanted to get their own lands back. Only natural. But that couldn't happen in Banda because there aren't any Bandanese left. And you know how tribal these chaps are; they wouldn't all mob together simply because they were all brown. They've got no common . . . aims; no . . . no . . . rallying ground.'

He ended with his familiar fumble for words. He knew what he wanted to make the young man understand, but the actual expressions seemed to dodge his tongue.

'That may be true,' the officer said, nodding his head sagely. 'I hope to God it is. But there's a fellow at Headquarters who's making a study of these things.' He hesitated, and then with a frown of anxiety and concentration on his face, plunged on. 'Actually the Board commissioned him to make a report about native labour and conditions as a reply to some of the tales that have been getting about. I gather that some of the shareholders had a fit of conscience. . . . Well, this chap's report will put them at their ease. But that wasn't the point, some of the things he turned out were very surprising and interesting, and didn't go into the report. As I said, he's a friend of mine and we often have an argument over what he shall include and what he shall leave out. That's all by the way. The point I'm thinking of now is this . . . All the Bandanese didn't get killed, and they didn't all get away to Banda Elat and Banda Elu as most people believe. A whole lot of women ended up in Java, and it is a fact that a great number of them got sent back to Banda, when the plantations started again, as slaves.' His eyes narrowed. 'That seems to me a pretty brutal thing . . . but then I'm one of those who think Coen was a brute. Maybe I shouldn't say that; maybe he's a hero of yours.' He hesitated again.

'He's just a name to me,' Piet said truthfully. 'I'm no scholar you know.' The young man looked surprised again, and Piet added, 'Seems to me only scholars care whether a dead man did good or evil. He subdued Banda for the Company, and so I go to Banda for nutmegs. That's all Coen, alive or dead, means to me. See? But go on with what you were saying.'

'Well, those women married, or had children, anyway. And probably the children don't count as Bandanese. But don't you think that they might be dangerous. Now. If you look back, sir,' he gracefully paid verbal tribute to Piet's seniority in years, 'wasn't it your mother who put most of your ideas into your head? Not your father. Have you noticed that most men imitate their father's behaviour, but tend to think like their mothers?'

Even Piet recognised the profundity of this simple observation. Damned true. He could prove it by himself. And by Evert. They were both, in size and shape, Jakob Kressle's sons; they smoked and drank and whored after his fashion; but their minds were their mother's. Sophe Odshoorn liked the Van Goens; so did her son. Jannetje Haan had hated them; and her son had hated them until he had married one. Oh, in a thousand things you could see the truth of the young man's words.

'That's one of the truest things I've ever heard,' he announced. 'It makes you think. It bears looking into. It'd make people think twice about who they married.'

'Well, bearing that in mind, wouldn't you think it very likely that there's more . . . how shall I put it . . . national feeling among those mixed-looking chaps in Banda, than there might seem to be?'

Piet's heart turned over again.

'But I take it they know what they're doing,' he said, putting up a feeble defence against his own thoughts. 'If my kinsman is a fair sample, the planters are pretty wide awake. I mean to

269

say, if you and me can see the danger, surely they will too, and be on their guard.'

Oh, Evert, use your head now, and all your cunning; be alert for Annabet's sake.

'Oh well, there's no use worrying,' said the young officer, using his favourite phrase, the favourite phrase of all congenital worriers. 'There may be news in Batavia. These prahaus, skirting the coast-lines and doing short relay trips, travel very quickly. Or, if things went really wrong they'd send a schooner back. *Greta*'s the fastest of the three; she'd move landward of us all the way and could be in Batavia now, this minute. If anything went really wrong they'd send *Greta* back for help.' He seemed to take comfort from the thought of the beloved schooner's speed. Then his brow darkened. 'Unless of course the English have rigged that cannon,' he said gloomily.

From that moment Piet did not draw a completely easy breath, taste anything he ate, or think a comfortable thought. Over and over again he saw Annabet with her gown and her long hair afire; he saw her with her throat cut; he saw her raped. The whole business of the war, which had been at first merely a secret to be kept, and then a secret to be confided—in order that Evert might wriggle out of any connection with it—became suddenly the most urgent and personal problem of his life. It was he who was directly responsible for taking Annabet to Banda; and this consciousness of responsibility, which had hitherto been mild, semi-romantic, concerned with a man's behaviour and a woman's happiness, now became savage and practical, concerned with wounds and pain and danger and life and death, things which Piet's mind understood.

The crowded lively harbour of the capital presented a picture from which one would have thought it difficult for any man to pick out, instantly, any particular detail; but the young naval officer, eagerly leaning out over the rail of the *Eastern Venture*, had a lover's eye. His cry, 'There she is. There's the *Greta*,' was compounded of relief and anxiety and triumph. At least the beloved schooner was safe and sound; but her presence here implied ill news from Banda; and he had been right in saying that she could outsail the big East Indiaman. Piet could share in one emotion only. The six words fell like lead upon his spirit. Bad news from Banda. Bad news. What news? What news? How bad?

The young man, politely trying to conceal his impatience, made his adieux. 'I'll get your fellow to wait,' he said, moving towards the boat which was just about to be lowered, 'and I'll send you word how things are.'

'—— you will,' Piet said roughly. 'I'm coming with you.'

The young man looked at him, startled, and saw that, just above the line where the golden growth of beard began, an edging of dirty pallor showed on the broad tanned face. Of course, he thought, tolerantly, he spoke of a kinsman in Banda; naturally he's anxious. He said with an attempt at lightness which sat uneasily upon him:

'Don't attach too much importance to her being here, sir. Maybe the whole thing was over in half a day, and she's brought the good news.'

'Don't talk bloody rot,' said Piet. 'We both know what it means.' He dropped into the boat.

'I know where to get the news, that's one comfort,' said the young officer, leaping shore and starting to run. Piet lumbered after him, across the quay, round a corner, down a narrow cut between two warehouses and in at a little low doorway. They clattered up a flight of dirty wooden stairs and burst into a small room, with a wide, inkstained counter dividing it into two. Behind the counter on the far side, another young naval officer, with his cuffs pushed back nearly to his elbows, his fair hair in wild disarray and a smear of ink on his forehead, sat hunched on a high stool, laboriously scribbling away with a squeaky quill.

'For God's sake . . .' he exclaimed irritably, finishing a line at great speed. Then he looked up. 'Why, Hein! You. Stand there a minute, don't speak. I thought you were some swine come for the copies. I won't . . .' He ducked his head and scribbled madly, threw down the quill, dashed sand over the wet ink, and then, suddenly leisurely, read through what he had written. Bundling the papers together he opened a little hatch in the further wall and pushed them through. 'Take them along,' he said, and slammed the hatch. 'Why, oh why did I join the Navy?' he said lugubriously, smoothing his hair with inky fingers. 'Six copies in half an hour. It isn't human. What they want is a writing machine.' He turned a brilliant sunny smile upon his friend, and Piet. 'It's good to see you again.'

'What about *Greta*? When'd she get in? What news?' Hein asked abruptly.

'About an hour ago. That's what all the hurry was about. She brought a report from Colonel Knoel; and somebody thought it would be a good idea to send a copy of it home. Some damned ship was expected to put in to-day for a few minutes. They don't care if I get hunchbacked and blind.'

'What was in the report?'

'Oh, nasty news, as usual. Knoel's wounded, but he wrote the report himself and it made me squint-eyed to read it. They went to Lu first, found it deserted, went on to Gadia, found that deserted too, proceeded to Ay and found that apparently deserted; and then hell broke loose apparently. The English swine had got platforms in trees and fired down, and pits in the ground and fired up; they'd got God knows how many

271

cannon, all hidden in bushes. They sank the *Margarete* and hit the *Sanje*. They cut the two landing parties to pieces. And when poor old Knoel got back to Banda, somebody'd started a little private fire and all the powder magazines had blown up. Write that out six times in half an hour and see if it doesn't make you dizzy!' he smiled disarmingly and rattled on.

'Looks as though you'll take *Greta* back, Hein, my lad. Poor old Albert lost half a hand—pity it wasn't half his head, I'll say it for you, you heartless rogue—and thought he'd rather go to hospital here than in Banda. Who wouldn't? And Van Holk is going to take Knoel's place. He didn't say how bad he was, but judging by his scrawl he's dead by now. They're going to cram fifty men on the *Greta* and send her back immediately, *Seabird* will follow with a hundred. Now is there anything else I can tell you and your friend? If not, you'd better skip. This is the very core and centre of our great administration; everything that goes on in this sanctum is very, very secret. I'll see you before you go, Hein, if you go.' He smiled, hopped on to his stool again and drew another sheaf of papers towards him.

'I'd better report at once, if I'm expected to take *Greta* back,' said Hein soberly, turning to the door.

'So had I,' said Piet, wooden-lipped. 'I reckon mine's the ship they want to take back that report. This is a bad business.'

'No worse than I expected, really. Thank God I got back in time. I'd have hated to hand *Greta* over again.'

Oh you and your *Greta*, Piet thought furiously, can't you see beyond your long nose!

They parted casually, each preoccupied with his own thoughts, at the mouth of the passage, and Piet hurried along to the Agent's office. The sunny street was filled with a crowd of chattering, jostling people. Piet hated them all because either they had not heard the news from Banda, or were undismayed by it. All right for them, snug in the centre of things, he thought; giddy, frivolous, like that young fool upstairs. If they'd left somebody ... somebody very ... somebody very ... somebody that they cared about in Banda. Oh God, two landing parties cut to pieces, that means practically all the standing force. And the powder magazines blown! And all the things gloomy young Hein had said about native Bandanese. ...

The Agent was frivolous and uncaring, too. He had sent out to the *Eastern Venture* for Piet, and now complimented him upon the promptness of his appearance.

'We want a report carried,' he explained, offering a chair and thrusting a glass of Marsala into his hand. 'It's bad news from Banda to-day, but a bad start is a good augury in any campaign. And it won't do the Directors any harm to realise that we have our difficulties out here. Make yourself comfortable, Captain Odshoorn. I won't keep you long. The report should be here any minute.'

The Agent's office seemed as busy as a street. Men came in and out. And here, within the circle of the initiate, Banda was on every man's tongue. Some came in search of news, others, already informed, came to discuss it. The general tone was lighthearted. Obviously Knoel had bungled the thing. The English would find what they had tackled when Van Holk set about them. He should have been sent in the first place; it was silly to play about with such an affair, even when victory looked certain; mustn't let anything interfere with the nutmegs.

One stout, and to Piet's mind, very over-dressed gentleman, did express a more pessimistic view. 'I don't like the look of it,' he said. 'It was supposed to be a strict secret, but by all accounts the English had got wind of it. How? That's what I want to know. It looks to me as though there'd been a leakage. After all, somebody's smuggled out nutmegs. Maybe information travelled the same road.'

Eventually somebody bustled in importantly and handed over one of the copies which Piet had seen in the making a few moments earlier. The Agent read it through, made some trifling alteration in the punctuation, enclosed it in a bundle of papers which he had ready and sealed the cover.

'These were to go by the *Indian Star*, but they'll get there a fortnight sooner if you take them. She'll carry better news, I hope.'

Piet took the bundle and put it into his inside pocket. He set down the glass which he was surprised to find empty, for he had no memory of drinking the wine. He found his hand being shaken; heard his voice replying to the Agent's good wishes for the voyage. Then he was in the street again, alone with his thoughts.

He tried to make them rational. He told himself that every woman in Banda was in equal danger with Annabet, and that every woman in the island had been taken there through somebody's agency. If anyone were to be blamed for Annabet's presence there, it was Evert. He himself had opposed the idea from the very beginning. A man couldn't be held responsible for a few words, spoken in jest, when he was drunk. But logic and common sense could not soothe the frenzied anxiety of his spirit or lighten the sense of heavy responsibility which lay on his heart. In a few moments now he would be on his way to the West. Not another breath of news from Banda would reach him for six months at the very least. Six months of this suspense. I can't bear it, he said simply, I can't bear it.

His stomach had sickened as the frivolous young man had given the gist of Knoel's report; now he found that the single innocuous glass of Marsala had turned to acid in his throat and lay sour and uneasy behind his collar-bone. As he stood looking across the crowded harbour, picking out his own ship and looking at her for the first time in his life without fondness, he belched violently, and some low level of his mind, immune from the anxiety, noted dispassionately that what he needed was a glass of schnapps. The door of a tavern, invitingly open upon a shadowy interior suggestive of coolness, was close at hand. Thrusting aside resolutions and scruples he entered.

The first measure eased the sour discomfort in his chest, but did nothing to disperse the agony in his mind. He contemplated ordering a second, but discarded the idea. Drinking wouldn't help. If he soaked in schnapps until he was unconscious his last thought would be of Annabet and the dangers around her. If he got roaring drunk he'd ... he knew what he'd do. He'd turn the damned ship back to Banda. The *Eastern Venture* was a peaceable trading vessel, but she was no negligible fighting craft. A good crew ... do anything he told them ... pistols ... cutlasses ... and the cannon. Aw, that's what he'd do if he were drunk. So he mustn't get drunk. By Heaven, did he need to get drunk?

He was stunned by the daring and the violence of his thought. He stumbled out of the tavern and stood again in the blinding sunshine, shaking his head a little, like a man pestered by a cloud of insects. Gradually his face hardened. The healthy colour seemed to drain out of it. All expression—even bewilderment—deserted his eyes. Slowly, like a man walking in his sleep, he turned towards the place where his boat waited. Behind the set, wooden, doomed, mask of his face, a tide of half-petulant tears came pressing. What a way to go downhill, when the climb had been so long and arduous.

Not lightly are the loyalties and disciplines of twenty-five years discarded.

BOOK FOUR

ANNABET had gone down to the quay with Evert to see the schooners set sail. Evert insisted upon it. He had been strangely excited during these last few days, boisterous and noisy to an extent which sometimes threatened to undermine his dignity. Was it, she wondered, that the midnight scene had pleased him, set his mind at rest, restored his pride? Or was that too personal, too feminine a view to take? Were his high spirits actually due to the nervous excitement which radiates from the prospect of war as heat radiates from a fire? On the morning when the expedition set out she inclined to the latter view, for almost every man and woman upon the quayside seemed to share in Evert's mood. Annabet, immune from the contagion by virtue of her secret knowledge, was an interested spectator at a scene the like of which she had never witnessed before. The planters, the merchants and their wives usually conducted themselves with an almost oppressive dignity; easy living, the absence of any mental stimuli, a relaxing climate and intermittent bouts of fever combined to make all the white people in Banda slothful, slow-spoken, ponderous. Part of Evert's charm for his fellows lay in the fact that with his greater resistance to circumstances he had retained a healthy vigour and bluster which would have passed unnoticed in his native Holland. But this morning they were all Everts; the women waved flags and flung flowers; the men slapped one another's backs, shook hands vigorously, threw up their hats and cheered lustily. And doubtless, Annabet thought, to anyone who did not know that the English islands had been left to the jungle, the monkey and the birds for a full fortnight, the scene was a stirring one. Knoel's miniature army was smartly turned out and well equipped; brown and white, the men bore themselves well; and the new draft, with its stiffening of trained soldiers, did vast credit to its fortnight's training. The inexpert eye could not have told which group was about to embark, and which was to turn back for holding duty at the Fort, as, with fife and drum at its head, the brightly-coloured column wound down to the shore.

Annabet thought comfortably—and they'll all come back. No ghastly wounds; no dead. Does anyone else know that? She scanned the faces about her. Here and there a woman wept, furtively, or openly; here and there a man looked serious. But there was no sign that anyone else knew the thing for a farce,

275

a concerted action whose reason had been quietly cancelled. Shal Ahmi? But he was not there. Gariz? She could not identify him apart from his painted prahaus. Did he know the import of the message he had taken?

'Lu to-day; Gadia to-morrow; Ay the day after,' a man shouted in her ear. Oh, thank God that Christy had told her how to find him; thank God that she had enough credulity to believe Shal Ahmi's story of the impending arrests. Suppose she were now as ignorant as all these laughing, flower-flinging, weeping women were ignorant. What unthinkable torment, what agony of mind she would have been enduring now.

Trudi Van Heem threaded her way though the crowd and put her plump warm arm through Annabet's.

'Come up and visit with me. You'll be tired with standing, and I can do with your company.'

This morning, between the downward beating light of the sunshine and the upcast glare from the sparkling water, Trudi's wide plump face looked grey; and the corner of one of her heavily-lidded eyes twitched regularly, a little beating pulse. She was conscious of it for she laid a finger against it as she talked.

'I'd like to do that,' said Annabet. 'I'll just tell Evert.'

They walked up to Trudi's house, past the little Hindu temple, deserted at this hour, with its images, its little dishes of rice, its wilted flowers and bits of rag in the forecourt. Walking like this with Trudi reminded Annabet of their visit to the gaol. Only a fortnight ago; yet the whole of life had undergone a subtle change in the short time. There had been the public announcement of the war and her own dazed realisation of the fact that Shal Ahmi had lied to her and used her. But she had quickly resigned herself to that thought. If it were good for Christy and his fellows to run from a mere arresting party, how much better that they should escape from a serious war.

The other difference which the fortnight had brought was in the relationship between herself and Evert. Evert was happy now and content. Perhaps rightly so. For the moment when she had realised that there was nothing left in life for her but to be Evert's wife had coloured the whole of her attitude towards him. Not that she did anything now which she had refrained from doing before, not that she had altered her behaviour in any way; but her spirit no longer looked beyond the bounds of Coenpark for happiness. Evert knew the difference.

She was aware, when she stood in the hall of the Van Heem house that she had spent the walk in silent thought, utterly undisturbed by Trudi, usually so garrulous. And that grey tinge under her sallowness; and that poor twitching eye which made one's own try to flicker in sympathy. Was Trudi ill?

As they took off their hats and loosened their damp flattened hair, she asked gently, 'Are you feeling quite well, Trudi? Was standing in the sun too much for you? Would you like to lie down?'

'God forbid. I'm glad to be up. I didn't sleep last night, that's all.' She put her finger to the twitch again. For a moment she stood still, staring, blankly at the wall; then she roused herself.

'We'll have some tea, shall we?'

She rang the bell and the house-boy, an elderly Chinese, appeared. He came in very quietly, and Trudi gave a kind of startled jerk, and swallowed audibly before she gave the order. Is she ill? Annabet wondered. Or has she had bad news? Has she found out about her husband's coloured girl that Evert thinks such a joke? I'd have expected her to be either angry, or quite humorously indifferent about that. Ought I to ask what is the matter? She asked me up for company, perhaps she wants to talk to me but is too shy to start. But could one imagine Trudi being shy?

The tea came, and Trudi lifted the pot and put it down again.

'You pour, dear. I'd only spill it.' She held her right hand out straight before her and Annabet saw that it was shaking with a steady, rhythmical vibration, not exactly a tremor, more like the form of palsy seen sometimes in the heads of very old people.

'Trudi, something is wrong with you. Has anything happened? Would you like to tell me about it? Is there anything I can do?'

Trudi stared at her for a moment, and then, horribly, her face crumpled, she put her hands over it and began to cry.

'I'm a coward,' she said in a voice of the bitterest self-contempt. 'I'm a coward, and I'm frightened out of my wits.'

'What of, Trudi? What's frightened you?'

Trudi did not answer. She drew a long shuddering breath and checked her sobs. She took a handkerchief out of her sleeve and dabbed at her face. There were queer dusky patches on her cheeks and forehead. Her humorous long-lipped mouth was loose and tremulous.

Annabet turned towards the tea-tray and poured a cup, hot and strong.

'This will help,' she said. 'Shall I hold it for you?'

Trudi nodded. She gulped at the liquid like a child, her loose lips wet and slippery, her eye twitching, her face blubbered with tears. Repulsive ... no, you must not think that. A woman who was kind to you, now in need of kindness.

'I'm sorry, Annabet,' Trudi said at last, pushing the cup aside and dabbing at her face again. 'I didn't want to frighten *you*. But I have to pretend in front of Gert. I don't want him to despise me. But sometimes I feel as though I must give way or go utterly mad.'

'You can give way with me, Trudi. Tell me what is wrong. Even if I can't do anything it may make you feel better to tell me.'

'It's just that I'm frightened. You see, I was here ... at least not here, in Lonthoir, when Kraemer went to Sulaya. It was just like this morning, Annabet. The flags and the flowers and the cheering ... it might have been the same morning all over again. And then ... you know what happened.'

Annabet nodded. There had been enough talk during the last fortnight of Kraemer and his unfortunate campaign to make her familiar with the story.

'It'll happen again,' said Trudi.

Despite herself, Annabet felt a cold prickle run along her spine and lift her hair.

'Oh no, Trudi. Things are so different now ...' She repeated, with all the confidence she could muster, the things she had heard Evert and other men say; neat little arguments about the contentedness and placidity of the coolies; their mixed nationalities and religions; their lack of leadership.

'But don't you see! That's what they said then. Gert says these things. All men say them. My father said them. I was twelve, Annabet. I can remember everything about that day. It began just like this one. And at night my sister and I—she was eight—were allowed to stay up to dinner, to celebrate, to mark the occasion. I heard my father saying those very things, and then men who dined with us said them too. To comfort my mother who was nervous. In twenty-four hours my father was dead. They cut off his hands before they flung his body in the fire. My mother was stabbed to death, but first ... Oh, it's too horrible to talk about.'

She put out her unsteady hand and snatched up the tea-cup. It shook so that a thin yellow stream slopped over her chin and on to the bosom of her gown.

'When I first heard about the war,' she went on in a slightly calmer voice, 'I wanted to go away. I wanted, oh, I know it sounds crazy, but I wanted to ask you and Rita Byskin to come with me to Batavia. I spoke to Gert and he laughed at me. At least, not laughed exactly, but he said things about running away and how it would look, and how there'd never be any spread of civilisation or any nutmegs grown or any trading posts or anything if people ran away. And why should three go and the rest stay, he asked. There isn't any answer. Except that my nerve is broken. I saw things so awful ... just like the worst kind of hell you can imagine.'

'You poor little thing,' said Annabet, speaking across the years to the small frightened child Trudi had been. Had been?

Rather was still. The years had added layer upon layer of fleshy growth, of wealth, of dignity and experience around the core of Trudi's being, but beneath them all cowered the frightened child, haunted by her nightmare memories.

'Oh, I was lucky, if being saved was lucky,' said Trudi bitterly. 'We had a Chinese houseboy. My father had bought him in Bandogar from a very cruel master who was trying to teach him acrobatic tricks. He was faithful and grateful. He carried me and my sister out of the house in a sack. Literally in a sack. All the natives who weren't killing and raping the whites were carrying off loot, so nobody noticed. The screams, Annabet. I hear them in nightmares still. There's one particular . . .'

'And afterwards, what happened to you afterwards?' Annabet asked quickly, trying to forestall that glazed look of horror.

'Afterwards? Oh, we got away in a prahau. To Java eventually.' For a moment the terror upon Trudi's mottled face was replaced with a sly, cautious look. Then with a gesture of her shaking hands that implied that nothing mattered any more, she said, 'We were orphans and penniless. The Company adopted us and sent us to school. And when we were sixteen they sent us East again. I'm a Company's Daughter. Nobody knows that in Banda, except Gert, of course.'

Even at that moment Annabet was conscious of surprise. Everybody had heard of the Company's Daughters, that sentimentally-named practically-exploited body of girls, raw human material of one of the Company's schemes for keeping men contented in the East Indies and for ensuring the continuity of the white race there. They were mostly girls of poor, or unknown origin, orphans, some of them picked up in the gutters, slums and stews of the ports and cities, given a little education, some smattering of social training and then despatched to marry any planter, merchant or clerk who had failed to provide himself with a wife. At a time when unrest and uncertainty in the islands had made it unlikely that any woman with an alternative to choose would want to go there, the scheme had had its advantages. Some of the marriages had turned out well and happily. But there had been scandals too. As the plantations became settled and marriage with a 'nutmeg prince' a thing to seek after rather than to avoid, the Company had adopted no more Daughters. There must have been, among the women in the islands, several who had been shipped out, like slaves or cattle, under the scheme; but Annabet had never heard of one until Trudi Van Heem, the most respected, the worst-feared woman in Banda, made her startling announcement. And nobody in Banda gave more clearly the impression of sound Dutch background and gracious upbringing. But then, her father had been a planter. More than any of them, perhaps, she was at home. That thought begot another.

'Didn't you hate coming back? Wasn't it rather cruel of them to send you?'

'I loathed and dreaded the idea.' Trudi's voice was harsh with remembered torment. 'I can't tell you what I suffered when they told me where I was bound for. I begged and prayed to be allowed to stay. I would have scrubbed floors in the Orphanage, done the meanest, hardest work all my life if only they'd let me stay. For the last six months there they kept me in the kitchen always, for fear I should say something that would frighten the others. Not that I would have. And once I tried to run away.... But, you see, they'd spent money on us. We were trade goods.' She paused, and then said in a softer voice, 'I was lucky to get Gert. He's been a very good husband to me. He laughs at me about my feeling against the natives, but he understands ... or at least he's humoured me. He found me Nina, because I couldn't bear a brown face in my bedroom; and all our boys indoors are Chinese. I don't like them either, really, which is very unfair. I can't help it. They remind me of Ho, and that night.' She shuddered. 'Not that I need anything to remind me. Even at home, where I was safe and never saw a brown face, I had those dreadful dreams.' She closed her eyes and two tears squeezed out and ran down her cheeks. 'I shouldn't talk to you like this. It's vile of me. Don't despise me too much.'

Suddenly Annabet knew the right thing to say. Why hadn't she thought of it before?

'Trudi, the past is over. You've outlived that, haven't you? What worries you now is the thought that it might happen again. To-day. Darling, I can assure you that Colonel Knoel isn't going to repeat Kraemer's campaign.'

'That's just what he will do. This morning was a ... an echo.'

'But I know something about this war that nobody else in Banda knows, Trudi. If you could promise not to ask me how I know, or to tell anybody what I tell you, I would tell you something that would make you feel a great deal happier.'

'What could you know about the war, Annabet? But tell me, tell me. I promise not to say anything, or to ask you questions.'

'Well ... I just happen to know that the soldiers and Colonel Knoel will come straight back home. Because the English have gone away from the islands. So there won't be time for anything to happen. Here, I mean. There, does that make you feel better?'

'It would if I could believe it, Annabet. But I don't see how you could know. I mean, dear, if anybody else knew, well, the men wouldn't have set out this morning. Have you been listening to compound gossip?'

'No. It's genuine fact, Trudi. They left a fortnight ago.'

'Then, my dear girl, if you have by some means got hold of a secret ... no, no. I'm not asking how you did it, but having done so, why in the name of wonder didn't you tell Colonel Knoel?'

'I don't know,' Annabet said slowly. 'I've thought about it a lot. For one thing, I doubt whether he'd have believed me— you don't quite believe me now, do you? And I couldn't give a soldier news like that without saying whence I had it myself. And that I couldn't tell. It was, it is, very awkward. Besides, it hasn't done the soldiers any harm. Going prepared to find an enemy and finding nothing isn't like expecting nothing and finding an enemy, is it? They'll just come home, all safe and sound.'

It was the first time she had put the argument into words, but the words had run along a well-worn groove in her brain. Night after night, ever since she had learnt that it was war, not arrests which had been planned and circumvented, she had debated the ethics of her position.

'The optimists,' Trudi said, 'were reckoning Lu to-day, Gadia to-morrow, and Ay the day after. If they did find Lu deserted they could easily reach Gadia to-day too. Then Ay to-morrow, with no fighting. Good Heavens, with any luck they could be back to-morrow afternoon.' She looked at Annabet with an expression which told how much she would have liked to believe her, how nearly, in fact, she did believe her, and yet how wide a gap lay between nearly and quite. But the news had brought her some relief; her skin was resuming something of its natural smooth sallowness, her eyes brightened, the twitch was less apparent. As the two women stared at one another, Annabet saw curiosity and speculation seep into Trudi's expression. But she could not resent it; who wouldn't be curious and full of speculations offered such news in such a way?

Trudi, less leaden-footed, went across to a bureau which stood between two windows, opened a drawer, and took out a map. 'I don't know,' she said meditatively, spanning a distance between her finger and thumb and then measuring it on the scale at the bottom. 'It is just possible, if the wind were right, and you were right about there not being any fighting, they might even be back to-night. Oh, Annabet, if only you could be right. If only I could go to bed to-night knowing that the soldiers were back in the Fort, how happy I should be. D'you know, when Gert built this house I chose the site. I wanted to be near the Fort. Our plantations lie on the other side, and it's often been inconvenient for Gert to live here. On the other hand, he doesn't have a journey into town, does he? So it works out.'

She laid the map back in the drawer, closed it, and moved to the left-hand window. Annabet, watching, saw her eyes go to the great black structure at the top of the artificially heightened mound. It was ugly from every point of view, stark and angular, with the grey dusty drill-ground sloping before it, and all sign of vegetation pruned away. But Trudi was looking at it with love.

'I know the Colonel's rooms,' she said, over her shoulder. 'I shall look out, to-night and to-morrow, to see if they are lighted.... Oh, Annabet, you have cheered me. I still can't quite believe, but I can hope now.' Her whole body stiffened suddenly, and she said in a different voice, 'Annabet, come here. Is that smoke?'

Annabet hurried across and stood shoulder to shoulder with her hostess. The window gave a full, foursquare view of the Fort, and little else, but by standing at the side and craning one's neck one could also see a portion of the town, the white and pink and yellow houses with the hyacinth blue of the harbour behind them.

She looked at the Fort, and then at as much of the town as was visible. She could see no smoke.

'Where, Trudi? Where d'you mean?'

'Straight ahead. Low on the Fort wall. That sticking-out piece at the foot. Yes, it's the gaol. Can you see it now? There ... now you can. It's blazing.' As she spoke, Annabet, to whom the drift of smoke had been invisible against the black bulk of the main building, saw the red and yellow spears of the flame shoot upwards.

'Oh yes, I see it now,' she said. Trudi Van Heem swung away from the window, blindly grasping at the back of a chair for support. Her face was ashen; her white lips parted as she panted. Annabet moved forward to support her, to help her into the chair, but she shook herself free. 'The door,' she gasped. 'Lock it. Lock it.' Better humour her; she was beyond reason; almost dead of terror. Annabet turned the key in the door. As she did so Trudi stumbled to the window and tugged at the long white shutters. Her breathing was rapid and noisy.

'I'll close them,' Annabet said, and ran across the room. Before she fastened the shutter she looked out and saw the Van Heem gardener placidly taking the dead heads from the roses.

'It really is nothing, Trudi,' she said. 'There's your gardener at work just as usual. And the fire is out now. Yes, they're taking away the buckets. It was just an accident. They cook their own food in gaol, don't they? On those ricketty little charcoal stoves. Probably one overturned.' As she spoke she

282

saw a thin streak of fire, like a comet, race across the drill-ground before the Fort and dart downhill, towards the town. What was that? Was she wrong, and Trudi right? Was something queer afoot? As though in answer there came a short sharp rattle of musket fire, ping, ping, ping. Hastily she closed the shutter and the room was dimmed, lighted only by the thin lines of sunlight which stole in at the tops and bottoms of the long windows and the place where the halves of the shutters met.

'That was shooting,' Trudi panted. 'Now was I right?'

'It still could be nothing, Trudi. Perhaps in the confusion of the fire a prisoner got away.'

'I want to move this chest in front of the door,' said Trudi, refusing to be comforted. She staggered over to a great Chinese lacquered chest which stood against the wall, six feet or more from the doorway.

'I don't think we could move it,' said Annabet, running to help her. For answer Trudi heaved with all her might and the chest moved about six inches. Darkness made the room seem abnormally hot, and by the time the heavy object was pushed and pulled athwart the doorway, Annabet was sweating and almost as breathless as Trudi.

'Now Gert might get here with help before they could break in,' Trudi said. 'If he hasn't been killed first.' She sank into a chair and fought for breath for a moment, and then said, in a small, calm voice that was more frightening than hysteria:

'I've just remembered. In my dreams it's always this room. The worst, the most dreadful thing, always happens in this room. And now I am here and I daren't move to leave it.'

'Darling, I'm sure nothing is going to happen. It's just that you've had this awful experience, and I've had no experience at all, so we've taken fright at nothing and locked ourselves in. The men will laugh at us!' The abject misery and fright upon Trudi's face did not lighten. Annabet tried again.

'You've never dreamed of being frightened in this room with me here, have you? So that shows. If you believe in your dreams, Trudi.' That was an argument on a level within the frightened creature's present reach.

'No. That's true. That's very true, Annabet. Oh, I am so glad you're here. If ever we get out of this . . . Listen.'

A fresh burst of musket fire, this time from the direction of the town. 'Oh, my God,' said Trudi Van Heem, almost soundlessly.

Was the town ablaze?

'Trudi, I'm just going to open one shutter a tiny crack and have a peep. I want to see if your gardener is still there. It gives me confidence to see him.'

'Be careful. For God's sake be careful,' said Trudi. But she got out of her chair and went with Annabet towards the window, and took hold of the shutter's edge, wary, frightened, ready to slam it home at a second's notice.

The old man was still at work. Craning her neck. Annabet looked beyond him, sideways, at the town. Yes, a great cloud of smoke now hung over the houses, blotting out the line of the sea. Despite the comforting evidence of the gardener's placid plodding figure something was wrong in Banda. She was just about to close the shutter again to hide the smoke pall from Trudi when she saw a little boy, naked save for a strip of loincloth, vault the gate and come flying towards the house. He bore every sign of having urgent news.

'There's a little boy,' she said, over her shoulder. 'I should think he has a message.'

'Telling them to start here,' said Trudi instantly. 'Close the shutter.' She tried to push Annabet's hands from the shutter with her own shaking ones.

At that moment the front-door bell emitted a jangling peal. Trudi started violently and gripped Annabet by the wrist.

'It's only the little boy I told you I could see, Trudi. He has got a message.'

The muted sound of voices came from the hall; then there was a tap on the door, the handle was tried and the tap was repeated.

'Don't speak. Don't answer. It's a trick,' Trudi whispered.

Annabet began to feel that the position was ridiculous. Not entirely immune from fear herself, she was reasonable enough to have taken courage from the sight of the gardener working, the little boy vaulting the gate, from the ordinary mundane sound of the door bell, the tapping at the inner door. Her patience with Trudi's fears frayed slightly.

'If we don't answer,' she whispered back, 'they'll be justified in breaking down the door to see what has happened.'

'Mevrouw,' said a voice from the other side of the door. And the handle was tried again. Annabet rose and walked over to the door. The great chest prevented her getting very near it, but she leaned forward and called.

'The door has stuck. Something wrong with the handle. What is it you want?'

'Mevrouw, I can't open the door.'

'No. It's stuck. What do you want?' she shouted.

'Mevrouw, is anything the matter?'

'This is ridiculous,' she said, and turned to look at Trudi who sat shaking in her chair, not at all comforted by this comic and mundane conversation between two people separated by a thick teak door and a great Chinese chest.

'I'll go out by the window and talk to them,' Annabet said.

'For God's sake don't. That's what they want you to do. It's a trick. That bell was a sign.'

'Trudi, don't be silly. It was the little boy.'

'Little boys don't come to the front door. Annabet, don't open that window. You don't know ... you couldn't believe how treacherous they are.'

'You can shut it behind me. Trudi they will break in in a minute. Your boy sounded really concerned.'

Trudi got up and clutched at Annabet with shaking, impotent hands. Annabet, pushing her off, thought irrelevantly, she's mad; I'm the one who should be frightened, locked in here with a mad woman. She opened one half of the shutter, pushed open the window behind it, and stepped through the narrow opening into the garden. To the last moment Trudi had followed her, clutching, imploring, past coherent speech, mouthing, gibbering. The garden was full of drifting smoke and the acrid scent of burning. From the window it looked as though the whole of Banda were ablaze. Trudi, as Annabet stepped out of the window, caught sight of the smoke, smelt the old nightmare scent of unleased fire. She slammed the shutter with a scream. Annabet heard the bar fall into place.

She hurried round the side of the house. The little boy, breathing deeply, stood on the top step. He began to gabble as she came in sight. 'Just a minute,' she said, and went into the cool wide hall. Trudi's house-boy was on his knees, trying to look through the keyhole of the drawing-room door, tapping and calling as he knelt. She touched him on the shoulder and he jumped up, startled.

'Mevrouw has a headache,' she said. 'And something's gone wrong with the door-handle. I did call. I could hear you, but you couldn't hear me. So I came out by the window. What does the boy want?'

'He has a message from Mynheer, Mevrouw. For Mevrouw.'

'I'll deliver it. Well?'

The little boy drew a deep breath which made his ribs start out like the furrows on a freshly-ploughed field. Then he rattled off his message. 'Mynheer says Mevrouw is not to be alarmed at the fires and the shooting. It is only three bad men trying to get their brother out of gaol. Mynheer will be home in an hour. Mevrouw is not to worry.'

'You may go,' said Annabet. What had this attempt at gaol-breaking to do with the town being ablaze? No good asking the child. He turned and sped across the garden, vaulted the gate again, and disappeared.

She went back and tapped on the window and called loudly, 'Trudi, it's me, Annabet. The boy brought a message from Gert. Everything's quite all right. He sent word you were not to worry.' Not a sound came from behind the shutters. She cried again, shouting the news of comfort. Still no sound, nor

285

any sign of life.

For Trudi Van Heem had realised as soon as she barred the shutter behind Annabet's back that now the very worst had happened. She had seen the smoke and the flames, and heard the shots, and she had deliberately barred her friend, a woman who had been kind to her, out into the world of danger. And the worst was not that she herself should be killed or maimed or frightened; the worst, the thing she had always dreaded, the thing that for years had lain just upon the other side of nightmare, was that she should know that she had acted like a coward, selfish, treacherous. The last faint remnant of sanity and reason reared its head in her demented brain, the last voice of self-preservation made itself audible. It was Annabet's fault, she thought. Annabet would insist on opening the window and being a party to what Trudi knew was a trick. It was Annabet's fault; she might have stayed in the dubious safety of the barred and barricaded room. Ah, but that thought was no good. She shouldn't have barred the shutter. At the very least she should have stood with it in her hand, so that Annabet, tricked and aware of the trick at last, could have had a path of retreat.

With that thought in mind she staggered to the window again and lifted her arms to the bar of the shutter; and her heart, insiduously weakened by years of nervous strain, and now racing madly with terror, refused the effort. She dropped where she stood, collapsing like a bundle of cloth upon the floor at the foot of the window. And so lay, never to be frightened of anything again.

Evert's reception of the news of Mevrouw Van Heem's death showed Annabet how straight and confined were the limits of his sympathy. He had never liked her. As the vainest man in Banda he had suffered most from her little barbed speeches. Of no great humour he had often failed to see the point of many of her witty words, and often found an insult lurking where none was intended. And now, when eternal silence had fallen upon her, he was not disposed, on account of that fact, to display any sentiment he did not feel. So, although he made the conventional remarks of sorrow and sympathy to Gert Van Heem, as soon as Annabet and he were alone, he threw off all pretence at grief and obviously expected his wife to do the same and to join him in his jubilant mood.

The morning's occurrence had excited him. He had played a foremost part in putting out the fires on the quayside, and had, spectacularly, but at some real risk to his life, entered a blazing building and dragged out a clerk who had been trapped and overcome by smoke fumes. Afterwards men had slapped his back and wrung his hands and said the incoherent, complimentary things which come easily even to the inarticulate when

286

moved by some display of courage or skill. When the situation was completely controlled there had been a good deal of talk and a great deal of drinking, and Van Heem's promised hour had run to three before he and Evert walked uphill to his house. Evert, not sure that Annabet would not by this time have returned to Coenpark, chose to go to the Van Heem house on the chance that she might still be there because he felt that once he entered his own remote and quiet home the great day would be over. He couldn't very well tell Annabet exactly how brave and reckless he had been, or relay the compliments that had been paid him. And as he walked uphill by Van Heem's side he hoped that Annabet would have prolonged her visit so that Van Heem could tell her and he himself could modestly say, 'Oh, it was nothing, shut up, Gert, you make me feel a fool.'

To find Trudi Van Heem dead and Annabet ugly with weeping and declaring that it was all her fault, she should have stayed inside no matter how silly it looked, was a poor end to an exciting day. As soon as he decently could he left Gert to his empty house and his sorrow and hurried Annabet away.

'Look here,' he said, almost at once, 'that's all nonsense about it being your fault. I can't think what induced you to say that in front of Van Heem. He'll believe it. He's too upset to see reason, and he'll damn well believe you could have done something different and kept his darling Trudi alive.'

'But, Evert, it's true. While I was with her she was calmer. You see...' She told Evert about Trudi's dreams, and how her mere presence had robbed them of their full threat. Evert listened with an impatience which found vent in snorts and clearings of the throat; as soon as she ceased speaking he said scornfully:

'What utter nonsense. Nobody ever died of fright. Trudi Van Heem was a fat old woman, accustomed to have her own way in everything. Shut in like that without a breath of air, and then, being disobeyed by you, threw her into a fit. And half Gert's frenzy is due to his conscience. I could see that with half an eye. He'll feel better when it dawns on him that now he can have his little brown girl in the house.'

He spoke with complete complacency. Hadn't he foresworn little brown girls since his marriage? He was in a position to judge other men's morals.

'How can you be so cruel, Evert? Trudi wasn't in a temper. She was senseless with fear. I oughtn't to have opened the window. She gave a dreadful scream when she saw the fires, and slammed the shutter to...'

'Shutting you out! A fine action. If she thought the slaves were rioting and there was danger outside she shouldn't have shut you out in it. The least she could have done was to hold it

287

open so you could get back!' He was in a position to judge courage, and correct behaviour in danger too, wasn't he? 'Look here, Annabet, if you go on howling your eyes out about a woman who didn't give a rap for what happened to you I shall be really angry.'

'I can't help it, Evert. I just keep remembering how utterly distraught she was, and thinking if only I'd stayed with her...'

'Nobody dies of fear. If they did, what would happen to soldiers when they're under fire for the first time? I was sixteen when I was in my first battle. I was scared senseless, so was everybody else. But we didn't *die*. Trudi Van Heem always over-ate. She'd got fat round the heart. The room was hot. And when you went out of it, against her orders, she lost her temper and had a stroke. And I shall be careful to put Gert right about it not being your fault. My God, the next thing'll be him saying that you ran away from her or something like that!' He whisked his big white handkerchief out of his pocket and handed it to her. 'Here, for Heaven's sake wipe your face and blow your nose and be sensible. You look like a Hindu widow about to commit suttee.' He spoke brusquely, but not unkindly, and Annabet saw that he was prepared to overlook her behaviour if she mended it at once. She wiped, and blew, and tried to force her mind away from the woman who had been, first slowly and then swiftly frightened to death, and said in a small thick voice:

'While we were breaking into the room, I heard some explosions. What were they, Evert?'

'All the powder stores,' he said more cheerfully. Ah, she was making an effort; blood would tell in any emergency, he thought. He had gathered enough from Annabet's stumbling, self-accusatory story to realise that from first to last she had behaved with sense and courage. And now she was rallying from the shock of finding herself in a strange house with a dead woman and ten demented servants to deal with. But for her silliness in blaming herself in front of Van Heem, he was proud of his wife. They were a well-matched pair. Presently he would find a way to tell her, without immodest boasting, of his own exploits.

'The silly brutes fired the gaol, you see, thinking that in the confusion they'd get this brother of theirs out. But it didn't work. That'd be the fire you saw, and you saw for yourself how smartly the soldiers put it out. Then two of the mad beggars ran with their torches into the town, setting light to places as they went. One was shot almost at once, the other started about a dozen fires before they shot him. But the third did the most damage. He crept round the Fort, setting fire to anything combustible, and one fire touched off a powder store.

There're several magazines, scattered about, some distance apart, in case of accident; but you can't stop sparks flying once explosions start, you see. They just went off one after the other.'

'Yes, I heard them. Does it matter? Losing the powder stores, I mean.'

Talk about anything, think about anything except that moment when the houseboy tried the key which did fit, and the key upon the inside fell with a clatter to the floor, and the door opened by inches, pushing the chest aside, and you saw Trudi lying there by the window, and the first of the crackling booms shook the shutters as you fell on your knees and tried to lift her.

'It's a loss, of course,' Evert said cheerfully. 'But it doesn't matter much. Knoel has got enough for his job.'

'But, Evert, suppose what Tr ... Trudi feared *did* happen, and the few soldiers that're left hadn't anything to shoot with.' Her fingers, lying lightly on his forearm, closed suddenly in a nervous grip. 'Suppose she was right, Evert. This might be the beginning of something ...'

'My *dear* girl, you've spent the day with a crazy woman and had a nasty shock, or surely you'd see that you're talking nonsense. There isn't a brown rascal in the islands who could ever think up anything so clever. There'll be no slave-rising here, believe me. They're over; things of the past. But when they happened they didn't begin with clever foresighted planning. Three or four silly bastards would lose their heads, generally at a religious festival and go for the nearest white man with whatever happened to be in their hands. Then the rest would follow. The idea of blowing up the powder stores on one day and then attacking some time later is one that no native mind could possibly conceive. I know 'em.'

Perhaps fear *was* catching. Or was it merely because Trudi was dead that the thing which had lain behind her fear now seemed so actual and possible. Anyway, even as Annabet thought of the argument against what Evert had just said, her heart jolted and she wished she had not thought of it.

'Shal Ahmi is clever,' she said, and her voice was small.

'That I grant you.' He glanced at her with indulgence, as though she had been a petted child who had uttered some words of precocious wisdom. 'Fancy you thinking of that. Real smart. I must tell Knoel that. You see he had the same idea. And for safety's sake, some days ago, before the war was made public, in fact, he raked up some excuse and put Shal Ahmi under lock and key for the duration.'

He broke off as they stepped into the open space between the line of offices and warehouses and the jetty. There, just ahead, was the shell of the burnt-out house where he had made his

289

rescue that morning. He wanted to tell Annabet about it, but his vanity was too complicated to allow him to say simply, 'I saved a man's life in that house this morning.' It wasn't enough that she should think him brave; his modesty must exact tribute too. And at that moment he had another proof of his own astonishing luck. From the doorway of Vehmeer's office, Vehmeer, Hoogenbeet and Vanderbosch, in the hilarious stage of inebriation, emerged. They hailed Evert with loud excited cries and bowed so low to Annabet that their unstable balance was threatened. Vanderbosch, who had only an hour before arrived from Lonthoir in a state of pitiable apprehension, must offer his congratulations and thump Evert upon the back. Vehmeer must recount, in meticulous detail, the story of Evert's valour. Hoogenbeet, far from brave himself, must tell how the noise of the explosions and rumours of risings in Banda had brought Vanderbosch into town to see whether soldiers couldn't be sent to Lonthoir as a precaution.

'If I'd been as fr-frightened as you're making out, you ass, I sh-shouldn't have come to the s-seat of trouble, sh-should I?' Vanderbosch asked good-naturedly. 'I came to ob-blige my wife. She was practically demented.'

And that reminded Evert of Van Heem's wife. With a glance at Annabet to warn her not to embark upon another bout of self-accusation, he composed his beaming face and broke the news.

'Now my wife will be sorry to hear that,' Vehmeer said. 'Look, we can't keep Mevrouw standing here. Come along to my house. Perhaps you, Mevrouw, will be kind enough to break the news to my wife, while we toast the hero. We've got a hero among us, you fellows, I hope you realise that.' He thumped Evert again, violently. And Evert moved out of reach, saying—for one must be modest, all truly great men are modest—things like, 'I just happened to be nearest. By God, if I'd known what an inferno it was I shouldn't have ventured. Anybody else would have done the same...' All the proper things.

Evert called to his man, saying they wouldn't be long, and the four men, all offering their arms and jostling and pushing like schoolboys escorted Annabet to the Vehmeer house. And there Jahane Vehmeer, pretty, vapid little woman whom Annabet had never liked very much, partly because she never listened to anything that wasn't flavoured with scandal, partly because she always tried to make other women look silly in front of men, cried unrestrainedly for five minutes upon hearing of Trudi's death, and then recovered and showed a disgusting avidity for details.

'I don't want to talk about it,' Annabet said. And thought, how completely untrue! To the right person I could talk about

290

it. I long to talk about it … sensibly, understandingly … probing the mystery of how a person who dreads something can be frightened to death by quite another thing which happens to resemble it. Like a person who fears ghosts being driven to an extremity of terror by what anybody else would see is only a stick with a sheet over it. But I couldn't make Evert understand. Is that because he is a man? Would Christy have understood? Could I have talked to him about it? I don't know. I never really knew anything about him, as a person. He was concerned for my welfare; but then so is Evert. Evert was just angry with Trudi for shutting me out. So might Christy have been. And Mevrouw Vehmeer is just curious, slimy with curiosity. I'd hate to tell her how Trudi died, and why. I hope nobody will ever tell her.

'The men sound merry, don't they?' said Jehane Vehmeer, tiring of her gloomy companion. 'And of course they have reason. Perhaps we ought to bury our grief … it can't do Trudi any good, poor dear … and join them. I hardly took notice of what my husband said about yours, but it sounded marvellous. I think I shall put my sad thoughts aside, just for to-night, and go in and offer my congratulations properly.'

She sprang to her feet, very visibly putting her sad thoughts aside; and Annabet, thinking, at any rate, the men won't ask ferreting questions, rose and followed her into the room where the four men were making merry. They were drinking schnapps, but Vehmeer poured wine for the ladies, and everybody toasted Evert again. Jehane Vehmeer, who was very susceptible to alcohol, grew almost deliriously vivacious and shrill. Evert joined the others in encouraging her, hiding his private scorn, and his delight that he had married a woman who could drink a glass of wine and remain a lady. And Annabet, watching and listening, came suddenly to the conclusion that she and poor Trudi had not been the only frightened people that day. If there had been no real threat, why all this wild celebration? Evert she excepted … his wild mood was probably the natural result of excitement. He had become the focus for his fellows' admiration, and was happy. But the others were excited because something which had looked threatening had turned out to be nothing. Was it possible that their rejoicing was premature; that the three dead natives who had flung their torches and finally been shot down, had had another, more sinister purpose than an attempt at gaol-breaking. She thought of the numbers of brown, brownish, almost white people in the islands and compared them with the white, taking Coenpark, its house and compound as a measuring-rod. She thought of Trudi Van Heem's father.

Evert noticed her growing pallor, and since he had now extracted his full meed of pleasure from his companions' flattery, moved to end the party.

'My wife's had a tiring day,' he reminded everybody. And at once an echo of melancholy fell upon the sensitive alcoholic mood.

'I'll walk down with you,' Vanderbosch said, belatedly remembering his demented wife, left alone with two stalwart sons and three brace of loaded pistols on his Lonthoir estate.

'Time I was home, too,' Hoogenbeet said.

Jehane Vehmeer saw that the evening, the most hilarious and exciting one she had enjoyed since she came to Banda, was over, and was reluctant to end it.

'We'll come to the quay with you,' she cried, jumping from the table upon which she had perched herself. 'It's full moon, and I love to see it make that silver path on the water.'

They emerged upon the waterfront just as Knoel, with his broken arm supported in the front of his jacket and a bloody clout tied about his head, stepped from the boat which had brought him from the *Greta*. In the eerie white light of the moon his wrinkled brown face was a mask of anguish and fury, and the evidence of his wounds was plain. So there had been fighting after all. The English hadn't gone away. They had stayed and fought. Christy!

Suddenly Evert felt her whole weight sag upon the arm on which her hand had rested so lightly, so conventionally.

'Hi, hold up,' he said, slipping his other arm around her. 'It's nothing to faint about. He isn't hurt, much.' The Vehmeers, Hoogenbeet and Vanderbosch surged forward crying. 'What news?'

Knoel said briefly, 'Bad. One of you fetch the Governor; and you, Vehmeer, give me a hand to Kaerko's. I can't manage to get to the Fort.' One of his legs had been injured too, Evert saw. And he was being led off to the Agent's house, and in a few minutes the Governor would arrive and the door would be shut. He must, he simply must know what the bad news was, how bad. He looked down at Annabet indignantly, and then, on an impulse, swung her into his arms and walked to where the prahau waited. He bundled her in unceremoniously and told the man to wait. Then he ran towards Knoel and elbowed Hoogenbeet aside. 'You're hardly capable of supporting yourself,' he said rudely. Then, well in the centre of things, with his strong arm around Knoel's battered little body, he asked:

'What happened, Colonel?'

'They were warned, and armed. And we were ambushed. That's all. And what in God's name has been happening here?' He jerked his bandaged head towards the shell of the house where Evert had effected his rescue.

Vehmeer, Hoogenbeet and Evert began simultaneously to tell

292

him what had happened. Evert was the one who checked the spate.

'What does it matter, Colonel? This morning's affair was mere—in the sea. What happened to *you*?'

'I'll tell you when we're all together,' said Knoel faintly. Evert felt the body stiffen within the circle of his arm. 'This wasn't going to be worth calling a war. This was a punitive expedition against unarmed men! I tell you, Haan, it'll take six months and a major campaign to root out that rattlesnake's nest.'

At the very back of his mind Evert was conscious of Annabet. Poor little thing, she'd had a shattering experience, and there was no doubt that Trudi Van Heem had bequeathed her a legacy of fear. She'd be very scared if she came to and found herself alone with the boatman, not knowing how she came there. But he couldn't, he just couldn't turn back now and go to her without hearing all Knoel's story, and learning what steps the Governor intended to take, faced with this reverse. Annabet must wait.

And when, only three-quarters of an hour later he pounded across the quay and jumped into the boat, Annabet, conscious again, gave no sign of thinking herself ill-treated. She did not mention the moment of extreme panic which she had known when she opened her eyes and found a brown face leaning above her. She spoke to Evert as though she had herself despatched him in quest of news.

'What had happened? What did he say?'

Evert put his hand on her arm and pressed it, lightly, warningly. 'Oh, splendid news. A good fight and a great victory. The Colonel looks a bit battered, but all his wounds are superficial. He says our casualties have been very light.'

He was not speaking from natural caution. The words had been put into his mouth by Knoel himself. For in Kaerko's office, after the whole dismaying story had been told, Vanderbosch, struck sober, had reverted to the state of terror in which he had arrived in Banda earlier in the evening, and had voiced his fears as to the effect such tidings would have upon the natives. Nobody, just then, not even green-gilled Hoogenbeet, had found his terror ludicrous. Knoel had said bluntly, 'Best not to tell them. If the *Greta* goes back at once, we'll have reinforcements and fresh powder before any rumours can be confirmed. I'll have my wounded taken into hospital and absolutely segregated. They'd better be landed to-night.' He looked at the Governor and then at Kaerko. 'Perhaps you could see to that for me. Lieutenants Voss and de Klerk will handle it. I'm done in. And I must send a report by the *Greta*. I want to make something clear.'

They looked at him inquiringly.

'I know,' he said heavily. 'I know what you're thinking; what they'll think in Batavia and everywhere else, and go on thinking and saying long after I'm dead. But it isn't true. The third landing was conducted as carefully as though we had had the enemy in sight. Two blanks hadn't made us careless or over-confident. But they'll blame me till the end of time.' His voice quavered, and every man in the room felt uncomfortable, the more so because every man recognised the truth of the statement. Knoel steadied himself and went on. 'I'm not whining. The ambush was fair enough, and the fight was fair enough. What sticks in my craw is the fact that we've an enemy in our very midst. Somebody had warned them. Those pits and platforms and cannon hadn't been rigged in a day....' He broke off as Doctor Van de Lijn entered and bustled forward, full of professional importance. 'No Dutchman,' he said, in a lower voice, 'and that leaves only natives under suspicion. And the secret was so well kept. There was so short a time...' He mused for a moment, grey-faced, gnawing at a finger. 'And I had Shal Ahmi, who I'd suspect of anything, safe under lock and key....'

Van de Lijn began to remove the bloody bandage, and Evert, feeling that he had leaned as much as there was to be learned at the moment, unostentatiously took his leave.

So now, following Knoel's advice, he spoke with false cheer and squeezed Annabet's arm to warn her not to ask any more questions. She sat quietly thinking. The English had not gone from the islands. There had been fighting after all. Christy might be wounded, or dead. Had that folded paper never reached him? Had he and the others ignored the warning which Shal Ahmi said it carried?

As soon as they had left boat and boatman at the landing-place, she burst out with her questions. 'What really happened, Evert? What did Colonel Knoel have to tell? Was there much fighting?'

'Wait till we're in the house,' said Evert cautiously.

Never had the distance seemed so long. But at last they were safely inside, with the door closed, and then, without further prompting, Evert burst out, 'Knoel was fooled. Completely fooled. Cover it up as he may, he can't hide that fact. And he knows it. Any commander worth his salt would have smelt the trick a mile off ... and landed on the other side, taken them from the rear and *surprised* them.'

'What happened exactly?'

'I'll tell you. But we must have something to eat first. You're so empty you faint, and I'm yawning my head off. If Jehane Vehmeer was anything but a giggling trollop she'd have known

294

it was her duty to give us something to eat if we were in her damned house at dinner-time.' He clapped his hands and roared for Josef. When the boy appeared he ordered a meal, some sort of meal, any sort of meal, something to eat, immediately. The ill news had not marred his appetite, on the contrary he felt more hungry, more vigorous, more active, more himself altogether.

'You do look mortally ill,' he said, leading Annabet to a chair in the dining-room. 'This has been a bloody fine day one way and another, hasn't it?'

'I'm all right, Evert. I'm not even hungry. I just want to know what happened to Colonel Knoel and the soldiers.'

'You shall hear,' said Evert, snatching up a piece of bread from the trencher in the centre of the table and breaking a crust. 'They went to Lu first; it's nothing but a speck of an island; it was deserted, but there were signs that the English had been there at some fairly recent date. They sailed across to Gadia and reached it before noon. That was deserted too. Not a soul, but again signs that the English had been there and had apparently left in a hurry. Knoel says there was a lot of stuff, some of it quite valuable, left about. Even some food, not much decomposed. In less than half an hour they'd combed the place thoroughly and were on their way to Ay. He *says* that he landed at Ay, after some preliminary cannon fire, as carefully and suspiciously as he had landed at the other islands. I doubt that. I'd wager that by that time the men were laughing and joking about a day's outing, walking anyhow and not looking for anything except loot. There was the usual ramshackle collection of huts, there were the signs of men having left hurriedly. Behind the huts, inland, there was a clearing, and beyond that, Knoel says, evidence that somebody had tried to start a nutmeg grove; a fifty-feet belt of saplings about shoulder high. Behind that again, the jungle. Not a sight or sound of human life. Just as he and his men reached the nutmegs, bullets began to hail out of the jungle ... literally hail, because they came from above. They'd got properly-built platforms up in the trees. And then firing began from underground, they'd got trenches running through the nutmeg grove. And then, behind them, all the huts burst into flame, and cannon began to pound away at the schooners. You see what had happened. They'd had warning of the attack, somehow, from somewhere, and they'd all gathered in Ay. They'd got plenty of muskets, plenty of ammunition, *and* cannon. Voss, the second in command, took every man he could collect, and made a second landing party and found himself between two concealed cannon and the blazing huts, just as Knoel was between the musket fire and the huts on the other side. Devilish clever. I oughtn't to say so, I suppose, but it was a piece of strategy worthy of old Gomarus himself. I can remember...'

The arrival of the food interrupted him. He insisted upon Annabet piling her plate high with the rizplatzen, and helped himself greedily. He dismissed Josef with a wave of his hand and would probably have proceeded to regale Annabet with some story of his former, idolised commander, had she not asked breathlessly:

'And were many English killed, too?'

'They never saw them. Never got near them. At least that's how I understand it. Those who could run or crawl made for the boats, some of them, like Knoel, had to cross the red-hot ashes of the huts to reach them. And the English never even pursued them. When those who could get away were on the schooners, there was more cannon fire, and the *Margarete* was sunk, and the *Sanje* hit. And so, back they came home.... Don't look like that, my darling. It's only a temporary setback. Eat your food. It's been kept waiting too long. But it's good.'

Only a temporary setback! What had Trudi said, Gert says those things. All men say them. This morning men had been talking about a punitive expedition that would last three days; this evening, after a bloody beating, they were talking of a temporary setback.

That would have been all right; that would have been admirable if it had concerned only the fight between the English and the Dutch in the islands. Cut off as they were on their tiny island, the English (remember, with a shudder of apprehension that that means Christy, too!) were bound to be defeated sooner or later. From Batavia would come fresh troops, supplies of ammunition, other schooners with their bright brass cannon. So far as open warfare was concerned, men were right to take the optimistic view, to think and speak about a temporary setback. But what of the enemy at home? The enemy who had sent that warning message. The enemy that only she knew by name. The enemy whom she had aided and abetted. What of him? Wasn't a temporary setback just what he had desired, and planned?

Her head was heavy and dizzy from the turmoil of her thoughts. She pushed away the hardly-tasted plate of rizplatzen and looked at Evert with sick eyes. She had felt, at the moment when the moonlight showed up the bloody bandage upon Knoel's head, that the time had come for her to make a cruel, a shattering decision; and inch by inch the trap had closed in on her. Remain silent and preserve your secret and jeopardise the lives of all the white people in Banda, or tell what you know and give them a chance, at least a chance, to defend themselves against the real enemy.

The dizziness in her head increased as her thoughts whirled

round like the axis of a cyclone. Why should this happen to me? I'm just Annabet Van Goens who got ill and so had to choose between Ireland and Banda; who was so ugly that Evert couldn't bear to look at me, so he went away till I was cured, and I got entangled with Christy and Shal Ahmi. I meant no harm. I just didn't want the patrols to pounce on Christy and hang him. So I passed on the message. I was just a pawn in a wicked man's evil game. But now I'm not a pawn. I can see what his game was. It is in my power partly at least to defeat it; if I speak now. If I pay the price of earning Evert's scorn and hatred.

I don't love him. I knew, on the night when he came back from Bandogar, that I should never love him. I oughtn't to put the false, hollow value of our smooth married life before the lives of all these people, many of whom have been kind to me, made me welcome, remembered my birthday. Even if they had been my personal and social enemies, I should consider them. They are my countrymen. They are white. The brown men cut off Trudi's father's hands and burned him; they raped and stabbed her mother. They killed Trudi, too. I must speak.

'Come along,' said Evert, starting up from his chair, the last piled forkful of food still on his mouth. 'If you won't eat, you must go to bed. I'm sorry I told you so much of what Knoel said. But I thought you were plucky. There's no need to take this business to heart. There's no idea of the English attacking *us*. They couldn't if they wanted to. They've no craft that would carry a cannon. The folks in Batavia won't see us come to harm, we're too valuable. They'll have fresh troops and powder here in no time. So there's not a thing in the world for you to worry about. Come on. You're exhausted, and upset about Trudi, naturally. A good night's rest'll set you right.'

He spoke brusquely, but kindly, concerned for her well-being. Still munching vigorously he came to her end of the table and slipped his hand under her elbow. A sick pang went through her as she realised that her next words would be an end to everything but loathing upon his part. She let him pull her to her feet, and then, twisting free of his hand, she seized the back of her chair and leaned on it for support as she gasped out the dreadful words.

'Evert . . . I know who sent that message. Shal Ahmi wrote it and I despatched it for him.' Brutal, irrevocable.

Evert looked as though somebody had struck him a stunning blow in the face. He actually stepped backwards, recoiling from her as he would have done from a self-confessed leper.

'Are you raving?' But he knew the answer to that.

'I wish I were. I had to tell you, Evert, because it means that he wished us harm, here in Banda. You must warn everybody.'

'Why in God's name did he pick on you?'

Cutting the story to the bone, without explanations or excuses, remembering that time was short, she told him the whole truth. When she reached the point where Shal Ahmi sent for her to go to the gaol, Evert, unable to keep silence any longer, broke in with, 'That'll do. So you went. To save Ayrton's hide.'

The hatred and fury in his face and in his voice surpassed anything she had imagined.

'But I didn't know anything about the war,' she said shrilly. 'I did wrong, I know. But Evert I love him. I couldn't let the patrol take him and hang him. Shal Ahmi said the patrol was after him because of the smuggling. I didn't know about the war, Evert, I didn't know about the ...'

Evert had forgotten the war; had shoved aside the impersonal significance of her story; overlooked the reason for telling it at this moment. His curiously single-tracked mind had seized only fact, and the name 'Christy Ayrton' danced in a red mist before his eyes. Annabet had not spoken the name, but he knew the one Englishman who would have found his way to Coenpark in an emergency and he had heard that Ayrton had been hurt in an unfortunate brush with the patrol. It had been Ayrton all the time.

In blind fury he reached out towards Annabet who leaned, trembling, frightened, half-fainting, yet relieved that the moment of speech was over, and laid his hands on her shoulders. He shook her as a child, mad with temper, might shake a rag doll. He shook her until she hung between his hands, her mouth open, her head lolling and her last fragment of consciousness ebbing away in the thought that he would kill her. But he mustn't forget Shal Ahmi. She clawed at his iron wrists with weak, desperate hands, and tried to find breath enough to utter the two words loud enough to be heard through the stream of awful words Evert was shouting at her. 'Don't forget Shal Ahmi,' she gasped, and the sound was shaken out of her as the last few drops might be shaken out of a bottle.

'I'll attend to him too,' said Evert, and pulling her once more towards him, thrust her away violently, at the same time loosing his hold so that she fell backwards, tried to catch at the chair, missed it and crashed to the floor, striking the side of her head on the table as she fell.

The madness seemed to go out of Evert then. He stood for a second looking down at her. Then she heard his tread, heavy and rapid and purposeful in the hall, and the thud of the door behind him.

She lay on the floor, too spent and battered to make the effort to rise yet. This was the end of everything. But she had done what she could to undo the evil she had unwittingly done. Evert would know what to do, and whatever it was Shal

Ahmi had planned might be forestalled. It might even be that on picking on her to help him, Shal Ahmi had committed a fatal mistake. If he could have found a brown accomplice ... But he couldn't. So there was no solace in that thought. If she hadn't carried the letter Colonel Knoel would have surprised the English. No getting away from that. Evert was justified in his anger. She remembered, without surprise or rancour, the names he had called her. Most of them were outside her comprehension, but he had said 'Whore' several times. Untrue; a word chosen for its hurtfulness rather than its accuracy. Evert must know that. Yet was it so ill-chosen? Wasn't it rather that Evert in blind fury, had spoken the judgment of Jean Marie, could he have known everything. To him and to anyone who held the spirit to be of equal importance with the flesh she was as soiled as any prostitute. She had lusted after Christy with her mind; she had accepted Evert with her body. And there had been those subtle, shaming moments of ecstacy when she had lain in Evert's arms and held Christy to her heart. Ah, the words of abuse Evert had flung at her were not bad enough; they implied something too simple and easily fathomed.

And again she wondered, why should all this have happened to me. Brought up so coolly and correctly, trained to do and say and even think the right things. I came here with such good intentions; meaning to repay Evert for saving me from Ireland, by being a model wife. The whole thing seemed so simple then. Life lay out as smooth and plain as a skein of silk; now it is spoiled and tangled, as though an idiot's fingers had been in it, knotted and complicated and useless, past any human skill to put it right.

And empty. Trudi, my one dear friend, dead. Christy dead, or doomed. Evert estranged.

She gripped the edge of the table to pull herself to her feet; and then suddenly she was on her knees, her arms along the table edge, her head bowed down upon them. And she was praying, not in the formal set phrases of happy childhood and easy church-going, but in the bitter, self-accusatory outpourings of the soul that feels it has lost alike its way in this world and its hold upon the one invisible.

The violence with which he had handled Annabet had relieved some of the pressure of anger within Evert's mind. Ten minutes of hard walking eased him still further, and before he reached the first pale glimmering house in the town he was able to push Annabet and Christy Ayrton to the back of his mind and to think about his errand.

He must go carefully now, not make a fool of himself, not appear to have caught Vanderbosch's terror, not betray Annabet. It was going to be difficult. His pace slackened as he thought, and by the time he had reached Kaerko's house he was walking slowly and ponderously.

Lights were bobbing about on the quay. The wounded from the *Greta* had already been brought ashore, the report had been taken aboard her and now she was headed for Java, her white sails catching the moonlight as she breasted each wave. The wounded from the *Sanje* were being unloaded and taken to the hospital within the Fort. Voss and de Klerk were in charge of the business, and it was being conducted in silence and as speedily as possible. By morning all the injured men and all those who had seen them would be immured within that frowning fortress, cut off utterly from the outer world. There would be rumours, naturally. Evert's own boatman, for instance, would whisper that he had seen the Colonel back in the island with a bloody bandage on his head; but until fresh troops and ammunition arrived no native would know for certain that the Dutch arms had met with a defeat, and before they had time to act upon this information—if they actually intended to act—the English would be defeated and the troops back to deal with any sign of insurrection. What then, asked Evert, coming to a standstill and watching the wounded stumbling along on their own legs, or being helped along by comrades, or being carried upon improvised stretchers, what are we worrying about. Even if Shal Ahmi did warn the English, even if he is planning some deep devilment, what can he do from his cell in the gaol, while the rest of the brown swine are kept in ignorance?

Once again he decided to feel his way very carefully.

Kaerko was still up and about. Perhaps in deference to the Governor who had not stopped to dress when summoned to the office, Kaerko had removed his coat and donned a long thin dressing-robe of brightly-coloured silk. His nondescript features were twisted into a mask of anxiety and his greeting of Evert's return betrayed his expectation of further bad news.

'Come in,' he said, opening the door. 'The Governor is still here and the doctor. What brings you back? More trouble?'

'That depends,' said Evert cautiously. 'How is Knoel?'

'Very poorly. He insisted upon writing his report himself and fainted as soon as he'd finished. Van de Lijn is with him now. He's given him opium and hopes he'll sleep.'

The Governor, looking very old and brittle, was seated in Kaerko's most comfortable chair. A tray nearby bore signs of an impromptu meal having been served and picked at without much relish.

'I had to hurry away earlier,' Evert explained, 'because my wife was waiting. But there was one little matter I wanted to bring up.' He divided his glance fairly between the Agent and the Governor. 'When we heard of the ambush, and were discussing from whence the warning might have been sent, why did no one think of Shal Ahmi?'

Kaerko's face reddened slightly and took on a truculent expression.

'Why Shal Ahmi?' he asked. 'I've said before, and I say it again, that Shal Ahmi, without position or salary, is one of the most loyal servants the Company possesses, in these islands or anywhere else.'

'Shal Ahmi,' said the Governor dispassionately, 'was safely in gaol before I made the announcement which conveyed to you the Company's intention. Colonel Knoel preferred a charge against him, fowl-stealing, a very trumped up charge. There is no harm in my telling you that, for the Colonel himself would be the first to admit it. He should have been released, but, with this matter brewing and Knoel feeling so strongly upon the subject, I decided to let the charge stand. So you see, unless he really owns the magical powers he lays claim to he could hardly have sent the message.'

'Perhaps not,' said Evert, humouring Kaerko who was bristling like a turkey cock. 'On the other hand, messages have been got out of gaols before this. And it sticks in my mind that gaol-breaking was attempted this morning. Because Seth Aranda's kin carried the fire we all assumed that it was Seth Aranda's escape that was intended.' He took one of the blind leaps in the dark which had so often landed him at a desired point, and turning to Kaerko, said sharply, 'I suppose he is still? I suppose he didn't get out in the general confusion?'

'How should I know? I am not the keeper of the gaol. If I were...' He remembered the Governor's presence and checked himself. 'With all due deference, your excellency, the man should never have been imprisoned at all. In a thousand ways he has served the Company, and just because Knoel is prejudiced...'

'Send up and ask,' Evert cut in abruptly.

'But even if he isn't there. If he did escape this morning,' Kaerko said, 'does that prove that he warned the English? That was your original suggestion, wasn't it, Haan? That the English had been warned by Shal Ahmi. If—and we'll soon find that out—he did take advantage of this morning's rumpus to escape from unwarranted confinement, does that make him guilty of the other charge?' He rang a little bell furiously, and to the sleepy servant who came in answer, gave an order to run to the gaol immediately and ask after Shal Ahmi.

'No ... wait,' said the Governor, rising stiffly. 'Go back to your bed.' As soon as the man had retired he explained, 'We agreed, didn't we, to keep the wounded away from the natives? They may not all be in yet. I'll go myself. I was only waiting for Doctor Van de Lijn to come down and tell me about the Colonel. I shall be glad of the walk. But before I go, Haan, I must say that I agree with Kaerko. Shal Ahmi's disappearance wouldn't prove anything.'

Smug and stupid, Evert thought; two officials sticking together against a mere planter! Oh, if only my information had come to me, with equal certainty, but from a different source, how I should enjoy ramming it down their throats.

'No,' he said, quite pleasantly, 'even his disappearance from the gaol wouldn't prove anything. But allied to what I heard this evening, it might point the way to something. I don't as a rule pay much attention to women's gossip, but my wife was with Mevrouw Van Heem to-day, just before she died, and ...'

'Mevrouw Van Heem dead?' asked the Governor in an astounded voice.

Evert nodded. 'She died this morning. My wife was with her, and swears that she died of fear. And before she died she told my wife something ... I think you will both admit that Mevrouw Van Heem was shrewd enough. And her house overlooks the Fort.' He paused.

'Well?'

'Mevrouw Van Heem says that she saw Shal Ahmi intercept, on the slope up to the Fort, the coolies who were carrying what looked to be musical instruments and tools. After he had inspected these burdens he seemed disturbed in his manner and proceeded to the waterfront where he was seen in conversation with a boatman who immediately put out to sea, though it was just on dark. In the light of what we know, does that seem to you a significant story, gentlemen?'

'I'll go and see what Shal Ahmi has to say about that,' said the Governor.

'He'll lie,' said Evert.

'He may lie, but we do have methods of extorting the truth.'

'Oh that ...' said Evert, lightly dismissing the thought of the instruments of torture, known to be rusting away in the Fort dungeon. 'So many other lies will come out with the truth, your Excellency, that we shall probably all find ourselves implicated.'

Even then Kaerko put up a feeble, but loyal defence. 'I have never caught Shal Ahmi out in a lie,' he said solemnly.

Evert laughed.

Almost as soon as the Governor had gone, Van de Lijn entered the room, pulling down his sleeves and shaking his head.

'His injuries are such as would make it seem incredible that he could have walked from the beach, talked to us and written

302

his report,' he said gravely. 'I have done what I could, but I fear for his life. Especially as his heart is broken as well as his head. I find it very significant that he wrote his report and then fainted, as though his spirit had braced itself to make his defence and then succumbed.'

'Did he include in his report the fact that he was now useless?' Evert asked brutally.

'His Excellency added a word or two to that effect. The Colonel merely mentioned that he had been wounded. His Excellency was anxious that another experienced man should be sent . . . in case of accident.'

'Huh,' Evert made a noise that showed that he was not impressed by this piece of forethought. 'That'll mean either Van Holk or Boender. Neither of 'em, to my mind, the right man for the job. What we want is an adventurer; not a soldier, hidebound with rules for conducting a campaign. I was thinking a little while ago, if Gomarus had been in charge to-day, he'd have guessed two deserted islands meant a trap on the third. He'd have landed in the unlikely place and attacked from the rear. By God,' he said, warming to his subject, 'I could do it myself. To-night. A hundred good men, that's all I'd ask. I'd make an attempt with fifty. To-night, when they're patting themselves on the back and talking about their victory. I've got no patience with these tactics, going to the front door and ringing the bell and saying, "Would you like to have a little battle this afternoon?" '

The doctor, who was not one of Evert's admirers, listened coldly. A professional man himself, he distrusted inspired amateurs; but Kaerko naturally timid and unenterprising, found his blood moving more warmly as he heard the bold words. Haan was pigheaded on the subject of Shal Ahmi, but otherwise he was admirable; he lived, perhaps, a little out of his proper period, he would have been an excellent pioneer, overlooking his nutmegs for four days a week and engaging in guerrilla warfare on the others.

'There's a good deal in what you say,' he said, thoughtfully.

Van de Lijn yawned. 'Well, I'll just have another look at my patient. Then I'll get along to the hospital. There'll be work for me there,' he said grimly. He disappeared, and in a moment was back in the doorway. 'He seems to be sleeping. I'll come back when I've dealt with the worst up there. Good night.'

Evert wandered over to the tray of food, and without waiting for an invitation, selected a pasty and set his teeth into it.

'I'd had nothing since breakfast, and then my supper was disturbed by what my wife told me about Shal Ahmi,' he explained. Inwardly he was a little surprised by the upwelling of vigour and spirit within him. Bad news all round; bad news from Ay and shattering news at Coenpark, and yet he was far from feeling dispirited. The spell with which Annabet had bound him had snapped, and he realised that for more than a year he had been in danger of limiting his world and his outlook to the narrow radius of a swaying petticoat. He had wanted Annabet and hated whoever, whatever it was that had barred him from full possession. Now he knew, and he could hate both Annabet and her lover. It was easy now; for the knowledge that Annabet had hankered for a man whom she had met after she had seen Evert Haan, stung his vanity. Christy Ayrton! Well, he could have her. If it hadn't been for the war he'd have tied a label round her neck, stripped her to her shift, and told a boatman to row her over to Gadia. He couldn't do that now ... but he had a very sweet revenge in mind. As soon as this business was settled he would go back and put it into action. And he would be avenged, not only for her mental unfaithfulness, but for all the weakness with which he had treated her in the past.

The Governor returned. Bless the man, he had been running! He was blown, and it took him so long to recover his breath that both Evert and Kaerko knew what he would say when he regained his voice.

'He's gone?' Evert said. Not as one who asks a question, but as one who answers it.

The Governor nodded, gasped, broke into speech.

'Somebody's been very remiss,' he said. 'Until I asked after the rogue nobody had noticed that his cell was empty. One gaoler swore that he was there at ten o'clock this morning, and that's the last anyone saw of him. He's gone now. I've sent a party to his house, but he'd hardly be there, would he? As soon as it's light we'll comb every house and compound in the island.'

'And I trust, your Excellency, that the searchers will be given orders to shoot at sight. I don't suppose he'd dare show his face at Coenpark; I've never encouraged his mumbo jumbo in my compound, but if I see him I shall shoot first and let him explain afterwards.'

'Such hasty and unwarranted action might easily precipitate the very situation we hope to avoid,' said the Governor, but his voice was uncertain, unrebuking.

'If what's afoot is what we think it is,' said Evert, flicking away a crumb, 'there'd be no situation with him dead. Shoot at the head is always a sound rule.' He swept his eye over the Governor and the Agent. Neither of them useful, neither of them men of action, neither of them men at all by his standard. 'Well, what other steps are we going to take?'

'There isn't much that we can do, is there? Until Shal Ahmi

304

is found and brought in for questioning.'

'With all due deference,' said Evert, and his tone made the perfunctory phrase almost insulting, 'I should suggest that word be despatched immediately to every planter. Tell them what we suspect, and ask them, not only to keep a sharp lookout for Shal Ahmi himself, but to look over anybody with whom he had any connections ... any slave he's doctored, or been seen talking to, or had any business with. You ...' he turned towards Kaerko, 'could help there. All these thousands of loyal actions he has performed, whom have they concerned? Who's been the source of any information he's given you? Who's been entangled in any muddle he's straightened for you. Those are the men he'll use now.'

'Very cogent suggestions,' said the Governor, looking at Evert with half-resentful admiration and then shifting his gaze to Kaerko who looked frightened and baffled and stubborn. 'Do you, Mynheer, keep a record of such happenings, or do you rely upon your memory?'

'Come along, Kaerko,' said Evert jovially. 'You've been foxed by the old——; but so have other people. It's beyond being a matter of prejudice or policy now. Give us a list of the people you *know* have reason to be grateful to him. Blast it, man, if half what we suspect is true, it's a matter of life and death for all of us. This expedition has started like Kraemer's, we don't want it to go on.'

'What Haan says is only too true,' said the Governor. 'If you have any information ...'

Kaerko went slowly to the big desk, juggled with some keys and opened the bottom drawer, from the back of which he took a small notebook, bound in black and red and ruled like an account book. The front page bore, in excellent copper-plate handwriting, the words:

'Account of Moneys paid out to Shal Ahmi in return for Services Rendered.'

With it in his hand Kaerko stood still for a moment. 'You will understand, your Excellency, that these sums were paid out of my private purse. No penny of the Company's money is involved. I have kept the account as a matter of interest.'

He handed the book to the Governor, and Evert, taking another pasty as he passed the tray, came and stood behind the chair in which His Excellency sat, and read over his shoulder. The little record covered several years, and although never, for any service, had Shal Ahmi received more than two guilders, the sum involved, in the aggregate, was quite considerable. The entries were varied.

'For information leading to the recovery of Mevrouw By-

305

skin's necklace without scandal.'

'For keeping watch on Captain Moeller for four days.'

'For reporting conversation overheard at Park Helgers.'

'Sick women hidden at the Dyke; suspect plague?'

And under each heading, as though prepared against just such an occasion as had caused the little book to be brought to the light, was inscribed, in Kaerko's beautiful hand, a list of people, Dutch and native, who were involved in each case. Evert caught sight, before the page flicked over, of an entry which concerned him, although his name was not mentioned.

'For information averting the arrest of Captain Piet Odshoorn on the charge of smuggling unlimed nuts aboard the *Eastern Venture.*

Manuelo Cortez.

Ramjit Sita Singh.'

A wry smile curved his mouth as he noted it. Shal Ahmi had asked only two guilders, one apiece for Manuelo and Ramjit; he himself had received, according to the book, two more from Kaerko's private purse. Four guilders had changed hands, and Piet had carried the papers! How cheap. But dear at any price!

'If this had been prepared for such an eventuality it could not have served the purpose better,' said the Governor, handing back the book. 'But the names are confusing. So many Mahommets and Alis and Juans and Hassans. Can they all be traced?'

'The nature of the business in which they were involved will guide me. My memory is excellent,' Kaerko said. He was relieved to have the book back in his hands; glad that the Governor, so unsatisfactory in so many ways, was at least lacking in vulgar curiosity.

'You'd better make a copy,' said His Excellency. 'This information will be invaluable, both in the search for Shal Ahmi's person, and as a guide to those who are likely to be his tools.'

'Well,' said Evert, coming out from behind the official chair, 'with that all settled, I will go home. I pass Byskin's and Jenner's on my way. I think I'll wake them and warn them of what we know and what we suspect. Good night, your Excellency. Good night, Kaerko.'

When he had concluded both his errands he stood on the path back to Coenpark and laughed to himself. All this fuss about warning the fellows, really, it wasn't necessary at all. They were all not only aware of, but definitely looking for, danger. Byskin had greeted his nocturnal visitor by poking a loaded blunderbuss through an upper window and bellowing, 'I'm armed. What do you want?' And at Jenner's Evert had found the house patrolled by two enormous hounds, one of whom bayed loud enough to wake everyone within a mile, while the other walked menacingly beside him, ready to take his arm in its jaws at the slightest provocation. And by Heaven he had provoked it. He had brought his fist down on its muzzle and snarled, 'Get away. Don't you know a white man from a coolie?' And the animal had retreated, growling. He'd tease Jenner about his hounds next time they met.

Well, that was Shal Ahmi and the rebellion disposed of. Now for Mistress Annabet.

The amusement faded from his eyes. In the waning moonlight they took on a cold frosty glitter. Walking slowly he reviewed, in great detail, the history of his married life. He skirted around the first episode, her arrival, his shock, the calling in of Shal Ahmi, tossing self-accusation aside and thinking eagerly, well, that cured her, didn't it? He dwelt lovingly upon the material things he had lavished upon his bride; upon his abandonment of all his ancient plans for humiliating her and so getting his own back upon the Van Goens. Damn it, he thought, if I'd been a raw schoolboy in love for the first time, living with the woman I'd chosen from a thousand, I couldn't have given her more, or treated her better. He dismissed the memory of those nights when he had emerged unsatisfied from her embrace and attempted to wring from her the name of the phantom. I tried, he told himself, I tried to understand her, I was patient, kind, tolerant. And when I thought I'd found the man, that cousin of hers, and she told me that the past was over and she'd try again, by God, I met her more than halfway.

The sweetness of the days and nights which had followed, he regarded now with distaste. It was the sweetness of rottenness. Then, more than at any other time, he had been deceived. That was true. You're not really, wholly cheated when you feel that you are being defrauded. It is when the cheating is subtle and sweet that the real deception begins. If for nothing else he owed her a grudge for this last month.

He followed the main road out on to the quay. The lights had gone now, it was all deserted and silent, save for the soft hiss of the rising tide. He turned into a narrow passage between two warehouses and stopped by a little low house, the whole of its frontage occupied by a wide, unglazed window, now closed by cane shutters, and a door over which projected a sign gaily painted with Chinese letters. He rapped on the door and waited. After two minutes he rapped again, more loudly. Suddenly impatient he cursed, and would have made a more violent assault upon the door had a little shutter let into

307

its upper half not opened. Wang Fu's wizened yellow face, fitfully lighted from below by the rays of a tiny oil-lamp which he had waited to kindle, showed in the aperture. Without greeting or a word of apology for rousing the old man from his bed at such an hour, Evert stated the nature of his errand. The Chinese unbolted the door and Evert stepped inside.

Katje had found her mistress in the dining-room and escorted her to bed. Mevrouw had been weeping a great deal, and was talking to herself in a very strange voice when Katje, impatient for her own bed and anxious because of the silence in the lower part of the house had crept down to investigate. Her earlier suspicion, abandoned some months ago, returned. Mevrouw was a little mad. She had let herself be undressed like a child, weeping again, and hardly speaking at all. The few words she did utter did not make sense enough to assuage the maid's curiosity or to explain the master's absence so late at night. Katje retired to her bed with many interesting speculations to entertain her last conscious moments.

In the morning Annabet, waking from the deep, sluggish slumber that follows a wakeful night, opened her eyes to find Katje, bearing the breakfast tray, with tears running down her brown impassive face.

She braced herself against the onslaught of misery which was launched with her first return to wakefulness and asked kindly:

'What is the matter, Katje?'

'I am dismissed, Mevrouw.'

'Dismissed? Who said so?'

'Mynheer. Josef was waiting when I entered the door and said Mynheer wished to see me. He dismissed me. I am to go to-day.'

'Did he give any reason?'

Katje shook her head. 'Except that you would have no further need of me and he would ask Mevrouw Byskin to take me into her service.' She gulped and fixed her beady, red-rimmed eyes upon Annabet's face.

'Mevrouw did not know of Mynheer's intention?'

Be careful now. Every word of this conversation would be repeated in the Byskins' kitchens and compound before the day was out.

'I didn't know that you were to go to-day, Katje. But for some time now, Mevrouw Byskin has wanted you for her maid. And I ... well, I never thought you seemed very happy here. And there ... are a number of maids in that household. So many young Juffrouws, and the daughter-in-law, Mevrouw Elie. I thought the change would please you, Katje.'

'It would have done,' Katje said with unflattering frankness,

308

'until three months ago.' She raised the hem of her little frilled apron and sobbed behind it. 'Now it is different. Since Ramjit's wife died. I shall never see him again,' she said in a shrill crescendo.

'Oh, yes you will, Katje. Listen. I'll speak to Mynheer Byskin at the first opportunity. I'll ask him to exchange a man for Ramjit. He's very good-natured, he'll arrange it with Mynheer. It'll be all right, I promise you. So stop crying.'

No need to tell Katje to stop crying. The tears had been turned off as briskly as though they flowed from a tap. The Byskin house was near the town and full of giggling chattering women of her own kind and status. If Mevrouw could find a way to place Ramjit in the Byskin compound her cup of happiness would be overbrimmed.

'You will remember, Mevrouw.'

'I shall remember.'

'Mynheer said I was to go at once. He is writing a letter for me to carry with me, now. But,' she added magnaminously, since Mevrouw had promised to do her a favour, 'I will lay out the dress for the morning, if Mevrouw will tell me which one. And Juan and Abbas will carry the bath.'

'Oh yes, Katje. I shall manage, thank you. I'll have the lilac dress with the plain collar. Thank you ... I hope you'll be happy, Katje. Good-bye.'

'When Ramjit comes I shall be happy, Mevrouw. Good-bye.'

So ended a relationship of peculiar intimacy. Annabet had a swift vision of Trudi's Nina, howling like a bereaved dog as she crouched by her mistress' body. I have failed even to endear myself to Katje, she thought dully. Not that it matters now. Nothing does.

She drank some coffee and set the tray aside. She missed Katje's aimless fidgeting around the room, much as it had sometimes annoyed her. The silence seemed to grow oppressive. Each of her thoughts was as uncomfortable as the one that went before it. The war, Christy, Evert, Trudi. Especially did she dread facing Evert again. Nights like last night should really be the end of things. When she fell against the table she should have died. Or she should have died as she knelt by the table, praying for forgiveness for her sins and for Christy wherever, in this world or another, he might be. Nights like that should not be followed by a bright morning, with the sun streaming in at the window and the doves cooing in the nutmeg grove and the scent of flowers coming up from the garden. Once a life had ended the person who lived it should not be left alive and sentient, given breakfast, asked what dress she would wear, just as usual.

She heard Evert's step in the gallery and leaped from the bed, pushing her arms into the sleeves of her dark blue wrapper. He opened the door abruptly and stood in the doorway, not speaking at first, just looking at her, coldly. She forced herself to return his stare, but the attempt failed. Her gaze wavered and averted itself.

'Evert ... please, don't look at me like that. I'm sorry. I was wrong, I know. But I am sorry. ...'

'You're going to be sorrier,' Evert said gloatingly. 'I've sent Katje away. I engaged her to attend my wife, not Ayrton's mistress.'

'Evert, I was not his mistress. You know that.'

'I'd have respected you more if you'd gone the whole hog,' he said untruthfully. 'Don't wag your virginity in my face, Madam. Whatever you care to call yourself you played the traitor to save his hide. Perhaps there's a word to describe you, but I don't know it.'

'I wasn't deliberately a traitor. I didn't even know about the war. I thought I was sending a warning about the patrols.' She was conscious of a wild impulse to add that she was no more than the people who had smuggled out the nutmegs to the English and then left them to the mercy of the patrols. But there was no point in angering Evert further, and nothing to be gained by argument.

'Will you collect the things that you brought from Heydberg, nothing more, and carry them to the room at the end of the gallery? This room, also, was intended for my wife.'

He had expected some protest. From things she had said out of a desire to please him in the early days of their marriage he had gathered that the room and the pretty things in it and the unique, incomparable bathroom were dear to her. He was disappointed to see no flash of resentment in her eyes; angered afresh by her meek words.

'Very well. I will do that.'

'You bet you will,' he said roughly. 'You'll further oblige me by staying in that room except when I ask you to come out. You'll come to know which side your bread was buttered, my fine lady, My God, when I think how I've pampered you. Get along now. ...'

He stood, overlooking her hasty, muddled effort to sort out what remained of the things she had brought from those he had provided in the first place or subsequently bestowed. The pile of belongings, when finally assembled, was pitiably small. Dresses rotted so quickly during the rains, and she had rashly given so many things away. After each of Evert's munificent offerings Katje had carried away a bundle of superseded garments, to wear, to give away, or to sell. There remained of Mevrouw's secretly grudging but honourably just provision merely a night-gown and a change of underclothes, saved and cherished for sentiment's sake, for Klara and Maria and

310

Mamma and Truitje had all had a hand in their making, and a gown of yellow muslin sprigged with little green sprays. The colour had reminded her of the primroses in the woods beyond Whitwater, and although it was faded and rotting she had hung it in the back of her cupboard and had looked at it sometimes when her eyes were tired of the brighter colours and more flaunting blossoms of this new home.

Apart from the silver articles upon the dressing-table she did not possess even a brush and comb. She had given her own to Katje, who had, craftily, expressed vast admiration for them.

She refrained from mentioning this deficiency. She gathered the few things into her arms and said 'I am ready.'

'Come along then,' said Evert, resolutely repressing his surprise that she should own so little.

He moved the key from the inside to the outside of the door and locked it. He didn't feel so elated as he had expected, and he attributed that fact to her behaviour. Too proud to show that she minded, pretending not to care about possessions. Wait till to-night. She'll be stung into speech then. And I shall have something to say as well.

He stepped ahead of her and opened the door of the room he had mentioned. It was nothing more than the dressing-room of the room next door. The communicating door was locked and Annabet's new domain was a narrow oblong, nine feet long, five feet wide, with a little truckle bed pushed against the inner wall. There was a cupboard and a chest of drawers upon which had been set a basin and ewer and a tiny, heart-shaped swing mirror, no bigger than a plate.

'It's luxury compared with what Ayrton could have given you,' Evert said. 'The boys will bring you food at midday, and I shall hope for your company at dinner.'

He closed the door, but did not, as she had expected, lock it. Annabet laying her possessions on the bed, remembered, with a stab of irrepressible irony that both the night-gown and the wrapper which she wore had been given her by Evert ... if he had thought of it would he have made me walk along the gallery stark? Oh dear, was that anything to be amused about?

Evert found Josef clearing away the breakfast things. He pushed the door shut with his foot and signed to Josef to stop fidgeting with the dishes.

'Listen to me,' he said brusquely. 'Katje's gone, and unless you want to follow her you'd better swear by your Prophet's beard or anything else you hold holy not to mention a word about some other changes I'm going to make in this house.'

'Mynheer, have I ever ...'

'I'm not talking about the past, I'm talking about the future.

311

Are you going to swear?'

'But certainly, Mynheer. By the beard of the Prophet I swear not to mention any of Mynheer's affairs.'

'All right. I'm having Isa back to-night.'

Josef gave no sign of his unbounded astonishment or of his sharply pricking curiosity.

'Yes, Mynheer.'

'She'll help you with the work. Abbas and Juan are not to come inside the house again. If there isn't enough to occupy them in the kitchen they can start work outside. They're both too old and neither of them good enough to be houseboys, anyway. So if a breath of this business gets abroad I shall know where it comes from, and you'll be sorry. Do you understand?'

'Perfectly, Mynheer. But ...'

'But what?'

'Katje, Mynheer. Is she not to be replaced?'

'No, except by Isa. Mevrouw is persisting in a very foolish course of action, Josef, and I must show her that I am not a man to be trifled with. You would do well to remember that, too.'

'Yes, Mynheer.'

Business in Banda that day was at a standstill. Behind the closed doors of offices and in corners of quiet warehouses, out of the hearing of clerks and porters, men gathered in little groups to talk over the news and voice their opinions, the cheerful trying to encourage the pessimists, the pessimists endeavouring to discourage the cheerful. Within an hour of leaving his house, Evert had forgotten both Annabet and Isa. As the person who had been present at the moment of Knoel's return, and present also at that midnight meeting in Kaerko's house, his contribution to every conversation was eagerly welcomed, his opinion constantly invited, his blustering, sanguine view of the situation extremely popular.

The news itself was bad. Knoel had died at dawn. Shal Ahmi had not been traced. Twelve, then fifteen, then nineteen, and finally twenty-three of the wounded men, hastily operated upon by Van de Lijn in the reeking hospital inside the Fort, succumbed during the day. Their names were sent down to Kaerko so that he might register them in his book of deaths, and he made no attempt to keep the white population in ignorance. He was anxious himself and willing for others to share his burden.

Evert called upon him shortly before noon and asked bluntly whether his suggestion of following up the people mentioned in his account book had borne any results.

'So far nothing,' the Agent replied, with less complacency than Evert would have expected. 'At least,' he consulted a slip of paper, 'on the Vanderbosch estate—following a clue presented by the fact that one of the coolies had begged Shal Ahmi's intervention in a matter of criminal carelessness—the man, Manuelo Cortes, was found to be in possession of a pistol. At first we thought we had made a discovery, but he swore that Mevrouw Vanderbosch herself had entrusted him with it. And that was the truth. Mevrouw Vanderbosch, apparently, had taken it upon herself to select six men and arm them in case of trouble. If many other ladies have taken similar precautions, the natives know more about our fears and suspicions than we do ourselves. I took it upon myself to point that out to her and Vanderbosch, to my surprise, was most offensive. He said that if the performance of the soldiers yesterday was any gauge there was little to be hoped for in the way of protection from official sources and it was every man for himself.' Kaerko swallowed and his Adam's apple jumped convulsively. 'Haan, where *could* Shal Ahmi *be*? I'd have gone bail on his loyalty and integrity. But you must admit that his getting out of gaol and disappearing just now looks very fishy.'

'*I* admit it! My good fellow, it was I who first pointed it out to you.'

'Oh yes, yes of course. Last night. Really, I'm so confused I hardly know where I am or what I am doing. This is a horrible business. Did I tell you that poor Knoel's funeral was arranged for to-night? In the Fort burial-ground, privately. His Excellency did suggest that those of the wounded who could walk, and the few soldiers who are uninjured should attend, quite informally. It didn't seem right that a soldier who, after all, died in the service of his country should be shovelled away like a dead dog.' He looked at Evert miserably. 'What's the matter with this place, Haan? On the whole they're well-treated. I don't have much to do with the plantations I admit, but the natives who come into Banda on errands, and the ones who live and work here always seem happy enough. They laugh and sing and loaf about at the slightest opportunity. Now the moment when we're in trouble we've got to treat them as if they were enemies too. It's like building your house on what looks like solid rock and then seeing it turn into a quagmire.'

'No, no,' protested Evert cheerfully. 'It's not quite so bad as that. It's like having a straw stack near your back door. Perfectly harmless so long as nobody throws a taper at it. All we're doing is seeing that nobody gets a chance to throw a taper . . . and keeping a bucket of water handy.'

'I'd feel better if I knew that Shal Ahmi were under lock and key. D'you know, Haan. It struck me last night. After you and the Governor had gone I sat down and added up what I'd paid him. Our association has lasted for six years—I came here in the same season as poor old Knoel, you'll remember. That's by the way. Six years. I've never paid him more than two guilders for any single service and it was quite a year before I discovered how very useful he was. But what do you think the sum totted up to? One thousand, two hundred and fourteen guilders. What's he done with it? He lives in a hovel, he owns nothing, he has no dependants, he lives so meagrely that he's always glad of a bite at the back door. Where's one thousand two hundred and fourteen guilders gone? That's what I should like to know.'

Evert, who had sometimes paid Shal Ahmi twice that sum in a single year and sometimes asked himself the same question, gave voice to a supposition with which he had often satisfied his own curiosity.

'I believe he owns property in Bandogar. Once, after that tornado, he asked me on my next trip to place an order for a new roof to a house there. That's all I have to go on. He may have been acting as a landlord, or as a charitable friend. Or the people in the house may have been his relatives. I don't know.'

'No. That's just it, Haan. Nobody knows anything about him, really. It seems incredible that he should have lived in the midst of a small community like ours, so open to inspection and so ridden with gossip and yet retained his mystery. Isn't it queer?'

'Everything about him is queer if you ask me. And the sooner he's found and locked away again the better.'

'Yes,' Kaerko nodded his head and looked miserable. 'On the other hand, with Knoel dead, I'm in an awkward position. Or at least I should be, if he were brought back. That charge of fowl-stealing was very shaky; I shouldn't have locked him up on it. Therefore it follows that he wasn't so wrong in seizing a chance to get away and ...'

'Nonsense,' Evert interrupted rudely. 'That's all water under the bridge. We want him now on suspicion of communicating with the enemy. We're at war, man. We've suffered a serious reverse, and our backs are to the wall. We can't afford any sentimental twaddle about justice and such like. We'll give him a fair trial when we've won the war.'

Kaerko looked relieved. Outside the routine duties of his post he liked being told what to do. Now Knoel, who had enjoyed directing and even mildly bullying him, was dead; and the Governor wasn't positive enough. In a world where so many things had gone wrong at once, and where so many decisions had to be taken, it was quite a comfort to find someone who could rap out 'Nonsense' and state a firm, even if misguided, opinion. From that morning dated Kaerko's dependence upon Evert. More frequently during the next days and nights was he to say, 'Let's send for Haan,' or, 'I should like Haan's opinion on that.'

Evert spent a longer day than usual in Banda and did not attempt to return to Coenpark until dusk. Nothing of note had happened since his visit to Kaerko; Shal Ahmi had not been found; no further signs of revolution had been uncovered. At four o'clock in the afternoon the Governor had issued a proclamation, forced out of him by the flying rumour that Colonel Knoel, seriously wounded, had been carried ashore during the previous evening. The proclamation, written in Dutch, Malay, Chinese and Tamil, merely stated that the war was going well. Colonel Knoel had returned to Banda in order to report upon the day's fighting in Lu, and had then proceeded to Gadia as arranged. Further bulletins would be issued as soon as reliable news arrived, and in the meantime it would be to the advantage of everybody if work went forward as usual.

Evert, passing the door of a warehouse upon which a copy was nailed, halted and stood at the edge of a little knot of coolies, porters and minor clerks and boatmen who had gathered round it. A honey-coloured boy with so severe a squint as one would have thought would have precluded him from reading at all, had just gabbled out the Dutch version and had started upon the Malay, showing off, very proud of himself, pausing now and then to shush, with great firmness, those of his elders, and betters who, having profited by the Dutch reading, were now trying to discuss it to the detriment of those of his hearers who still awaited the translation.

'Bravo,' said Evert loudly, when for the second time the boy raced through the final sentence and spread his hands to show that he had finished. 'Very clever, my boy,' he said, with the geniality which so often sweetened his casual contacts. 'I'll wager a guilder you can't twist your nimble young tongue round the next lot.'

'Mynheer will lose his guilder,' said the boy with a cheeky smile which, momentarily obliterating the squint, made him oddly attractive. Hardly looking at the paper, trusting his memory, and with his crooked gaze shifting between Evert and the Chinese members of his audience, he rattled through the proclamation again in fluent Chinese.

'Splendid,' said Evert, tossing the coin expertly. 'Five, if you can master the Tamil.' He looked around and noted the faces of those few who were still waiting, patient, unenlightened.

'Five, Mynheer? Never in my life did I earn money so easily. Listen.'

This time he turned his back to the paper and in a loud clear voice gabbled the Governor's message for the fourth time. Evert saw one or two of the hitherto blank faces lighten with understanding. The boy wasn't cheating.

Good-humouredly he handed over the money.

'I doubt if there's another boy in Banda who could have

315

done it,' he said.

'Necessity loosens the tongue, Mynheer. My mother is Malay, my father from Cormandel, my master is Chinese, and my native tongue is Dutch.' His good eye looked at Evert and his other seemed to turn a derisive glance at the oblong of paper. 'What is more, Mynheer, a lie is a lie in any language.'

'Hi. What's that? What the devil do you mean by that?' Evert demanded. But the boy, with a final pert glance, had slipped through the little gabbling crowd and gone.

I shall know him again, that eye and the Chinese master will make him easy to find, Evert thought. I'll have him safe by ten o'clock to-morrow morning. Cheeky little devil. Maybe I ought to do something about it now. But I told Isa sunset. And though he seemed to be looking at the paper when he said 'lie,' that may have been just his affliction. And the damned natives love to make wild wide sweeping statements like that. He may not have meant anything. All the same, I wish I'd got my hands on him.

The memory rankled in him half-way to Coenpark. Then he forgot it. The sweet treat he had prepared for himself was about to begin.

A whole day, spent in complete silence and solitude, in a room nine by five with nothing but a loathsome bit of embroidery and one's thoughts for company, is a wonderful clarifier of one's mind. By the time when Evert returned, Annabet had settled exactly what she must say to him, with dignity and restraint, but with assurance; and for quite a long time she had been looking forward to his arrival. She was not frightened of him any more.

She heard him enter; there was nobody else who would come straight in at the front door, and nobody else ever pushed the door closed with such a careless, backward thrust. But some time elapsed before he flicked his fingers across the door of her dressing-room and called, in quite a cheerful voice, 'Are you ready for dinner? Don't keep me waiting. I'm hungry.'

Annabet herself was empty rather than hungry. She had had no dinner, no breakfast, and the boys had not arrived with the promised midday meal. No one had come near her all day, and she was too miserable as well as too proud to go out and demand attention.

Now she smoothed her hair as well as she could with her hands, pinched up the pleats and the sleeves of the old faded, rotting yellow dress and stepped out on to the gallery. Despite her cultivated calmness of mind her heart began to thud quickly and audibly as she made her way down the stairs. All the flowers in all the tubs and vases had been changed; they

316

were all scarlet now, some kind of lily, with stiffly-curving petals and great yellow stamens, thick with dusty pollen. She had never seen, or smelt, anything like them before. Their perfume was overpowering, heavy and sweet and languorous.

The candles were lighted in the dining-room and the door was open, an oblong of warm yellow light. She could see the middle section of the table from where she stood on the stairs, and it held more silver and more flowers and more candles than usual. Evert surely wouldn't have asked guests to-night ... knowing that she must come to the table in this old gown, without even having been able to brush her hair. Or ... wasn't that just the kind of thing he was capable of? If this were part of her punishment, she must bear it.

She straightened her back and lifted her head and walked into the room with that peculiar gentle dignity which had made Piet prefer her to Klara in the church at Heydberg all those months ago.

Evert was sitting at one end of the table, his plate already piled, his glass filled. Josef, with his back to the room, was moving dishes about on the sideboard. And somebody was sitting in Annabet's chair, at the other end of the table. A third place was laid in the centre of one of the longer sides. As his wife halted just inside the doorway, Evert pointed to it with an oddly uncouth movement of his knife-handle.

The situation needed no explanation. This is one of the things I must bear, Annabet thought. It doesn't matter. To fuss would be ridiculous. Having forfeited all claim to Evert's esteem, I mustn't mind his behaviour.

She slipped into her place, saying quietly. 'Good evening.' The little golden-brown girl choked over a mouthful of food. Evert took a noisy gulp from his glass. Josef's usually careful hands let a plate fall with a clatter.

Everybody is as uncomfortable as I am myself, Annabet thought.

Josef placed a plate of food before her, and she applied herself to it for a moment or two, not knowing, despite her hunger, what she was eating.

The silence in the room became a pain. Desperately, irrationally, she sought for some word which would end it. But what could she say? Was there a single phrase that would be acceptable? And was it for her to speak at all? Neither hostess nor guest ... When Evert had planned this, for planned it must have been, had he envisaged the possibility that her intended discomfiture would be shared by everyone, even by Josef? Evert himself seemed to be trying to cover the silence by noisy manipulations of his knife and fork; the little brown girl ate like some dainty animal, sometimes using her fingers. Her small pretty face wore a look of frightened malevolence such

317

as might, indeed, have been seen upon the face of a small wild creature held captive in unnatural surroundings.

Josef, tray in hand, went out of the room. Had he to fetch the next course of the meal himself? Where were the boys?

As soon as he had gone Evert brought his heavy mocking look to bear upon the girl.

'Well,' he said, 'you're making slow work of it. What's the matter? Isn't it to your liking?'

'Is very good. But I am not hungry.'

'And you,' said Evert, switching his glance to Annabet, 'have you lost your appetite as well as your tongue?'

'I was hungry,' Annabet said, laying down her knife and fork, 'but I am satisfied now. I think, if you don't mind, I'll go back to my room. I had ... something I wanted to say to you, but it will do later on.'

'You'll oblige me by staying where you are and taking a little notice of my guest. You were always one to point out the beauties of nature, and you've hardly looked at her. Look at her. Don't you think she's pretty?'

Isa, after another flashing look of malevolence, stared down at her plate. Why, Annabet wondered, was Evert so anxious for her to study the girl? One glance had been enough to reveal all that was of significance ... that she was a woman, that she was attractive, that she was brown, and that she was in the place of honour at the table. Probably most women, after that one glance would have turned and walked away; and they would have been wise. Was that what Evert had expected and wanted? And if she had retreated would he have ordered her back, made a scene?

Then she realised why Evert had ordered her to look at the girl. Hung in the little brown ears were the emerald and diamond ear-rings, the matching necklace sparkled upon the slender, round, honey-brown neck, the ring flashed from the thumb of the little brown hand—too big for any of the slim, red-tipped fingers.

Oh, Evert, she thought, how pitiable, how puerile! As though I would mind. And again she wondered what had he hoped for, what had he expected. Was she supposed to scream now, or rave, or fling herself upon that little childish creature and try to snatch back her possessions?

Isa raised defiant eyes. Annabet looked straight at her and said quietly, 'You are very, very pretty. And the trinkets suit you extremely well.'

The bitch, Evert thought furiously. All pose, all pretence. At heart, of course, she would like to dash at Isa and scratch her eyes out. But she wouldn't give him the pleasure of knowing that he had provoked her; too proud; too much a Van Goens.

318

Subtlety was wasted on their thick-hided conceit. He should have taken a stick and given her a damned good thrashing.

And the other little trollop was pretty well equally annoying; instead of sitting up and making the most of herself and throwing herself in madam's pasty, sick-looking face, there she sat, looking like a cornered monkey, half scared, half savage.

Josef, with the vast, devout, injured dignity of a high priest condemned by circumstances to scour the floor of his sanctuary, bore in a tray of food and began to change the plates. The strained silence lay hold upon the room again. But the crisis was past. Annabet knew now what Evert had hoped for. Evert knew that his plan had failed in its purpose. And she won't flinch—he thought—at the idea of Isa and me in that room. Goddamn her, she's had me jealous for two years, but she'll never be jealous of me. Not that I care, he told himself, ignoring a strange stab at his vitals. I've finished with her. And I shall have Isa....

He looked along the table and let his eyes dwell upon the brown girl, trying by anticipation and the memory of past delights to spur himself into a comfortable state of about-to-be-gratified lechery. But there was no response. In his mind he could strip Isa naked, no nerve, no muscle moved. With something very much like dismay he realised that Isa had lost her power.

Against his will he looked at Annabet. Yellow hair a little tousled, pale face a little sunken, eyes reddened with tears; long neck and fingers unadorned, body quiescent within the faded shabby dress....

With a blinding flash of revelation he saw what had happened to him; knew what had lain behind his tolerance, his patience, his discontent, his jealousy, behind last night's fury and spurious sense of freedom, behind the glee with which he had planned his revenge. Stunned and dumb, he realised that in one respect he was no more immune than other men, and no luckier. Too late he knew that he could no more humiliate Annabet than he could possess her. He could only love her.

His new knowledge, once assimilated, served only to infuriate him further. When the wretched meal was at last over he sent Isa away, dismissing her with a few brusque words. Then he turned towards Annabet and said in much the same tone, 'Well, you said you wanted to speak to me. Out with it; but I warn you, if you're thinking a few soft words will put you back where you were, you're going to be disappointed.'

'I wasn't thinking of that, Evert. I've been over and over in my mind all day, and I just wanted to explain something to you, and then ask you to let me go back to Holland.'

'You can go back to Holland when you can pay your own passage,' Evert said brutally, and was lashed to further anger to find that hurling insults into that sad white face brought pain as well as pleasure. 'I've wasted enough money on you,' he added.

'Then perhaps I could go elsewhere; or perhaps I could find someone who would take me. I could ... cook and mend.' She brought out the last words with extreme diffidence. So small and uncertain tools. 'You mean that if I can find a way to go you would allow me? You don't want me here any longer?'

'What I want or don't want has never been your first consideration in the past. We won't discuss my feelings now. I am waiting to hear what you please to call an explanation.'

'It is more an apology. Evert, if I talked for an hour I couldn't tell you how sorry I am that it has turned out like this. I was so very ignorant. I'd no idea what love meant when I came to Banda. When I was very young I imagined that I was in love with my cousin, but that was just girlish fancy, and then he became a priest. It was he, in a way, who sent me here, although he didn't know it. When I first realised what had happened to me, I was almost mad, and then he came and told me things that are half true and half false about the spirit being more important than the body. And then there was Mamma, she said no husbands and wives were in love before they married, and that if I tried to please you, and minded my manners and kept your house well, everything would be all right. And I might get better. I didn't come to you in the wrong spirit, Evert. And what Mamma said might well have been true ... if Christy hadn't come.' Her fingers moved in the pleats of her faded dress, wrenching and plaiting nervously; the red colour washed over her pale face; but she went on steadily, aware that Evert was, at least, listening attentively. 'Honestly, Evert, I couldn't help falling in love with him. It's the last thing I would have chosen. I never ... you know, Evert, you must know that I ... that we ... I only kissed him before he went; and I knew really then, in my heart, that I should never see him again. It was mad of me to tell you what I did. But I was grateful because you'd had me cured and I wanted you not to be disappointed, because, you see, knowing how I felt about Christy I knew I should never feel like that about you or any other man. I did give you the chance to send me home then. Didn't I?' Evert stared unspeaking. 'And about what I did for Shal Ahmi. I'd no idea then that it was war he was warning them of. I couldn't do nothing and let Christy be killed when I had the means to warn him in my hand. Evert, if you've ever been fond of anyone in your life, put yourself in my place and try to understand. I'm not asking you to take me for your wife again. I realise how horrible I seem to you. But if we could ...

part ... without hatred. If I needn't feel that I'd ruined your life as well as my own....'

'And that's all you have to say?'

Annabet nodded. There had been other things, little frail silly things that could not be spoken in the face of Evert's cold, scornful stare.

'You make out a very good case for yourself, poor little innocent. But you must know in your heart that it's all sentimental rubbish. Look at my side for a moment. I married you, beggared, crippled, a bag of skin and bones; I overcame my own prejudices in order to give you the last chance of recovery, I gave you everything you wanted, and a lot that you'd never have thought of; I treated you with respect; I was faithful. In two whole years I never gave a thought or a glance to another woman. And what is my reward? You turned my house into a stew; day and night you were pining and fretting for your lover, and finally you turned traitor to save his worthless hide.' The words seemed to wake an echo, and he realised that they were just a repetition of what he had said before. A kind of sick weariness came over him; round and round we go, over and over the same bit of ground, getting nowhere, he thought; it's like a fencing match against somebody who will stay out of reach. If only she'd acted like as I thought she would when she saw Isa, we'd have had a blazing row and I could have thrown her own jealousy in her face as proof that she did care. But it's no use. She doesn't. Nothing will make her. And arguments are just a waste of time.

'Colonel Knoel died this morning; twenty-three soldiers died during the day. There'll be more deaths to-morrow. Half those men would be alive, celebrating the shortest and best-planned campaign in history, but for you. Take that thought to bed with you. Your friend Shal Ahmi is still at large, and God only knows what devilry is going on under the surface. Maybe we'll all perish in our blood before this thing is done. But perhaps you think that a small price to pay for the safety of Christy Ayrton's carcass. Love like yours must be worth having, my lady. You make me sorry that I could never attain to it. Good night.'

That did break her. She turned and went stumbling out of the room like an old woman, her hands over her face, her shoulders shaking with sobs.

He had an irrational impulse to call her back, to say—that's all rot, soldiers expect to die in a battle, it's what they're paid for, and as for Shal Ahmi, he'll rot in gaol; and reinforcements will come and we'll grind the English into powder. They were the things he would have said if she had brought this tragic situation about through any other reason than a desire to save Ayrton. How stoutly he would have comforted her! How

321

madly and unreasonably he longed to do it now, even now, knowing why she had acted. Really, he must be a little crazy. And could you wonder?

The sun was quite high next morning when Isa tapped on the dressing-room door and called softly, 'Mevrouw, I have brought your breakfast.'

So there was another day to face. She had spent most of the early hours of the night in tears and frantic prayers, at first for forgiveness and then for death. When at last she had lain down upon the outside of the little truckle bed she had felt so ill and so utterly exhausted that it had seemed possible that her later request might be granted. Of forgiveness she had no sign. Mevrouw Van Goens, who had abandoned the practice but retained the ideology of her own faith when she left Brussels to marry her Protestant cousin, and Father Vincent who had seen in young Annabet's earthly affection an opportunity to sow seeds which might later come to flower, would have been pleased, perhaps, to know that in this extremity her distracted mind had adopted a strongly Catholic bias. She had prayed for the souls of all the men for whose deaths she felt responsible. That they had died with their sins upon them she begged might be reckoned against her, not against them. She had prayed, not only to God but to the Virgin, and those of the Saints whom she could remember by name. For herself she had begged forgiveness, not only for unchaste thinking and worldly behaviour but for having voluntarily abandoned the opportunity of leading a devout and dedicated life. Not going to Ireland was the first and the most heinous of her offences, all the others stemmed directly from that. And when at last she had fallen into exhausted, leaden slumber whose precincts were like the precincts of death, she had expected to wake to the pains of Purgatory which must not be thought of as the sterile process of punishment but as a blessed chance of the ultimate attainment of forgiveness.

And now there was Isa with a breakfast tray.

She opened the door and stood in the shaft of light from the gallery. She had slept in the yellow dress. Her unbrushed yellow hair was wild and tangled, her face more hollow and whiter than it had been even on the previous evening, and her eyes were sunk in lilac-coloured shadows. She looked ill, and mad, Isa thought.

The little brown girl was bright and flowerlike in her scarlet jacket and a sarong of clear apple-green. Her own gold earrings were in her ears this morning, and her jingling collection of coloured bangles glinted upon her slim arms. But her beautiful brown dove's eyes were heavy-lidded, and she wore an expression that was at once sulky and troubled.

Annabet said, 'Thank you,' and put out her hands to take the tray. Isa did not relinquish it, however. She entered the room, and pushing back the basin and ewer on top of the chest of drawers set down the tray, taking in every detail of the cramped apartment as she did so. It was rather strange, Annabet thought, that Evert's new favourite should be waiting upon her, and she said 'Thank you' again, humbly. Isa flashed her one of those queer glances and then looked at the tray.

'I hope I have done it right. There was no one to ask except Josef, and he was busy and would not help.'

'It looks just right,' said Annabet gently. 'You won't ... you mustn't mind if I leave some. I'm not hungry. But I am grateful for the coffee. It smells lovely.'

Isa backed away from the chest of drawers and stood in the tiny space between the foot of the bed and door.

'Mevrouw,' she said, and the word was jerked out nervously. 'I want to say something. It is this. I did not ask to return. It is not because of me it has happened thus.'

'Oh no. I know that. I never imagined for a moment ...'

'In some way you have made him very angry, Mevrouw.' Difficult to tell whether that was a question or a statement. The girl's lilting little voice made either possible. If it were a question perhaps one ought not to reply. There was such a thing as dignity, though in the circumstances ...

'Yes. I have made him very angry.'

'And it was for your punishing that he brought me back.' Again that doubt as to whether she was bent upon giving or extracting information. But this time Isa did not wait for an answer. She rushed on, and as she spoke something very curious seemed to happen within, or rather behind her eyes, it was almost as though a red flame had waved back and forth and then gone out. 'That was a bad thing. And to give me the jewels and pretend they were for me alone. And to pretend that it would all be as it was before, but better. Mevrouw, that is what he did. I did not know. I would not have come to be made sport of.'

There was nothing that one could say to that. To offer pity might seem insulting; one knew too little of her circumstances to say, well, why not go home? She might not have a home. Her whole past life and her background were beyond the reach even of imagination. At some past time she had lived at Coenpark and been Evert's mistress, that much was clear; and then she had disappeared so entirely that Annabet had never heard even a breath of rumour as to her existence. Now, out of that obscurity, she had emerged again, a tool in Evert's hand for Annabet's punishment. And human enough to feel the ignominy of her position. Not to be blamed, or pitied, or advised.

The silence had fallen again. Annabet moved to the tray and poured a cup of coffee. Standing there she caught a glimpse of herself in the tiny heart-shaped mirror and was appalled, first at her own appearance and then by the greatness of her horror. Having renounced the world and prayed to die it did seem ridiculous to feel so violently about one's hair. Quite clearly there was something peculiarly worldly about hair; in Convents they cut it off! Her eyes turned towards the little case which held her needles, her thimble and the sharp-pointed scissors which had been old Truitje's parting present. For a moment the balance of her mind hung undecided. A sense of guilt, despair, exhaustion, self-abnegation upon the one side, nothing but youth and vanity upon the other. Then, impulsively, she turned to Isa:

'Do you think you could lend me a comb? Your own comb.'

'I have none of my own, Mevrouw. He said I need nothing. Everything, he said, I should find in the place prepared for me. And that was true. I did not know then that all the things were yours. But I will fetch it.'

'But I ... perhaps...' Oh, wasn't it an awkward thing to put into words. Isa flashed a look of complete understanding.

'Just the same, I will fetch it.'

Was that anything to be amused at? Wasn't it the awful final proof of her entirely graceless and degenerate nature that at such a moment she should find anything funny? But it was. And as Isa petered in with the silver comb and the silver-backed brush as well, Annabet gave vent to something that was very like the conspiratorial giggle which had so often sounded through the bleak Heydberg house; and Isa's silky sulky lips parted in a smile that held more malice than amusement. In that moment a bond, frail, frangible but real enough, was forged between them. Except in moments of rivalry over a man there is a curious freemasonry among women.

Von Holk arrived in Banda in a mood of self-confidence and self-importance calculated to restore cheerfulness to a community far more shattered than that of the islands actually was. He laid—foolishly, since no man can foresee the future with certainty and what he has said against a predecessor may so easily be said again against himself—the whole blame of the original expedition's failure at Knoel's door. Knoel was dead, and apart from the few sentences written when his eyes were dimming and his hand failing, he had no defence, and deference to this pitiable defencelessness took the form of referring to him perpetually as 'poor Knoel,' or, by those who had known him well, 'poor old Knoel.'

Von Holk, during the voyage down from Batavia had had ample opportunity to study the dead man's report. It proved conclusively in his opinion that the late Colonel was a fool, unfit to be trusted with any mission of importance. No numbers were given, or even suggested, no directions, no times. 'In the afternoon' ... 'inland, behind the huts' ... vague, unprofessional. And of course the culmination was just what might have been expected from a campaign headed by a vague and unprofessional person. 'Some English opened fire...' the kind of thing any layman would write.

Convinced that Banda's premier soldier had been stupid and lacking in precision, Von Holk did not expect much from the Governor and the Agent; and he saw in them exactly what he expected to find. The Governor was dithering, indecisive, nervous, and the Agent was fussy, nervous, dithering and indecisive. Voss, whom Knoel's death had left in command of the remaining soldiers was, in his new superior's opinion, little short of imbecile. Instead of drilling his new draft and getting them ready for action he had spent his time hunting for some wretched native who had broken out of gaol. And not even found him. In an island the size of a pocket handkerchief: it was ludicrous; it was pitiable. And if the English were half as strong as Knoel's written and Voss' verbal report made out, the wonder was that they hadn't swooped down on the island and followed up their victory in Ay by the conquest of Banda, where the poor silly sods had even let their powder reserves be blown up by three natives with torches. This last fact stuck in Von Holk's mind like a burr in a sheep's fleece. Again and again he referred to it, sometimes as a joke, sometimes seriously. And when, within a short time of his arrival he discovered that the chief men of Banda were at least equally concerned with the possibility of a native rising as they were with the English war, his immediate mental reaction was to think—and no wonder! If they let three coolies destroy all their powder, how can they hope to hold down thousands?

He himself, straight from long-settled Batavia, regarded the settlers' fear as grossly exaggerated. He—to use his own expression—got to the root of the business about Shal Ahmi, within his first twenty-four hours of control. Why had Voss, with so much of importance to do, wasted his time combing through the alleys of Banda Neira and the compounds of the plantations? Voss explained; Kaerko explained; His Excellency explained. In each explanation the name of Evert Haan was prominent. Von Holk sent for Evert, and within five minutes had angered him so profoundly that only the most iron self-restraint prevented Evert from bursting out with the stark, awful truth. How would Von Holk's boiled pudding face with its gooseberry eyes look if Evert rapped out, 'I know Shal Ahmi warned the enemy because my wife carried his message. Ask her, if you doubt my word.' Not to be able to say it. God,

325

it was enough to make a man mad. It is like holding a master card in a game and not being able to play it. But he stuck to his story about Mevrouw Van Heem's last words to Annabet, and made much of the significance of Shal Ahmi's escape from gaol under cover of the raid which was supposed to free Seth Aranda, and relieved his temper by barking at the great man in a manner which even the Governor himself did not dare to use.

'If you're so clever, then, tell us poor fools who the hell did send the warning if he didn't?'

'I don't think they were specifically warned,' Von Holk replied, not in the least offended. 'It's so fashionable to underrate the English that if they show the slightest bit of cunning everybody imagines that someone of another nationality has had a hand in it. The English themselves encourage this supposition. They like to be thought simpletons. They laugh in their sleeves. I haven't the slightest doubt that they guessed what would happen to them, sooner or later, and probably had assembled themselves and their weapons in a strategic position months ago. Because Knoel didn't find them at breakfast, you all begin to talk of treachery, and Voss wastes his time hunting the supposed traitor. And what is more, some idiot from Lonthoir ... what was his name, Banderbosch or something like that, actually forced his way into my presence this morning demanding that before I move against the English I make sure that everything is safe at home. He suggested that I leave a posse of picked men to patrol the islands. I sent him off with a flea in his ear.'

Evert, who had actually no patience with Vanderbosch, and no fears for himself, and no doubts as to the docility of the Coenpark natives, belied his own feelings and retorted:

'Vanderbosch is old enough to remember Kraemer's campaign. And he knows more about native behaviour than you and I will ever learn.' He looked into Von Holk's face as he delivered this rebuke, and then, satisfied that he had done his duty by his fellow planter, added truculently, 'Not that we want any men left. Vanderbosch happens to be nervous. You go ahead and pound Ay into powder and we'll take care of things at home.'

Von Holk, for some reason, liked Evert better than he liked anyone he had met so far in Banda.

'Leave that to me,' he said in a friendly way. 'I'm leaving Voss in charge here. I've replenished his powder stores. If you can keep the natives from running amok with torches, you've ample supplies to keep order.' He grinned sardonically, and Evert squirmed. If Von Holk knew what he, Evert Haan, knew, of Shal Ahmi's resource and cunning, he wouldn't find anything funny in three natives blowing up the entire powder reserve. But alas, that source of information was also sealed. Nobody in Banda, except Evert Haan, knew the depths and reach of Shal Ahmi's guile; and he, Evert Haan, was battling against it, single-handed.

The fresh powder had been stored, all together, at Von Holk's suggestion, in the ground floor of one of the gatehouses of the Fort. The place had two prime advantages: it was easily accessible from the inside of the Fort, and from the outside it was under the constant surveillance of the sentries who guarded the gate. In his last interview with Voss—who felt very shamed and sore at being left behind this time—Von Holk had said in the jibing manner which covers the greatest insults, 'Don't, even if the Governor himself suggests it, go chasing any gaol-breakers; and if you see any natives with torches hanging around the gatehouse, set your terrier on them.'

Voss, who had been aboard the *Margarete* when the previous powder stores were fired, resented this jibe, and with youthful lack of caution retorted in a manner which was going to do him a very ill-service when Von Holk returned to Head-quarters. And then, because he was young, and had failed with his second landing party to extricate Knoel, whom he had idolised, from that death hole between the musket barrage and the blazing huts, and had failed again in his search for Shal Ahmi, and had failed yet a third time when he tried to per-suade his new commander to take him on the next expedition, went back to the Fort, and straight to the board which bore the list of the names of the trusted white soldiers who were picked for sentry duty. He scratched out the name of one of every two on night duty and substituted his own. Then he had his hard camp bed moved into the doorway of the powder store. He would go on guard all night; he would work from eight in the morning till two; from two until six he would sleep in such a position that if the powder were blown up he would be blown up with it, and Von Holk, returning victorious—as he would, his sort always did, and he had poor old Knoel's experience to profit from—shouldn't have any chance to taunt him.

Von Holk sailed at sunset. He planned a dawn attack. This time, by his own orders, there was no crowd upon the beach to see the *Greta,* the *Seabird* and the refitted *Sanje* set sail; and the new bulletin from the Governor, in Dutch, Malay, Chinese and Tamil, informed the islanders that evening that fresh forces under General Von Holk had gone to relieve the vic-torious soldiers of Colonel Knoel from the wearisome task of rounding up the English survivors who had taken to the jungle. The squint-eyed boy with his Pentecostal gift of ton-gues was no longer there by the warehouse door to delight his listeners with his virtuosity. Evert had reported him first thing in the morning after his performance, and when the new paper was nailed to the door he was safely in gaol.

At two o'clock in the morning after Von Holk's departure, Lieutenant Voss and the sergeant who had admitted Trudi Van Heem and Annabet to Shal Ahmi's cell were on guard together. The sergeant, usually an amiable man, was sulky. Night guard was boring and deadly at any time, but generally you knew perfectly well that at midnight and perhaps—but not certainly—again at about four o'clock, the officer on duty would stick his head out of the gateway and inquire whether all was well. Between those two moments you and Dirk (it was generally Dirk, that wasn't too difficult to arrange) were able to sit down in comparative comfort, backs against the wall, and talk, or play 'Nobbin,' or drowse as the fancy took you. Now, instead of Dirk, Lieutenant Voss, bolt upright, deadly serious, was sharing the night duty, and the eight-hour spell, long enough at any time, stretched out interminably.

There was no moon that night, but the stars, except when hidden by scudding clouds, were brilliant; and there were two lanterns, one on either side the main gate. At intervals, to ease the tedium of standing and to keep themselves awake, Voss and the sergeant turned right, or left, and marched to the end of the wall and back again. They took turns and the gate was never for a second left unguarded.

The sergeant took his turn, walked to the end of the wall, and since Voss stood in the circle of light thrown by the lanterns and a cloud just then blotted out the star glimmer, was momentarily lost to sight. Voss found himself almost automatically counting in time to the man's paces, just as he counted his own, for lack of something better to do, when he walked his beat. Ninety-six, turn, and ninety-six back again. But this time, after the ninety-sixth pace there was a pause, a moment, perhaps a little more, it might be less, it was difficult to reckon exactly. Then the steady pacing footsteps began again and the sergeant walked back to the edge of the circle of light and took up his regular position. It was not difficult to account for that momentary pause, and it went through Voss' head that he would make similar use of his next second of privacy. Might as well go now. He turned; and immediately a heavy body hurled itself upon his back, and there was an excruciating sharp pain in the back nape of his neck. He opened his mouth to shout and no sound, only a gush of blood came from it. He fell forward on his face.

Seven minutes later there was a great blinding flash and a roaring explosion that seemed to shake the whole island. Von Holk, with his scorn of what he called 'piddling little dumps, impossible to guard properly,' had, by insisting upon housing the new powder all in one place, played straight into the hand of whoever it was who was so anxious that there should be no ammunition in Banda Fort. And this time the damage was not confined as on the previous occasion to the powder and the isolated buildings which had housed it. All the main gateway of the Fort was blown up; the Governor, whose palatial suite was immediately over it, was killed in his bed; and the hospital, which was directly behind the place where the powder had been stored, was entirely wrecked.

Voss' body, with its head half severed from behind, was not recovered until long after when a new Governor, planning a new front to the Fort, ordered the heaps of stone from the old one to be moved. The flesh had all gone from the bones by that time, but the knife which had killed him—a curved Malay kris—was still there bedded into the vertebrae of his skeleton. The sergeant's body, however, stripped of its distinctive yellow shirt but clad in its breeches, was found at the end of the wall. And nearby was a worn and shabby coat of rust-coloured velvet, old-fashioned even when judged by the standard of the gentleman of Banda who must wait a year for any news of a change in cut, and then perhaps five more before they could take advantage of it. But it was not the old-fangledness of the garment, nor its worn silver-gilt buttons and obstinately clinging shreds of tarnished lace, all so suggestive of past glory which made it significant in the horrified eyes of those planters and merchants privileged to see it. For the coat had three pockets, two in its skirts, one in its torn and dirty lining. And in each pocket there was something which only a very careless person—or a very cunning one—would have discarded with the coat. In one was an English Book of Common Prayer, in the edition sanctioned by Archbishop Laud and made the subject of one of his Acts of Uniformity; in another a simple leather purse, greasy from long usage, and containing fifteen shillings and fourpence in English money; and in the small inner pocket, was a letter, also greasy, and frayed and worn very thin in the folds. It bore a date, January, 1648, and began, 'My Own Dear Edward.'

When Evert saw the coat and the contents of its pockets, they were laid out on the biggest desk in Kaerko's office. It was still very early in the morning and the room faced west, but Kaerko had drawn the shades over the window because he had been crying and wished to hide the red rims of his eyes. But this morning everyone's eyes were red-rimmed, for nobody had slept much after that explosion, and certainly nobody was in a mood to be critical.

'Well, what d'you make of that?' Kaerko asked; and although Vehmeer and Van Heem and Lieutenant de Klerk were all in the room together with half a dozen others, he looked straight at Evert.

'I can tell you what I'm intended to make of it,' Evert said. 'It's all laid out as plain as print. I'm to think that an Englishman came ashore last night, stabbed the sergeant, put on his shirt and chucked away this coat, disposed of Voss, somehow, and touched off the powder. I know English money when I see it, and according to you the book and the letter are in the English lingo. All the same ...'

'Well?'

'I may sound daft, but to my mind it's a little *too* plain. As though somebody said, "Look in all my pockets and you'll see the same thing!" Do you see what I mean?'

'That it was put there deliberately to mislead us. That the guard was killed and the powder fired by ... a native. But where, in the whole of Banda, would any native find these?' Kaerko pointed to the things upon the desk.

'They're all old,' Evert said. 'And we haven't always been at war with the English.' He pondered for a moment and went off on another tack. 'There's no sign of what happened to Voss. If, as de Klerk says, he would stand by the gate while the sergeant walked, it's easy to guess that he's now under the stones. But suppose the sergeant cried out and Voss ran to him ... has the ground around there been searched?'

'Thoroughly,' said de Klerk. 'There isn't cover for a rabbit, and the ground is sandy. There was no sign of a scuffle or of a body being dragged. I thought of that,' he went on defensively. 'As soon as I found the one body and knew that Voss was missing, I searched with that in mind. Voss was my friend as well as my comrade in arms.'

'Yes, yes, of course. Well, Voss is either under the stones, or kidnapped. And if he was kidnapped by the English he's gone; but if it was a native job he's in the island somewhere. We must search.'

'Shal Ahmi, by all accounts, is in the island somewhere,' said Van Heem.

'But there is this difference. Shal Ahmi wants to remain in hiding. Voss, I take it, doesn't. I suggest that, just for the sake of making sure, we beat over the island again, and yell his name in every alley, every compound. It may seem just a waste of time, it may *be* just a waste of time. But if Voss were alive and could be found he could tell us what we want to know.'

Well, he thought, looking at Kaerko, if we're all agreed on that, give the order. Send me, go yourself, but for God's sake do something.

'Well,' said Kaerko, 'are we agreed on that? Then perhaps ...'

'Perhaps Lieutenant de Klerk would collect a party and set

out at once.' Evert smiled at the smart young soldier and said, disarmingly, 'You must forgive me if I'm taking too much on myself, Lieutenant, it isn't for me to give you orders. But all at sixes and sevens as we are and poor Kaerko here with everything on his hands. . . .'

'You couldn't have given me a job more to my liking. If Voss is alive and in Banda, I'll find him.'

'I'd like to say we'd get the stones moved and make sure that way,' Evert said. 'But it'd take a week no matter how many men we turned on to it. And if he's under there he's dead, and can't tell us anything.'

De Klerk hurried away. A curious silence fell upon the roomful of men. Kaerko fingered the velvet of the coat and stared at it as though he hoped to learn something from its texture. Then suddenly he lifted his head and spoke.

'I suppose,' he said, 'the Company never imagined a situation like this when they sent us here. But now you see the weakness of their arrangements. You've all been busily and profitably employed growing and shipping nutmegs, that's what you were here for. I was here to count nutmegs and keep tallies and tell you what the Company wanted in cargo and . . . in a way . . . behaviour; Knoel, God rest him, was here to keep order and assure us that we were protected against danger; His Excellency, God rest *him*, was here to. represent the Company's dignity and to see that neither Knoel nor I got above ourselves. But there wasn't any form of government, gentlemen. And now we're realising it, too late. Our world has fallen apart. We're at war with the English and have horrible reason to suppose that all is not well at home. The military authority, vested first in Knoel and then in Von Holk, is busy elsewhere; the civil authority, in the person of His Excellency, has been blown to pieces. What is left? We're worse off than the meanest village at home. That has its old, established orders, its known precedences. We have nothing. Sometimes I think,' he said with a wild glance at Evert, 'that I shall go mad.'

The silence which he had so suddenly broken, fell again. So much of what he said was so terribly true. Every man in the room had been obsessed with the production or the marketing of nutmegs. Planters and merchants—farmers and hucksters. Cut off from the old ways of life, where the Padroon ruled the village and the Burgermaster ruled the town. A new growth. Without real roots or shape. Now in the face of danger left without a rallying point. Dogs without a master. Sheep with no shepherd. Votaries of the sacred guilder, learning for the first time that money was nothing but a symbol.

'Nonsense man,' Evert said heartily. 'We've lost our figure-heads . . . but what are they except a decoration? We all had a

331

shock last night, but we're none the worse for that. The Governor, poor soul, is dead, and so are those poor crocks in the hospital. But all the real men are still alive. We've had sense enough to ask ourselves about *that*,' he tapped the velvet coat with his finger. 'If last night's business was the work of the English Von Holk is paying them for it now; and if it was the work of the natives we're ready and waiting for them. We're here, Kaerko, all of us, to plan the best means of defence. We're all free Dutchmen ready to defend ourselves. Isn't that so? We don't need anybody to tell us what to do or how to do it.'

'I grant you,' said old Cornelius Byskin in his reedy voice, 'that the Governor and the wounded men in the hospital are no great loss, materially. But the powder! Evert, doesn't your heart fail you when you realise that *twice* in so few days we have lost our powder?'

'Our powder? The public supply. The soldiers' powder, you mean. Did you ever stop to think, Cornelius, that if the Fort had been stuffed solid with powder and riots had broken out at places as far apart as say, Vanderbosch's place and mine and Hansen's, the soldiers, for all the good they'd be, might as well be armed with snowballs. Haven't you got powder of your own? And muskets? And pistols? Haven't you *three* men you could trust? Didn't you come out here with an idea that you might have to fight, as you worked, for yourself and your own? Don't think I can't see danger as clearly as any man. I'm not a fool. Shal Ahmi warned the English; he broke gaol; he's still at large; and that coat with all its paraphernalia stinks of him, to my mind. *But*, I've made sure that there isn't a firearm anywhere in Coenpark except in my house, and if the whole lot come against me with sticks and knives and torches, I'm ready for them. They'll get a warm welcome. And if you all go home and take the same precautions we shall hang out until Von Holk comes back.'

Cambellis, a merchant who lived in Banda Neira and who had actually been the first to throw himself into Kaerko's house demanding wildly, 'Now what shall we do?' spoke up in desperation.

'That's all very well for you, Haan, but we haven't all got compounds full of trustworthy natives. What about the town rabble? Did you happen to notice as you came along? Mobs of them, gossiping and staring. The secret is out now. They know that our backs are against the wall. All riots start in towns.'

'I'll give them something to riot about,' Evert said after a moment's reflection. 'They can start clearing up that mess outside the Fort. A good day's work stone-carrying for everybody who shows his face in the street. What d'you think of that for a cure?'

332

Every member of the hastily assembled council approved of the idea, but it was Evert who went out into the burning day and shouted the orders.

Panic mounted by steady, almost imperceptible stages all through that day. De Klerk, drawing blank after blank in search for Voss, sent a report to Kaerko from time to time, and the Agent was secretly relieved that this new combing of the island had revealed nothing which called for immediate action. As the day wore on he went, at shortening intervals, to an upper room of his house where the window looked out over the harbour, and with his glass to his eye scanned the glittering dancing waters for some sign of Von Holk's return. It had only taken Knoel sixteen hours to visit three islands and lose a battle; how long would it take Von Holk to attack one island and gain a victory?

By mid-afternoon the wretched little man was facing a new problem. From the outlying plantations of Lonthoir and other islands, a trickle, and then a growing crowd of frightened people began to pour into Banda Neira. The story of the finding of an English coat had spread rapidly, and gathered a snowball layer of rumour and supposition as it travelled. The later arrivals fully believed that the Von Holk's forces had been dispersed, that the English had attacked the town during the night and been beaten off, but would shortly attempt another landing at some unfortified spot. Planters, with their wives and their families, most of them accompanied by houseboys and maids, stewards and foremen known to be faithful, besieged Kaerko's house, avid for information, for advice, for comforting words. Kaerko was not without sympathy for them, but as the Company's Agent, he was much concerned for the safety of the plantations they had abandoned. Even at a moment like this, he could not happily resign himself to the thought of work stopping in the groves, of ripe nuts falling to the ground to rot, or being left to the rapacious doves. And apart from that, a compound full of idle natives, left without direction or discipline, constituted a special danger at such a time.

Putting aside his ordinary human feelings, he forced himself to speak as Agent to planter. 'But the house and the plantation is your property, held in trust from the Company. It is your duty to protect it. Who will, if you don't?' Several of the men, relieved to find the true situation less serious than flying rumour had portrayed it, regretted their precipitancy, and said they would go back as soon as they had found accommodation for their families. Then their womenfolk would cry and some would refuse to be parted, and some said they would go home too, if they could leave their children in safety, and at that the children would cry too. And Kaerko would scamper up the stairway and look out towards the harbour again and pray that he might catch a glimpse of the returning schooners. If only Von Holk could come back with news of a smashing victory, and take charge!

By sunset, when Evert gave the signal for the stone-carrying work to cease, even he was exhausted. Four times during the long hot day he had gone home to Coenpark and found everything going on as usual. He was not surprised by that. Behind his cheerful, blustering, confident exterior, he was suffering from a curious schism of mind. He *knew*, better than anyone in the islands, that Shal Ahmi was up to something, was in league with the English, was hidden somewhere and doubtless planning fresh devilry. Yet he could not, for the life of him, believe in the logical outcome of Shal Ahmi's plans and actions. The blessed lack of imagination which had been such an asset to his career in the past, prevented him, as he looked upon his placid slaves going about their work, from seeing them as anything but peaceful slaves. He had gone through all the motions of credulity and preparation. Josef, Hassan, the foreman Toeg, and half a dozen others had been partly taken into confidence and armed; Isa, pretending to be taking Katje's place, went to and fro between house and compound, warned to keep eyes and ears open. Not even the most frightened, most suspicious man, not Vanderbosch himself, could have done more. Yet, as he looked at his big, lovely, silent house dreaming away the afternoon within its circle of shrubs and flowers, Evert could no more imagine it with its windows smashed, its doors battered in, its walls charred by fire, than he could have imagined himself as a feeble drooling invalid.

All the same, his own sense told him that Shal Ahmi hadn't organised that ambush on Ay, or twice had the powder reserve destroyed in order that everything in Banda should go on as usual. It behoved a man, even if he couldn't quite believe in a threatened danger, to be wary and careful. But as after his fourth visit Evert had himself rowed swiftly back to town, intending to send his mob of labourers home—too tired, if he knew anything, to get into much mischief during the night— and pay a last visit to Kaerko and then return to look after his own house and plantation, he found himself wishing that something definite and irrefutable would happen. Something to clear the air. Something which would point to a focus for attack. The nervous strain to which even he had been subjected in the last few days took the form of impatience, unlike Kaerko's, which evidenced itself in a prayer for delay, for the deferment of the moment when the threat ceased to be academic.

He dismissed his gang of involuntary labourers cheerfully, yelling at them in Dutch and Malay that they had worked very well, and that there was food for all who wanted it at the bottom of the drill-yard. He had commissioned Van Heem and Vehmeer to collect food during the day. 'Good stodgy stuff, as much as possible,' he had said. 'And no liquor. We don't want an orgy. I reckon that tired limbs and a full belly'll keep 'em quiet till morning, anyway.' Van Heem and Vehmeer had amassed a great quantity of food, and as Evert saw the men, women and children trail away, tired, grateful, cheerful, he thought—and *they* don't look dangerous either! Then he looked behind him, across the drill-yard to the Fort, smashed like a honeycomb and felt another stab of impatience at the intangibility of the danger.

'Let's go and see Kaerko,' he said, laying a heavy arm on his companions' shoulders.

'There's no news,' Van Heem said heavily. 'I looked in less than an hour ago. The Hansens were there then, the whole family. Kaerko was suggesting that you should put them up, but Mevrouw Hansen said she hadn't left the Dyke in order to go to Coenpark which was just as isolated. So they're up at my place now. That makes sixteen.'

'We've got twenty-two,' said Vehmeer. 'Old Graef of Lonthoir arrived. He'd remembered all his bastards and rounded them up from the compound. Twelve of them. You never saw such a collection of dirty, ugly-looking little devils. Jehane is madder than a pi-dog. But when old Graef tackled me he'd got just his wife and his white lot with him then, the rest were round the corner somewhere. I offered him hospitality, and he went off. Then, just as I was weighing out the rice, Jehane sent for me to go home at once, and there were all those little brown beggars. What could I do? The poor old chap had tears in his eyes. "They're as much mine, Mevrouw, as these," he kept saying. Nice for Mevrouw Graef with her own pretty little brood! And the old beggar old enough to be her father. Funny though, how blood counts for more than colour at a moment like this.'

Evert's elbow jerked against Vehmeer's ribs and Vehmeer remembered, a moment too late, that though Trudi had borne Gert no children, Gert had known the joy of fatherhood. Evert said:

'I can't understand these fellows at all. As soon as I've seen Kaerko I'm going home, and if there's any trouble that's where I shall stay. I look after Coenpark and Banda must look after itself.'

'That's senseless. You'd do far better to bring your wife in and stay here until it's all over. Here, at least, we might hold out until Von Holk returns, if we all stick together. One man, even a bold one, Evert, doesn't stand a chance all alone.'

'I shan't be alone,' said Evert shortly. 'And I'm not sure yet that anything *will* happen. I've been thinking about things all day, and I ... By God I believe I see through it.' He brought his hand down on Van Heem's back in a blow that almost felled him. 'I see, now. It *is* the English at the back of it all ... not Shal Ahmi. He's just a tool. Their tool. I'll bet they fooled the old boy who boasted that he couldn't be fooled. They told him they were going to land and drive us out of here and promised him everything under the sun if he dropped them a word in season, and saw that the powder was kept short. And here we've been thinking of nothing but bloody rebellion. Slave rebellion my backside! Where'd we get that into our heads from?'

'From past history,' said Van Heem dryly.

Evert gave a grunt of scorn and disgust. 'Folks remember too much, too long,' he said, and releasing his hold upon his companions leaped ahead of them up the steps of Kaerko's house, eager to lay the result of his cogitation before somebody who would be glad to hear it.

De Klerk was with the Agent. His round boyish face was drawn and tired and flushed with dark dry heat. Kaerko, who seemed to have grown smaller and greyer in the few hours since the morning, was perched upon the edge of his desk, his feet in the seat of his chair. De Klerk was blurting out some story in a hasty, shamefaced manner.

'Ah,' said Kaerko, 'I was going to send for you as soon as de Klerk had finished. Go back to the beginning now, will you?'

'News of Voss?' Evert asked, as the young soldier hesitated.

'Not a sign. I've just made an utter ass of myself and stirred up trouble. That's all. I can't think why I was such a fool, but I really thought I'd got him. I was *sure*.'

'Shal Ahmi?'

'Yes. It was at the Horn—Vasser's place. You know how crazy he is; I didn't seem as though I could make him understand either what had happened or what we were looking for. He could only talk about nutmegs and thought we were looking for contraband. He wouldn't even come into the compound with us. So we went by ourselves. Myself, six men. And I saw an old, fat, bald woman peep out of a hut and go back in again, hastily. And I thought to myself, now why do you look familiar to me and then I realised. Gentlemen, that old woman was the very spitting image of Shal Ahmi himself. You know how Voss searched until it didn't seem possible that the man could be still on the island and not be found. I thought, I have it! That old woman is Shal Ahmi, disguised! I stopped looking for Voss. I told my men to surround the hut, and I went to the door. She sat on the floor, just inside, but by that time she'd

336

got on a red sari and all the coins were dangling over her eyes. Then I was sure. I felt a bit awkward, but I told her, first in Dutch and then in Malay to strip to the waist so that I could see she was a woman. She pretended not to hear, or not to understand, and somehow I got the idea that she was laughing at me. I know now, gentlemen, that I acted like a fool, but it just came over me that poor old Voss had spent his last days in the search and got nothing but a reprimand and a lot of jibing for his pains, and now he was dead, and here, within reach of my hand ... I just took hold of her clothing and ripped it off. She was a woman, no doubt about that, and she started to yell the place down. A couple of men came running out of the grove shouting and waving their gai-gais; my chap nearest the door put his musket across lengthways and one of the men brought his gai-gai down on his skull. They don't look as if they'd make much of a weapon, but by Heaven, my chap's head split like an apple. And before I could utter an order another of my fellows fired. You can't blame him. What he saw was not a native gone mad trying to get to his mother or aunt or something; he just saw his mate brutally assaulted, and he had his musket all ready primed ...'

'Yes, yes ...' his listeners all nodded, understandingly.

'By that time I'd left the old hag, clutching her rags and still yelling, and had got out and was just getting some sort of order when who should appear but Mynheer Vasser with a couple of pistols in his hands. D'you know what he did? Fired 'em both off, just blind, like that, right, left. Killed Dirk Brader outright, and shot Jan Heoke through the teeth.... I don't think he'll live. Two of my best men. And God knows I have few enough. That was sheer murder, gentlemen. He hadn't asked a question or looked, except to take aim. That's three good men lost on a search party, and all because I thought ...'

He broke off, and the four other men saw his short upper lip begin to quiver and his prominent brown eyes mist with tears.

'Vasser's been mad for ten years,' Evert said. 'You can't blame yourself for his behaviour. And by Heaven, if I saw an angel with wings, or a devil with horns that looked like Shal Ahmi just now, I'd strip 'em off just to make sure. I can't see that you have any cause to upset yourself.' He narrowed his eyes. 'You are quite positive that it *was* a woman? You weren't disturbed by the row? You did take a good look?'

'Oh yes, I am positive. It wasn't ... really ... a very pretty sight. But I looked.'

'Where's Vasser now?'

'In what remains of the gaol,' Kaerko answered the question.

'I brought him back with me,' said de Klerk eagerly. 'It was

337

murder ... and honestly, if I hadn't taken it seriously my remaining three would have probably ... I mean they really were horribly upset. I'm afraid he was in a bit of a mess when I handed him over. He didn't seem to understand what he'd done, you see, and they weren't very patient and he didn't come willingly. And it's a long way from the Horn.' He looked miserably at Evert and Van Heem and Vehmeer. 'I'm glad you understand; I was a bit afraid that I'd started a kind of civil war on top of everything else.'

'Oh, nobody cares about Vasser,' Evert assured him. 'He just could grow nutmegs, so the Company tolerated him. Isn't that so, Kaerko? But he's mad, and now he's a murderer. He can hang for all me.'

'Or me,' said Van Heem.

'And unless the English actually land here,' said Evert, going back to his own inspired train of thought, 'I don't think we need worry about the natives or Shal Ahmi. I can't think there's riot planned, we'd have found some sign during all these searches. If there were any chance of an English landing, maybe we might be stabbed in the back. But Von Holk will see that doesn't happen.'

'He's already been away longer than Knoel was,' said Kaerko drearily.

'Burning them out. Knoel simply bounced back. There's the difference,' said Evert, cheerfully, forgetting that he disliked Von Holk intensely. 'Well, if that's all, I'll get home. Look, I came by prahau, but I'll walk back. If anything should happen, of interest, shall we say? one of you give my man the word and send him home. Thanks. Good night, Kaerko, get some sleep, you look as though you could do with it. Good night, Vehmeer, I hope your lodgers behave themselves. If you see Cambellis, Van Heem, tell him that we've overworked and overfed his mob, and they're all sleeping like pigs. Good night, de Klerk, and don't you worry—or dream of your fat woman.' He nodded and grinned to each as he spoke, and strode away, slamming the door as was his habit; and something of cheer and confidence went with him. Every one of the four men he left was conscious for a moment of the length and the loneliness of the path to Coenpark ... and it was dark now ... and things unsettled, to say the very least.

Before Evert entered his house he made a round of the compound. Everything was just as it had been on a thousand nights before. He looked in upon Toeg, ostensibly to give some orders about the work in the morning, and heard, with his ears, what his eyes had already seen; everything was peaceful and quiet. He stopped Josef on his way to the kitchen and told him to serve dinner at once. And then he entered the house. And at

338

once a curious feeling of flatness came upon him.

In the old days Isa had always been waiting like a faithful, yearning little dog, or like a child. She would hide behind a bank of flowers, or just within a room, or on the curve of the stairs, and then call, or jump out upon him, welcoming him with little cries and clasps and kisses. In more recent times there had been Annabet, beautiful, silky, smooth and scented, waiting for him in the drawing-room, or coming downstairs towards him, with a smile and words of welcome, with a readiness to hear his news.

To-night—as for several nights past—there was no welcome. Isa had changed, probably she was jealous and couldn't understand why he kept Annabet in the house if he had finished with her, or, more likely, she was shy of showing her feelings before the white woman. And Annabet was like somebody dead. Last night he'd kissed Isa at the dining-table and Annabet hadn't even looked away. He could neither hurt, nor provoke nor shame her. She looked like a dead woman too. In another few days, if this state of affairs went on, she'd be as scraggy as she had been on her arrival.

All day he had been too busy, both in mind and body, to give a thought to his domestic cares. But now, coming into the quiet house, he knew that he wanted somebody to talk to. There was so much to tell. His own cleverness about the English coat; his day's work; his final seeing through the whole business; the joke about de Klerk and the fat old woman.

And Isa was no good as a listener.

He mounted the stairs more slowly than usual. He was very tired. All this business was a strain on a man—and when things were wrong at home too! And everywhere he went there were the miserable beggars gaping at him, wanting to be cheered and bolstered up.

He was conscious of a sudden, unfamiliar feeling of depression. What's the matter with me? He asked himself. I've been in worse straits than this and never felt downhearted. Short of sleep, and empty-bellied, that's what it is. Feel better when I've fed.

He went into his own room and washed his hands and splashed the cool water against his face. Something tinkled in the next room—Isa at the dressing-table. Surly little beast, prinking her damned face and letting him come into a house that felt like a tomb.

He sat down on the side of his bed and his eye lighted upon the brandy flask on the bedside table. A good drink, that was what he needed. If Kaerko weren't a watery-blooded codfish he'd have seen to it that there was some liquor in his damned office. We do his work. Evert thought crossly, and he won't even wet our whistles for us. And he'll get all the credit.

He drank from the flask and waited for a moment, hoping to feel better. Then he rose and went out on the gallery, halting outside the door of the blue-and-white room. 'What's the matter with you? Are you sick?' he shouted. 'You've had all day to get ready.'

Isa opened the door and stood there, sulky, seductive, a little defensive as she always was these days. Why in hell, he demanded of himself, had he been fool enough to think that he could get any pleasure out of putting her in Annabet's place?

The door of the little room at the end of the gallery opened quietly and Annabet stepped out. She looked ill, very pale and wasted, but her hair was smooth and shining and the old rag of a dress had been washed and pressed during the day.

'So you're ready too,' he said roughly, angered by his own mixed feelings. 'Nobody to greet me, oh no. But both of you ready at feeding-time. Worse than a couple of dogs. Even monkeys'd show some signs of welcome.'

Isa flashed one of her curious inscrutable glances and did not speak. Annabet, after a second's hesitation, said quietly:

'I was, actually, very anxious to see you, Evert. Is there any news?'

'Maybe,' he said grudgingly. Why should the prospect of telling her about his day give him pleasure? Did she deserve to be taken into the confidence of decent men? He looked at her, and all at once felt quite sick with self-pity. At a moment like this when there was danger and uncertainty outside, if only he'd been sure of his wife. I'd have shed my last drop of blood for her, he thought melodramatically.

The odd trio went down the stairs and into the dining-room in silence. Then something in the quality of Evert's speechlessness told Annabet that he was longing to talk. As she lifted her knife and fork she called up the memory of Mamma's training. Pretend that Evert is a stranger, she thought, pretend that there is nothing between us save the necessity of dining together and making agreeable conversation.

It worked. Her voice came out clear and steady and gracious.

'What have you been doing all day, Evert? What has been happening in Banda?'

He told them both about the English coat; about the killing of the guard and the destruction of the Fort—all the things which everyone on Banda knew by that time. Then with a cold imperative glance he dismissed Isa. 'Go and help Josef make the coffee, Isa. You do it better than he does.'

And then, with a sweet sense of relief and homecoming which he did not recognize for what it was, he told Annabet about Voss and the fat woman, and his own inspiration as

340

to the true position between the English and Shal Ahmi. Almost against his will he went on:

'I reckon that if you hadn't helped him it would have made no difference. He'd have found somebody else.'

It was no longer an impersonal discussion of outside news; no longer a mere dinner-table conversation. How could it be? The very silence cried 'Christy Ayrton' in a voice louder than thunder. Evert wanted to shout, 'Oh, why did you do it? Why must you love somebody else? Why wasn't I enough for you?'

Isa sidled in with the coffee.

A meal and a rest restored Evert's body, and talking to Annabet had disturbed his mind and he decided not to go to bed. His boatman might come back with news—that was the excuse he gave himself. Twice before midnight he walked down to the little jetty and stood staring along the narrow inlet of water between the nutmeg trees. To-night there was a slip of moon like a tendril of hair in the sky, and no clouds over the multitudinous stars; and the little night wind with its burden of spices crept about in the open spaces. Evert's incongruous susceptibility to beauty was heightened and quickened by the tension of his nerves. As he walked he dreamed. Von Holk would come back victorious and all this nonsense would be forgotten. All the English would be killed, and that would dispose of Christy Ayrton. He would punish Annabet for a little while longer, and then he would send Isa away. All would be well.

Each time as he turned back from the inlet of sea he took the path which led to the compound. Everything there was quiet. Before the huts the little fires or the smouldering charcoal braziers which had been used for the cooking of the evening meal were damped down under handfuls of leaves whose smoke kept the voracious insects at bay. It was all as he had seen it on a thousand nights before. There was even the baby wailing softly in the cabin nearest the cluster of kendri trees. For a full five years there had always been a baby there.

He went back to the house, snuffed the candles, drank a glass of schnapps and chewed a hard biscuit, visualised for a moment both his women sound asleep upstairs, Isa snuggled in the luxury of the blue-and-white bed, Annabet stretched upon the hard mattress of her tiny one. Once again he was surprised to find that he felt no pleasure in the contrast; once again he admitted to himself that fetching Isa back had been a mistake.

But in this state of unusual physical exhaustion, awake alone in this unfamiliar night hour, he realised that he had been mistaken in his treatment of Annabet from the very beginning. He should have sense enough to see that in the ugly scarecrow thing which the *Java* had brought him, something very special and precious lay hidden. She'd been friendly and intelligent then, eager to please, his for the taking. If only he'd waited. I was as much to blame for things going wrong as she was, he thought, and on the day when she says she loves me I'll tell her so.

He pulled the branching candlestick closer and looked once more to the priming of his pistols. Thinking of those days after Annabet's arrival had brought Shal Ahmi into his mind. He fingered over his belief that Shal Ahmi was harmless unless the English came to Banda, which they could never do, never in a thousand years. But at the same time he thought, with comfortable assurance and some pride of his own canny arrangements in case of trouble. Of Josef and the four picked men sleeping in the kitchen beside the harmless looking bread-bin packed with arms and powder; of Hassan and Toeg and his two brothers, armed and warned in the cabin in the very centre of the compound; of himself, so wary and clever.

One more prowl round, he thought, and then he would try to get a little sleep.

There was still no sign of Tas, the boatman. But no news, in this case, was good news, because if Von Holk had run into trouble as Knoel had done, they'd have heard in Banda by now. He waited by the jetty for some moments, more in idleness than expectation; then for the third time he walked through the compound and saw nothing, heard nothing. He looked into the kitchen, which seemed for a moment to be in inky darkness, but which presently lightened into shades of grey of varying density. He could distinguish the five sleeping forms. As a test he said, 'Josef,' quite softly, and instantly one body stirred, rose on an elbow and said, 'Mynheer?' in the same suppressed tone.

'Everything is all right, Josef. I'm just having a last look round.'

He went back into the house and dragged a long chair into the passage that ran between the living-rooms and the kitchen. He set his little oil lamp beside the chair and laid his pistols beside it. He kicked off his boots and loosened his collar and the top of his breeches. He intended to doze lightly, keeping one ear open for any sound of Tas whom he had told to come to the back door.

He was just about to stretch himself in the chair when the handle of the door moved. Tas! News of Von Holk! Bootless, empty-handed, he ran to the door and wrenched it open. As it swung back a musket went off in his face. In less than a second he had time to feel a scorching, searing pain somewhere in the region of his right ear, to think, so it's started, and to know

342

that he was not much hurt. His hands shot out and closed upon bare warm flesh. A musket clattered as it fell. The man within his grasp wriggled and Evert felt the point of a knife pierce his left arm at the wrist. He freed his right hand and swung it in a great blow. He felt his knuckles split against hard bone and heard, with atavistic pleasure, a sharp crack. The body he held turned heavily and slumped downwards almost dragging him with it. He let it fall.

Ah, he could see now. He snatched up the musket and brought the butt of it down twice upon the face of the man who lay at his feet. Try to kill me, did you? he thought. Wonder who it was; ought to have looked first, can't recognise him now, just a bloody mash. Where're my brave chaps in the kitchen; must have heard the shot. Ah, they're moving now. Must get my boots on; a man's helpless without boots if he's used to them. Damn this blood, you'd think I'd been pig-killing.

He stamped his feet into his boots, took up his pistols, remembered the dead man's musket and tucked it under his arm. One more. One more, he thought, gift from Heaven.

As he turned towards the kitchen Josef came out. He had a musket under his arm, a pistol in one hand.

'Mynheer, it has begun.'

'I know, somebody just tried to kill me. Come on.'

'Yes, Mynheer.'

Josef's voice and manner were as calm as though Evert had merely asked him to put some forgotten thing upon the dining-table. They belied the secret sickness of his heart. Josef was not brave, he had not even the optimistic recklessness of youth, he had always lived softly, and he hated the sight and the thought of blood. But the whole of his life had been spent in obedience to the white men, and for fifteen of those years Evert had been his master, and now, in war as in peace, he was prepared to come and go and do and speak exactly as Evert directed. Of the four men with him, two were old and had lived at Coenpark ever since Evert had owned it, and two were boys whom Evert had once destined for the draft and then withdrawn. Disappointed of being soldiers in the ordinary professional sense, they were keen to prove their value as amateurs. These four, with Hassan, Toeg and his two brothers across the compound, comprised the whole of Evert's secret force. He had argued that the more people let into a secret the less the chance of its remaining a secret, and that nine men, all trustworthy and properly armed, were better than a mob.

In this, although he did not know it, Evert's instinctive common sense had led him to precisely the same conclusion as Shal Ahmi's wily, convolvulated reasoning. There were at that moment in the Coenpark compound, only nine revolutionaries. There had been ten, but the tenth lay now, dead on the path outside the house door, his mission unfulfilled. Shal Ahmi had depended more upon strategy than upon numbers. The numbers were there, a vast horde of stupid coolies, flaccid as seaweed, ready to sway with the tide. But everyone of Shal Ahmi's selected men was a fanatic, carefully chosen, sternly tested; and every one was a direct descendant, either son or grandson, or great-grandson of one of those women Piet's young officer had spoken of, those pure-blooded Bandanese women who had been brought back from Java to work as slaves upon the soil that their fathers had owned and died to retain.

Out of this revolutionary nucleus one man had been chosen, on every plantation, to perform the most dangerous and difficult task of all, the striking of the first blow. And there again Shal Ahmi's and Evert's utterly dissimilar minds had shown a kinship. Evert had said, 'I believe in shooting at the head.' Shal Ahmi had arranged for the quiet assassination of every planter. Once that was done his few tried adherents could take charge, overcome any dissentients, and stop the outbreak of trouble between the ill-united factions, who, as soon as the white control was removed would take the opportunity of avenging their age-old grievances and grudges.

The methods for the assassinations varied and had been left fluid. Evert, whose house-servants slept apart, was to be killed indoors if entry could be gained to the house. Byskin, whose slaves slept all over the house, even along the upper passages, was to be killed on his regular night visit to the earth-closet in the shrubbery. Van Heem's intelligent, embittered bastard son had been entrusted with the task of avenging his discarded Bandanese mother's wrong and the slur of his own birth. Boender's death blow was to be struck by a house-slave, who, five years earlier, had been whipped and temporarily degraded to plantation work for stealing. He was not a thief and when the truth was discovered Boender, a sentimentalist where natives were concerned, had made a public proclamation, restored the man to his old position, and bought the Chinese girl whom he wanted for a wife. But the injustice had rankled, and Shal Ahmi had taken advantage of it. Nothing had been arranged hastily; no trouble had been spared. Over the whole of Banda and Lonthoir his nets had been spread, and some of them had taken years to lay. Since the day when he had conspired with Mynheer Haan to smuggle nutmegs to the English, Shal Ahmi had known that the day of vengeance would dawn; but it would not be only, as the Dutch fondly imagined, the vengeance of Dutch upon English.

But Evert, alienated from Annabet and tired of Isa, had

344

chosen to sleep on a chair in the passage and had been expecting Tas the boatman with news. The door which his assassin had softly tried had opened unexpectedly, the musket had been fired wildly, the knife-blade had only provoked reprisal. And the nine conspirators, awake, waiting for Fernando's return with word that the job was done, had still to reckon with Evert himself.

The compound was humming like a beehive. The single shot had wakened a number of the lighter sleepers and they had wakened the others. Here and there men had come to the low doorways, here and there women had lighted the little oil lamps. Shal Ahmi's men with their brand new muskets and pistols and knives stood ready in their secret, separate places. Tani Amani, malaria-ridden, an old man at fifty, whose mother had served a princess in the Palace upon whose ruins Kaerko's office now stood, and who had been appointed the chief of the Coenpark revolutionaries, drew long deep breaths and counted them, waiting for the moment of glory.

But it was Evert's voice which roared through the compound; roared in Dutch, and then in the Malay which he had never mastered properly that the first person to poke a head out of a hut would have his brains blown out. Roared for Ramjit Singh to step outside and ordered that everything he said should be repeated in Tamil, clearly, audibly. Roared for four little boys from the cabin under the kendri trees to throw twigs upon the smouldering smoking braziers.

Then Tani Amani knew that the moment of glory had come, but in shape other than he had hoped. As soon as the flames leaped and the starlight was dimmed by the glow of the little fires, he pushed aside the mat that covered his doorway, lifted his musket and fired at his master. The bullet actually tore away a piece of shirt-sleeve. I'm lucky, Evert thought. Aloud he said, 'Get him' to his two young men. 'Don't give him time to reload.'

But Tani Amani had a new pistol, too. He waited until the young men were within a few paces and then fired it into the face of the taller one. The young man's cheek was blown away. He was stunned for a second, and then remembered that his master's face had been horribly injured too, but that hadn't stopped him. His hands were sharing the burden of Tani Amandi when they brought him over to Evert.

'We'll be scarred on the same side,' Evert said, and whipped round like a snake to fire into the unglazed window of another hut from which one of Tani Amandi's confederates was taking aim. Evert had felt, with the seventh sense of an old soldier, the danger behind him, and turning had seen the glint of light upon the barrel of the musket.

'Get him,' he said to Josef and the other older man. And to

the two youngsters, 'Chuck Tani into the well.' Then, seeing them hesitate, 'Go on. He tried to kill you, didn't he?'

Tani made no outcry, but as the splash sounded a woman somewhere began to scream, and in several huts the noise was taken up.

Josef and his companion made for the hut from which the threatened rebel shot had failed to be fired. And then, for a few seconds it did seem that hell had broken loose in the compound. No one human eye could take note of all that happened, and the noise confused the ear. From the hut upon which Josef was bearing down a frightened screaming woman emerged and threw herself on the ground clutching at the houseboy's knees. Simultaneously three shots rang out from the other side of the compound and the boy with the wounded face fell flat, squealing. Evert took the unfired pistol from his hand and aimed it at the man who had shot the boy. Toeg and his brothers closed around a third hut, while from a fourth a man emerged on his belly, crept like a snake to the rear of it, and from there fired at Evert again. The bullet struck the front of his leg and emerged at the back, missing the bone and the main artery by a hair's breadth. Stung by the pain and mad with lust of battle Evert yelled 'Missed me. Try again,' and though the words were lost in the tumult the man seemed to obey him. He showed half his face around the hut, taking aim with one eye. Evert fired and blew his hand off.

And then suddenly it was all over. In the grove the birds, disturbed by the tumult, settled down again with a flutter of wings and little cries. In the compound there was only the sound of screaming women and the yelling of frightened children. The smoke and the stench of the gunpowder sullied the spicy air.

Evert sat down upon the wall of the well and lifted his leg to the same level. As an old soldier he knew the danger of leg wounds. Expertly, with steady hands, he took out his knife, slit the seam of his breeches and pulled the cloth aside and tied his handkerchief tightly about the wound. Then deliberately he looked over his little force. The boy whose face had been hurt lay where he had dropped felled by his second wound. Josef had been shot through the shoulder and dark streams of blood were streaking his brown chest, but he was holding fast on to his prisoner. One of the older men stood with his foot on the small of the back of a fellow who lay supine, but alive and groaning. The younger man held a wriggling captive by the neck. Three. One down the well. One still lying behind the hut from whose cover he had shot Evert. Five. There had been more than five enemy shots.

'Turn out every hut from which a shot was fired,' said Evert to Hassan. 'Down the well with those. Then reload. There may be more trouble.'

Two of the prisoners screamed as they went over. Evert, sitting within a foot of their passage from life to death, never even looked their way. He was reloading his pistols and at the same time keeping his eyes upon the huts in which he suspected rebels still to be lurking.

'Now,' he said. 'Everybody out of there, and there, and there.' He pointed. 'Go boldly. I'm covering you.'

Only one of the four remaining showed any fight. He shot Hassan as he kicked the door open, and immediately after was picked off by Evert. The other three allowed themselves to be led out. One man was followed by a little crowd, two young women, an old one and a horde of children. As they were rounded into the centre of the compound, towards the well and the cold-eyed man who sat upon its rim, the women and children screamed like banshees and threw themselves upon the ground. The man to whom they belonged, ran forward, not waiting to be kicked and prodded towards his doom. With clasped hands he flung himself at Evert's feet. 'Mercy for my women and little ones. They knew nothing. They had no share.'

'I may consider that. On conditions,' said Evert stonily. 'Stand aside with your brood. Over with the others, Hassan.'

Even the screaming women fell silent, listening to the splashes. Even the children hushed. There was a deadly, horrified silence in the compound.

'Now,' said Evert, 'make up the fires. All the fires. And you, Ramjit, repeat this order. Everybody is to come out and sit on the ground immediately in front of his cabin.' He bellowed the order in Dutch and Malay himself.

One by one the cabins opened and the neutral crowds who had crouched within doors listening to the shots and screams and the orders crept out silently and seated themselves exactly as Evert had bidden them.

'Now, listen to me, all of you,' said Evert loudly. 'There has been a plot afoot. But for my vigilance and the valour of these few with me, you and I, with our families and dear ones would have been slain in our sleep before this night was out. Ten of your comrades, ten of my people have been possessed by the devil and were bent upon murdering us all. Repeat that, Ramjit.'

The man who had so far been spared, moved and looked as though he were about to speak. Evert glanced significantly at the cluster of women and children and then at the gaping mouth of the well. The man stiffened.

'I will now find out for you the name of the devil who planned this thing. Kari Adoad will tell us.' He lowered his voice, but in the tense silence every word which he addressed

347

to the man in an almost genial, conversational tone, was clearly audible. 'Kari Adoad, who inspired this foul deed? Who made this devilish plot?'

'Mynheer, I do not know. I never saw or spoke with him. Tani Anandi carried the orders. . . .'

'Come here,' said Evert gently. 'Look into the well. See the end of Tani Anandi, the fitting end of all who carry the devil's orders. Would you join him? Who gave the orders? *I* know, Kari Adoad. I could speak the name now. But I want your fellows to hear it from your lips.'

'Mynheer, I do not . . .'

'Lift the youngest child, Josef. Here,' he jerked his head significantly over his shoulder. The youngest and prettiest of Kari's women screamed and grabbed at the child. Josef pushed her aside.

'I will speak, Mynheer,' said Kari Adoad in a dead voice.

'Turn then to the others and speak clearly. Who gave orders for the murder of us all?'

'Shal Ahmi, but Mynheer, he never . . .'

'That will do. You all heard what the man says, and remember the truth, when wrung out of a man is always the simple truth. Shal Ahmi he says, ordered the massacre.' He repeated the statement in Malay, and Ramjit Singh echoed it in Tamil.

'And what did he promise you and these,' he jerked his thumb into the well, 'when we should all be dead? With what promises did he bribe you to wickedness?'

'Mynheer . . .'

'I wait, Kari Adoad, and the water waits.'

'Mynheer, he promised that things should be as they were in the days of our forefathers. He spoke of peace and plenty and said that we should be kings and princes as were our fathers before us.'

'You hear,' said Evert. 'For the benefit of a handful of those whose forebears lived in the islands the rest of us were to be slain. You and you and you,' he pointed to a few men selected at random, 'and me,' he touched his own breast. 'Our lives were of no importance if by dying we gave back the glory of ancient Banda. You and your wives and children, me and my wife must die that Kari Adoad might be a king and a prince.' He allowed this piece of information to sink in and then turned back to Kari.

'Where is Shal Ahmi now?'

'Mynheer, that I do not know. By the graves of my ancestors I swear I do not know. Mynheer, be merciful. If you dropped them all into the well one by one before my eyes and then tore out my eyes, I could not tell. I do not know.'

'Try it,' said Evert, and signalled to Josef.

348

The youngest child was a little girl. Great black eyes, wide with bewilderment, shone in her little brown face. Her long black hair streamed over Josef's hands as he lifted her. Her mother screamed again and called wildly to Kari to tell everything, anything, to think of nothing but the child. Tears and sweat poured down the father's face and body. As Josef held the little creature over the well mouth, waiting the final signal, Kari made a convulsive movement. 'I cannot tell you what I do not know,' he cried in a terrible voice, and lunged forward. Evert, aware of his precarious position upon the well edge, moved to set his injured leg to the ground. Toeg made a dive for Kari, and caught him, but at the same time Josef put out a hand to steady Evert and the child, feeling some support withdrawn, screamed and twisted, trying to put her small arms around Josef's neck. She slipped and with another piercing, dreadful scream disappeared into the water. Her mother, with a cry that set all the birds in the grove fluttering from their perches again, pushed her way through the ring of guards and jumped into the well herself.

Nobody in the outer circle moved or made a sound. Kari sobbed aloud. Evert put his leg up again and adjusted the handkerchief which had been disturbed.

'That was your doing, Kari Adoad,' he said calmly. Then, sweeping his eyes around the compound, he went on: 'There are now ten bodies in this well; you see the fate of those who aim to be kings and princes. Be warned. The devil is strong and still at large; to-morrow or the next day he may be here again, promising to make kings and princes of more of you who will pay the price in blood. On that day remember the end of Tani Anandi and of Kari Adoad, for as I live I swear that such shall be the end of any man who dares to take an order from anyone but me.' He signalled to his men again, and Kari went to join his wife and his former conspirators.

He rose then, concealing with difficulty a grimace of pain as he put his foot to the ground. 'Nail up the well,' he said to his foreman. 'They must fetch water from the spring until we can dig anew. The old will serve to keep the memory of this night alive.'

He turned and was hobbling away when a middle-aged woman ran out from the seated ranks and knelt before him. She was the mother of the boy who had been first wounded and then killed.

'I may take his body, Mynheer?' she asked, and pointed.

'Assuredly.' He put his heavy hand on her shoulder. 'Your son died honourably, having fought like a good soldier.' He peered at her in the firelight. Hindu. 'There is no doubt that in his next life he will be a great warrior. As for you and any other of his kin, the bread of idleness shall be spread for you in my compound for the rest of your days. May they be many.'

Annabet had heard the first shot and leaped out of bed without any very clear idea of where to go or what to do. As she dragged on her gown and thrust her feet into her slippers, she heard a door open along the gallery and a series of heavy bumps. She tore open her door, expecting to find Evert dragging out muskets and powder pouches. But it was only Isa, quite calm, surrounded by bundles of various sizes which she was carrying a short distance towards the stairs, dropping, and then going back for more. Incongruously Annabet thought of backstitching.

Isa stiffened when she saw Annabet, but she did not pause.

'They were given to me,' she said defensively. 'And now that this has come you will never need them again.'

She threw a heavy bundle wrapped in a towel towards the head of the stairs and dashed back for another, slightly smaller, knotted in one of Annabet's silk petticoats.

Annabet had seen that Evert's door stood open; a glance showed her that the room within was empty. Ignoring Isa, she ran towards the stairs thinking, I could load muskets if I were shown ... I must help ... I must help....

Downstairs the house was darkness and she felt her way along the hall and as far as the door at the head of the passage kitchen. It was locked. She imagined that upon the further side she could hear movement and voices and she beat on the door and shouted 'Evert' at the top of her voice. But Evert was at that moment mustering his men and had forgotten her very existence. She heard, as she stood there, the outer door slam. She turned and felt her way into the hall again, turned down the shorter passage which led to Evert's little office and found its door locked.

The hall was dimly lighted when she returned. Isa had set a candle at the stair top and was now getting her bundles down. Some she merely threw, and they fell, limp and heavy, like dead bodies. Others she carried down, and then raced lightly up the stairs again.

'I don't think you'll get them any further,' said Annabet. 'We're locked in.'

Isa paused, half-way up the stairs. 'Every door?'

'Yes, look.' Annabet tried the door of the dining-room and of the parlour. 'The office, too, and the door behind the stairs.'

'Then I shall throw them out of the window and jump out myself,' said Isa; and she ran down the stairs and seized the towel-wrapped bundle in arms which looked too frail to lift anything a quarter of its size.

A burst of musket and pistol fire sounded from the compound.

'They'll be here,' said Isa, anxious, but not frightened. 'They'll take some of my things.' She looked at her scattered bundles as a flustered mother hen might look at her chickens. And then suddenly her face changed.

'Mevrouw! They will rob me. But they will kill you.' She clutched the bundle to her body and over it looked at Annabet. Her face was like a flower. 'I would not wish them to kill you,' she said simply.

'I'm prepared to be killed,' said Annabet truthfully. And wildly melodramatic as the statement sounded, it was nothing more than the truth. Her recent moods of self-hatred, despair and resignation had seen death as the inevitable, indeed desirable, thing. And although, at this moment, there was sickness in her stomach, and a cold crepitation pervading her flesh, they were only the physical reactions to threatened danger. In her mind she was as calm and detached as Isa. 'I'm prepared to be killed. But I should like to help Evert first.'

'Oh, no one can help him now,' said Isa, without emotion, but with great certainty. 'They are too many. All day I have gone about the compound spying and caught no word. That means that all are in it since, without sign, it comes. He is dead now, Mynheer Haan. Listen.'

There was another burst of firing and then silence. 'All is over. Soon they will remember the house.' She dashed to the top of the stairs and threw the bundle along the gallery. Then she ran back and looking down, said, 'The thought has come to me. Help me to carry away the things that were given me, and you shall be safe. Come, come quickly.' She slipped down the stairs again and dragged Annabet by the hand, up, and into the blue-and-white room where now nothing seemed to remain except the immovable pieces of furniture and a few discarded native clothes tossed into a corner. Her little red-tipped fingers which looked so indolent and helpless, fell upon Annabet, hard and rapid as a monkey's paw. Off with the dressing-gown and the night-robe, and on with the tattered, dirty finery which Isa had not thought worth while to carry with so many more valuable things to care for.

Annabet stood neither helping nor hindering the flying hands. She had not thought of escape. She had wanted to help Evert, but every door had been locked. My life will end as it has been led, she thought, in futility. Nothing I ever started has reached its appointed end. Even my death will be silly. And if Isa but knew it she will be bound to lose every bit of loot she entrusts to me. But let it go. Christy is dead by this time, and Evert. Let me serve as packhorse to a little native girl. . . .

Isa slit a garment with a sound like a shriek. 'It'll cover your face,' she said, dropping it upon Annabet's unresisting head. 'Pretend to be old, stoop. That is if anyone sees us. Now.' She

351

abandoned her dressing of Annabet in native clothes as abruptly as a child might cease dressing a doll. 'Help me with the bundles!' She ran to the open window and flung back the curtains.

Annabet picked up the towel-wrapped bundle and dropped it into the rosebed beneath the window. How often had the scent of those short-lived roses come up into the room while she was dreaming of Christy ... or trying to give Evert his dues ... or confusing one with the other....

There was no sound now from the compound, but there were fires. Trudi Van Heem had spoken of the shots and the screams and the fires; she said that it was like hell. Perhaps hell started without any loud announcement, like love, or growing up. Perhaps this was hell itself, silly and meaningless. Perhaps one's hell was like one's life, silly and meaningless without being really bad. Dressed like a native girl, throwing bundles out of a window, with Christy dead and Evert. Christy and Evert, linked together at last in the chains of death. And she soon, uncaring, to join them. 'No marriage nor giving in marriage.' The preacher had said that in Heydberg Church. Suppose, Purgatory passed, she should meet Christy and Evert again, stripped of their bodies, clad in their souls. I wouldn't know either of them, she thought, dismayed. And they would not know me. All along it's been body, body, body. Hair, eyes, mouths, hands, voices. All perishable as the petals on my cherry tree.

'It'd be quicker if I just handed you the parcels and you dropped them out,' said Isa. Her voice was quite sharp and authoritative. 'There, that's as much as we can hope to carry,' she said, throwing across a bundle of what felt like shoes. 'Now we must jump.'

'I don't think I could,' said Annabet, voicing the conviction that had seized her as she dropped out the first bundle.

'You must,' said Isa. 'There's no other way out. You'll be killed if you stay here. And I want your help.' She came and stood by the window. 'It's not far. Get up on the sill and put your feet out, then drop.' Short of putting up violent resistance, Annabet could see that she would be pushed out as unceremoniously as one of the bundles. Just then a door slammed heavily in the lower part of the house. 'Oh, be quick,' said Isa, 'they're coming, they're coming.' She spoke with such urgency that one would have thought it was her life, not her loot which was in jeopardy. She weighed the problem of whether to jump herself and run to and fro with the bundles, or whether to spend a few valuable seconds forcing the stupid white woman through the window and have the advantage of her services as a porter. She chose the latter, and had actually heaved Annabet on to the sill and was about to thrust her forth when the voice that neither of them expected to hear again, rang through the house. From the bottom of the stairs Evert was calling imperatively.

'Mynheer. He is alive still,' said Isa, with surprise, but little joy in her voice. She stepped back, and Annabet lost her balance and fell into the room. Isa stood undecisive for a second while Annabet pushed past her and out on to the gallery.

'I'm coming. Evert. I'm coming. What's happened? Are you hurt?' She sped down the stairs calling as she ran. He wasn't dead. There was still a chance that she could do something, help in some way.

'Yes, I'm hurt,' said Evert, quite cheerfully. He put his grimy right hand over the wound at the side of his face, sparing her the first shock. 'Not badly. I'm all right. Don't go fainting, now. I want you to see to me. Josef has got enough to attend to or I wouldn't have bothered you.'

'I'm glad you did. Let me look. Oh! And your arm too. And your leg. Oh Evert!'

'I can't manage the stairs. You'll have to get water and bandages here.' He hobbled to the door of the dining-room and unlocked it with the key he took from his pocket. He sat down heavily in his usual chair and lifted his leg, setting his booted foot upon the edge of the table. A little pool of blood gathered immediately upon the shining wood.

'The others are nothing, but this might bleed me to death. Get some cold water and a stout bandage. Edge off a sheet if you've nothing else handy.'

She ran upstairs and fetched down her own ewer, the sheet from her bed and her scissors.

'Light some more candles and set them here,' said Evert, pointing to the table. 'It's all right. Take your time. That's the way. It went clean through, didn't it? That's a good thing. By God, I've had luck to-night,' He looked at her as she held the wet cold cloth to each wound in turn, and passed his hand over his eyes and looked again. 'What're you doing in those clothes?'

The makeshift veil had fallen off as she tumbled back from the windowsill, and Isa's little jacket, being too small, did not meet across her breast. And she couldn't spare a hand to pull it. She said, a little shamefacedly, 'It was Isa's idea. She was so sure the worst had happened. . . .'

'A damned good idea, too. I'm afraid I hadn't thought about what you'd do. But then I didn't really expect anything like this.' His voice was rueful for a moment. Then he went on, 'Anyhow, the worst didn't happen. Though by God it was a near thing. If that swine had stopped to take aim. . . . Pull it tighter. You won't hurt me. That's the way. Now, look at this.'

353

He turned the side of his head towards the light. 'It's still numb, I can't feel it much. Did he take my ear off?'

'Not ... not the whole ear. The lobe and some of the ...' It was silly but the mutilation which Evert said was not serious was worse to look at than the two holes in the leg had been.

'I shall look as though I've been cropped for thieving,' said Evert. 'Here, give me that rag. This isn't your job, I can see. Pour yourself some brandy. Give me some, too. With plenty of water in mine.'

'No, I'm all right, Evert, really. It was just your poor ear ... and a great long gash along your jaw. You'll have a scar, I'm afraid.'

'I shall grow a beard from ear to ear and wear my hair long. No. You can't bandage that to do any good without throttling me. It'll dry off by itself. Or I've got some alum somewhere, when I can remember where to look for it. Annabet ... I'll have to have that brandy, you keep going a mile away and then coming close again.'

She ran to the sideboard, and as she was pouring the brandy Josef came in, bringing with him a pungent scent of ointment. His chest was swathed in a piece of cloth dripping with yellowish-brown fluid.

'Mynheer. There is someone at the back door.'

'Tas?'

'He says so, Mynheer.'

'Then why didn't you let him in?'

'I thought I would ask you first.'

'You could have told Tas by his voice, I should think,' said Evert, lifting his leg from the table and cursing.

'I know his voice, Evert. Sit still. I'll know in a minute.'

'I'll go. I'm all right,' said Evert, snatching the glass from her hand and gulping from it. Tas might have good news. And by Heaven that would make the whole thing practically perfect.

'Lean on me then,' said Annabet. He put his hand on her shoulder and hobbled across the hall, down the long passage, and stopped at the door which, only an hour earlier, he had opened so carelessly.

'Who's there?'

'Tas, Mynheer. Let me in. Mynheer. Let me in, please.'

Evert opened the door, cautiously this time, and Tas, the boatman, fell into the passage. He took one horrified look at his master and said, 'Here too?' Evert put his bulk between Tas and Josef and manoeuvred the boatman along into the hall. As Tas walked he produced a crumpled piece of paper and kept trying to hand it backwards to Evert. Annabet followed Evert, and as soon as they reached the hall pulled forward a chair. With the paper still unfolded in his hand, Evert sat down

354

and stretched out his leg stiffly.

'Have you seen any trouble, Tas?'

'Yes, Mynheer. Mynheer Kaerko's clerk brought me the paper and said that Mynheer Kaerko himself had been shot at in his office. And there was shooting everywhere.'

The few lines of scribble across the sheet of paper could not have been recognised as the Agent's meticulous hand, it was so nearly illegible that Evert guessed rather than read its import. He crushed the paper in his fist when he had scowled at it for a moment or so, and then said, easily and cheerfully, 'Ah well, that's all right, Tas. Not so bad as it looks. Like me! Go along to the kitchen and get something to eat and send Josef and Toeg here to me.'

'Is it bad news?' Annabet asked timidly.

He stared at her without speaking, and she realised that for the first time he was discouraged about the state of affairs. He had been exhilarated when Knoel left for the war, and cheerfully confident and resourceful when the first bad news came in; he had been boastful and angry, derisive and optimistic in turn during the interval of waiting; to-night, wounded and tired, he had shown admirable resolution and fortitude; but now, for the first time, she saw desperation on his face.

'By God, yes,' he said at last, clenching his fist on the paper, 'the worst news yet. Von Holk's defeated and dead. Kaerko's most trusted houseboy tried to stab him over a cup of coffee. Byskin's killed, and Van Heem. All Banda is in uproar. But the soldiers held, and Kaerko wants me to go and take charge.' His face darkened with fury and the patches of pallor around his nose and mouth were engulfed in a fevered flush.

'That's always the way. I've looked after my own. I stopped the nonsense here before it got under way. All these goddamn fools. Fancy Kaerko writing at such a time, "My houseboy handed me the coffee and then tried to stab me," doesn't that show? Fancy mentioning coffee! My God, if I . . .' He broke off as Josef and Toeg appeared.

'Well,' he said cheerfully, 'everybody didn't have the luck we did. In one or two places that old devil's followers got the best of it. We've got to call out the army, and I, as an old soldier, am going to be commander-in-chief. How do you fancy coming with me Josef and showing the youngsters how to shoot, eh?'

'Me also, Mynheer?' asked Toeg eagerly.

'But if I take you, who's going to look after the nutmegs, Toeg. And the house, and Mevrouw?'

Josef and Toeg exchanged a long, significant look.

'Mynheer,' Josef said, 'at Coenpark I shoot well because I know what I am about, but for fighting in other places I have little stomach. But Toeg . . .'

'Toeg is like me, he likes a fight for its own sake. Is that so?' The big foreman nodded and grinned. 'Very well. I'll take Toeg and leave you, Josef. Mind, if Toeg goes, you've got to keep everybody at work and out of mischief.'

'My brother will help, Mynheer,' said Toeg.

'Very well,' said Evert again. 'Now Toeg, apart from those in the kitchen and us, who're the best six men on the place?'

Often in the past, in moments of bitterness, Annabet had attributed Evert's popularity to his unscrupulous use of humbug. 'Here's the old ass, now,' he'd say, as the guest arrived, and the next second he would be in the hall greeting the man with every sign of affection and esteem. Or sometimes for two full days before they were due to be guests themselves he would complain of the impending boredom, deriding his host and raking up bits of malicious scandal about his hostess, yet during the visit he would be the most charming guest that ever stepped across a threshold. He never attempted to hide his double-facedness from Annabet, and sometimes she was flattered and sometimes frightened by the fact. On the one hand, it implied a peculiar intimacy; on the other, it announced clearly that he had little regard for her opinion of his honesty. But to-night, watching his swift change from despair to cheerfulness, hearing that carefully chosen but carelessly spoken, 'and us,' she was bound to respect his tactics. He was clever. A list of his other virtues slipped into her mind. He was brave. He was generous. When not provoked, he was very kind. He was good company. Ninety-nine women out of a hundred would be madly in love with him. Why had she to be the hundredth? If Christy had never come to Coenpark, I suppose I should be in love with Evert now, she thought. After all, I wasn't hard to please. I nearly kissed Jean Vehk. If Evert had come back that night. . . .

But he hadn't, and now, though she remembered his virtues, and thought that he might be killed, and was conscious of all the wrongs she had done him, she knew, with a flat, deadly certainty that held a tinge of regret as well as great bewilderment, that she would not feel, as he left, one tithe of the emotion she had felt when the door closed behind Christy.

'All right,' said Evert, ending the confidential talk with Toeg. 'Fetch them. We'll take all the arms and powder we have. And tell Tas to have the boats ready. Now, you, Josef, you chose to stay behind, and believe me you've picked the hard job. When I come back I shall expect to find . . .'

But feeling wasn't everything. There were obligations and duties. And penances. She waited until Evert had told Josef exactly what he must do in his absence, and then she said quietly:

'Don't add me to Josef's responsibilities, Evert. Let me go

with you. Honestly, I'm not frightened, and I might be able to help. I'd rather go with you. Really. Truly.'

Evert waved Josef away. Then, turning stiffly in his chair, he looked at her.

'I'd rather take you,' he said heavily. 'But I dare not. Here the thing is squashed. Everybody who had a shot to fire in Coenpark fired it to-night. In Banda the thing got out of hand and the fighting is still to come. And we may have to fight our way in. I don't say you'll be safe here. But I will say that you're safer here than anywhere else in the islands. I'm leaving Josef and several good men in charge. And I'll leave Tas, too. He's proved his faithfulness to-night. If the worst should happen, he'll get you away in his prahau.' He looked wildly around the hall and up the stairs and along the gallery. 'God knows,' he said vehemently, 'I never thought of this when I brought you here.'

'If I hadn't helped Shal Ahmi,' said Annabet, beginning to sob, 'if Captain Knoel hadn't been ambushed . . .'

'Don't talk bloody rot. If you hadn't helped him he'd have found somebody else. Stop crying, Annabet, and listen to me. My will's in the iron safe in my office. Take it out, here's the key, and keep it, whatever happens. I may be killed. Every white man in Banda may be killed. But if Tas gets you away, and you have my will, the Company'll see you get your rights. They'll never give up Banda, and you have a stake in it. And there's money in the bank at Amsterdam as well. Remember, you can trust Josef and you can trust Tas, and there'll be no trouble in the compound unless Shal Ahmi's people overrun the island.' He stopped abruptly. A spasm went over his face. 'Even then . . . he might remember that you . . .'

She screamed at him, 'Don't say it, Evert. I know it's true. I know it's all my fault. But don't say it. I wouldn't . . . Evert, please let me come with you. You could show me how to load muskets, even if I couldn't shoot. I don't want to be safe. I don't deserve to be safe.'

'But I want you to be safe, that should be sufficient. Besides, you'd be a nuisance. I've made everything here as safe as possible in the circumstances, and I want you to stay here until the worst happens, and then trust to Tas.' Another spasm convulsed his face. 'And now, fetch me a little brandy please. And then, if you don't mind, my shaving things and a clean shirt. I won't attempt the stairs.'

'How're you going to walk?' she asked, when she came back with the brandy. 'Couldn't you be carried? Between two men, on a chair.'

'It may come to that. But not to-night. It'd be a bad example for one thing. My fellows are all wounded, more or less, and they've got to come because really, they're all I have. Those

Toeg is collecting now are only for show. The others have been taught to shoot, and to-night they've been under fire. And if I walk they will. Help me into this shirt, will you?'

There was a sound of voices and of men mustering in the passage beyond the door at the back of the stairs. 'Hurry,' said Evert, hindering her efforts by his struggles. 'Where's Isa? I'll tell her to keep you company.'

'She's gone. If you hadn't come back just when you did, I should have gone too. She wanted me to help carry her things.'

'Your things, I suppose.' He backed away from her and un-aided tucked the shirt into the top of his breeches. 'I'm sorry, Annabet.' He gave a bark of mirthless, half-hysterical laughter. 'For two years you've driven me crazy. You're my wife, and you sold me and everybody else in Banda to save another man's hide. And here am I apologising to you for the loss of your truck.' He swung round and put his hands on her shoulders. 'Maybe I am crazy. I've got to go now. But I shall come back. We'll settle everything then. Kiss me before I go.'

With his good arm he hugged her to him; his hard mouth moved over her face, eyes, hair, cheek and lips.

'Be careful, Evert. Take care of yourself.'

'I will. Don't worry. I'm coming back.'

He released her so suddenly that she fell back against the wall. She watched him hobble to the passage doorway, saw him brace himself before he opened it, saw, as it swung open, the dim lamp-lighted passage, full of brown faces and the barrels of muskets slung at curious angles.

Then it closed, and she was alone with Josef, who said softly, 'There are good men in the kitchen, Mevrouw. And I myself will sleep here at the foot of the stairs. Mevrouw need have no fear. Is there anything Mevrouw would like before she goes to bed. A cup of tea, perhaps?'

She looked at him blankly, and then shook her head. 'Don't worry about me, Josef. I'm not frightened and I'll ask you for anything I want. You give all your attention to looking after things.'

Over Banda Neira, all night long an orangy-pink haze hung, and now and then a fresh column of blue-black smoke shot into the glow as a new fire started below. Then as the last-fired building was consumed the smoke column faded and was absorbed, the haze regained its colour and hung unstained until another conflagration broke out.

Annabet spent the night at her window, at first standing and then kneeling. Some time before dawn she dropped her head on to her folded arms and slept a little. When she woke, stiff

358

and cramped, the fire haze was fading into the rosy dawn light.

The sun rose, just as usual, and as usual the tong-tong sounded. Hundreds of doves rose with a soft flutter of wings as the coolies went to work in the groves.

Annabet went downstairs, and was met as usual by the scent of freshly-made coffee. Josef was just bringing the tray through the passage door.

'Could we send and find out how things are going?' she asked.

'Mynheer gave no orders about that, Mevrouw.'

'But I am anxious, Josef. Wouldn't one of the boys run? A boy could slip in unnoticed, whatever happened, surely. Send Abbas to me.'

When the boy came she explained what she wanted him to do. To run into Banda and gather all the news possible. To find Evert if he could, ask after his health, tell him that all was well at Coenpark, and see if he had any message for Mevrouw.

Abbas seemed to be delighted with his errand. He grinned and nodded and scampered off. But an hour passed and then another. He did not return. Annabet's suspense became unbearable. At eleven o'clock she sent Juan on the same errand, and when, at the end of another hour the midday tong-tong sounded and neither boy had returned, she despatched a third messenger, this time a boatman, who was to take a prahau and try to get into Banda from the seaward side. She was angry with the boys rather than anxious about them. She had a fixed idea that natives could move with impunity anywhere, no matter what had happened. The boys had simply forgotten their errand and were hanging about among the crowds, or looking at the fire damage.

But the boatman, old and steady, did not return either. The hot drowsy afternoon wound its way along, slowly, and Annabet, unable any longer to remain still, wandered about the house, looking out of every window, listening at every door. If night set in without news arriving she knew she would go mad. What had happened to Evert? If things had gone well, surely he would have sent word. Was he dead? Was every white person in Banda dead? And she cut off here, isolated, just waiting and waiting.

Towards the end of the afternoon she wandered into her ravished bedroom, and noticed, close to the windowsill the length of material which Isa had ripped and arranged over her head. She picked it up, pushed her hair back from her face and set the makeshift veil in place. If she rubbed earth into her skin and walked with down-bent head, could she, in the darkness, make her way into Banda, and find out for herself what had happened? If they were all dead she must die with them.

359

She folded the veil and hung it over her arm and went downstairs again, intending to gather a handful of soil from the garden while it was still light enough to see. Just as she set her foot on the bottom stair pandemonium broke out, both inside the house and without. A kind of muffled roaring, pierced with screams from the compound, and from the back of the house, shouts and the sound of blows and then six shots fired in rapid succession. The door at the back of the stairs was torn open and Josef flung himself through it, closely pursued by a tall native whom Annabet had never seen before. Josef screamed 'Mevrouw, Mevrouw,' and Annabet thought that he was running to her for refuge and was filled with wild pity. In the next second she thought that Josef had turned traitor, for as his eyes found her he levelled his pistol and pointed it straight at her breast. But he screamed, in a terrible voice, 'Mynheer's order,' just before he fired. The bullet passed over Annabet's shoulder, ricochetted off the banister behind her and struck one of the large pottery jars full of dead flowers. Water and fragments of pottery and bits of twig rained down on Annabet's head. The man who was following Josef shot him through the back of the neck.

Annabet held the newel post at the foot of the stairs and looked at the stranger. He held his musket and looked at her. Then he turned his head indecisively and looked over his shoulder. Another burst of gunfire and the sound of shrill demented screaming came from the compound. Josef lay in his blood on the tiles at her feet, the fingers of one of his outspread hands twitching a little.

'Why don't you kill me?' Annabet asked at last in a shrill cracked voice.

'Shal Ahmi's order, Mevrouw,' said the man, and turned his head again to watch the door. She heard him draw a deep breath of relief as another native, an old man with grizzled hair and lined hollow cheeks, came forward from the passage door.

'You have her? That is good,' he said, nodding his head with an air of satisfaction. He turned Josef's body over with his foot, callously as one would roll a billet of wood from one's path. He nodded again. 'It is over,' he said, and Annabet wondered whether he referred to Josef's life, or to the fighting in the compound. Certainly a deathlike silence had followed the last outbreak.

'Take her to the others. I remain,' the older man ordered. The man who had shot Josef shifted his musket and took Annabet by the arm.

For the first few hundred yards of the walk into Banda she tried to question him, but to every question he returned only one answer, 'I do not know, Mevrouw,' spoken in a civil, quiet voice.

As they drew nearer to the town evidence of fierce fighting met Annabet's horrified, fascinated eyes. Dead bodies lay huddled in grotesque attitudes under the charred walls, among the broken bushes, in the midst of trampled flowerbeds. The big houses, with all their windows broken and their doors gaping, stood like empty shells in the last slanting light of the sun. A curious, almost an enchanted silence lay over the precincts of the town. Nobody stirred. And with the detached, active part of her mind Annabet noticed that although the houses with their open doors and windows were stuffed with possessions, nothing appeared to have been touched or moved.

On the waterfront itself, when they reached it, some activity was in progress. Little groups of men, moving quietly and resolutely and obviously under orders, were collecting the bodies of the dead and dividing them into two heaps. One sort they handled reverently and gently, the other they tumbled roughly together. Ours and theirs, Annabet thought sickly. How could they tell? By what means did a dead native show to which side he had belonged? But her deduction had been right, for before her guard urged her forward with a gentle but relentless pressure on her arm she saw the body of a white man, clad in shirt and russet-coloured breeches, thrown on to the heap of roughly-handled dead.

Evert's breeches had been blue, but there was no comfort, no hope in the thought. Either he was dead, defenceless as the body she had just seen cast aside, or he was captured. And with Banda in Shal Ahmi's hands it was better to be dead.

They stopped by the doorway of Rykshalt's warehouse. The men on guard at the doorway watched them approach and grinned and spoke to the man who held Annabet's arm. He spoke in Malay, but her guide was as uncommunicative in that tongue as in Dutch. He replied in two monosyllables which made the man on the door shrug his shoulders. He raised the bar of the door, opened it about a foot and pushed Annabet inside.

The lower floor of the warehouse had been cleared of its contents. It smelt of dust and nutmegs and mace and of overcrowded humanity confined in airlessness and heat. At first all the pale faces swam together in the gloom, and then, here and there, Annabet recognised somebody. Jehane Vehmeer, old Rita Byskin and her daughters and daughter-in-law, pretty Marie Graef with her little children clinging to her skirts, Elsa Hassen wearing nothing but a nightdress and a shawl.

They crowded about her, beginning to weep afresh, as though her appearance deepened their sense of calamity. Well, may you cry, she thought. If you knew all you would fall on me and tear me to pieces. I helped to bring you to this.

Now that there could be no good news, no hope in any news, there was news in plenty. True, some of the women had been struck silent with grief and terror, but others were voluble. They crowded about her, asking questions, not waiting to be answered, speaking with hysterical tears, or bitter calm, of their own losses and experiences. Jehane Vehmeer and Marie Graef had actually seen Evert. The Vehmeer house had been fired, and they had been trying to get the children away to Van Heem's when the battle had broken out in the street. Between the blazing house and the turmoil in the street they had been trapped, obliged to shelter as well as they could in the bushes of the garden.

'I saw Evert quite clearly.' Jehane said. 'He was fighting to get through to some soldiers who were surrounded between our house and Van Heem's. He was magnificent, Annabet, but of course it was hopeless. . . .'

'What happened to him?'

'I didn't see. Some natives came searching through the bushes and found us and brought us here.'

'All the men are dead,' said Marie Graef positively. She looked with tear-swollen eyes at her children and added, 'I wish to God we were all safely dead too.'

There were no words of comfort. The bitter, despairing words were echoed in the heart of every woman in the room.

Annabet looked at the children. Tear-stained and dishevelled, they were still more beautiful than flowers. And because Knoel had not been able to carry out his surprise attack and return triumphant they were all . . . The load of shame and self-hatred became insupportable. I must tell them, she thought wildly; I can't live here with them, accepted as a fellow-sufferer, when it is all my fault.

The door opened noisily and two men entered, pushing before them two of the low open barrows used for transporting the sacks of nutmegs. One was piled with food, a miscellaneous collection evidently the spoil of several larders; the other held about two dozen cups and two vast jugs of coffee. As one of the men straightened himself and released the handles of his barrow, he said in an inquiring tone, 'Mevrouw Haan?' Annabet stepped forward.

'You will come with me, if you please.'

The women crowded about her again, with renewed tears. They believed that she was being singled out for special, more speedy vengeance, because Evert had so nearly made contact with the soldiers and won the street battle. She pulled herself free of their hands and said in the wild shrill voice over which she seemed to have no control, 'Oh please don't worry about me. Don't give a thought to me, I do beg of you. Whatever happens to me isn't half what I deserve.'

The man interposed his body between her and the rest of the women and she stepped quickly through the door which the guard bolted again immediately. Her new guide was more communicative.

'You may be calm, Mevrouw. No harm is intended.'

'Where are you taking me?'

'Only to the Fort, Mevrouw. To Shal Ahmi himself.' I'll ask him, she thought, to have me shot. Or, if he won't do that, to have me shut up alone in the darkest, foulest place he can find. I can't go on living among those innocent ones.

The gaping void where the great gateway had been, and the heaps of stones which had been the gatehouse and the wall, had been fenced off, and her guide led her through another entrance, far to the seaward side. There were guards there, and more at some of the inner doorways, but that same strange quiet prevailed. There was none of the running to and fro, none of the bustle and transmission of orders which one would have expected to find in the headquarters of a man who had just organised a bloody and successful revolution and made himself head of the island. Nor, when finally the tall double door of the Justice room opened and she stepped inside alone, was there any sign of success about Shal Ahmi himself.

He sat behind the table across which the Governor and his attorney had so often dispensed Dutch justice. Two wrought-iron candle-stands, each holding twelve candles, stood, one on either side his chair. Behind him his own little brazier, or one exactly similar, glowed under a handful of aromatic herbs. The polished table-top held only a few sheets of paper, a silver inkstand and some quills in a little silver pot, and a small rough pottery bowl containing rice balls, smoking hot, at which he was picking with his fingers.

He looked up as she entered.

'Ah, Mevrouw. We meet again. Come in and be seated.'

He nodded towards a chair on the opposite side of the table. She sat down, thankful for the support. Seeing him again, so exactly as he had been in the gaol during that fatal interview, unnerved her so that her knees quivered and she could not have spoken if she had wanted to. She could only sit and stare at him with sick eyes.

'I mean you no harm,' he said gently. 'On the contrary.' He lifted a rice-ball, and then, with it poised half-way to his mouth, remembered something. 'I disturbed your supper, Mevrouw.' He dropped the rice-ball back in the bowl and clapped his hands together so sharply that her half-whispered

'It doesn't matter' was drowned. The door opened smartly and Shal Ahmi said quietly:

'Fetch some cakes and a bottle of wine for Mevrouw.'

'I couldn't swallow it,' she said.

'Nonsense. You look to be upon the verge of collapse, and you need strength, Mevrouw. We have a great deal to do.'

'We? You mean you want me to do something? To help you again? I won't do it, Shal Ahmi. I wouldn't lift a finger to do anything you suggested ... not if you ... not if you cut off my hands. ...'

He looked at her with calm interest. 'Your hands, Mevrouw? How strange that you should mention them. Your hands have for me a significance beyond all the other hands in the world.' He looked at them, thin and white and tremulous, clasped against the front of Isa's soiled little jacket. 'Why do you speak so vehemently?'

'Because I listened to you once; and I shall regret it to the last day of my life.'

'To me, Mevrouw? Was it not rather to your own heart that you listened. And when you have heard what I have to say your heart will speak again. This time with many voices, not with one only.' His eyes narrowed slightly. 'You speak of regret. That is unnecessary and foolish of you. In the first place you were deceived by me, and in the second place, although Gariz arrived with his message safely, it was only one of three, and not even the first come. From the very heart of affairs in Batavia a like warning had been sent, by whom, who can say? No, no, Mevrouw, I am not speaking from a desire to comfort you. Why should I? The days when I must lie and fumble my way are past. Ah well, cry if you wish, you will feel better afterwards.'

'I should have liked Evert to know,' she sobbed.

'Well, it may be that he does,' said Shal Ahmi, biting his rice-ball at last. 'There are many who hold that after death great wisdom comes. Mynheer Haan is dead. A slippery man, Mevrouw, but one of great courage. Ah, thank you. Set it down here.' His smooth brown fingers busied themselves with the cork of the bottle, but his eyes rested on Annabet, without impatience, without sympathy, but with close interest, as though he had never seen a woman in tears before and had no idea of their meaning. He poured some of the wine into one of the glasses which bore the Company's badge, as did almost everything the Governor had used, and then said gently:

'Mevrouw, are you crying because of the crime you did not commit, or for the husband you did not love?' She made no answer and went on crying, helplessly. 'Look at me,' he said, with insistence. 'Now, stop crying. Come, drink your wine and listen to what I want you to do.'

364

'I'm not going to do anything.'

'You may think differently when you have heard my proposal. You have spent a little time among my prisoners. Did you count them?'

'No.'

'There are twenty-eight women and thirty-four children. Sixty-two in all. There are also six or seven men in another place, but they are all badly wounded and need not, I think, be considered. But the sixty-two women and children are very important. There is at this moment,' he changed to a casual conversational tone, 'a little ship on her way to Batavia with news of the defeat of the great Von Holk and of the beginning of trouble in Banda. She bears a charmed life, that little ship. Twice she has escaped, twice she has carried back bad news. But this time, before she reaches port a humble prahau, dodging among the islands and shallow waters will outstrip her and carry bigger news to Batavia. And if I have reckoned rightly, the little *Greta* will not, this time, return with fresh men and fresh arms. Because my prahau will carry word that I have won back my islands and that twenty-eight women and thirty-four children, all of the purest Dutch blood, are in my hands. You see, Mevrouw? With the firing of the first shot against me, sixty-two innocent lives will end bloodily.' His voice took on edge. 'This among other things I wish to make quite clear to the authorities. And the trouble is that though I speak Dutch at least adequately, I write it very ill. The spoken word is easily acquired, but for writing one needs a teacher, a copybook, some leisure. And I would not have the authorities in Batavia dismiss my ultimatum thinking me an ignorant native of no account. I must make it very clear that I am a man to be reckoned with; no shade of meaning must be overlooked because the word which carries it is ill-spelt or unclearly written. Therefore, Mevrouw, you must write the letter for me.'

'I couldn't do that without the consent of the others.'

'What others? The women in Mynheer Rykshalt's warehouse. Mevrouw, you have been among them. You know, better than I, that they would agree to any measure that ensured their safety and the safety of their children. Is it not written in your own Holy Book, "All that a man has will he give for his life." Are women less reasonable than men?'

'The women with children would probably endorse your letter.' She reckoned rapidly, Marie Graef had six children, Sanje Byskin four, Corrie Byskin three, Anna Rykshalt four; the children were accounted for before half the women were counted. 'Those who have lost their men and have no children here might, very probably, choose death rather than deny everything their men died for. Besides, Shal Ahmi, the authorities in Batavia would not leave you in control of the islands for

365

the sake of a few women and children.'

Shal Ahmi moved aside a paper and touched the one thus brought uppermost. 'Perhaps not, Mevrouw. I am not in a position to argue about the humanity of your people. But here I have other arguments, and I think, very powerful ones. Today I went into Mynheer Kaerko's office and studied all his books. The best year that the Company has ever known was six years ago, in 1653. In the rough draft of the letter I wish you to write I have promised that exactly the same amount of nutmegs, mace and kendri oil shall, without fail, be produced every year henceforth, and so long as I remain in control of Banda. And I have pointed out that the administration will cost them nothing. No Governor, no Agent, no soldiers to pay. Will that move those who have no scruple against the shedding of innocent blood? Moreover, I offer them a monopoly—that is the sacred word, is it not—twice as valuable as the one they now hold. I can swear that not one single nut will ever be smuggled out of the islands. And I offer security too. Four times in each year they may send their inspectors to look everywhere and to see everything, as a proof that I am not deceiving them. You will agree, Mevrouw, that such proposals will at least halt the progress of hostilities. The authorities in Batavia will consider them worthy of being referred to the supreme authority. And that will gain me almost a year. Openly and with a free hand, I can do much in a year.'

Despite herself, she was interested and impressed. 'But wasn't that kind of arrangement tried, long ago? I've heard men speak of the old days, at dinner-parties. Contracts ... that was the name. Weren't there bargains between the people in the islands and the Company? And didn't they all fail?'

'That was so, indeed. And all the contracts were broken, and all the peaceable agreements failed because my people were always looking backwards upon the old lazy days of leisure and easy living; and the Company was always looking forward to days of greater effort and greater power. How then could they hope to agree? Now the trial has been made. My people know that the easy days have gone for ever; your people know exactly what richness the powerful days have brought them, and what burdens. I offer to match the richness and diminish the burden. I think that now we may come to a better understanding—if you write it all as clearly as I speak it, Mevrouw.'

She stared at him, half-hypnotized by his confidence, by the boldness and scope of his plan. And as she stared she realised why it was that there was a difference about his appearance. On the folds of his spotless white clothing, above his left breast, glittered an enormous jewel. A single diamond, as large as a walnut, wide and rounded at one end, tapering at the other. It rose and fell with his breathing, flashing, sparkling, combining in itself the elements of fire and water.

Shal Ahmi saw the direction of her eyes. 'Ah,' he said, and touched the stone with the tip of one finger. 'You are admiring my diamond. It was once the centre-piece of my father's crown. You are seeing, Mevrouw, what no other white person has ever seen, the Sacred Raindrop of Banda. I could not bring myself to sell it with the others. For sentiment's sake I have preserved it through many vicissitudes.' His hand dropped back on to the edge of the table and his tone changed. 'We must not dwell upon the past. The future is ours. You will write the letter.' He pushed some of the sheets of blank paper, a red-feathered quill, and the ink-pot across the shining table.

'I won't write it,' she said steadily. 'You deceived me before. You said then that by acting as you told me I should save lives. Now you say it again.'

'This time it is true. Sixty-two lives lie in the hollow of your hand, Mevrouw.'

'Go to your prisoners,' she said, 'ask them if they agree to your plan. If they do get one of them to write the letter.'

He leaned forward against the edge of the table and spoke with extreme earnestness.

'I will tell you something. I will explain why you, and you only, must write for me. Mevrouw, do you remember the time when you arrived in Banda. On the night of that day the man who had married you came to me for aid. Like all vain men he imagined that the eyes of all his world were upon him; like all vain men he feared, above everything else, the ridicule of his fellows. And because you had come to him, twisted and ugly, in the place of the beautiful bride about whom he had boasted, he came to me, pitiable, abject, distraught in his despair. He said to me, in simple words, "Rid me of her." ' He paused and studied her, watching for some effect of his words and was disappointed to find none. She was listening to a story that was empty of all personal meaning, a story of two dead people, long ago. 'Mevrouw, all white men and all white women are born my enemies. The life of one of them is less to me than the life of any leaf on any tree in the jungle. I could have killed you then, so very easily, without danger to myself, without the slightest remorse. But on that evening I was most strangely aware of being upon the brink of an important decision, so I did what I always do at such a time. I appealed directly to the gods. When Mynheer Haan left me to go and make the way clear I took out my tela, the sacred stones which, when they fall, fall from the gods' own fingers, and I cast them for you. Astonished, incredulous, hardly able to believe my eyes, I read in the signs which can neither lie nor be misunderstood, that you, a white woman, as yet unseen by me, would serve me and my cause. The tela told me clearly that by your hand you would help me.' His bright, almost hypnotic stare bored into her. 'When you came to the gaol and the letter of warning was taken into your hand, Mevrouw, I thought, there, it is done, the will of the gods is fulfilled, and I was willing then that you should go your way in peace. As clearly as I might then, I told you to fly from the danger that was to come. But later, when the gaol was broken for me and I reached Ay, I learned, again with astonishment, that the action of your hand had been unimportant. You had not, since a previous message had already arrived there, served me, or borne out the prophecy of the gods. There are many gods, Mevrouw, and it may well be that their plans may overlap. But my gods had told me that it was by your hand that my triumph would be finally established. Therefore it was plain to me that your action was still to be performed. Now I understand. You did not flee to Batavia; the shot which should have killed you this afternoon, though fired at close quarters, went astray. *Because* you were to write that letter for me. Written by your hand it will meet with the reception that I plan for it. You are young and foolish, Mevrouw, I am old and wise in these matters, and I say to you, very solemnly, the gods are not mocked. We may delay and deny, ah, we may protest and weep, but in the end we do their bidding.'

'But your gods are not mine, Shal Ahmi. I have served my God very ill, but He allows me what He allows all His followers, free-will. And I will not write the letter that will help you to keep Banda, which my husband and all the men I knew have died to save from you.'

'Would that be so evil a thing, Mevrouw?' he asked with the patience which he had learned through thirty tedious years. His smooth bland face took on an expression of passionate intensity. 'Since the very dawn of time, these islands have always belonged to my people, the happy, harmless, laughing people of Banda. We interfered with nobody, we desired nothing save to live as our fathers lived, to adhere to the old customs, to raise our children as we had been raised, and to die, and go to our fathers. But we lived where the nutmegs grew. We did not grow the nutmegs, they grew around us, making shade for our houses, wood for our fires and the substance of friendly trade with our neighbours. Then the white men came, deeming the nutmeg precious, demanding ever more and more. We did not resist them, Mevrouw, we laughed and said: take the nutmegs you deem so precious and leave us alone. But that they could not do. They must have our nutmegs, and then they must have our bodies, bound in contracts to labours that our fathers never conceived. Then they must have our souls. Even our gods we must abandon. First in favour of the white virgin goddess and her baby, and then in favour of the strict old man god and his rules written in the stone. But always the nutmeg was behind the altar, Mevrouw. Then, and then only, when we saw our gods, the laws of our fathers, everything we held sacred in jeopardy, did we resist. Hold, we said, this is too much. With what result? Mevrouw, the blood shed last night is but a drop in the ocean to that which Coen and Gomarus shed. Even those desperate ones who took to the hills were hunted out or lured down with false promises and slain, not in anger, but as goats and sheep in the slaughterhouse. For the sake of the little nutmeg which can neither heal a broken bone, stop a flux or cure a sickness of the soul, the Dutch were willing to kill and kill until not one man of the Bandanese blood remained alive.' He folded his arms in his sleeves and leaned forward, resting his elbows on the table. 'One did, Mevrouw. I escaped from Coen's bloody hands. I remained alive. I remembered. And I waited. The men of my own race, of my own age had gone to their fathers untimely, and I must wait until the sons of the women who were driven screaming into the slave markets of Batavia and Bandogar were brought back to live as slaves on the very soil where they had lived as the children of free men. I waited until they had borne children of their own. Their fathers were of all colours, of many beliefs and of many races. But I claimed them as my own, Mevrouw. I trained them, I armed them, and I waited. Had I time I would tell you of the thousand little dirty shameful things I have done for a guilder, of the great dangerous thing I did for many guilders. My children had children, and I claimed them too. Not one escaped my notice. To every one I offered the chance to avenge his mother's shame, to reclaim his grandsire's cherished, bloodstained land. I have borne scorn, and calumny, shame, hunger and imprisonment. And I have won back my islands.' He paused, and then with a wave of his hand, one of his rare gestures, dismissed the subject. 'Mevrouw, when you have written the letter you shall have your reward.' He turned his hands back upwards and studied them intently. 'I was in Ay, among the English, so lately as yesterday afternoon. Your man still lives. He has been shot in the foot and will probably limp for the rest of his days. But what is that? When the letter is written I will send you to Ay.'

Still ostensibly studying his hands, he glanced at her shyly from under his lowered, hooded eyelids. He had the—for him—almost unique experience of seeing one of his offhand momentous statements ignored. No melting warmth came to the frozen pallor of her hard little face, no light quickened in her sick eyes. For a moment he wondered whether she had heard, or hearing, understood. And he did a thing which he rarely did, rarely had cause to do. He repeated himself.

'When the letter is written, Mevrouw, you will be free. I will send you to Ay.'

Some submerged, moribund feeling stirred in her feebly, tried to resuscitate itself, and failed. Up to so short a time ago the idea of one day going to Christy had lain behind all thought, all action, all hope. And now, by means that she had never dreamed of, the idea had become an actuality. She had only to write a few words, be patient for a few minutes more, and she would be free to go to Christy.

But there was no resurrection of hope and desire. Appalled and astonished she regarded her own lack of emotion. It was too late. One could not wrest one's own heart's desire out of a holocaust; one could not step across the bodies of all those dead men, light of spirit because one man was still alive. With her world, Banda, happy and secure and thriving, with Evert alive and arrogant and possessive, it had been possible to toy with the idea of going to Christy and setting personal happiness and fulfilment before everything else. But Banda was ravaged and burned; Evert and the other men whom she had known, were dead, and in that crowded, airless prison twenty-four women were weeping for their loss. The mere contemplation of personal happiness against such a background was obscene.

And Christy? She had understood once, when she had held him in her arms, the terrible significance of one person. Now, sadly, but with an overpowering assurance, she knew that it was not paramount. There were things for which even love must stand aside. Or rather there were loves more urgent and embracing than the love between men and women.

The songs and the poems and the books denied that. If she had been a woman in a poem she would have been crying with joy now, ready to do anything, say, write, do anything that would give her the chance to see Christy again. But I'm not, she thought steadily. I'm just an ordinary, wretched, bewildered woman, bound to admit that Christy counts for less to me at this moment than those sad women, those pretty, innocent children. Is that because I didn't love him enough? I shall never know. Such things have no measure. I would have left Evert and all the security and comfort of Coenpark; I would have gone hungry and barefoot with him anywhere. But I can't leave those women and children for him. I don't even want to. There is no feeling left in me. Only my mind remains.

'And the rest of your hostages?' she asked, breaking the long silence.

'They must remain, naturally. Until I have my assurance from Holland itself, and have rebuilt the Fort and armed myself against the perfidy which the Company might show.

They shall be treated well, Mevrouw. I may kill to rule, thereby following the example of those who call themselves my superiors, but I do not rule to kill. Moreover, strange as it may sound, I bear no grudge against the women of your race. Women are not, of themselves, dangerous. Even among your people there has never been a woman explorer, a woman soldier, or a woman perkinier. Also, of course, it is to my advantage to keep them alive. A dead hostage is no argument.'

'In Batavia they will not know whether your hostages are alive or not. Or the numbers.'

'They will have my word.'

'They could have mine as well. It might count for more.'

He looked at her sharply. 'What are you suggesting, Mevrouw?'

'A bargain. Send those women to Matu, Shal Ahmi. Then, when they have been gone for one hour I will write your letter and another as well. I will write a letter purporting to come from all your hostages, and signed by me, begging the authorities in Batavia to consider your terms and save our lives. They have no means of knowing that of the sixty-three only one will remain in your power. It will take months for the women to make their way from Matu to Batavia, and even then no one will know they are not women who have escaped naturally. So many are dead that you might still hold sixty-three hostages.'

She remembered what he had said about her hands, and as she spoke she folded them together ostentatiously and placed them upon the edge of the table. She saw his eyes follow them.

'My husband was esteemed by the Company. They will remember the name in Batavia. And you will have your answer before the women get back to Java. Matu is so small. Hardly one ship in a hundred stops there.'

Shal Ahmi leaned back in his chair and his smooth brown fingers moved slowly over the blazing jewel on his breast. After a long pause he said in a voice which, though smooth and bland as ever, held something cold and menacing.

'You are daring to offer me terms, Mevrouw?'

She felt her breath catch with fear. One's mind might be prepared for death; one might be so desperate, so sickened, that one longed and even prayed for it. But it was easy, painless death the mind envisaged. A cessation of being. The frail, shrinking flesh, so vulnerable, so susceptible, had strong instincts and dreads of its own. She had said wildly, 'Not if you cut off my hands...' But suppose he took her at her word and said, write, or with this knife I will sever your hands at the wrists. He was capable of it. Remember little Jean Vehk who had offered no provocation at all.

'You will lend your aid so soon as these women are out of

Banda?'

'Yes, Shal Ahmi. That is my condition.' Thank God her voice was under control again, and rang out with firm assurance.

'Mevrouw, such a suggestion shows regrettable lack of faith in my integrity.'

'Does that surprise you, Shal Ahmi? Remembering how you tricked me before. Since the moment when I realised what I had done I have not passed an hour without wishing myself dead. You are not yet strongly established; an attack from Batavia could brush you aside. If I helped you to postpone such an attack, and those women remained in your hands and you dealt evilly with them; or if, a year hence, an unfavourable reply came from Holland and you wreaked your vengeance upon your prisoners, the torments I have felt in these last weeks would be as nothing to those I should know. I understand you now. All your time, all your endeavours have been devoted to the restoration of Banda, nothing else matters to you. So you will be able to understand me. All my care now is to save the poor remnant of my people. When they are safe, I will help you. Not till then. Apart from their safety, nothing matters to me.'

'Not even the young Englishman?'

'No. I will write your letter, and my own letter. I will stay here and be your sole hostage. If things go wrong you may wreak your vengeance on me. One body or sixty-three, what does it matter?'

'Give me your right hand, Mevrouw,' he said gently.

Unsuspecting she stretched it across the expanse of shining mahogany. He turned it in his own for a moment, looking at it with interest. Then he bent her little finger, pressing the top joint down upon the bottom one and then gradually increasing the pressure until the full force of his strength was brought into play. She had had no idea that such a simple thing could cause such excruciating agony. The taut muscles cracked, the stretched nerves sent arrows of pain along her arm and into her neck. She wanted to scream; but she set her teeth into her lower lip and held back the sound. Jerkily she shook her head at him, dumbly informing him that if he broke all her fingers one after the other she still would not give in.

There was, mercifully, a limit to the amount of pain that could be consciously accepted. Still fast in the torturing vice, she felt her arm growing numb, Shal Ahmi's face with its expression of fiendish interest was washed over by a wave of darkness. She began to sag forward as she sat.

He released her finger suddenly, and straightened it, quite gently, between his own.

'One should always test one's opponent,' he said pleasantly, and then sat silent for a moment, thinking, while Annabet stretched and rubbed the pain-paralysed, rapidly-swelling finger.

'Very well,' he said at last, abruptly. 'They may go. I will give the orders.'

'No. Not you. You could so easily tell the men to row for an hour and then bring the boats back.'

'How then shall we arrange it?'

'Send a man with me with orders to do exactly what I say, and then to bring me back.'

He clapped his hands again.

'Go with Mevrouw Haan and see that all her orders are carried out, Julendi. She understands that she is not to go with the others. She is to come back here with you. I, Mevrouw, will snatch a few minutes sleep. For four days I have been awake without intermission.' He lay down, as simply as a dog might do, upon the thick silky rug upon which the Governor's table stood and to all appearances was asleep before Annabet and her guard were out of the room.

Out of his presence, freed from the conflict of wills in which, miraculously, she had gained a victory, she could sort out her thoughts. There was a shred of hope now for the women and children at least. There were sufferings ahead of them, but once in Matu they would be among friends and on the first stage of their journey to Batavia. She fingered that thought gladly. There was less complete joy in the knowledge that, even if she had never visited Shal Ahmi in the gaol, never carried that message to Gariz, the course of the war would not have been altered, the rebellion not averted. But her sense of guilt in that matter was too deeply ingrained to be removed by a few words. She still felt like a traitor.

About Christy she could feel nothing at all, except an impersonal relief that he was still alive—as though he had been a stranger whose life had been in danger; and a kind of muted sorrow that an emotion which had been so vivid and so engrossing should have been so mortal.

Over the piece of information which Shal Ahmi had thrown at her about Evert's intention towards her on her arrival, she skimmed without investigation. They had both been wrong, so often; and now he was dead.

There was one other thing which stood out from that interview in the Justice Room, and it was this: Impregnable as Shal Ahmi appeared to be to ordinary human feelings, there was one noticeable chink in his armour. He was superstitious. And of that one weakness she had taken full advantage. It might even be that she could find some other way of using the weapon so suddenly and surprisingly placed in her hand. In her hand. Literally. She looked down at her own hand wonderingly. The little finger stood out stiff and distorted.

They had reached the warehouse again.

'See me safely locked in here, Julendi. Then go and find six seaworthy prahaus, large ones. Man them with reliable men, three of whom at least have been to Matu before. Find somebody to help you and provision the boats—rice and water will do, enough to keep seventy people alive until they reach Matu. Do you understand?'

The man looked at her with wild astonishment. But Shal Ahmi, the master, had said that she must be obeyed, it was not for him to question or hesitate.

The air within the prison room was almost unbreathable by this time. A little office opening off it had been provided with two buckets for the sanitary needs of sixty-two people; but the small room had no proper door, just a swinging screen which started a foot from the top and ended a foot from the ground and the noisome stench had pervaded the whole place. A brass oil lamp hung upon the inner was flickering to extinction and exuding its own peculiar odour of burnt wick, rancid oil and hot metal.

Most of the women were sitting on the bare floor, resting their backs against the wall. Some had their children's heads in their laps or pressing against their shoulders. Older children either leaned against the wall, or lay in the centre of the floor, their heads supported upon rolled shawls or petticoats. Almost all the children and some of the women were asleep when the guard opened the door, but a startled stir, among the women at least, testified to nervous alertness.

Jahane Vehmeer, whom Annabet had never liked, threw herself forward and cried, 'Oh, you're back. I'm so glad. I never hoped to see you again. What happened? Why were you sent for?'

'Shal Ahmi has decided to send us all to Matu. The prahaus are being got ready now. It means days in open boats, in the sun. And they'll be overcrowded and short of food and water, but there'll be safety in the end.'

He had been right, of course. Safety ... the preservation of their own bodies from death and torment ... that was what was uppermost in their minds. Relief shone on every face, even those upon which the tears of mourning were scarcely dry. In the final issue life itself was a very precious thing, the most important thing of all.

The barrow of food, with a good deal remaining in it, had been pushed into one corner.

'Eat before you go,' Annabet said. 'There will be little enough afterwards.'

374

Those who had no appetite before, were hungry now. Nobody wondered why Annabet Haan should be telling them all what to do. Nobody noticed that Annabet Huan who said 'Eat' now stood aside eating nothing. The children, hastily roused, stood about, sleepy-eyed, hardly troubling to lift to their mouths the food which their mothers almost fought to secure for them.

Old Rita Byskin hobbled forward. 'Why is he sending us to Matu, Annabet darling? That's turning us loose.'

'He did not explain anything. He sent a man to see to the prahaus and me to tell you. That is all.'

A babble of speculation broke out. Shal Ahmi didn't want the trouble of feeding them. He couldn't spare men to guard them. He was clever enough to see that the presence of a group of white women, some of them young and pretty, would cause trouble among his men. 'Every native, in his heart, wants a white woman *that* way.' Annabet stood aside, silent, and looked at her hand. 'It was by your hand, by your *hand*, Mevrouw, that my triumph would be finally established.' Obviously he believed it implicitly. There was no living breathing creature who did not believe something implicitly. How very, very fortunate for these women, flicking their tongues after stray crumbs. . . .

'Mevrouw, the prahaus wait.'

'Tell the guard to open the door.'

They tumbled out into the sweet, spice-scented, breeze-fanned air. They rushed towards the boats, a pale-coloured frail line like a wisp of foam which the tide had flung inland and was now drawing out again. The nutmeg tide of Banda.

'Some women and some children in each prahau, please,' said Annabet, running among them like an anxious sheep-dog among a distracted flock. 'Mevrouw Graef, this way. If you travel with Corrie there will be only two adults to ten children. We must even the loads.'

They were so meek, so anxious to be told what to do.

'Julendi, tell the men that it is Shal Ahmi's order that the boats are to go, with their best speed, straight to Matu. Tell each one that and then tell them to start, one by one.'

Out of the orderly confusion a voice cried here and there, 'What about you, Annabet? Come with us. See, there is a place here.' But she pretended that she had a place in another boat, always in another boat. As the last one shot out into the moon-silvered water she stepped backwards behind Julendi and the three men who had helped him to provision the prahaus so quickly. The men talked together for a moment in Malay, and she listened to the tone of their conversation. It was difficult to assess, but she was curiously sure that there was no anger and no criticism in it. Shal Ahmi had commanded and the thing was done. Julendi turned back to her, 'And now Mevrouw, I will take you back to the Fort.'

'In exactly one hour from now,' she said, and went and sat on the steps of the deserted warehouse. She watched the prahaus grow smaller until they were mere dots in the moonlit water. Then, dot by dot, they were lost over the shining horizon.

Shal Ahmi was awake and waiting when they returned to the Fort. The rice bowl had been removed and the brazier sprinkled with a fresh handful of herbs; but the bottle of wine and the glass and the little dish of cakes still stood on one corner of the table.

'We have wasted almost two hours, Mevrouw,' he said in an unhurried manner. 'Head the letter as I suggested before, "From the Justice Room in the Fort of Banda." And to-day's date by your Dutch reckoning. So. Now we will make no claim to titles and honours which would cause amusement and lead to disputation. On the next line write, "From Shal Ahmi, who has this day won back what his fathers lost." And then, "Your Excellencies ..."'

He leaned over her and studied the clear Italianate hand-writing which the governess from Brussels had taught to little four-year-old Annabet in the schoolroom of the great house at Janshaven.

'That is beautifully done, Mevrouw. Now I will tell you what I want said and you will put it into good Dutch in that beautiful writing.'

His arguments and his suggestions fell smoothly, following one another like the beads of a Rosary.

As she set down sentence after sentence, giving great care to punctuation, which had always been her weak point, Annabet could feel no doubt as to the letter's reception. 'At the first sign of hostility from you,' she wrote, 'the sixty-three hostages will be killed, and axe and fire will be loosed in the groves. The first white man to visit Banda uninvited will find no single tree in flower.' That threat alone showed the inassailability of his position. By their own act the Company had concentrated the trade within the limit of these few tiny islands; the loss of the Banda groves would strike the Company a death-blow. For the sake of the nutmeg groves alone the islands must be left to Shal Ahmi for as long as his power lasted.

And she had seen enough of the quiet, deadly orderliness of his revolution to know that his power would last as long as he did. After that?

She rested her pen and looked up. 'I'm curious about one thing, Shal Ahmi. Who will rule Banda when you are dead?'

'It is queer you should ask that question,' he replied amiably, without any sign of that superstitious shrinking from the thought of his own demise which would have shown itself in almost any normal man at such a moment. 'In my quiet times to-day I have thought about that, too. I could not get a son, Mevrouw, until the land was mine again. Could I condemn my own flesh and blood to walk humbly, like a slave, to be eaten up alive by the hunger for power which I have known? But now I shall look about me and find some healthy young woman of the purest Bandanese blood remaining. And she will bear me a son.' His supreme confidence pervaded the room. 'I am not yet an old man, Mevrouw. I was but a boy when Coen came. I shall live to see my son reach manhood; and I shall rear him like a prince of Banda; but I shall teach him, too, the lessons of patience and industry and cunning which I myself learned so hardly. If that answers your question, Mevrouw,' he said pleasantly, 'let us proceed. We have almost done.'

She set the quill in motion again, obediently putting each sentence into the clearest form, the plainest writing. But part of her mind moved independently. Without leadership the natives were useless, she thought. If Evert had been at Coenpark this afternoon, Shal Ahmi's men would have been routed. In his absence the faithful ones had been overcome with hardly a struggle. Even the revolutionaries were meek, schooled in obedience, looking to Shal Ahmi for guidance in everything. If he could be removed . . .

Faced with that thought she felt weak and futile, and wished fervently that she had been other than she was. One brave, clever woman, or even a stupid one, sufficiently resolute, might turn the tide of fate even now. He trusted her implicitly, saw in her nothing but the useful tool the gods had prepared and tempered for him long ago.

We're like Sisera and Jael in the Old Testament story, she thought. But Jael drove the tent peg through Sisera's temples. If I were Jael this letter would never reach Batavia. The *Greta* and other ships would sail back, and the island might be retaken.

But she had never, in all her life, entertained a really violent impulse, and as she looked at Shal Ahmi's hairless head shining in the candlelight the idea of inflicting a physical injury upon him made her feel sick.

Yet the man had killed harmless, kind little Jean Vehk, treacherously; treacherously he had dealt with Evert and all the other white men in the islands, even Kaerko, who had risked unpopularity by his support of him, had been killed. And he had tricked her into an act which had caused her such remorse that it had killed her self-esteem and her will to live and her will to love. He was ruthless and pitiless. And if one had an obscure feeling that his singlemindedness and con-

377

fidence were somehow admirable, that was only because squeamish, weak-nerved, muddling people were bound to admire qualities they lacked themselves.

His blood, shed now, would save much bloodshed later on. But he had only one real enemy in the island, Annabet Haan, who had never killed anything bigger than a fly, and avoided that as often as not.

'My name, at least, I can write clearly,' said Shal Ahmi, taking the papers from her and plunging a second quill into the ink-pot. 'Write now your letter from the sixty-three hostages. You may add, in all truth, Mevrouw, that your husband died like a hero in the defence of the town. It may add weight to your appeal, and is no more than his due. Had there been ten like him ... Yes, Julendi?'

The door at the far end of the room had opened, and the native came in, soft-footed.

'Wan Tau has collected the bodies,' he said, addressing Shal Ahmi without preamble, but in a tone of such complete respect that no title known to man could have enhanced it. 'There are four score and six of the white men and their slaves. He asks what shall be done with them.'

'Burn the heap as it lies,' said Shal Ahmi shortly.

'And Pua asks if the six wounded may be taken elsewhere. The well in the square is hidden under wreckage and it is far for Pua to fetch the water. All the time they demand water.'

'Tell Pua to cut their throats and throw them on to the pile with the others.'

Annabet heard her own little whimpering sound of horror. Shal Ahmi looked at her. 'Mevrouw, they cannot recover. Doctor Van de Lijn is dead, and they suffer.' He turned back to Julendi.

'The prahau I ordered is ready?'

'It waits.'

'Carry the orders to Wan Tau and Pua, and then come back for the papers.'

He watched while Annabet, with a hand growing less and less steady, wrote the last sentences of her false appeal.

Shal Ahmi studied it carefully. 'It is very well written, Mevrouw. So long as you remain in Banda playing the part of sixty-three hostages, you shall write all my letters.'

He opened a drawer of the table and took out a stick of sealing-wax and the Governor's official seal. Very carefully he folded his own letter, and hers, and enclosed them in a sheet of stout paper, folding over the ends and pressing them flat.

She watched him, while a process too swift, too urgent, too incoherent to be called thinking took place in her brain. Those three words, 'cut their throats' had been like a flash of lightning, making clear in half a second what had been vague and misty. They showed the whole mind of the man. His plans were reasonable, his arguments were plausible, but they all led to one end, complete and absolute power of a kind which no man, even a good man, could possess without danger. Nobody could pretend that the white people were perfect, there were bad men, cruel men, fake men among them, but their powers for evil and cruelty and falsity were curbed by something which would not exist in Shal Ahmi's Banda, the force of public opinion, the tenets, however lightly held of Christianity, the vague, faltering, faulty but vital concept of justice. Coen and Gomarus had been cruel, but they had been open to censor, and there were many Dutchmen who refused even to recognise the brilliance of their leadership on account of their faults of character. That didn't wipe out the cruelties, but it would lay a foundation for merciful dealings in the future. There had been cruel perkiniers; but in Holland there were men who, drawing their incomes from the dividends which the Company paid, had yet been just enough and disinterested enough to register their protests against practices which it would have paid them to ignore. There were Dutchmen who might conceivably have said of six helpless wounded men, 'cut their throats'; but there would always be, near at hand, some other Dutchmen who would raise a voice in protest. There was, always, among free white people a will to good, though it might be too feeble or too late to avert evil. It came plodding along, and one day it would win. But the thing Shal Ahmi stood for left no room for that. One could see, very easily, what Banda would be like, left to him, and to the son he intended to rear and train. A slave community. And if anybody were a nuisance, or useless, 'cut their throats.' ... He stood, for all his suavity and plausibility, for the old, dark, evil things.

He had risen and was holding the wax to the flame of one of the candles when the door opened again, very abruptly, and Julendi, not waiting for a word of recognition, padded rapidly across the floor. Shal Ahmi looked at him with displeasure.

'Close the door, Julendi.'

The man halted, opened his mouth to speak, thought better of it, and turned and closed the door, quietly. Then, half-way back to the table where Shal Ahmi was pressing the seal to the warm wax, the urgency of his news overcame his awe and he said breathlessly:

'There is a Dutch ship coming in. A fishing boat brought news.'

Shal Ahmi turned the paper about and calmly sealed the other end before speaking.

'Did the fisherman note the name?'

'It is the *Eastern Venture*, lately here.' The control imposed

379

upon Julendi by his master's will cracked a little. 'She should be on her way to Holland now. What is she doing here?' he asked in a voice of excited foreboding.

'Since when have such matters been your concern, Julendi? Am I not to be trusted to deal with a solitary Dutch ship? Even to turn her arrival to advantage? Is she visible yet from the quay?'

'Her topsails only. But the tide and the wind are with her. She comes in fast.'

'Even so there will be time to spare before they land. Tell Hassim to have his men ready. I myself will bring out the Dutch flags when I come. Hold yourself ready to hoist them.'

His calmness was contagious. Julendi who had rushed into the room in a state of nervous excitement, left at his ordinary pace and as quietly as usual.

Annabet had heard the news with a thrill of jubilation, fast followed by one of deadly apprehension. She knew—for she had travelled in one of them—the fighting capacity of the tall East Indiamen. Given a fair chance Piet and his crew might retake the island—but only if Shal Ahmi were dead before the boats were lowered. Already he was planning another tricky victory. He would hang out the Dutch flags, and Piet and his sailors would see them in the moonlight and imagine they were flying to celebrate a victory. They would come ashore all unsuspecting. Piet Odshoorn, so kind and honest would be added to Shal Ahmi's long list of victims, unless . . . unless . . .

Her heart faltered; even her breathing seemed to stop. But her mind was relentless. She had seen for herself how utterly the natives depended upon leadership; she had seen for herself how completely Shal Ahmi had vested himself with all power and all control. His death would throw his followers into such helpless panic and consternation that Piet—if he were firm— could put an end to the rebellion.

Such a violent fit of trembling seized her that even her head was palsied. If I knew what to do, she thought wildly, I couldn't do it.

Shal Ahmi, as though he were alone in a timeless world, placidly cleared the top of his table. The bottle and the wine-glass he pushed to its extreme edge so that she had only to put out her hand to reach them. She made the action with jerky abruptness and poured some wine into the glass. Some of it spilled over, and even when she had lifted it and set it to her mouth a convulsive movement of her head rattled the rim against her teeth and some more wine spilled down the front of Isa's jacket. The feel of the cool hard bottle within the grip of her damp palsied hand remained after she had released it; and the feeling was somehow urgent and significant, but with what meaning she did not know.

Now Shal Ahmi was fumbling within the bosom of his robe and drawing out a little greasy leather bag. She heard the chink of stones and remembered, with a stab of superstitious terror what he had said earlier in the evening about his tela. If he had spoken truly it might well be that at the first glance he would read a warning of her hatred, of her determination to do him harm if only she could think of a way.

But Shal Ahmi did not immediately look at the stones. He tossed them on to the table-top and moved his hands over them blindly, his eyes staring straight ahead, blank, unfocussed.

The tela had told him that with her hand he would seal his triumph. Her hand. Her hand, where the touch of the wine-bottle lingered, its meaning—ah, its dreadful meaning—now bursting through the barriers of reluctance and incredulity.

And simultaneously with the flash of inspiration came the memory of Cousin Jean Marie, Father Vincent. It was the spirit that mattered. And God knew—oh God, You must know and pity me and strengthen my heart and never my hand—that the evil she was about to do was to be done in the cause of mercy and justice, in the right spirit, to prevent greater evil.

She drew a long, steadying breath. Shal Ahmi gathered the stones into his hand and let them fall. He leaned forward, studying their message. There crept over his face an expression of bewilderment.

Annabet, all conscious thought suspended, took the wine bottle in her hand again, casually, as though to refill her glass. Shal Ahmi never raised his eyes. He gathered his stones and flung them again, and again leaned forward. Annabet, softly and swiftly as a cat, rose to her feet and moved until she stood behind him. Her very loathing of what she did made the blow one of unimaginable violence. Chance, or something less blind, guided it truly. It struck the bowed bald skull at its base, just where it joined the neck.

Shal Ahmi fell forward like a broken puppet. Blood and wine ran out over the stones of the tela which had spoken so truly. For with her hand she had established his triumph. Established it beyond all chance of reverse or slow decay.

Still moving as though obeying some other will than her own, she lifted the sealed packet of letters and held it to the candle-flame. The last embodiment of Shal Ahmi's plans and dreams and perfidies flared, shrivelled, blackened between her fingers.

The door opened, and Julendi, nervous and anxious again, entered hastily. The *Eastern Venture* with the tide and the wind behind her and a demented Piet Odshoorn at her helm, was coming in at phenomenal speed, and Julendi thought his master should be told.

He had actually uttered a word or two before he saw what had happened in his short absence. He whipped out his short, curved knife. Annabet, with a wild memory of Shal Ahmi's words about the gods and their overlapping plans, knew, in that last moment, why she had come to Banda.

THE END

NORAH LOFTS' GREAT HOUSE TRILOGY NOW IN CORGI BOOKS

600 years in the history of a House from mediaeval times to 1955. The poignant record of the lives, loves, frustrations and tragedies of generations of occupants all seeking to restore their shattered lives in the timeless shelter of OLD VINE.

☐ **THE TOWN HOUSE** 08185 x 6/–
Martin Reed, young blacksmith and serf, strikes his lord and is obliged to flee the Manor with the girl he wishes to marry. Truly a 'from rags to riches' magnificent beginning to the saga.

☐ **THE HOUSE AT OLD VINE** 08186 8 6/–
In novel 2, Maud, Martin's granddaughter, is now a grandmother. Time, 1496 to 1680. The house has mellowed.

☐ **THE HOUSE AT SUNSET** 08187 6 6/–
In this, the final volume, 'the House today' is threatened by demolition order—but is dramatically saved at the 11th hour!

Other Outstanding Works by Norah Lofts:

☐ **THE DEVIL IN CLEVELY** 08202 3 5/–
Autocrat Sir Charles ruled his villagers firmly but kindly. When he died the new Squire came with odd ideas and odder friends . . .

☐ **OUT OF THIS NETTLE** 08203 1 5/–
Following the massacre of the clans at Culloden, Colin Lowrie of the clan Lowrie was forced to flee. He journeyed the world. This is the story of his wild life and of his eerie love affair with an eccentric heiress.

☐ **THE LUTE PLAYER** 08249 x 5/–
The 12th century! Richard Coeur-de-Lion leading his knights on to Saracen battle fields—his ill fated union with Berengaria and his strange relationship with Blondel, the Lute Player—

TWO GREAT WORLD-FAMOUS CLASSICS FROM BRIGITTE VON TESSIN AND KATHLEEN WINSOR

THE BASTARD
Volume I 5/-   552 07921 9
Volume II 7/6   552 07922 7

Brigitte von Tessin

From the wild, brutal, romantic world of 17th-century France, a story of intrigue and passion—the story of Gaston, Comte de Racon, arrogant and lecherous—married to a young Huguenot heiress—and father of THE BASTARD, Martin Saint-Jean.

THE BASTARD, Volume II, continues the story of the savage, tumultuous Racon family. . . . Here is Madeleine, the Comte de Racon's wife, barring her husband from her bed, yet longing to be the victim of his savage desires, and Martin Saint-Jean, THE BASTARD, carving love, name and fortune for himself with a sword . . .

FOREVER AMBER
Volume I 5/-   552 07116 1
Volume II 5/-   552 07117 X

Kathleen Winsor

This magnificent novel has, in the twenty years of its life, been an enormous bestseller throughout the world. Set against the obviously authentic background, its unforgettable heroine, Amber St. Clare, is surely one of the best-known characters in fiction. Abandoned on the streets of London and soon to have a child, sixteen-year-old Amber managed, by her wits, beauty, and courage, to climb to the highest position in the land: the favourite mistress of Charles II.